THE MAN
IN
THE MOSS

PHIL RICKMAN

THE MAN IN THE MOSS

PAN BOOKS
IN ASSOCIATION WITH MACMILLAN LONDON

First published 1994 by Macmillan London

This edition published 1994 by Pan Books Ltd
a division of Pan Macmillan Publishers Limited
Cavaye Place, London SW10 9PG
and Basingstoke
in association with Macmillan London

Associated companies throughout the world

ISBN 0 330 33784 X

3 5 7 9 8 6 4 2

A CIP catalogue record for this book is available from
the British Library

Typeset by CentraCet Limited, Cambridge
Printed and bound in Great Britain
by Cox & Wyman Ltd, Reading, Berkshire

The author is indebted to the Dawber family and South Pennine Press for permission to reproduce sections of the text of *Dawber's Book of Bridelow*, a short guide to the village and its environs first published in 1896 and still updated every four or five years.

PROLOGUE

I

A cold midwinter fogbank lay on the Moss.
It lay like a quilt on the black mattress of the peat, and nothing moved.

Not even the village schoolteacher standing on the promontory at the end of a ragged alley of graves where the churchyard seemed to overhang the bog's edge.

Damp January was clamped across the teacher's mouth and nose like a chloroform pad. He'd only been an hour out of bed, but the cold made him tired and the sight of the Moss only made him feel colder.

It was, as he'd explained to countless generations of pupils, the biggest surviving peatbog in the North of England, a gross product of violent death and centuries of decay . . . vast forests burned and torn down by the barbarian invaders . . . soaring greenery slashed and flattened and transformed by time into flat, black acres bounded by the hills and the moors.

The peat was dead. But, because of its acids, the peat had the power to preserve. Sometimes fragments of the ancient dead were found in there, from iron-hard limbs of trees to the arms and legs of corpses (which were taken away by the villagers and quietly buried).

Inside his long, deeply unfashionable overcoat, the teacher suddenly shivered.

Not at the thought of the corpses, but because he was waiting for the piper.

The piper on the Moss.

The sad, swollen drone, the bleak keening of a lost soul, had reached him on a sudden, spiked breeze during his habitual morning walk before school.

And he'd stopped, disquieted. The air had been still, weighted by the fog; no breeze at all except for this single, quick breath. As if it had been awoken only to carry the message that the piper was on the Moss.

This worried him, for the piping was never heard in winter.

3

As a rule, it came on summer evenings, when the Moss was firm and springy and the sound would be serene, rippling along the air currents, mingling with bird cries . . . plaintive enough to soften the clouds.

But the piper did not come in winter.

Seeking reassurance, the teacher turned around, looking for the soft blue eye of the Beacon over the village. But the fog had closed the eye; he could not even make out the outline of the Norman church tower.

And while his back was turned, it began. A distant, drifting miasma of music. Notes which sounded ragged at first but seemed to reassemble somehow in the air and harmonize eerily with the atmosphere.

Cold music, then, with a razor-edge of bitterness.

And more. An anger and a seeping menace . . . a violence, unsuppressed, which thrust and jabbed at the fog, made it swirl and squirm.

Trembling suddenly, the schoolteacher backed away from it; it was as if the fog and the frozen stillness of winter had combined to amplify the sound. And the sound made vibrant, pulsing images in his head.

It was as though the sky had been slashed and the rain bled from the clouds.

As though the cry had been physically torn from the ruptured breast of a bird in flight.

Or the morning itself had been ripped open, exposing the black entrails of another kind of night.

And then the piper himself came out of the fog with the black bladder like a throbbing tumour under one arm, and the sound exploded around him, a sound as dark as the peat under his plodding boots.

A black noise. The piper in a black mood.

'Why can't you keep away?' the teacher whispered. 'Why do you have to haunt us?'

He pulled his hat over his ears to muffle the piping and hurried away from it, back towards the church until the Beacon's ghostly disc emerged from the fog and he could see the vacant smile on the face of Our Sheila who fingered and flaunted her sex on the church porch.

4

He rushed past her and into the church, shutting the great oak door behind him, removing his hat and clamping it to his breast, staring up at the Winter Cross, all jagged branches, blunted thorns, holly and mistletoe.

He couldn't hear the pipes any more but felt he could *taste* the noise – that the oozing sound had entered his ears and been filtered down to the back of his throat where it came out tasting sourly of peat.

'Doesn't mean owt, does it?' he called out to the Winter Cross. 'We'll be all right, won't we? Nowt'll change?'

And nothing *would* change for more than fifteen winters of fog and damp. But fifteen years in the life of a Moss was barely a blink of the eye of God, and when the Moss revealed what it had preserved . . . *then* the changes would come, too many, too quickly and too horribly.

And the teacher, in retirement, feeling the kiss of the eternal night, would remember the first time the piper had appeared on the Moss in winter.

Meanwhile, later that week, the fog would lift and there would be snow.

then . . .

II

They were all around her at the stage door, like muggers in the night. She could smell the sweat and the beer . . . and a sour scent, like someone's rancid breath, squirting out of the darkness and straight to the back of her throat.

Coughing. Coughing at nothing. For as long as she could remember, hostility had occasionally come to her like this . . . like a single, piercing puff from a poisoned perfume spray.

But nothing there, really.

There were maybe twenty of them, but it was mostly OK,

wasn't it, mostly warm wishes and appreciation? Just never happened to her before. One of them had his jacket off, eyeing her. He was grinning and mumbling.

'Sign your *what*?' she said.

'Get used to it, lass.' Matt Castle grinning too. 'This is only the start of it. For you.'

Now the guy was rolling up a chequered shirt-sleeve in the sub-zero night, handing her this thick black felt-tip pen.

'Oh, your *arm*.' She tried to smile, printing her name all the way up the soft, hairless underside of his forearm.

M o i r a   C a i r n s.

Usually it would be just a handful of enthusiasts, harmless as train-spotters, chattering learnedly about the music and mainly to Matt. Dropping away as they headed for the car park. Shouting, See you again . . . stuff like that, mostly to Matt.

You should be loving this, hen, she told herself. Real fans. Can you believe that? You're a star.

Willie and Eric were loading the gear into Matt's old minibus, wanting to be away – more snow on the way, apparently. Two girls in leather jackets held open the back doors for the tea chest Willie kept his hand-drums in.

She felt it again, back of her throat. Nearly choked on it.

'Ta,' Eric said. Moira saw Little Willie sizing up the girls for future reference. Tonight, she knew, he was worried he wouldn't get home Across the Moss, if the snow came down.

Matt got into the driving seat, Eric slammed the back doors and climbed in on the passenger side. One of the girls in leather – buxom piece – opened a rear side door for Willie. Willie rolled his eyes at her, gave her his most seductively innocent grin. 'See you sometime, eh?'

Moira's throat was burning up.

The girl said, 'Yeah, I'll be around.' She held on to the open door. 'Gina,' she said. The wire-caged light over the back-stage exit threw a grille of shadows on to her pale, puffy cheeks.

Willie, five and a bit feet tall, liked his women big. 'Gina. Right,' he said, 'I'll remember.'

The first sparse snowflakes hit the wet black asphalt and dissolved. Moira, tucking her long hair down her coat collar, smiled at the girl, put out a foot to climb into the van next to Willie.

And then the moment froze, like life's big projector had jammed.

Moira turned in time to see the girl's eyes harden, glazing over like a doll's eyes as she whirled – a big, clumsy dancer – and flung the door. Like the door was a wrecking hammer and Moira was the side of a condemned building.

Snarling, '*Traitor!*' Discoloured, jagged teeth exposed. 'Fucking bitch!'

Willie had seen it. With both hands, he had pushed her back. She stumbled, fell over the kerb, the door connecting with a shuddering crunch and this girl Gina snarling, '*Bitch* . . .', voice as deadly cold as the grinding metal.

And then the door reopened and Willie was hauling her in and snatching it shut behind her, the girl screaming, 'Go on . . . feather your own nest, fucking cow!' And beating on the panel into Moira's ear as Matt started the engine and pulled urgently away into the unheeding, desultory night traffic.

'Jesus,' Willie Wagstaff said. 'Could've had your fingers off.'

'Screw up ma glittering career, huh?' White face in the streetlight and a rasp of Glasgow giving it away that Moira was pretty damn shocked. 'Couldny play too well wi' a hook.'

Matt said mildly, 'Don't let it bother you. Always one or two. Just jealous.' The snow heavy enough now for him to get the wipers going.

'Wasny about envy.' Moira had her guitar in her arms. 'I'm no' exactly popular with your fans any more is the problem.'

'You're in good company,' Matt said. 'Look how the purists shunned Dylan when he went over to rock and roll.'

'Called me a traitorous cow.'

'Yeah, well,' Matt said. 'We've been over this.' So damned *nonchalant* about it. He seemed so determined she shouldn't feel bad that she felt a sight worse.

Eric, the mournful one who played fiddle and twelve-string, Eric, the mediator, the peacemaker, said, 'Weren't a bad gig though, were it?'

'Was a grand gig,' Moira said. Good enough, she thought, heartsick, to be the start of something, not the end.

Least her throat wasn't hurting so bad. The guitar case was warm in her arms. The snowflakes began to stick and cluster on the side windows as Matt drove first to Eric's house at Ashton Under Lyne, where Willie had left his Mini van. They switched the drum chest to the back of the little grey van, and Willie said, 'I won't mess about. If it's snowing like this down here it'll be thick as buggery over t'top.' He hung his arms around Moira's neck and gave her a big kiss just wide of the lips. 'Ta-ra, lass. Don't lose touch, eh?'

Then Eric kissed her too, mournfully, and by the time she got into the front seat next to Matt she was in tears, both arms wrapped around the guitar case for comfort.

'This is the worst thing I ever did, you know that, Matt?'

There was silence. Just the two of them now, for the last time. Time for some plain talking.

'Don't be so bloody daft.' Still his tone was curiously mild.

'She was right, that slag, I should have ma fingers chopped off.'

'Listen, kid.' He tapped at the steering-wheel. 'You made one sacrifice for this band when you threw up your degree course. That's it. No more. Don't owe us nowt. It's been nice – cracking couple of years, wouldn't've missed it. But you're not even twenty-one. We're owd men, us.'

'Aw, Matt . . .' Could anybody be this selfless?

'Gone as far as we're going. Think I want to be trailing me gear around the country when I'm sixty? No way. It's a good get-out, this, straight up. For all of us. Eric's got his kids, Willie's got his . . .'

Matt didn't finish the sentence, covering up the break by changing down to third, swinging sharp right and taking them through Manchester's Piccadilly: bright lights, couples scurrying through the snow. Snow was nice in the city, Moira thought. For a while. When it came by night.

Think about the snow. Because Matt's got to be lying through his teeth.

But the silence got too heavy. 'OK,' she said, to change the subject. 'What *do* you want to be doing?'

'Eh?'

'You said you didny wanna be trailing your gear around when you were sixty. What would you like to be doing?'

Matt didn't answer for a long time, not until they were out of the city centre.

'I'm not sure,' he said eventually. 'We're all right for money, me and Lottie. Thanks to you.'

'Matt . . .' *I can't stand this*.

'All right. I don't know. I don't know what I want to do. But I'll tell you this much . . . I know where I want to *be*.'

Moira waited. The snow was heavy now, but they were not too far from Whalley Range, where she lived, and it wouldn't take Matt long to get to his bit of Cheshire and Lottie.

'What I want,' he said, 'is to be out of these sodding suburbs. Want to go home.'

'Across the Moss?' The words feeling strange in Moira's mouth.

'Yeah,' Matt said.

Across the Moss. Willie and Matt would often slip the phrase to each other, surreptitiously, like a joint. Across the Moss was Over the Rainbow. Utopia. The Elysian Fields.

'Lottie likes it fine where we are. All the shops and the galleries and that. But it's not me, never was. Don't belong. No . . . echoes. So. Yeah. I'm going home. Might take a year, might take ten. But that's where I'm ending up.'

Which didn't make her feel any better. Twenty years older than her and here he was, talking about ending up. Did this happen to everybody when they turned forty?

'This is Willie's village, up in the moors?'

'Yeah. And Willie stayed. Willie's got family there. My lot moved to town when I was a lad. You never get rich up there, not even the farmers. But we were happy. We were *part of it*. Willie's still part of it. Drops down to town to play a gig or two, get his leg . . . go out with a woman.'

Moira smiled. Matt tended to be kind of proper, like a father, when they were alone.

'But he keeps going back. And his mother . . . she's never spent a night away, his ma, the whole of her life.'

'Some place, huh?'

9

'Special place.' He was staring unblinking through the windscreen and the snow. 'It's quite lonely and primitive in its way. And the Moss – biggest peatbog in the North.'

'Really?'

'Vast. And when you get across it – it's weird – but there's a different attitude. Different values.'

'Isn't that what everybody says about the place they were brought up?'

'Do you?'

She thought about this.

'No,' she said. 'Maybe not.'

The world outside was a finite place in the thickening snow. Matt was somewhere far inside himself. Across the Moss.

She glanced at him quickly. Thickset guy, coarse-skinned. Nobody's idea of a musician. Brooding eyes the colour of brown ale. Most times you thought you knew him; sometimes you weren't so sure. Occasionally you were damn sure you *didn't* know him, and couldn't.

After a while she said, 'What's it called? I forget.'

'Bridelow,' Matt said in a deliberate way, rounding out all the consonants. 'Bridelow Across the Moss.'

'Right,' she said vaguely.

'Dramatic place. To look at. Never saw that till I started going back. I take the little lad up there sometimes, of a weekend. When he's older we're going to go hiking on Sundays. Over the moors.'

'Sounds idyllic. Like to see it sometime.'

'But mostly I go alone.' Matt pulled up under the streetlamp in front of the Victorian villa where Moira had her apartment. 'Me and the pipes.'

'You take the *pipes*?'

Bagpipes. The Northumbrian pipes, played sitting down, had been Matt's instrument. Then he'd started experimenting with different kinds of bag, made of skins and things. He called them the Pennine Pipes, claiming they'd been played in these parts since before the Romans came to Britain.

The Pennine Pipes made this eerie, haunting sound, full of a kind of repressed longing.

'Releases me,' Matt said.

She didn't want to ask him what it released him from.

'Takes it away,' Matt said.

She didn't want to ask him what it was that piping took away.

'On the Moss,' Matt said. 'Only on the Moss.'

The tips of her fingers started to feel cold.

'The Moss takes it away,' Matt said. 'The Moss absorbs it.'

He switched off the engine. Snow was settling on the bonnet.

'But the Moss also preserves it,' Matt said. 'That's the only drawback. Peat preserves. You give it to the peat, and you've got rid of it, but the peat preserves it for ever.'

He turned and looked at her; she saw something swirling in his eyes and the truth exploded in her mind. *Oh, Christ, don't let me taste it. God almighty, don't let it come. Was the girl, what's her name, Gina . . . it was the girl, it wasny you, Matt, wasny you . . . please, don't let it be you . . .*

In the silence, the kind which only new snow seemed to make, they looked at each other in the streetlight made brighter by the snow.

'This is it then,' Matt said flatly.

'Think I might cry again.' But *she* was lying now. There was the residue of something unpleasant here, something more than sadness swirling in Matt's eyes.

Matt had his door open. 'Pass us your guitar.'

'Huh? Oh. Right. Sorry.'

The street was silent, snow starting to make the three- and four-storey houses look like soft furnishings. Lights shone pastel green, pink and cream behind drawn curtains. Matt took the guitar case, snowflakes making a nest in his denim cap. He pushed it back. He said, just as relaxed, just as mild and just as offhand as he'd been earlier, 'One thing I've always meant to ask. Why do you always take this thing on stage with you?'

'The guitar?'

'No, lass. The case. This old and cracked and not very valuable guitar case. You never let the bloody thing out of your sight.'

'Oh.' How long had he been noticing this? She looked at

11

him. His eyes were hard. He'd never asked her questions; everything he knew about her was stuff she'd volunteered. Matt was incurious.

And because of that she told him.

'There's . . . kind of a wee pocket inside the case, and inside of that there's, like, something my mother gave me when I was young.'

He didn't stop looking at her.

'It's only a comb. Kind of an antique, you know? Very old. Too heavy to carry around in your pocket. It means a lot to me, I suppose.'

'That's your mother, the . . . ?'

'The gypsy woman. Aye. Ma mother, the gypsy woman.' She shook snow off her hair. 'They're big on good luck tokens, the gypsies. Throw'm around like beads.'

Matt said roughly, 'Don't go making light of it.'

'Huh?'

'You're trying to make it seem of no account. Traditions are important. Sometimes I think they're all we have that's worthwhile.' He propped the instrument in its stiff black case against the wide concrete base of the streetlamp.

Moira said, 'Look, you're gonny get soaked.'

He laughed scornfully, like the noise a crow makes.

'Matt,' she said, 'I'll see you again, yeh?' And she did want to, she really did. Sure she did.

He smiled. 'We'll be on different circuits now, lass. You in a suite at the Holiday Inn, me over the kitchen at the Dog and Duck. Tell you what, I'll buy all your records. Even if it *is* rock and roll. How's that?'

She took a step towards him, hesitant. He was only a wee bit taller than she was.

This was it. The final seconds of the last reel.

Two years in the band, building up her reputation on the back of his. Matt watching her with some pride. A touch supervisory at first, then graciously taking half a pace back until even the wee folk clubs were announcing 'The Matt Castle Band with Moira Cairns'. And a couple of times, to her embarrassment, Moira Cairns in bigger letters.

And now she was leaving. Off to London for the big money.

12

Traitorous bitch.

'Matt . . .' It was the worst moment. She should kiss him too, but that would seem perfunctory, demeaning and pretty damn cheap.

Also, for the first time, she didn't want to go that close to him.

He'd pulled down his cap; she tried to peer under the peak, to find out what his eyes were saying.

Nothing. His eyes would show no resentment, no disappointment. She was leaving the band which had changed her life, made her name. Leaving the band just when she was starting to put something back, and Matt felt . . .

He felt nothing.

Because . . . Jesus . . .

'Did you go on the peat today?' she asked him in a very small voice, the snow falling between them. 'Did you go on the peat with the pipes? Did you let the damn peat absorb it?'

And then the projector stuttered and stalled again, images shivering on the screen of the night, and she saw him suddenly all in white. Maybe just an illusion of the snow. He was very still and framed in white. It wasn't nice. The white was frilled around him, like the musty lace handkerchiefs in the top dresser drawer at her gran's house.

And a whiff of soiled perfume.

Death?

For the first time, there was a real menace to him. Too transient to tell whether it was around him or *from* him. Her throat swelled. She coughed and the tears came, the wrong kind of tears. She felt the snow forming on the top of her own head; it was almost warm. Maybe she looked like that too, shrouded in white.

Matt held out his right hand and she gripped it like a lifeline, but the hand was deathly cold. She told herself, Cold hands, warm heart, yeah? And tried to pull him closer – but all the time wanting to keep him away and hating herself for that.

He dropped her hand and then put both of his on her shoulders. His arms were rigid, like girders, but she felt they were trembling, his whole body quivering with some titanic tension, something strong holding out against something potentially stronger, like a steel suspension bridge in a hurricane.

Then he said, 'Going to show me?' Voice colder than the snow.

She wanted to squirm away; she made herself remain still, trying to find his eyes. No. Please. Don't spoil this. I'll buy it. You're a selfless, self-sacrificing guy. I don't want to know any more.

'This famous comb,' he said with a smile that was faintly unpleasant.

'It's no' famous,' she said quickly, almost snapping.

His brown eyes were steady. Hey come *on* . . . this is Matt Castle. What's he gonna do, steal it off you, snatch it out your hand and drive away?

Keep it safe. Never take it out for show . . . Never treat it as a trinket or a wee souvenir. You understand, child?

No, see, all it is, right, he's decided in his own mind that we aren't going to meet again. He wants there to be no space for future recriminations. But he needs something to hold on to, right? A link.

That's all it is. He wants a link. A special moment, something between us and no one else.

You owe him. You owe him that.

You owe him nothing.

She stopped searching for his eyes, didn't want to know what they might have to tell her about Matt Castle, the kindly father figure, that Matt Castle who'd said, Take your chance, grab it while you can, lass. Never mind us. We're owd men.

Dumbly, Moira laid the guitar case on the pavement in the snow, and – hands shaking with the cold and the nerves – flipped up the chromium catch.

It was like opening someone's coffin.

Only the guitar lay in state. In a panic, she felt beneath the machine-heads for the velvet pouch which held the ancient metal comb.

I have to. I owe him, Mammy. I'm sorry, but I owe him.

PART ONE

THE SPRING CROSS

From *Dawber's Book of Bridelow*:

INTRODUCTION

THIS LITTLE BOOK bids you, the visitor, a cordial welcome to Bridelow Across the Moss, a site of habitation for over two thousand years and the home of the famous Bridelow Black Beer.

Bridelow folk would never be so immodest as to describe their tiny, lonely village as unique. But unique it is, both in situation and character.

Although little more than half an hour's drive from the cities of Manchester and Sheffield, the village is huddled in isolation between the South Pennine moors and the vast peatbog known as Bridelow Moss. So tucked away, as the local saying goes, 'It's a wonder the sun knows where to come of a morning . . .'

A spring morning. A hesitant sun edging over the moor out of a mist pale as milk. Only when it clears the church tower does the sun find a few patches of blue to set it off, give it a bit of confidence.

The sun hovers a while, blinking in and out of the sparse shreds of cloud before making its way down the village street, past the cottage where Ma Wagstaff lives, bluetits breakfasting from the peanuts in two mesh bags dangling from the rowan trees in the little front garden.

The cats, Bob and Jim, sitting together on Ma's front step – donkeystoned to a full-moon whiteness – observe the bluetits through narrowed green eyes but resist their instincts because Ma will be about soon.

And while Ma understands their instincts all too well, she does not appreciate blood on her step.

Milly Gill, shedding her cardigan at the Post Office door, thought the mist this morning was almost like a summer heat-haze, which wasn't bad for the second week in March.

It made Milly feel excited, somewhere deep inside her majestic bosom. It made her feel so energetic that she wanted to wander off for long walks, to fill up her reservoirs after the winter. And to go and see the Little Man. See what he had in *his* reservoir.

And of course it made her feel creative, too. Tonight she'd be pulling out that big sketch pad and the coloured pencils and getting to work on this year's design to be done in flowers for the dressing of the Holy Well. It was, she decided, going to reflect everything she could sense about her this morning.

Milly Gill thought, I'm forty-nine and I feel like a little girl.

This was what the promise of spring was *supposed* to do.

'Thank you, Mother,' Milly said aloud, with a big, innocent grin. 'And you too, sir!'

*

The Moss, a vast bed, hangs on to its damp duvet as usual until the sun is almost overhead. Behind temporary traffic-lights, about half a mile from the village, a Highways Authority crew is at work, widening the road which crosses the peat, a long-overdue improvement, although not everybody is in favour of improving access to the village.

It's close to midday before the foreman decides it's warm enough to strip to the waist.

This is the man who finds the chocolate corpse.

The splendour of the morning dimmed a little for the Rector when, on getting out of bed, he felt a twinge.

It was, as more often than not, in the area of his left knee. 'We really must get you a plastic one,' the doctor had said last time. 'I should think the pain's pretty awful, isn't it?'

'Oh.' The Rector flexing his creased-up Walter Matthau semi-smile. 'Could be worse.' Then the doctor ruefully shaking his head, making a joke about the Rector being determined to join the league of Holy Martyrs.

'I was thinking of joining the squash club, actually,' the Rector had said, and they'd both laughed and wondered how he was managing to keep this up.

The answer to this was Ma Wagstaff's mixture.

Standing by the window of his study, with sunshine strewn all over the carpet, pleasant around his bare feet, the Rector balanced a brimming teaspoonful of Ma's mixture, and his eyes glazed briefly at the horror of the stuff.

It looked like green frogspawn. He knew it was going to make his throat feel nostalgic for castor oil.

The bottle, as usual, was brown and semi-opaque so he wouldn't have to see the sinister strands and tendrils waving about in there like weed on the bottom of an aquarium.

But still, it worked.

Not a 'miracle' cure, of course. Ma Wagstaff, who promised nothing, would have been shocked at any such suggestion. 'Might just ease it a bit,' she'd say gruffly, leaving the bottle on his hall table, by the phone.

19

Through the study window the Rector saw sun-dappled gravestones and the great Norman tower of St Bride's.

He rubbed his feet into the sunshiny carpet, raised his eyes to heaven, the spoon to his lips, and swallowed.

Out on the Moss, the foreman stands in the middle of the trench, in front of the JCB, waving his arms until the driver halts the big digger and sticks his head inquiringly round the side of the cab.

''Owd on a bit, Jason. I've found summat.'

The trench, at this point, is about five feet deep.

'If it's money,' says the JCB driver, 'just pass it up 'ere and I'll hide it under t'seat.'

'Well,' said Mr Dawber, 'as it's such a lovely day, we'd best be thinking about the spring. Now – think back to last year – what does *that* mean?'

Some of them had the good manners to put their hands up, but two little lads at the back just shouted it out.

'THE SPRING CROSS!'

Mr Dawber didn't make an issue of it. 'Aye,' he said. 'The Spring Cross.' And the two troublemakers at the back cheered at that because it would get them out of the classroom, into the wood and on to the moors.

'So,' said Mr Dawber. 'Who can tell me what we'll be looking for to put in the Spring Cross?'

The hands went up as fast and rigid as old-fashioned railway signals. Ernie Dawber looked around, singled out a little girl. 'Yes . . . Meryl.'

'Catkins!'

'Aye, that's right, catkins. What else? Sebastian.'

'Pussy willows!'

'Ye-es. What else? Benjamin.'

'Acorns?'

They all had a good cackle at this. Benjamin was the smallest child in the class and had the air of one who found life

20

endlessly confusing. Ernie Dawber sympathized. He'd always reckoned that the day he retired he'd be able to sit back, job well enough done, and start to understand a few basics. But everything had just got hazier.

With them all looking at him, giggling and nudging each other, Benjamin seemed to get even smaller. Mr Dawber had a little deliberation about this while the class was settling down.

'Now then . . .' he said thoughtfully. 'Who can tell me when we find acorns?'

'AUTUMN!' four or five of the cleverer ones chorused scornfully.

'That's right. So, what I'm going to do – and don't forget to remind me when the times comes, lad – I'm going to put Benjamin, because he knows all about acorns . . . in charge of making the *Autumn* Cross.'

The clever ones looked aghast, unable to find any justice in this, and Ernie Dawber smiled to see it. Coming in just a few hours a week, to teach the children about nature, at least gave him more time to consider the psychology of the job.

'Now then.' He clapped his hands to change the mood. 'What else do we need for the Spring Cross? Tom.'

'Birds' eggs.'

Mr Dawber's voice dropped an octave.

'We most certainly do *not* take birds' eggs to put into the Spring Cross, or for any other reason, Thomas Garside. And if it comes to my notice that any of you have disturbed any nests there's going to be TROUBLE.'

There was silence.

'And don't anybody think I won't find out about it,' said Mr Dawber.

And they knew he would, because, one way or another, Mr Dawber found out about *everything*. And if it was important enough he put it in *The Book of Bridelow*.

The foreman tells the JCB driver to switch his engine off. His voice is shaking.

'Come down a minute, Jason. Come and take a look at this.'

21

The driver, a younger man, swings, loose-limbed, to the ground. His boots shudder on the surface of the Moss. 'What you got?'

'I'm not sure.' The foreman seems reluctant to go back in the trench.

The driver grinning, shambling over to the pit and balancing expertly on the rim. Can't make it out at first. Looks like a giant bar of dark chocolate.

Then, while the foreman is attempting to light a cigarette and nervously scattering matches over the peat, the driver suddenly realizes what he's staring at, and, when the thought lurches into his head, it's eerily echoed by the foreman's fractured croak.

'Looks like a dead 'un to me, Jason.'

The driver falls over backwards trying not to topple into the trench.

Just Eliza Horridge and Shaw now, and the drawing room at The Hall was too big.

He was taller but slighter than his father, who used to stand, legs apart, in front of the fireplace, lighting his pipe, belching dragon's breath and making it seem as if the room had been built around him. When Arthur Horridge spoke, the walls had closed in, as if the very fabric of the building was paying attention.

'The w-w-w-worst thing about all this . . .' Shaw's thin voice no more emphatic than the tinkling of the chandelier when a window was open, '. . . is that when der-der-Dad wanted to expand ter-ten years ago, the bank wouldn't back him, and now . . .'

'We'll ride it,' Liz Horridge told him firmly. 'We always have. We've got twenty-three people depending on us for an income.'

'Ter-ter-too many,' said Shaw. 'Fer-far . . .'

'No!' The first time ever that she hadn't waited politely for him to finish a sentence. 'That's *not* something your father would have said.'

She turned away from him, glaring out of the deep Georgian-style window at the brewery's grey tower through the bare brown treetrunks. Its stonework badly needed repointing, one more job they couldn't afford.

'When sales were sagging,' Liz said, as she'd said to him several times before, 'Arthur always blamed himself, and it was our belt – the family's – that was tightened. I remember when he sold the Jag to—'

'It was der-different then!' Shaw almost shrieked, making her look at him. 'There was no competition to ser-speak of. Wh-what did they need to know about mer-mer-market forces in those days?'

'And it's all changed so quickly, has it, in the six months since your father's death?'

'It was cher-changing . . . yer-years before. He just couldn't see it. He didn't w-want to ser-see it.'

'He knew what his duty was,' Liz snapped, and her son began to wring his hands in frustration.

The sun shone through the long window, a cruel light on Shaw, the top of his forehead winking like a feeble flashlight. If baldness was hereditary, people doubtless asked, why had Arthur managed to keep most of his hair until the end, while Shaw's had begun to fall out before he turned twenty?

Behind the anger, Liz felt the usual sadness for him, while acknowledging that sympathy was a poor substitute for maternal pride.

'Mother,' Shaw said determinedly, 'listen to me. We've ger-got to do it. Ser-soon. We've got to trim the workforce. Ser-ser-some of them have ger-got to go. Or else . . .'

'Never,' said Liz Horridge. But she knew that such certainty was not her prerogative. Shaw was the owner of the Bridelow Brewery now. He glared mutinously at her, thin lips pressed tight together, only too aware of how much authority he lost whenever he opened them.

'Or else what?' Liz demanded. 'What happens if we *don't* trim the workforce?'

She looked down at herself, at the baggy jeans she wore, for which she was rather too old and a little too shapeless these days. Realizing why she was wearing the jeans. Spring cleaning. An operation which she would, for the first time, be undertaking alone, because, when Josie had gone into hospital, she hadn't taken on another cleaner for economic reasons. Thus trimming her own workforce of one.

'The ber-ber-brewery's not a charity, Mother,' Shaw said pleadingly. 'Jim Ford says we could be out of ber-business inside a year.'

'Or else what?' Liz persisted.

'Or else we sell it,' Shaw said simply.

Liz laughed. 'To whom?'

'Ter-ter-to an outside . . . one of the big firms.'

'That's not an option,' Liz said flatly. 'You know that. Beer's been brewed in Bridelow since time immemorial. It's part of the local heritage.'

'And still cer-could be! Sell it as a going concern. Why not?'

'And you could live with that, could you?'

He didn't answer. Liz Horridge was shaking with astonishment. She faced him like an angry mother cat, narrowing her eyes, penetrating. 'Who's responsible for this? Who's been putting these thoughts in your head?'

'Ner-nobody.' But he couldn't hold her gaze. He was wearing a well-cut beige suit over a button-down shirt and a strange leather tie. He was going out again. He'd been going out a lot lately. He had no interest in the brewery, and he wasn't even trying to hide this any longer.

'And what about the pub? Is this fancy buyer going to take that on as well?'

'Ser-somebody will.' Shaw shrugged uselessly, backing towards the door. 'Anyway, we'll talk about it later, I've got to . . .'

'Where are you going?'

'I . . . I'm . . .' He went red and began to splutter. Pulled out a handkerchief and blew his nose, wiped his lips. For years she'd worried because he didn't go out enough, because he hadn't got a girlfriend (although this had hardly been surprising). Now at last, at the age of thirty-one, he was feebly groping for control of his own destiny . . . and floundering about, unbalancing *everything*.

Liz Horridge turned away from him and walked to the

other window, the one with the view of Bridelow, which summer would soon obscure. She could see the humped but still sprightly figure of Mrs Wagstaff in the distance, lugging a shopping basket across the cobbles to Gus Bibby's General Stores.

Her breast heaved and she felt tears pumping behind her eyes.

Arthur . . . it's not my fault.

Mrs Wagstaff stopped in the middle of the street and – although it was too far away for Liz to be certain – seemed to stare up through the trees at the Hall . . . at this very window.

As though the old girl had overheard Liz's thoughts. As though she could feel the agony.

When Liz turned around, wet-eyed, she found she was alone; Shaw had quietly left the room.

Although he'll be cool enough when the Press and the radio and TV reporters interview him in a few hours' time, the County Highways foreman is so shaken up right now that he has to be revived with whisky from the JCB driver's secret flask.

What he's discovered will come to be known as the Bridelow Bogman. Or the Man in the Moss. Important people are going to travel hundreds of miles to gaze with reverence upon its ancient face.

'And what was your reaction when you found it?' asks one of the reporters. 'What did you think it *was*?'

'Thought it were a sack o' spuds or summat,' the foreman says, quotably. His moment of glory. But out of his hands soon enough – so old and so exciting to the experts, like one of them Egyptian mummies, that nobody else seems to find it upsetting or horrifying, not like a *real* body.

But, though he'll never admit it, the foreman reckons he's never going to forget that first moment.

'And what did you think when you realized what it was?'

'Dunno, really . . . thought it were maybe an owd tramp or summat.'

'Were you shocked?'

'Nah. You find all sorts in this job.'

But that night the foreman will dream about it and awake with a whimper, reaching for his warm missus. And then fall asleep and wake again, his sweat all over both of them and his mind bulging with the moment he bent down and found his hand was gripping its cold and twisted face, his thumb between what might have been its teeth.

PART TWO

BLACK GLOW

From *Dawber's Book of Bridelow*:

THE FIRST-TIME VISITOR to Bridelow is strongly urged to approach it from the west, from which direction a most dramatic view of the village is attained.

From a distance of a mile or two, Bridelow appears almost as a craggy island when viewed from the narrow road which is virtually a causeway across Bridelow Moss.

A number of legends are attached to the Moss, some of which will be discussed later in this book.

CHAPTER I

In early summer, Bridelow hopefully dolls herself up, puts on a bit of make-up and an obliging smile for the sun. But the sun doesn't linger. On warm, cloudless evenings like this it saves its final pyrotechnics for the moor.

Sunset lures hues from the moor that you see at no other time – sensual pinks and melodramatic mauves which turn its stiff and spiky surface into velvet.

. . . a delusion, thought Joel Beard, soon to leave theological college. A red light tenderizing the face of an old whore.

He had his back to the sinking sun. To him, it seemed agitated tonight, throwing out its farewell flames in a long, dying scream. As well it might.

Most of the lonely village was below the moor, and the sun's flailing rays were missing it. The stone houses hanging from the hill were in shadow and so was the body of the church on its summit. Only the spikes of the church tower were dusted with red and gold.

Joel dismounted from his motorbike.

In the centre of the tower was a palely shining disc. Like a rising full moon, it sent sneering signals to the sun: as you fade, it promised gleefully, I'll grow ever brighter.

Joel glared at the village across the sullen, scabby surface of the Moss. He imagined Bridelow under moonlight, stark and white as crow-picked bones.

Its true self.

The disc at the centre of the tower was actually an illuminated clockface, from which the hands had long ago fallen. Often said to be a friendly face which turned the church into a lighthouse at night, across the black ocean of the Moss.

. . . you see, at one time, Mr Beard, very few people dared cross the Moss . . . except those for whom the Devil lit the way – have you heard that legend?

It was no legend. On a dark night, all you would see of the village would be this silver disc, Bridelow's own, permanent full moon.

Was this how the Devil lit the path? Was this the Devil's light, shining from the top of the stairs in God's house, a false beacon for the weak, the uncertain and the disturbed?

Joel's black leathers straightened him, like armour, and the hard white collar lifted his eyes above the village to the luminous moor. Its lurid colours too would soon grow dull under the night, like a harlot's cheap dress.

From the village, across the barren Moss, he heard voices raised, a shriek of laughter.

The village would be alive tonight. A new landlord had installed himself at the decrepit local inn, The Man I'th Moss, thus saving it from closure, a side-effect of the widely condemned sale of the Bridelow brewery.

Joel waited, astride his motorbike, his charger, until the moor no longer glowed and the illusion of beauty was gone.

Everyone saw shadows in the blackened cities, those obvious pits of filth and fornication, where EVIL was scrawled in neon and the homeless slept with the rats. And yet the source of it was up here, where city-dwellers surged at weekends to stroll through the springy heather, picnic among the gorse . . . young couples, families, children queuing at the roadside ice-cream vans, pensioners in small cars with their flasks of tea.

It's all around you, Mr Beard . . . once you know what you're looking for. Look at the church, look at the pub, look at the people . . . you'll see the signs everywhere.

Beneath him, the bike lurched into life, his strong, gauntleted hands making the engine roar and crackle, spitting holy fire.

He rode away from the village, back into the hills.

'Shades,' Ma Wagstaff would say later that night. 'Them's what's kept this place the way it is. Shades of things.'

Of all Ma's famous sayings, these were the words that would keep coming back at Ernie Dawber during the short, anxious days and the long, chill nights of the declining year.

And when, as local historian, he tried to find the beginning (as in, What exactly started the First World War? What caused the first spark that set off the Great Fire of London?), he'd keep coming back to this particular evening. A vivid evening at the end of May. The evening he'd blithely and thoughtlessly told Ma Wagstaff what he'd learned about the death of the bogman . . . and Ma had made a fateful prediction.

But it started well enough, with a big turn-out for the official reopening of The Man, under its new proprietor. The two bars couldn't hold all those come to welcome him home. So several dozen folk, including Ernie Dawber – best suit, waistcoat, watch-chain – were out on the cobbled forecourt, having a pint or two and watching the sun go down over the big hills beyond the Moss.

A vivid evening at the end of May. Laughter in the streets. Hope for the future. Most enmities sheathed and worries left at home under the settee cushions.

A real old Bridelow night. That was how it ought to have been enshrined in his memory. All those familiar faces.

A schoolteacher all his working life, Ernie Dawber had known at least three-quarters of this lot since they were five-year-olds at the front of the school hall: eager little faces, timid little

31

faces . . . and a few belligerent ones too – always reckoned he could spot a future troublemaker in its pram.

He remembered Young Frank Manifold in the pram, throttling his panda.

'Well, well . . .' Twenty-odd years on, Young Frank strolling up to his boss, all jutting chin and pint mug clenched like a big glass knuckle-duster. 'It's *Mr Horridge*.'

Shaw said nothing.

'What's that you're drinking, *Mr Horridge*?' Sneering down at Shaw's slim glass.

Shaw's smile faltered. But he won't reply, Ernie thought, because if he does he'll start stuttering and he knows it.

There'd been a half-smile on Shaw's face as he stood alone on the cobbles. A nervous, forced-looking smile but a smile none the less. Ernie had to admire the lad, summoning the nerve to show himself tonight, not a month since Andy Hodgson died.

Especially with more than a few resentful brewery employees about.

'Looks like vodka,' Frank observed. 'That what it is, *Mr Horridge*? Vodka?' A few people starting to look warily at Frank and Shaw, a couple of men guiding their wives away.

''Course . . . I forgot. Bloody Gannons make vodka on t'side. Gannons'll make owt as'll sell. That *Gannons* vodka? That what it is . . . *Mr Horridge*?'

Shaw sipped his drink, not looking at Frank. This could be nerves. Or it could be an insult, Shaw pointedly pretending Young Frank was not there.

Whichever, Ernie decided he ought to break this up before it started to spoil the atmosphere. But somebody better equipped than him got there first.

'Where's your dad, Frank?' Milly Gill demanded, putting herself firmly between him and Shaw, like a thick, flowery bush sprouting between two trees.

'Be around somewhere.' Frank staring over the postmistress's head at Shaw, who was staring back now. Frank's knuckles whitening around the handle of his beermug.

'I think you'd better find him, Frank,' Milly said briskly. 'See he doesn't drink too much with that diabetes.'

32

Frank ignored her, too tanked-up to know his place. 'Fancy new car, I see . . . *Mr Horridge*. Porsche, int it? Andy Hodgson'd just got 'isself a new car, day before he fell. Well, I'm saying "new" – Austin Maestro, don't even make um no more. He were chuffed wi' it. Easily pleased, Andy, weren't he, Milly?'

'It was an accident,' Milly said tightly. 'As you well know.'

'Aye, sure it were, I'm not accusing Mr Horridge of *murder*. Only, why don't you ask him why Andy were suddenly ordered to reconnect a bloody old clapped-out pulley system for winching malt-sacks up to a storeroom right at top of t'building as isn't even *used* no more except by owls. You ask this bastard that, Milly.'

'We've had the inquest,' Milly said. 'Go and see to your dad.'

'Inquest? Fucking whitewash. I'll *tell* you why Andy were sent up. On account of place were being tarted up to look all *quaint* and *old-fashioned* for a visit from t'Gannons directors. Right, *Mr Horridge*?'

'Wasn't c . . . Not quite like that,' said Shaw quietly.

'Oh aye. How were it different? Lad dies for a bit of fucking *cosmetic*. You're all shit, you. Shit.'

The air between them fizzed. Shaw was silent. He'd been an expert at being silent during the three years Ernie had taught him before the lad was sent to prep school. And still an expert when he came back from University, poor bugger.

'And this Porsche.' Young Frank popped out the word with a few beery bubbles. 'How many jobs Gannons gonna axe to buy you that, eh?'

'Frank,' Milly Gill told him very firmly, big floral bosom swelling, 'I'll not tell you again!'

Careful, lass, Ernie thought. Don't do owt.

'You're a jammy little twat,' Frank spat. 'Don't give a shit. You never was a proper Horridge.'

A widening circle around them, conversations trailing off. 'Right.' Milly's eyes went still. 'That's enough. I'll not have this occasion spoiled. Am I getting through?'

'Now, Millicent,' Ernie said, knowing from experience

what might happen if she got riled. But Shaw Horridge startled them all. 'It's quite all right, Miss Gill.'

He smiled icily at Young Frank. 'Yes, it is a per-Porsche.' Held up his glass. 'Yes, it is vodka. Yes, it's mer-made in Sheffield by a s-subsidiary of Gannons Ales.'

He straightened up, taller than Frank now, his voice gaining strength. 'Gannons Ales. Without whom, yes, I wouldn't have a Porsche.'

And, stepping around Millie, he poked Young Frank in the chest with a thin but rigid forefinger. 'And without whom *you* wouldn't have a job . . . *Mr Manifold*.'

Ernie saw several men tense, ready to hold Young Frank back, but Frank didn't move. His eyes widened and his grip on the tankard slackened. Lad's as astonished as me, Ernie thought, at Shaw Horridge coming out with half a dozen almost fully coherent sentences one after the other.

The red sun shone into Shaw's eyes; he didn't blink.

The selling of the brewery was probably the worst thing that had happened to Bridelow this century. But not, apparently, the worst thing that had happened to Shaw Horridge.

He lowered his forefinger. 'Just remember that, please,' he said.

Looking rather commanding, where he used to look shyly hunched. And this remarkable confidence, as though somebody had turned his lights on. Letting them all see him – smiling and relaxed – after perpetrating the sale of the brewery, Bridelow's crime of the century. And indirectly causing a death.

Took some nerve, this did, from stuttering Shaw.

Arthur's lad at last. Maybe.

'Excuse me,' Shaw said dismissively. 'I have to meet someone.'

He turned his back on Young Frank Manifold and walked away, no quicker than he needed to, the sun turning the bald spot on the crown of his head into a bright golden coin.

'By 'eck,' Ernie Dawber said, but he noticed that Milly Gill was looking worried.

And she wasn't alone.

*

'Now then, Ernest. What's tha make of that, then?'

He hadn't noticed her edging up behind him, although he'd known she must be here somewhere. She was a Presence.

Just a little old woman in a pale blue woollen beret, an old grey cardigan and a lumpy brown woollen skirt.

'Well,' Ernie Dawber said, 'Arthur might have been mortified at what he's done with the brewery, but I think he'd be quite gratified at the way he stood up for himself there. Don't you?'

'Aye,' said Ma Wagstaff grimly. 'I'm sure his father'd be right pleased.'

Ernie looked curiously into the rubbery old features. Anybody who thought this was just a little old woman hadn't been long in Bridelow. He took a modest swallow from his half of Black. 'What's wrong then, Ma?'

'Everything.' Ma sighed. 'All coming apart.'

'Oh?' said Ernie. 'Nice night, though. Look at that sun.'

'Aye,' said Ma Wagstaff pessimistically. 'Going down, int it?'

'Well, yes.' Ernie straightened his glasses. 'It usually does this time of night.'

Ma Wagstaff nodded at his glass. 'What's that ale like now it's Gannons?'

'Nowt wrong with it as I can taste.' This wasn't true; it didn't seem to have quite the same brackish bite – or was that his imagination?

Ma looked up and speared him with her fierce little eyes. 'Got summat to tell me, Ernest Dawber?'

Ernie coughed. 'Not as I can think of.' She was making him uneasy.

'Anythin' in the post today?'

'This and that, Ma, this and that.'

'Like one of them big squashy envelopes, for instance?'

'A jiffy-bag, you mean?'

'Aye,' said Ma Wagstaff. 'Wi' *British Museum* stamped on it.'

Ernie fumed. You couldn't keep anything bloody private in this place. 'Time that Millicent kept her damn nose out!'

'Never mind that, lad, what's it say?'

'Now, look . . .' Ernie backed away, pulling at his waist-coat. 'In my capacity as local historian, I was able to provide Dr Hall and the British Museum with a considerable amount of information relating to the Moss, and as a result, following their examination of the body, they've kindly given me a preview of their findings, which . . .'

'Thought that'd be it.' Ma Wagstaff nodded, satisfied.

'. . . which will be published in due course. Until which time, I am not allowed . . .'

'If *you* know, why shouldn't *we* know?'

'I'm not *allowed*, Ma. It's what's called an embargo.'

'Oh.' Ma's eyes narrowed. 'That's what it's called, is it?' Means educated fellers like you get to know what's what and us common folk . . .'

Common folk? Ma Wagstaff? Ernie kept backing off, looking around for friendly faces. 'Please, Ma . . . don't push me on this. You'll find out soon enough.'

But the nearest person was a good ten yards away, and when his back hit the wall of the pub's outside lavatory block, he realized she'd got him into a corner in more ways than one.

'Now then,' Ma said kindly. 'How's that prostate of yours these days?'

'Nowt wrong with my prostate,' Ernie replied huffily.

Ma Wagstaff's eyes glinted. 'Not yet there int.'

CHAPTER II

'This is mer-madness,' Shaw said.

'No,' said Therese, 'it's exciting.'

'You're exciting,' he mumbled. 'That's all.' He pushed a hand through her sleek hair, and she smiled at him, tongue gliding out between her small, ice-white teeth. He was almost crying; she had him on the edge again. He pushed his back into the car's unfamiliar upholstery and clenched both hands on the wheel.

'Shall we go, then?'

'I can't.'

'I promise you,' Therese said, 'you'll feel so much better afterwards.'

And he would, he knew this from experience. Once, not long after they'd met, she'd made him go into a chemist and steal a bottle of Chanel perfume for her. *I'll buy it for you*, he'd almost shrieked. But that wasn't good enough. He was rich . . . buying her perfume – what would that demonstrate?

So he'd done it. Stolen it. Slipped it into the pocket of his sheepskin jacket and then bought himself two bottles of the shop's most expensive aftershave as an awkward sort of atonement.

But the awkwardness had just been a phase. He remembered lying awake all that night, convinced someone had seen him and the police would be at the door. *Don't worry*, she'd said, *it'll get easier*.

Jewellery next. Antique jewellery from a showcase, while Therese had distracted the manager.

You'll feel better, she'd say.

She was right. For the first time ever he was getting whole sentences out without stammering. Although his mother hadn't said anything, it was obvious she'd noticed. And been impressed. He'd felt quite wonderful, couldn't wait to see Therese again to tell her.

His confidence had increased daily. Soon he'd found he could speak openly to groups of men in the brewery like his father used to do, instead of slinking into his office and only communicating with the workers through the manager.

And when Gannons had made their approach, he'd found it surprisingly easy to make his decision – with a little help from Therese.

'Do you want really to stay in Bridelow all your life? Couldn't bear it, myself. Couldn't live here for a *week*.'

And he knew it was true. She wouldn't spend any time here. If they went for a walk, it had to be up on the moors. If they went for a drink, it had to be at some pub or club in Manchester or somewhere.

He wanted desperately to show her off, to show that stuttering Shaw Horridge could get himself a really beautiful girlfriend. But she seemed to find Bridelow beneath her.

37

'Dismal little place,' she said. 'Don't you think? I like lights and noise and people.'

So it hadn't been difficult, the decision to let Gannons have the brewery. Biggest thing he'd ever done and all over in a couple of weeks. All over before anyone in the village knew about it. *Fait accompli*.

'You'll feel better,' she said. And he had. He always did.

Sometimes the terror of what was happening would still flare and, for a moment, it would blind him. He'd freeze, become quite rigid. Like tonight, facing the oaf Manifold, who'd wanted to fight, wanted to take on stuttering Shaw, beat him publicly to the ground. Make a point in front of all his mates.

And Shaw had thought of Therese and felt his eyes grow hard, watched the effect of this on the thug Manifold.

'Start the car, Shaw,' Therese said softly.

Shaw laughed nervously, started the engine.

'Good,' she said. 'Now pull away gently. We don't want any screeching of tyres.'

It was a Saab Turbo. A black one. She'd blown the horn once and he'd known it was her.

It was a different car, but he wasn't unduly surprised; she'd often turn up in quite expensive ones. Her brother's, she'd say. Or her father's. Tonight she'd stopped the Saab in a lay-by the other side of the Moss, saying, 'I feel tired; you drive.'

'Would I be insured?'

Therese laughed a lot at that.

'Who owns it exactly?'

'How should I know? I stole it.'

'Interferin' devils.' Be unfair, perhaps, to say the old girl was xenophobic about Southerners, but . . . No, on second thoughts, it wouldn't be unfair; Ma was suspicious of everybody south of Matlock.

'Aye,' Ernie said, 'I know you don't think he should have been taken to London, but this was a find of enormous national, nay, international significance, and they *are* the experts after all.'

He chuckled. 'By 'eck, they've had him – or bits of him, anyroad – all over the place for examination . . . Wembley, Harwell. And this report . . . well, it really is rather sensational, if you ask me. Going to cause quite a stir. You see, what they did . . .'

Putting on his precise, headmasterly tone, Ernie explained how the boffins had conducted a complete post-mortem examination, submitting the corpse to the kind of specialized forensic tests normally carried out only in cases of suspicious death.

'So they now know, for example, what he had for dinner on the day he died. Some sort of black bread, as it happened.'

Ma Wagstaff sniffed, obviously disapproving of this invasion of the bogman's intestinal privacy.

'Fascinating, though, isn't it,' Ernie said, 'that they've managed to conduct a proper autopsy on a chap who probably was killed back when Christ was a lad . . . ?'

He stopped. 'What's up, owd lass?'

Ma Wagstaff had gone stiff as a pillar-box.

'Killed,' she said starkly.

'Aye. Ritual sacrifice, Ma. So they reckon. But it was all a long time ago.'

Ma Wagstaff came quite dramatically to life. Eyes urgently flicking from side to side, she grabbed hold of the bottom of Ernie's tweed jacket and dragged him well out of everybody's earshot, into a deserted corner of the forecourt. Into the deepest shadows.

'Tell us,' she urged.

The weakening sun had become snagged in tendrils of low cloud and looked for a minute as if it might not make it into the hills but plummet to the Moss. From where, Ernie thought, in sudden irrational panic, it might never rise again.

He took a few breaths, pulling himself together, straightening his jacket.

'This is not idle curiosity, Ernest.'

'I could tell that, Ma, when you were threatening to bugger up my prostate.' How much of a coincidence had it been that he'd shortly afterwards felt an urgent need to relieve himself which seemed to dissipate as soon as he stood at the urinal?

'Eh, that were just a joke, Ernest. Can't you take a joke any more?'

'From you, Ma . . .'

'But this is deadly serious,' Ma said soberly.

The sun had vanished. Ridiculously, Ernie thought he heard the Moss burp. 'All right,' he said. From the inside pocket of his jacket he brought out some papers bound with a rubber band and swapped his regular specs for his reading glasses. Be public knowledge soon enough, anyroad.

Ernie cleared his throat.

'Seems our lad,' he said, 'was somewhere around his late twenties. Quite tall too, for the time, 'bout five-five or six. Peat preserves a body like vinegar preserves onions. The bones had gone soft, but the skin was tanned to perfection. Even the hair, as we know, remained. Anyroad, medical tests indicate no reason to think he wasn't in good shape. Generally speaking.'

'Get to t'point,' Ma said irritably.

'Well, he was killed. In no uncertain manner. That's to say, they made sure of the job. Blunt instrument, first of all. Back of the head. Then, er . . . strangulation. Garotte.'

'Eh?'

'Garotte? Well . . .' He wondered if she ever had night-mares. Probably wouldn't be the usual kind if she did.

Little Benjie, Ma's grandson, had wandered across the forecourt with that big dog of his. 'Hey.' Ernie scooped a hand at him. 'Go away.'

He lowered his voice. 'They probably put a cord – leather string, sinew – around his neck and . . . inserted a stick in the back of the cord and, as it were . . . twisted it, the stick. Thus tightening the sinew around his . . . that is, fragments of the cord have been found actually embedded. In his neck.'

Ma Wagstaff didn't react like a normal old woman. Didn't recoil or even wince. 'Well?' she said.

'Well what?' said Ernie.

'Anythin' else?'

Ernie went cold. How could she know there was more to

it? He looked over her head at the bloodied sky. 'Well, seems they . . . they'd have pulled his head back . . .'

His throat was suddenly dry. He'd read this report four times, quite dispassionately at first and then with a growing excitement. But an *academic* excitement. Which was all right. Emotionally he'd remained unmoved. It had, after all, happened a good two thousand years ago – almost in prehistory.

'So the head'd be sort of pulled back . . . with the . . . the garotte.'

When they'd brought the bogman out, a little crowd had assembled on the edge of the Moss. Ernie had decided it would be all right to take a few of the older children to witness this historic event. There'd been no big ceremony about it; the archaeologists had simply cut out a big chunk of peat with the body in the middle, quite small, half his legs missing and his face all scrunched up like a big rubber doll that'd been run over. Not very distressing; more like a fossil than a corpse. They'd wrapped him in clingfilm and put him in a wooden box.

Ernie was staring into Ma Wagstaff's eyes, those large brown orbs glowing amber out of that prune of a face, and he was seeing it for the first time, the real horror of it, the death of a young man two thousand years ago.

'He'd be helpless,' Ernie said. 'Semi-concussed by the blow, and he couldn't move, couldn't draw breath because of the garotte . . .'

Ma nodded.

'That was when they cut his throat,' Ernie said hoarsely.

Ma nodded again. Behind her, out on the pub forecourt, a huge cheer suddenly went up. The new landlord must have appeared.

'You knew,' Ernie said. He could feel the blood draining out of his face. 'You *knew* . . .'

'It were the custom,' Ma Wagstaff said, voice very drab. 'Three times dead. See, Ernest, I were holding out the hope as this'd be just a body . . . some poor devil as lost his way and died out on t'Moss.' She sighed, looking very old. 'I knew really. I knew it was goin' t'be what it is.'

41

'A sacrifice?' It was growing dark.

'Not just any sacrifice. We're in trouble, Ernest.'

Sometimes Shaw wanted to say, I feel like just *being* with you is illegal.

Some mornings he'd be thinking, I've got to get out of this. I'll be arrested, I'll be ruined.

But then, all through the day, the longing would be growing. And as he changed to go out, as he looked in the mirror at his thin, pale face, his receding hairline and his equally receding jawline, he saw why he could never get out . . . not as long as there was anything she wanted from him. Not as long as he continued to change.

They drove to a country pub and parked the Saab very noticeably under a lighted window at the front, being careful to lock it and check the doors. He wondered how exactly she'd stolen it and how she'd obtained the keys, but he knew that if he asked her she would simply laugh at him.

In the pub, as usual, he couldn't prise his hungry eyes from her. She sat opposite him, wearing an old fox fur coat, demurely fastened to the neck. Shaw wondered if, underneath the coat, above (and inside) her black tights, she was naked.

With that thought, he felt his desire could lift their heavy, glass-topped, cast-iron table a good two inches from the floor.

'You could arouse the dead,' he said, almost without breath.

'Would you like to?' Therese's lips smiled around her glass of port.

'Pardon?'

'Arouse the dead?'

He laughed uncomfortably. Quite often she would say things, the meaning of which, in due course, would become devastatingly apparent.

Later, two miles out of Macclesfield town, Shaw driving again, she said, 'All right, let's get deal with this, shall we?'

'What?'

But she was already unzipping his trousers, nuzzling her

head into his lap. He braked hard, in shock, panic and uncontainable excitement. 'Yes, Shaw,' she said, voice muffled, 'you *can* stop the car.'

'Somebody . . . somebody might see us . . . you know, somebody walking past.'

'Well,' Therese said, burrowing, 'I suppose somebody might see *you* . . .'

Five minutes later, while he was still shivering, she said, 'Now let's get rid of the car.' She had the interior light on, re-applying lipstick, using the vanity mirror. Her fur coat was still fastened. He would never know if she was naked underneath it.

'How are we going to get home?'

'Taxi. There's a phone box across the road. I'll ring up for one while you're dispensing with the car.'

A shaft of fear punctured his moment of relief. 'Disp . . . ? How?'

'I seem to remember there's a bus shelter along here. What . . . about a quarter of a mile . . . ? Just take it and ram it into that.'

He just stared at her. Through the windscreen he could see high, evergreen, suburban hedges, sitting-room lights glimmering here and there through the foliage.

Shaw said weakly, 'Why don't we just leave it somewhere? Parked, you know . . .'

'Discreetly,' Therese said. 'Under a tree. With the keys in.'

'Yes,' he said inadequately.

She opened her door to the pavement, looked scornfully back at him. 'Because it wouldn't do anything for you. Your whole life's been tidy and discreet. I'm trying to help you, Shaw.'

His fingers felt numb as he turned the key in the ignition. A car slowed behind them.

'What if there's somebody in the bus shelter?'

Therese shrugged, got out, slammed the car door. Shaw dug into his jacket pocket, pulled out a handful of tissues and began feverishly to scrub at the steering-wheel and the gear-lever and the door-handle and anything else he might have touched.

He'd been doing this for a couple of minutes when a wetness oozing between his fingers told him he was now using the tissue he'd employed to clean himself up after Therese had finished with him. And they could trace you through your semen now, couldn't they, DNA tests . . . genetic fingerprinting . . . oh, no . . . Banging his forehead against the steering-wheel . . . no . . . no . . . *no* . . .

The passenger door clicked gently open.

The police. The police had been surreptitiously following them for miles. That car going slowly, creeping up . . . He'd be destroyed.

Shaw reacted instinctively. He flung open his door, threw his weight against it, hurling himself out into the middle of the road, a heavy lorry grinding past less than a couple of feet away.

Across the roof of the Saab he looked not into a police uniform but into Therese's dark, calm eyes.

'I'll be listening out,' she whispered, 'for the sound of breaking glass.'

CHAPTER III

Matt Castle was standing on the pub steps with an arm around the shoulders of Lottie, his wife. Looked a bit awkward, Ernie noticed, on account of Lottie was very nearly as tall as Matt.

Lottie Castle. Long time since he'd seen her. By 'eck, still a stunner, hair strikingly red, although some of that probably came out of a bottle nowadays. Aye, that's it, lad, Ernie encouraged himself. Think about sex, what you can remember. Nowt like it for refocusing the mind after a shock.

How had she known? Was the bogman part of the Bridelow Tradition? Was that it? By 'eck, it needed some thinking about, did this.

But not now.

'I'll stand here.' Matt Castle was smiling so hard he could

hardly get the words between his teeth. 'So's you can all hear me, inside and out. *Can* you hear me?'

'What's he say?' somebody bleated, to merry laughter, from about three yards in front of Matt. Ernie noted, rather disapprovingly, that some of this lot were half-pissed already.

'Yes, we can,' Ernie called helpfully from the edge of the forecourt.

'Thank you, Mr Dawber.'

Ernie smiled. All his ex-pupils, from no matter how far back, insisted on calling him Mr Dawber. When they'd first met, he was a baby-faced twenty-one and Matt Castle was eleven, in the top class. So he'd be fifty-six or seven now. Talk about time flying . . .

'I just want to say,' said the new licensee, shock-haired and stocky, 'that . . . well . . . it's bloody great to be back!'

And of course a huge cheer went up on both sides of the door. Matt Castle, Bridelow-born, had returned in triumph, like the home team bringing back the cup.

Except this was more important to the community than a bit of local glory. 'Looks well, doesn't he?' Ernie whispered to Ma Wagstaff, who didn't reply.

'Always wanted a pub of me own,' Matt told everybody. 'Never dared to dream it'd be *this* pub.'

The Man I'th Moss hung around him like a great black overcoat many sizes too big. Ernie hoped to God it was all going to work out. Draughty old pile, too many rooms . . . cellars, attics . . . take a bit of upkeep, absorb all the contents of your bank account by osmosis.

'To me, like to everybody else, I suppose, this was always Bridelow Brewery's pub.' Matt was dressed up tonight, suit and tie. 'We thought it always would be.'

At which point, quite a few people turned to look for Shaw Horridge, who'd long gone.

'But everything changes,' Matt said. 'Fortunes rise and fall, and this village owes the Horridge family too much not to make the effort to understand why, in the end, they were forced to part with the pub . . . and, of course, the brewery.'

We've all made the effort, Ernie thought, as others murmured. And we still don't understand why.

'Eeeh,' Matt said, his accent getting broader the more he spoke. 'Eeeh, I wish I were rich. Rich enough to buy the bloody lot. But at least I could put together enough for this place. Couldn't stand seeing it turned into a Berni Inn or summat.'

No, lad, Ernie thought. Left to rot.

'But . . . we got ourselves a bit of a bank loan. And we managed it.' Lottie Castle's fixed smile never wavering, Ernie noted, when Matt switched from 'I' to 'we' covering the money aspect.

Matt went on about how he didn't know much about running a pub but what he did know was music. They could expect plenty of that at The Man I'th Moss.

Matt grinned. 'I know there's a few of you out there can sing a bit. And I remember, when I was a lad, there used to be a troupe of morris dancers. Where'd they go to?'

'Orthopaedic hospital,' somebody said.

'Bugger off,' said Matt. 'There's to be no more cynicism in this pub, all right? Anyroad, this is open house from now on for dancers and singers and instrumentalists. If there aren't enough in Bridelow we'll ship 'em in from outside . . . big names, too. And we'll build up a following, a regular audience from the towns . . . and, brewery or no brewery, we'll make The Man I'th Moss into a going concern again.'

At which point, somebody asked, as somebody was bound to, whether Matt and his old band would get together in Bridelow.

'Good point,' Matt accepted. 'Well, me old mucker Willie's here, Eric's not far off. And I'm working on a bit of a project which might just interest . . . well, somebody we used to work with . . . eeeh, must be fifteen years ago. Late 'seventies.'

Everybody listening now, not a chink of bottle on glass or the striking of a match. Outside, the sun was just a rosy memory.

Matt broke off. 'Hey up. For them as can't see, Lottie's giving me a warning look, she thinks I should shut up about this until we know one way or t'other . . .'

Lottie smiled wryly. Ernie Dawber was thinking, What the 'eck was her name, the girl who used to sing with Matt's band

and then went off on her own? *Very* popular she used to be, or so he'd heard.

'But, what the hell,' Matt said. 'If I'm going to do this right, I'll need your help. Fact is . . . it was this business of the bogman got me going. Lottie reckons I've become a bit obsessed.' He laughed self-consciously. 'But the thing is . . . here we are, literally face to face with one of our forefathers. And it's my belief there's a lot he can teach us . . .'

Ernie Dawber felt Ma Wagstaff go still and watchful by his side.

'I mean about ourselves. About this village. How we relate to it and each other, and how we've progressed. There's summat special about this place, I've always known that.'

Moira Cairns, Ernie remembered. That was her name. Scottish. Very beautiful. Long, black hair.

'Right.' Matt bawled back over his shoulder, into the bar, 'Let's have a few lights on. Like a flamin' mausoleum in there.'

Ma Wagstaff stiffened and plucked at Ernie's jacket.

The sun wasn't ever going to get out of that low cloud, he thought. Won't know till tomorrow if it's made it to the hills or if the Moss has got it.

'By 'eck,' he said ruefully, as if his fanciful thoughts were printed on the misting, mackerel sky where Ma Wagstaff could read them, 'I'm . . .'

'Getting a bit whimsy?'

Ernie laughed through his discomfort. She made it sound like a digestive problem.

'Not before time,' Ma said. 'Never any talking to you when you was headmaster. Jumped-up little devil. Knew it all – what teacher ever don't? Still . . . better late than not. Now then, Ernest Dawber, I'll try and teach thee summat.'

He let Ma Wagstaff lead him away to the edge of the forecourt, from where terraced stone cottages plodded up to the high-towered church, a noble sentinel over the Moss.

'What do you see?'

'This a trick question, Ma?'

Now, with the sun gone, all the houses had merged. You couldn't tell any more which ones had fresh paintwork, which had climbing roses or new porches. Only a few front steps stood out, the ones which had been recently donkey-stoned so they shone bright as morning.

'To be honest, Ma, I can't see that much. Can't even see colours.'

'What *can* you see, then?'

'It's not light,' Ernie said, half-closing his eyes, 'and it's not dark. Everything's melting together.'

'Go on.'

'I can't see the individual houses. I suppose I can only see the people who live in them. Young Frank and Susan and the little lad. Alf Beckett. Millicent Gill at the Post Office . . . Gus Bibby, Maurice and Dee at the chip shop. And I suppose . . . if I look a bit harder . . .'

'Aye, you do that.'

'If I look harder I can see the people who lived in the houses before . . . The Swains – Arthur Swain and his pigeons. Alf Beckett's mother, forty-odd years a widow. I can bring them all back when I've a mind. Specially at this time of day. But that's the danger, as you get older, seeing things as they were, not as they are.'

'The trick,' said Ma, 'is to see it all at same time. As it was and as it is. And when I says "as it was" I don't just mean in your lifetime or even in my lifetime. I mean as far back as yon bogman's time.'

Ernie felt himself shiver. He pushed the British Museum papers deeper into his inside pocket. Whatever secret knowledge of the bogman Ma possessed, he didn't want to know any more.

Ma said, 'You stand here long enough, you can see it all the way back, and you won't see no colours, you won't see no hard edges. Now when you're out on t'Moss, Brid'lo don't look that welcoming, does it? All cold stone. You know that, you've written about it enough. But it's not cold to us, is it? Not when we're inside. No hard edges, no bright colours, never owt like that.'

'No.'

'Only shades,' Ma said, almost dreamily. 'Them's what's kept this place the way it is. Shades of things.'

'Shades?'

'Old colours all run together. No clashes. Know what I'm telling you, Ernest?'

'Harmony?' Ernie said. 'Is that it? Which is not to say there's no bickering, or bits of bad feeling. But, fundamentally, I s'pose, Bridelow's one of those places where most of us are happy to be. Home. And there's no defining that. Not everybody's found it. We're lucky. We've *been* lucky.'

'Luck?' Something was kindling behind Ma's eyes. Eighty-five if she was a day and still didn't need glasses. '*Luck*? You don't see owt, do you?' Ernie'd had glasses full-time since he was thirty-five. 'What's it got to do wi' luck?'

'Just a figure of speech, Ma.'

'Balls,' said Ma. 'Luck! What this is, it's a balancing act. Very *complicated* for t'likes of us. Comes natural to nature.'

Ernie smiled. 'As it would.'

'Don't you mock me, Ernest Dawber.'

'I'm sorry, Ma.' She was just a shade herself now, even her blue beret faded to grey.

'Beware of bright, glaring colours,' she said. 'But most of all, beware of black. And beware of white.'

'I don't know what you mean.'

'You will,' said the little old woman. 'You're a teacher.' She put a hand on his arm. 'Ernest, I'm giving you a task.'

'Oh, 'eck.'

'You've to think of it as the most important task you've ever had in your life. You're a man of learning, Ernest. Man wi' authority.'

'Used to be, Ma. I'm just a pensioner now . . .' Like you, he was going to say, then he noticed how sad and serious she was looking.

'Get that man back.'

'Who?' But he knew. 'How?' he said, aghast.

'Like I said, Ernest. Tha's got authority.'

'Not that kind of authority, for God's sake.'

*

Nobody there. He swallowed. Nobody. Not in or near the bus shelter.

It was on his nearside, which was no good, he might get hurt, so he drove further along the road, reversing into someone's drive, heading back slowly until he could see the glass-sided shelter, an advertisement for Martini on the end panel, lit up like a cinema screen in the headlights: a handsome man with wavy hair leaning over a girl on a sofa, topping up her glass.

He was mentally measuring the distance.

What am I *doing*? *What am I bloody doing?*

I could park it just here. Leave it. Walk away. Too far, anyway, for her to hear the impact.

In his mind he saw Therese standing by the telephone kiosk, about to phone for a taxi. In his mind she stopped. She was frowning. She'd be thinking what a miserable, frightened little sod he was.

He *could* say there *had* been somebody in the bus shelter, two people. Get angry. Was he supposed to kill them? Was he supposed to do that?

But she would know.

He stopped the car, the engine idling. The bus shelter had five glass panels in a concrete frame. The glass would be fortified. He would have to take a run at it, from about sixty yards.

If he didn't she would know.

He remembered the occasions she'd lost her temper with him. He shivered, stabbed at the accelerator with the car in neutral, making it roar, clutching the handbrake, a slippery grip. Too much to lose. Gritting his teeth until his gums hurt. *Too much to lose.*

And you'll feel better afterwards.

Took his foot off. Closed his eyes, breathed rapidly, in and out. The road was quiet now, the hedges high on either side, high as a railway embankment.

Shaw backed up twenty or thirty yards, pulled into the middle of the road. Felt his jaw trembling and, to stiffen it, retracted his lips into a vicious snarl.

He threw the Saab into first gear. Realized, as the stolen car spurted under him, that he was screaming aloud.

On the side of the bus shelter, the handsome man leaned over the smiling girl on the sofa, topping up her glass from the bottle. In the instant before the crash, the dark, beautiful girl held out the glass in a toast to Shaw before bringing it to her lips and biting deeply into it, and when she smiled again, her smile was full of blood.

You'll feel . . . *better*.

The big lights came on in the bar and were sluiced into the forecourt through the open door where Matt Castle stood grinning broadly, with his tall red-haired wife. Behind them was the boy – big lad now, early twenties, must be. Not one of Ernie's old pupils, however; Dic had been educated in and around Manchester while his dad's band was manhandling its gear around the pubs and clubs.

'Happen he *will* bring a bit of new life,' Ernie said. 'He's a good man.'

'Goodness in most of us,' Ma Wagstaff said, 'is a fragile thing, as you'll have learned, Ernest.'

Ernie Dawber adjusted his glasses, looked down curiously at Ma. As the mother of Little Willie Wagstaff, long-time percussionist in Matt Castle's Band, the old girl could be expected to be at least a bit enthusiastic about Matt's plans.

Ma said, 'Look at him. See owt about him, Ernest?'

Matt Castle had wandered down the steps and was still shaking hands with people and laughing a lot. He looked, to Ernie, like a very happy man indeed, a man putting substance into a dream.

Lottie Castle had remained on the step, half inside the doorway, half her face in shadow.

'*She* knows,' Ma Wagstaff said.

'Eh?'

'I doubt as she can see it, but she knows, anyroad.'

'Ma . . . ?'

'Look at him. Look hard. Look like you looked up t'street.'

Matt Castle grinning, accepting a pint. Local hero.

'I don't understand,' said Ernie Dawber. He was beginning to think he'd become incapable of understanding. Forty-odd years a teacher and he'd been reduced to little-lad level by an old woman who'd most likely left school at fourteen.

Ma Wagstaff said, 'He's got the black glow, Ernest.'

'*What?*'

On top of everything else she'd come out with tonight, this jolted Ernie Dawber so hard he feared for his heart. It was just the way she said it, like picking out a bad apple at the greengrocer's. A little old woman in a lumpy woollen skirt and a shapeless old cardigan.

'What *are* you on about?' Ernie forcing joviality. Bloody hell, he thought, and it had all started so well. A real old Bridelow night.

'Moira?' Matt Castle was saying. 'Aye, I *do* think she'll come. If only for old times' sake.' People patting him on the shoulder. He looked fit and he looked happy. He looked like a man who could *achieve*.

'The black glow?' Ernie whispered. 'The *black glow?*'

What had been banished from his mind started to flicker back: images of the piper on the Moss over a period of fifteen, twenty years. Echoes of the pipes: gentle and plaintive on good days, but sometimes sour and sometimes savage.

'Black glow?' his voice sounding miles away.

Ma Wagstaff looked up at him. 'I'm buggered if I'm spelling it out for thee.'

PART THREE

BOG OAK

From *Dawber's Book of Bridelow*:

BRIDELOW MOSS IS A two-miles-wide blanket of black peat. Much of its native vegetation has been eroded and the surface peat made blacker by industrial deposits – although the nearest smut-exuding industries are more than fifteen miles away.

Bisected by two small rivers, The Moss slopes down, more steeply than is apparent, from the foothills of the northern Peak District almost to the edge of the village of Bridelow.

In places, the peat reaches a depth of three metres, and although there are several drainage gullies, conditions can be treacherous, and walkers unfamiliar with the Moss are not recommended to venture upon it in severe weather.

But then, on dull wet days in Autumn and Winter, the gloomy and desolate appearance of the Moss would deter all but the hardiest rambler . . .

CHAPTER I

OCTOBER

With the rain hissing venomously in their faces, they pushed the wheelchair across the cindered track to the peat's edge, and then Dic lost his nerve and stopped.

'Further,' Matt insisted.

'It'll sink, Dad. Look.'

Matt laughed, a cawing.

Dic looked at his mother for back-up. Lottie looked away, through her dripping hair and the swirling grey morning, to where the houses of Bridelow clung to the shivering horizon like bedraggled birds to a telephone wire.

'Mum . . . ?'

In the pockets of her sodden raincoat, Lottie made claws out of her fingers. She wouldn't look at Matt, even though she was sure – the reason she'd left her head bare – that you couldn't distinguish tears from rain.

'Right.' Abruptly, Matt pushed the tartan rug aside. 'Looks like I'll have to walk, then.'

'Oh, Christ, Dad . . .'

Still Lottie didn't look at the lad or the withered man in the wheelchair. Just went on glaring at the village, at the fuzzy outline of the church, coming to a decision. Then she said tonelessly, 'Do as he says, Dic.'

'Mum . . .'

Lottie whirled at him, water spinning from her hair. 'Will you just bloody well *do it*!'

She stood panting for a moment, then her lips set hard. She thought she heard Dic sob as he heaved the chair into the mire and the dark water bubbled up around the wheels.

The chair didn't sink. It wouldn't sink. It wouldn't be easy to get out, even with only poor, wasted Matt in there, but it wouldn't sink.

Maybe Matt was hoping they wouldn't *have* to get it out. That he'd be carried away, leaving the chair behind, suspended skeletally in the Moss, slowly corroding into the peat or maybe preserved there for thousands of years, like the Bogman.

'Fine,' Matt said. 'That's . . . fine. Thanks.'

The chair was only a foot or so from the path, embedded up to its footplate in Bridelow Moss. Dic stood there, tense, arms spread, ready to snatch at the chair if it moved.

'Go away, lad,' Matt said quietly. He always spoke quietly now. So *calm*. Never lost his temper, never – as Lottie would have done – railed at the heavens, screaming at the blinding injustice of it.

Stoical Matt. Dying so well.

Sometimes she wished she could hate him.

It was Sunday morning.

As they'd lifted Matt's chair from the van, a scrap of a hymn from the church had been washed up by the wind-powered rain, tossed at them like an empty crisp-packet then blown away again.

They'd moved well out of earshot, Lottie looking around. Thinking that on a Sunday there were always ramblers, up from Macclesfield and Glossop, Manchester and Sheffield, relishing the dirty weather, the way ramblers did. If it belonged to anybody, Bridelow Moss belonged to the ramblers, and they made sure everybody knew it.

But this morning there were none.

The bog, treacle-black under surface rust, fading to a mouldering green where it joined the mist. And not a glimmer of anorak-orange.

As if, somehow, they knew. As if word had been passed round, silently, like chocolate, before the ramble: avoid the bog, avoid Bridelow Moss.

So it was just the three of them, shadows in the filth of the morning.

'Go on, then,' Matt was saying, trying to pump humour into his voice. 'Bugger off, the pair of you.'

Lottie put out a hand to squeeze his shoulder, then drew

back because it would hurt him. Even a peck on the cheek hurt him these days.

It had all happened too quickly, a series of savage punches coming one after the other, faster and faster, until your body was numbed and your mind was concussed.

I don't think I need to tell you, do I, Mrs Castle.

That he's going to die? No. There were signs . . . Oh, small signs, but . . . I wanted him to come and see you weeks . . . months ago. He wouldn't. He has this . . . what can I call it . . . ? Fanatical exuberance? If he felt anything himself, he just overrode it. If there's something he wants to do, get out of his system, everything else becomes irrelevant. I did try, doctor, but he wouldn't come.

Please – don't blame yourself. I doubt if we'd have been able to do much, even if we'd found out two or three months before we did. However, this business of refusing medication . . .

Drugs.

It's not a dirty word, Mrs Castle. If you could persuade him, I think . . .

He's angry, doctor. He won't take anything that he thinks will dull his perceptions. He's . . . this is not anything you'd understand . . . he's reaching out for something.

'Go on,' Matt said. 'Get in the van, in the dry. You'll know when to come back.'

And what did he mean by *that*?

As they walked away, the son and the widow-in-waiting, she saw him pull something from under the rug and tumble it out into his lap. It looked, in this light, like a big dead crow, enfurled in its own limp wings.

The rain plummeted into Matt's blue denim cap, the one he wore on stage.

Dic said, 'He'll catch his dea—'

Stared, suddenly stricken, into his mother's eyes.

'I don't understand any more,' he said, panicked. 'Where he is . . . I've lost him. Is that . . . I mean, is it any place to be? In his state?'

'Move.' Lottie speaking in harsh monosyllables. 'Go.' The

only way she could speak at all. Turning him round and prodding him towards the van.

'Is it the drugs? Mum, is it the drugs responsible for this?'

Lottie climbed into the van, behind the wheel. Slammed the door with both hands. Wound the window down, keeping the rain on her face. She said nothing.

Dic clambered in the other side. He looked more like her than Matt, the way his dark red hair curled, defying the flattening rain. Matt didn't have hair any more, under his blue denim cap.

'Mum?'

'No,' Lottie said. 'There's no drugs. Listen.'

It was beginning.

Faint and fractured, remote and eerie as the call of a marsh bird, familiar but alien – alien, now, to *her*.

But not, she was sure, to the Moss.

She saw that Dic was crying, helpless, shoulders quaking. An aggressive thing, like little kids put on: I can't cope with this, I *refuse* to cope . . . take it away, take it *off* me.

She couldn't. She turned away, stared hard at the scratched metal dashboard, blobbed with rain from the open window.

Because she didn't understand it either. Nor, she was sure, was she meant to. Which hurt. The sound which still pierced her heart, which had been filtered through her husband, like the blood in his veins, for as long as she'd known him and some years before that.

It had begun. For the last time?

Please, God.

She looked out of the window-space, unblinking, cheeks awash.

Fifty yards away, hunched in the peat, bound in cold winding-sheets of rain, the black bag under his arm like a third lung . . .

. . . Matt Castle playing on his pipes.

Eerie as a marsh bird, and all the birds were silent in the rain.

The tune forming on the wind and falling with the water, the notes pure as tears and thin with illness.

Dic rubbed his eyes with his fingers. 'I don't know it,' he

said. 'I don't know this tune.' Petulant. As if this was some sort of betrayal.

'He only wrote it . . . a week or so ago,' Lottie said. 'When you were away. He said . . .' Trying to smile. 'Said it just came to him. Actually, it came hard. He'd been working at it for weeks.'

Lament for the Man, he'd called it. She'd thought at first that this was partly a reference simply to their pub, The Man I'th Moss, adrift on the edge of the village, cut off after all these years from the brewery.

But no. It was another call to *him*, wherever he was. As if Matt was summoning his spirit home.

Or pleading for the Man to summon him, Matt.

'I can't stand this,' Dic said suddenly. Dic, who could play the pipes too, and lots of other instruments. Who was a natural – in his blood too, his dad more proud than he'd ever admit, but not so proud that he'd encouraged the lad to make a profession of it.

'Christ,' said Dic, 'is this bloody suicide? Is it his way of . . . ?'

'You know him better than that.' Figuring he just wanted a row, another way of coping with it.

'It's not as if he's got an audience. Only us.'

'Only us,' Lottie said, although she knew that was wrong. Matt believed – why else would he be putting himself through all this? – that there had to be an audience. But, it was true, they were not it.

'All right, what if he dies?' Dic said sullenly, brutally. 'What if he dies out there now?'

Lottie sighed. What a mercy that would be.

'What I mean is . . . how would we even start to explain . . . ?'

She looked at him coldly until he subsided into the passenger seat.

'Sorry,' he said.

The piping was high on the wind, so high it no longer seemed to be coming from the sunken shape in the wheelchair, from the black lung. She wondered if any people could hear it back in Bridelow. Certainly the ones who mattered wouldn't be able to, the old ones, Ma Wagstaff, Ernie Dawber. They'd be in church. Perhaps Matt had chosen his time well, so they wouldn't hear it, the ones who might understand.

Dic said, 'How long . . . ?'

'Until he stops. You think this is easy for me, Dic? You think I believe in any of this flaming stupid . . . Oh, my God!'

The piping had suddenly sunk an octave, meeting the drone, the marsh bird diving, or falling, shot out of the sky. Lottie stopped breathing.

And then, with a subtle flourish of Matt's old panache, the tune was caught in mid-air, picked up and sent soaring towards the horizon. She wanted to scream, either with relief and admiration . . . or with the most awful, inexcusable kind of disappointment.

Instead she said, briskly, 'I'm going to call Moira tonight. I've been remiss. I should have told her the situation. He wouldn't.'

Dic said, 'Bitch.'

'That's not fair.' He was twenty, he was impulsive, things were black and white. She leaned her head back over the seat. 'I can understand why she didn't want to get involved. OK, if she'd known about his illness she'd have been down here right away, but at the end of the day I don't think that would have helped. Do you?'

The end of the day. Funny how circumstances could throw such a sad and sinister backlight on an old cliché.

Dic said, 'It would have taken his mind off his condition, maybe.'

Lottie shook her head. 'It's an unhealthy obsession, this whole bogman business.' They'd never really spoken of this. 'She'd have made things worse. She probably knew that.'

He said sourly, 'Why? You mean . . . because of his other unhealthy . . .'

Lottie suddenly sat up in the driving seat and slapped his face, hard. '*Stop it.* Stop it *now.*'

She closed her eyes on him. 'I'm tired.'

The pipes spun a pale filigree behind her sad, quivering eyelids, across the black moss where the rain blew in grey-brown gusts.

Take him, she prayed. To God. To the Man. Away.

Was this so wrong? Was it wrong, was it sinful, to pray to the Man?

God? The Man? The Fairies? Santa Claus? What did it matter?

A thrust of wind rattled the wound-down window, pulling behind it an organ trail from St Bride's, the final fragment of a hymn. It lay for a moment in strange harmony upon the eddy of the pipes.

No, Lottie decided. It's not wrong.

Take him. Please.

Anybody.

CHAPTER II

Three hours.

Three hours and he hadn't touched her. Chrissie had heard of men who paid prostitutes just to sit on the edge of the bed for half the night and listen to them rambling on about their domestic problems.

Maybe she should demand overtime.

'The other one,' Roger said, 'the one they found in Lindow, I mean, they christened him Pete Marsh. They had this instant kind of affection for the thing.'

Chrissie had been Dr Roger Hall's temporary admin assistant for nearly a fortnight and was a lot more interested in *him* than bog people. She poured coffee, watching him through the motel mirror. Unfortunately, he looked even more handsome when he was worried.

'Well, I mean, there's no way,' Roger went on, 'that I feel any kind of *affection* for *this* one. It's about knowledge.'

'So why not just let him go? After all, he must be pretty bloody creepy to have around,' said Chrissie, who shared an office at the Field Centre with a woman called Alice. She tried to imagine the situation if Alice was a corpse.

'It's not *creepy*, exactly.' Roger sat up in bed, carefully arranging the sheet over his small paunch.

'Spooks *me*,' Chrissie said, 'to be honest. And I never have to see him, thank God.'

'No, it's just . . . it's as if he knows how badly I need him. How much I need to *know* him, where he's coming from.'

'You're getting weird. You tell your wife stuff like this?'

'You're kidding. My wife's a doctor.'

That was a novel twist, Chrissie thought. My wife doesn't understand me – she's too intelligent. Chrissie didn't care for the underlying message Roger was sending out here. OK, he was tall, he had nice crinkles around his eyes, everybody said how dishy he looked on the telly. And OK, *she* was seducing *him* (with a bit of luck). But, in the end, one-to-one was the only kind of relationship Chrissie was basically interested in.

'No need to pout,' he said. 'I wasn't suggesting you were a bimbo. Just that a corpse is a corpse to Janet, regardless of its history.'

She brought him coffee. Outside, coming up to 7 p.m. on an autumn Sunday evening, traffic was still whizzing up the M6. Roger said he felt safe here: the one place he could count on people he knew not showing up was the local motor lodge. Chrissie had booked in; he'd arrived later, leaving his car on the main service area, away from any lights.

He was a very cautious man. He was supposed to be in London until tomorrow evening, on Bogman business. They were re-examining the stomach-lining or something equally yucky.

'Roger, look . . .' Chrissie lit a cigarette. 'I know how important he's been to you – for your career and everything. And I take your point about him giving the Field Centre a new lease of life – obvious we *were* being wound up, the amount of work we were actually *doing* . . . I mean, I've been wound up before.'

'I bet you have,' Roger said, looking at her tits, putting down his coffee cup. But he still didn't reach out for her.

Chrissie tried to find a smile but she'd run out of them. 'Sunday,' she said sadly.

'Didn't know you were religious.'

'I'm not.' She'd just suddenly thought, What a way to spend a Sunday evening, in a motel no more than two miles

63

from where you live. With a bogman's minder. 'Do you touch him much?'

'You make it sound indecent. Of course I touch him. He feels a bit like a big leather cricket bag. You should pop in sometime, be an experience for you.'

Chrissie shuddered.

He grinned. 'Not that you'd get much out of it. He hasn't got one any more.'

'What, no . . . ?'

'Penis.'

Chrissie wrinkled her nose. 'Dissolved or something?'

'No, they must have chopped it off. And his balls. Part of the ritual.'

'Oh, yucky.' Chrissie wrapped her arms around her breasts and eased back into bed, bottom first.

'What I like best about your body,' Roger said, not moving, 'is that it's so nice and pale. All over.'

'Actually, I had quite a deep tan in the summer. Still there, in places.'

'Not as deep as *his* tan, I'll bet. That's what you *call* being tanned. Literally. Tanned and pickled. It's what it does to them. The acids. I like you. You're pale.'

It's not healthy, Chrissie thought, the way he brings everything back to that ancient thing. It's like 'Love me, love my bogman'. Oh, well . . . 'Roger,' she said hesitantly, looking at the gap between them, probably just about the size of the bloody bogman. 'Can I ask you something . . . ?'

'Sure,' he said tiredly, 'but if you want me to do anything complicated, you'll have to . . .'

'Don't worry. I just want to know something about you and . . . *him* . . . Just to clear the air. Then maybe we can relax. Thing is, there've not been all that many bogmen found, have there? All right, that Pete Marsh, and before him a bunch of them in Denmark. But when one's discovered in this country, it's still a major find, isn't it?'

'In archaeological terms, he's worth more than the average Spanish galleon, yes.'

'Hot property.'

'Very.'

'So what,' said Chrissie very slowly, 'is he *really* doing in a little-known university field centre behind a school playing-field in the North of England? Why did the British Museum experts and all these London people . . . why did they let you bring him back?'

Roger's eyes closed in on one another. This is where he starts lying, Chrissie deduced. The more university degrees a man had, she'd discovered, the more hopeless he was at concealing untruths.

'What I mean *is*,' she said, airing the bits of knowledge she'd rapidly absorbed from the Press cuttings file, 'they like to keep these things, don't they? They go to Harwell and Oxford for this radiocarbon dating, and then . . .'

'Well, he's been to Harwell. He's been to Oxford. And he's been to the British Museum.'

'And he's come back,' said Chrissie. 'Why's that?'

The Archdeacon poured himself a cognac, offered the bottle to the Rev. Joel Beard but wasn't entirely surprised when Joel declined.

Only we poor mortals have need of this stuff, the Archdeacon thought. He's above all such vices.

Sadly, he thought.

Between them on the leather three-seater Chesterfield sat a shining white dome, like a strange religious artefact.

It was Joel's crash-helmet.

He's deliberately placed it between us, the Archdeacon thought. He's heard about me. 'And so you know the place quite well, I gather,' he said hoarsely. 'You know Hans. And his family.'

'Well, I remember his daughter, Catherine,' Joel said. 'A wilful girl.'

All right, thought the Archdeacon. So you're one hundred per cent hetero. I can take a hint, damn you.

He edged back into his corner of the Chesterfield and looked into his drink, at the pictures on the wall, out of the window at the bare front garden, sepia under a Victorian streetlamp. Anywhere but at Golden Joel, the diocesan Adonis.

'Of course,' Joel said, 'he's been in better health.'

'Erm . . . quite. And it isn't, you know, that we think he's *failing* in some way. He's been an excellent man. In his time. He's a very . . . *tolerant* man. Perhaps that's part of the problem. Ah . . . not that I'm *decrying* his tolerance . . .'

The Archdeacon snatched a sip of his brandy. Oh dear. Why did he let Joel Beard do this to him?

Joel smiled. Or at least he exposed both rows of teeth. 'Look, perhaps I can clarify some of this, Simon. I don't think tolerance *is* such a fundamental virtue any more. I think we've been tolerant for so long that it looks as if . . . I mean, what, increasingly, is the public's idea of a typical Anglican clergyman?'

You dare, you brute, the Archdeacon thought. You *dare* . . .

'A ditherer,' said Joel. 'An ineffectual ditherer.'

'Oh.' The Archdeacon relaxed. 'Quite.'

'There's a big game going on, you know, Simon. We – the Church – ought to be out there. But where are we?'

'Ah . . . where indeed?'

'We aren't on the pitch. We aren't even on the touchline.'

'Perhaps not.'

'We're in the clubhouse making the bloody tea,' said Joel Beard.

'Well, I . . .'

'There's real evil about, you know. It's all around us and it's insidious. A burglary somewhere in Britain every thirty seconds or so. An assault. A rape. A husband beating his wife, sexually abusing his small children. We talk of social problems. Or if we use the word evil, it's *social* evil . . . We're making excuses for them and we're excusing ourselves. When I was a gym teacher . . .'

Oh, please . . . The Archdeacon saw beneath the cassock to the tensed stomach and the awesome golden chest.

'. . . before every rugby lesson, there'd be the same pathetic collection of little notes. "Dear Sir, Please excuse my son from games, he has a minor chest infection." This sort of nonsense. Same ones every other week. The wimps. Well, I'm afraid that's what *we* look like sometimes. "Dear People, Please excuse me from confronting Satan this week, but my steeple's developed stone-fatigue and I have to organize a garden party." This is what we've come to. We've reached the point where we're ashamed to wield the weapons forged for us by God.'

The Archdeacon refused to allow himself to contemplate the weapon God had forged for Joel Beard. He took a mouthful of cognac and held it there while Joel talked of the Church's manifest obligation to confront the Ancient Enemy again. Lord, but he was a magnificent sight when fired-up – that profile, hard as bronze, those rigid golden curls . . .

Upstairs, in his 'files', the Archdeacon kept seven photocopies of the famous picture of Joel in the *Sheffield Star* – the one of him brandishing his outsize pectoral cross. At the time this dramatic pose had only reinforced the Diocesan consternation expressed when Joel, still at college, had been on local radio threatening physical disruption of certain Hallowe'en festivities planned by the university students' union.

The Archdeacon had managed to placate the Bishop, who'd been suggesting immediate efforts ought to be made to interest this turbulent mature student in a period of foreign missionary work – the Colombian jungles or somewhere equally dangerous. Known his type before, the Bishop fumed. More trouble than they're worth, these self-publicists. Nonsense, said the Archdeacon. With respect, men like Beard must be considered the Church's Future . . . if the Church is to have one.

During these discussions about his future, Joel had apparently received a series of telephone calls alerting him to inbred evil in a small village in the Southern Pennines.

Anonymous, of course. But weren't they always? And wasn't the Archdeacon himself becoming just a little tired of Hans Gruber, the old-fashioned rural priest treading his own sheep-tracks, totally immersed in his parish, oblivious to the Diocese?

'. . . mustn't be afraid to get *physical*.' Joel thumped the back of the Chesterfield, and the Archdeacon almost fainted. 'Or, indeed, *meta*physical . . .'

'Well, then . . .' The Archdeacon's hand was shaking so much he had to put down his glass. 'If you're determined to face this thing head-on, we'll delay no longer. There's just this question of accommodation in Bridelow. Not had a curate for so long we let the house go.'

'I understand,' said Joel, 'that there's accommodation in the church itself.'

'In the ch . . . ? You don't mean this . . . priest's hole sort of place under the floor? You're not serious.'

'Well,' said Joel. 'Short-term, I see no reason why not. It was originally intended as emergency accommodation for visiting clergy, I gather. And how often does a priest get the opportunity to experience a night in the House of God?'

'Quite,' said the Archdeacon. 'Quite.' He was remembering the old story about an itinerant Bishop of Sheffield a century or so ago, who'd spent a night under the church at Bridelow and was supposed to have gone potty. Silly story. But still, was it wise for Joel to sleep down there? Alone?

The Archdeacon tingled.

Finally Chrissie said, 'Admit it, you're getting a bit obsessed.'

'That's ridiculous.' Not much conviction *there*. 'I'm just . . . stressed, that's all. I'm not good at deception.'

'No, you're not.'

'I meant with Janet. Look, would you mind putting that thing out.' He reached over her, took the cigarette from between her fingers and dropped it in an ashtray on the bedside ledge.

Well!

'Honestly, it's not an obsession,' he said. 'Not the way you think. Look, I'll tell you, OK. But you've got to keep it to yourself. Not a word, OK? Thing is, I've . . . I've had approaches.'

'Lucky you.' When, a few minutes ago, he'd put a hand experimentally on her thigh, it had felt like a lukewarm, wet sponge.

He said, 'When you were young . . .'

'Thank you very much, Roger.'

'No, no . . . I mean, when you were a child . . . Did you ever read Stanage's books?'

'Sta . . . Oh, *John Peveril* Stanage.' She felt a mild stirring of interest; not his usual type of stultifying archaeological tome. 'Well, who didn't?'

'He wanted to see me,' Roger said. 'Or rather he wanted me to go and see him.'

'Good God, is he still alive?'

'Very much so. Not yet sixty, I'd guess. 'Course, he's been a published writer since his early twenties, which makes him . . .'

'Very rich, I suppose,' Chrissie said.

'You wouldn't know it to see where he lives – end of one of those run-down Georgian terraces in Buxton. Sort of seedy – palatial inside, but I'm assured he's loaded. You remember much about his stuff?'

'I wasn't much of a reader,' Chrissie admitted. 'But you didn't need to be much of a reader to get into his books. Really exciting . . . and *interesting*, you know? Because they were usually about places we knew. King Arthur in Manchester, I remember that one – *Castle Fields*, it was called. I think. That right?'

'That's right.'

'And *The Bridestones*!' Chrissie sat up in bed. 'Gosh, yes. And *Blue John* . . . *Blue John's Way*? God, I remember when I was . . .'

'Yes, thank you, Chrissie. Anyway, turns out Stanage is quite a serious antiquarian, in an *amateur* sort of way. Obsessed for a long time with the Celtic history of the North-West – albeit in a fanciful, *mystical* fashion.' Roger sniffed. 'So naturally he's quite excited about our friend from the peat.'

God, Chrissie thought. Another one. What is it with this corpse?

'. . . and he's talking about establishing some sort of foundation . . . through the University . . . to set up an official Celtic museum . . . Keep this under your hat, won't you, Chrissie?'

I'm not wearing a bloody hat, she thought. I'm not wearing anything, in case you haven't noticed.

'. . . with the bog body as a centrepiece.'

'Oh.' She was starting to see. 'Money?'

'*Big* money,' said Roger. 'And Stanage's foundation would also support continued research, which would . . .'

'Keep us all in work.'

'To say the least. So, naturally, I'm keeping him to myself. We're going to work out the logistics of it between us and then present a complete package, an arrangement nobody – not the University, nor the British Museum – can afford to turn down.'

'And what does *he* get out of it? Stanage? I mean, what does the great man get out of dealing exclusively with you and keeping it all under wraps until you're ready to turn it to your advantage?'

'Er . . . He just likes being in on it, I think,' Roger said, trying to look as if this aspect hadn't occurred to him before. 'He gets access to the bogman pretty much whenever he wants.'

Which explained why Roger had been so keen to bring the body back to the Field Centre. Chrissie gave him a wry look he didn't appear to notice.

'So I'm having to keep all these balls in the air . . . juggle Stanage, the University, the British Museum . . . and now those sodding Bridelow people, who want the bloody thing *put back*!'

'Sorry?' Chrissie had been thinking ruefully about balls in the air. 'Who wants it back?'

Roger snorted. 'They're superstitious. We know that our friend . . . *him* . . . that he was sacrificed for some reason. Maybe to persuade the gods to keep the Romans at bay, after the Celts were driven out of the fertile lowlands of Cheshire and Clwyd and into the hills.'

'Barbaric times,' Chrissie said, thinking of Arnold Schwarzenegger in skins and a headband.

'So – incredible as it may seem that serious archaeological research in this day and age should still be complicated by this kind of crap – it appears some people in Bridelow feel that by taking the thing away we'll bring bad luck down on the village. As simple and as primitive as that.'

'Sort of like Tutankhamun's tomb?'

'If you like.'

Chrissie wanted to laugh. It was *pre*-Schwarzenegger. More

70

like one of those old Hammer films, Peter Cushing as Roger Hall.

'Keep getting pestered by this man Dawber. Who, admittedly, was quite useful at first. Used to be head teacher at the local school. Sort of . . . amateur historian.'

Roger said the words 'amateur historian' like other people would say 'dog turd'.

'Oh, of course, I know him,' Chrissie said. 'Mr Dawber. Tubby little chap. Rather cute. I suppose you think he's an eccentric, whereas Stanage . . .'

'Stanage *knows*,' Roger said strangely. He seemed to remember his coffee. It was cold. He put the cup down. Looked uncomfortable. 'Dawber's trouble. He says we should – get this – now we've done all our tests and found out everything we can, we should put the thing back in Bridelow Moss, in a secret location of *their* choosing – this is the bloody villagers – on the scientific basis that if the peat has preserved him for two thousand years it's probably the best way of keeping him in good nick for another two thousand . . .'

He laughed bitterly. 'The crackpot elements you have to deal with when you unearth something that catches the public imagination.'

Oh, you'll deal with crackpots, Roger, Chrissie thought. You'll deal with crackpots if there's something in it for you.

After about half an hour, Roger tried again.

Disastrously.

Stress, he explained. The stress of keeping your balls in the air.

They lay in the dark and talked some more. Talked about her ex-husband, who drank. Talked about his wife, who was brilliant and capable and seemed to power an entire hospital on an average of twenty-eight hours' sleep per week.

Talked about him, Roger . . . and him, *him*.

'Look . . . what I said about Stanage . . . forget it, will you? Forget I even mentioned Stanage.'

'All right,' Chrissie said.

A few minutes later, with a stagnant kind of sweat on his

forehead, Roger said to the ceiling, 'Sometimes . . . when Janet's on nights at the General . . . I wake up in the early hours, feeling really sort of cold and clammy.'

Which didn't exactly augur well, Chrissie thought, for the next few hours.

'And you know . . . I can almost feel it in the bed with me. Lumps of it.'

Jesus. She said, 'Lumps?'

'Peat. Lumps of peat.' Roger slid a damp and hopeless hand along her left thigh. 'That's stress for you.'

CHAPTER III

CENTRAL SCOTLAND

The Earl's place was nineteenth-century Gothic, a phoney Dracula's Castle with a lofty Great Hall that stank, the American thought, of aristocratic bullshit, domination and death.

He could tell the woman hated it too. Especially the skulls. Or maybe she had something else on her mind. She was worried; he could tell that much. Still, he wasn't about to miss this opportunity.

He'd kept glancing at her over dinner at the long baronial table, a couple of hours ago. All that wonderful long black hair, with the single streak of grey. He'd never seen her before, not in concert, not even on TV, but he knew the face from the album covers, and he'd know the voice.

She was standing alone over by the doorway, frowning at the gruesome trophies on the walls. Not talking to anyone, although there were people all around her, expensively dressed people, crystal glasses hanging from their fingers like extra jewellery.

He supposed she'd be a couple years older than he was, which only added to that mysterious, lustrous glamour. Pretty soon she'd pick up her guitar, take her place on the central dais to sing for them all. Which didn't leave him much time.

What he needed was a neat, elegant opening line. Kind of imagining – her general aura being so magical – that one would come naturally.

He carried his glass across, stood alongside her, following her gaze around the overloaded walls.

He said, 'Uh . . .'

And followed up with something so dumb he could only hope to attribute it to the impact of fifteen-year-old malt on an uncultured brain.

'Impressive, huh?' he said.

She looked at him. Coldly. Looked at him like she was thinking, Yeah, well you *would* have to be impressed by this kind of Victorian shit. Where you come from, pal, this most likely is what passes for ancient, right?

'After its fashion,' she said mildly.

From the middle of a cluster of people, the Earl was watching them. Or rather, watching *him*, because he was American and therefore could maybe buy this place and everything else of its kind between here and Pitlochry many times over.

The Earl was a sleek man, English all the way down to the tip of his sporran. But the Earl wanted to be a real Celt and no doubt was counting on the American wanting that too, all the way down to the deepest part of his wallet.

A discreet buff-coloured card, handed to him several weeks ago by his mother – who also, unfortunately, was his boss – had said:

THE CELTIC BOND: A major conference of politicians and poets, writers, broadcasters and business people, to establish an international support-mechanism for the regeneration of a submerged European culture. Hosted, at his Scottish family seat, by . . . .

'Shit,' he'd said in some dismay. 'You're kidding, aren't you?'

She wasn't. Since she lost the use of her legs, the single most important element in his mother's life had become her Scottish ancestry. 'We are Celts, Mungo,' she'd say. 'Above all, never forget *that*.' By which she meant *her* side of the family; hence he bore *her* family name rather than that of his long-gone, long-forgotten father.

'If I can say this,' he said now, politely, trying to recover some credibility, 'you don't seem too relaxed.'

'No?' She wore a long, black dress, very plain. He could sense no perfume.

'I mean I can't imagine you'd be nervous about performing.'

She wasn't looking at him. She was still looking at the heads. Huge sets of antlers protruding from bleached fragments of skull, all over three walls, from just above head-height to within a couple of feet of the lavishly moulded ceiling.

'And I guess you aren't the nervous kind, anyway,' he said. 'So . . .'

Wherever you sat, the remains of three or four dozen butchered stags were always in view. On the central wooden dais, where she'd sit to sing, she'd probably feel herself constricted by some kind of grisly necklace of bone.

Gross.

'I was just wondering,' she said at last, when it must have been clear he wasn't about to go away, 'why people should think this is really such an essential part of being a Celt. Killing things for fun and showing off about it.'

A good word popped up in the American's head, like somebody had flashed him a prompt-card.

'Pantheistic,' he said. 'The old Celts were highly pantheistic. So I'm told.'

'That means they had *respect* for animals,' she said scornfully. She had a soft Scottish voice but not too much of an accent. 'A bit like your Red Indians.'

'Native Americans.' He smiled. 'To be politically and ethnically correct.' The smile was supposed to say, I may be devilishly attractive, with my untamed curly black hair, this cool white tuxedo, thistle in the buttonhole. But you can trust me. I'm a sincere guy. 'Can I get you another drink?'

'No,' she said. 'No, thank you.'

'I . . . ah . . .' He hesitated. 'I have a couple of your albums.'

'Oh?' She didn't seem too interested. 'Which ones?'

'Well, uh, my favourite, I guess, is still the one you did with The Philosopher's Stone. That'd be quite some years ago.'

'Oh.' She glanced away, as if looking for someplace else to put herself.

'Uh, I also have your first solo album,' he said quickly. 'How I recognized you. From the sleeve. You haven't changed.'

'Oh, I've changed, believe me. Look, I . . .'

'You never did cut your hair, though,' he said, urbanely displaying his knowledge of the album's prime cut.

'What?'

'"Never let them cut your hair,"' he quoted, '"or tell you where . . ."' Listen, I . . . I just wanted to say it's real good to meet you . . . Moira. No one said you'd be here. Makes me glad I came after all.'

She said, 'I'm a last-minute replacement. For Rory McBain. He's sick. We have the same agent.'

A flunkey needed to come past with a tray of drinks, and he took the opportunity to manoeuvre her into a corner, unfortunately under two pairs of huge yellowing antlers. He said, 'Listen, that album – with the Stone – it had some magic.'

'He has bronchitis,' Moira said.

'Huh?'

'Rory McBain.'

He smiled. 'See, when I hear you sing, it always sounds to me like . . .'

'That album,' she said with an air of finality, 'was a mistake. I was too young, too stupid, and I never should have left Matt Castle's band.'

'Huh?'

She shook her head, wide-eyed, like she was waking up.

'Matt Castle?' He had his elbow resting on a wooden ledge below another damned antlered skull.

'He was . . . He was just the guy who taught me about traditional music when I was a wee girl. Look, I don't know why I said that, I . . .'

Her poise wavered. She looked suddenly confused and vulnerable. Something inside of him melted with pure longing while something else – something less admirable but more

75

instinctive – tensed like a big cat ready to spring. The album cover hadn't lied. Even after all these years, she was sensational.

'Traditional music,' he said, looking into her brown eyes. 'That's interesting, because that's all you do these days, right? You used to write all your own songs, and now you're just performing these traditional folksongs, like you're feeling there's something that old stuff can teach you. Is that this, uh, Matt Castle? His influence?'

'I . . . no . . . No, Matt was a long time ago, when I was in Manchester. He . . . Look, if you don't mind . . .'

He was losing her. He couldn't bear it. He tried to hold her eyes, babbling. 'Manchester? That's the North of England? See, why I find that interesting, this guy was telling us, at the conference this afternoon, how the English are the least significant people – culturally, that is – in these islands. Unlike the Scottish, the Welsh, the Irish, the English are mongrels with no basic ethnic tradition . . .'

She smiled faintly. 'Look, I'm sorry, I—'

'See, this guy, this Irish professor – McGann, McGuane? – he said there was nothing the English could give us. Best they could do is return what they took, but it's soiled goods. At which point this other guy, this writer . . . No, first off it was this Cornish bard, but he didn't make much sense . . . *then*, this writer – Stanton? Stanhope? – he's on his feet, and is he *mad* . . . This guy's face is *white*. I thought he was gonna charge across the room and bust the first guy, the professor, right in the mouth. He's going, Listen, where I come from we got a more pure, undiluted strain of, uh, heritage, tradition . . . than you'll find anywhere in Western Europe. And this guy, this Stanfield, he's from the North . . .'

Moira Cairns said, 'I'm sorry, I really do have to make a phone call.'

And she turned and glided out of the doorway, like the girl in the Irish folksong who went away from this guy and mov'd through the fair.

'. . . the North of England,' the American said to the stag's head.

This wasn't a *new* experience, a woman walking away from

76

him, but it was certainly rare. You blew it, he told himself, surprised.

She could feel him watching her through the doorway, all the way down the passage.

Was he the one?

She took a breath of cool air. The man was a fanatic. Probably one of those rich New Yorkers bankrolling the IRA. Surely there was some other unattached female he could find to sleep with tonight. Why were fanatics always promiscuous?

And was he the one whose examination she could feel all over her skin, like she was being touched up by hands in clinical rubber gloves?

'Phone?' she said to a butler-type person in the marble-tiled hallway.

'Next to the drawing room, madam, I'll take you.'

'Don't bother yourself, I'll find it.'

Dong.

She'd found herself, for no obvious reason, while this smoothie American was trying to come on to her, hearing the name Matt Castle, then saying it out aloud apropos of nothing . . . and then . . .

Dong.

This was the *dong*. The hollow chime. Not the *tink*, not the *ping*.

Aw, hey, no, please . . .

The phone turned out to be in the room where she'd left her guitar, where it would be safe – the black case lying in state, like a coffin, across two Jacobean chairs. Safe here, she'd thought, surely. This is a *castle*. But she'd take it with her when she'd made her call.

She stood in front of the phone, picked it up and put it back a couple of times. She didn't know who to ring.

Malcolm. If in doubt, call Malcolm. She was planning, anyway, to strangle the bastard for tonight. 'You'll enjoy it,' he'd insisted. 'You'll find it absolutely fascinating. Rory's mortified.'

She rang him at home in Dumbarton. 'Malcolm,' she said,

'I may never convince myself to forgive you for this. I may even cast about in the shark-infested waters you inhabit for a new agent.'

He didn't say a word. Had he heard all this before from her? More than once? Was she becoming querulous? Creeping middle age? She felt tired, woozy. She shook herself, straightened her back, raised her voice.

'Listen, there are so-called Celts here not only from Ireland and Wales and Brittany, but from Switzerland and Italy – with Mafia connections, no doubt – and America and some wee place nudging up to Turkey. And they are – to a man, Malcolm – they are a bunch of pretentious, elitist, possibly racist wankers.'

'Racism?' Malcolm said. 'I thought it was about money. EC grants. Minority languages. EC grants. Cultural exchanges. More EC grants . . .'

'Aye, well . . .'

'Is it not a good fee for you?'

'Is it the same fee as Rory's fee would've been?'

'Oh, Moira, come now . . .'

'Forget it. Listen, the real reason I disturbed you on the sabbath . . .'

'Not my sabbath, as it happens.'

'. . . is my answering-machine is on the blink and I suspect someone's trying to get hold of me, and it's no' my daddy because I called him.'

'Nothing urgent I'm aware of, Moira, don't you worry your head.'

'No messages?'

'None at all.' He paused. 'You aren't feeling unwell again, are you?'

'I'm fine.' Her left hand found the guitar case, clutched at it. She had that feeling again, of being touched. She shivered. She felt cold and isolated but also crowded in, under detailed examination. Too many impressions: the hollow chime, the eyes, the touch – impersonal, like a doctor's. Too much, too close. She had to get out of here.

'It's none of my business, of course,' said Malcolm, who

78

believed in the Agent's Right to Know, 'but what was it exactly that made you think someone wanted to contact you?'

'Just a feeling.'

'Just a *feeling*?'

'Aye,' she said wearily. There was nothing touching her now. The room was static and heavy, no atmosphere. The furniture lumpen, without style. A museum. Nothing here.

Nothing . . . right?

He said, 'You are a strange, witchy woman, Moira.'

'Malcolm,' Moira said. 'Go fuck yourself, huh?'

From *Dawber's Book of Bridelow*:

RELIGION (i)

BRIDELOW IS DOMINATED by the ancient church dedicated to St Bride and built upon a small rise, thought to be the remains of the 'low' or burial mound from which the village gets the other half of its name.

The tower is largely Norman, with later medieval embellishments, although there was considerable reconstruction work to this and to the main body of the church in the eighteenth and nineteenth centuries. The clock was added to the tower following a donation by the Bridelow Brewery in 1889 and was subsequently illuminated, enhancing the role of the tower as a 'beacon' for travellers lost on Bridelow Moss. The churchyard offers a spectacular view over the Moss and the surrounding countryside, which, to the rear, gives way to a large tract of moorland, uninhabited since prehistoric days.

CHAPTER IV

During evensong, though he still didn't know quite what had happened with Matt, the Rector said a short prayer for the dying landlord of The Man I'th Moss.

Holding on to the lectern, eyes raised to the bent and woven branches of the Autumn Cross, he said carefully, 'Grant him strength, O Lord, and . . . and a peaceful heart.'

Not sure quite what he meant, but he felt it was the right thing to say; you learned to trust your instincts in Bridelow. Sure enough, several members of the congregation looked up at him, conveying tacit approval. Briefly, he felt the warmth of the place again, the warmth he'd always remember, a quite unexpected warmth the first time he'd experienced it.

Unexpected because, from the outside, the church had such a forbidding, fortress-like appearance, especially from a distance, viewed from the road which traversed the Moss. He remembered his first sight of the building, close on thirty years ago. Not inspiring, in those days, for a novice minister: hard and grey-black with too many spiky bits and growling gargoyles. And Our Sheila perpetually playing with herself over the porch.

This was the 1960s, when what a young clergyman dreamed of was a bright, modern church with a flat roof and abstract stained-glass (after ten years, it would look like a lavatory block, but in the sixties one imagined things could only get better and better).

'Amen,' the congregation said as one. The old schoolmaster, Ernest Dawber, glanced up at the Rector and gave him a quick, sad smile.

The warmth.

Sometimes it had seemed as if the church walls themselves were heating up under the pale amber of the lights – they were old gas-mantles converted to electricity, like the scattered streetlamps outside. And at Christmas and other festivals, it felt as though the great squat pillars either side of the nave had become giant radiator pipes.

But the warmth was rarely as apparent now. The Rector wondered if it would even be noticeable any more to a newcomer. Perhaps not. He'd gone to the expense of ordering more oil for the boiler and increasing the heat level. Knowing, all the same, as he went through the motions, that it couldn't be that simple.

There'd been a draught in the pulpit today; he certainly hadn't known that here before. The draught was needle-thin but it wasn't his imagination because, every so often, the Autumn Cross would sway a little over his head, rustling.

It rustled now, as he read out the parish notices, and something touched his hair, startling him. When he reached up, his fingers found a dead leaf. It crackled slightly, reminding him of the furious flurry of leaves blasted against his study window at dusk, like an admonishment: *you must not watch us . . . you must turn your face away*.

A strikingly cold autumn. October frost, nearly all the trees gone bare. His arthritis playing up.

Giving him a hard time tonight. Difficult keeping his mind on the job, wanting only to get it over and limp back to his study – even though, since Judy's death, this had become the loneliest place of all.

'. . . and on Wednesday evening, there'll be a meeting of the morrismen in the Function Room at The Man, that's 7.30 . . .'

The congregation numbered close on seventy tonight, not a bad turnout. A few regular faces missing, including several members of the committee of the Mothers' Union, but that wasn't too surprising, they'd been here this morning. Couldn't expect anyone to attend twice, even the Mothers.

He rounded off the service with a final hymn, accompanied as usual by Alfred Beckett on the harmonium – a primitive, reedy sound, but homely; there'd never been an organ in Bridelow Church, despite its size.

'Well done, lad,' Ernie Dawber said at the church door, patting his shoulder. 'Keep thi chin up.' Fifteen years his senior, Bridelow born and bred, Ernie Dawber had always called him 'lad'. When the Rector had first arrived, he'd expected a few problems over his name. It had still seemed too close to the War for the locals not to be dubious about a new minister called . . .

'. . . Hans Gruber,' the schoolmaster had repeated slowly, rolling it round his mouth like a boiled sweet.

'Yes.'

'That's German, isn't it?'

Hans had nodded. 'But I was actually born near Leighton Buzzard.'

Ernie Dawber had narrowed his eyes, giving the new minister a *very* hard look. 'Word of advice, lad. Keep quiet about that, I should. Thing is . . .' Glancing from side to side. '. . . there's a few folks round here who're not that keen on . . .' dropping his voice, '. . . southerners.'

The Rector said now, thinking of his lonely study, 'Come back for a glass, Ernie?'

'I don't think so, lad.' Ernie Dawber pulled on his hat. 'Not tonight.'

'I'll never forgive you for this.'

He was gripping the stiffened edge of the sheet like a prisoner clutching at the bars of his cell, his final appeal turned down.

'We should never have let you go home, Mr Castle,' the nursing sister said.

'Matt, please . . .' Lottie put her cool hand over his yellowed claw. 'Don't say that . . .'

'You never listen.' Feebly shaking his head, inconsolable.

All the way here in the ambulance, Lottie holding his hand, he'd been silent, away somewhere, still on the Moss perhaps.

His eyes shone with the tears that wouldn't come, no moisture left in his body.

The nurse said, 'I think he should have some sleep, don't you, Mrs Castle?'

'Sleep?' Matt was bleakly contemptuous. 'No real sleep in here. Comes out of the bloody . . . drug cabinet . . . only sort of sleep you can get in here.' He looked past the nurse. 'Where's Dic?'

'I told you, Matt,' Lottie said gently. 'He wouldn't come in. He's too confused. He's probably walking round the grounds, walking it off. He'll come in tomorrow, when he's . . .'

'Might be too late, tomorrow.'

Lottie smiled at him. 'Don't be soft.' There was a small commotion behind her, a nurse and a young porter putting screens around a bed opposite Matt's.

'Another one gone,' Matt grunted.

'Bath-time, that's all,' the nurse said unconvincingly.

'Give you any old crap in here. Look, tell Dic . . .' His faltering voice forming words as dry and frail as an ancient cobweb. '. . . Tell him, he can be in the band. If he wants to. When . . . when Moira comes, he can play. But you won't, will you? You never do owt I say.'

'You tell him,' Lottie said. 'Tell him when you see him in the morning.'

Matt Castle made no reply. He seemed too dehydrated to sweat or to weep. It was as though somebody had talcumed his face, like a . . .

Lottie swallowed hard.

'Useless . . . bitch.'

Matt fell asleep.

Shrivelled leaves, unseen, chattered on the window-pane.

The dead leaves said, *Go away, draw the curtains, put on the light.*

It's not your affair, the dead leaves said.

The Rector didn't move, just as he hadn't moved in the late afternoon, at dusk, when the warning flurry had hit the pane, as if flung.

At the top end, the vicarage garden almost vanished into the moor. When the light faded, the low stone wall between them dissolved into shadow and the garden and the moor became one. On the other side of the wall was a public footpath; it was along this they came, and sometimes, over the years, around dusk, the Rector had seen them, had made himself watch them.

Tonight, resting up before evening service, sitting in the window of the darkening study, wedged into a hard chair, his swollen foot on the piano stool, he'd watched three of them enter the churchyard from the footpath, passing through the wooden wicket gate. They were black, shapeless, hooded and silent. A crescent moon had wavered behind smoky cloud.

It was all over, though, as was usual, when he walked out across his garden, through the gate and into the churchyard half an hour before the evening service.

Now he was back in his study, listening to the leaves with the lights out. All he could see through the window was the reflection of two bars of the ineffectual electric fire. When Judy, his wife, was alive there'd been a coal fire in the study every night from the end of September until the end of April.

The Rector was cold. Eleven years now since Judy's death.

Where had all the warmth gone, the warmth which before had only increased with the drawing-in of the days? Where had the smiles gone, the smiles which lit the eyes while the mouths stayed firm?

And why, for that matter, had Ma Wagstaff's herbal preparation had so little effect this time on his arthritis?

He stood up, hobbled close to the window, cupped his hands to the pane and peered through.

At the garden's edge, a few graves lurched giddily on the slope, and then the church loomed like an enormous black beast. Lately, Hans Gruber had been wondering if life would not have been a good deal simpler in one of those modern churches, where one's main headache was glue-sniffing behind the vestry. Us and Them. Good and evil. God and Satan.

Hans thought, Wouldn't that be wonderful?

After his wife had left, they'd wheeled Mr Castle's bed into a side ward where, unless anyone was brought in suddenly, he'd be alone, until . . .

'Until morning,' the young nurse whispered, reassuring herself.

Mr Castle was sleeping. She was glad; she was still afraid of people who were dying, who were in the actual process of it. She wasn't yet sure how to talk to them, how to *look* at them. And the awful suspense – what it would be like, the atmosphere in this small, comparatively quiet space, in the moment, the very second when *it* happened.

She was never going to get used to this. She was supposed to comfort the dying, but more often than not it was the dying who comforted her – old ladies, all skin and bone and no hair, patting her hand, one actually saying, *Don't worry, luv, I won't keep you long*.

Less bothered, it often seemed, than she was. Sometimes it was like they were just waiting for a bus.

She sat at the desk by the door, under the angled, metal-shaded lamp, the only light in the room. There were four beds on the side ward, three of them empty. It was the only part of this hospital where you could usually count on finding a couple of spare beds, it being the place where terminal patients were often brought in the final stages so they wouldn't distress other patients who were not quite so terminal.

Tamsin, the other nurse, a year or two older, was out on the main ward. Sister Murtry would pop in occasionally, see they were all right.

Sister Murtry had been very firm with Mrs Castle, who was a tall, strong-looking woman – only Sister Murtry would have dared. 'Come on now, he needs his sleep and you need yours.' . . . Mr Castle waking up suddenly and chuckling in a ghastly, strangled way when she said *he* needed sleep.

(She looked across now at his face on the pillow; his skin

was like cold, lumpy, wrinkled custard. He wasn't so very old: fifty-seven, it said on his chart, not even elderly.)

'Will you be sure to . . .' Mrs Castle had been in the doorway. Sister Murtry's hands on her shoulders, pushing her out.

'Yes, I'll ring you myself if there's any change. But there probably won't be, you know . . . Just go and get your sleep, or we'll be seeing you in here too . . .'

She imagined Mrs Castle lying wide awake in a cold double bed, waiting for the phone to ring. The wind howling outside – they lived up by Bridelow Moor, didn't they? The wind always howled up there.

He was quite a famous man, Mr Castle. There'd been dozens of Get Well cards when he was in last year for tests and things. Dr Smethwick, the registrar, who was a folk music fan, had been thrilled to bits to have him in. 'Pioneer of the Pennine Pipes,' she remembered him saying, and Dr Burt had said, dry as a stick, 'Oh, he works for the Water Authority, does he?' And she'd rushed out, scared to giggle because she was still a student then, and Dr Smethwick was senior to Dr Burt.

Dr Smethwick had moved on, to a better job in Liverpool. Now there was nobody left who knew anything about Mr Castle or the Pennine Pipes. All he had tonight was her, and she was afraid of him because he was dying.

She wondered how many folk had died here, in this small space, over the years. Passed away, they still preferred you to say that to the relatives. She said it to herself.

Passssed . . . awayyyy. Soft, like a breath of air.

She jumped. Mr Castle had released a breath of air, but it wasn't soft. It was . . . *phtttt* . . . like a cork popping out of a bottle or like a quiet fart (one of the regular noises of the night here).

'Mr Castle . . . ?' Whispering, rising rapidly to her feet with a rustle of the uniform, bumping her head on the edge of the metal lampshade.

'All right, Mr Castle . . . Matt.' A hairgrip, dislodged by the lamp, fell to the desk, she felt her hair coming loose at the back. 'I'm here.'

But when she reached the bedside he was breathing normally again – well, not *normal* normal, but normal for a man who . . . for a man in his condition.

Holding her hair in place with one hand, the grip in her teeth, she went into the main ward to collect her mirror from her bag.

Plenty breathing out here, and snoring, and a few small moans, everything hospital-normal. Up the far end of the ward, Tamsin was bending over Miss Wately's bed, Miss Wately the retired headmistress who wouldn't be called by her first name, which was Eunice. Tamsin straightened up, saw her and raised a hand to her lips, tilting her head back as if the hand held a cup.

She nodded and smiled and pointed over her shoulder to the side ward, and Tamsin nodded and held up five fingers.

'Ger . . . yer owd bugger . . .' an old man rasped in his sleep. It was supposed to be a mixed ward but because of the attitude of patients like Miss Wately, the men tended to be at one end and the women at the other. Best, really, at their age. No kimono-style dressing-gowns and baby-doll nighties on this ward.

She found the mirror, slipped it into her pocket, went back into the side ward and sat down, her eyes moving instinctively from bed to bed, four beds, all empty.

'Moira?'

All *empty*.

'Oh!' She spun round, her hair unravelling down below her shoulders.

He said, 'You've come then, eh?'

God help us, he was hanging over her . . . like bones in pyjamas.

'Mr Ca—'

What was holding him up? She'd seen his legs, his muscles all wasted, gone to jelly. Been in a wheelchair weeks and weeks, they'd said to watch him, he might even die in the night, and here he was *standing up*, oh God, his lips all pulled back and frozen into a ric-rictus?

'Tam . . .' trying to shout for the other nurse, but her voice was so dry the name just dropped out of her mouth like a piece of chewing gum '. . . sin.' Hardly heard herself.

His eyes were far back in his head, black marbles, like the eyes had already died.

Then one of his hands reached out, it was all shrivelled and rigid, like a chicken's foot, and he started . . . he started playing with her hair, pulling it down and fingering it, looking down at it in his fingers, mumbling, *Moira . . . Moira*.

Eventually she managed to say, 'I'm not your wife, Mr . . . Mr Castle . . .'

But remembered Sister Murtry saying, 'Her name's Charlotte, I think.' And then, later, 'Come on, Charlotte, let's be having you, can't stay here all night. Not good for either of you.'

She couldn't move. The metal bars on the bedheads made hard shadows on the walls, the little ward was like a cage. If only Sister Murtry would come now, bustling in, short and dynamic. Nobody Sister Murtry couldn't handle.

Oh, God, this was the wrong job, she hated dying people, their stretched skin, their awful smell, especially this one – the damp stench of ripe, putrid earth (the grave?). She began to shiver and tried to stand up, drawing back, away from him, but there was nowhere to go, her bottom was pressed into the edge of the desk, and Mr Castle was still hanging over her like a skeleton in a rotting sack and smelling of wet earth.

How could he smell of earth, of *outside*?

'Tam . . . sin . . .' Her scream was a whisper, but her mouth was stretched wide as his greenish chickenfoot hand whipped out and seized her throat.

CHAPTER V

CENTRAL SCOTLAND

The scuffed sixteen-year-old Ovation guitar, with its fibreglass curves, was a comfort. Its face reflected the great fire blazing on the baronial hearth.

'Ladies of noble birth . . .' Adjusting the microphone. 'In those days, they didn't have too much of a say in it, when it came to husbands. This is . . .' thumbing an A-minor, tweaking the top string up a fraction, '. . . this is the story of a woman who's found herself betrothed to a titled guy much younger than she is. However . . .' gliding over a C, 'I doubt if we're talking toy-boys, as we know them. This is like . . . nine or ten, right?'

Tuning OK. 'I mean, you know, there's a limit to the things you can get from a boy of nine or ten.'

No reaction. You bastard, Malcolm. And you, Rory McBain – one day you really will be sick.

'Anyway, she's stuck with this kid. And she's standing on the castle walls, watching him playing down below, working out the dispiriting mathematics of the situation and wondering if . . .'

Shuffling on the stool, tossing back the black wings of her hair, the weight of it down her back pulling her upright so that she could see the audience and the gleaming stag skulls all around. The walls of neatly dressed stone, with spotlit banners and tapestries. The black eye-holes in the skulls, and the eyes of the conference delegates looking, from five or so yards away, just as opaque and unmoving.

'Anyway, don't expect a happy ending, OK? This is a traditional song. You don't get many happy endings in traditional songs. It's called . . . "Lang a-growin"'.'

The bastard McBain would have handled this better. For the sake of ethnic credibility, he'd do a couple of songs in the Gaelic, of which he understood scarcely a word. What *she* had these days was a different kind of credibility: sophistication, fancy nightclub ethnic, low and sultry vocals, folk tunes with a touch of jazz guitar, strictly rationed to what she could handle without fracturing a fingernail.

'He's young . . .' Hearing her own voice drifting vacuously in the air, the words like cigarette smoke. '. . . but he's daily . . . growin' . . .'

Over an hour ago, she'd called Lottie's number. A guy answered, obviously not the boy, Dic. The guy'd said Lottie was at the hospital in Manchester. Muffled voices in the background – this was a pub, right? She'd asked no more questions. She'd call back.

The hospital. In Manchester. Oh, hell.

The Great Hall was huge, the acoustics lousy. When the song was over, applause went pop-pop-pop like a battery of distant shotguns. The stags' heads gathered grimly below the ceiling, so many that the antlers looked to be tangled up. 'Splendid,' she heard the Earl call out magnanimously. How many wee staggies did you pop yourself, my lord, your grace, whatever? Maybe you invited members of the Royal Family to assist. Traditional, right?

Moira did a bit of fine tuning on the guitar. She was wearing the black dress and the cameo brooch containing the stained plaid fragment that was reputed to have been recovered from a corpse at Culloden. Credibility.

'This song . . . You may not know the title, most of you, but the tune could be slightly familiar. It's . . . the lament of a girl whose man's gone missing at sea and she waits on the shore accosting all the homecoming fishermen as they reach land. The song's called "Cam Ye O'er Frae Campbelltoon". It's, er . . . it's traditional.'

Traditional my arse. Me and Kenny Savage wrote it, still half-pissed, at a party in Kenny's flat in 1982 – like, Hey, I know . . . how about we invent a totally traditional Celtic lament . . .

She told them, the assembled Celts, 'The chorus is very simple . . . so feel free to join in . . .'

And, by Christ, they *did* join in. Probably with tears in their eyes. All these Scots and Irish and Welsh and Bretons and the folk from the wee place up against Turkey . . . writers and poets and politicians united in harmony with a phoney chorus composed amidst empty Yugoslav Riesling bottles at the fag end of Kenny Savage's Decree Absolute party in dawn-streaked Stranraer.

What a sham, eh? I mean, what am I *doing* here?

And Matt Castle dying.

Tears in her own eyes now. Last year he'd told her on the phone that he'd be OK, the tests had shown it wasn't malignant. And she'd believed him; so much for intuition.

The damn tears would be glinting in the soft spotlight they'd put on her, and the Celtic horde out there, maudlin with malt, would think she was weeping for the girl on the shore at Stranraer – and weeping also, naturally, for the plight of Scotland and for the oldest race in Europe trampled into the mud of ages.

'Thank you,' she said graciously, as they applauded not so much her as themselves, a confusion of racial pride with communal self-pity.

And that makes it nine songs, over an hour gone, coming up to 10.30. Time to wind this thing up, yeh? Lifting the guitar strap out of her hair. Let's get the hell out of here.

At which point someone called out smoothly, 'Would it be in order to request an encore?'

She tried to smile.

'Maybe you could play "The Comb Song"?'

It was him. It would have to be. The New York supplier of Semtex money to the IRA.

'Aw, that's just a kiddies' song.' Standing up, the guitar-strap half-off.

'Well, I don't know about the other people here,' the voice said – and it was *not* the American, 'but it's the song I most associate with you, and I was rather disappointed not to hear it.'

'Oh, hell, it's a good long time ago, I don't think I even remember the words . . .' Who the fuck was this?

'If you go wrong, I'm sure we could help you out.' She couldn't make out his face behind the spotlight. She looked up, in search of inspiration, but her gaze got entangled in antlers.

'Also,' she said miserably, 'it isn't exactly traditional. And it's awful long. See, I don't want to bore your friends here . . .'

'Miss Cairns . . .' The Earl himself took a step towards the dais, into the spotlight, the light making tiny dollar-signs in his eyes. 'I doubt if any of us could *possibly* be bored by any of your songs.' A touch of threat under the mellifluousness? Some flunkey had replaced the empty Guinness glass by her stool with a full one. She picked it up, put it down again without drinking. There were murmurings.

What the hell am I going to do now? She felt their stares, the more charitable ones maybe wondering if she was ill. Aw, *shit . . .*

What she didn't feel any more were the eyes of the Watcher. This had maybe been a mistake. Sometimes you made mistakes. It probably had been the American and it probably was no heavier than lust.

'I warn you,' Moira said, as the Ovation's strap sank back into her shoulder, 'this is the longest song I ever wrote.'

And to the accompaniment of a thin cheer from the floor her fingers found the chord, and she sang the rather clumsy opening lines. Trying not to think about it, trying to board up her mind against all those heavyweight memories tramping up the stairs.

> *Her father works with papers and with plans,*
> *Her mother sees the world from caravans . . .*

The song telling the story of this shy, drab child growing up in the suburbs of a staid Clydeside town with the ever-present feeling that she's in the wrong place, that she really ought to be some other person. Bad times at school, no friends. Brought up at home by the grandmother, restrictive, old-fashioned Presbyterian.

> *I wish to God you hadna been born,*
> *Your hair's a mess, get it shorn,*
> *Get it shorn . . .*

Then the song becoming a touch obscure – one night, around the time of her adolescence, the child seems to be in this dark wood, when the moon breaks through the clouds and the trees, and she finds she's holding . . . this curious, ancient comb. It's a wonderful magic comb and apparently is the key to the alternative reality which for all these years has been denied to her. She runs it through her hair and becomes electrified, metamorphoses into some kind of beautiful princess. Fairytale stuff.

> *. . . She sees herself in colours and*
> *She weighs her powers in her hand . . .*

Dead silence out there. She had them. Oh, it had its magic, this bloody song which intelligent people were supposed to think was all allegorical and the comb a metaphor for the great Celtic heritage. Most likely this was how the American saw it, and the other guy who'd demanded the song.

A bastard to write, the words wouldn't hang together – sign of a song that didn't want to be written.

The song knew from the start: some things are too personal. Chorus:

> *Never let them cut your hair*
> *Or tell you where*
> *You've been,*
> *Or where you're going to*
> *From here . . .*

Couple of twiddly bits which, after all these years, she fluffed. Then dropping down to minor key for the main reason she hadn't wanted to perform this number, the creepy stuff, the heavy stuff.

> *And in the chamber of the dead*
> *Forgotten voices fill your head . . .*

Sure, there they are . . . tinny little voices, high-pitched, fragmented chattering, like a cheap transistor radio with its battery dying. Tune it in, tune it in.

Who is this? Who is it?

No.

No, no, NO!!!!!!!!!!!!!!!!!!

Oh, shit, please, don't die, Matt, don't die on me now . . . you have no *right* . . .

Singing on, through her wild tears, an awed silence in the room like a giant cavern, hall of ages, caged in bones. You think you know this song, these words, Mr New York Irishman . . . ?

> *. . . for the night is growing colder*
> *and you feel it at your shoulder . . .*

Icy-bright singing now, purged of that phoney, Guinnessy growl. One or two women out there shivering and reaching for their cardigans. The song rippling across the night sky, down the dark years, and you're watching its wavering passage from a different level, like an air traffic controller in a tower late at night. Something flying out to meet it, on a collision course.

> *Give up, you fool, there is no heat.*
> *The Abyss opens up beneath your feet . . .*

Here he is again, uncertainly into the spotlight, looking around. Hello again, Earl, something wrong is there, my lord, your grace . . . ? Is it cold for you in here? Will you get some servant to turn up the heating, throw more peat on the fire? And all the while, will you listen to these wee voices, chattering, chattering, chattering . . .

> *The comb is ice, it's brittle, oh,*
> *You cannot hold it, must let go . . .*

Yes, let it go. It's a trinket, it's worthless, it takes your energy. Let it drift. Let the night have it. Let . . .

These – Christ – these are not my words. These are somebody else's words.

I'm singing somebody else's goddamn words!

And the comb is being pulled away now in a deceptively soft silver haze, gently at first, just a tug. Then insistent, irritable – *let it come, you bitch* – and slender hands, slender like wires, scalpelling into her breast. Feeling delicately – but brutally and coldly, like a pathologist at an autopsy – for her emotional core, for the centre of her.

somebody . . .

In a frenzy, she's letting go of the song, she's groping wildly at the air, feeling her spirit straining in her body as the big lights come on, huge shimmering chandeliers.

Moira has fallen down from the stool.

She's lying twisted and squirming on the carpeted dais, both arms wrapped around the guitar. From miles away, people are screaming, or is it *her* screaming at *them* . . . Stop it! Catch it! Don't let it go from here! Help me! Help me!

She can hear them coming to help her, the army of her fellow-Celts. But they can't get through.

They can't get through the walls of bone.

The walls of jiggling, swelling bone. Not just the skulls any more; the plaster's fallen from the walls and the walls are walls of bone, whole skeletons interlocking, creaking and twisting and the jaws of the skulls opening and closing, grisly grins and a clacking laughter of teeth, right up against her face. She's trapped, like a beating, bloody heart inside a rib-cage.

She sees the comb and all it represents spinning away until it's nothing but a hairline crack of silver-blue. She watches it go like a mother who sees her baby toddling out of the garden gate into the dust spurting from the wheels of an oncoming articulated lorry.

Mammy!

But you can't hear me, can you, mammy? The connection's broken.

I'm on my own.

But no.

There is a man.

A tall, thin man, with a face so white it might be the face of some supernatural being.

No, this is a real man. He's wearing an evening suit, a bow-tie. He has a small voluptuous mouth and an expanse of white forehead marked with greyish freckles, and the white hair ripples back from the forehead; not receding, it has always been that way. She ought to know him; he knows *her*.

And where she keeps the comb.

This person, unnoticed in the hubbub by everyone but her, is lifting the black guitar case from the steps of the dais and examining it to see how it opens. He looks at her, furiously impatient, and the air between them splinters like ice and when she tries to see into his eyes, and they are not there, only the black sockets in a face as white as any of the skulls.

Their eyes meet at last. His have projected into the sockets from somewhere. They are light grey eyes. And there's a whiteness around him, growing into arms like tree-branches above his head. No, not arms, not branches.

Antlers.

★

95

Moira shrieked, flinging the guitar away from her. It made a mangled minor chord as it rolled down the steps of the dais. She threw herself after it, headlong into the glass-spattered Guinness-sodden tartan carpet, clawing at the pair of shiny, elegant evening shoes, the air at first full of swirling, unfocused energy.

And then, for a moment, everything was still.

Most of those in the room were still seated at their tables, with drinks in front of them, the men and women in their evening wear, white shirts and black bow-ties, jewellery and silk and satin. The American half out of his seat, dark Irish hair tumbling on to his forehead. The Earl on his feet; his expression . . . dismay turning to disgust: was this woman having a *fit*? In his castle?

Everybody shimmering with movement, but nobody going anywhere.

Projector-jam.

Until the first skull fell.

It was possibly the smallest of them, so comparatively insignificant that Moira wondered briefly why anyone would have admitted to having shot it, let alone wanted to display it. She watched it happen, saw the antlers just lean forward, as if it was bowing its head, and then the wooden shield it was mounted on splintered and the poor bleached exhibit crashed seven or eight feet on to a table, crystal glasses flying into the air around it.

'God almighty!' a man blurted.

The white, eyeless head toppled neatly from the table into the lap of a woman in a wine-coloured evening dress, the antlers suddenly seeming to be sprouting from her ample Celtic cleavage.

For a whole second, the woman just looked at it, as though it was some kind of novelty, like a big, fluffy bunny popped on her knees by an admirer at a party. Her glossy red lips split apart into what appeared for an instant to be an expression of pure delight.

It was this older woman next to her, whose ornate, red-brown coiffure had been speared by an antler, she was the one who screamed first.

More of an escalating gurgle actually. Both women jerking to their feet in quaking revulsion, clutching at one another, chairs flying . . .

. . . as, with a series of sickening ripping sounds, several other skulls cracked themselves from the walls, all at once . . .

('*Look!*' Some guy grabbing the Earl by the shoulders, shaking him.)

. . . and began to descend in, like, slow motion, some so old they fell apart in the air and came down in pieces.

Moira's audience in cowering disarray. 'Stop this!' the Earl commanding irrationally, limbs jerking in spasms, semaphoring incomprehensible fear, like a spider caught in its own web. 'Stop it! Stop it *at once!*'

This tumultuous rending and creaking from all the walls. Even the great fire looking cowed, burning back, low and smoky as though someone had thrown muffling peat at it.

Next to the fireplace, this severe and heavy lady – a matriarch of Welsh-language television, it was said – just sitting there blinking, confused because her spectacles had been torn off and then trodden on by a flailing bearded man, some distinguished professor of Celtic Studies, eyes full of broken glass, one cheek gashed by a blade of bone.

And, pulling her gaze away from this carnage, in the choking maw of the great fireplace Moira thought she saw a face . . . so grey it could only have been formed from smoke. The face swirled; two thrashing arms of smoke came out into the room, as if reaching for her.

Moira whispered faintly, 'Matt?' But it was smoke, only smoke.

The butler guy weaving about helplessly in the great doorway as the stag skulls fell and fell, this roaring, spitting avalanche of white bone and splattering glass, battered heads and scored skin, people yelping, moaning, hurling themselves under collapsing tables, craving shelter from the bone-storm.

She caught the black guitar case as it fell towards her. Caught it in her arms.

Come to mammy.

She sat bewildered on the bottom step of the dais, in the refrigerated air, in the absurdly shocking mess of glass and antlers.

I have to be leaving, she thought.

Hands on her shoulders. 'You OK? Moira, for Chrissake . . . ?'

'Get the fuck off me!'

But it was only the American, Mr Semtex.

'Please . . . You OK? Here, let me take that . . .'

'No! Let it alone, will you?'

She saw the white-faced man on his knees, not six feet away. He was holding one of the skulls, a big skull, one antler snapped off halfway, ending in a savage point, a dagger of bone. There was blood on the point.

And blood welling slowly out of his left eye, blood and mucus, a black pool around the eye.

The other eye was very pale, grey going on pink. He was staring at her out of it.

Moira clutched the guitar case defiantly to her throbbing breast.

'Just hang on in there, pal,' the American said to the white-faced man. 'We're gonna get you a doctor.'

Ignoring the American, the man with the injured eye said (and later the American would swear to her that he hadn't heard this, that the guy was too messed up to speak at all) . . .

The man said, very calm, very urbane, 'Don't think, Miss Cairns, that this is anything but the beginning.'

CHAPTER VI

I n Matt Castle's band, Willie Wagstaff had played various
hand-drums – bongo-type things and what the Irish called
the *bodhran*, although Matt would never call it that; to him
it was all *Pennine* percussion.

This morning, without some kind of drum under his hands,
Willie looked vaguely disabled, both sets of fingers tapping
nervously at his knees, creating complex, silent rhythms.

Lottie smiled wanly down at him. They were sitting on
wooden stools at either end of the kitchen stove, for warmth.

'Can you finish it, Willie? Can it be done?'

Willie looked up at her through his lank, brown fringe, like
a mouse emerging from a hole in the wall. Lukewarm autumn
sunbeams danced with the dust in the big kitchen behind the
public bar. Such a lot of dust. She'd been neglecting the
cleaning, like everything else, since Matt had been bad. Now it
was over. Dust to dust.

Willie said, 'We got two or three instrumental tracks down,
y'know. The lament. It all got a bit, like . . . half-hearted, as
you can imagine. Me and Eric, we could see it weren't going to
get finished. Not wi' Matt, anyroad.'

'I want it finished,' Lottie said crisply. 'It was his last . . .
I'm not going to use the word obsession, I've said it too much.'
She hesitated. '. . . I'm not religious, Willie, you know that,
not in any . . . any respect.'

Willie gave three or four nods, his chin keeping time with
the fingers on his knees.

'But I just feel that he won't be at peace . . . that it won't
be over . . . until that music's finished.'

'Aye.' Willie's fingers didn't stop. Nerves.

'So what about Dic?' Lottie said.

'Will Dic want to do it?'

Lottie said grimly, 'He'll do it. Is he good enough?'

'Oh, aye,' Willie said without much difficulty. 'I reckon he
is. With a bit of practice, like. But really, like, what we could

do with is . . .' He beat his knees harder to help him get it out.
'. . . Moira.'

'She rang me,' Lottie said. 'Last night.'

Willie's eyes lit up, expectant. Dear God, Lottie thought,
they're all in love with her.

'Actually, it was early this morning. I mean very early.
Gone midnight. The kind of time people don't ring up unless
it's an emergency.'

'Oh,' Willie said, and his hands were suddenly still.

'She asked me about Matt. She said, was he ill? I told her,
yes, he was very ill. I told her it was close to the end. I told
her . . .' Lottie stood up and put her hands on the warm metal
covers over the hot-plates of the kitchen stove, pressing down
with both hands, hard. 'I didn't *need* to tell her.'

Willie was quiet.

'We didn't say much. She started to explain why she'd put
him off when he wrote to her. I stopped her. I said we'd discuss
it some other time.'

There was a new kind of silence in the room.

'I put the phone down,' Lottie said. 'It was about twenty-
five past twelve. I waited for a minute or two, in case Dic had
heard the phone, but he was fast asleep. I thought, I'll make
some cocoa, take it up with me. But I didn't move. I knew. I
mean, why should she suddenly ring after all these years at that
time of night? And sure enough, not five minutes had passed
and the phone rang again, and it was Sister Murtry at the
hospital. And I just said, He's gone, hasn't he?'

There was more silence, then Lottie said, 'I've not slept
since. I've just sent Dic to bed for a few hours. I'm not tired,
Willie. I'm not using up any energy – not thinking, you
know?'

Lottie sat down again. 'I shan't be staying here. Only until
it's done. His *bloody* project. I think coming back here, buying
the pub, the whole bit, that was all part of it. The project. All
I want is to draw a line under it, do you see? I mean, I hope somebody'll buy the pub, somebody sympathetic, but if not . . .'
She shrugged. 'Well, I've got to get away, regardless.'

Willie nodded. Fingers starting up very slowly. 'Um . . .
what about Moira?'

'I'm not inviting her to the funeral, that's for sure.' Lottie folded her arms, making a barrier. 'If she wants to help complete these songs, that'd be . . . I'll not be *begging*. No more of that. And another thing, Willie – tell whoever needs to be told, tell them I'm not having anything to do with these stupid . . . traditions. You know what I'm saying? Matt might've accepted it, I don't. All right?'

'Aye, all right,' Willie said, not sounding too happy. But that was *his* problem, Lottie thought. 'Yeh,' he said. 'I'll tell her.'

When Willie had gone, Lottie pushed her hands on to the hot-plate covers again, seeking an intensity of heat, needing to feel something. Something beyond this anaesthetized numbness.

Wanting pain – simple pain. Loss. Sorrow.

Not any of this confusion over the gratitude that he was gone and the wanting him back . . . but back as he used to be, before all this. Before his *project*.

A blinding sun through leafless trees ricocheted from the windscreens of cars on the forecourt. A perky breeze ruffled the flags projecting from the motel's awning and lifted tufts of Chrissie's auburn hair. She thought she probably looked quite good, all things considered.

That, she told herself, was what a good night's sleep could do for you.

Ha!

Roger Hall paused, gripping the door-handle of his Volvo Estate. Don't say it, Chrissie thought. Just don't give me that, *I still can't understand it, this has never happened to me before* . . .

He didn't. He merely put on an upside-down, pathetic grin. 'Can we try again sometime?' Eyes crinkled appealingly, full of silly morning optimism, and she felt herself falling for it – even if she knew he still wasn't telling the half of it.

'Why not,' she said, daft bitch. She squeezed his arm. 'How long will you be gone?'

'Oh, only until Tuesday. That is, I'll be back late tonight so I'll see you tomorrow morning. Have lunch together, shall we? Would that be . . . ?'

'Of course,' she said. She would have wangled the day off and gone to London with him. They'd been too close to the Field Centre last night, that was probably the problem. Too close to *him*.

'I'm really only going down there,' Roger said, 'to make sure we get all the stomach returned. Don't want them trying to pinch him back, bit by bit.'

Shut up! Just shut up about that fucking thing!

'Don't worry about it, Roger. Just drive carefully.'

As the Volvo slid away past the Exit Southbound sign, two commercial traveller types came out to their twin Cavaliers and gave her the once-over. Chrissie found herself smiling almost warmly at the younger one. It would be two years in January since her divorce.

She got into her Golf. She looked at her face in the driving-mirror and decided it could probably take a couple more years of this sort of thing before she ought to start looking for something . . . well, perhaps *semi*-permanent.

Sadly, Roger's marriage was now in no danger whatsoever. Not from her, anyway.

All the trouble he'd gone to to deceive his wife. Was that for her? Was that really all for her? And then he couldn't do it. Because of 'tension'.

She imagined him driving like the clappers to London, where he was supposed to have spent the night, and then driving determinedly back with the bogman's peaty giblets in a metal samples case.

There was his real love. And there was more to it.

After the way he'd been talking last night, she'd half-expected to wake up in the early hours to find him all wet and clammy and moaning in his sleep about lumps of the stuff in the bed.

But that hadn't happened either. Indeed, the only thing to remind her of soft, clammy peat was the consistency of Roger's dick.

Chrissie got out of the motel compound by the service entrance and drove to work.

Not to worry.

Later that morning, little Willie Wagstaff went to see his mother in her end-of-terrace cottage across from the post office.

'Need to find a job now, then,' the old girl said sternly before he'd even managed to clear himself a space on the settee. Ma was practical; no time for sentiment. Dead was dead. Matt Castle was dead; no living for Willie playing the drums on his own.

'Can't do owt yet,' Willie said. ''Sides, there's no work about.'

'Always work,' said Ma, 'for them as has a mind to find it.'

Willie grinned. Rather than see him relax for a while, Ma would have him commuting to Huddersfield or Chorlton-cum-Hardy to clean lavatories or sweep the streets.

'Devil makes work for idle hands,' she said. Her as ought to know – half the village reckoned she'd been in league with the bugger for years.

'Aye, well, I've been over to see Lottie this morning.'

'Oh aye? Relieved, was she? Looking better?'

'Ma!'

'Grief's one thing, our Willie, hypocrisy's summat else. She's done her grieving, that one.'

'I've to tell you . . .' Willie's fingers were off . . . dum, dum de-dum, side of his knees.

Ma's eyes narrowed. Her hair was tied up in a bun with half a knitting-needle shoved up it.

'Er . . .' Dum, dum, dum-di-di, dum-di-di . . .

'Gerrit out!' Ma squawked.

'No messing about,' Willie mumbled quickly. 'Lottie says, none of that.'

'What's that mean?' Making him say it.

'Well, like . . . well, naturally he'll be buried in t'church-yard. First one. First one since . . .' His fingers finding a different, more complicated rhythm. 'What I'm saying, Ma, is, do we *have* to . . . ? Does it have to be Matt?'

103

Ma scowled. She had a face like an over-ripe quince. She wore an old brown knee-length cardigan over a blue boiler-suit, her working clothes. The two cats, one black, one white, sat side-by-side on the hearth, still as china. Bob and Jim. Willie reckoned they must be the fourth or fifth generation of Ma's cats called Bob and Jim, and all females.

Willie liked his mother's cottage. Nothing changed. Bottles of stuff everywhere. On the table an evil-looking root was rotting inside a glass jar, producing a fluid as thick as Castrol. Comfrey – known as knitbone. And if it didn't knit your bones at least it'd stop your back gate from squeaking.

'Rector come round,' Ma told him. 'Said was I sure I'd given him right stuff for his arthritis.'

'Bloody hell,' said Willie. 'Chancing his arm there.'

'No, he were right,' said Ma surprisingly. 'It's not working. Never happened before, that hasn't. Never not worked, that arthritis mixture. Leastways, it's always done *summat*.'

She reached down to the hearth, picked up an old brown medicine bottle with a cork in it; Ma didn't believe in screw-tops. 'Full-strength too. Last summer's.'

Willy smiled slyly. 'Losing thi touch, Ma?'

'Now, don't you say that!' His mother pointing a forefinger stiff as a clothes-peg. 'Think what you want, but don't you go saying it. It's not lucky.'

'Aye. I'm sorry.'

'Still . . .' She squinted into the bottle then put it back on the hearth behind Bob or Jim. 'You're not altogether wrong, for once.'

'Nay.' Willie shook his head. 'Shouldn't've said it. Just come out, like.'

'I'm not what I was.'

'Well, what d'you expect? You're eighty . . . three? Six?'

'*That's* not what I'm saying, son.'

Ma's brown eyes were calm. She still didn't need glasses, and her eyes did wonderful things. In Manchester, of a Saturday, all dolled up, she could still summon a waitress in the café with them eyes, even when the waitress had her back turned. And Willie had once seen this right vicious-looking street-gang part clean down the middle to let her through; Ma had sent the eyes in first.

But now the eyes were oddly calm. Accepting. Worrying, that. Never been what you might call an accepter, hadn't Ma.

'*None* of us is what we was this time last year,' Ma said. 'Ever since yon bogman were took . . .'

'Oh, no,' Willie stood up. 'Not again. You start on about that bogman and I'm off.'

'Don't be so daft. You know I'm right, our Willie. Look at yer fingers, drummin' away, plonk, plonk. Always was a giveaway, yer fingers.'

'Nay,' Willie said uncomfortably, wishing he hadn't come.

'I'm telling you, we're not protected same as we was.' Ma Wagstaff stopped rocking. 'Sit down. Get your bum back on that couch a minute.'

Willie sat. He was suddenly aware of how dim it was in the parlour, despite all the sunlight, and how small it was. And how little and wizened Ma appeared. It was like looking at an old sepia photo from Victorian times. Hard to imagine this was the fiery-eyed old woman who'd blowtorched a path through a bunch of Moss Side yobboes.

'We've bin protected in this village,' Ma said. 'You know that.'

'I suppose so.'

'We're very old-established, y'see. Very old-established indeed.'

Well, this was true. And the family itself was old-established in Bridelow, at least on Ma's side. Dad had come from Oldham to work at the brewery, but Ma and her ma and her ma's ma . . . well, that was how it seemed to go back, through the women.

'But we've let it go,' Ma said.

Willy remembered how upset she'd been when her grand-daughter, his sister's lass, had gone to college in London. Manchester or Sheffield would've been acceptable, but London . . . *It's too far . . . ties'll be broken. She'll not come back, that one . . .*

He said, 'Let it go?'

105

Ma Wagstaff leaned back in the rocking-chair, closing her eyes. 'Aye,' she said sadly. 'You say as you don't want to hear this, Willie, but you're goin t'ave to, sooner or later. You're like all the rest of um. If it's up on t'moor, or out on t'Moss, it's nowt to do wi' us. Can't do us no harm. Well, it *can* now, see, I'm telling thee.'

All eight of Willie's fingers started working on his knees.

Ma said, 'They're looking for openings. Looking for cracks in t'wall. Been gathering out there for years, hundreds of years.'

'What you on about, Ma?'

'Different uns, like,' Ma said. 'Not *same* uns, obviously.'

'Yobboes,' Willie said dismissively, realizing what she meant. 'Bloody hooligans. Always been yobboes and hooligans out there maulin' wi' them owd circles. Means nowt. Except to farmers, like. Bit of a bugger for farmers.'

'Eh . . .' Ma was scornful. 'Farmers loses more sheep to foxes. That's not what I'm saying.'

Her eyes popped open, giving him a shock because there was no peace in them now, no acceptance. All of a sudden they looked just like the little white marbles Willie had collected as a lad, shot through with the same veins of pure, bright red.

She stabbed a finger at him again. 'I can tell um, y'know. Couldn't always . . . Aye. Less said about *that* . . .'

Willie's own fingers stumbled out of rhythm, the tips gone numb. 'Now, don't upset yourself.'

'But there's one now,' Ma said, one hand clutching an arm of the rocking-chair like a parrot's claw on a perch. 'Comes and goes, like an infection. Looking for an opening . . .'

'Shurrup, Ma, will you. Whatever it is, Lottie doesn't want . . .'

'Listen,' Ma said without hesitation. 'You tell that Lottie to come and see me. Tell her to come tomorrow, I'm a bit busy now. Tell her I'll talk to her about it. Just like we talked to Matt. Matt knew what had to happen. Matt were chuffed as a butty.'

'Aye.' Matt and his mate, the bogman. Together at last.

'Only we've got to protect the lad,' Ma said.

'I don't like any of this, Ma. Lottie'll go spare.'

'Well, look.' Ma was on her feet, sprightly as a ten-year-old, moving bottles on the shelf. 'Give her this.'

'What is it?'

Daft question.

'Aye.' Accepting the little brown bottle. 'All right, then, I'll give it her. Tell her it'll calm her down. Make her feel better. But I'll not tell you're going ahead with . . .' Willie gave his knee a couple of climactic thumps. 'No way.'

He didn't tell Ma what Lottie had said about them finishing Matt's bogman song-cycle.

Because, when it came down to it, he didn't like the thought of that himself. And he had a pretty good idea how Ma would react.

I warned him not to meddle with stuff he knows nowt about, she'd say. And I don't expect to have to warn me own son.

So, in a way, Willie was hoping Lottie would have forgotten about the whole thing by the time the funeral was over.

A funeral which, if she'd any sense, she'd be attending with a very thick veil over her eyes.

CHAPTER VII

The man with two Dobermanns prowling the inside of the wiremesh perimeter fence was clearly too old to be a security guard. His appallingly stained trousers were held up by a dressing-gown cord with dirty gold tassels; a thinner golden cord was draped around the crown of his tattered trilby.

However, the dogs looked menacing enough, and when the man flung open the metal gate, they sprang.

For just a few seconds, the dun-coloured sky disappeared as the Dobermanns rose massively and simultaneously into the air. And then they were on her, both heads into her exposed face, hot breath pumping and the great, savage teeth.

'Oh, my God!' Moira shrieked as the rough tongues sliced through her make-up. 'Do you guys know what this bloody stuff *costs*?'

She threw an arm around each of the dogs, trapping the four big front paws to her tweed jacket, and they all staggered together through the gate and on to the site, knocking over an empty grey plastic dustbin.

The elderly man in the black trilby caught the bin as it fell. 'Moira!' he yelled. 'Hey!'

'Donald,' Moira said, arms full of black and gold paws. 'You all right?'

'Well, damn.' He pulled his hat off. 'We wisny expecting ye today, hen, the Duchess didny say . . .'

'That's because she didn't know,' Moira said. 'I hope she's not away from her van . . . Down, now . . .'

The dogs obediently sat at her feet. 'Ye've still got the way, all right,' Donald said admiringly.

'They've grown. Again. I swear I've never seen Dobermanns this big. What d'you feed them on?'

Donald didn't smile. 'Public health officials.'

'My daddy,' she reminded him gently, 'was a public health official.'

'Aye, I know. But yer daddy wisny like the hard-faced bastards they send round these days.' Donald turned his head and shouted at a woman pegging baby-clothes to a washing line outside a lilac-coloured caravan. 'Hey, Siobhan, the Duchess, she in now?'

'Oh, sure . . .' The woman stumbled and dropped a nappy in a puddle. She picked it up, wrung out the brown water and hung it on the line. 'Leastways, I haven't seen no red carpet goin' down today.'

'Tinkers,' Donald said disparagingly. 'They're all bloody tinkers here now, 'cept for the few of us.'

Moira followed him and the dogs through the site, with its forty-odd vans on concrete hard-standings and its unexpectedly spectacular views of the Ayrshire coast. It might have been a holiday caravan site but for the washing-lines full of fluttering clothes and the piles of scrap and all the kids and dogs.

They passed just one perfect old Romany caravan, bright

red and silver, originally designed for horses but with a tow-bar now. A man with a beard and an earring sat out on the step whittling chunks out of a hunk of dark wood. He wore a moleskin waistcoat trimmed with silver. Moira stared at him, amazed. 'Who the hell's that?'

Donald turned his head and spat. One of the Dobermanns growled. 'Oh,' Moira said. 'I see.'

'Bloody hippies. Call 'emselves *New Age* gypsies. Wis a time this wis a *select* site. All kindsa garbage we're gettin' now, hen.'

He stopped at the bottom of six concrete steps leading to the apex of the site, a flat-topped artificial mound with the sides banked into flowerbeds.

Nothing changes, Moira thought. Wherever she's living it's always the same.

Evergreen shrubs, mainly laurel, sprouted around the base of the shining silver metal palace which crowned the mound like the Mother Ship from *Close Encounters*. The old man mounted the bottom step. 'Hey, Duchess!'

It wasn't what you'd call a traditional Romany caravan. Few like it had been seen before on a statutory local authority gypsy site. Only movie stars on location lived quite like this.

Donald stayed on the bottom step, the Dobermanns silent either side of him. There were antique carriage lamps each side of the door, a heavy door of stained and polished Douglas fir, which slid open with barely a sigh.

She came out and stood fraily in the doorway, a soft woollen evening stole about her bony shoulders. The day was calm for the time of year, no breeze from the sea.

Donald said, 'Will you look who's here, Duchess.'

From the edges of the stole, the Duchess's hair tumbled like a cataract of white water almost to her waist. She looked down at Moira and her face was grave.

Moira said, 'Hullo, Mammy.'

'You OK?'

He'd looked anxious, his tuxedo creased, the thistle lolling from his buttonhole.

Well, actually, it was more than anxious; the guy had been as scared as any of them in the room full of splintered bone – twisted antlers across the tables on beds of broken glass, and one pair still hanging menacingly among the glittering shards of a chandelier.

Moira had said, 'You ever see bomb damage in Belfast?'

'Huh?'

She was up on her knees now, examining the guitar for fractures.

'Bomb damage,' she said, not looking at him.

He was silent. He crouched down next to her, the two of them by the dais, all the others, the multi-national Celts, brushing each other down, sheltering in groups in the corners of the Great Hall.

The pale man had been helped away by the Earl and some servants. He'd looked just once at Moira with his damaged eye.

There were no cracks in the body of the guitar, although its face was scratched and it looked to be very deeply offended.

'What's your name?' Moira turned to the American.

'Huh?'

'What are you called?'

'I, uh . . .' He grimaced, the suaveness gone, black curls sweated to his forehead. He looked as limp as the thistle he wore. 'I don't believe this has happened. Some kind of earthquake? Or what? Uh . . . Macbeth.'

'That's your name? My God. Here, hold this a second.' She passed him the guitar while she untangled her hair.

He held the instrument up by the neck, gripping it hard. 'You *have* earthquakes in these parts?'

'What?' She'd started to laugh.

'Earthquakes. Tremors.'

She said, 'Macbeth. I thought you were going to be Irish, despite the thistle. New York Irish.'

'Just New York. Born and raised. Mungo Macbeth. Of the Manhattan Macbeths. My mother said I should wear the kilt.' He straightened the thistle. 'We compromised.'

'That's a compromise?'

He said, 'You really are OK now?'

110

'Oh, I'm fine. Just fine.' Feeling like she'd come through a war – a whole war in just a few minutes.

Mungo Macbeth had been looking around at all the wreckage, where the stags' heads had fallen. Then up at the ceiling.

'There isn't one of them left hanging,' he'd said, awed. 'Not a goddamn one.'

He was right.

What have I done?

'I mean, is that weird?' Mungo Macbeth said. 'Or is that weird?'

'And what was it that made you think,' the Duchess said contemptuously, 'that it was you?'

She didn't sound at all like Moira. Her voice was like the refined *tink* you made when you tapped with your fingernail on crystal glass of the very highest quality. A most cultured lady who had never been to school.

'Not me on my own,' Moira said. 'Someone . . . something was . . . you know, like an invasion? I felt threatened. This guy . . . Also, I didn't like the setup anyway, generations of stalkers' trophies, and all these elitist folk, like "we are the Celtic aristocracy, we're the chosen ones . . ."'

The Duchess lifted her chin imperiously. 'What nonsense you talk. Do you seriously think that if you began to suddenly resent me or something, you could come in here and break everything on my walls?'

Virtually all the wallspace in the luxurious caravan had been decorated with fine china.

'Your walls, no,' Moira said.

'I should think not indeed.'

'But this place, I felt very threatened.'

She kept seeing, like on some kind of videotape loop, the man unfastening her guitar case. But it was all so dreamlike, part of the hallucination summoned by the song and the strangeness of the night. She couldn't talk about it.

'I'm mixed up, Mammy.'

'Don't whine,' the Duchess said mildly.

111

'I'm sorry.' And the smoky form in the fireplace? The sensation of Matt – and yet *not* Matt?

And the *knowing*. Confirmed by the call.

Lottie? Lottie, listen, I know it's late, I'm sorry . . . Only it's Matt. I've been thinking about Matt all night . . .

The Duchess said, 'Have you the comb with you?'

'Surely.' Moira pulled her bag on to her knee.

'Show me.'

The Earl had said he couldn't explain it; the heads had been accumulating on the walls for four or more generations, none had ever been dislodged before. Some sort of chain-reaction, perhaps, the domino effect. He had suggested everyone go through to the larger drawing room, and the servants had been dispatched for extra chairs and doctors to tend the injuries, none of them apparently major.

Uninjured, Moira and the American called Macbeth had gone outside into the grounds.

'Clear my head,' he said.

The house behind them was floodlit, looked like a wedding cake. A narrow terrace followed the perimeter of the house, and they walked along it, Moira carrying the guitar in its case. 'Why are you here?' she said, drifting. 'What do you do? Or are you just rich?'

'TV,' Macbeth said. 'I make lousy TV shows. But, yeah, also we're rich, the Macbeths. Which is why they let me make my lousy TV shows, and also why I'm here. That is, my mother . . . she was invited. She owns the company.'

'Uh huh.' Moira nodded, as if she was interested. White flakes of bone were still silently spattering her vision, like TV static.

'They sent me,' Macbeth said, 'on account of, A – I'm just about the most expendable member of the family, and B – she figured it was time I reconnected with my, uh, roots.'

'Roots sometimes need to stay buried,' Moira said. 'You dig up the roots, you kill the tree.'

'I never thought about it like that.'

'It's probably just a clever thing to say. You *found* your

roots? Have you been to where Birnam Wood came to Dunsinane?'

'No,' he said. 'But I think I just found one of the three witches.'

'Really?' Moira said coldly.

'Only these days they come more beautiful.' Macbeth stopped suddenly and threw up both hands. 'Ah, shit, I apologize. I don't mean to be patronizing, or sexist or anything. It was, uh . . . The hair . . . your wonderful, long, black hair . . .'

Oh, *please* . . .

'With that lonely grey strand,' Macbeth said. 'Like a vein in onyx. Or something. I recognized it soon as you came into the room tonight. See, I don't know much about Celtic history, but rock music and folk . . . I mean, I really do have those albums.'

'Would that you didn't,' Moira said quietly. Then she shook her hair. 'Sorry. Stupid. Forget it.'

Standing on the edge of the terrace overlooking a floodlit lawn, he cupped both palms around his face. 'I am such an asshole.'

No way she could disagree.

Macbeth hung his head. 'See, I . . . Aw, Jesus, I'm in this party of seriously intellectual Celtic people, and, like . . . what do I know? What's my contribution gonna be? What do I *know*? – I know a song. So I go – showing off my atom of knowledge – I go, how about you play The Comb Song? Just came out. Dumb, huh?'

She looked hard into his dark blue eyes. 'So it *was* you asked for the song.'

'Yeah, it just came to me to ask for that song. Then someone else took it up. It was confusing. I coulda bit off my tongue when it came clear you didn't want to do that number. I'm sorry.' He sat down on the paved area, legs hanging over the side of the terrace. He rubbed his eyes. 'All those stag heads. Like it was orchestrated.'

'You think it was somehow down to the song? Hence I'm a witch? You connect that with *me*?'

'Uh . . .' Macbeth looked *very* confused. 'I'm sorry. Whole

113

thing scared the shit out of me. You feel the atmosphere in there? *Before* it happened?'

Headlight beams sliced through the trees along the drive. The ambulance probably. Maybe two. Maybe a whole fleet, seeing this was the Earl's place.

'Cold,' Macbeth said. 'Bone-freezing cold. I mean . . . shit . . . it isn't even cold *out here . . . now.*'

Moira had said, 'Can you excuse me? I need to make a phone call.'

She didn't know how old the comb was. Maybe a few hundred years old, maybe over a thousand. She'd never wanted to take it to an expert, a valuer; its value was not that kind.

The comb was of some heavy, greyish metal. It was not so very ornate and half its teeth were missing, but when she ran it through her hair it was like something was excavating deep furrows in her soul.

The Duchess weighed the comb in fingers that sprayed red and green and blue fire from the stones in her rings, eleven of them.

'My,' the Duchess said, 'you really are in a quandary, aren't you?'

'Else why would I have come.'

'And someone . . . You've not told me everything . . . I can sense a death.'

'Yes,' Moira whispered. Feeling, as usual, not so much like an acolyte at the feet of a guru, more like a sin-soaked Catholic at confession.

'Whose?'

'Matt Castle.'

'Who is he?'

'You know . . . He was the guy whose band I joined when I left the university in Manchester. Must be . . . a long time . . . seventeen years ago.'

'This was before . . . ?'

'Yes.'

The Duchess passed the comb from one hand to the other and back again. 'There's guilt here. Remorse.'

'Well, I . . . I've always felt bad about leaving the band when I did. And also . . . three, four months ago, he wrote to me. He wanted me to do some songs with him. He was back living in his old village, which is that same place they found the ancient body in the peat. Maybe you heard about that.'

'A little.' The Duchess's forefinger stroking the rim of the comb.

'Matt was seriously hung up on this thing,' Moira said, 'the whole idea of it. This was the first time . . . I mean, when we split, his attitude was, like, OK, that's it, nice while it lasted but it's the end of an era. So, although we've spoken several times on the phone, it's fifteen years last January since I saw him. Um . . . last year it came out he'd been to the hospital, for tests, but when I called him a week or so later he said it was OK, all negative, no problem. So . . . Goes quiet, we exchange Christmas cards and things, as usual. Then, suddenly – this'd be three, four, months ago – he writes, wanting to get me involved in this song-cycle he's working on, maybe an album. To be called *The Man in the Moss*.'

'And you would have nothing to do with it?'

'I . . . Yeh, I don't like to bugger about with this stuff any more. I get scared . . . scared what effect I'm gonna have, you know? I'm pretty timid these days.'

'So you told him no.'

'So I . . . No, I couldn't turn it down flat. This is the guy got me started. I owe him. So I just wrote back, said I was really sorry but I was tied up, had commitments till the autumn. Said I was honoured, all this crap, and I'd be in touch. Hoping, obviously, that he'd find somebody else.'

She paused. Her voice dropped. 'He died last night. About the same time all this . . .'

The Duchess passed the comb back to Moira. 'I don't like the feel of it. It's cold.'

The comb is icy, brittle, oh . . .

Her mother was glaring at her, making her wish she hadn't come. There was always a period of this before the tea and the biscuits and the Duchess saying, How is your father? Does he ever speak of me? And she'd smile and shake her head, for her

115

daddy still didn't know, after all these years, that she'd even met this woman.

The Duchess said, 'That trouble you got into, with the rock and roll group. You dabbled. I said to you never to dabble. I said when you were ready to follow a spiritual path you should come to me. It was why I gave you the comb.'

'Yes, Mammy, I know that.' She'd always call her Mammy deliberately, in a vain effort to demystify the woman. 'I'm doing my best to avoid it. That's why . . .'

'The comb has not forgiven you,' the Duchess said severely. 'You have some damage to repair.'

'Aye, I know,' Moira said. 'I know that too.'

She'd returned from the phone floating like a ghost through a battlefield, blood and bandages everywhere – well, maybe not so much blood, maybe not any. Maybe the blood was in her head.

'You all right, Miss Cairns? You weren't hit?'

'I'm fine, Your . . . I'm fine.'

'You're very pale. Have a brandy.'

'No. No, thank you.'

All this solicitousness. Scared stiff some of his Celtic brethren would sue the piss out of him. She was impatient with him. Him and his precious guests and his precious trophies and his reputation. What did it matter? Nobody was dying.

Yes, Moira. Yes, he is. I'm sorry . . . No, not long. I'll know more in the morning. Perhaps you could call back then.

She had to get out of this house, didn't want to see wounds bathed and glass and antlers swept away. Didn't want to know what had happened to the pale man.

Outside, Mungo Macbeth, of the Manhattan Macbeths, still sat with his legs dangling over the edge of the terrace.

Moira joined him, feeling chilly now in her black dress, stiff down by the waist where it had soaked up spilled Guinness from the carpet.

And because he was there and because he was no threat any more, she began to talk to Macbeth. Talked about many things – *not* including Matt Castle.

116

In fact she was so determined not to talk about Matt – and, therefore, not to break down – that she blocked him out, and his dying, with something as powerful and as pertinent to the night: she found she was telling Mungo Macbeth about the Comb Song.

'Everybody thinks it's metaphor, you know?'

'It exists?'

'Aye. Sure.'

Then she thought, *Only person I ever told before was M . . .*

She said quickly, 'Your family make regular donations to the IRA?'

'. . . *what*?'

His eyebrows went up like they'd been pulled on wires and she stared good and hard into his eyes. They were candid and they were innocent.

'Sorry,' she said. 'I forgot. You aren't even Irish.'

'Moira, let's be factual here. I'm not even Scottish.'

She found herself smiling. Then she stopped. She said, 'Every year these gypsies would camp on the edge of the town, derelict land since before the War. Only this year it was to be redeveloped, and so the gypsies had to go. My daddy was the young guy the council sent to get rid of them. He was scared half to death of what they might do to him, the gypsy men, who would naturally all be carrying knives.'

Some night creature ran across the tiered lawn below them, edge to edge.

'My gran told me this. My daddy never speaks of it. Not *ever*. But it wasn't the gypsy men he had cause to fear, so much as the women. They had the poor wee man seduced.'

Macbeth raised an eyebrow, but not much.

'Like, how could he resist her? This quiet Presbyterian boy with the horn-rimmed spectacles and his first briefcase. How could he resist this, this . . .' Moira swung her legs and clicked her heels on the terrace wall.

'I can sympathize,' Macbeth said.

'She was a vision,' Moira said. 'Still is. He'd have laid down his beloved council job for her after the first week, but that wasn't what they wanted – they wanted the camp site until the autumn, for reasons of their own, whatever that was all about.

117

And they got it. My daddy managed to keep stalling the council, his employers, for reasons of *his* own. And then it all got complicated because she wasn't supposed to get herself pregnant. Certainly not by *him*.'

She'd glossed over the rest, her daddy's ludicrous threats to join the gypsies, her gran's battle for custody of the child, the decision by the gypsy hierarchy that, under the circumstances, it might be politic to let the baby go rather than be saddled with its father and pursued by *his* mother.

And then her own genteel, suburban, Presbyterian upbringing.

'And the rest is the song. Which you know.'

The American, sitting on the wall, shook his head, incredulous. 'This is prime-time TV, you know that? This is a goddamn *mini-series*.'

'Don't you even think about it, Mr Macbeth,' Moira said, 'or Birnam Wood'll be coming to Dunsinane faster than you can blink.'

'Yeah, uh, the wood. I was gonna ask you. The scene in the wood where you get the comb . . . ?'

'Poetic licence. What happened was, the gypsies were in town, right, just passing through. Two of them – I was twelve – these two gypsies were waiting for me outside the school. I'm thinking, you know . . . run like hell. But, aw . . . it was . . . intriguing. And they seemed OK, you know? And the camp was very public. So I went with them. Well . . . she'd be about thirty then and already very revered, you could tell. Even I could see she was my mother.'

'Holy shit,' said Macbeth.

'We didn't talk much. Nobody was gonna try and kidnap me or anything. Nobody offered me anything. Except the comb. She gave me that.'

'And is it a magic comb?'

'It's just a comb,' Moira said, more sharply than she intended.

'He's close to you,' the Duchess said.

'Who?'

'The departed one.'

'Still?'

'We'll have some tea,' the Duchess said in a slightly raised voice, and a young woman at once emerged from the kitchen with a large silver tray full of glistening white china. 'One of my nieces,' the Duchess said, 'Zelda.' There would always be nieces and nephews to fetch and carry for the Duchess.

She lifted the lid of the pot and sniffed. 'Earl Grey. Never mind. You should take a rest, Moira. Unravel yourself.'

'Maybe I'd rather not see what's inside of me.'

The Duchess stirred the tea in the pot, making it stronger, making the Earl Grey's rich perfume waft out. 'Maybe you should get away, and when you get back your problems will be in perspective. Go somewhere bland. St Moritz, Barbados . . .'

'Jesus, Mammy, how much money you think I'm making?'

'Well, England then. Tunbridge Wells or somewhere.'

'Tunbridge *Wells*?'

'You know what I mean.'

'Yeah. You're telling me it's something I'm not gonna get away from no matter where I go.'

'Am I?'

'You said there was damage to repair. You think I *damaged* Matt Castle?'

'Do *you*?'

'I don't kn . . . No! No, I don't see how I could have.'

'That's all right, then,' said the Duchess. She smiled.

Moira felt profoundly uneasy. 'Mammy, how was he when he died? Can you tell me that?'

'Moira, you're a grown woman. You *know* this man's essence has not returned to the source. I can say no more than that.'

Moira felt the weight of her bag on her knees, the bag with the comb in it. The bag felt twice as heavy as before, like a sack of stolen bullion.

She said in a rush, 'Mammy, somebody was after the comb. I had to fight for it.'

'Yes. That happens. The comb represents a commitment. Sometimes you have to decide whether or not you want to renew it.'

'So it was this struggle which caused . . . See, I'm confused. I feel exhausted, but I feel I made it through to a new level, a new plateau. But that usually means something heavy's on the way. Well, doesn't it?'

The Duchess blinked. 'How is your father?' she said brightly. 'Does he speak of me often?'

She said goodbye to Donald at the gate and patted the Dobermanns. Her old BMW was parked about fifty yards away near a derelict petrol station. Parked behind it was a car which had not been there before, a grey Metro with a hire-firm sticker on the rear window.

Leaning against the Metro was a man wearing a dinner jacket over a black T-shirt. On the T-shirt it said in red, I ♥ Govan. The remains of a thistle hung out of one lapel of the jacket.

His face fumbled a grin.

'Uh, hi,' he said.

Moira was furious.

'You followed me! You fucking *followed* me!'

'Listen . . . Moira . . . See, this has been . . . Like, this was the most bizarre, dramatic, *momentous* night of my life, you know?'

'So? You've had a sheltered life. Is that supposed . . . ?'

'I can't walk away from this. Am I supposed to like, push it aside, maybe introduce it as an anecdote over dinner with my associates?'

Moira stood with her key in the door of the BMW. She wanted to say, OK, while you're here maybe you can tell me something about a tall, pale man with white hair.

Instead, she said, 'Macbeth, you shouldn't believe everything a woman tells you when she's in shock.'

'I . . . Goddamnit, I *saw*. And I tried to sleep on it and I couldn't, so this morning . . .' Mungo Macbeth looked sheepish and spread his hands . . .

She gave him a cursory glance intended to wither, fade him out.

'I figured maybe you could use some help,' he said.

'OK,' she said. 'You see those gates? Behind those gates is a guy with two huge and ferocious dogs. The dogs'll do anything the guy says. And the guy – he'll do anything I say. You got the message?'

'Couldn't we go someplace? Get a bite to eat?'

'No, we could not.' Moira opened the driver's door of the BMW and got in, wound down the window. 'You think I need a strong male shoulder to lean on, that it? Or maybe a bedpost?'

Macbeth said helplessly, 'I just think . . . I just think you're an amazing person.'

'Macbeth . . .' She sighed. 'Just go away, huh?'

He nodded, expressionless, turned back to his hire car. He looked like he might cry.

This was *ridiculous*.

'Hey, Macbeth . . .' Moira leaned back out of the window, nodded at his T-shirt. 'You ever actually *been* to Govan?'

'Aw, hell . . .' Macbeth shrugged. 'I cruised most of those Western Isles. Just don't recall which is which.'

Moira found a grin, or the grin found her. Hurriedly, she put the car into gear, drove away, and when she looked back there was only a bus, a long way behind.

From *Dawber's Book of Bridelow*:

THE BREWERY

FINE BEERS HAVE BEEN brewed in the Bridelow area since time immemorial, the most famous being the almost-black Bridelow Bitter.

This, or something similar, was first produced commercially, on an extremely small scale, by Elsie Berry and her sons in the late seventeenth century, using a species of aromatic bog-myrtle as a preservative. The Berry family began by providing ale for the Bridelow pub, The Man I'th Moss, but demand grew swiftly in communities up to fifteen miles away.

The Bridelow Brewery as we know it today was founded in the early nineteenth century by Thomas Horridge, a businessman from Chesterfield who bought out the Berry Family and whose enterprise was to provide employment for many generations of Bridelow folk. He at once began work on the construction of the first proper road across the Moss to facilitate the movement of his brewery wagons.

Descendants of Thomas Horridge continued to develop the industry, and the family became Bridelow's greatest benefactors, building the village hall, enabling major repairs to be carried out to the ancient church and continuing to facilitate new housing as recently as the 1950s.

However . . .

CHAPTER VIII

I n the bar at The Man I'th Moss, lunchtime, Young Frank Manifold said, in disgust, 'Bloody gnat's piss!'
And angrily pushed his glass away.

'I'll have draught Bass next time,' Young Frank said. 'Never thought I'd be saying that in this pub. *Never*.'

'Eh, tha's just bitter, lad,' said Frank Manifold Snr, who preferred Scotch anyway. 'Tha's a right to feel bitter, mind, I'm not saying tha's not . . . Know what they've done, now, Ernie? Only paid off our drivers and replaced um wi' their own blokes.'

'Ken and Peter?'

'Gone! Paid off! Cut down lorries from five to two – bigger uns, like. Needed experienced HGV drivers, *they* reckoned. Makes you spit.'

Ernie, who also was on whisky, had a sip out of Young Frank's beer glass. 'Lad's right, I'm afraid,' he said. 'It's gone off.'

'Well, thank you!' Young Frank said devoutly. 'Thank you very much, Mr Dawber.'

'Only just don't go shouting it around the place,' Ernie muttered. 'Lottie's got to sell the stuff and she's enough problems.'

'No, she doesn't,' said Young Frank, back-row smart-arse in Ernie's top class fourteen years ago. 'Doesn't have to sell it at all no more. Free house, int it?'

Lottie wasn't here this lunchtime. Stan Burrows, who'd also been made redundant from the brewery, was minding the bar. Stan said, 'I heard as how Gannons was kicking up,

123

claiming they'd been sabotaged, not given proper recipe, like. Threatening legal action, what I heard.'

'Balls,' said Young Frank, glaring at his discarded glass. 'They don't give a shit.'

Ernie Dawber, on his usual stool at the end of the bar, by the telephone, pondered this. The way he saw it, there was no way the Horridge family could have got away with not providing Gannons with the correct recipe. And why should they want to, with Shaw Horridge on the Board?

Yet it was a fact. Since the brewery had been taken over, the stuff had been slowly shedding its distinctive flavour. Surprising, because it was well known that Gannons, whose bestselling product was a fizzy lager with a German name produced down Matlock way, had been anxious for some time to acquire their own genuine, old-established Real Ale – and would therefore be expected to treat Bridelow beer with more than a modicum of respect.

Ernie decided he'd better go up to the Hall one night and have a bit of a chat with Shaw Horridge or his mother. Bridelow Black Bitter had a reputation. Even if the brewery was in new hands, even if there'd been this swingeing 'rationalization', which meant firing half the lads, it was still *Bridelow* beer.

Gnat's piss! By 'eck, he'd never thought to hear that.

When his daughter rang from Oxford, in the early afternoon, the Rector barely made it to the phone in time.

'Were you in the garden?' Catherine asked him suspiciously, and Hans didn't deny it. It had taken him almost a minute to hobble from the kitchen to the study.

Pointless, however, trying to conceal anything from Cathy. 'How's the knee?' she demanded at once and with a certain menace.

'Oh,' Hans said, as airily as he could manage with clenched teeth. 'Could be worse, you know.'

'I've no doubt that it could, Pop. But worse than *what* is what I'd like to know.'

Hans tried to keep from screaming out loud as he fell into the window chair, pulling the phone on to his knees.

Cathy said, 'I don't suppose you'd even tell me if you'd had to have a Zimmer frame screwed into the back of the pulpit.'

The still-aggressive sun, having gouged chunks out of the church wall, began to attack the study window, and when the Rector twisted away from it, his left knee felt like a slab of volcanic rock with a core of molten lava.

'Well, actually,' he said, abandoning pretence with a sigh, 'it couldn't be a *lot* worse.'

'Right,' his daughter said. 'I'm on my way, Pop. Expect me for supper.'

'No, no, no. Your studies . . . whatever they are.'

Cathy said crisply, 'In a post-graduate situation, as I keep explaining, you get a fair bit of leeway. I'm coming up.'

'No. Listen. You don't understand.' Raising his voice, trying to shout down the pain as much as her. 'I'm getting a lot of help. The Mothers' Union . . . terribly kind, and . . . Look, when I need you, I promise I'll be in touch. You know I will.'

He swallowed a great slab of breath and bit his tongue, jamming his palm over the mouthpiece just in time. Change the subject. Talk about something else. 'Erm, Matt Castle . . . Poor Matt died on Sunday night.'

'Oh, no.'

'It was a mercy, Catherine.'

'Yes, I suppose it would be. Did . . . ?'

'Oh, very quick. In the end, he spent no more than a few hours in hospital. Kept signing himself out, you see. Determined to die in Bridelow. He was even out on the Moss yesterday morning, I'm told, with Lottie and the boy. Brave man. Poor Matt.'

'What's going to happen to the pub?'

'She'll stay on, I imagine. For a while. You know what she's like. Terribly independent. Old Mrs Wagstaff sent one of her special potions across, to help her sleep. Lottie bunged it back at once, with Willie. She's very resistant to all that.'

'When's the funeral?'

'Friday afternoon.'

'You're going to have difficulty, aren't you? Especially if it gets colder.'

Putting her finger on it, as usual. So Hans had to come out with what, apart from the pain, was on his mind. 'Cathy, they've given me a curate.'

'Oh,' she said, surprised. 'Well, you certainly could do with the help. But it, er . . . that could be a headache, couldn't it?'

'It was only a matter of time,' Hans said, 'parish this size. Suppose I've been holding out. Putting it off. That is, I realize this sort of thing – new chaps – has always taken care of itself in the past. I mean, I myself was not . . . well, not, perhaps, the man they would have chosen at the time. But one gets acclimatized. Headache? Hmm . . . let's hope not.'

'Anybody I know?'

'Oh, a young fellow, few months out of college. Simon's very keen . . . Well, actually not *that* young. Late twenties, I suppose. Used to be a teacher. Joel Beard, his name. Pleasant enough lad. Slightly earnest, but so many of them are, aren't they?'

Cathy said, 'Jesus Christ.'

Hans didn't say anything. His daughter never blasphemed for effect.

'I was at the high school with him.' Hans could hear her frowning. 'For a year or two. That is, he was four or five years in front of me. He was Head Boy. One of those who takes it seriously. Very authoritative, very *proper*. Seemed more of a grown-up than some of the teachers, do you know what I mean? Most of the girls were crazy about him. But I was never into Greek gods.'

She stopped. 'Pop, listen, you *do* know he was at St Oswald's, don't you?'

Yes, he did. He was surprised, though, that *she* knew the significance of this. 'It's not necessarily a drawback, you know, Cathy.'

He tried to straighten his right leg and, although there was no great pain in this one, the right knee fought him all the way. Both knees now. God save us. Wheelchair job soon. Or one could go into hospital and leave Joel Beard in charge.

'Simon thinks he's a star,' he said. 'Which means, I suppose, that the silly sod's fallen in love with him. He used, apparently . . . Joel, this is . . . he used to be some sort of

126

Born Again Christian. Before he decided to go straight, as it were.'

'You call two years at St Oswald's going *straight*? The most notoriously fundamentalist theological college in the country?'

'I like to think I'm broadminded,' Hans said.

'Sure, but how broadminded is Ma Wagstaff?'

'Look,' Hans said, 'people adjust. *Bridelow* adjusts people. I'd rather have a fundamentalist or a charismatic than some clerical bureaucrat with a briefcase and a mobile phone. Anyway, the Diocese likes him. "He's tough, he's athletic" – this is Simon talking – "and he's bringing God back into the arena." Bit of muscle. They're into that these days. The anti-pansy lobby. Even Simon, ironically. I mean, all right, I could refuse him, I could tell them to take him back, say he doesn't fit it . . . but somebody's going to ask, *why* doesn't he fit? And anyway, who's to say . . . ? They might not be . . . orthodox here, but they have a strong faith and strong, simple principles. Ma Wagstaff? *Very* broadminded in some ways.'

'Hmmm,' said Cathy, unconvinced.

'However, rest assured, I won't let him take Matt's funeral. I suspect the ladies have plans.'

'God, no, you mustn't let him do that.'

'So if I have to go out there on a pair of crutches . . . or a Zimmer frame.'

'Don't you go talking about Zimmer frames, Pop.'

'*You* did.'

'That's when I'll come,' Catherine decided. 'I'll come on Wednesday night. I'll get you through the funeral. I won't have you talking about Zimmer frames.'

'Now, look . . .'

'I'm not going to argue, my phone bill's getting ridiculous. I'll see you Wednesday night.'

And she hung up on him.

'Thank you,' the Rector said with resignation into the dead phone. 'I suppose.'

The Hall had once been surrounded by parkland, although now it just looked like ordinary fields with a well-ordered assembly of mature trees – beech and sycamore and horse-chestnut.

The trees were higher now, but not yet high enough to obscure the soaring stone walls of the brewery, four storeys high, an early Victorian industrial castle, as proud and firm in its setting as St Bride's Church.

She hated it now.

You could not see the brewery from the drawing room. But with all the trees nearly bare again, Eliza Horridge, from her window seat, could see the village in detail. She supposed she'd always preferred autumn and winter for this very reason: it brought her closer to Bridelow.

The sad irony of this made her ache. On the night the redundancies had been announced, she'd gone – rather bravely, she thought – down to the post office to buy some stamps which she didn't need. She'd just had to get it over, face the hostility.

Except there hadn't been any. Nobody had screamed Judas at her, nobody had ignored her or been short with her.

But nobody had said a word about the jobs either. They didn't blame her personally. But Liz Horridge blamed herself and since that night had never been back into Bridelow.

Self-imposed exile in this warm and shabby-luxurious house with its pictures and memories of Arthur Horridge. *Self*-imposed; could go out whenever she wanted. Couldn't she?

She snatched up the phone on its second ring to wrench her mind from what it couldn't cope with.

'Yes?' The number was ex-directory. There were too many people down there with whom she could no longer bear to speak.

'Yes? Hello? Is that you, Shaw?'

Something told her she was in for a shock, and her eyes clutched at the view of the village for support, following the steep cobbled street past the pub, past the post office, past a line of tiny stone cottages to the churchyard.

'Liiiiiz . . .' Mellifluously stretching the word, as he used to, into an embrace. 'Super!' Shattering her.

'Thought I saw you last week, m'girl, in Buxton. Was in a wine bar. Thought you came up the street. No?'

'Couldn't have been,' she scraped out. 'Never go . . .'

'Thought you *sensed* me . . . turned your head so *sharply*.'

'. . . to Buxton.' Her voice faded.

'And looked at the window of the wine bar, with a sort of yearning in your eyes. Couldn't see me, of course.'

She stared down at the village, but it was like watching a documentary on the television. Or a soap opera, because she could identify most of the people and could map out the paths of their lives from their movements, between the post office and the pub and the church.

'But perhaps it wasn't you, after all,' he said.

She could even hear their voices when the wind was in the right direction. And yes, it was a lot like the television – a thick glass screen between them, and she was very much alone, and the screen was growing darker.

'Or perhaps it was you as you *used* to be. Those chestnut curls of yore.'

Her hand went automatically to her hair, as coarse and dry now as the moorland grasses. She grabbed a handful of it to stop the hand shaking.

'One wonders,' he mused. 'Your hair grey now, Liz? Put on weight? Or angular and gaunt? I'd so much like to see.'

'What do you want?' Liz croaked.

'If you were with me, I suppose you'd keep in trim, dye your hair, have your skin surgically stretched. Probably wouldn't work, but you'd try. If you were with me.'

'How dare you?' Stung at last into anger. 'Where did you get this number?'

He laughed.

She felt alone and cold, terribly exposed, almost ill with it. 'What are you trying to do?'

He said, 'How's dear old Ma these days? Is she well?'

She said nothing.

'Perhaps you don't see her. Or any of them. The word is you've become something of a *recluse*. All alone in your rotting mansion.'

129

'What nonsense,' she said breathlessly.

'Also, one hears the Mothers' Union isn't as well supported as it was. Sad, secular times, Liz. What's it all coming to? Silly old bats, eh?'

'They had *your* measure,' Liz said, with a spurt of spirit. 'They saw you off.'

'Oh, *long* time ago. Things change. Barriers weaken. Look, old sweetheart, I've been thinking, why don't we meet up?'

'*Certainly not!*'

'Love to be able to come to Buxton, wouldn't you? Love to be smart and sprightly and well-dressed. Give anything to have those chestnut curls back. Perhaps it was you after all, sitting in your emotional prison and *day-dreaming* of Buxton. Perhaps *that's* what I saw. Perhaps you *projected* yourself. Ever tried that, Liz? Should do. Could be a way out – send the spirit, give the body the bottle to go for it. Perhaps I'll drop in on you. Like that, would you?'

'You can't! They won't let you!'

'Times change, m'girl, times change.'

'What do you mean?'

'Will you tell dearest Ma I called?'

She said nothing.

'Of course you won't. Don't see her any more, do you? You don't see any of them. Do you . . . *Liiiiiz?*'

'Leave me . . . !'

She crashed the phone down, and she and the phone sat and trembled.

'Alone,' she said, and began to weep.

'I thought perhaps I might leave early,' Alice said. 'I've got a check-up at the dentist's in Buxton at six and I've got some stuff to pick up at Boots, and I don't like the look of the weather. Is that all right?'

'Suppose so,' Chrissie said, bending over the filing cabinet. Roger had arrived mid-morning, seeming preoccupied, and had not even mentioned their lunch-date, just sloped off to some appointment. Now Chrissie would have to check everything, switch off the lights and lock up.

'You don't mind being alone with . . .' Alice giggled. '. . . *him?*'

'Couldn't be safer,' Chrissie said. 'Rog . . . Dr Hall was telling me he hasn't got one.'

'Hasn't he?' Alice was putting her stuff away in her calfskin handbag. She flicked a card across the desk at Chrissie. 'See, there's my appointment.'

'What for?'

'The dentist's. Just to show you I'm not making it up.'

'I never thought you were making it up, Alice, OK?'

'Why hasn't he got one?' asked Alice without much interest. She was a good ten years older than Chrissie, had grown-up kids and a big house. Didn't need the job but Chrissie supposed that in Alice's circle it was nice to say you worked for the University, even if it was only as a number two secretary in an overgrown Portacabin outside Congleton.

Chrissie said, 'Part of the ritual, apparently, when he was sacrificed.'

'I suppose that would be *quite* a sacrifice for a man,' said Alice, pretending to shudder.

'Actually, it's possible they just cut it off after he was dead.'

'I see.' Alice shrugged into her sheepskin coat. Hard luck, Chrissie thought. Now you'll never know how big they were in pre-Christian times.

Alice took her car keys out of her bag, stuck the bag under an arm. 'So it's all right then, if I leave now?'

'Yes,' Chrissie said. Yes, yes, *yes!* she screamed to herself.

But when Alice had gone, she decided it *wasn't* all right. Bloody fat-arsed cow got away with too much. Spends most of the day experimenting with this disgusting sea-green nail varnish, then pisses off to sprawl on the sofa and moan to her husband about how overworked she is.

Chrissie picked up the dentist's appointment card which Alice had left behind. It looked authentic enough, if you didn't happen to know Alice's eldest daughter was a dental receptionist.

It was 4.30. A dim grey afternoon, with all the lights on. She couldn't herself go in case somebody (Roger) rang, or one of the research students came in to raid the files.

She stared across the office at a double-locked metal door.

131

'Just me and you, chum, and you've got no dick.' Chrissie laughed.

Under the laughter, there was a soft noise from behind the metal door.

Chrissie breathed in hard. 'Who's that?'

There was silence.

Yes, that was it – just a *soft noise*. Not a thump, not a clang. She looked around and over her shoulder. The room had three desks, seven filing cabinets and two big metal-framed bookcases. It was garishly lit by fluorescent tubes and the windows had Venetian blinds. Between the blinds she could see the deserted college playing-fields and, beyond, the tops of container-lorries on the motorway.

She was alone in the Field Centre and there was nobody apparent outside. 'Now, look,' Chrissie said, 'this is not on. This is not bloody *on*.'

It was going dark out there.

The soft noise came again, like a heavy cushion – an old-fashioned one, with brocade – being tossed on to a sofa.

Bravely, Chrissie slipped off her shoes and moved quietly to the metal door.

Should she check this out? *Dare* she?

Although she'd never been in there alone, she knew where there was a key.

She put her ear to the door.

There was silence.

Shaw's Porsche was coming up the drive, black as a funeral car – did it *have* to be a black one? She could tell by the speed that it wouldn't be stopping at the house but continuing up to the brewery. There was a new link road for the brewery lorries, so they never grumbled past the Hall these days, and no local vehicles, except for Shaw's Mercedes and his Porsche, ever laboured up from Bridelow any more.

So the Hall, sealed off from both the brewery and village, irrelevant now to both, might as well not exist.

'Nor me,' Liz Horridge whispered into the empty, high-ceilinged room with its bland Regency-striped wallpaper and its cold, crystal chandelier. 'I've become irrelevant to everybody.'

Even Shaw – famous mother's boy – had quite casually replaced her in his life. Always away at meetings, in Matlock, Buxton, Sheffield, London even. Or with his girlfriend, the mysterious Therese.

With whom Shaw appeared obsessed. As well he might. The girl was far too beautiful for him – at thirty-one, he was at least ten years older, losing his hair, conspicuously lacking in style despite his costly education. But being seen with Therese (Therese *Beaufort*, no less) had done wonders for his confidence, and his lifelong stutter had virtually disappeared.

Her delight had turned to a damp dismay. Years of speech therapy, of love and patient coaxing at the fireside. And what was it that finally killed Shaw's stutter?

Sex.

She could weep. *Had* wept.

And wept and wept.

Last week he'd made her position quite appallingly clear. 'If I were you, Mother,' he'd said in passing – everything Shaw said to her these days appeared to be in passing – 'If I were you I'd be off. Out of here. Somewhere warm. The Channel Islands. Malta.'

She clung to the sofa. 'But I don't *want* a holiday, Shaw.'

'No, not a holiday. I mean, for good. To live. Why not? It's warm, it's civilized. And absolutely everyone would want to come and stay with you.'

'What are you *saying*?'

Shaw had smiled affably and dashed off to his 'meeting'.

Every day since, she'd sat here, by this bay window, and listened to his voice in her head saying so smoothly, without a hint of impediment, *Somewhere warm. The Channel Islands. Malta* . . .

And envisaged Therese Beaufort, in some slinky designer costume, drink in hand, languid in this window, gazing out on *her* property.

Liz Horridge thought she could see old Mrs Wagstaff waddling up the main street of Bridelow towards the church. Or maybe it wasn't. Maybe she just needed to see the old girl.

How's dear old Ma these days? Is she well?

Three decades ago, in the crowded parlour full of bottles, two cats on the hearth, Ma Wagstaff cradling Liz's head. Sleeping in the little bedroom. *If he comes to you . . . scream. Don't matter what time.*

And now, *Perhaps I'll drop in. Wouldn't you like that?*

You can't. She'll stop you.

Things change. Barriers weaken.

She looked out at the village, willing it closer. She'd give anything to be able to shatter that damned glass screen before it all went black.

Well, look at it this way – there was no way anyone could have got in there without her or Alice knowing about it. Therefore there was no one in there, except for . . . well, yes.

The spare key was filed in the third filing cabinet. Under K, for key.

The problem was, suppose something was amiss in there? Suppose a rat or something had got in? Suppose something electrical had malfunctioned, threatening the bogman's welfare? And therefore Roger's. And hers.

Tentatively, she unlocked the third filing cabinet and located the key. It was smoky-coloured steel, about four inches long.

Who would Roger blame if something had gone wrong with the bogman, his future? Who was in charge of the office in Roger's absence?

Filed under B was a second and longer key for the double lock to the inner room, the specimen room, the bogman's bedroom.

She just rather wished, as she pushed in the first key, that she hadn't acquiesced so readily to Alice's 'request' to leave early.

Chrissie slipped on her cardigan. It would be cold in there, wouldn't it? Mustn't get the shivers, that would never do.

The metal door opened with a soft vacuum belch.

'Sorry to intrude,' Chrissie said softly.

Behind the door was a small hallway where two new

Portacabins had been pushed together. This was where the white coats were kept, and there were a couple of lavatory cubicles and a washbasin. Then there was another, unlocked door leading to an anteroom with a desk. And then the innermost metal door, with a double lock through which minions like her and Alice were not supposed to venture.

So there couldn't possibly be anybody in there.

Anybody *else*.

She'd been in there a couple of times, but only with Roger and not for very long. So she knew what *he* looked like, no problem about that.

The second key turned easily, twice, and Chrissie walked into an almost complete but alarmingly pleasant darkness which hummed faintly.

She didn't move. Apart from the hum, it was very, very quiet. Nothing scurried away. She'd left the door open behind her to allow a little light in there, but the velvety darkness absorbed it all within a yard or two of the opening and she had to fumble about for switches.

It was not cold. This was it. Well, of course, this was why it seemed so pleasant. The temperature was controlled to body heat. *Bog* body heat. He'd apparently been freeze-dried and then maintained in a controlled environment. She rather hoped he was packed away or at least covered up with something.

. . . do you touch him much?

Chrissie's hand found a switch, and the lights came on, flickering blue laboratory light, white on white tiles.

Mortuary light. Chrissie tensed, breathed in sharply.

But, of course, she was right. There was absolutely nobody here.

Nobody *else*.

. . . of course I touch him. He feels like a big leather cricket bag. You should pop in sometime, be an experience for you.

Actually he was rather smaller than the cricket bags Chrissie had seen when her ex-husband used to play.

He was lying on his table in his heat-regulated bubble, looking like somebody who'd spent far too long in a solarium.

Yes, he had a lovely tan.

Still hard to think of him as an actual corpse. He was too

135

old. But still, ancient as he was, when you thought about it, he was probably in a better state of preservation than Chrissie's late grandad was by now.

Chrissie laughed at her stupid self.

She leaned over the bogman, curled up under his plastic bubble.

'All right then, chuck?'

She wondered what he'd sound like if he could reply, what language he spoke. Welsh, probably.

She looked around. There were a couple of wires, naked rubber, emerging from the bottom of the container. Pretty primitive. The British Museum boffins would probably have a fit.

But nothing seemed amiss.

'I'll leave you, then,' Chrissie said. She tried to see his face. His nose was squashed, like a boxer's. There were whiskers around his contorted lips, which were half open, revealing the brown stumps of his teeth.

There was a fold in the side of his neck, a flap, like another lip. She thought, God, that's where they cut his throat, poor little devil.

Beaten over the head, garrotted, throat cut and then they chopped his dick off.

Oh, yuck.

Automatically, she glanced down to where his groin ought to be, where the body was bent.

And then Chrissie made a little involuntary noise at the back of her throat.

She glanced back at his face.

His twisted lips . . . leering at her now.

Her eyes flicked rapidly back to his groin, back to his face, back to his groin. She felt her own lips contorting, and she made the little noise again, a high-pitched strangled yelp, and she began to back off towards the door.

But she couldn't stop looking at him.

. . . *what, no* . . .

. . . *penis* . . . *must have chopped it off. Part of the ritual.*

Chrissie's hands began to tingle as they scrabbled frantically behind her back for the door-handle.

Get me *out* of here.

Far from being emasculated, the bogman, under his bubble, had the most enormous erection she had ever seen.

From *Dawber's Book of Bridelow*:

NATURAL HISTORY

BRIDELOW MOSS IS believed to be over four thousand years old, but there has been considerable erosion over the past two centuries and the bog appears to have been affected by pollution from industry twenty or more miles away, with much of the vegetation being destroyed and the surface becoming even darker due to soot-deposits.

Erosion is gradually exposing the hills and valleys submerged under the blanket bog, and many fragments of long-dead trees, commonly known as 'bog oak', have been discovered. Because of the preservative qualities of peat, wood recovered from the Moss is usually immensely strong and was once considered virtually indestructible . . .

CHAPTER IX

There was frost on the morning of the day Matt Castle was to be buried, and the heaped soil beside the prepared grave looked like rock.

The grave was in the highest corner of the churchyard, and the Rector could see it from the window of his study. A shovel was set in the soil, a stiff, scarecrow shape against the white morning.

Hans turned back to the room and to the kind of problem he didn't need, today of all days.

'I didn't know who else to come to,' the young farmer said, the empty teacup like a thimble in his massive hands. 'I've got kids.'

'Have you told the police?'

'What's the point?' The farmer wore black jeans and a torn leather jacket. He wasn't a churchgoer but Hans had christened his second child.

'If you've been losing stock . . .'

'Aye, one ram. But that were months ago. I told t'coppers about that. What could they do? Couldn't stake out whole moor, could they? Anyway, like they said, it's not a crime no more, witchcraft.'

'Devil worship,' Hans said gently. 'There's a difference. Usually.'

'All bloody same to me. With respect. Like I say, it's not summat they warn you about at agricultural college, Vicar. Sheep scab's one thing, Satanism's summat else.'

'Yes.' Hans didn't know what to do about this. The man wasn't interested in counselling, sympathy, platitudes; he wanted practical help.

'So I've come to you, like.' His name was Sam Davis. This was his first farm. A challenge – seventy acres, and more than half of it basically unfarmable moorland, with marsh and heather, great stone outcrops . . . and the remains of two prehistoric stone circles half a mile apart.

''Cause it's your job, really, int it?' said Sam Davis, thrusting out his ample jaw. A lad with responsibilities. Two kids, a nervy wife and no neighbours. 'T'Devil. An' all his works, like.'

And there he really had put his finger on it, this lad. If this was not a minister's job, what was? Hans tried to straighten his leg. Some minister *he* was, took him half an hour to climb into the pulpit.

'Tell me again,' he said. 'There was the remains of a fire. In the centre of the circle. Now . . . on the previous occasion, you actually found blood. And, er, the ram's head, of course. On the stone.'

'Just like they wanted me to find it,' Sam Davis said. 'Only it weren't me as found it, it were t'little girl.' He set his cup down in the hearth, as if afraid he was going to crush it in his anger.

'Yes. Obviously very distressing. For all of you. But you

138

know . . . It's easy for me to say this, obviously, I'm not living in quite such an exposed . . .'

'Hang on now, Vicar, I'm not . . .'

'I know . . . you're a big lad and well capable of taking care of your family. The actual point I was trying to make is that it's easy to get this kind of thing out of proportion. Quite often it's youngsters. They read books and see films about Satanism, they hear of these ritual places, the stone circles . . . not in Transylvania or somewhere but right here within twenty miles of Manchester and Sheffield . . .'

'So you think it's youngsters, then.'

'I don't know. All I'm saying is it's *often* kids. The kind, if you saw them, you could probably tuck a couple under each arm.'

'Aye, well, like I say, it's not me . . . so much as the wife. I wanted to wait up there, maybe surprise 'em, like, give 'em a bloody good hiding, but . . .'

'I think your wife was right,' Hans said. 'Don't get into a vendetta situation if you can help it. It's probably a phase, a fad. They'll go off and find another circle in a week or two, or perhaps they'll simply grow out of it. You've told the police, and apart from the, er, the ram . . .'

'I've not told coppers about last night. Only you. There's nowt to see. Only ashes. No blood. No bits.'

'How far is the nearest circle from where you live?'

'Half a mile . . . three-quarters. But it's a tricky climb at night, can't do it wi'out a light, and wi' a light they'd see me comin'. Jeep's no bloody use either, on that ground.'

'So you saw the fire . . .'

'Bit of a red glow, that were all.'

'And your wife heard . . .'

'She *thought* she heard. Like I say, could've bin a sheep . . . fox . . . owl . . . rabbit.'

'But she thought it was . . .'

'Aye,' said Sam Davis. 'A babby.'

'There's a dragon,' the boy said, and his bottom lip was trembling. 'There *is* . . .'

'Gerroff,' said Willie Wagstaff.

He'd been for his morning paper and didn't plan to bugger about on a day as cold as this, wanted to get home and put a match to his fire.

'You go an' look, Uncle Willie.'

This was Benjie, nearly eight, Willie's youngest sister Sally's lad. Tough little bugger as a rule. He had The Chief with him, an Alsatian, Benjie's minder.

Willie folded up his paper, stuck it under his arm. 'What you on about at all?'

'. . .'s a dragon, Uncle Willie . . .'s 'orrible . . .'

He was about to cry. Pale too. Cheeks ought to be glowing, morning like this. Especially with having the day off school, to go to Matt's funeral.

Then again, could be that was at the bottom of this. Death, funerals, everybody talking hushed, a big hole being dug in the churchyard for the feller he called Uncle Matt. And Benjie trying to understand it all, seeing this great big dragon.

'All right,' Willie said, pretending he hadn't noticed the lad was upset. 'I'll buy it. Where's this dragon?'

'On t'Moss.'

'Oh, aye. And what were *you* doin' on t'Moss on your own then, eh?'

'I weren't on me own, Uncle Willie. T'Chief were wi' me. An' 'e dint like it neither.'

The big dog flopped his mouth open, stuck his tongue out and looked inscrutable.

'Gerroff,' said Willie. 'That dog's scared of nowt. All right, lead the way. But if you're havin' me on, you little Arab, I'll . . .'

When the farmer had gone, Catherine came in with a mid-morning mug of tea for Hans, and he asked her, 'You hear any of that?'

'Bits.' His daughter sat on the piano stool. She was wearing a plain black jumper and baggy, striped trousers with turn-ups. 'Got the gist. What are you going to do about it, Pop?'

'Well,' said Hans, 'I don't really know. Obviously I don't like the sound of this baby business. And I'm not one to generalize about hysterical women. But still, I think if a child had gone missing virtually anywhere in the country we'd have heard about it, don't you?'

Cathy looked serious, as she often did these days, as if she'd suddenly decided it was time to shoulder the full responsibility of being an adult, as distinct from a student.

'No,' she said. 'Not necessarily.'

'What do you . . . ?' Hans looked puzzled. Then he said, 'Oh. That.'

'It's been exaggerated a lot, of course, but that doesn't mean it doesn't go on, Pop.'

'You're beginning to sound like Joel Beard.'

'Oh, I don't think so.'

'Well,' said Hans, 'if there really is a possibility of something of that nature, then he should tell the police, shouldn't he? But where's his evidence? His wife thought she heard a baby crying. As he said, it could have been any one of a dozen animals, or the wind or . . .'

Cathy said, 'A friend of mine at college did a study of so-called ritual child abuse. What it amounts to, in most of the cases which have been proved, is that the ritual bits – the devil-masks and the candles and so on – are there to support the abuse element. Simply to scare the children into submission. So in most cases we're not talking about actual Devil worship . . .'

'Just extreme evil,' Hans said. 'Where's the difference exactly?'

'I'm not an expert,' Cathy said, 'but I rather think there *is* a difference.' She grinned slyly. 'I think it's something Ma Wagstaff could explain to you if you caught her in the right mood.'

Cheeky little madam. Hans smiled. 'I'm the accredited holy man in these parts, in case you'd forgotten. Anyway, why didn't young Sam go to Ma Wagstaff for advice?'

'Because he hasn't lived around here very long. He doesn't know the way things operate yet.'

141

How they changed. There'd been a time, not so long ago, when Cathy had been dismissive, to say the least, of Ma Wagstaff and all she stood for.

'And you do, do you?' Hans said. 'You know how things operate.'

'I'm getting an inkling.'

'Perhaps we should discuss this sometime.'

'I don't think so,' Cathy said.

Hans frowned.

'I don't think words can really pin it down,' she said. 'Or that we should try to.'

She looked at him blandly. All open-faced and pain-free. Twenty-three years old, a light-haired, plain-faced girl – even Hans had to admit she was no great beauty. However, there was a knowingness about her that he hadn't been aware of before.

He felt old. Suddenly she was starting to look wiser than he felt. How they changed. Every time they came home from University they'd grown stronger and more alien. Catherine studying archaeology at Oxford and Barney, her twin (who he'd rather imagined would follow him into the Church) at the London School of Economics and now researching for a prominent Conservative MP – Barney, the one-time Young Socialist.

'Have you got a boyfriend, Cathy?' he asked suddenly.

'Why do you ask?'

'Because I'm your only surviving parent.'

Her nose twitched mischievously. 'And you'd got around to wondering if I was gay, I suppose.'

He felt his eyes widening. Was this indeed what he'd been wondering? One of those forbidding, shapeless lumps that lay in the mental silt.

Cathy swivelled suddenly on the piano stool, lifted up the wooden lid to expose the keys, and began to beat out the opening bars of 'Jerusalem'.

'I don't think I'm queer,' she said, addressing the keys. 'But some people find me a bit strange.'

*

The frosted peat was quite firm where he walked. Didn't even need his wellies today.

Fifty yards out, Willie stopped.

Bog oak, he told himself, that's all. Probably passed it hundreds of times, but they get turned around by the wind, bits break off.

The Moss looked like a dark sea sometimes. You came down from the village, across the road, and it was like clambering over the rocks to get to the bay. That was on a misty day, when the Moss stretched quickly to the horizon. But on a bright morning, like now, you could see how the bog actually sloped gently upwards, then more steeply towards the mountains, Kinder Scout in the distance.

On a beach there was driftwood. In a moss, bog oak, great chunks of blackened wood coughed up by the peat. Made good, strong furniture.

Benjie wouldn't cross the road to the Moss, but The Chief had followed Willie, reluctantly, big paws stepping delicately over the black pools at the edge, where it nearly met the tarmac.

Now, fifty yards into the Moss, The Chief stopped too and made a noise at the back of his throat that was half-growl and half-whine.

'Bog oak,' Willie said to the dog. 'You never seen bog oak before?'

Point was, though, he personally had never seen owt like this before. The size of it. The fact that it had suddenly appeared in a place where there were no trees, save a few tatty pines.

He walked up by the side of it, and its shape began to change, but it still didn't make you think of anything scarier than half an oak tree with its branches all crushed up and twisted.

But when he got around it, looking back through the branches towards the village, this was when his breath got jammed up in his throat, when he felt like he was swallowing half a brick.

Willie backed off to where the dog was crouching and

143

snarling, his black lips curled back over his teeth. 'All right, Chief,' Willie said hoarsely.

He looked back to where Benjie stood, forlorn in his red tracksuit.

'You're going t'ave to explain this,' Willie told himself, his right hand building up a rhythm on his hip pocket where there was a bunch of keys. 'Lad's countin' on you. Better come up wi' summat a bit quick.'

He straightened up.

'Bog oak.'

He'd stick to his story. The fact that he'd never seen bog oak like this before was *his* problem. Just had to make it sound convincing for the lad.

Willie marched boldly up to the thing, grabbed hold of the end of one of its branches to snap it off, about nine inches of it. 'Strewth!' It was like trying to snap a crowbar. It came though, all at once. 'Go on,' he said to The Chief. 'Fetch it.'

And he threw it as hard as he could, glad to get it out of his hand if truth were told. It felt cold and hard, just like iron or stone. But it was wood all right, nowt fossilized about it, too light – he'd hurled it into the wind and it landed barely ten feet away.

'Well, go on then!' Bloody hell, he'd thrown dozens of sticks for this dog over the years.

The Chief didn't move; the thick fur on the back of his neck was flattened, his eyes were dull and wary, his tail between his legs.

'You soft bugger,' Willie said.

What this was, the dog was close to Benjie, they'd grown up side by side. Only natural he'd picked up on the kid's fear. Aye, Willie thought, and it'd've put the shits up me too, at his age.

Then he thought, admitting it to himself, What do you mean, *at his age* . . . ?

He tried to look at the thing dispassionately. It was amazing, like a work of art, like bloody *sculpture*.

But it didn't make him think of a dragon. Dragons were from fairy tales. More than that, dragons were animals. All

144

right, they had wings and long scaly tails, but they were animals and there was nowt scary about animals.

Willie wanted to back off further, until he couldn't make out the details. He wanted to crouch down at a safe distance and growl at it like The Chief.

Basically he didn't want to see it any more, wished he'd never seen it at all because it was the kind of shape that came up in your dreams. This was stupid, but there was no getting round it.

The tangle of branches wrapped round, woven into each other like pipes and tubes, like a human being wearing its intestines on the outside.

And out of all this, the head rearing up on a twisted, scabby neck, and the head was as black as, as . . . as peat. It had holes for eyes, with the daylight shining through, and a jagged, widely grinning mouth, and on either side of the head were little knobbly horns.

And where one of the horns went into a knob, there was even the beginnings of another face, like one of them gargoyles on the guttering at St Bride's.

But what was worse than all this was the way the thing thrust out of the peat, twelve feet or more, two big branches sticking out either side of the neck-piece, like hunched shoulders, and then smaller branches like dangling arms and hands and misshapen fingers, like they had arthritis in them, like the Rector's fingers.

And when a gust of wind snatched at it, the whole thing would be shivering and shaking, its wooden arms waving about and rattling.

Dancing about.

Willie remembered something that used to scare the life out of him when he was little. The teacher, Ernie Dawber's uncle, telling them about Gibbet Hill where hanged men's skeletons used to dangle in chains, rattling in the wind.

'Oh, come on . . . !' Willie said scornfully. He was shivering himself now – cold morning, coldest this year, not expecting it, that's all there is to it, nowt else.

'Come on.'

Walked away from it across the Moss, towards the little lad and the village, wanting to run, imagining Benjie screaming, *Run, Uncle Willie, run! It's come out of t'bog and it's after you . . . ! Run!*

He kept on walking steadily, but the fingers of both hands were drumming away, going hard and steady at his thighs.

'Bog oak,' Willie made himself shout. 'Bog oak!'

PART FOUR

THE BURIAL

CHAPTER I

Across the border, heading south, Moira ignored all the big blue signs beckoning her towards the M6. Motorways in murky weather demanded one-track concentration; she had other roads to travel.

You should take a rest, Moira. The Duchess. *Unravel yourself.*

Well, sure, nothing like a long drive to a funeral for some serious reflection . . . for facing up to the fact that you were also journeying – and who knew how fast? – towards your own.

The countryside, getting rained on, glistening drably, looked like it also was into some heavy and morose self-contemplation. It was almost like she'd left Scotland and then doubled back: there were the mountains and there were the lochs. And there also was the mist, shrouding the slow, sulky rain which made you wet as hell, very quickly.

Cumbria. She stopped a while in a grey and sullen community sliding down either side of a hill. Wandered up the steep street and bought a sour, milky coffee in a snack-and-souvenir shop. A dismal joint, but there was a table where she could spread out the map, find out where she was heading.

Many places hereabouts had jagged, rocky names. Nordic-sounding, some of them. The Vikings had been here, after the Romans quit. And what remained of the Celts? Anything?

She looked out of the café window at a ragged line of stone cottages with chalet bungalows, Lego-style, on the hillside behind.

She watched a couple of elderly local residents stumbling arm-in-arm through the rain.

English people.

. . . this guy was telling us, at the conference this afternoon, how the English are the least significant people – culturally, that is – in these islands . . . mongrels . . . no basic ethnic tradition.

And what the hell, Moira wondered, were New Yorkers?

149

Mungo Macbeth, of the Manhattan Macbeths. Could you credit it?

Moira had another go at the coffee, made a face, pushed the plastic cup away.

She sighed. Poor Macbeth. Poor glamorous, superficial Macbeth. Who, back home, through the very nature of his occupation and his connections, would likely have whole queues of mini-series starlets outside his hotel room. Who, in New York, would have been chasing not her but his lawyer, wondering if a bonestorm was an Act of God or maybe worth half a million in compensation.

But who, because this was Scotland, the old ancestral muckheap, and because of the night – the crazy, surrealistic, Celtic night – had behaved like a man bewitched.

Moira took her plastic cup back to the counter, which was classic British stained-glass – stained with coffee, congealed fat, tomato ketchup.

'On your own?' the guy behind the counter said. He was lanky, late-twenties. He had a sneery kind of voice out of Essex or somewhere. Nowhere you went these days in Britain, did the people running the tourist joints ever seem to be locals.

She said, 'We're all of us alone, pal.' And, slinging her bag over her shoulder, headed for the door.

'You didn't finish your coffee,' he called after her. 'Something wrong with it?'

'It was truly fine.' Moira held up the back of a hand. 'Got all my nail varnish off, no problem.'

About half an hour later, she surrendered to the blue signs. On the motorway the rain was coming harder, or maybe she was just driving faster into it. At a service area somewhere around Lancaster, she found a phone, stood under its perspex umbrella, called her agent in Glasgow and explained where she was.

'Previous experience, Malcolm, told me not to call until I was well on the road, or you'd instantly come up with a good reason why I wasn't to cross the border.'

150

'Never mind that. I have been telephoned,' Malcolm said ponderously, the Old Testament voice, 'by the Earl's man.'

Oh, shit.

'Hoping you were fully recovered.'

'Right . . .' she said cautiously.

'And most apologetic about the abrupt termination of your performance the other night by the inexplicable precipitation from the walls of approximately a hundred stags' heads. Now, was that not an extraordinary thing to happen?'

'Bizarre.'

'Several people had to be treated for minor lacerations, and there were two broken arms.'

'Oh, dear.'

'So naturally the Earl wanted to reassure himself that you had not been damaged in any way.'

'I'm fine. Just fine.'

'Because you seemed to have disappeared. Along with one of his guests, a gentleman called, er, Macbeth.'

'Sorry,' Moira said. 'No more money.' She hung up and ran back into the rain, black hair streaming behind her, before he could say anything about witchy women.

The psychic thing.

A millstone, a fucking albatross.

She started the car, the eight-year-old BMW with a suitcase in the boot, the suitcase jammed up against the Ovation guitar sleeping in its black case like Dracula in his coffin – we only come out at night, me and that guitar, together. With sometimes devastating results.

The damned psychic thing.

If you really could control it, it would be fine. No, forget fine, try bearable. It would be *bearable*.

But going down that old, dark path towards the possibility of some kind of control. Well, you took an impulsive step down there, the once, and you found all these little side-paths beckoning, tiny coloured lanterns in the distance – follow *me*, I'm the one.

You dabbled. I said to you never to dabble.

The coloured lanterns, the insistent, whispering voices.

The comb has not forgiven you. You have some damage to repair.

Yes, Mammy.

She drove well, she thought, smoothly, with concentration. Down into England.

The way – many years ago, a loss of innocence ago – you travelled to the University in Manchester for all of four months before, one night, this local folk group, Matt Castle's Band played the student union.

Matt on the Pennine Pipes, an amazing noise. Growing up in Scotland, you tended to dismiss the pipes as ceremonial, militaristic.

Matt just blows your head away.

The Pennine Pipes are black and spidery, the bag itself with a dark sheen, like a huge insect's inflated abdomen. Matt plays seated, the bag in his lap, none of this wrestling with a tartan octopus routine.

'Where d'you get these things?'

'Like a set, would you, luv?'

'I wouldn't have the nerve, Mr Castle. They look like they'd bite.'

An hour and a couple of pints later he's admitting you can't buy them. There are no other Pennine Pipes. Perhaps there used to be, once, a long, long time ago. But now, just these, the ones he made himself.

How to describe the sound . . .

Sometimes like a lonely bird on the edge of the night. And then, in a lower register, not an external thing at all, but something calling from deep inside the body, the notes pulled through tube and bowel.

'The Romans brought bagpipes with them. The Utriculus. Whether they were here before that, nobody knows. I like to think so, though, lass. It's important to me. I'm an English Celt.'

Within a month you're singing with the band, trying to match the pipes . . . which you can't, of course, could anyone?

But the contest is productive: Matt Castle's Band, fifteen years semi-professional around the Greater Manchester folk clubs, is suddenly hot, the band offered its first nationwide tour – OK, just the small halls and the universities, but what it could lead to . . . maybe the chance – the only chance they'll ever get at their time of life – to turn full-time professional.

Only this tour, it has *got* to be with Moira Cairns, eighteen years old, first-year English Lit. student. Oh, the chemistry: three middle-aged guys and a teenage siren. No Moira and the deal's off.

Typically, the only pressure Matt applies is for you to take care of your own future, stick with your studies. *'Think about this, lass. If it all comes to nowt, where does that leave you . . . ?'*

And yet, how badly he needs you to be in the band.

'I can go back. I can be a mature student.'

'You won't, though. Think twenty years ahead when me and Willie and Eric are looking forward to our pensions and you're still peddling your guitar around and your looks are starting to fade off . . .'

Blunt, that's Matt.

About some things, anyway. There was always a lot going on underneath.

Moira shifted uncomfortably in her seat and caught sight of herself in the driving mirror. Were those deep gullies under her eyes entirely down to lack of sleep? She thought, Even five, six years ago I could be up all night and drinking with Kenny Savage and his mates and I'd still look OK.

More or less.

The further south she drove, the better the weather became. Down past Preston it wasn't raining any more and a cold sun hardened up the Pennines, the shelf of grey hills known as the backbone of England.

Some way to go yet. Fifty, sixty miles, maybe more. If she was halfway down the backbone of England, then Bridelow must be the arse-end, before the Pennines turned into the shapelier, more tourist-friendly Peak District.

Moira switched motorways, the traffic building up, lots of

153

heavy goods vehicles. Like driving down a greasy metal corridor. Then the Pennines were back in the windscreen, moorland in smudgy charcoal behind the slip-roads and the factories. Somewhere up there: the peat.

I have to do this, Matt had written. *It's as if my whole career's been leading up to it. It just knocked me sideways, the thought that this chap, the bogman, was around when they were perhaps playing the original Pennine pipes.*

Time swam. She was driving not in her car but in Matt's old minibus, her last night with the band. Matt talking tersely about piping to the Moss, how the experience *released* him.

And he'd written, *It was as if he'd heard me playing. I don't know how to put this, but as if I'd played the pipes and sort of charmed him out of the Moss. As if we'd responded to something inside us both. Now that's a bit bloody pretentious, isn't it, lass?*

And Moira could almost hear his cawing laugh.

She came off the motorway and ten minutes later, getting swept into naked countryside that was anything but green, she thought, Shit, what am I doing here? I don't belong here. I walked out on the guy fifteen years ago.

. . . traitorous cow . . .

Hadn't escaped her notice that one thing Lottie had not done was invite her to the funeral.

Always a space between her and Lottie. Never was quite the same after Moira found the nerve to get her on one side during her second pregnancy and warn her to take it easy, have plenty of rest – Lottie smiling at this solemn kid of nineteen, explaining how she'd carried on working until the week before Dic was born.

Never was quite the same with Lottie, after the termination and the hysterectomy.

The road began to climb steeply. It hadn't rained here, but it was cold, the tops of stone walls and fences sugared with frost.

Jesus, I am *nervous*.

It was gone 2 p.m., the funeral arranged for 4.30. Strange time. At this point in the year they'd be losing the light by then.

Her mouth was dry. She hadn't eaten, or drunk anything

154

since the two aborted sips of the filthy coffee in the Lake District, and no time now for a pub lunch.

The sky was a blank screen, the outlines of the hills now iron-hard against it.

Lottie was jealous back then, though she'd never let it show.

The countryside was in ragged layers of grey, the only colour a splash of royal blue on the side of some poor dead sheep decomposing by the roadside, tufts of its wool blown into a discarded coil of barbed wire. The sky harsh, blanched, without sympathy.

Unquintessential England. As hard and hostile as it could get. No water-meadows, thatched cottages or bluebell woods.

No reason for Lottie to be jealous. Was there? Well, nothing happened, did it? Matt was always the gentleman.

Was.

Can't get used to this. I *need* to see him buried.

In front of her, a reservoir, stone sides, a stone tower. Cold slate water. She followed the road across it, along the rim of the dam, slowing for a black flatbed lorry loaded with metal kegs, the only other vehicle she'd seen in three or four miles. Across the cab, in flowing white letters, it said,

BRIDELOW BEERS

The road narrowed, steepened. It was not such a good road, erosion on the edges, holes in the tarmac with coarse grass or stiff reeds shafting through. No houses in sight, no barns, not even many sheep.

And then suddenly she crested the hill, the horizon took a dive and the ground dipped and sagged in front of her, like dirty underfelt when you stripped away a carpet.

'Christ!' Moira hit the brakes.

The road had become a causeway. Either side of it – like a yawning estuary, sprawling mudflats – was something she could recognize: peatbog, hundreds of acres of it.

There was a crossroads and a four-way signpost, and the sign pointing straight ahead, straight at the bog, said BRIDE-LOW 2, but there was no need, she could see the place.

Dead ahead.

'Hey, Matt,' Moira breathed, a warm pressure behind her eyes. 'You were right. This is something.'

Like a rocky island down there, across the bog. But the rocks were stone cottages and at the high point they sheered up into the walls of a huge, blackened, glowering church with a tower and battlements.

Behind it, against a sky like taut, stretched linen, reared the ramparts of the moor.

Unconscious of what she was doing until it was done, her fingers found the cassette poking out of the mouth of the player.

She held her breath. There was an airbag wheeze, a trembling second of silence, and then the piping filled up the car.

Moira began to shiver uncontrollably, and it shook out all those tears long repressed.

She let the car find its way across the causeway.

On the other side was a shambling grey building with a cobbled forecourt. The pub. She took one look at it and turned away, eyes awash.

So she saw the village through tears. A cliff face resolved into a terraced row, with little front gardens, white doorsteps, houses divided by entries like narrow, miniature railway tunnels. Then there were small dim shops: a hardware kind of store, its window full of unglamorous one-time essentials like buckets and sponges and clothespegs, as if nobody had told the owner most of his customers would now have automatic washing machines; a fish and chip shop with some six-year-old's impression of a happy-looking halibut painted on a wooden screen inside the window; a post office with a stubborn red telephone box in front – British Telecom had now replaced most of them with shoddy, American-looking phone booths, but, thankfully, had forgotten about Bridelow.

The streetlamps were black and iron, old gaslamps. Maybe a man would come around at night with a pole to light them.

Well, it was conceivable. Much was conceivable here.

Moira saw an old woman in a doorway; she wore a fraying grey cardigan and a beret; she was as much a part of that doorway as the grey lintel stones.

Peat preserves, Matt had said.
Peat preserves.

From *Dawber's Book of Bridelow*:

RELIGION (ii)

Stone Circle
(upper moor)

E Dawber

THAT BRIDELOW WAS a place of pre-Christian worship is beyond doubt. As has already been noted in this book, there are a number of small stone circles dating back to Neolithic times on the moor less than a mile from the village. The original purpose of these monuments remains a matter for conjecture, although there have been suggestions that some are astronomically-oriented.

As for the village itself, the siting of the church on a presumed prehistoric burial mound is not the only evidence of earlier forms of worship. Indeed . . .

CHAPTER II

'Steady, Pop, just take it *ve* . . . ry steady.'

'No, leave me, please, I'll be fine, if I can just . . .'

'God, I never realized. How could you let it get to this and say nothing? How *could* you?'

Hans hissed, '*Shut up!*' with a savagery that shocked her. He pulled away and ducked into the church porch, and Cathy was left staring at Our Sheila who was grinning vacuously, both thumbs jammed into her gaping vagina.

Cathy turned away and saw why her father had been so abrupt: a large man was bearing down on them, weaving skilfully between the gravestones like a seasoned skier on a slalom.

'Catherine!' he roared. 'How wonderful!'

'Joel,' Cathy said wanly.

'So. You've come all this way for Matt Castle's burial. And you're looking well. You're looking . . . *terrific*. Now.' He stepped back, beamed. 'Did I spot your esteemed father . . . ?'

'In here, Joel.'

He was slumped on the oak bench inside the porch looking, Cathy thought, absolutely awful, the pain now permanently chiselled into his forehead. Joel Beard didn't appear to notice.

'Hans, I've been approached by two young chaps with guitars who apparently were among Matt Castle's many protégés in Manchester. They say they'd like to do an appropriate song during the service, a tribute. I didn't see any problem about that, but how would the relatives feel, do you think?'

Cathy's father looked up at his curate and managed to nod. 'I'll . . . Yes, we must consult Lottie, obviously. Perhaps, Cathy . . .'

Cathy said, 'Of course. I'll ring her now. And I'll come and tell you, Joel, OK?' Why couldn't the big nerk just clear off? But, no, he had to stand around in the porch like some sort of ecclesiastical bouncer, smiling in a useful sort of way, his head almost scraping the door-frame.

'Can we expect any Press, do you think? Television?'

Cathy said, 'With all respect to the dead, Joel, I don't think Matt Castle was as famous as all that. Folkies, no matter how distinguished, tend to be little known outside what they call Roots Music circles.'

'Ah.' Joel nodded. 'I see.' With those tight blond curls, Cathy thought, he resembled a kind of macho cherub.

'Staying the night, Catherine?'

'Probably. The roads are going to be quite nasty, I gather. Black ice forecast. In fact,' she added hopefully, 'I wouldn't hang around too long after the funeral if I were you.'

'Not a problem,' Joel said. 'I have accommodation.'

'Oh?' Damn. 'Where?'

'Why . . .' Joel Beard spread his long arms expansively. 'Here, of course.'

Hans sat up on the oak bench, eyes burning. 'Joel, I do wish you wouldn't. It's disused. It's filthy. It's . . . it's damp.'

'Won't be by tonight. I've asked the good Mr Beckett to supply me with an electric heater.'

'Hell,' Cathy said. 'Not the wine-cellar.' It was a small, square, stone room below the vestry where they stored the communion wine and a few of the church valuables. It was always kept locked.

'Ah, now, Catherine, this is a latter-day misnomer. The records show that it was specifically constructed as emergency overnight accommodation for priests. Did you know, for instance, that in 1835 the snow was so thick that the Bishop himself, on a pastoral visit, was stranded in Bridelow for over two weeks? When he was offered accommodation at the inn he insisted he should remain here because, he said, he might never have a better chance to be as close to God.'

'Sort of thing a bishop *would* say,' said Cathy.

'Ah, yes, but . . .'

'And then he'd lock himself in and get quietly pissed on the communion wine.'

Avoiding her father's pain-soaked eyes, but happy to stare blandly into Joel Beard's disapproving ones, Cathy thought, I really don't know why I say things like that. It must be you, Joel, God's yobbo; you bring out the sacrilegious in us all.

The digital wall-clock in the admin office at the Field Centre said 14.46.

'Er . . .' Alice murmured casually into the filing cabinet, 'as it's Friday and Dr Hall's not likely to be back from that funeral and there's not much happening, I thought I might . . .'

'No chance,' Chrissie snapped. 'Forget it.'

Alice's head rose ostrich-like from the files. 'Well . . . !' she said, deeply huffed.

Done it now, Chrissie thought. Well, bollocks, she's had it coming for a long time. 'I'm sorry, Alice,' she said formally, 'but I don't think, for security reasons, that I should be left alone here after dark.'

Alice sniffed. 'Never said that before.'

'All right, I *know* the college is only a hundred yards away and someone could probably hear me scream, but that's not really the point. There are important papers here and . . . and petty cash, too.'

She'd caught one of the research students in here when she returned from lunch. The youth had been messing about in one of the cupboards and was unpleasantly cocky when she informed him that he was supposed to have permission.

'Nothing to do with *him*, of course.' Alice smirked. 'Because you're not silly like that, are you?'

'I *beg* your pardon?'

'Him! In there. The one with no . . . personal bits.'

'Don't be ridiculous,' Chrissie mumbled, head down so that Alice would not see her blush. How stupid she'd been the other night, thinking . . .

'It was just a thought,' Alice said. She opened the bottom drawer of the smallest filing cabinet and brought out her make-up bag.

. . . when obviously it couldn't have been . . . what you thought. You were just more frightened than you cared to admit, going in there on your own . . .

'Going anywhere tonight?'

. . . it was just the way the thing was lying, and the projecting . . . item was just some sort of probe or peg to hold it together . . .

'What? Sorry, Alice . . .'

'I said, are you going anywhere tonight?'

'Oh, I thought I'd have a night in,' Chrissie said. 'Watch a bit of telly.'

She didn't move. She was still aching from last night. Roger had taken her to dinner at a small, dark restaurant she'd never noticed before, in Buxton. And then, because his wife was on nights, had accompanied her back to her bungalow.

Roger's eyes had been crinkly – and glittering.

His 'stress', as experienced at the motel, had obviously not been a long-term problem. Gosh, no . . .

'I wonder,' Alice said, 'if *Mrs* Hall will be with him at the funeral.'

'I think he likes to keep different areas of his life separate,' Chrissie said carefully.

Lottie said, shaking out her black gloves, 'To be quite honest, I wish he was being cremated.'

Dic didn't say anything. He'd been looking uncomfortable since the undertakers had arrived with Matt's coffin. For some reason, they'd turned up a clear hour and a quarter before the funeral.

'I don't like graves,' Lottie said, talking for the sake of talking. 'I don't like everybody standing around a hole in the ground, and you all walk away and they discreetly fill in the earth when you've gone. I'd rather close my eyes in a crematorium and when I open them again, it's vanished. And I don't like all the flowers lying out there until they shrivel up and die too or you take them away, and what do you *do* with them?'

Dic, black-suited, glaring moodily out of the window, his hands in his hip-pockets. Lottie just carried on talking, far too quickly.

'And also, you see, in a normal situation, what happens is the funeral cars arrive, and they all park outside the house, with the hearse in front, and all the relatives pile in and the procession moves off to the church.'

'Would've been daft,' Dic said, 'when it's not even two minutes' walk.'

'Which means . . . I mean, in the normal way, it means the coffin doesn't leave the back of the hearse until it reaches the church door. Not like this . . . it's quite ridiculous in this day and age.'

The two of them standing alone in the pub's lofty back kitchen.

Alone except for Matt's coffin, dark pine, occupying the full length of the refectory table.

'But I mean, what on earth was I supposed to say to them?' Lottie said. 'You're early – go and drive him around the reservoirs for an hour?'

The relatives would be here soon, some from quite a distance, some with young children.

'I keep thinking,' Dic said, his voice all dried up, 'that I ought to have a last look at him. Pay my respects.'

'You had your chance,' Lottie said, more severely than she meant to. 'When he was in the funeral home. You didn't want to go.'

'I couldn't.'

Her voice softened. 'Well, now's not the time. Don't worry. That's not your dad, that poor shell of a thing in there. That's not how he'd want you to remember him.'

God, she thought, with a bitter smile, but I'm coping well with this.

Of course, half the Mothers' Union had been round, offering to help with the preparations and the tea and the buffet. And she'd said, very politely, No. No, thank you. It's very kind of you, but I can look after my own. And the old dears had shaken their heads. Well, what else could they expect of somebody who'd turn down Ma Wagstaff's patent herbal sedative . . .

Yes. She was coping.

Then Dic shattered everything. He said, 'Mum, I've got to know. What happened with that nurse?'

Lottie dropped a glove.

162

'At the hospital. The night he died.'

'Who told you about that?' Picking up the glove, pulling it on, and the other one.

'Oh, Mum, everybody knows about it.'

'No, they don't,' she snapped.

'They might not here, but it was all round the Infirmary. Jeff's girlfriend knew, who's on Admissions in Casualty.'

'They've got no damn right to gossip about that kind of thing!'

Dic squirmed.

'God, you choose your bloody times, my lad.'

'I'm sorry, Mum.'

'Not as if she was hurt. She had a shock, that was all. He didn't know where he was. He was drugged up to the eyeballs. She was a young nurse, too inexperienced to be on a ward like that, but you know the way hospitals are now.'

'They said he attacked her.'

'He *didn't* attack her. God almighty, a dying man, a man literally on his last legs . . . ?'

Dic said, unwilling to let it go, 'They said he called her, this nurse, they said he called her . . . Moira.'

Lottie put her gloved hands on the pine box, about where Matt's head would be, as if she could smooth his hair through the wood, say, Look, it's OK, really, I understand.

'Leave it, will you, Dic,' she said very quietly. 'Just leave it.'

'She's not coming today, is she? The Cairns woman.'

'No,' Lottie said. 'She's not.'

'Good,' said Dic.

Cautious as a fieldmouse, little Willie Wagstaff peeped around the door, sniffed the air and then tiptoed into the dimness of Ma's parlour.

The curtains were drawn for Matt, as were the curtains in nearly all the houses in Bridelow, but at Ma's this was more of a problem, the place all cluttered up as usual with jars and bottles and big cats called Bob and Jim.

He crept over to the table. In its centre was a large aspirin bottle, the contents a lot more intriguing and colourful than aspirins.

The principal colour was red. In the bottom of the bottle was a single red berry, most likely from the straggly mountain ash tree by the back gate. All the berries had vanished from that bugger weeks and weeks ago, but this one looked as bright and fresh as if it was early September.

Also in the bottle was about a yard of red cotton thread, all scrimped up. One end of the thread had been pulled out of the bottle and then a fat cork shoved in so that about half an inch of thread hung down the outside.

The bottle had been topped up with water that looked suspiciously yellowish, the tangle of red cotton soaked through.

'By the 'ell,' Wille said through his teeth. 'Nothin' left to chance, eh?'

'*You put that down! Now!*'

Willie nearly dropped it. Ma's eyes had appeared in the doorway, followed by Ma. Too dim to see her properly; she was in a very long coat and a hat that looked like a plate of black puddings.

'Bloody hell, Ma, scared the life out of me.'

'Coming in here wi'out knocking. Messing wi' things as don't concern you.'

'*Me* messing!' He gestured at the bottle. 'I bet that's not spring water, neither.'

'Used to be!' Ma glared indignantly at him. 'Been through me now. That strengthens it.'

'Oh, aye? I thought you were losing your touch.'

Ma stumped across to the table, snatched up the bottle and carried it over to the ramshackle dresser where her handbag lay, the size and shape of an old-fashioned doctor's bag. She was about to stow the bottle away then stopped. 'Who's carrying him, then?'

'Me. Eric. Frank Manifold Senior. Maybe young Dic. Why?'

'That Lottie,' Ma said. 'She's a fool to herself, that girl. If she'd let t'Mothers' Union give her a hand, we'd all be sleeping easier.'

'Eh?' He watched Ma passing the aspirin bottle from hand to hand, thoughtfully. 'Oh, now look, Ma . . . just forget it. I am not . . . Anyway, there'll be no chance, Lottie'll be watching us like a bloody hawk.'

'Aye, p'raps I'll not ask you,' Ma said, to his relief. The thought of opening Matt's coffin turned his guts to jelly.

'And anyway, why d'you need a thing like that? I thought it were all sorted out.'

'You *thought*.' Ma was contemptuous. 'Who're you to think, Willie Wagstaff?'

'Ma, I'm fifty-four years old!' Willie's fingers had started up a hornpipe on the coins in the hip pocket of his shiny black funeral pants.

'And never grown up,' Ma said.

'This is grown-up?'

Ma bent and put the bottle down on the edge of the hearth. The fire was just smoke, no red, all banked up with slack to keep it in until Ma returned after the funeral. She straightened up, wincing just a bit – not as sprightly as she was, but what could you expect – and faced him, hands clamped on the coat around where her bony old hips would be.

'It's like damp,' Ma snapped. 'Once you get an inch or two up your wall, you're in trouble. If your wall's a bit weak, or a bit rotted, it'll spread all the faster. It'll feed off . . . rot and corruption. And sickness too.'

'Ma . . .' Willie didn't want to know this. He never had, she knew that.

Ma picked up his thoughts, like they'd dropped neatly in front of her dustpan and brush. 'Comes a time, Willie Wagstaff, when things can't be avoided no longer. He were a good man, Matt Castle, but dint know what he were messing with. Or *who*.'

'Probably dint even know he were messing wi' owt.'

'And that wife of his, she were on guard day and night, nobody could get near. He were crying out for help, were Matt, by the end, and nobody could get near. Well . . .'

'Matt's dead, Ma,' Willie said warningly.

165

Ma picked up the aspirin bottle. 'And that,' she said, ramming the bottle deep into the bag, 'is why he needs protection. And not only him, obviously. This is *crucially* important, our Willie.'

'Oh, bloody hell,' said Willie. It had always been his way, with Ma, to pretend he didn't believe in any of this. Found it expedient, as a rule.

'A time ago, lad, not long after you left school, we had some trouble. D'you remember? Wi' a man?'

'I do and I don't,' Willie said evasively. Meaning he'd always found it best not to get involved in what the village traditionally regarded as woman's work, no matter how close to home.

Ma said, 'He were clever. I'll say that for him. Knew his stuff. Knew what he were *after*. But he were bad news. Wanted to use us. Had to be *repelled*.'

Willie *did* believe, though, at the bottom of him. Most of them did, despite all the jokes.

'What about him?'

Ma's lips tightened, then she said, 'They're allus looking for an opening, and this one stood out a bloody mile. And Matt Castle dint help, chipping away at it, making it bigger.'

'Eh?'

'This musical thing he were working on. T' Bogman.'

'Oh . . . aye . . .'

'Another way in, Willie. Weren't doing *that* on his own, were he?'

Willie went quiet. He knew Matt had been consulting with some writer, but the man never came to Bridelow, Matt always went to the man. Until the final few weeks when he couldn't drive himself any more.

He looked at his mother with her big, daft funeral hat and dared to feel compassion. She didn't need this, her time of life. 'Look, don't get me wrong, Ma . . .'

Ma Wagstaff's fearsome eyes flared, but they couldn't hold the fire for very long nowadays.

'. . . but you've bin at this for a fair few years now . . .'

'More than fifty,' Ma said wistfully.

'So, like . . . like I were saying to Milly . . . don't you ever get to, like . . . *retire*? I mean, is there nobody else can take over?'

Ma straightened her hat. 'There is one,' she said biblically, 'who will come after me.'

'But what 'asn't come yet, like,' Willie said, stepping carefully. You could push it just so far with Ma, and then . . .

The eyes switched from dipped to full-beam. 'Now, look, you cheeky little bugger! When I need your advice, that's when they'll be nailing me up an' all.'

Willie held up both hands, backed off towards the door.

'Which is not *yet*! Got that?'

'Oh, aye,' said Willie.

Outside in the hard, white daylight, he looked across at the church.

'On me way, Matt,' Willie said with a sniff and a sigh, rubbing his hands in the cold. 'I hope they've nailed *you* down, me old mate. Good and tight.'

CHAPTER III

GLASGOW

S hit, could this be the right place?

Realistically – no.

First off, there was no elevator. The stairway, when he managed to find it, was real narrow, the steps greasy. He didn't even like to think what that smell was, but if he was unfortunate enough to be accommodated in this block he'd surely be kicking somebody's ass to get the goddamn drains checked out.

Hardly seemed likely she'd trust her fortunes to a guy working out of a dump like this. But when he made the third landing, there was the sign on the door, and the gold lettering said,

THE M. W. KAUFMANN AGENCY.
PLEASE KNOCK AND ENTER.

Which he did, and inside it was actually a little better than he'd guessed it would be. Clean, anyhow, with a deep pink carpet and wall-to-wall file-cabinets. Also, one of those ancient knee-hole desks up against the window. And the knees in the hole were not, he noticed, in there because they needed to be concealed.

She was about eighteen, with ringlets and big eyes. She swivelled her chair around and looked at him the way, to his eternal gratitude, women always had.

'I . . . uh . . .' He stood in the doorway for a couple of seconds, trying to salvage some breath. This guy Kaufmann had to be pretty damn fit, working here.

'Mr Macbeth, is it?'

He nodded dumbly.

'Do excuse the stairs,' she said. 'Mr Kaufmann represents quite a number of singers.'

'Huh?' Doubtless there was some underlying logic here concerning singers and breath-control, but he was too bushed to figure it out. He hung around in the doorway while she went off to consult with M. W. Kaufmann in his inner sanctum.

Thinking, So you did this again, Macbeth. Put on a suit and tie this time, cancelled your lunch appointment, got busted for speeding by a cop with an accent so thick it sounded like he hadn't got around to swallowing his breakfast. You really did all of this. Over a woman. Again.

Maybe, he thought, as the kid beckoned him in, maybe this is what they call a mid-life crisis. Sure. Like all the other mid-life crises I been having since I turned twenty-nine.

'Mr Macbeth,' M. W. Kaufmann said. 'I am Malcolm Kaufmann.'

They shook hands, and, waving him to a chair, Kaufmann said, 'This all seems rather, er, irregular.'

'I'm an irregular kind of guy,' Macbeth said winningly.

Malcolm Kaufmann looked less than won. He was a small, foxy-eyed person with stiff hair the unnatural colour of light-tan shoes.

The secretary was hanging around, eyeing up Macbeth without visible embarrassment. 'Thank you, Fiona.' Kaufmann waved her out, eyeing up Macbeth himself but in a more discriminating fashion.

'So,' he said. 'You're in television, I understand.'

Macbeth confessed he was, planning to build up the image a little. Then he changed his mind and built it up a lot. How he was over here for the international Celtic conference, but also on account of his company was tossing around an idea for a major mini-series . . . piece of shlock about this American guy, doesn't know his ass from his sporran, comes over to Scotland to look up his Celtic roots and before he knows it he's besotted with this, uh, mysterious Scottish lady.

'I see,' Kaufmann said.

Yeah, I guess you do at that, Macbeth was thinking. Besotted with a beautiful, mysterious lady who sings like a fallen angel and has wild, black hair all down her back with just one single, long-established strand of grey. Under the spell of an enchantress who can make the earth move, *and* the walls and the ceiling, and after you meet her you don't sleep too good any more.

He said, 'Did Moira ever act?'

'Ah.' Kaufmann leaned back in his chair, tilting it against the wall, tapping his rather prominent front teeth with a ballpoint pen. 'Well, her first love, naturally, is her music, but I do believe . . .' Clearly searching his memory for the time she'd done a walk-on for some local soap.

Macbeth helped him out. 'Certainly has the charisma, don't you think?'

'Indeed, indeed. The same, er, quality, perhaps, as that apparent in . . . who shall I . . . ? Cher . . . ? Does that comparison do her justice, would you say?'

'Spoken like a good agent, Malcolm.'

Kaufmann's eyes narrowed. 'Don't be deceived by the surroundings, Mr Macbeth. I *am* a good agent. You say . . . that you encountered Moira at the Earl's recent Celtic gathering. That would be on the evening when her performance was unaccountably disrupted.'

'Right,' Macbeth said. 'Unaccountably disrupted.'

'By what appears to have been an earth tremor.'

'Which, when it happened, I don't recall having felt.'

'Really.'

'Maybe I'm insensitive that way,' Macbeth said.

'But you don't really think so.'

Macbeth shrugged. 'Like you say, she has charisma.'

They both nodded.

'Of course,' Macbeth said, 'this is early days. See, first off, what I'd really like is to meet with Moira over lunch before I leave here . . . discuss things informally.'

'And how long will you be here?'

'Two weeks, at the outside.'

'Well, I shall no doubt be in touch with her very shortly.' Kaufmann smoothed down his unconvincing hair. 'And I shall naturally inform her of your interest. Then perhaps the three of us might . . .'

'Yeah, that'd be, uh, that'd be just . . . She in town right now?'

'I fear not.'

'See, I thought if she was doing a gig someplace, I'd kind of like to be in the audience.'

Kaufmann smiled. 'This sudden interest in Moira . . . this is entirely professional, of course.'

'I'm a very professional kind of guy. However, I've long been a fan. Of the music. But also . . . Malcolm, this is kind of sensitive . . .'

'Which, as you pointed out to me a few moments ago, you are not.'

'Yeah, well, when I, uh, encountered the lady that night, I was a mite overwhelmed, I guess, by the essential, uh, Celtish-ness, if that's the word, of the occasion and, if I'm being honest, by the experience of Moira herself, and so . . . well, I believe I said a few things left her thinking – as you doubtless are thinking right now – what a Grade A dork this person is.'

'Oh, yes,' said Kaufmann. He paused. 'She can certainly be quite disconcerting.'

'Thank you for that. So I'd like to meet with her informally and maybe convince her that, in less-inhibiting circumstances . . .'

'I see. Well, sadly, Moira is *not* working tonight. Or in the city at present. She has a personal matter to attend to. And though, as her agent, I am obviously aware at all times of her whereabouts, no, I'm afraid I can't tell you where she is. That really *would* be irregular.'

'Ah . . . right,' Macbeth said.

'Perhaps you could leave a number with Fiona, where we can contact you.' The agent's face was blank.

'Right,' Macbeth said gloomily.

CHAPTER IV

Joel Beard had been standing there for a couple of minutes, over by the window in the Rector's study, his mouth slightly open.

'Hans,' he said urgently, as if the church was on fire, 'Hans, quickly, who on earth is that?'

The Rector couldn't manage anything quickly any more, but, yes, he too had seen the hooded figure. It had vanished now behind the church tower.

'I'm sorry, Joel?'

'Over there. Didn't you see it?'

'No. I mean . . . all kinds of women pass through that gate.'

Joel turned to him, a 'Got you' smile on his large, unlined face. 'I don't think I mentioned the gate, did I, Hans? And I don't think I mentioned a woman.'

'Well, obviously I assumed . . .' Hans grimaced and bent to his worse knee, feigning pain for once. *Bloody* man. Joel had spent three half-days with Hans, being shown around, shaking a few hands. Big, cheerful, amiable character, anxious to learn. But suddenly . . .

'I wouldn't be surprised,' Joel said in his flat, calm York-shire voice, 'if there weren't quite a lot of things you haven't noticed. Things that go on, hereabouts.'

'. . . the hell are you talking about?'

'Hell?' said Joel. 'Yes. I think I *am* talking about hell. For instance, Sam Davis, the young chap who was here this morning . . .'

Hans stared at him. 'How do you know about that?'

'When he came out, his Land Rover wouldn't start.' Joel flashed his teeth. 'I was around. I fixed it. We had a chat.'

'Mechanic too, eh?' the Rector said. 'You're obviously an endlessly useful man to have about the place.'

Joel, deaf to all sarcasm, said, 'I told Sam I'd go along to the farm, talk to his wife. And perhaps . . . perhaps do what I can to protect them.'

'Joel, if there's any protecting to be done in this parish . . .' God in heaven, this was the man's first full day in Bridelow, and he was taking over!

'Oh, I realized, of course, that you'd be along there yourself if it wasn't for your, er, leg. I explained all this to Sam, of course I did.'

'Made my excuses, did you?'

'Hans . . .' Joel Beard wore a hefty gold-plated crucifix on his chest. Joel, the avenging angel. For the first time, Hans was getting an inkling of how disruptive this man could turn out to be.

'Hans, I'm only trying to help,' Joel said, like a social worker addressing some uppity pensioner.

'The problem is, Hans, people sometimes don't realize the amount of sheer legwork involved in ministering to a rural parish. Admit it, now, you've needed help for quite some while, and been too proud to ask for it. Well, naturally, we all admire you for that, but there's a job of work to be done here, you know that.'

The Rector said coldly, 'I really don't know *what* you're talking about.'

'Perhaps,' Joel said gently, 'that's because you're too close to it. You know what I think? I think these filthy rites on the moors are only the tip of the iceberg.'

He glanced back out of the window to the place where the hooded woman had disappeared. *Stay away*, Hans pleaded inside his head. *Stay out of sight . . . for God's sake . . . whoever you are.*

'There's been talk, you know,' Joel said into the glass pane.

'I have to be frank, it's the only way I can be. And I think it's only fair you should know. A good deal of talk. At diocese level.'

Hans sat down suddenly, carelessly, in his armchair – and felt the pain might hurl him at the ceiling. 'Listen,' he gasped, gripping the chair arms, holding himself down. 'Has it ever occurred to you for one blessed moment that perhaps there are things *you* don't understand? I know you were at St Oswald's. I know the sort of bull-at-a-gate Christianity they go in for . . .'

'I only know what's in my heart.' Joel almost chanting, his eyes squeezed to slits, Joel the seer, Joel the prophet. 'I know that God is living in my heart, and therefore what I feel to be right and good must *be* right and good because it is His Word.'

God save us, Hans thought, from Born Again Christians cunning enough to get into the business proper. And God help me to restrain this man's excesses.

Leave him alone! Can't you see what you're doing to him?

Cathy, in the hall, ear to the study door. Dressed for the funeral, black jumper and skirt, coat over her arm.

Half an hour ago she'd sneaked down to the wine-cellar to discover that Joel had set up a camp bed on the stone flags and a card-table with candles, like a makeshift altar.

A bit eerie. A lot disturbing.

What the hell was this bloke trying to achieve, digging himself in, like a big mole, under the very heart of Bridelow?

'Talk,' Hans said. 'You say there's been talk. What kind of talk?'

Joel walked back to the centre of the room, stood in front of the piano, his hands behind his back, the polished cross flashing from the black of his cassock. Like a cheap medallion, Hans thought from the sour darkness of his pain.

'I'm not a humble man,' Joel said.

Hans, coughing, nearly choked.

'I know this,' Joel said. 'And I pray one day Almighty God will let me come to humility in my own way. But not . . . *yet.*'

His hands whipped round from behind his back. One was an open palm and the other a fist. They came together with a small explosion in the still, fusty air of the Rector's study.

'Not yet,' Joel Beard said softly, turning back to the window. Still, presumably, no sign of the woman in black. Whichever of them it was, Hans thought, she would do well to depart quickly and discreetly, the way they could when they wanted to.

'It's not the time, you see, for humility.' Joel standing behind Hans's chair now, blocking his light. 'The clergy's been humble and self-effacing for so long that it amounts to downright indolence. It's time, I believe, to remember the other Christ. The one who ejected the traders and the money lenders from the temple. There's worse than that here. Isn't there?'

'Look . . .'

Joel spat out, 'It's the Devil's lair!'

'It's . . .' Hans tried to get out of his chair, felt suddenly dizzy.

'That's what the talk's about.' Joel's eyes burning in the afternoon gloom. 'Satan walking openly in the street. Satan walking, bold as brass, to the very door of this church, where that filthy whore parades her . . . her parts.'

'No.' Hans felt old and ineffectual. 'It's not true.'

'Yes! There's a cult of Satan, making blood sacrifices on the moors, and this is where it's emanating from. God only knows how long it's flourished here.'

Cathy breathed in, hard.

Half an hour ago, Joel had caught her spying. Stood and watched her coming up the steps from the cellar, smiling at her from the vestry doorway. Cathy, red-faced, mumbling, 'Just seeing if there was anything I could do. To, er, to make you a bit more comfortable down there.'

Could have bitten her tongue off. She supposed lots of women would find him awfully attractive, with the tight golden curls, the wide smile – and that physique. Perhaps she really *was* gay.

174

Certainly she hated the man now. How could he say these things?

. . . that filthy whore parades her parts . . .

Our Sheila?

You're insane! She wanted to fling open the study door and scream it at him.

Joel said reasonably, 'We're not asking you to do anything yourself. Obviously, you've had to live with these people for a very long time. Big part of your life. And we all realize you're not well . . .'

'And who?' Hans asked wearily, as if he didn't know, 'are *we?*'

Joel, for once, was silent.

'The Bishop? Our newly appointed archdeacon? Perhaps he fancies you, Joel, have you thought about that?'

Joel Beard turned away in distaste. 'Christ says . . .'

'But . . . but *you're* not Christ, Joel,' Hans said, horrified at the hollow weakness of his own voice. He slumped back into the chair, into the endless cavern of his pain, his eyes closed.

The Rev. Joel Beard laughed agreeably. 'We'll crack this thing together, Rector. You and me and God.'

Hans heard him rubbing his hands. 'Well. Time's getting on. Funeral to conduct. Though I can't think *why* you left it until so late in the day.'

'Family request,' Hans mumbled, lying. 'Some relatives had . . . long way to travel.'

'Hmm. I see. Well, come on, old chap.' Joel's strong Christian hand on his shoulder. 'Soon be over.'

From behind the door, Cathy scurried away, pulling on her coat. He'd caught her once today. He'd never catch her again.

The two of them stood at the bottom end of the churchyard, not far from the lych-gate. There was a monument here on its own, stark and pointed, like an obelisk, one word indented on a dressed-stone plaque.

HORRIDGE.

'It was always pretty scary,' Shaw said, 'to think that one day I'd be under that too.'

Therese, in her ancient fox-fur coat, walked all round the monument. 'Is it a vault?'

'Something like that. I didn't take too much notice when they stuck my father in there. I'm sure that one of the reasons I was determined to unload the brewery was to avoid being buried here. I mean, I didn't think about it at the time, but it must have been at the back of my mind. To break the family ties with Bridelow, get the hell out of here. For good. I mean . . . not have to come to people's funerals who you hardly knew, because you're a Horridge. I reckon the old man would have sold out himself if he'd had half a chance.'

'Where would you *like* to be buried?'

'Somewhere warm. If it has to be in this country I'd prefer to be cremated.'

'I wouldn't mind.'

'Being cremated?'

'Being buried here,' Therese said. 'I like vaults.' She smiled, her eyes glinted. 'You can get out of them.'

Shaw shuddered, a feeling he was growing to enjoy. She looked very edible today, as ever. However, for the first time, he rather hoped she was *not* naked under that coat. It was so cold, though, that he didn't really imagine she could be. She'd attached a scarf-thing to it today, with the fox's head on the end. Shaw, who'd ridden to hounds two or three times whilst staying with friends, didn't find this offensive but suspected there were people in Bridelow who would; they appeared to have strong views about killing animals for pleasure.

She said, 'Have you ever seen him, your father?'

He knew her well enough by now to know exactly what she meant by that, but he pretended he didn't. 'Of course I've seen him. He didn't die until I was twenty-five. Come on, let's get a drink before the show starts.'

'It's your family vault, after all,' Therese said. 'You've got rights of access. Why don't we pop in and visit him one night?'

'For God's *sake*, Tess . . .' Not his bloody father, the sanctimonious old sod.

'I've told you before,' she said coldly. 'I don't like to be called Tess.' Then she turned her head and looked up into his face, and the fox's glass eyes were looking at him too. 'We could ask him, you see.'

He felt the chill wind raising his hairline even more, wished he'd worn his stylish new Homburg. She was playing with his mind again. Sometimes it was difficult to sleep.

'We could ask him if you were right. That he really did want to get out of Bridelow. That he would've had no objections at all to Gannons taking over the brewery. Give your mother something to think about.'

'I'd rather not, if you don't mind,' Shaw said. He was thinking about last summer, a warm day in August, when he'd found out about another side of Therese.

Over dinner one night in Manchester, he'd giggled nervously and said to her, 'You know, I'm beginning to think you must be some sort of vampire, only ever coming out at night.'

'Would you like that – if I was a vampire?'

'I don't know. What would it mean?'

'I could make you undead, couldn't I?'

'Er . . . haven't you got to be dead before you can be undead?'

She'd put down her glass and looked at him, red wine glistening on her lips, face still and golden in the moving candlelight, like a mask from some Egyptian tomb.

'And what,' she said, 'makes you think you aren't?' And he began to shake with desire, a new kind of desire which began at the bottom of his spine.

But he'd kept on at her in the car – it was a Range Rover this time, belonging, she said, to a friend – as she whizzed them down Deansgate around 1 a.m. What did she do at weekends, in the daytime? Social work, she said.

'*Social* work?'

And it was true; two days later they were out on the moors. He was following Therese in gloriously tight jeans and there were two friends called Rhona and Rob and a bunch of people Therese described loosely as 'offenders'.

Rhona, who was quite attractive, despite having a sort of crewcut, was apparently a professional social worker with the local authority. Rob, a lean, hard-looking man, was – amazingly – a policeman, a detective sergeant. You had to admire her cheek, being friends with a copper after all the cars and things she'd stolen.

They'd parked their vehicles in a long lay-by off the Sheffield road and after two hours of hard walking, Shaw's legs were starting to ache.

'Where are we going exactly?'

'Not far now,' Therese assured him. The six 'offenders', who were of both sexes and ranged in age from teens to about sixty, were fairly silent the whole way.

After a further few minutes, Therese stopped. They were on a kind of plateau, offering a magnificent view of miles of sunlit moorland and, more distantly, a huge expanse of darkness which he assumed was the Moss, with the hills behind it reaching up to Kinder Scout.

'Gosh, look,' Shaw said, 'there's the Bridelow road. We've come a hell of a long way round. If we'd just gone through the churchyard and carried on up the moor we'd have been up here in about half an hour.'

'It was better to come this way,' Therese said. 'Don't whinge, Shaw.'

There were stubby stones around where she was standing, arranged in a rough sort of circle, or maybe an egg-shape; it was hard to tell, they were so overgrown.

One of the older offenders was on his knees. He was probably exhausted. He had his arms around one of the bigger stones, a thing about two and a half feet high, and he seemed to be kissing it.

'What sort of offenders are they?' Shaw whispered.

'Just people who society considers maladjusted,' Therese said. 'It's stupid. They all have special qualities nobody seems to want to recognize.'

Rob said, 'We're helping to rehabilitate them.'

Therese had taken a few objects from Rob's backpack –

odd things, photographs in frames, a small pair of trainers, a large penknife – and arranged them around the circle, up against the stones.

They had a rough sort of picnic outside the circle of stones, with a whole cooked chicken, which everybody pulled bits off, and red wine. Afterwards, they all sat around in the springy yellow grass, not talking, the sun going down, Shaw starting to feel a little drunk, a little sleepy.

He was aware that Rob and Rhona had entered the circle and were murmuring to themselves in low voices. They seemed to have taken all their clothes off. They began to touch each other and then to have sex. Shaw was deeply shocked but kept quiet about it. It went on for some time. Until suddenly, dreamily, a plump, spotty, middle-aged woman called Andrea stood up and joined Rob and Rhona in the circle and began to behave as though there were some other people in there too.

'Hello, David,' she said joyfully, the first time she'd spoken all afternoon. 'All right, Kevin?'

She giggled. 'Yes,' she said. 'Me too. Do you like it here? It's nice, isn't it?'

At that stage Rhona and Rob left her and came out and sat with Therese and Shaw. Flies and midges buzzed around Andrea in the dusk. Shaw seemed to fall asleep. When he awoke he saw Andrea on her knees in the circle with her arms around what looked like two dusty shadows.

'Isn't it heartwarming?' Therese was whispering, as if they were watching a weepy from the back stalls. 'She's becoming reconciled to the loss of her brothers.'

'What happened to them?'

'They died,' Therese said. 'A long time ago. She killed them. With a penknife. They were only little. 'Course she was only a child herself. It was such a shame, they put her away for a long time.'

He didn't remember how they got back to the cars except that it was dark by then and it didn't seem to take nearly as long as it had taken them to get to the circle.

*

In the churchyard, Therese said, 'Is *she* here – your mother?'

'No, she . . . she thinks she's got that Taiwanese flu. I've tendered her apologies.'

'Funny, isn't it, the way she won't come into Bridelow.'

'She should leave. She's no connections here.'

'Why won't she leave?'

'I don't know,' Shaw said, but he did. His mother couldn't bear to be supplanted by Therese. His mother did not like Therese. This was understandable. Sometimes he wasn't sure that the word 'like' precisely conveyed his own feelings.

Her dark hair, swept back today, was mostly inside the collar of the fur coat. She wore a deep purple lipstick.

Nor, he thought, was 'love' appropriate. So *why* . . .

Therese nodded back towards the village. Shaw looked at his watch: three minutes to four, and the light was weakening.

. . . *why* . . .

Therese said, 'It's coming.' Meaning the funeral procession.

Shaw shuddered again, with a cold pleasure that made him afraid of her and of himself.

'You know,' Therese said, 'I think it's time you met *my* father. Properly.'

'Is he dead?' Shaw asked fearfully.

CHAPTER V

Everything that happened, the dreadful inevitability of it all, Ernie Dawber would remember in horribly exquisite detail. Like a series of grim cameos. Or the meticulously etched illustrations in the pre-war picture-book from which he used to tell stories to the youngest children on Friday afternoons, enjoying the measured resonance of his own headmasterly tones and then holding up the book to what was left of the light so they could all see the pictures.

Cosy, back then. Friday afternoons in mid-autumn, with Mr Dawber and The Brothers Grimm. Home to buttered toast for tea.

Now it was another Friday afternoon. But this time the text was being read to Ernie and *he* could see all the pictures, the pages turning over in a terrible, considered rhythm, until he wanted to leap up from his seat in the back row, crying out, *Stop . . . stop!*

He didn't leap up much any more. Sometimes, lately, he felt unsteady and disconnected in his head. But when he went to the doc's for some pills for it, the doc had made him have tests. Sorry he'd gone now.

No leaping up, anyroad. Nowt he could do except to witness it, for this was all he was now: the observer. The local historian, dry and factual. Not for him to comment or to judge.

Nothing that happened on this day would ever be recorded, anyway, in *The Book of Bridelow*. And so was best forgotten.

As if ever he could.

Cosy, too (the first picture) in the bar at The Man before the funeral, having a whisky for the cold, with his half of Black, his mind charting the changes from that warm evening when Matt Castle had brought them hope.

Although, unknown to him at the time, the Change must have begun on the bright March morning when the roadmen found the bog body.

Hand clenching on his glass of Black, now condemned as gnat's piss by them as knows. The only light in the bar is greenish-blue, from the old gas-mantle Matt Castle reinstated, childishly happy when he found it could still be made to work. Such small things seemed to delight Matt, painstakingly patching up frail memories of his childhood.

Unaware that he, too, was part of the Change.

Behind the bar, Stan Burrows in a black waistcoat, says passively, 'Tough about Gus Bibby, eh?'

'Why? What's up?'

'You not heard, Ernie? He's closing up the Stores.'

'No!'

'I could see it coming, me. Just not up to it no more. Bent double half the time. I went in for a bucket last week, had to climb up and get it meself. 'Sides which, he's selling nowt. What can you buy in Gus's you can't get in Macclesfield twenty per cent cheaper?'

'It's a matter of principle, Stan. We're glad enough to shop at Gus Bibby's when there's snow or floods and you can't get across the Moss. Anyway, what about his son?'

'How many days a year can't you get across t'Moss since they've built that road up? Nay, it's price of progress, int it?'

'*Progress*?' Ernie nearly choking on his so-so half of Black.

Stan saying, 'Nay, Bibby's'll shut and it'll stay shut. Who's going t'buy that place?'

'What about his son?'

'He'll not come back, will he? Got a good job wi' Gas Board in Stockport. Would you come back?'

'Aye,' said Ernie. 'I would.'

'How many's like you, though, Ernie? Any more. Be honest. How many?'

Second picture.

Halfway up the street, church behind him, looking down towards The Man. From up here, the pub looks as if it's built on the Moss itself.

A bitter wind has blown through Bridelow, snatching the leaves from the trees and bleaching the colour from the faces inside the front porches. The faces hovering, ghostly in the shadows, the bodies invisible in black.

The villagers start to step from their doorways; the coffin's coming.

A fair turn-out, thanks to Matt's folk-music friends from the Manchester circuit and outsiders with an interest in Bridelow like Dr Roger Hall. And the former brewery workers who failed to find employment in Buxton, Macclesfield, Glossop, or even Manchester and Sheffield; they're all here, except for the ones hunched over their fires with their Beecham's Powders and a bad case of Taiwanese flu, the like of which would never have got Across the Moss in the old days.

Ernie fancies he can hear wretched coughing from behind

the drawn curtains, as if the virus has spread to the stones themselves.

Turn the page, lad.

Up by the arched lych-gate now, watching people stepping down to the cobbles to join the ragged tail of the procession.

The blinds are down at the Post Office, soon to be the only shop remaining in Bridelow. Ernie hardly recognizes black-clad Milly Gill, who normally looks like a walking botanical garden. Is she in mourning just for Matt Castle, or for Bridelow itself?

The coffin's at a funny angle because of the respective heights of the men carrying it, from little Willie to gangling Frank. Are Willie and Milly Gill back together? Ernie hopes so; they need each other, time like this.

Lottie Castle follows immediately behind and, by 'eck, mourning becomes her, she's never looked as fine, the red hair swept back under a neat, black pillbox hat with a little veil, generous mouth set hard. With her, half a pace behind, is the lad, Dic, a leather case under his arm.

Go on, turn over, you've got to look . . .

The coffin on a wooden bier beneath the Autumn Cross, the Rector hunched stiffly before it, his strong hair slumped over his forehead, not quite hiding pearls of sweat, and the lines in his face like an engraving.

Behind the Rector bobs the new curate, curly-haired lad, built like a brick privy. Bit of a firebrand, by all accounts.

He'll be all right. He'll settle down. Won't he?

At the side, by the choir stalls, is Hans's lass, Catherine, who seems all of a sudden to have lost her youth. Anxiety on her firm, plain face; worried about her dad, and with good reason. Needs a long rest, that lad.

Two youngsters with guitars who Ernie doesn't recognize sing a wistful but forgettable ballad, stop and look around afterwards before realizing congregations aren't supposed to applaud, especially at a funeral.

Then the Rector gets down to it.

'Lord, we're here to thank you for the life of Matthew Castle, and to pray that his soul might . . .'

Ernie, in the centre of the rearmost pew, locates Ma Wagstaff without much difficulty – that's quite a hat Ma's got on, with those big black balls on it. Anyway, it's through Ma that he spots . . . *the mystery woman*. Otherwise he never would have noticed her, all in black like that and in the shadow of the pillar.

Ma turns around just once, with that famous penetrating stare. Thought at first the old girl was looking at *him*. And then he sees the black, hooded figure to his left, on the little seat wedged up against the stone pillar.

By 'eck. They're not usually as public as *this* about it, these women.

Pretty place, this church. Norman, was it, those huge archways? And candles here and there, like in a Catholic church. Warm stained glass with Garden of Eden-type pictures full of flowers and fruit.

And the cross that hung above the carved wooden screen dividing the nave from whatever the altar area was called.

The cross was of green wood. Or at least wood that *had* been green last summer. Woven boughs, some with shrivelled, dead leaves still hanging from them. A cross from the woods and the hedgerows. Yeah, nice. And strange. One of several strange things in here – like the German Shepherd dog sitting stoically on a pew next to a small boy.

Well, why not?

But still just a wee bit weird.

Jesus, she'd be feeling at home here next. But she still kept the cloak about her; it was pretty damn cold in here and going to be a good deal colder outside, when the darkness came down.

Underneath the cloak, the jeans and jumper she'd travelled down in. No place to change. Wouldn't worry Matt how she looked, but jeans might not be viewed as entirely respectful at a funeral in these parts; keep them covered.

Also . . . *I don't want this place to know me. Don't want to be identified by Lottie or Willie or Eric or anybody who ever bought a Castle Band album.*

Not yet, OK?

Locking the car, she'd glanced up into the thickening sky, and thought, Before this burial's over, it's going to be fully dark. Matt Castle going out of the dark and into the last black hole, and the peaty soil heaped upon him under cover of the night.

But no bad thing, the dark.

I can't face anybody, she'd thought, standing alone in the muddy parking area behind the church, pulling up the deep hood until her face was lost, *traitorous cow*, I'll stay at the back, out of sight, I'll pay my respects in my own way. And then I'll get the hell out, and nobody'll be the wiser.

And yet . . .

She'd stared up at the church, at its dour, crenellated walls, at its Gothic stained-glass windows showing their dark sides to the sky, taking the light and giving out nothing. At all the pop-eyed stone gargoyles grinning foolishly down on her.

. . . *somehow* . . .

Followed the walls to the tower and the edge of the churchyard where the moor began in ochre tufts and gorse bushes, and in the distance there was a clump of rocks like a toad, and if you blinked the toad would be quivering, having leapt and landed five yards closer.

. . . *there's something here that knows me already.*

No people around at that time, only the sensation of them behind the drawn curtains. *Not* peering through the cracks at the stranger and the stranger's dusty BMW, nothing so obvious.

'This is a *knowing* place,' she'd found herself saying aloud.

Then, all too damn conscious of looking very like an extremely witchy woman, she'd passed through a wooden wicket gate under a steep, stone archway, to walk a while among Bridelow's dead.

There, at the top of the churchyard, was the hole awaiting Matt, the area immediately around it covered with bright emerald matting, luridly unconvincing artificial grass. She stood on it, on the very edge of the hole, staring down into the black, rooty soil. And saw again the smoke-choked mouth of the great fireplace at the Earl's castle, the clawing thing her mind had constructed there.

Mammy, how was he when he died, can you tell me that?

Backing away from the open grave, thinking, There are people here who can tell me that. And I can't ask.

Standing several yards from the church doorway now and feeling strongly that someone was watching out for her. But knowing from experience that this feeling of being watched wasn't necessarily a case of some*one* but some*thing*. That the watcher could be something in the air, something that existed purely to watch.

Spooking herself. Down here in England, where she had no heritage and there should be no reverberations.

'Aw, fuck this,' she'd said aloud, turning towards the church doorway, looking up . . . directly into the massively exaggerated, gaping pussy of the *Sheelagh na gig*.

'Shit,' Moira said. 'Was you, wasn't it?'

The *Sheelagh*. The exhibitionist. The stone effigy of a woman, compressed to the dimensions of a gargoyle. Thrusting out her privates and leering about it. A blatant fertility symbol (or something) almost always found in the stonework of churches, mostly in Ireland.

But rarely as prominent as this.

'Got yourself a prime spot, here, hen,' said Moira. She'd walked under the *Sheelagh na gig*, through the porch and into the church, feeling better now she knew who'd been watching her. This was OK, this was not the white-haired, white-faced man who'd tried to steal the comb and (maybe . . .) brought the bloody house down. This was something older, more benevolent (maybe . . .).

She'd been the first in church. She'd sat here alone inside her own dark shroud, concealed by a pillar, until . . .

Until Matt arrived.

'. . . we'll all of us remember the day Matt returned,' the Minister said. 'The gratitude felt by the whole village that its *second* most important institution was to be saved . . .'

He's not well, this minister, Moira thought. And he's

worried. A real sense of oppression coming off him. And there shouldn't be that in here. This is abnormal.

The old lady knows, the one in the really bizarre hat.

Hans leads them out into the churchyard, the pace all the more funereal because he can hardly walk.

As they near the doors, Ernie Dawber, standing up in his pew, sees the curate, Joel Beard, stride forward to take the Rector's arm. Then there's a rush of footsteps down the aisle and he sees Catherine squeeze past the coffin resting on the shoulders of Willie and Eric, Frank Senior and Young Frank and practically *throw* herself between the two clergymen, dashing the curate's hand aside and snatching her father's arm, clasping it.

By 'eck. No love lost there and she doesn't care who knows it.

The pews are emptying from front to back, which means Ernie will be the last out, except for the Mystery Woman. He glances behind just once, as he joins the end of the procession, but she's not there.

Sometimes they just disappear, these people.

The next picture is so black at first, because of the sky, that it's almost like a woodcut.

The graveyard packed like a dark fairground. But a circle of space at the top, where the moor looms above the rectangular hole in the soil, which, when the lamplight flares, is like the opening of a shaft.

Alfred Beckett, verger and organist, has lit a metal paraffin lantern which he holds up on a pole, hanging it over the grave as Hans completes the burial rite, his own version, some of it turned about, but all the old lines there.

'Man born of woman hath but a short time . . .'

As the phrases fade, like a curlew it begins.

The piping.

Ernie gasps, muffling his mouth with a leather-gloved hand, clutching a Victorian marble cross for support. A hush enclosing the churchyard as the cold and homeless notes roam the air.

He straightens up against the cross, brushing in relief at his overcoat. It's the lad. Dic. Matt's coffin on the ground at the edge of the grave and Dic standing by it, the Pennine Pipes under his arm and the wilderness music swirling up into the cold.

Only the lad. For just a few seconds . . .

Ernie moving closer. The lad plays well. His dad'd be proud. Tries to see Lottie's face, but her head's turned away. Someone weeping behind him.

Can't see the coffin any more. The four bearers lined up on either side of Dic, concealing the grave. Lamplight shows him the fingers of Willie Wagstaff's left hand starting to move against his thigh, a slow beat, in time with the piped lament.

Ernie finds he's standing next to the lamp-bearer, Alf Beckett, when somebody – likely a woman – whispers, 'Put it out, Alf.'

'Eh?'

'Put lamp out.'

Silently, Alf Beckett lowers the pole to the ground, unhooks the lantern, lays it on the grass at his feet, shuffling around to put himself in front of it so that no light is cast into the grave.

'That do?'

'Fine. Ta, lad.'

Oh, hell.

Quite soon, behind the pipes, there's a scraping and a scuffling on the ground, like mice or rats. Ernie tries to shut it out. He's not *supposed* to hear this. He looks up, away from it, and the only face he can see clearly is the Rector's, upturned to the sky, to what light remains.

The Rector also knows he is not supposed to hear or to see. He has his eyes tightly closed.

'*Get it over with,*' Ernie hisses. '*Get it bloody done!*'

Raises his eyes above the little graveside scrum but doesn't close them. Sees the black shapes of the sparse trees on the edge of the churchyard, where it meets the moor. The trees trembling. Has this withering, shrivelling sensation of something blowing towards them, off the moor, off the Moss. Irrational. His nerves. Like the night when he was scared the Moss would swallow the sun and it would never come up again. Come on, settle down, calm yourself, there's nowt you can do except keep your mouth shut and your eyes averted. Nowt here for the Book of Bridelow.

Dic keeps on piping, the same melancholy tune, over and over again, but erratic now, off-key; he's getting tired . . . but the noises behind him go on, the scuffling on the ground, and now a jarring creak and an intake of breath.

And then all hell . . .

'*Stop! Let me through!*'

Rough hands thrusting Ernie aside.

'Mr Beckett, where's the lamp? Stand back, will you. Stand *back*, I said, or somebody . . . will . . . get . . . hurt.'

The lantern snatched up, its gassy-white flame slanting, flaring in the furious eyes of the Rev. Joel Beard, smoke rolling from the funnel.

Hands grab at him to hold him back from the grave, but Joel, snarling, is big and fuelled-up with rage, the metal cross swinging as his cassocked chest swells and his elbows slam back.

The lamp flies up into the night and Joel catches it by its base as it falls, pushing Alf Beckett so that Alf spins sideways into Dic Castle and the Pennine Pipes make a squirming, ruptured noise, subsiding into empty, impotent blowing and wheezing.

The Rev. Joel Beard steps to where the coffin of Matt Castle lies at the grave's edge, and he lifts the lantern high.

CHAPTER VI

She was not among those weeping when the Pennine Pipes began.

It got to her in other ways . . .

Hanging back behind the crowd, still as the headstones around her, Moira felt confused, puzzled . . . the pipes plucking at something inside her, starting this small, familiar tingle in her lower abdomen.

OK, she would have known anyway that it wasn't Matt she could hear, there wasn't the same lilting, light-as-air technique, the inimitable *agility*. Would have been no mistaking that.

And yet . . .

The Roman numerals on the church clock, lit-up, said 5.30. It *would* be dark at 5.30 this time of year. But the darkness had the icy, velvet quality of midnight, and whoever had organized this service had *known* it was going to end like this.

Why?

Sure as hell was the strangest funeral she'd ever been to, the minister and the principal mourners in a distant lamplit huddle, the freezing air over the entire churchyard somehow electric with this almost feverish, dreamlike tension, and the piping going on and on and *on*, like in a time-loop . . . so that you wound up mentally pinching yourself, asking, *is this real?*

. Like, where am I? Did I drive across these unknown hills into some dream dimension?

Needing at last to break through, maybe talk to someone, hear the sound of her own voice, anybody's voice, she moved closer, symbolically tossing back the hood of her cloak . . . at the moment the lantern went down.

She saw the big shapes of the trees at the end of the churchyard. Below them, shadows intertwined. The amorphous tableau at the top of the small rise where Matt's grave was to be. From whence came the insistent, never-ending piping but no sounds of a funeral service, no suggestion of anyone leading the proceedings.

Only – under the pipes, as she drew close – a whispering, as if there was more than one person whispering but they weren't listening to each other, the voices rustling together like wind-dried leaves.

And she caught a passing perfume, a sick, sad smell.

Then, to her left, a small commotion. An expulsion of breath from a yard or so away, a dragging on her cloak and she was almost pulled down.

'*Stop!*' A man's voice, strong, authoritarian. '*Let me through.*' For just a second everything froze, and then there was this instinctive communal resistance, a tightening of the clutch of bodies around her. The whispering intensified, new urgency in it, the dead leaves really crackling now.

A scrabbling now, by her feet; some guy had been pushed over, rolled on to the cloak. He found his feet, she reclaimed the cloak. Somewhere nearby there was a struggle going on.

She didn't move. The lamp appeared again, bouncing wildly in the air, like some will-o'-the-wisp thing. In the spinning light she got a split-second picture of . . . must be Matt's boy, Dic Castle, playing the pipes, the bag trapped in an elbow, his face red with effort, and Willie Wagstaff next to Dic, Willie's eyes flitting anxiously, from side to side, and she could almost feel the rhythm of the little guy's famously impressionable fingers in her head, thud, thud . . .

Thud, thud. . . . And then the oil-lamp went up again, was held steady.

And Moira looked down, oh, Jesus, into Matt Castle's face framed in quilted white.

The smell. The perfume of the dead. The coffin lid off. His hair gone. Grave-dirt spilled on his closed eyes.

The way you never want to see them, the way you can't bear to remember them. And still you can't turn away your head; it won't move.

What have they *done* . . . ?

Moira began to shiver. She closed her eyes, and this was worse, like waking up in the fast lane, her senses lurching out of control, cracked images oscillating in the steamy half-light between perceived reality and illusion, the place where the whispers went.

. . . vaporous arms reaching from the smoky maw of a great fireplace . . .

. . . the splintering white of a skull-storm . . .

. . . dancing lights on the moor . . . a rock like an encroaching toad . . . pop-eyed gargoyles belching blood . . . an eruption of steaming intestine on stone . . .

All these reflecting one to another like in the shards of a

191

shattered mirror, while tiny, vicious, chattering voices gnawed at her eardrums and she felt something sucking around her shoes pulling her down, and she knew that if she didn't open her eyes she'd be screaming like a loony.

But when she did it was no better. She blinked in pain.

He lay there in his coffin. Matt Castle, not in a shroud but a plain, white T-shirt. And his grey-white hands, crossed over his chest, were fumbling at it.

Oh, God, oh, Jesus, his damned hands were . . .

'How dare you! How *dare* you!'

The man holding up the lantern, the big cleric she'd seen in the church earlier, this man's face bleached in the lamplight with rage and shock.

Below him, the old lady with the bizarre hat, sleeves pushed up and both arms in the coffin, pressing something into the dead hands of Matt Castle, crossed over his breast.

It was her hands moving, not his.

Moira saw a frightened, angry glazing in the eyes of the big man as he bent roughly down with the lamp; forced himself between the old woman and the body in the coffin.

She thought she heard him sob, or it might have been her.

The big minister guy had put his own hand in there . . . *Holy Christ, is this real . . . ? . . .* and brought it out, something clutched into a fist.

'Put that *back* . . .' The old woman's eyes flashing green-gold, like a cat's, in the lantern-light.

'This is . . . *unpardonable* . . .' Yeah, he *was* sobbing, the big man; sickened, shattered, furious at what he was doing.

'Joel . . .' The minister, the Rector, was there, on the other side of the grave, his face all twisted up, the fair-haired girl still holding on to his arm. 'Please. Put it back. I'll explain to you, I promise . . .'

'How . . . How *can* . . .'

'Turn away, Joel. Please. It isn't what you . . . Just *turn away*.'

The big clergyman lifted his left hand to the lamp. He was holding up a small bottle. Something moved in it, liquid. Moira glimpsed red.

'Joel . . . Give it to me . . . You don't know what . . .'

She saw that Joel was breathing rapidly now, a kind of wild, petulant hysteria there. She saw him rise to his full height, saw his arm pull back.

The Rector screamed, 'No!', shook out of the girl's grip, threw himself across the empty grave, one shoe reaching the phoney nylon grass mat on the other side, inches from the coffin . . .

. . . as Joel, breathing violently, hurled the bottle above all the heads towards the moor beyond the trees. Then he turned, put down the lamp and stumbled back into the crowd, his hands flailing.

Heard him clumping away, his outraged breathing. His sobs.

'Grab him, somebody, please . . .' The girl, and she meant the Rector. People pushing past Moira, reaching out for the minister as the false grass slid from under his shoe and he almost rolled into the open grave.

Several minutes later, the graveyard had quietly emptied, except for the group around the empty coffin. Mostly women and not whispering any more. At the centre was the one with the hat. She was the oldest of them. Two of the others replaced the coffin lid.

Moira had backed beyond the lamplight, was a short distance away, leaning up against this tall cross in the Celtic style. Trying to breathe.

Oh, God. Oh, Holy Jesus. What the fuck am I into here?

One of the women at the graveside was Lottie Castle.

Lottie's voice was very quiet, very controlled, carefully folded up tight. 'I can't believe . . . that any of this has happened.'

'Lottie . . .' It was Willie, coming up behind her.

'And *you* . . .'

'I know,' Willie said. 'I'm sorry.'

'I'll never forgive you, Willie. Or that . . . *her*.'

'She only wanted . . . Oh, Jesus Christ,' Willie wailed. 'This is awful. This is a right bloody mess. I can't tell you. Oh, God, Matt . . . Why'd it have to be Matt?'

'Willie,' the old girl in the hat demanded. 'Stop that skrikin' and fetch me that bottle back.'

'Ma, nobody's going to find that bloody bottle tonight. If ever.'

'Then we'll have t'do what we can.' She placed both hands on the coffin. 'Pass us me bag, Joyce, it's down behind that cross.' Moira tensed; at her feet was a thick vinyl shopping bag.

Lottie's leather boot slammed down hard on the coffin between the old woman's hands. 'You,' Lottie said, 'have done about enough for one day.'

The old woman's hat fell off. She looked startled. Like nobody ever spoke to her this way.

'You don't understand, girl.'

Moira sensed an even further drop in the temperature of the night air between them. 'No,' Lottie said. 'You're right. I don't understand any of this. I don't want to. Matt thought he did. He thought he *should*. Well, what good did it do him? Tell me that. I thought you'd try something. I told Willie to warn you off. It goes against everything I . . . everything I don't believe.'

'Please, lass,' the old woman coaxed. 'Let us get on with it, best we can. Let's try and put things straight before . . .'

'No. That's it. Finish. You've blown it, Mrs Wagstaff. You've turned the burial of my husband into a bloody circus. You even . . . involved my son in your pathetic, superstitious . . . Anyway, that's it. It ends here. Willie, you and Eric and the Franks are going to put that poor man in the ground.'

The old woman looked up at her. 'I beg of you, Mrs Castle . . .'

'Ha! The famous Ma Wagstaff begging? Don't make me laugh. Don't make it worse. Just get out of my way, you *silly* old bag.'

Lottie stood on the fake grass behind the coffin and raised a boot. 'Now. Have I got to push it in myself?'

She stopped. 'Where's Dic?'

Willie said, 'I told him to help them get Rector home. I thought it'd be best. Lad'd 'ad enough.'

One of the other women with Ma Wagstaff said hesitantly, 'Is he all right? Rector?'

'I don't know,' Willie said. 'Lottie, look . . . what Ma's on about . . . I know how bloody awful it seems. Hate it meself . . .'

'Then put my husband in the ground, Willie Wagstaff. And you . . .' Lottie stared contemptuously at Ma Wagstaff. 'If I ever see you near this grave again, I swear I'll wring your stringy old neck for you.'

She stood and folded her arms and waited. Moira knew she wouldn't move until the last shovelful was trampled down. When Ma Wagstaff looked at her she turned her back.

'Right, then.' Willie had a rope. He threw one end across the grave and another man caught it. 'OK, Frank. Where's t'other rope? Let's do this proper. I'm sorry, Ma, she's right. Nowt else you can do now. Let's get it filled in.'

Ma Wagstaff stood up, put on the hat with the black balls, dented now. She said, 'Well, that's it. It's started.'

'What has?'

'There were more of um here. At least one. I could tell. I could feel um. Like black damp.'

'Go home, Ma. Stoke thi' fire up, make a cuppa, eh? I'll be round later. See you're all right. Now, don't you look at me like that, I'm not a kid no more, I'm fifty-four . . . going on seventy, after today.'

'Black seed's sown,' Ma Wagstaff said ominously. 'Bury him tight and pray for us all.'

The old woman walked unsteadily away, her back bent. Like she'd been beaten, mugged, Moira thought. Several other women followed her silently down the cemetery path.

The church clock, shining bluish in the sky, said 5.42.

When the women reached the shadow of the cross where Moira stood, Ma Wagstaff stopped, stiffened, stared up at her. As Moira silently handed her the shopping bag, old embers kindled briefly in Ma's eyes. Neither spoke. Moira didn't know her.

And yet she did.

*

195

Hans lay stiffly on the old sofa in the Rectory sitting room. They'd put cushions under his knees, taken off his dog-collar. His eyes were wide open but Ernie Dawber could tell they wouldn't focus.

Hans kept trying to tell them something, but his mouth wasn't shaping the words.

'Can't fee . . . fee . . .'

'Pop, stay quiet. Let's put your overcoat over your legs. How's that? Mr Dawber, don't you think we should get the doctor to him?'

'I do. You go and make us some tea, Catherine. Dic, ring for an ambulance.'

When they'd gone, Ernie leaned over Hans. 'Don't try and talk, just nod, all right? Are you trying to say there's bits of you you can't feel? Hey up, you don't have to nod that hard, just tilt your jaw slightly. Is it your arm? Your shoulder?'

Hans pushed an elbow back into the sofa, trying to raise himself. 'Chest. Shoulders.'

'Now, then . . .' Ernie raised a warning finger. 'Listen, lad, we've known each other a long time, me and thee. I'll be frank with you. I'm not a doctor, but my feeling is you've had a bit of a heart attack.'

The Rector squirmed in protest.

'Ah, ah! Don't get alarmed, now, I've seen this before. It's nowt to get panicked about. What you are is a classic case of a man who's been pushing himself too far for too long. I know this is not what you'd call an easy one, this parish, for a clergyman, and you've handled things with tremendous skill, Hans, and courage, over the years, anybody here'll agree with that . . .'

The Rector's eyes flashed frustration.

'Aye, I know. It's not the best of times to get poorly, what, with . . . one thing and another. And that Joel . . . by 'eck, he's a rum bugger, that lad. Impetuous? Well . . . But, Hans, be assured, they'll *cope*, the Mothers' Union. They *will* cope. They've had enough practice. Over the years.'

Wished he felt half as confident as he sounded. The trouble with Bridelow was so much had been left unsaid for so long that nobody even questioned the way the mechanisms operated any more. It was just how things were done, no fuss, no ceremony, until there was a crisis . . . and they found the stand-by machinery was all gunged up through lack of use.

When they heard the warble of the ambulance, Hans grabbed hold of Ernie's wrist and began to talk. 'I've buggered things, Ernie.'

'Don't be daft. Don't worry about Joel. This time next week he'll think it was all a bad dream.'

The Rector's dry face puckered.

'Don't think so? Oh, aye. Folk do, y'know. Things heal quick in Brid'lo. The thing about it . . . and I've been thinking about this a lot – and writing it down. Started a book – don't say owt about it, God's sake – Dawber's *secret Book of Bridelow*. Not for publication, like, Ma Wagstaff'd have a fit . . . just to bring all the strands together, reason it out for meself . . .'

'No, look . . .' Hans blinked hard.

'No, the thing about Bridelow . . . it's so *prosaic*. Know what I mean? Not sensational. No dressing up . . . or dressing down, for that matter. Nowt to make a picture spread in the *News of the World*. Joel? Nobody'd believe him, would they? You think about it.'

He patted the Rector's hand. 'No, better still, *don't* think about it. Get yourself a bit of a rest. *I'll* handle things. Brid'lo born, Brid'lo bred. Leave it to Uncle Ernie.'

This had been his forte as a headmaster. Getting the kids to trust him. Even when he hadn't the foggiest idea what he was doing.

As the ambulancemen crunched up the path, Hans said, 'Shurrup, you old fool and listen. It's Joel.'

'Like I said, we'll handle him.'

'No. You don't understand. Know where he's . . . where he's going to spend the night. Do you?'

'Back in Sheffield if he's got any sense.'

'No. He's . . . made up a bed. Little cellar under the church. Ernie . . . Don't let him. Not now. Not after this.'

'Oh,' said Ernie. 'By 'eck. You spent a night down there once, didn't you?'

'Only once,' said the Rector.

CHAPTER VII

GLASGOW

She told him that not only had she never eaten here, she'd never even been inside the joint before. And he, having stayed in better hotels most of his life, felt – as usual – like an overprivileged asshole.

She had the grouse, first time for that too. (Didn't Scots eat grouse on a regular basis, like Eskimos and sealmeat?) He joined her, a new experience for him also. The grouse wasn't so great, as well as which, it looked like a real bird, which made him feel guilty.

Afterwards, looking up from the sweet trolley, she said, 'I suppose you'll be wanting your pound of flesh, then.'

'Aw, come on, Fiona. I can buy a girl dinner without the question of flesh coming into it.'

'I should be so lucky.' She smiled enticingly. 'I was referring to Moira. You'll want to know about Moira.'

'Well,' he said, 'yeah. But only if this isn't gonna get you into any kind of, uh . . .'

'Shit?' said Fiona. 'I don't think so. I see all Mr Kaufmann's receipts, he never comes here. Anyway, it's nice to live dangerously for a change. I bet you live your whole life dangerously.'

'Me?' For one and a half years after leaving college he'd been a trainee assistant-director. The very next day he was an executive producer. Mom's company. 'Uh, well, not so's you'd notice.'

'You do *look* kind of dangerous, Mungo.'

'Looks can be deceptive.' Last thing he planned was to seduce this one.

'Irish,' she said. 'You look Irish, somehow.'

'So people keep telling me.'

'Mungo,' she said. 'Aw, hey, that's really incredible. Mungo Macbeth.'

'Of the Manhattan Macbeths. My Mom's real proud of that.' Giving her the condensed autobiography. 'From being a small kid, I learned how the actual King Macbeth was really a good guy whose name was unjustly blackened by this English hack playwright.'

'That's true, actually,' Fiona said. 'He wisny a bad guy.'

'I'm told they also used to play pipe-band records to me in my cradle,' Macbeth said, screwing up his nose. 'But that made me cry, so they hired this genuine Scottish nanny, used to sing me Gaelic lullabies. That part I remember. That was great. That was how I got into the music.'

'My dad used to sing me Tom Jones,' Fiona said glumly. '"The Green Green Grass of Home". *Not* so great.'

'*My* dad never got to sing me anything,' Macbeth said. 'He didn't last that long. He was kind of jettisoned by my mother's family before I was born. *They* are the Macbeths. My dad's name was Smith. I mean, Smith? Forget it. So, anyhow, this trip came up, she said, Go . . . go feel the true power of your Celtic heritage.'

'You feeling it?'

'I'm feeling a jerk is what I'm feeling. I won't say she was expecting a delegation from the clan Macbeth to turn out for me at the airport in full Highland costume, but you get the general picture.'

'Out of interest, have you actually seen anybody in a kilt since you got here? Apart from at the Earl's do?'

'Nope.'

'So what'll you tell her when you get home? Hey, would it be OK for me to have the profiteroles?'

'And just a coffee for me,' he said to the waiter. 'Make that two – I'll wait. What do I tell Mom? I'll say I had a peculiarly Celtic experience. I'll say it was too deep and personal to talk about.'

'Oh, wow,' Fiona said, rolling her big eyes. Problem was that tonight she didn't look eighteen any more. She was in a tight red dress – well, some of her was in it. Macbeth thought hard about Moira Cairns to take his mind off this comparatively minor but far from discountable temptation.

'I'll tell her I met a real witch,' he said. 'One of the weird sisters.'

'Aw, she's no' a witch,' Fiona said scornfully.

'No? What is she?'

'She's what my granny used to call *fey*. OK, maybe a bit more than that. Like, one day she was very annoyed with Mr Kaufmann . . . I mean she's usually *quite* annoyed with him but this was something . . . Anyway, here they are, raging away at each other, and she's about to storm out the door and then she just turns round, like she's gonny say something else, only she canny find the words. And *then* . . . one of the damn filing cabinets starts to shake and . . . I'm no' kidd'n' here . . . all four drawers come shoot'n' out at once. Really incredible. Awesome silence afterwards.'

'Coulda been an earth tremor.'

'That was what Mr Kaufmann said. But he still went all white, y'know? I mean, that filing cabinet was locked, I'm certain it was.'

'I can sympathize.' Macbeth shuddered, his mind making a white skull out of the tureen on an adjacent table. 'Listen, Fiona, I'm a little shaky on Moira's early career. She was at college in Manchester which is where she joined this local band, right?'

'Matt Castle's band. Matt Castle just died.'

'Oh, shit, really?' Remembering something mindlessly insulting he'd said about Matt Castle just after they met. What a shithead. A wonder she spoke to him at all after that.

The waiter brought Fiona's profiteroles. 'Hey, great,' Fiona said. 'So then she was approached about joining this rock band. Offered a lot of money, big money even for the time, to make two albums.'

'The Philosopher's Stone,' Macbeth said. 'But they only made one album.'

'Right. She split before they could get around to the second one. But, see, the word is that the reason they wanted her, apart from her voice, was that . . . You remember Max Goff, who owned Epidemic Records?'

'He was murdered, year or so ago. Some psychopath kid with a grudge.'

'Right,' Fiona said.

'I didn't know she was with his outfit. It was CBS put out the album in the States.'

'Well, the word *is*, Mungo . . .' Fiona leaned conspiratorially across the table, '. . . that the real reason Max Goff wanted her in the band was he'd heard she was psychic. He was very into all that. Like, he already had a couple of guys signed to Epidemic who were also psychics and he wanted to put them all together in a band, see what happened. Of course Moira didny know this, she thought the guy just liked the way she sang, right?'

'And what happened? I mean, that first album, that was terrific. I wore mine out.'

'Aye, but it all got very heavy, with drugs and stuff, and Moira broke her contract, came back to Scotland, went solo. Signed up with Mr Kaufmann, who's . . . well, he's no' exactly part of the rock scene.'

'I wondered about that.'

'The other singers on Mr Kaufmann's books are, like, mostly, y'know, nightclub or operatic or kind of Jimmy Shand type of outfits.'

'Who?'

Fiona dug into a profiterole; cream spurted. 'See, Moira made it clear she wisny gonny have anything to do with the rock scene ever again. And that's how it's been. She just does traditional folk concerts and selected cabaret-type dates. Really boring. Hell of a waste.'

'It's very intriguing. What do you think happened?'

Fiona shrugged. 'Most likely she just got in with a bad crowd. I used to think, well, maybe she was doing drugs in a big way. Heroin or something. And realized it was, like, a one-way street, y'know?'

'But you don't think that now?'

She shook her head. 'I know her better now. She's too strong. She widny touch drugs – not the kind that might get any kind of hold on her, anyway. I think it's more likely she

201

just rejected the psychic stuff, the way they were fooling about, Max Goff and these guys. She knows what it can do, right? Like, if one person can shoot all the drawers out of a filing cabinet, what's gonny happen wi' four or five of them . . . ?'

'This is fascinating, Fiona.' The kid was smarter than he'd figured. 'You're saying maybe she came back to Scotland to, kind of, put herself in psychic quarantine. Maybe scared of what she could do.'

'I'm only guessing,' Fiona said, 'but how come she'll no play any of the old songs any more? I think she wants to put all that stuff behind her. But can you do that? Being psychic, I mean, it's no' like a jumper you can take back to Marks and Spencer. Drink your coffee, Mungo, 's gonny get cold.'

He drank his coffee, not tasting it. He'd been fooling himself that this thing about Moira was purely . . . well, more than physical . . . romantic, maybe. She was beautiful and intelligent, and he loved her music from way back. But maybe it went deeper. Maybe this was a woman who he'd instinctively known had been closer to . . . what? The meaning of things? Things that having money and influence and famous friends couldn't let you into?

Time of life, he thought, staring absently into Fiona's cleavage. Or maybe I really do have Celtic roots.

'Mungo,' she said. 'Can I ask you something?'

'Go ahead.' He could guess.

'All this stuff about a mini series . . .'

'Kaufmann told you about that?'

'I keep my ear to the ground.'

Or the door. He grinned. 'Yeah?'

'Was that on the level?'

'You mean, are we gonna go ahead with a film about, uh . . .'

'An American guy who comes over here to trace his roots and . . .'

'OK, OK . . .'

'. . . falls in love with this beautiful . . .'

'You're embarrassing me, Fiona.'

'Aw, hey,' she said. 'I think that's sweet.'
'So maybe you'll help me.'
'How?'
'Tell me where I find her.'
'I don't know,' Fiona said. 'Really.'

PART FIVE

OUR SHEILA

From *Dawber's* Secret *Book of Bridelow* (unpublished):

THE OLDEST WOMAN in Bridelow commands, as you would expect, considerable respect, as well as a certain affection.

Ma Wagstaff? No, I am afraid I refer to Our Sheila who displays her all above the church porch.

The so-called *Sheelagh na gig* (the spelling varies) is found – inexplicably – in the fabric of ancient churches throughout the British Isles: a survival of an older religion, some say, or a warning against heathen excess. Usually it is lazily dismissed as 'some sort of fertility symbol'.

The shapes and sizes vary, but the image is the same: a female shamelessly exposing her most private area. Pornography, I am glad to say, it isn't. The faces of these ancient icons are normally grotesque in the extreme, their bodies compressed and ludicrous.

Our Sheila, however, is a merry lass with an almost discernible glint in her bulging stone eyes and a grin which is more innocent than lewd.

Do not dismiss her as a mere 'fertility symbol'. She has much to say about the true nature of Bridelow.

CHAPTER I

Round about 6.30, Chrissie had got a phone call from the police. Would she mind popping over to the Field Centre?

When she'd arrived the place was all lights. Police car and a van outside, an unmarked Rover pulling in behind her.

When the two CID men from the Rover walked across, they looked as if they'd been laughing. Now, facing her across her own desk, they were straight-faced by not exactly grim. 'I'm Detective Inspector Gary Ashton,' the tall one said. 'This is DS Hawkins' – waving a hand at the chubby one in the anorak. 'Now . . . Miss White.'

'Chrissie,' she said.

'Lovely.' He was a fit-looking bloke, short grey hair and a trenchcoat. Fancy that . . . even with policemen, fashion goes in circles.

'If you've been trying to get hold of Dr Hall,' she said helpfully, 'he went to a funeral, but it should be well over by now.'

'Thank you. We know,' Ashton said. 'He left early, apparently, and went home. He's on his way. Now, just to get our times right, when exactly did *you* go home?'

Oh, sugar, Chrissie thought. 'We finish at four forty-five,' she said.

Actually she'd left at 4.15. Just before four, Alice had fallen back on the irrefutable – claiming she had one of her migraines coming on. Chrissie had stuck it for fifteen minutes on her own and then thought, sod it, and gone to fetch her coat.

'Four forty-five,' Ashton said. 'Right.' They could tell when you were lying, couldn't they? If he could, he didn't seem too concerned.

'Now,' he said. 'You're responsible for locking up, are you?'

'I do it if there's nobody else. I wouldn't say I'm *responsible*. There's the caretaker, he comes on at five. And then a private security firm comes round a few times at night . . . that's just since *he's* been here. They were worried there might be a few, you know . . . weirdo types, wanting to have a look. Or something. What's happened, then? Has there been a break-in?'

'So when you left, everything was locked up. What d'you do with the keys?'

'The front and back door keys we drop off at the caretaker's office at the main college building. The keys to the bogman section . . . we keep those in here, I'm afraid. Is that bad? In one of the filing cabinets – but that's always locked at night, of course.'

If this chap's an inspector, she realized, it's got to be more than just a break-in.

'And the big doors at the back?'

'We never open them. Well, only when . . . when the bogman arrived in a van. They brought him straight in that way.'

'Do you go round and check those doors, Chrissie, before you leave? Round the outside, I mean.'

'Do I buggery,' said Chrissie. 'I'm an office manager, not a flaming night watchman. Look, come on, what's this all about? What's happened?'

Ashton smiled. 'So you didn't see or hear anything suspicious before you left?'

'No. Not tonight.' Oops.

'What d'you mean, not *tonight*?'

'Well . . . I thought I heard a noise in there, where . . . he is . . . a couple of nights ago, but it was nothing. Probably a bird on the roof.'

'You didn't raise the alarm?'

'What for? It was locked. I knew nobody could get in through those doors without making a hell of a racket, so there didn't seem . . .'

'Somebody got in tonight, Miss White.'

'Oh, hell,' said Chrissie. 'They didn't damage him, did they? Roger'll go hairless.'

*

She was cold. The BMW beckoned.

She could, after all, simply drive away from this.

Nobody invited you, girl.

Frost on the cobbles. No one else on the street. Curtains drawn, chimneys palely smoking.

Ah, the burden of guilt and regret. All he'd done for you, all he meant to you, and the thought that you'd never see him again.

Well, you saw him.

She shivered.

Problem with this place was there was nowhere you could even get a cup of coffee . . . except the pub.

She stood and stared at it from across the road. It was a large, shambling building set back from the street, with a field behind it and nothing behind that but peat. Dark sooty stone. Windows on three floors, none of the upper ones lit. Outside was a single light with an iron shade, a converted gaslamp, quite a feeble glow, just enough to light up the sign above the door: The Man I'th Moss. In black. No picture.

Didn't look like Lottie Castle's kind of place. Lottie was big sofas and art-nouveau prints.

Moira stepped lightly across the cobbles, peered through the doorway. Only a dozen or so people in the bar, Lottie not among them. Willie was there, with Eric Marsden. The big dollop of hair over Eric's forehead had gone grey but he looked no more mournful than he always had. Eric: the quiet one. In every band there was always a quiet one.

Go in then, shall I?

Why, it's Moira . . .

Come to help us re-form the band?

Just one problem. We had to bury Matt.

Never mind. Have a drink, lass.

She turned away, gathering her cloak about her. Moved quietly across the forecourt to the steeply sloping village street.

There was a guy leaning against the end wall of a stone terrace, smoking a cigarette. She kept her distance, walked down the middle of the street, along the cobbles.

Nothing for you here. Go back to what you know. The fancy

clubs and the small halls. You can play that scene until you're quite old, long as the voice holds out. Save up the pennies. In twenty years you can retire to a luxury caravan, like the Duchess. Sea views. All your albums collected under the coffee table.

As she came abreast of him, the guy against the wall turned and looked at her, muttered something. Sounded like 'Fucking hell'.

Then he tossed his cigarette into the road at her feet. 'And they tell me,' he said, 'that this used to be a respectable neighbourhood.'

'Who's that?' Too dark to make out his features.

'You don't know me.'

'But you know me, huh?'

'Yeah,' he said. 'But not nearly as well as my dad did.'

'Oh,' Moira said.

His voice had sounded different when she last heard it. Like high, pre-pubertal.

She sighed.

'Dic,' she said. 'You want to go somewhere and discuss all this?'

He laughed. A short laugh. Matt's laugh. A cawing.

'Well?' she said.

'I'm thinking,' he said from deep within his shadow.

''Cause I don't mind,' Moira said. 'I'm easy.'

'Yeah,' he said, 'we all knew that.'

Moira paused. 'That was your chance, Dic. I threw you that one. You gave the predictable, adolescent answer. So go fuck yourself, OK?'

She turned away, moved quickly up the street, clack, clack, clack on the cobbles. As good a way as any to do your exit. Grabbing the chance to go out angry; it helped. On either side of her were the gateposts of the stone cottages, a black cat on one, watching her like it knew her well. Lights behind curtains, lights from an electrified gaslamp projecting from an end wall, and over them all, like another moon, the illuminated church clock. Take it all in, you won't see it again. Bye-bye, Bridelow.

'All right!' It rang harshly from the cobbles like an iron bar thrown into the street.

It didn't stop her.

'Yeah, OK!' Running feet.

She carried on walking, turned towards the lych-gate, the corpse gate, but passed it by and entered the parking area behind the church, where it was very dark.

She was taking her keys out of her bag when he caught up with her.

'I'm sorry. All right?'

'Good. You'll be able to sleep.' Fitted the key in the car door. 'Night, Dic. Give my love to your mother.'

'Look . . .'

'Hey,' she said gently. 'I'm leaving, OK? You know your dad was screwing me, what can I say to that?'

'I want to talk about it.'

'Well, I'm no' talking here, it's cold and I'm no' going to the pub, so maybe you should just go away and *think* about it instead, huh? Call me sometime. Fix it up with my agent. I'm tired. I'm cold.'

'Where will you go?'

'And what the fuck does that have to do with you? I shall find a nice, anonymous hotel somewhere . . .'

'Look,' Dic said. 'There *is* somewhere we can talk. Somewhere warm.'

'Cosy.' Moira got into the car. 'Goodnight.'

'Moira . . .'

She started the engine, switched on the lights, wound down the window. 'By the way. Your playing, it was . . . Well, you're getting there.'

'I don't want to get there,' he said without emotion. 'I just wanted to please him.'

'Aye,' Moira said.

'It never did, though.'

'No,' she said.

A dumpy, elderly man walked through the headlamp beams. He wore a long raincoat and a trilby hat, like Donald's, only in better shape. 'Good evening,' he said politely, as he passed.

★

212

The lights were on in the church, ambering the pillars in the nave. A suitcase stood by the font.

Ernie Dawber watched the new curate manhandling a metal paraffin stove into the vestry.

'All right, lad?'

Joel Beard, alarmed, set down the stove with a clang.

'Ernie Dawber, lad. We met the other day, with Hans.'

'Ah, yes.' The curate recovered, stood up straight. He was wearing his cassock and the huge pectoral cross. 'Look, I'm sure you mean well, Mr Dawber, but I'd rather not discuss anything tonight, *if* you don't mind.'

'Beg your pardon?'

'The funeral, Mr Dawber. What happened at the funeral. You were about to tell me how innocuous it all was. I'm saying I'd rather not discuss it.'

'Well, I think we *should* discuss it, Mr Beard. Because it looks like you're in charge now.'

Joel Beard looked bewildered. He'd obviously rushed away from the graveside, dashed down to his little cell to recover and didn't yet know about Hans.

Ernie told him.

'Oh,' Joel said. 'Oh, my Lord.'

'Aye.'

'Is he going to be all right?'

'Happen,' said Ernie. 'If he gets some rest. If he doesn't spend all his time worrying what the bloody hell's going on back in Bridelow.'

Joel Beard gave him a hard look for swearing in church.

'Now look, lad,' Ernie said. 'Pull yourself together. You're not really going to kip down there?'

'I am.' Joel rested an arm on the edge of the font. 'It's quite clear to me that it's become even more important now for me to sleep in God's pocket. You were there today, I think, Mr Dawber. You saw what went on.'

'I saw a big, soft bugger making a bloody fool of himself,' said Ernie stoutly. 'Now, come on, it's getting cold. Pick up your suitcase; you can stay in my spare room for tonight, and we'll have a bit of a chat.'

Joel Beard made no reply. He stood very tall and very

213

still, the amber lights turning his tight curls into a golden crown.

'Good night, Mr Dawber,' he said.

The double doors crashed back. Roger Hall burst in, and he was white to the edges of his beard.

Chrissie was sitting at her desk, the senior detective, Ashton, casually propping his bum against it, hands deep into his trenchcoat pockets, the detective-sergeant playing with the zip on his anorak.

Roger just stood in the doorway breathing like a trainee asthmatic. He was wearing casual gear, the polo shirt and the golfing trousers. 'All right, what's happened?' Staring all round the room and finally noticing her. 'Chrissie . . . ?'

'Don't look at *me* like that, Dr Hall. I know less than you.' Obviously. Being the minion.

'How much *did* they tell you on the phone, Dr Hall?' Ashton asked, coming to his feet.

'Just . . . Just that . . . Is this on the level? It's not a joke?'

Ashton shook his head. 'Doesn't look like it, I'm afraid, sir.'

Roger glared across the office at the metal door. It was shut. 'It's unbelievable.' Shaking his head. 'What happened to the so-called security patrol?'

'We'll be talking to the company, sir, have no doubts. Meantime, we didn't like to touch anything until you got here, so if you'd be good enough to take us through . . .'

Roger nodded dumbly. Chrissie was almost feeling sorry for him. His face was like a crumpled flour bag. He looked like a parent who'd just learned his child had been found on a railway line. In fact, to him, if somebody had vandalized his beloved bogman, this was probably worse.

Which was why Chrissie didn't *quite* feel sorry for him.

The two detectives, Ashton and the chubby one in the anorak, waited while Roger went to unlock his personal high-security cabinet. He brought out both keys. The detectives followed him to the ante-room and then all three of them went through to the inner lab.

Chrissie stayed behind, both elbows on her desk, chin

propped in her hands, waiting for the eruption. She didn't know whether to laugh or cry on his behalf.

'No . . . !' Roger's voice echoing back. 'Look . . . Inspector, is it?'

'Gary Ashton, sir. Greater Manchester.'

'I'm . . . I just can't *believe* this has happened. What I . . . Look, let me do some checks. It's possible . . . unlikely, but possible . . . that there's a rational explanation. I've been away for a few days this week. It's conceivable, I suppose, that something was arranged and by some incredible oversight I wasn't informed.'

'You mean whoever it was forgot to inform the caretaker they'd be dropping in, sir? After dark?'

'No. You're right. Clutching at straws, I suppose. God almighty, this is . . . How did they actually get in?'

'Quite professionally done, sir. The rear doors were forced, both sets, but forced by somebody who knew how, if you see what I mean.'

'It's . . . unbelievable.'

Chrissie heard a clang. Roger's fist hitting the metal table.

'If you wouldn't mind, sir . . . fingerprints.'

'Sorry. It's just . . . if anything, any one thing, had been specifically calculated to fucking *ruin* me, this . . .'

'Ruin you, Dr Hall?'

'I . . . We had a lot riding on it. You don't get your hands on one of these very often.'

'How valuable would you say? I mean, I realize you can't . . .'

'*In*valuable. And yet not valuable at all to most people. You could hardly stick it in your hall like a Rodin. It's beyond me, the whole thing. And yet . . .'

Chrissie's head shot up out of her hands. *Never!*

'Well, sir, I expect you've got photographs. I'll also need to know what kind of vehicle would be required, assuming it's been removed from the immediate area.'

Bloody *hell*! Chrissie stood up. She found she was shaking.

'We'll obviously be searching the grounds pretty thoroughly. But if you wanted to get it away without damaging it . . . would it need any special conditions? Refrigeration?'

'It's in peat, Inspector. Peat's a preservative. That's how he survived for two thousand years.'

'Of course. Sorry. Stupid of me. Anyway . . . We're clearly not looking for young tearaways here, so have you any idea, any notion at all, who in the wide world would go to so much trouble to . . .'

'Steal a two-thousand-year-old corpse.'

'Old as that? Well. Wouldn't be much use for medical research then? So what are we looking for? Bit of a nutter? A rich eccentric collector? I'll be honest, Dr Hall, I've not come across anything quite like this. It's a one-off.'

'It's unbelievable,' Roger said for about the fifteenth time, and Chrissie heard him pacing the echoing empty lab.

CHAPTER II

The girl who opened the Rectory door was sipping red soup off the top of an overflowing mug. She watched both of them cautiously over the rim.

'Sorry,' Dic said. 'It's an awkward time.'

She swallowed hot soup, winced. 'No problem. I'm on my own.'

'That's what I thought. We, er, we needed somewhere to talk . . . Sorry . . . your dad, is he . . . How is he?'

'They say it's a minor heart attack.' Tomato soup adhering to her lips. 'I'm not allowed to see him until tomorrow, he has to have rest. Ma Wagstaff says not to worry. He'll be OK.'

She sounded like this was supposed to be a reliable medical opinion. 'This is Moira Cairns,' Dic said.

'Hello,' Catherine Gruber said limply.

Moira sensed she was worried sick.

The porch light was a naked bulb. Above it, the gaping orifice, spread by stone thumbs, was deepened by the hard, unsubtle shadows it threw.

The *Sheelagh na gig*, lit for drama, grinning lasciviously at

216

Joel Beard. And he was appalled to think that everyone entering the church to worship God should have to pass beneath this obscenity.

Tradition, the antiquarians said. Our heritage. Olde Englande.

Joel Beard saw beyond all this, saw it only as symbolic of the legacy of evil he had been chosen to destroy.

A few minutes ago, he'd telephoned the Archdeacon from the kiosk in front of the Post Office, giving him a carefully edited summary of the evening's events in Bridelow. Not mentioning the appalling incident at the graveside with the bottle – which the Archdeacon might have judged to be, at this stage, an over-reaction on his part.

'Well, poor Hans,' the Archdeacon had said easily and insincerely. 'I think he should have a few months off, don't you? Perhaps some sort of semi-retirement. I shall speak to the Bishop. In fact I think I'll go and see him. Meanwhile you must take over, Joel. Do what you feel is necessary.'

'I have your support?'

'My support spiritually – and . . . and physically, I hope. I shall come to see you. Drop in on you. Very soon. Meanwhile, tread carefully, Joel. Will you live at the Rectory now?'

'The girl's still there, Simon. Hans's daughter. She'll have to go back to Oxford quite soon, I'd guess. But then there's Hans himself, when he leaves hospital.'

'Don't worry. We'll find him somewhere to convalesce. Meanwhile . . .'

'. . . I shall sleep in the church. In the priest's cell.'

'All alone down there? My God, Joel, you're a brave man.'

'It's God's House!' Joel had said, even he feeling, with a rare stab of embarrassment, that this was a naive response.

And *was* it God's House?

And which God?

As he entered the church of St Bride under the spread thighs of the leering Sheelagh, he experienced the unpleasant illusion of being sucked into . . .

No!!

*

217

'Long-haired girls,' Dic Castle said bitterly. 'Always the long, dark hair.'

Moira said, 'I can't believe this.'

'No?'

'*No*,' she said firmly.

The minister's daughter had left them alone in the Rectory sitting room. Dic had wanted her to stay, like he needed a chaperone with this Scottish whore, but she wouldn't. They could hear her banging at a piano somewhere, ragtime numbers, with a lot of bum notes. Letting them know she wasn't listening at the door.

'He never touched me sexually,' Moira said. 'He never came near. On stage, it was always him on one side, me on the other, Eric and Willie in between but a yard or two back. That was how it was on stage. That was how it was in the van. That was how it *was*.'

Somewhere, walls away, Catherine Gruber went into the 'Maple Leaf Rag', savaging the ivories, getting something out of her system.

'And you clearly don't believe me.' Moira was sitting on a cushion by the fireplace. Paper had been laid in it, a lattice of wood and a few pieces of coal.

Dic said, 'Followed him once. After a charity gig. She was waiting for him in the car park. About twenty-one, twenty-two. About my age. Long, dark hair.'

'When was this?'

'Fucking little groupies,' Dic said. He was semi-sprawled across a sofa, clutching a cushion. 'At his age. Er . . . 'bout a year ago, just before he . . . before it was diagnosed.'

Dic had a lean face, full lips like Matt. Dark red hair, like Lottie. Still had a few spots. 'And, yeah,' he said, 'I do know she wasn't the first.' Staring at Moira in her jeans and her fluffy white angora sweater, hands clasped around her knees, black hair down to her elbows.

'Because you still think the first was me. Sure. And you know something . . . Gimme a cigarette, will you?'

He tossed the cushion aside, got out a crumpled pack of Silk Cut and a book of matches. 'Didn't know you smoked.'

'Tonight,' she said, taking a cigarette, tearing off a match, 'I smoke.'

The minister's daughter was playing 'The Entertainer', sluggishly.

Moira said, 'Just answer me this. Earlier tonight, at your dad's funeral, at the graveside . . . I mean, how'd you feel about that?'

His face closed up, hard as stone. 'I just played the pipes. Badly. I didn't see anything.'

She nodded. 'OK.'

'So I don't know what you're talking about.'

'I understand. We'll forget that, then.'

He lit his own cigarette, said through the smoke, 'Mum said you wouldn't be coming anyway.'

'She didn't know.'

'You seen her?'

'No. And that's not because . . . Listen, I'm gonna say this. There was a time when I felt bad. Twenty, fifteen years ago. When I felt bad *because* I never came on to him, not even after a gig in some faraway city when we were pissed. And I felt bad that I was twenty years younger and I was taking off nationally, and he was maybe never going to.'

'I bet you did.' Dic sneered. 'I bet that really cut you up.'

She ignored it. 'I was thinking, if we'd slept together, just the once, to kind of get it over, bring down that final barrier . . . You got the vaguest idea what I'm saying?'

He just looked at her through the smoke.

'Anyway,' Moira said, 'we didn't. It never happened. Maybe that's another piece of guilt I'm carrying around. I don't know.'

The piano music stopped. Dic lay back on the sofa, hands clasped behind his head. Outside, the wind was getting up, spraying dead leaves at the windows.

There was a polite knock on the door and Cathy came in. 'I'm making some tea, if . . .'

'Oh, yeah, thanks.' Dic sitting up, looking sheepish.

'Be ten minutes,' Cathy said.

Moira said, as the door closed, 'Lottie. Your mother. She know about this?'

'We never discussed it.'

'But you think she knows, right?'

Dic shrugged.

'This girl. This so-called girl of Matt's. You know who she was?'

'No. I tried to find out from people at the folk club – The Bear, you remember the joint? Nobody seemed to know her.'

'So how do you know they were . . . ?'

'Because they went straight into this shop doorway. Would've taken a jack to prise them apart.'

'Right,' Moira said sadly. 'And she looked . . . like me?'

'Yeah. Superficially. Like you used to look.'

'Thanks a lot.'

Dic picked up the cushion and hurled it with all his strength at a bare wall. 'I didn't mean it like that, OK? I don't mean a fucking thing I say. I just like insulting people, yeah?'

'Sure,' Moira said. This wasn't getting either of them anywhere. She wished she'd stuck to her original plan and never agreed to come here with him. So he had problems. They'd made him stand there playing the pipes while they messed with his dad's body in its coffin. She could feel the confusion and the rage billowing out of him.

'Dic . . .' She was going to regret this.

'Yes?'

No, she wasn't. She wasn't going to say anything either of them might regret. She gathered up her cloak from the carpet. 'I'm away, all right?'

'Yeah.'

The hissing sound disturbed him. And the occasional popping. And the blue glow.

It came from the circular wick of the paraffin stove. Intense, slightly hellish, ice-blue needles pricking the dark, the close stone walls shimmering like the inside of a cave lit by a cold and alien sea-glare.

Joel turned the flame up fully until it was flaccid and yellow, and then he blew it out. The stove was having little or no effect anyway. His original plan had been to bring an electric heater down here, but there was no power point, and the nearest one in the church was too far away for Alfred Beckett's extension lead to reach.

Joel lit a candle.

With the stove out, the temperature must be plunging, but at least it didn't *look* as cold.

He sat on the side of the camp-bed, with the double duvet wound around him.

Cold he could live with, anyway, insulated by years of refereeing schoolboy rugby matches. Cold he could almost relish.

He'd taken off his boots but added an extra pair of rugby socks. When he lay down, his feet – projecting from the bottom of the bed – would touch the stone blocks of the far wall. That was how cramped this cell was.

But discomfort was good. It was a holy place. Above him the nave of St Bride's, around him its ancient foundations. Rock of Ages. A blessed place, a sanctuary where bishops – well, at least one bishop – had passed the dark, cold hours in sacred solitude.

If he hadn't been so bone-tired, so sated with righteous rage, Joel might have spent the night in holy vigil, on his knees on the stone floor, like some medieval knight. Praying for divine aid in the deliverance of Bridelow from its own dark dragon.

But his body and his mind were both demanding sleep . . . a state often at its most elusive when most needed. He was also rather appalled to find his loins apparently yearning for the comfort of a woman.

Before his conversion, Joel had exploited his God-given glamour at every opportunity – and there had been many. Now he did not deny himself the yearning, only its habitual, casual assuagement.

He told himself this unseemly erection in the House of God was merely a side-effect of the cold and the pressure of the duvet.

His watch told him it was not yet 10 p.m. But tomorrow, he felt, would be a long day. So he would allow his body sleep.

221

When he blew out the candle and lay back, the paraffin stench hung over him like a chloroform cloth. He must not sleep in this air. Clutching the duvet around him, he arose into the absolute darkness, followed his nose to the stinking heater and pulled it two yards to the oaken door. Bent almost double, he carried the appliance into the little tunnel which led to the stairway.

And then, leaving it out there, shuffled back to his cell. Locking the thick and ancient door of his sanctuary against the pagan night. Falling uncomfortably into the rickety bed.

Tread carefully, Joel.

What did the Archdeacon mean by that? Joel would tread with the courage and determination of the first Christians to walk these hills. Those who had driven the heathens from their place of worship and built upon it this church.

And whose holy task, because of the isolation of the place and the inbred superstition of the natives, had yet to be completed.

With God's help, Joel Beard would drive out the infidel. For ever.

Cathy was pouring boiling water out of a big white teapot, down the sink. 'Forgot to put the bloody tea in. I'm a bit impractical.'

'Well, don't bother for me,' Moira said. 'I have to go.'

'You're the singer, aren't you?' Cathy filled the kettle, plugged it into an old-fashioned fifteen-amp wall-socket. It was that kind of kitchen, thirty years out of date but would never be antique. Moira said wearily, yes, she was the singer.

Cathy said, 'Still, I bet you don't play the piano as good as me.'

Moira grinned. 'How long you known Dic?'

'Years. On and off. He'd come up to Bridelow with his father at weekends. I used to fancy him rotten at one time.'

'Used to?'

Cathy shrugged. 'That was when we were the same age,' she said elliptically.

Moira looked at her. A little overweight; pale, wispy hair

pulled back off a face that was too young, yet, to reflect Cathy's cute sense of irony.

'When we came in, you said you thought your father was knackered. You said it'd do him good to get out of this place for a while.'

'I said that, did I?'

Try again. 'You were born here?'

'So they tell me. I don't live here at present. I'm in Oxford.'

'Doing what?'

'Studying,' Cathy said. 'The principal occupation in Oxford, next to watching daytime telly and getting pissed.'

'What are you studying? Oh, hey, forget it. I'm tired of walking all around things. What I really want to know is what happened at Matt's funeral that fucked your dad up so bad. And who's the other minister, the big guy, and how come you don't like him. Also, who's the crone who fumbles in coffins, and why was your daddy letting it go on. That's for starters.'

Cathy straightened up at the sink. 'You can't do that.'

'Huh?'

'You can't just come into Bridelow and ask questions like that straight out.'

'Oh. Really. Well, I'll be leaving then.'

'OK,' Cathy said lightly.

The avalanche of liquid peat hit him like effluent in a flooded drain and then it was swirling around him and he was like a seabird trapped in an oil-slick, his wings glued to his body. If he struggled it would tear his wings from his shoulders and enter his body and choke him. He could taste it already in his throat and his nose.

But, even as it filled his dream, he knew that the tide of peat was only a metaphor for the long centuries of accumulated Godless filth in this village.

He knew also that he *did* have wings that could carry him far above it.

For he was an angel.

And if he remained still and held his light within him the noxious tide could never overwhelm him.

Joel dreamed on.

Although the stone room around him was cold, the black peat in the dream was warm. He remained still and the peat settled around him like cushions.

Inside his dreaming self, the light kept on burning. Its heat was intense and its flame, like the one inside the paraffin heater, became a tight, blue jet arising from a circle. It heated up the peat too.

In his dream he was naked and the peat was as warm and sensuous as woman-skin against him.

Moira waited for her by the Rectory gate.

It was bitterly cold. She imagined the walls of the village cottages tightening under the frost.

Cathy came round the side of the house, a coat around her shoulders. 'How'd you know I'd come after you?'

Moira shrugged.

'You're like old Ma Wagstaff, you are. You know that?'

'That's . . .'

'The crone, yes.'

'I hope not,' Moira said. Well, dammit . . . Willie's old mother? And he never said. All those years and he never said a word.

'I'm trying to understand it all,' Cathy said. 'Somebody has to work it all out before we lose it. Most people here don't bother any more. It's just history. I suppose that's been part of the problem.'

Moira realized she was just going to have to do some listening, see what came together. The church clock shone out blue-white and cold, as if it was the source of the frost.

'The old ways,' Moira said. 'Sometimes they don't seem exactly relevant. And people get scared for their kids. Yeh, you're right, they don't want to understand, most of them. But can you blame them?'

'It's not even as if it's particularly simple. Not like Buddhism or Jehovah's Witness-ism,' Cathy said. 'Not like you can hand out a pamphlet and say, "Here it is, it's all there." I mean, you can spend years and years prising up little stones all over the place trying to detect bits of patterns.'

Cathy fell silent, and Moira found she was listening to the night. The night was humming faintly – a tune she knew. People like me, she thought, we travel different roads, responding to the soundless songs and the invisible lights.

It's all too powerful . . . the heritage . . . maybe you should go away and when you get back your problems will be in perspective . . . go somewhere bland . . . St Moritz, Tunbridge Wells . . .

Bridelow?

Ah, Duchess, you old witch.

She said, 'So what *is* the history of this place? I mean, the relevant bits.'

'You need to talk to Mr Dawber. He's our local historian.'

'And what would he tell me?'

'Probably about the Celts driven out of the lowlands by the Romans first and then the Saxons.'

'The English Celts? From Cheshire and Lancashire?'

'And Shropshire and North Wales. It was all one in those days. They fled up here, and into the Peak District, and because the land was so crap nobody tried too hard to turn them out. And besides, they'd set up other defences.'

'Other defences?'

'Well . . . not like Hadrian's Wall or Offa's Dyke.'

'The kind of defences you can't see,' Moira said.

'The kind of defences *most* people can't see,' corrected Cathy. She looked up into the cold sky. Moira saw that all the clouds had flown, leaving a real planetarium of a night.

Cathy said, 'She'd kill me if she knew I was telling you all this.'

'Who?'

'Ma Wagstaff, of course.'

'And what makes you so sure she *doesn't* know?'

'Oh, *God*,' Cathy said. 'You *are* like her. I knew it as soon as I saw you at the door.'

'It's the green teeth and the pointy hat,' said Moira.

'I don't know what it is, but when you've lived around here for a good piece of your life you get so you can recognize it.'

225

'But your old man's the minister.'

'And a bloody good one,' Cathy snapped. 'The best.'

'Right,' Moira said. 'I'd like to meet him when he's feeling better.'

'We'll see.' Cathy walked past her, out of the Rectory gates, stood in the middle of the street looking up at the church. 'It's a sensitive business, being Rector of Bridelow. How to play it. And if it's working, if it's trundling along . . . I mean, things have always sorted themselves out in Bridelow. It's been a really liberal-minded, balanced sort of community. A lot of natural wisdom around, however you want to define wisdom.'

The moonlight glimmered in her fair hair, giving her a silvery distinction. Then Moira realized it wasn't the moonlight at all, the moon was negligible tonight, a wafer. It was the light from the illuminated church clock.

'They call it the Beacon of the Moss,' Cathy said.

'Huh?'

'The church clock. That's interesting, don't you think? It's not been there a century yet and already it's part of the legend. That's Bridelow for you.'

'You mean everything gets absorbed into the tradition?'

'Mmm. Now, Joel Beard . . . that's the big curate with the curly hair, the one and only Joel Beard, *Saint* Joel. Now, Joel's really thick. He thinks he's stumbled into the Devil's back yard. He thinks he's been called by God to fight Satan in Bridelow because this is where he can do it one-to-one. In the blue corner Saint Joel, in the red corner The Evil One, wearing a glittery robe washed and ironed by Ma Wagstaff and the twelve other members of the Mothers' Union.'

'The Mothers' Union?' Moira laughed in delight.

'Thirteen members,' Cathy said. 'There've always been thirteen members. I mean, they don't dance naked in the moonlight or anything – which, bearing in mind the average age of the Mothers, is a mercy for everyone.'

'Oh, Jesus,' said Moira, 'this is wonderful.'

'It *used* to be rather wonderful,' Cathy said. 'But it's all started to go wrong. Even Ma's not sure why. Hey, look, have you anywhere to stay tonight? I mean, you want to stay here? There's a spare room.'

This kid would never say she didn't want to be in the house alone.

'Thank you,' Moira said. 'I think I'd like that.'

Dic, who didn't drink much, had gone back to his father's pub and sunk four swift and joyless pints of Bridelow Black, sitting on his own at the back of the bar.

At one stage he became aware of Young Frank pulling out the stool on the other side of his table. 'Steady on, lad.' Tapping Dic's fifth pint with the side of a big thumb. 'It's not what it were, this stuff, but it'll still spoil your breakfast.'

Dic said, 'Fuck off, Frank.'

Frank got his darts out of his back pocket. 'Game of arrows?' Dic shook his head, making Frank's image sway and loom like something on a fairground ride.

'Come on, lad.' Frank's grating voice rising and fading out of the pub hubbub like a radio coming untuned. 'Life's gorra go on. You can't say you weren't expecting it. He were a good bloke, but he's better off dead than how he were, you got t'admit that.'

'Frank!' Dic clambered to his feet, sank the rest of his pint, most of it going into his shirtfront. 'Fucking leave it, will you?'

And then he was weaving and stumbling between the tables and out into the night.

He stood in the doorway a while, getting his breath together, then he strode across the forecourt and on to the street. The cobbles gleamed, frosty already, in the light of the big clock in the sky, shining like the earth from the moon in those old space pictures.

Dic began to moonwalk up the street, taking big strides, crashing into the phone box outside the post office, giggling like a daft sod. Coming up by the church, where he'd talked to Moira Cairns – there was her BMW, still parked there. Moira Cairns . . . Wouldn't mind poking that sometime, give her one for his old man. Maybe she owed him one, part of his inheritance.

He wished he had his pipes with him. Give them a fucking tune. Give them a *real* tune. Bastards. What were they at?

What were they fucking at down there? Hands in Dad's coffin, sick bastards.

Standing by the lych-gate with its cover like a picture-postcard well and a seat inside. Went in, sat down. Out of the blue light in here, anyroad. Right under the church but the sloping roof blocked it out. Dic nestled in the darkness, feeling warm. Closed his eyes and felt the bench slipping under him, like dropping down a platform lift into a velvet mineshaft. Dic threw his arms out, stretched his head back, accepting he was pissed but feeling relaxed for the first time since he didn't know . . .

He giggled. There was a hand on his thigh.

It moved delicately up to his groin like a big spider.

'Feels good,' Dic said, pretty sure he'd fallen asleep on the bench. Lips on the side of his neck and his nostrils were full of the most glorious soiled and sexy perfume.

The hand sliding his zip down, easing something out.

He pulled in his arms, hands coming together around the back of a head and soft hair. Hair so long that it was brushing the tip of his cock.

'Moira,' Dic whispered.

From *Dawber's* Secret *Book of Bridelow* (unpublished):

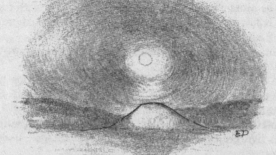

ALTHOUGH THERE HAS never been any excavation, it is presumed that the 'low' or mound on which St Bride's Church is built was a barrow or tumulus dating back to the Bronze Age and may later have been a place of Celtic worship.

Similar mounds have been found to enclose chambers, which some believe to have been used not so much for burial purposes as for solitary meditation or initiation into the religious mysteries. Some tribes of American Indians, I believe, fashioned underground chambers for similar purposes.

There has been speculation that the small cell-like room reached by a narrow stairway from the vestry occupies the space of this original chamber. The official explanation for this room is that it was constructed as overnight accommodation for itinerant priests who came to preach at St Bride's and were unable, because of adverse weather, to return that night across the Moss. However, there are few recorded instances of this being necessary, and when, in 1835, a visiting bishop announced his intention of spending the night there 'to be closer to God' he eventually had to be found a room at The Man I'th Moss after being discovered naked and distressed in the snow-covered churchyard at three o'clock in the morning!

CHAPTER III

The Moss was like a warm bath, and he left it with regret. Knowing, all the same, that he must. That there was nothing to be accomplished by wallowing.

So he strode out. And when he glanced behind him, what he saw took away his breath.

For it was no longer a black and steaming peat bog but a vast, sparkling lake, an ecstatic expanse of blue and silver reaching serenely to the far hills.

Its water was alive. Quiescent, undemanding, but surely a radiant, living element. No, not merely living . . . *undying. Immortal.*

And the water was a womanly element. Light and placid, recumbent. Generous, if she had a mind to be. If you pleased her.

He felt tufts of grass crisp and warm under his wet feet and was embarrassed, thinking he would surely besmirch it with filthy peat deposits from his bog-soiled body. But when he looked down at himself he saw that his skin was fresh and clean – not from the bog, but from the lake, of course.

And he was naked. Of course. Quite natural.

He stood at the tip of a peninsula. He thought at first it was a green island because the mound which rose, soft as a breast, from its centre was concealing the hills behind. But as he ascended the rise, new slopes purpled into being, and when he reached the summit the surrounding hills were an amphitheatre.

In the middle of which he stood.

Naked.

Appraised.

'Shade the light! Shade it, damn you!'
  'What with?'

'*Your hand, jacket, anything . . . You poor little sod, you're really frightened, aren't you . . . ?*'

'*No, it's just . . .*'

'*Don't be . . . Easier than you expected, surely, wasn't it? Soil's lovely and loose, obviously replaced in haste, everyone shit-scared, like you. Look, why don't you get the ropes? We can have this one out and into the Range Rover before we start on the other, OK?*'

'*All right. Now?*'

'*Got a firm grip, have we? You let it go and – I promise you, cock – we'll put you down there and bury you alive.*'

'*Yes, all right, yes, I've got it.*'

'*OK, now. Pull.*'

'*Oh . . . agh . . . Where shall I . . . ?*'

'*Just at the side will do. Right. Fine. Now, let's have the lid off.*'

'*What . . . ?*'

'*Have a little look at him, eh? Hah! See that . . . not even nailed down, they really were in a panic, weren't they? To think I was once almost in awe of these little people. How wrong can . . . Oh, now . . . Oh, look at that.*'

'*Oh!*'

'*Go on. Have a better look. Get closer. Put your fingers on his eyes.*'

'*I can't, I . . . Oh, God, how did I get into this?*'

'*No good asking Him, my friend, you've cut all your ties in that direction . . .*'

Ernie Dawber was soon aware of Something Happening in the churchyard.

A light sleeper, Ernie. Eyes and ears of the community, twenty-four hours a day. The headmaster's house overlooked the playground on the one side, and from the landing window there was no hiding-place at all for a pair of eight-year-olds sharing a packet of Embassy Gold.

Ernie's replacement as head teacher came from Glossop and had not been prepared for such dedication. In fact he'd said, more or less, that if they made him live over the shop, as it were, they could stick the job. He was a good lad, though, generally speaking, so the Education Authority had accepted his terms, allowed him to commute from Across the Moss . . . and sold the house to Ernie.

Who couldn't have had a better retirement present. He was always on hand – and more than pleased – to take groups of kids on nature rambles or do a spot of relief teaching in the classroom in an emergency.

And he could still watch the generations pass by. Through the landing window . . . the schoolyard. While through the back bedroom window, on the other side of the house . . . the graveyard. Full circle.

So all it took was the clink of a shovel, and Ernie Dawber was awake and up at the window.

They were being very quiet about it – as usual. He couldn't see much, just shadows criss-crossing through torchbeams, up at the top end, where the churchyard met the moor. Where Matt Castle had finally been planted and the earth piled at last on top of him.

Ernie watched for just over half an hour, and then the torches were extinguished.

'By 'eck,' he said, half-admiringly, hopping over the freezing oilcloth back to bed, 'tha's got a nerve, Ma.'

He remembered Joel Beard. What, really, could he have done? If their stupid curate was determined to spend the night in the little cellar under the church, how could he stop him?

Maybe the Rector's fears were unfounded. Maybe his experience and that of the Bishop all those years ago . . . Well, they were sensitive men. Not all clergymen were, by any means, and this lad certainly looked, well, not *dense* exactly, that wasn't quite the word. Dogmatic, set in his beliefs. Blind to other realities.

But at least, tucked up in his cell, he wouldn't be aware of what was happening up in the churchyard.

And that was a small mercy, Ernie thought, getting into bed. He felt a trifle dizzy but decided to disregard it.

*

He thought he recognized the naked woman on the hill. There was *something* about her, the way she looked at him, the way she smiled.

The way she seemed to say, *Are you man enough?*

He stood above her. Confident of his superior strength, his muscular limbs, his halo of golden curls. Their power over women. Oh, he was man enough.

For had he not fallen into the black peat and emerged from clear water, as clear as the Sea of Galilee? And had not the peat been washed from him?

Now the female lay in the grass before him, close to the summit of the green mound, her legs spread. He knew what she wanted.

Her wild hair was spread over the grass. Hair which reflected the light, changing like water. Hair which rippled like the lake.

He smiled his most superior smile. 'I know what you want.' Disdainful.

And if there was no disdain in the reaction of his body, this was another demonstration of his power. Proof that he certainly was man enough.

But, gently, she shook her head.

First, you must recognize me for what I am. And then worship me.

The lights were tiny, some distance away, a short procession of them. Torches, lanterns, Tilley lamps; whatever, people were carrying them, and they were carrying them openly across Sam Davis's farmland, and Sam gripped the bedroom window-ledge, bloody mad now.

'Right!'

'No!'

'I'm gettin' shotgun . . .'

'Sam, *no* . . . !'

'Shurrup,' he rasped. 'You'll wake kids.'

'I'm not letting you.' He heard her pull the cord to the light over the bed.

233

'Look . . .' Sam turned his back on the window. Esther, all white-faced and rabbit-eyed, sitting up in bed, blankets clutched to her chin. 'They're makin' a bloody fool o' me, yon buggers,' he whispered. 'Don't even hide their bloody lights no more.'

'We should never've come here.'

'Oh, don't bloody start wi' that again.'

'Why d'you think it were so cheap? It's a bad place, Sam.'

'It's the best *we'll* bloody get.'

'Nobody wanted it, and I don't just mean the land.'

'Aye,' he said. 'I know you don't mean the bloody land, rubbish as it is.'

'I'm scared,' she said, all small-voiced. 'It's an awful thing t'be scared of your own home, Sam.'

He snatched a glance out of the window; the lights had stopped moving, they'd be clustered up there in a circle of their own around what was left of the stone circle.

'Sam!'

'*Shurrup!*'

'Aren't *you* scared? Really. Aren't y—'

'Listen. What it does to me . . . it just makes me tampin' mad. Been goin' on weeks, months . . . and what have I done about it? Tell me that? Am I going t'stand here for ever, like an owd woman, frickened t'dearth?'

'You went to the vicar. That new feller's coming tomorrow. You said he were coming tomorrow.'

'Waste of bloody time. *And* the coppers. I keep telling yer. Couldn't even charge um wi' trespass 'cause it's got to be trespass wi' intent to do summat illegal, and worshipping the devil int even a criminal offence no more – sooner bloody nick you for a bald tyre. Bastards. Useless bastards. All of um.'

Kept saying it. Kept repeating it because he could hardly believe it, the things you could get away with. Was he supposed to sit around, with his finger up his arse, while them bastards up there were shagging each other front and back and sacrificing his beasts? No bloody *way!*

'You go out there,' Esther said, 'and I'm ringing the police, and I'll ring the bloody vicarage too and tell um where you are, I don't care what time of night it is.'

'Oh, shit!' Sam advanced on the bed, spreading his arms wide, cold by now in just his underpants. 'Bloody *hell*, woman. What do *you* suggest I do, then?'

'Come back to bed,' Esther said, trying her best to smile through the nerves that were making her face twitch. 'Please, Sam. Don't look. Just thank God they're up there and we're down here. Please. We'll talk about it tomorrow.'

'Well, thanks very much for your contribution.' Sam sighed. '"We'll talk about it tomorrow." Fucking Nora.'

He took one last glance.

The circle of light did not move.

'I've had it wi' talk,' Sam said.

First you must recognize me. For what I am.

'Recognize you?' He laughed. 'For what you are?'

He stood above her, looking down on her. The elongated shadow of his penis divided her lolling breasts like a sword.

'I *know* what you are,' he said. 'I know *precisely* what you are.'

He saw a blue calm in her eyes that was as deep as the lake, and for a moment it threatened to dilute his resolve.

Then he heard himself say, 'How *dare* you?'

She lay below him, placid, compliant.

'You're just a whore. How dare you seek my recognition? You're just a . . . a cunt.'

In an act of explicit contempt he lowered himself upon her, and her hands moved to her crotch, thumbs extended, to open herself for him.

He's . . . quite small, isn't he? I somehow expected him to be bigger. More impressive.'

'Quite manageable, really. Oh my, earth to earth, peat to peat . . . it would have been rather less easy to get at him in a week or two. Watch it now, be careful of his eyes. Mustn't be blasé.'

'I'm not. It's just I'm actually not as worried about, you know, touching this one. It doesn't seem like a real body, somehow. More like a fossil.'

'Lay him gently. You've done well so far. I'm proud of you. But lay him gently, he's ours now. And remember . . . never forget . . .'

'I know . . . I'll feel so much better afterwards.'

'Shut up. Join hands. In a circle. Around the body.'

It was not a rape; she was a whore, and a heathen whore. When he plunged into her, he found her as moist as black peat and packed just as tightly around him.

Light into darkness.

Not to be enjoyed. It was necessary.

'Whore,' he gasped with every breath. 'Whore . . . whore . . . whore . . .'

Lifting his head to seek out her eyes, looking for a reaction, searching for some pain in them.

'Whore.' Saw her mouth stretched into a static rictus of agony.

'Wh . . .' Tighter still around him.

And dry.

'. . . ore . . .'

Dry as stone.

No.

Too late; he thrust again. Into stone.

The pain was blinding. Immeasurable. The pain was a white-hot wire driven through the tip of his penis and up through his pelvis into his spine.

His back arched, his breath set solid in his throat. And he found her eyes.

Little grey pebbles. And her mouth, stretched and twisted not in agony but ancient derision, a forever grin.

'. . . in the midst of death we are alive . . .'

'. . . WE ARE ALIVE!'

('Go on . . . two handfuls . . . stop . . . not on his face . . . shine the light . . . there . . .')

'Behold, I shew you a mystery. We shall not sleep, but we shall

236

be changed. In a moment. In the twinkling of an eye. At the last trump – for the trumpet shall sound. And the dead shall be raised.'

'. . . AND THE DEAD SHALL BE RAISED!'

('OK, now fill in the grave . . . quickly, quickly, quickly . . .')

'Dust to dust, to ashes, to earth.

'DUST TO ASHES TO EARTH!'

('Now stamp it down, all of you. Together . . .')

'And the dead shall be raised corrupted . . . and we shall be changed.'

'. . . WE SHALL BE CHANGED.'

('Douse the lights. Douse them!')

CHAPTER IV

Another hard, white day, and she didn't like the look of it. It had no expression; there was a threat here most folk wouldn't see.

Not good weather, not bad weather. Nowt wrong with bad weather; you couldn't very well live in Bridelow if you couldn't put up wi' spot or two of rain every other day or a bit of wind to make your fire smoke and your eyes water. Or blizzards. Or thunder and lightning.

But this was no weather. Just cold air at night and a threat.

Everything black or white. Black night with white stars. White day with black trees, black moor, black moss.

Cold and still. Round about this time of year there should be some colour and movement in the sky, even if it was only clouds in dirty shades of yellow chasing each other round the chimney pots.

Shades. There should be shades.

Ma Wagstaff stood in her back kitchen, hands on woollen-skirted hips.

She was vexed with them cats too. She'd washed their bowl, first thing, and doled out a helping of the very latest variety of gourmet cat food Willie'd brought her from that posh supermarket in Buxton – shrimp and mussel in oyster sauce. And the fickle little devils had sat there and stared at it, then stared at her. 'Well, that's it,' Ma growled. 'If you want owt else you can gerout and hunt for it.'

But the cats didn't want to go out. They mooched around, all moody, ignoring each other, looking up at Ma as if was her fault.

Bad air.

As Ma unbent, the cat food can in one hand, a fork in the other, her back suddenly creaked and then she couldn't stand up for the pain that started sawing down her spine like a bread knife.

Then the front door went, half a knock, somebody who couldn't reach the knocker. As Ma hobbled through the living room, the white light seemed to be laughing heartlessly at her, filling the front window and slashing at the jars and bottles.

The door was jammed and opened with a shudder that continued all the way up Ma's spine to the base of her skull.

'Now then,' Ma said.

On the doorstep was her youngest grandson with that big dog of his. Always went for a walk together before school.

Benjie said nowt, grinned up at her, gap-toothed, something clutched in one hand.

'Well, well,' said Ma, smiling through the agony. 'Where'd you find that?'

'Chief found it,' said Benjie proudly. 'Jus' this mornin', up by t'moor.'

'Ta.' Ma took the bottle and fetched the child in for a chocolate biscuit from the tin. The bottle wasn't broken, but the cork was half out and the glass was misted. The bit of red thread that hung outside for the spirit to grasp was soaked through and stuck to the bottle.

''Ey!' Benjie said suddenly. 'Guess what.'

'I'm too owd for guessin' games, lad.'

'Bogman's bin took!'

'Eh?'

'It were on radio. Bogman's bin stole.'

'Oh,' said Ma, vaguely, 'has he?'

The child looked disappointed. 'Are you not surprised?'

238

'Oh, I am,' Ma said. 'I'm right flabbergasted. Look, just get that stool and climb up theer and fetch us biscuit tin. Me owd back's playin' up a bit.'

Ma held up the bottle to the cruel light. Useless.

'Will it still work?' asked Benjie innocently, arms full of wooden stool. Ma had to smile; what did he know about witch-bottles?

'Would it *ever*'ve worked, lad?' She shook her head ruefully, wondering if she'd be able to stand up straight before teatime. 'That's what I keep askin' meself.'

Fine lot of use *she* was. She ought to be out there, finding out exactly what they were up against – even if it killed her – before two thousand and more years of care and watchfulness came to ruin.

Oh, she could feel it . . . mornings like this, everything still and exposed.

She looked down at young Benjie, chomping on his choc-olate biscuit. It *will* kill me, she thought. I'm old and feeble and me back's giving way. I've let things slip all these years, pottered about the place curing sick babbies and cows, and not seeing the danger. And now there's only me with the strength inside. But I'm too old and buggered to go out and find um.

It'll come to *me*, though, one night, Ma thought, with uncustomary dread. When it's good and ready.

But will *I* be?

Joel Beard awoke screaming and sweating, coughing and choking on the paraffin air.

He sat on the edge of the camp bed, with the duvet wrapped around him, moaning and rocking backwards and forwards in the darkness for several minutes before his fingers were suf-ficiently steady to find the candle on its tray and the matches.

He lit the candle and, almost immediately, it went out. He lit it again and it flared briefly, with a curious shower of sparks, before the wick snapped, carrying the flame to the metal tray, where it lasted just long enough for Joel to grab his cross, his clothes and his boots and make it to the door.

On his way through the tunnel to the steps, he knocked over the paraffin heater, with a clatter and crash of tin and glass, and didn't stop to set it upright.

At the top of the steps he was almost dazzled by the white dawn, awakening the kneeling saints and prophets, the angelic hosts and the jewel-coloured Christs in the windows.

Deliverance.

He dressed in the vestry, where he found a mildewed cassock and put that on over his vest and underpants. But he did not feel fully dressed until his cross was heavy against his chest.

The air in the nave felt half-frozen; he could smell upon it the bitter stench of autumn, raw decay. But no paraffin. And the cold was negligible compared with the atmosphere in last night's dungeon.

He unbolted the church door, stood at the entrance to the porch breathing in the early morning air – seven o'clockish, couldn't be certain, left his watch in the dungeon, wasn't going back for it – and he did *not* look up, as he said, 'You're finished, you bitch.'

And then went quickly down, between the graves, to the gardener's shed, up against the perimeter wall.

The shed was locked, a padlock through the hasp. He had no key. He shook the door irritably and glared in through the shed's cobwebbed window. He could see what he wanted, a gleaming edge of the aluminium window-cleaning ladder, on its side, stretching the length of the shed. He also saw in the window the reflection of a face that was not his own.

Joel was jolted and, for a moment, could not turn round.

The face was a woman's. It had long, dark hair, steady, hard eyes and black whore's lips. The lips were stretched in a tight, shining grin which the eyes did not reflect.

Cold derision.

Remembered pain speared Joel's spine as he turned, half-hypnotized by the horror of it, turning as he would turn to stare full into the face of the Gorgon knowing it would turn him into stone, like the angels frozen to the graves.

He saw the still figure of a woman on the other side of the church wall, the village street below her. Her back was turned to him. Slowly, she began to walk away, and because the wall blocked her lower half she seemed at first to be floating. Her long, black hair swayed as she moved, and in the hair he saw a single thin, ice-white strand.

Joel felt a twisted revulsion. Twisted because there was inside it a slender wafer of cold desire, like the seam of white in the hair of the woman who walked away.

He watched her, not aware of breathing. She was wearing something long and black. He watched her until she was no more, and not once did she turn round.

Joel sobbed once, felt the savage strength of rage. He bunched a fist and drove it through the shed window.

Ernie Dawber had heard about the bogman on the morning news. So he wasn't exactly surprised when, round about 10.30, he heard a car pulling up irritably in the schoolhouse drive.

Hadn't given much thought to how he was going to handle this one. Too busy making notes for a daft book that would never get published.

The page he was writing, an introduction, began:

Bridelow might be said to operate on two levels. It has what you might call an underlife, *sometimes discernible at dusk when all's still and the beacon is about to light up* . . .

He looked up from the paper and the room went rapidly in and out of focus and swayed. Bugger. Not again. Damn.

He pushed his chair back, swept all the papers from his desk into an open boxfile and went to let the man in.

'A raw day, Dr Hall.'

'A word, Mr Dawber, if you're not . . . too *busy*.'

Innuendo. It was going to be all innuendo this time, he could tell.

'I'm a retired man. I'm not supposed to be busy. Come in. Sit down. Cup of tea? Or something a little . . .'

'No, thank you. Nothing.' Oh, very starchy. 'It's interesting that you don't seem at all surprised to see me, Mr Dawber.'

'I'm not daft,' Ernie said. 'That's how I got to be a headmaster.'

Underneath Hall's open Barbour jacket was a suit and tie. An official visit.

'Well, at least shut the door,' Ernie said. 'It's the worst kind of cold out there.'

The archaeologist consented at last to come into the study. Ernie closed the boxfile and placed it carefully under his chair. 'Look around,' he said. 'You don't need a search warrant.'

'I haven't said anything to the police,' Hall said. 'Not yet. I'm giving you a chance either to bring it back or tell me where it is.'

Ernie didn't insult him by asking what he was talking about. 'Dr Hall, this is a very serious allegation.'

'Don't worry, I know enough about the libel laws not to make it in public. That's why I've come to see you. If we can keep it between the two of us and the, er . . . if it comes back undamaged, that'll probably be as far as it goes.'

'Now look, you don't really think . . . ?'

'Oh, I don't for one minute think you were personally involved. Besides, you were at the funeral, I saw you. Wouldn't have been time.'

'So I'm just the mastermind. The brains behind the heist. That it?'

'Something like that.'

'All right,' said Ernie Dawber. 'I'll be straight with you. Yes, I did come to you on behalf of the village and urge you to put that thing back in the bog. That was me, and I meant it. But – and I'll say this very slowly, Dr Hall – I do *not* know who stole the bogman from the Field Centre. I'll say it to you and I'll say it again before a court of law.'

And he truly didn't know. Nobody ever knew these things apart from those concerned.

Had his *suspicions*, who wouldn't have?

But nothing black and white. Ma Wagstaff was right. There was never anything in black and white in Bridelow, which was how it was that balance and harmony could always be gently adjusted, like the tone and contrast on a television set.

Shades of things.

Oh, aye, naturally, he had his suspicions. Nowt wrong with suspicions. Suspicions never hanged anyone.

Roger Hall had changed colour. His beard-rimmed lips gone tight and white. Dr Hall's tonal balance was way out.

'It's here, Dawber. I know it's here.'

'You're welcome to search . . .'

'I don't mean this house. I mean in Bridelow. Somebody has it . . .'

'Don't be daft.'

'That's if it hasn't already been put back in the bog. And if it has, we'll find it. I can have two coachloads of students down here before lunch. We'll comb that moss, inch by inch, and when we find the area that's been disturbed . . .'

'I wish I could help you, Dr Hall.'

'No, you don't.'

Ernie Dawber nodded. That was true enough. No, he didn't.

Joel lugged the ladder through the graveyard and into the church, dragging it along the nave, putting it up finally against a stone pillar next to the rood screen. He shook the ladder to steady it, then began, with a cold determination, to climb.

In his ankle-length black cassock, this was not easy. Close to the top, he hung on with one aching, bruised and blood-stained hand, the big, gilded cross swinging out from his chest, while he rummaged under the cassock for his Swiss Army knife, using his teeth to extract its longest, sharpest blade.

The topmost branches of the Autumn Cross were almost in his face. It was about six feet long, crudely woven of oak and ash with, mashed up inside for stuffing, thousands of dead leaves and twigs, part of a bird's nest, shrivelled berries and hard, brown acorns.

Disgusting thing.

Fashioned in public, he'd been told, on the field behind The Man I'th Moss, with great ceremony, and the children gathering foliage for its innards.

'Oh, Lord,' Joel roared into the rafters, 'help me rid your house for ever of this primeval slime!'

He leaned out from the ladder, one foot hanging in space, tiny shards of glass still gleaming amidst the still-bright blood on the hand gripping a rung. His fatigue fell away; he felt fit and supple and had the intoxicating sensation of grace in his movements.

Deliverance

Orange baling-twine bound the frame of the cross to a rusted hook sunk into a cross-beam. He swung his knife-arm in a great arc and slashed it through.

'Filth!' he screamed.

The Autumn Cross fell at once, and Joel watched it tumble and was glad.

A beginning.

The sapless, weightless artefact fell with a dry, slithering hiss. Like a serpent in the grass, he thought, satisfaction setting firm in the muscles of his stomach, his head filled with a wild light.

He did recoil slightly, throwing the lightweight ladder into a tilt, as the so-called cross burst apart on the stone flags, fragments of leaves and powdery dust rising all around until the belly of the church was filled up with a dry and brackish-smelling sepia mist.

Joel coughed and watched the filthy pagan detritus as it settled. A bigger job than usual for the women on the Mothers' Union cleaning rota.

He hoped the foul bitches would choke on the dust.

CHAPTER V

With a nod to Our Sheila, Moira slipped quietly into St Bride's church just before 10 a.m.

To be alone. To confront the spirit of Bridelow. Maybe find something of Matt Castle here.

Special place, Matt had said, a long, long time ago on a snowy night in Manchester. *It's got . . . part of what I've been trying to find in the music. That's where it is . . . where it was all along.*

Cathy Gruber had persuaded her to stay the night in the guest room. She'd slept surprisingly well, no awful dreams of

Matt in his coffin. And awoken with – all too rare these days –
a sense of direction: she would discover Matt, trace the source
of the inspiration. Which was the essence of the village.

Bridelow, last refuge of the English Celts.

*A more pure, undiluted strain than you'll find anywhere in
Western Europe.*

She stopped in the church porch.

Who said that? Who *said* that?

The American said it. Macbeth.

Macbeth?

Yeah, quoting somebody . . . some writer addressing the
Celtic conference. Stanhope, Stansfield, some name like that
. . . from the North of England.

Connections.

She felt like a small token in a board-game, manoeuvred
into place by the deft fingers of some huge, invisible, cunning
player.

And she knew that if she was to tap into Matt's imagination,
she was also going to have to confront his demons.

As she walked – cautious now – out of the porch, into the
body of the church, something whooshed down the aisle and
collided with her at chest-level.

'Hey!' Moira grinned in some relief, holding, at arm's
length, a small boy.

'Gerroff!' Kid was in tears.

'You OK? You hurt yourself?'

The child tore himself away from her, wailing, and hurled
himself through the door, an arm flung across his eyes, like
he'd been blown back by an explosion.

Moira's grin faded.

Something had changed.

The place looked bare and draughty. Even through the
stained-glass windows, the light seemed ashen and austere.
On a table near the entrance, next to the piles of hymn books,
all the lanterns and candlesticks had been carelessly stacked,
as if for spring cleaning. One of the slender, coloured candles
had rolled off the edge and lay snapped in two on the stone
flags.

She picked up the two halves, held one in each hand a

245

moment then placed them on the table and wandered up the central aisle of a church which seemed so much bigger than yesterday at Matt's funeral, so much less intimate, less friendly.

Something was crunched under her shoe. She looked down and saw curled-up leaves and broken twigs, shrivelled berries and bracken and acorns and all the rustic rubble of autumn scattered everywhere.

Like a savage wind had blown through the nave in the night. Looking up, she saw what was missing, what the mess around her ankles was.

Somebody smashed the Autumn Cross.

'No accident, this,' Moira said aloud. Shivered and wrapped her arms around her sweatered breasts. It was still cold, but after what she'd learned last night, she'd left the black cloak at the Rectory. This was obviously not a place in need of a spare witchy woman.

She stood by the rood screen and looked back down the naked church. She looked down at the mess all around her, on the stone floor and the scratched and homely pews. Saw, for a moment, a scattering of bleached white skulls. But she knew almost at once that it wasn't the same.

Or at least that *she* was not to blame this time.

This was a rape.

She experienced a moment of awe. *I walked into someone else's conflict.*

But it was not *quite* someone else's conflict. There was a connection, and the connection was Matt Castle.

Last night, she'd said to Cathy, just as abrupt as the girl had been, 'Why did they open Matt's coffin? What was in that bottle?'

'Ah.' Cathy's eyes cast down over the steaming mug of chocolate. 'You saw that.'

'Don't get me wrong, I'm not normally an intrusive person, but Matt meant a lot to me.'

'Dic obviously thinks so.'

'Oh. You heard that. I wondered if maybe you had one of those pianos that plays itself.'

'Those pianos don't play bum notes.' Cathy looked offended. 'No, I didn't have my ear to the door. Dic and I went for a drink the other night. I drove, he got a bit pissed. He said his father . . .'

'The boy's way off. There was nothing more complicated than friendship between me and Matt. He never . . .'

He never touched me.

Moira stumbled and fell into a dusty pew. Sat staring into the vaulted ceiling where the cross had been, but seeing nothing.

He never touched me.

That was true. Never a friendly kiss. Never a celebratory hug when a gig had gone down well or the first album had gone into profit. *Never touched me sexually.. He never came near.*

But he looked.

Often she'd feel his moody gaze and turn and catch his eyes, and she'd smile and he wouldn't, and then he'd look away.

She bent painfully over the prayer-book shelf.

Clink. From outside, the sound of a chisel on stone.

I was thinking, if we'd slept together, just once, to kind of get it over, bring down that final barrier . . .

No. Wouldn't have got anything over. Would have started something bad. You knew that really, just as you really knew what was going on inside Matt Castle and chose to ignore it. Just a crush; he'll get over it. He didn't. He couldn't. He made you leave the band, before . . .

The clinking from outside was coming harder. Maybe they were demolishing the joint entirely.

Too choked to think about this any more, stomach tight and painful, Moira stood up, made her way slowly down the aisle to the doors. But when she grasped the ring-handles, the doors wouldn't open.

'Owd on! You'll have me off.' Sound of someone creaking his way down a wooden ladder up against the doors.

She leaned her back against the doors, took a few deep breaths, and called out after a few seconds, 'OK?'

'Aye.' The porch doors opened, and there was a smallish guy in his sixties, flat cap and a boiler-suit. Big, soft moustache, like a hearthbrush. 'Sorry, lass, dint know there were anybody in theer.'

He held a mallet and a masonry chisel. There were chips of grey stone and crumbly old concrete around the foot of the step-ladder.

'Storm damage?' Moira said.

'You what?'

'You repairing storm damage?'

'Summat like that.'

But then, looking up at the wall above the porch, she saw where the chippings had come from.

From the stones supporting the Exhibitionist. The *Sheelagh na gig*. Our Sheila.

'You're taking her down?'

'Aye.' He didn't sound too happy.

'Why?'

He gave her a level look. 'Alfred Beckett, verger, organist, dogsbody. Who are you?'

She grinned. Fuck it, she was here now, in the open, uncloaked. 'Moira. Moira Cairns. Used to work with . . . Matt Castle.'

The name felt different. A different, darker Matt Castle.

'Matt Castle, eh?' said Alfred Beckett. 'Right. 'Course.' He seemed to relax a little. 'How do.' He stuck out a stubby hand and Moira took it, stone dust and all. He had a firm grip; it pulled her back into what people took for the real world.

'So, Mr Beckett . . .' She glanced up at the ancient woman squashed into a stone plaque, fingers up her fanny. A few strokes of the chisel away from a serious loss of status.

'Aye,' Mr Beckett said, like a ragged sigh, and Moira saw he wasn't far from tears. He said he was following instructions. Didn't *want* to do it. *Hated* doing it. But he wasn't in an arguing position, was he? Vergers being a good way down the ecclesiastical hierarchy.

'And if I don't do it,' he said, '*he'll* do it hisself. And he won't be as careful as me.'

'Mr Beard,' Moira said.

'Aye. He'll smash her, like . . .'

'Like the Autumn Cross.'

'I'll see she's all right,' Alfred Beckett said. 'I'll keep her safe until such time as . . .'

248

He sighed, fished a packet of Arrowmint chewing gum out of the top pocket of his boiler-suit. Moira accepted a segment and they stood together chewing silently for a minute or so.

Then Mr Beckett said, 'Aye. It's a bugger.'

A scrap of cement fell from Our Sheila.

Moira said, 'But isn't she – excuse me, I'm no' an expert in these matters – isn't she protected in some way?'

'No, lass, she's . . .'

'I meant, isn't she a feature of a listed historic building?'

'Oh,' said Alfred Beckett. 'Aye. Happen. But Mr Beard reckons she's not safe and could fall on somebody's head. Same as she's not done for the past umpteen centuries.'

'Aye,' Moira said eventually. 'It's a bugger all right.'

'Now then. Why aren't you at school?'

Benjie threw his arms around Ma's waist and burrowed his head into her pinny. He started to sob.

She pulled him into the kitchen, shut the back door. 'Now, lad. What's matter? Tell owd Ma.'

Ma Wagstaff sat her grandson on the kitchen stool. Spine still giving her gyp, she reached up for a bottle of her special licorice toffees. Never been known not to work.

When it was out, Ma said, 'The bugger.'

Benjie with his swollen eyes and his wet cheeks bulging with toffee.

'The unfeeling, spiteful bugger,' Ma said.

Biggest thing that had ever happened to Benjie, Ernest Dawber putting him in charge of the Autumn Cross – a whole afternoon, inspecting the twigs and branches, acorns, bits of old birds' nests and stuff the other kids had brought, saying what was to go into the cross, what was right for it, what wasn't good enough. Standing proudly, top of the aisle, the day Alfred Beckett had come with his ladder, and the cross, all trimmed and finished, had been hoisted into place, and everybody cheering.

Biggest thing ever happened to the lad.

'Leave him to me,' Ma said. 'I'll sort that bugger out meself, just you see if I don't.'

Benjie stared at her, wildly shaking his head, couldn't speak for the toffee.

'Gone far enough,' Ma said. 'Got to be told a few things. For his own good, if nowt else.'

'No!' Benjie blurted. 'Don't go near it, Ma.'

Ma was taken aback. 'Eh?'

'. . .'s getting bigger, Ma. Every day, 's getting bigger.'

'What is, lad?'

'The dragon!' The little lad started crying again, scrambling down from the stool, clutching Ma round the waist again, wailing, 'You've not to . . . You've *not* to!'

Eh?

Mystified, but determined to get to the bottom of this, Ma detached his small hands from her pinny, squatted down, with much pain, to his height. 'Now then. Summat you've not told me. Eh? Come on.' She held his shoulders, straightening him up, feeding him some strength, not that she'd much to spare these days. 'Come on. Tell owd Ma all about it.'

He stared into her face, eyes all stretched with terror.

'Bigger, Ma . . . 's *bigger*.'

'He might look big to you, Benjie,' Ma said gently. 'But he's only a man.'

'No. 's a dragon!'

'Mr Beard?'

''s a *dragon*.'

So the new curate was in combat with the Forces of Evil.

As represented by Our Sheila and the Autumn Cross.

And whatever Willie's Ma was doing inside Matt Castle's coffin.

Last night – early this morning – as the dregs of hot chocolate were rinsed from the mugs, she'd at last got it out of Cathy, what it was all about – or as much of it as Cathy knew.

'*So, the coffin's on the ground and the light's been lowered, and the lid is open . . .*'

'*I didn't see it!*'

'*And your friend, old Mrs Wagstaff has her hands inside . . .*

250

and I'm wondering if maybe the old biddy has a passing interest in necrophilia . . .'

'That's a terrible thing to say!'

'I know . . . so tell me. What's going on, huh?'

'It was . . . I think it was . . . a witch bottle.'

'I thought you said she wasny a witch.'

'It's just a term. It's a very old precautionary thing. To trap an evil spirit . . . ?'

'Matt's spirit . . . ?'

'No . . . I don't know. Maybe if there was one around. In there with him.'

'In the coffin?'

'I don't know . . . it's no good asking me. You're going to have to talk to Ma. If she'll talk to you.'

And Lottie. Today it was important to talk to Lottie, because Lottie was not part of this place, had not been returning, like Matt, to the bosom of a tradition which was older than Christianity.

. . . a more pure, undiluted strain . . . than you'll find anywhere in Western Europe . . .

Moira had come through the lych-gate, was standing at the top of the cobbled street, the cottages like boulders either side under a blank, unyielding sky – a sky as hard as a whitewashed wall.

. . . this writer . . . Stanton, Stanhope . . .

. . . he's on his feet, and is he mad . . . this guy's face is . . .

this guy's face is . . .

this guy's face is . . .

White.

251

CHAPTER VI

The plump woman in the village Post Office looked like a chief Girl Guide, whatever they called them now. Also, although she wore no wedding ring, she struck Moira as a member of the Mothers' Union.

'I wonder, um, could you help me? I'm looking for Willie Wagstaff.' She'd forgotten to ask Cathy where Willie lived, and Cathy had set out to drive fifteen miles to the hospital to visit her dad.

'Willie? Have you been to his house?'

Moira smiled. 'Well, no, that's . . .'

'Sorry, luv, I'm not very bright this morning.' The postmistress rolled her eyes. 'Go across street, turn left and after about thirty yards you'll come to an entry. Go in there, and you'll see a cottage either side of you and it's the one on the left.'

Moira bought ten postage stamps and two packets of Arrowmint chewing gum in case she ran into Alfred Beckett again.

There was no answer at Willie's house, a narrow little cottage backing on to other people's yards. Moira wondered if he lived alone. She squashed her nose to the front window. There was a bowl of flowers in it, with ferns. A woman's touch. Females had always been drawn to Willie, born to be mothered. In the old days, it used to be said that otherwise worldly mature ladies would turn to blancmange when little Mr Wagstaff smiled coyly and let them put him to bed.

Moira was not that mature, yet. The reason she needed Willie was to talk about Matt, and also to meet his mother. She came out of the entry, unsure what to do next. There was no one else in the place she knew, except . . .

At the bottom of the village street, Moira found herself facing the pub, the last building, apart from a couple of wooden sheds, before the street widened into the causeway across the peatbog.

This was the difficult one.

Against the white morning, the pub looked hulking and sinister, like a gaol or a workhouse. Stonework so murky that in places it might have been stained by the peat. Outside on the forecourt, a man in an apron was cleaning windows.

A red-haired woman appeared in the porch, handed the man a steaming mug of tea or coffee, stopped and stared across the forecourt. Waited in the doorway, watching Moira.

You ready for this, hen?

'They're not Ancient Monuments, these circles. Ancient, possibly. Monuments . . . well, hardly.'

Joel Beard kicked at a stubby stone.

'No signs pointing um out, anyroad,' said Sam Davis. 'Not even proper tracks.'

'That's because they're not in the care of any Government or local authority department. Unlike, say, Stonehenge, where you have high-security fences and tunnel-access. Which is why these places are so open to abuse.'

The Reverend Beard, in his dark green Goretex jacket and his hiking boots, striding through the waist-high bracken. Action priest, Sam thought cynically.

'Lights, you say?'

Although they were less than a hundred yards from the first circle, it wasn't even visible yet. This was the most direct route from Sam's farmhouse, but he reckoned that mob last night must have come in from behind, over the hill.

'Cocky bastards,' Sam said, breathing harder, keeping pace with difficulty, due to shorter legs. 'Bold as brass. If wife hadn't kicked up, I'd've been up theer last night.'

Sam bunched his fingers into fists. 'I'd give um bloody devil worship.'

'I know how you feel,' the minister said, 'but you did the right thing in coming to me. This is my job. This is what I'm trained for.'

Sam Davis watched the big blond man flexing his lips, baring his teeth, steaming at the mouth in the cold air. It was all Esther's fault, this, making him drag the Church into it. 'Look, Mr Beard . . .'

253

'Joel . . .'

'Aye. Thing is, I don't want to turn this into some big bloody crusade. All I want is these buggers off me property. Know what I mean?'

The Reverend Beard stopped in his tracks. 'Sam, have you ever had foot-and-mouth disease on your land?'

'God. Be all I need.'

'Swine fever? Fowl pest? Sheep scab?'

'Give us a chance, I've only been farming two year.'

'The point I'm making,' Joel Beard said patiently, moving on, as the bracken came to an end and the ground levelled out, 'is that when a farmer's land is infected by a contagious disease, it's not simply a question of getting rid of the afflicted livestock. There are well-established procedures. For the purpose of, shall we say, decontamination.'

'Aye, but . . . let's get down to some basic facts, Joel. Who exactly are these fellers? Your mate, the Vicar . . . now he reckoned it's just kids, right?'

. . . *could probably tuck a couple under each arm* . . .

'Kids?' said Joel Beard.

'For kicks,' Sam said. 'Like drink. Drugs. Shoplifting. Kicks.'

'Hans Gruber said that?'

Sam shrugged. 'Summat like that. Right, this is it.'

'I beg your pardon . . .'

'The main circle. You're in t'middle of it, Joel. Told you it weren't much.'

Around them, sunk into tufts of dry, yellow grass, were these seven small stones, stained with mosses and lichens, none more than a couple of feet high, in a circle about fifteen feet diameter. Sam found it hard to credit them being here, in this formation, for about four thousand years.

'Don't know much about these things meself,' Sam said. 'Some folk reckon they was primitive astronomical observatories. You could stand in um and see where t'sun were risin'. Or summat.'

Personally, he didn't give a shit. By his left boot were two flat stone slabs, pushed together. The ground had clearly been disturbed. There were blackened twigs and ashes on the slabs.

'. . . but what that's got to do wi' bloody sacrifices is . . .'

'Sam!'

The Reverend Joel Beard shot up, like a charge of electricity had gone through him, and then, yelling 'Get back!', seized Sam Davis by the shoulders and shoved him out of the circle.

'What the . . . ?' Sam struggled out of Joel's grip, stumbled back into the bracken.

Joel was still in the circle, swaying like a drunk, swallowing big, hollow breaths through his mouth. His body bent into a fighting stance, hands clawed, eyes blinking.

Sam Davis stared at him. He was going to kill Esther for landing him with this big tosser.

'There's evil here,' Joel said.

Stupid sod looked ready for war. All that bothered Sam was how close the battlefield was to his kids. Down below, half a mile away, his farmhouse and its barns and buildings looked rickety and pathetic, like matchstick models he could kick over with the tip of his welly.

Joel Beard had closed his eyes. The sun, shuffling about behind weak clouds, had actually given him a faint halo.

For getting on ten minutes, Joel didn't move, except, at one point, to lift up both hands, on outstretched arms, as if he was waiting, Sam thought, for somebody to pass him a sack of coal. Then he spoke.

'I give you notice, Satan,' Joel said in a powerful voice, 'to depart from this place.' He'd unzipped his jacket to reveal a metal cross you could have used to shoe a horse.

Then he raised his hands so that they were parallel to his body and began to push at the air like this mime artist Sam had once seen on telly, pretending he was behind a pane of plate-glass.

'Bloody Nora,' Sam muttered to himself, crouching down among the ferns, unnerved by the whole thing but determined not to show it, even to himself. 'Got a right fuckin' nutter 'ere.'

Shaw Horridge watched them through binoculars from the Range Rover. It was parked on a moorland plateau about half

255

a mile away. The binoculars, being Shaw's own, were very good ones.

The Range Rover belonged to a squat, greasy little man who lived in Sheffield and was unemployed. He called himself Asmodeus or something stupid out of *The Omen*.

'They're moving on, I think,' Shaw said.

Asmodeus had a beard so sparse you could count the hairs. He had the seat pushed back and his feet on the dashboard. 'Good,' he said, as if he didn't really care.

Shaw lowered his binoculars. 'What would you do if they came up here with spades and things?'

'I'd be very annoyed indeed,' Asmodeus said in his flat, drawly voice. 'I'd be absolutely furious. So would Therese, wouldn't you, darling?'

Therese was stretched out on the rear seat, painting her fingernails black. Shaw scowled. He didn't like Asmodeus calling her darling. He didn't at all like Asmodeus, who was unemployed and yet could afford a newish Range Rover.

And yet he was still in awe of him, having seen him by night, this little slob with putrid breath and a pot-belly, not yet out of his twenties and yet able to *change things*.

And he was excited.

'But what would you *do*?'

Asmodeus grinned at him through the open window. 'You're a little devil, aren't you, Shaw? What would *you* do?'

Shaw said, because Therese was there, 'Kill them.'

'Whaaay! You hear that, Therese? Shaw thinks he'd kill them.'

Therese lifted newly painted nails into the light. 'Well,' she said, 'we might need the priest, but I must say that little farmer's beginning to get on my nerves.'

Shaw tensed.

'Tell you what, Shaw,' Asmodeus said. 'We'll give you an easier one. How about that?'

They sat at one end of a refectory table, near an Aga-type kitchen stove, their reflections warped in the shiny sides of its hot-plate covers. Moira kind of jumpy inside, but Lottie pouring tea with steady hands, businesslike, in control.

And this was less than twenty-four hours after the set-to at Matt's graveside, Lottie laying into Willie and Willie's Ma and the other crones, while the minister was helped away into the vibrating night.

Over fifteen years since they'd been face to face. Lottie's hair was shorter. Her face was harder, more closed-up. Out on the forecourt, it had been, 'Hello, Moira', very nonchalant, like their meetings were still everyday events – no fuss, no tears, no embrace, no *surprise*.

No doubt Dic had told her Moira was around.

She sipped her tea and said Lottie was looking well, in spite of . . .

'You too,' Lottie said, flat-voiced. 'I always knew you'd become beautiful when you got past thirty. Listen . . . thanks.'

'For what?'

'For not coming when he wrote to you.'

'I was tied up.'

'Sure,' Lottie said. 'But thanks anyway. Things were complicated enough. Better this way.'

'This way?'

'His music,' Lottie said. 'His project. His beloved bogman. Now stolen, I believe.'

'Lottie, maybe I'm stupid, but I'm not with you.'

'It was on the radio this morning. Thieves broke into the University Field Centre out near Congleton and lifted the Man in the Moss. I find it quite amusing, but Matt would've been devastated. Like somebody kidnapping his father.'

'Somebody stole the bogman? Just like that?'

Lottie almost smiled. 'Hardly matters now, though, does it? Listen, I'll take you down in a bit, show you his music room. He left some stuff for you.'

'For me?'

'Tapes. Listen, I'm not pushing, Moira, but I think you should do it.'

'Do it?' She was starting to feel very foolish.

'Get together with Willie and Eric and Dic and record his

257

bogman music. I don't know if it's any good or not, I haven't heard much of it, but Matt saw it as his personal . . . summit? His big thing? Life's work?'

Moira looked hard at her, this austere, handsome woman, fifty-odd years old. Looked for the old indomitable spark in the eyes. Truth was, she was still indomitable, but the eyes . . . the eyes had died a little. This was not the old Lottie, this was a sad and bitter woman playing the part of the old Lottie.

'Then we'll do it,' Moira said. 'Whatever it's like.'

'Good. Thank you. But don't decide yet. You see – I'll be frank – if you'd come when he wrote to you . . . Well, he was quite ill by then, into the final furlong. He wasn't fit to record. Not properly. And then there was the other problem. And don't say, *what* other problem . . . let's not either of us insult the other's intelligence.'

'OK.' Moira leaned back and slowly sipped her tea. They sat there in silence, two women with little in common except perceived obligations to one man.

Mammy, how was he when he died? Can you tell me that?

This was the woman who could tell her. But Lottie had never had much patience with religion of any sort – organized or . . . well, as *dis*organized as whatever it was Ma Wagstaff was trying to do last night with her patent witch bottle.

'Lottie,' she said, 'I'm sorry. I didn't know. Well, maybe I knew inside of me, but I was young, too young to understand it. And nothing happened, Lottie, I swear it.'

Lottie shrugged. 'Better, maybe, if it had. Better for me, I can tell you, if he'd gone off with you. But after sticking with it, through all kinds of . . . Well, I wasn't prepared to have him spending his last days ignoring me, eaten up with old lust and regrets. So I'm glad you couldn't come.'

Lottie took her teacup to the sink, dropped it into a plastic bowl. The sink was a big, old-fashioned porcelain thing, pipes exposed underneath it with bits of rag tied around them. Not what Lottie's used to, Moira thought. Lottie is stainless-steel and waste-disposal.

'You've . . . had problems, then.' Christ, everything I say to this woman is just so fucking facile . . .

Lottie turned on the hot tap, held both hands under the

frenzied gush until the steam rose and her wrists turned lobster-red. 'You could say that.'

Eventually, turning off the water, wiping her hands on a blue teatowel, she said, 'I was married for twenty-eight years to a man who collected obsessions. The Pennine Pipes. The Mysteries of Bridelow. The Bogman . . .'

Moira said nothing. She was feeling faint. Her breath locked in her throat. She was getting a strong sense of Matt's presence in the room.

'. . . and you,' Lottie said.

In the lofty, rudimentary kitchen, Moira heard a roaring in her head, saw a flashing image of Matt in his coffin, white T-shirt, white quilted coffin-lining, before it was washed away by the black tide carrying images of a stone toad, dancing lights, the steam from writhing intestines liberated on to a flat stone . . .

'On the night he died . . .'

Moira swallowed tea, but the tea wasn't so hot any more and she was swallowing bile.

'On the night he died,' Lottie said, 'he sexually assaulted a nurse in the hospital.'

I'm not hearing this.

She started to look wildly around the kitchen. High ceiling with pipes along it . . . whitewashed walls with crumbling plaster showing through in places . . . stone-flagged floor like the church of St Bride . . . two narrow windows letting in light so white it was like a sheet taped across the glass.

And this awful sense of Matt.

'The nurse had long, dark hair,' Lottie said, almost wistfully. 'He addressed her as Moira.'

The silence was waxen.

She felt scourged.

Lottie said, 'I wanted you to know all this . . .'

Matt was dodging about under the table, behind the pipes, vibrant, shock-haired Matt reduced to a pale, fidgeting thing, hunched in corners, flitting, agitated, from one to another, giving off fear, hurt, confusion.

'. . . before you made a firm decision about the music. You see? I'm being open about it. No secrets any more.'

Moira looked up into the furthest corner, near the back door, and a cobweb inexplicably detached itself from the junction of two pipes and hung there, impaled by a shaft of white light, heavy with glittering flies' corpses.

'Come with me.' Lottie rolled down the sleeves of her cardigan and strode across the kitchen to the back door, with its long, gaoler's key.

PART SIX

MOTHERS

From *Dawber's* Secret *Book of Bridelow* (unpublished):

THE MOST WIDESPREAD and powerful Celtic tribe in Northern Britain were the Brigantes, whose territory – known as Brigantia – included much of Yorkshire, Lancashire and Southern Scotland and had its southern boundary in the lower Pennines. The mother goddess of the Brigantes was Brigid, and it is believed that many churches dedicated to 'St Bride' were formerly sites of pagan Celtic worship . . .

CHAPTER I

The bloody media.

Over twenty cars parked outside the Field Centre, and men and women pacing the concrete forecourt, most of them turning round when Roger Hall's car pulled in – where the hell was he supposed to park with all these bastards clogging the place? Three cameramen, all swinging round, shooting his Volvo Estate as it manoeuvred about seeking space, as if he might have the bogman himself laid out in the back.

'No . . . no, I'm sorry . . .' Ramming his way through jabbing hands holding pocket tape recorders.

'Dr Hall, have you any idea yet . . . ?'

'Dr Hall, do you know when . . . ?'

'Can you just tell us, Dr Hall, how . . . ?'

'*No!*' He held up both hands. 'There'll be an official Press statement later.'

Bastards. Leeches. One of the double doors opened a few inches and he was hauled in. Chrissie and the other woman, Alice, got the door closed and bolted behind him.

Inspector Gary Ashton was sitting on Roger's desk. 'Any luck, sir?'

'Blank wall.' Roger was brushing at his jacket, as if the reporters had left bits of themselves on him. 'However . . .'

'I must say,' Ashton said, 'it seemed a bit of a long shot to me, that a bunch of villagers from Bridelow would go to all this trouble.' He smiled hesitantly. 'Look, I've had a thought. I hardly like to suggest this, sir, but I don't suppose there's a University rag week in the offing?'

'Don't be ridiculous,' Roger said.

'Well, I don't honestly think,' Ashton said tautly, 'that it's any more ridiculous than your idea about superstitious villagers. Which sounds a bit like one those old Ealing comedies, if I may say so, *sir.*'

Roger said, 'I think you should listen to me without prejudice. I think I know how they've done it.'

Liz Horridge stood frozen with terror at the edge of the pavement.

She was sweating hard; there seemed to be a film of it over her eyes, and a blur on the stone buildings around her turning the cottages into squat muscular beasts and the lych-gate into a predatory bird, its wings spread as if it were about to hop and scuttle down the street and overwhelm her, pinning her down and piercing her breast with its cold, stone beak.

She was leaning, panting, against the back of a van parked

on the corner where the main street joined the old brewery road.

Oh, and by the way, Mother, the Chairman's hoping to drop by tonight.

Who?

The Chairman, Gannons. Been planning to come for ages, apparently, but, you know, appointments, commitments . . .

Will he come here?

We'll receive him in the main office, show him around the brewery. Then, yes, I expect I'll bring him back for a drink. A proper drink. Ha!

Go. Get out. Got to.

She'd thought that when she got so far the fear would evaporate in the remembered warmth of the village, but the village was cold and empty, and a blind like a black eyelid was down in the window of Gus Bibby's general stores, which always kept long hours and would always be lit by paraffin lamps on gloomy days.

But it was Saturday afternoon. Gus Bibby did *not* close on a Saturday afternoon. Saturday had always been firewood day, and there'd be sacks of kindling outside. Always. Always on a Saturday.

Liz felt panic gushing into her breast. Maybe it wasn't Saturday. Maybe it wasn't afternoon. Maybe it was early morning. Maybe the whole place had closed down, been evacuated, and nobody had told her. Maybe the brewery itself had been shut down for weeks and the village had been abandoned.

. . . Chairman's hoping to drop by tonight . . .

No!

How could I not have seen it? How could I have sat there, pretending to examine Gannon's proposals and estimates and balance sheets, and not see his name?

Because it wasn't there . . . I swear . . .

Liz Horridge pumped panicky breath into the still, white air. Not far now. Not fifty yards. She could take it step by step, not looking at houses, not looking at windows.

Someone's door creaked, opened.

'Ta-ra then, luv, look after yourself . . . You what . . . ?'

Liz scuttled back into a short alleyway, squeezed herself into the wall. Mustn't let anyone see her.

'Yeh, don't worry, our Kenneth'll be up to see to it in t'morning. Yeh, you *do*. Ta-ra.'

Door closing.

Footsteps.

Liz clung to the wall. She wore an old waxed jacket and a headscarf over the matted moorgrass that used to be chestnut curls.

She emerged from the entry into the empty street, like a rabbit from a hole. Wanting. Needing. Aching.

To sit again at Ma Wagstaff's fireside, a warm, dry old hand on her sweating brow. *If he comes . . . scream. Don't matter what time.*

Can't turn back now. If you turn back now you'll surely die. Believe this.

'How are you, Pop?'

He was out of bed, that was a good sign, wasn't it? Cathy found him wearing a dull and worthy hospital dressing gown, sitting at his own bedside in a shabby, vinyl-backed hospital chair. He was in the bottom corner of a ward full of old men.

'Bit tired,' he said. 'They've had me walking about. Physiotherapy. Got to keep moving when you've had a coronary.'

Cathy clutched at the bed rails. 'They never told me that!'

'Had to drag it out of them myself. Soon as they get you in hospital you're officially labelled "moron".' His features subsided into that lugubrious boxer-dog expression.

'What's it mean, Pop?'

'Coronary thrombosis? Means a clot in the coronary artery. Means I was lucky not to christen Matt Castle's grave for him. Means I have to *rest*.' Putting on a pompous doctor-voice. '"We have to get ourselves together, as they say, Mr Gruber." Tell me about Joel. Please tell me he didn't sleep under the church.'

Cathy said carefully that she hadn't seen him today. Not a word of what she'd heard about him rampaging around the place in his post-funeral fury, ripping down anything that hinted of paganism. Just that she hadn't actually *seen* him. And that she didn't know where he'd slept.

'Storm gathering inside that chap,' Hans said. 'Hurricane Joel. Wanted to make sure he was somewhere else when it blew.'

'Don't you think about it, Pop. Get some rest. Let them do their tests, try and endure the hospital food and don't refuse the sleeping pill at night.'

'Cathy . . .'

'I know, but it's not *your* problem.'

Hans's head lolled back into the hard vinyl chair. 'I keep the peace. It's taken me years to strike the right balance.'

'Don't worry, they'll sort him out, Ma and the Union. They'll deal with him.'

'But . . .'

'They sorted you out, didn't they?'

Cathy smiled for him. Trying to look more optimistic than she felt.

Hans said bleakly, 'Cathy, Simon Fleming came to see me. They want me to go to the Poplars "for a few weeks' convalescence".'

'Where?'

'The Church's nursing home in Shropshire. Ghastly dump. Full of played-out parsons mumbling in the shrubbery. Nobody gets out alive.'

Cathy felt desperately sorry for him but couldn't help thinking it might be the best answer, for a while. Let the Mothers handle it. Whatever there was to be handled.

He didn't seem to have heard about the disappearance of the bog body, and she didn't tell him. He had enough to worry about already.

'Look, all you need,' Roger Hall said, 'is an exhumation order. That's not a problem, is it?'

Backs to the doors, the Press people assembled on the other side, Chrissie and Alice looked at each other. Roger playing detective. Didn't suit him. Chrissie wondered idly if Inspector

267

Garry Ashton was married or attached. She thought this business was rather showing up Roger for what he was: pompous, arrogant, humourless – despite the nice crinkles around his eyes.

Ashton said, a little impatiently, 'You were convinced earlier that the body was hidden in Bridelow.'

'Still am,' Roger said smugly.

'Go on,' Ashton said, no longer at all polite. 'Let's hear it.'

Chrissie liked his style. Also the set of his mouth and the way his hair was razor-cut at the sides.

Roger said, 'I attended a funeral in Bridelow yesterday. Matt Castle, the folk musician.'

'So I understand,' Ashton said. 'Mr Castle a friend of yours, was he?'

With a tingle of excitement, Chrissie suddenly knew what Ashton was wondering: did *Roger himself* have anything to do with the theft? The police must have spoken to the British Museum by now, learned all about Roger's battle to bring the bogman back up North. And why was he so keen to keep pointing the police in other directions?

Gosh, Chrissie thought . . . And Roger's obsessive attitude! The bogman intruding everywhere. And when the bogman was in a state of, er, emasculation, Roger himself was . . . unable to function. And complaining of clamminess and peat in the bed and everything. And then suddenly Roger *could* . . . with a vengeance! And the bog body had acquired what appeared to be an appendage of its own.

Chrissie felt a kind of hysteria welling up. *Stop it!* I'm going bloody bonkers. Or somebody is.

Suddenly she didn't want him touching her again.

'Castle?' Roger said. 'Not what you'd call a friend, no. But he was always very interested in the bog body, as many people were. Kept ringing me up, asking what we'd learned so far. And actually turned up here twice, wanting to see the body, which, of course, was *not* available for public viewing. Although I did allow it the second time.'

'Why'd you do that?'

'Because . . . because he was with someone I judged to be more reliable.'

He didn't elaborate; Ashton didn't push the point either. Chrissie thought of the writer, Stanage.

'So, anyway,' Roger said, 'it was Castle's funeral yesterday, and I thought I ought to show my face. I only went to the church service. Left before they actually put him into the ground. But I very much wish I'd stayed with it now, seen him buried.'

'I might be thick,' said Ashton, 'but I'm not following this.'

'All right, let's approach it from another angle. We've all been assuming that the break-in took place last night, right?'

'Have we, Dr Hall?'

'Ashton, look – can we stop this fencing? I know you're an experienced policeman and all that, but I've been doing *my* job for over twenty-five years too.' Angrily, Roger drew his chair from under the desk, scraping the Inspector's legs.

'Look. Because of the funeral and one or two other things, I didn't come in here at all yesterday. And you only found out about the burglary before me because our normally lazy caretaker just happened to try the doors for a change. Correct?'

Ashton came slowly down from the desk, stood looking down at Roger. Interested.

'But if he'd bothered,' Roger said, 'to check the doors the night before – and if he says he did he's probably lying, I know that man – he'd probably have found them forced then. My strong suspicion is the break-in happened the previous night. And that the body wasn't here at all yesterday.'

'And what does that say to you?'

'What it says to me, Inspector – and I might have to spend a bit of time explaining this to you – but what it says to me is that my bog body is buried in St Bride's churchyard.'

'I see,' Ashton said thoughtfully. 'Or do I?'

'The funeral!' Roger raised his hands. 'The grave – it's a *double* grave! What I'm saying is, dig up Castle's coffin, you'll find our body lying underneath. Trust me.'

. . . and there it was.

Oh, Lord. Oh, Mother.

Ma Wagstaff could see the thing from the top of the churchyard, the highest vantage-point in Bridelow.

It hadn't been there a week ago, had it? There was a time when she knew this Moss better than anybody. Couldn't claim that now. Getting owd now. Letting it slide.

Ma leaned on her stick and wondered if she could make it all the way out there without some help. She'd have been able to yesterday, but yesterday was a long time ago. Yesterday, though she hadn't realized it at the time, she still had some strength.

She'd thought that sooner or later it would come to her, but instead it had sent her an invitation. Brought by a little lad who for no good reason had decided the dragon – because the dragon was *there* – was responsible for breaking up his Autumn Cross.

And in a way he was right.

Right about that thing out there; Ma could feel its black challenge. And looking across at it, she could tell why he thought it was a dragon – those little knobbly horns you could make out even from this distance.

Only an owd dead tree, as sometimes came out of the Moss when there was storms and flooding.

Bog oak.

Except there hadn't been a storm.

So it was black growth, like the blackness that grew in Matt Castle, and she had to gauge its strength.

Ma hesitated.

Not one to hesitate, wasn't Ma, but if she went out there she'd be on her own. As well as which, somebody needed her help this side of the Moss; she'd known this for days. Well, aye, people was always needing owd Ma's help, but this was somebody as didn't want to ask, hadn't for some reason been able to overcome a barrier, and until this barrier was overcome there was nowt Ma could do. Now she could feel the struggle going on, and when the plea came she must be there to answer it.

Pulled this way and that, between the flames and the torrent. Oh, Lord. Oh, Mother, which way do I turn? Let it slide for so long, losing me grip.

I'll walk out then.

Walk out there following the river, staying near the water, gathering what power I can. Happen I can deal wi' this quick, nip it in t'bud. Stare it down, give it the hard eye, reshape it, turn it back into wood and only wood.

Leaning heavily on her stick, Ma Wagstaff followed the old, steep narrow path down from the churchyard, meeting the thin river at the bottom of the hill where it went under the path – a little bridge, no more than a culvert – and there was a scrubby field to cross before they reached the Moss.

I can make it. I can. Can I lean on you, Mother?

The last few steps were going to be the hardest, by far.

From two yards away, Ma Wagstaff's front door looked like the golden gates of heaven: unattainable.

Liz Horridge was aware of her mouth being wide open, gulping, a fish out of water, metabolism malfunctioning.

Agoraphobia.

Say it!

AGOR . . . A . . . PHOBIA!!! Common-enough condition, always so hard to imagine, until it came upon you in panic-attacks, convulsions, stomach-cramps.

Yet this . . . more like *claustro*phobia . . . not *enough* air . . . lungs bursting.

She'd tried to do it in planned stages, like an invalid learning to walk again. The first stage had been waiting for the postman, whom she hadn't seen face-to-face for months. When the van drew up, she'd be watching from the dining-room window, and if the postman was carrying a parcel she would run to open the front door, leaving it slightly ajar, and by the time he was tossing the parcel on to the mat, Liz had taken cover.

Yesterday, almost sick with apprehension, she'd waited for the post van down by the main gate, rehearsing how she'd handle it. Just taking a walk. Normally go the other way. Yes, it is cold. Bright, though. Bright, yes. Thank you. Good morning.

When the postman didn't come, she was so relieved. It had

been foolish. Trembling, she'd returned to the house to make Shaw's breakfast. But Shaw had gone. To be with *her*. Whenever he went out without saying even vaguely where he was going, it would always be to be with *her*.

Therese Beaufort had come into the house only once, had been polite but dismissive, had shown a vague interest in everything, except Liz, at whom she'd looked once, with a chilly smile before reappraising the drawing room, as if sizing it up for new furniture. Now she merely parked outside and waited, expressionless, not looking at the house (yes, I've *seen* your mother now, thank you).

And now there was . . .

Look, Liz, why don't we meet up?

And

Chairman's hoping to drop by tonight.

Fear. Despair. She'd walked away, down the drive, down the road, into terror, knowing she could not go home tonight. To the village, to Ma Wagstaff, to plead for sanctuary.

Liz Horridge fell down, tearing her skirt, feeling the small, jutting stones of Ma Wagstaff's front path gashing her knees. She began to crawl towards the door, feeling the emanations of the stone buildings heavy on her back as if they would crush her into the little pointed stones beneath her.

The whitened donkeystoned step gleamed like an altar.

Liz rose on her knees, tried to reach the knocker but managed only the letter-box which snapped at her fingers like a gin-trap.

'Mrs Wagstaff,' she managed to wail. '*Please, Mrs Wagstaff . . . let me in . . .*'

But nobody came to the door.

'I'm sorry! I couldn't stop it! It wasn't my fault about the brewery. Please . . . He's coming back. Please let me in.'

And then the stones came down on her. The weight of the village descended on her shoulders, taking all the breath from her and she couldn't even scream.

CHAPTER II

'*D*idn't know I was coming back to die . . . I mean, that's what people do, isn't it, and animals, go back home to die? But I wouldn't have. If I'd known. Last thing they need here's any deadwood.'

The voice frail, but determined. Going to get this out, if it . . .

Killed him. Yeah.

'*Just as well, really. That I didn't know.*'

All Moira could see through the windscreen was the Moss. The vast peatbog unrolling into the mist like the rotting lino in the hall of her old college lodgings in Manchester, half a life away.

The BMW was parked in the spot at the edge of the causeway where yesterday she'd sat and listened to the pipes on cassette. Now it was another cassette, the one from the brown envelope inscribed MOIRA.

'*Funny thing, lass . . . this is the first time I've found it easy to talk to you. Maybe 'cause you're not there. In the flesh. Heh. Did you realize that, how hard it was for me? Lottie knew. No hiding it from a woman like Lottie. Shit, I don't care who knows. I'm dead now.*'

Matt laughed. The cawing.

She'd followed Lottie into a yard untidy with beer kegs and crates. Beyond it was a solid, stone building the size of a two-car garage. It looked as old as the pub, had probably once been stables or a barn.

'Matt's music room,' Lottie said.

She'd been almost scared to peer over Lottie's shoulder, into the dimness, into the barnlike space with high-level slit windows and huge, rough beams. Dust floating like the beginnings of snow.

Lottie silent. Moira, hesitant. 'May I?' Lottie nodding.

Moira slipping past her, expecting echoes, but there was carpet and rugs underfoot and more carpet on the walls to flatten the acoustics. She saw a table, papers and stuff strewn across it.

Shelves supported by cement-spattered bricks held books, vinyl records and tapes. Heavy old speaker cabinets squatted like tombstones and there was a big Teac reel-to-reel tape machine. Matt's scarred Martin guitar lay supine on an old settee with its stuffing thrusting out between the cushions.

Hanging over the sides of a stool was something which, from across the room, resembled a torn and gutted, old, black umbrella.

She'd walked hesitantly over and stared down at the Pennine Pipes in pity and horror, like you might contemplate a bird with smashed wings. It was as if he'd simply tossed the pipes on the stool and walked out, for ever, and the bag had maybe throbbed and pulsed a little, letting out the last of Matt's breath, and then the pipes had died.

Moira's throat was very dry. She was thinking about Matt's obsessions: the Pennine Pipes, the bogman and . . .

'Can't help your feelings, can you? Like, if you're a married man, with a kid, and you meet somebody and you . . . and she takes over your life and you can't stop thinking about her. But that's not a sin, is it? Not if you don't . . . Anyway, I never realized that you . . . I never realized.'

Matt's voice all around her now. Car stereos, so damned intimate.

Lottie had turned away, calling back over her shoulder, 'I'll be in the kitchen. Stay as long as you like. Lock up behind you and bring me the key. The parcel's on the table.'

And was gone, leaving Moira alone in the barn that was like a chapel, with the pipes left to die.

On the table, a thick, brown envelope which had once held a junk-mail catalogue for Honda cars. It had been resealed with Sellotape and

MOIRA

was scrawled across it.

Inside: the tapes, four of them, three of music. And this one, a BASF chrome, marked *personal.*

'Not a sin . . . if you don't do owt about it. But I always found it hard to talk to you. I mean . . . just to talk to you. Till it came time to tell you to get out of the band. That was easy. That was a fucking pushover, kid. I'm sorry the way that worked out, with The Philosopher's Stone. Sounded like a big opportunity. Like, for me too – chance to make the supreme sacrifice. But we can't tell, can we? We never can bloody tell, till it's too late.'

Rambling. He'd have been on some kind of medication, wouldn't he? Drugs.

'But when they told me I'd had me chips, I did regret it. Regretted it like hell. I thought most likely you'd just have told me to piss off, but there might have been a . . . Anyway, I'd have given anything for just one . . . just one time with you. Just one. Anything.'

Christ. Moira stared out of the side window to where half a tree had erupted from the Moss, like bone burst through skin.

'When you wrote back and you said you were too busy, I was shattered. I'd convinced meself you'd come. I just wanted to at least see you. Just one more time.'

Moira bit down on her lower lip.

'I'd tried to write a song. Couldn't do it. It was just a tune without words. Nothing. Best bloody tune I ever wrote, which isn't saying much – play it for you in a minute. Won't be much good, the playing, what d'you expect? Be the last tune I ever play. Gonna play it over and over again until I get it perfect, and then I'm gonna get Lottie to take me out and I'll play it to the fucking Moss. The Man in the Moss. That's what it's about. The Man in the Moss. That'll be me, too. Want to die with this tune in me head. This tune . . . and you.'

She felt a chill, like a low, whistling wind.

'It's called Lament for the Man. I want the Moss to take it. A gift. Lament for the Bridelow Bogman. Soon as I read about him, months ago, before it came out about the sacrifice element, I was inspired by him. Direct link with me own past. The Celts. The English Celts. Like he'd come out the Moss to make a statement about the English Celts. And I was the only one could interpret it – sounds arrogant, eh? But I believe it. Like this is what me whole life's been leading up to.'

275

Matt starting to cough. On and on, distorting because the recording level couldn't handle it. The car-speakers rattling, like there was phlegm inside.

'*Fuck it,*' Matt said. '*If I go back and scrub this I'll forget what I was gonna say. Sorry. Can you handle it? See, this was before they'd completed the tests on the bogman, before it was known about the sacrifice. Even then I was pretty much obsessed. I didn't care if we spent every penny we'd got. Lottie – she's a bloody good woman, Moira, I never deserved Lottie – she went along with it, although she loved that chintzy house in Wilmslow and she hated The Man I'th Moss, soon as she clapped eyes on it. But she went along with it. Sometimes I think, did she know? Did she know before me, that I was gonna snuff it? She says not. I believe her.*'

Across the Moss she could see the pub, a huge grey boathouse on the edge of a dark sea, its backyard a landing stage.

'*And then, soon after we came, the report came out about the bogman. About what he was. A sacrifice. To appease the gods so they'd keep the enemy at bay, make this community inviolate. Protect these Celts, these refugees from the fertile flatlands, the Cheshire Plain, Lancashire, the Welsh border. Invaders snatching their land, Romans, Saxons. And this, the old high place above the Moss – maybe it was a lake then. Bridelow.*'

Matt's voice cracked.

'*Bridelow. The last refuge. I cried. When I heard, I cried. He went willingly. Almost definitely that was what happened. Almost certain he was the son of the chief, everything to live for – had to be, see, to make a worthwhile sacrifice.*'

Voice gone to a whisper.

'*Gave himself up. Willingly. That's the point. Can you grasp that, Moira? He let them take him on the Moss and they smashed his head, strangled him and cut his throat, and he knew . . . he fucking knew what was gonna happen.*'

She stared through the windscreen at the Moss. Thick, low cloud lay tight to the peat, like a bandage on its putrefying, suppurating skin.

'*Hard to credit, isn't it? I mean, when you really think about it. When you try and picture it. He let the buggers do it to him. Young guy, fit, full of life and energy and he gives himself up in the*

276

*most complete sense. Can you understand that? Maybe it affects me
more because I've got no youth, no energy, and what life there's left
is dribbling away by the minute. But by God . . . I realized I
wanted a bit of that.'*

She thought about the bogman. The sacrifice. She thought
about Matt, inspired. Always so contagious, Matt's inspiration.
She thought, I can't bear this . . .

*'Can you get what I'm saying? Like, they took him away, these
fucking scientists, with never a second thought about what he meant
to Bridelow and what Bridelow, whatever it was called back then,
meant to him. So I wanted . . . I wanted in. To be part of that.
To go in the Moss, too. Lottie tell you that? Lottie thinks it's shit,
but it isn't. . . .'*

'No,' Moira whispered. 'It wouldn't be.'

*'. . . want some of me out there. With him. He's my hero, that
lad . . . I'm fifty-seven and I'm on me last legs – nay, not even that
any more, me legs won't carry me – and I've found a fucking hero
at last.'*

Matt starting to laugh and the laughter going into a choke
and the choking turning to weeping.

*'Me and Ma Wagstaff met one day. One stormy day. Ma
understands, the old bitch. Willie's Ma, you know? Says to me,
"We can help you help him. But you must purify yourself."'*

Out on the Moss, the dead tree like bone was moving. It
had a tangle of thin branches, as if it were still alive, and the
branches were waving, whipping against the tree.

'She says, You have to purify yourself.'

The tree was a bad tree, was about to take its place alongside
the encroaching stone toad on the moor, the eruption of guts
on an ancient, rough-hewn altar. Bad things forcing themselves
into Bridelow.

'And then you came to me . . .'

Moira's eyes widened.

*'I used to think she was . . . a substitute. Me own creation.
Like, creating you out of her, you know what I mean? An obsession
imposes itself on what's available. But I should've known.
Should've known you wouldn't leave me to die alone.'*

Her senses froze.

'So, as I go into the final round, as they say, I'm drawing

277

*strength from the both of you. The bogman . . . and you, Moira.
Tomorrow's Sunday. I'll be going out on the Moss, to play. Last
time, I reckon. I'll need Lottie and Dic, poor lad, to get me there,
but I'll send them away, then there'll just be the three of us.'*

'No,' she said. 'What *is* this?'

'Me and thee and him.'

Matt chuckled eerily.

Hard rain hit the Moss.

'No,' she said.

*'Thanks, lass. Thanks for getting me through this. Thanks for
your spirit. And your body. It was your body, wasn't it?'*

She wrapped her arms around herself, began to shake,
feeling soiled.

*'Ma said, You've got to purify yourself. But there's a kind of
purity in intensity of feeling, isn't that right? Pure black light.'*

'I'll play now,' Matt said, and she heard him lifting his
pipes onto his knees.

*'If you're listening to this, it means you're here in Bridelow. So
find Willie, find Eric. And then find me. You'll do that, won't you?
Find me.'*

The old familiar routine, the wheeze, the treble notes.

'I won't be far away,' Matt said.

And the lament began. At first hoarse and fragmented, but
resolving into a thing of piercing beauty and an awful, knowing
anticipation.

Out on the black Moss, as if hit by a fierce wind, the dead
tree lashed impatiently at its bones with its own sinuous
branches, like cords of gut.

Moira thought, There's no wind. No wind to speak of. The
Moss in the rain was dull and opaque, like a blotter. She didn't
want to look at the tree but a movement drew her eyes. Human
movement.

An old woman was hobbling across the peat; she had a
stick. A stringy shawl flapped around her head. She was
approaching the tree very deliberately, slow but surefooted.

She seemed to be wearing ordinary shoes, not boots or
wellingtons; she knew the peat, where to walk.

Cathy had said, *You're going to have to talk to Ma. If she'll
talk to you.*

It *is* her, isn't it?

The dead tree was about a hundred yards away. The old woman was walking around it now, poking experimentally at it with her stick and then backing away like a terrier.

A wavy branch lashed out, wrapped itself around the walking stick. Moira drew breath.

Another movement, quick and sudden, and the shawl was torn away from the woman's shoulders, thrown triumphantly up into the air on the tip of a wavy branch, like a captured enemy flag.

'Holy Christ!' Moira was out of the car, leaving the driver's door hanging open, stepping down from the causeway, hurrying into the Moss.

Where the sinewy, whipcord branches of the old, dead tree were writhing and striking individually at the old woman, Ma Wagstaff, pulsing like vipers. Moira running across the peat, through the rain, desperately trying to keep her footsteps light because she didn't know this Moss. There was no wind. The rain fell vertically. Behind her Matt's music on the car stereo was a dwindling whine.

'Mrs Wagstaff!' she screamed. '*Mrs Wagstaff, get away from it . . .*'

In the distance, over the far hills, behind the rain, the sun was a bulge in the white bandage of cloud and the flailing tree of guts and bones was rearing up against it; she was maybe sixty yards away now and the tree was tossing its head.

It had a head.

And its eyes were white; they were only holes in the wood, letting the sky through, but they burned white, and it was not a case of what you knew it to be, old and twisted wood, shrivelled, wind-blasted, contorted by nature into demonic, nightmare shapes – this was the old mistake, to waste time and energy rationalizing the irrational.

'Mrs Wagstaff, back off!'

What was the old biddy doing here alone? Where were the Mothers' Union, when she needed back-up?

'Mrs Wag . . . Don't . . . don't look . . .'

Moira stumbled.

'Don't look at it,' she said miserably, for Bridelow Moss had got her left foot. Swallowed it whole, closing around her ankle, like soft lips.

White eyes.

Black, horned head, white eyes.

'It's thee. It were always thee.'

Ma Wagstaff growled, stabbed at it one last time with her stick – the wood was so hard. that the metal tip of the stick snapped off.

'Mrs Wag—'

Woman's voice screaming in the distance.

Nowt to do wi' her. Ma's job, this.

She moved away, like an old, experienced cat. Bait it. 'Come on, show thiself.' A dry, old rasp, not much to it, but she got it out. 'What's a tree? What's a bit of owd wood to me, eh? Show thi face. 'Cause this is as near as tha's ever going to get to Bridlo'. We seen to thee once . . . and it'll *stick*.'

Backing away from it, and all the muck coming off it in clouds. She was going to need some help, some strength. It'd take everything she'd got – and some more.

And not long. Not long for it.

All-Hallows soon. The dark curtain thin as muslin.

Dead tree out of the Moss, and made to live, made to thresh its boughs.

Him.

Taunt it.

'You're nowt.' Words coming out like a sick cough. 'You're nowt, Jack. You never was owt!'

Dead tree writhing and slashing itself at her, and though she was well out of range by now, she felt every poisoned sting.

Get it mad.

'Ah . . .' Ma turned away. 'Not worth it. Not worth me time. Bit of owd wood.'

But her heart was slamming and rocking like an old washing-machine.

Black horned head, white eyes.

Dead, but living in *him*.
White eyes.

CHAPTER III

There was a metallic snapping sound followed by a faint and desperate wailing.

'*Mrs Wagstaff . . .*'

The voice was familiar. But it didn't matter.

This was a funny little house, bottles and jars on every ledge, even on the edges of individual stairs. Sprigs of this and that hung from the ceilings and circulated musty smells.

The witch's den.

He sat in silence at the top of the stairs. Unperturbed.

'*Please, Mrs Wagstaff . . . let me in . . .*'

Then silence. He smiled. As children, they'd clustered by the church gate and whispered about the witch's house, not daring to go too close. *See the curtain move . . . ? It's her. She's coming . . . !*

It hadn't changed; only his perspective on it. The wicked witch. Perspectives changed. Now it was cool to be . . . wow, *wicked*! But Ma Wagstaff wasn't authentically wicked, never had been. Ma Wagstaff, let's face it, wasn't quite up to it and wouldn't be now. She'd conned them, generations of them.

Now *I'm* really rather wicked, he thought. If there's such a thing. Or at least I'm getting there.

He didn't move. His body didn't move.

The reason it didn't move was he didn't want it to. Suddenly, he had true self-control, and this amazed him. Or rather it amazed him to reflect on what a bag of dancing neuroses he used to be, so untogether he couldn't even regulate the sounds coming out of his own mouth.

Sher-sher-Shaw. Ster- ster-stuttering Shaw.

Amusing to imagine what he'd have been like if he'd been given this present task even a month ago, when he was still unconvinced. When he used to say, It's, you know . . . *bad*, though, isn't it? It might be fun, it might be exhilarating, but it's bad, essentially. Surely.

And were you good before, Shaw? Were you good when you were stuttering and dithering and letting your father dominate you? Is that your idea of what it means to be good? In which case, how does it feel to be bad?

Terminology. Nowadays Bad was cool, like Wicked. A step in the right direction.

How's it feel? Feels good. Alive. Quite simply that. I didn't know before what being alive *meant*. I said to her, *haven't you got to be dead to be undead?* And she said, *what makes you think you aren't?*

So I was dead and now I'm alive. I know that when I pull the handles, turn the switches, press the buttons . . . something will *happen*.

They'd told him he'd seen nothing yet. They'd told him there would be a sign. And now there was. And *what* a sign. Once again, Shaw couldn't resist it. He allowed his right hand to remove its leather glove and brush its palm across the top of his head.

A delicious prickly sensation.

The first time he'd felt it, he'd wanted to leap up and squeal with joy. But there was no need to do this any more. He could experience that joy deep inside himself, knowing how much more powerful and satisfying the feeling was if he *didn't* allow it to expend itself through his body, dissipating as he hopped about like a little kid, punching the air.

So Shaw Horridge's body remained seated quietly at the top of the stairs in Ma Wagstaff's house while Shaw Horridge's spirit was in a state of supreme exultation.

His hair was growing again! He was alive and he had made it happen.

Just a fuzz at first, then thicker than a fuzz – almost a stubble. He'd heard of men going to Ma Wagstaff for her patent hair-restorer, some claiming it worked. A bit. But not actually sure whether it had or not.

Not like this. No doubt about this. Where there'd been no hair, now there was hair.

All around him were Ma Wagstaff's bottles full of maybes.

Maybe if the wind's in the right direction. If the moon's full. If there's an R in the month. Quite sad, really. A grey little world of hopes and dreams. No certainties.

Hair-loss was natural in some people, his mother said. But it had taken Therese to prove to him that you didn't have to accept something just because it was supposed to be *natural*. Acceptance was just spiritual sloth.

Being truly alive was about changing things. Changing people, situations. Changing your state of mind. Changing the 'natural'.

Being alive was about breaking rules with impunity. Men's rules. Also the rules men claimed they'd had from God. 'Natural' rules. This was what she'd taught him. Learn how to break the rules – for no other reason than to break them – and you become free.

Thou shalt not kill. But why? We kill animals to eat, we kill people with abandon in wartime. We kill for the Queen, we kill for the oil industry? Where does the taboo begin?

He stretched his arms and yawned. Settled down to wait, aware of his breathing, fully relaxed. How could bad be bad when it felt as good as this.

Eventually, kneeling messily in the rain, Moira pulled her shoe out of the bog.

The shoe was full of water; she shook it out and put it on. By this time the old woman had hobbled to the edge of the Moss, where there was a gate leading into a field, beyond which was the pub and, further up, the hill on which the church sat.

The dead tree was still. It looked hard, heavy, almost stone-like. Too dense to move in the wind, even if there'd been one. But it moved for me, she thought, limping back to the car. And it moved for Ma Wagstaff.

Such things were almost invariably subjective. Like, how often did two people see a ghost, at the same time, together? Ghosts and related phenomena were one-to-one. You saw it and the person with you said, hey, what's wrong with you, what are you staring at, why've you gone so pale?

But the tree moved for Ma Wagstaff. And it moved, no question, for me.

She climbed behind the wheel and sank into the seat, drained. The cassette tape had ended. She flipped it out of the player.

Ma Wagstaff understands, the old bitch. She says to me, 'We can help you help him. But you must purify yourself.'

I am not getting this, Matt. What were you into, you and Ma?

And then

. . . *whuppp.*

Moira reeled back in the seat as something hit the windscreen. Like a big bird, covering the sky, darkening the car, it flapped there, wriggling and beating at the glass.

'Holy Jesus.'

It was snagged in the wipers, but it wasn't a bird . . . only a dark blue woolly shawl. Ma Wagstaff's shawl, snatched from her by the devil-tree. Blown across the Moss. Blown hard, directly at the car, like it had been aimed.

Moira began to pant, closing her eyes tight, squeezing on the steering-wheel until it creaked.

When she opened her eyes the shawl had gone, and the vertical rain showed there was still no wind.

OK. Move.

She switched on the engine; slammed the BMW into reverse, pulled it back on to the causeway, pointing it at Bridelow. The sky was dirty now, but she wondered if it would still be white through the eyeholes in the thing of wood on the Moss.

Ma said, You've got to purify yourself. But there's a kind of purity in intensity of feeling, isn't that right? Pure black light.

Right. Get off my back, Matt. You're sicker than I figured. Just get the *hell* off my back.

Moira drove erratically into the village street, bumping carelessly along the cobbles and over the kerb. Nobody about. No sign of the old woman. The cottages featureless and damp, a huddle.

Pure black light.

Black light? White light? What is this shit? Wished she could call the Duchess, but the Duchess wasn't on the phone. The Duchess wants to contact anybody, she doesn't mess with phones.

Moira sat in her car at the bottom of the street, ploughing her fingers through her hair. Exposed. And scared?

Oh, yes.

And maybe half-deranged. Couldn't properly express in words what she was doing here. Like she'd been sucked into the smoking fireplace that night at the Earl's castle and gone up the chimney and been spit out cold on Bridelow Moss.

Now everything was pointing at Ma Wagstaff, but Ma Wagstaff had run away.

She left the car in the street, squelched to the Post Office, peatwater oozing out of her shoes.

'Willie's not in,' she panted at the big, flowery Girl-Guide postmistress. 'Where would I find his mother's place?'

Weak as a kitten, Ma felt. Weak as a day-old kitten, its eyes not open yet. Weak and blind.

Help me, Mother.

Ma followed the river back, gratefully leaving the Moss behind. There was a crack starting in her walking stick where the black tree had snapped off the metal tip. Soon the stick wouldn't support even a skinny, spidery owd thing like her, and what would she do then?

It got her to the churchyard, God alone knew how, and she propped her old bones up against a stone cross. Looked up at the church porch, and it hit her like an elbow in the ribs.

Desecrated!

Oh, Mother. Oh, Jesus!

Over the door . . . a mess of crumbling old cement.

That *vandal.*

The Goths and the Vandals and the Angles and the Saxons and the Romans and the so-called Christians. All them raiders Bridelow had fought off over the long centuries. And the buggers still at the door with their battleaxes.

285

Inside the church, little Benjie's Autumn Cross all smashed. And the vile thing growing out on the Moss, waving Ma's torn shawl like a banner. And the seeping sickness within that saps health and takes jobs. And now Our Sheila smitten from the wall, thrown away like she was nowt more than one of them dirty magazines.

Grinding, in pain, the few teeth she'd got left to grind, Ma Wagstaff staggered through the graveyard, up to the top end, where Matt Castle lay, the earth still loose on him, covered by wreaths, already bashed about by the weather, petals everywhere.

The witch bottle lay in her coat pocket. Dead.

Moving like an owd crab on a pebble beach, Ma staggered by Matt's grave without stopping. The earth loose around him – not buried proper, not yet. Still airholes in the soil. Poor bugger might as well be lying stretched out on top.

The rain had stopped, but the clouds still bulged like cheeks full of spit. Ma stumbled out on to the moor, through the top wicket gate, between two tattered gorse bushes.

This was not the real moor; this was still Bridelow. Until you got over the rocks.

Below the rocks was the holy well, the spring, water bubbling bright as lemonade into a natural-hewn stone dish. The well they dressed with flowers in the springtime to honour the Mother and the water. Long before she reached it, Ma could hear it singing.

A rock leaned over the spring, like a mantelpiece over a hearth, above it the moor, which was not Bridelow.

Carved out of the stone, a hollow, with a little shelf.

On the shelf a statue.

'Mother,' Ma said breathlessly.

The statue was plaster. She wore a robe once painted blue, now chipped and faded. Her eyes were uplifted to the sky beyond the shelf of rock, her hands turned palms-down to bless the water trickling from the rock below her feet.

'Oh, Mother.' Ma dropped her stick. She'd made it home.

She fell down upon the stone, the edge of her woollen skirt in the rock pool; began to cry, words bubbling out of her like the water from the rock. 'I've brought thee nowt . . . Forgive me, Mother. Not properly dressed. Dint know I were coming, see.'

She sat up, crossed herself, closed her eyes, all hot and teary. Cupped her hands into the pool and brought the spring water to her eyes. And when they were touched by the water, she saw at last, through her eyelids, a warm, bright light.

Ma lifted up her hands into the light, and felt them touch the hem of the radiant blue robe of the Mother, the material that felt like a fine and silken rain.

She began to mumble, the old words dropping into place, words in English, words in Latin, words in an olden-day language that was neither Welsh nor Gaelic, words from the Bible, power-words and humble-words. Words to soak up the light and bring it into her blood. Come into me, Mother, give me light and give me strength, give me the holy power to face your enemies and to withstand . . .

The shadow fell across her.

The bright blue gauze dissolved. Ma's eyes opened into pain.

The curate stood astride the sacred spring. Big and stupid as a Victorian stone angel.

'So,' he said. 'This is it, is it?'

He kicked a pebble into the pool. 'It's even more tawdry than I expected, Mrs Wagstaff.'

'Go away,' Ma said quietly, looking down into the pool. 'What's it to do wi' you? Go on. Clear off. Come back when you're older.'

'*What's it to do with me?*' He stood there thick and hard as granite. 'You can ask that? Where did you get this?' With a hand like a spade, he plucked the Mother from her stone hollow. 'One of these Catholic shops, I suppose. Or was it taken from a church? Hmm?'

He held the statue at arm's length. 'Hardly a work of art, Mrs Wagstaff. But hardly deserving of this kind of grubby sacrilege.'

Ma was on her feet, blinding pain ripping through every sinew. 'You put that *back*! That's sacred, that is! Put it back *now*! Call yourself a minister of God? You're nobbut a thick bloody vandal wi' no more brains than pig shit!'

287

'And you,' he said, tucking the statue under an arm, 'are a poor, misguided old woman who ought to be in a Home, where you can be watched over until you die.'

Ma Wagstaff tried to stand with dignity and couldn't.

Joel Beard bent his face to hers. 'You're a throwback, Mrs Wagstaff. A remnant. My inclination as a human being is to feel very sorry for you, but my faith won't allow me to do that.'

Behind his eyes she saw a cold furnace.

'Thou shalt not suffer a witch to live!'

The statue hefted above his head like a club. Ma cowered.

'Oh, no . . .' He lowered the statue to chest-height. 'Don't cringe, Mrs Wagstaff. I wouldn't hurt you physically. I'm a servant of God. I merely remind you of the strong line the Bible takes on your particular . . . sub-species.'

Joel Beard put out a contemptuous hand to help her up. She looked at the hand and its fingers became a bundle of twisted twigs bound roughly together, and the connection was made with the thing on the Moss, two opposing terminals, the black and the white, each as dangerous and Ma stranded in the middle.

'Gerraway from me!' She shrank back, feeling that if she touched his hand she'd be burned alive.

'What are you afraid of, Mrs Wagstaff?'

'I'm afraid of denseness,' Ma said. 'Kind of denseness as rips down a child's offering, smashes it on t'stones . . .'

'But . . . but it was evil,' he said reasonably. 'Can't you people see that? Primitive. Heathen. It insulted the true Cross.'

Ma Wagstaff shook her head. 'Tha knows nowt. Tha's big and arrogant, and tha knows nowt. Tha's not fit to wipe Hans Gruber's arse.'

Joel Beard raised the statue of the Mother far above his head. His face severe. His golden curls tight as stone.

'All right, then,' he said. 'Be your own salvation, Mrs Wagstaff.'

Ma grabbed at the air, eyes widening in horror. She began to whimper. Joel smashed the Mother down on the rocks and her head broke easily, pounded to plaster-dust.

Ma Wagstaff cried out. The cry of the defeated, the gutted, the desolate.

Gone. Nowt left. Gone to dust.

Beating the plaster from his hands and his green hiking jacket, Joel Beard strode away across the dirty-yellow moor-grass. Fragments floated in the centre of the pool until the springwater scattered them, making widening circles over the Mother's headless body.

CHAPTER IV

For the first time since all this had begun, Lottie's hands began to shake, and she pressed them against the hot-plate covers on the stove so that if the policeman had seen it he'd think she was simply cold.

It was a bad dream, switching from one dreadful scene to another until the horror was spinning about her like a merry-go-round of black shadow-horses, and whichever way she turned . . .

She turned back to the policeman, who, to give him his due, looked no happier about this than she felt. Steadying her voice, she said, 'You want to dig up my husband.'

'This is . . .' Inspector Ashton exhaled down his nose. 'Look, Mrs Castle, if there was any other way . . . It's not your husband we want to . . . see. It's the grave itself. Normally when there's an exhumation it's at the request of the coroner or the pathologist, to enable further examination of a body. In this case we don't want to touch the body, we don't even want to open the coffin. We . . . have reason to believe the grave may have been disturbed before your husband was placed in it.'

Lottie felt her face muscles harden. Somebody had blown the gaff on Ma Wagstaff and her primitive rituals. What the hell *else* had the old hag been up to?

'We have reason to believe,' Ashton said, 'that certain . . . stolen goods may be buried under your husband's coffin.'

'What goods?'

'I'd rather not say at the present time, if you don't mind, Mrs Castle.'

He'd turned up in the bar not long after Moira had left. On his own. Asked if he might have a word. All very casual and quiet.

Lottie thought about the implications. 'And what if I don't agree?'

Ashton sighed. 'It'll just take longer for us to get permission.'

'But you'll get it anyway.'

Ashton nodded. 'Between ourselves, what does bother me is that the person who's made the allegations about this . . . these stolen goods . . . has intimated that if we don't act on them quickly, he'll make his suspicions known to the media. I don't need to tell you what *that* would mean in terms of invasion of privacy, unwarranted intrusion into private grief, reporters all over your doorstep . . .'

'You mean,' said Lottie, 'that this man's blackmailing you?'

Ashton laughed. 'If only it was that simple. No, I was inclined to disbelieve him at first, but now I agree there's a strong basis for thinking something's down there as shouldn't be. And if we can handle our excavations discreetly, after dark, inconspicuous, no fuss . . .'

'Have you spoken to anyone else in the village?'

'No, I certainly haven't, and I'd be very much obliged if you'd keep this to yourself as well. Last thing we want is an audience. 'Course, we'll have to consult with the minister, but that won't be a problem, I shouldn't think.'

Lottie thought about Ma Wagstaff and her Old Ways and Matt's apparent acceptance of all this rubbish as part of the unique West Pennine tradition. Acknowledging, with much bitterness, Matt's part in all this.

'Right.' She pulled her hands from the stove. 'Go ahead. I'll sign whatever you want me to sign.'

'Thank you,' said Ashton. 'That's very brave of you, Mrs Castle.'

'Just one thing.'

He'd begun to button his trenchcoat; he stopped.

'Keep me out of it, Inspector. I don't want to know when you do it or what you find. I don't want to be involved.'

Ashton nodded, relieved. 'And you'll keep this to yourself?'

'Oh, I wouldn't want to alert anybody who might have cause to be . . . embarrassed.' Lottie smiled grimly. 'I certainly wouldn't.'

Suspicious, at first, as he came up the street. Fingers going on his thighs, nose twitching as if he had whiskers. Then he saw who it was, and she watched the sun come up in his cheeks and knew it was all right.

'Moira!'

More than ten years dissolved in the Pennine air.

'Willie, hey, I was looking for you the whole morning.'

'I were down me workshop. Doin' a bit o' bodgin' an' fettlin'.' He stepped back, put his hands on her shoulders like a dog on its hind legs. 'Eee, lass, I can't tell you . . . you're looking bloody grand.'

She thought he was going to lick her ears, but he backed off and they stood a couple of yards apart, inspecting each other. He hadn't changed at all: small and wary, brown hair down to his quick eyes. She didn't know what to say. So damn much to talk about, and none of it superficial.

It started to rain again. 'Once it starts,' Willie said, twitching his nose at the sky, 'it gets to be a bloody habit in Brid'lo.'

He smiled. 'Got time for a cup o' tea, lass?'

Did he think she was just passing through? 'Jesus, Willie,' Moira said, feeling close to collapse. 'I've got time for a whole damn pot.'

She would come in by the back door.

Same way he'd come in. It hadn't been locked, didn't even have a lock on it. He remembered how, as a child, he'd been dared to go in by other kids. Into the witch's den. He'd refused. He was afraid.

This time last year he'd still have been afraid. Even a couple of months ago he would.

He came to his feet and stood behind the balustrade, his hands around the wooden ball on top. It was sticky with layers of brown varnish. The paper on the walls was brown with age. There'd been flowers on it; they just looked like grease patches now.

Late afternoon dimness enclosing him. He'd have been afraid of that too, once. Afraid to open the bedroom doors, afraid of the ghosts within. Afraid of what he might disturb.

Afraid not to be afraid.

But not any more.

Willie had a teapot in a woollen tea-cosy made out of an outsize bobble hat.

'You make it yourself?'

'I have a friend,' Willie said, looking embarrassed about it, the way Willie had always looked embarrassed about women, although it never seemed to get in his way.

'You've a girlfriend here? In Bridelow?'

'More of an arrangement,' said Willie. 'Been on and off for years. What about you?'

'Oh. You know. Livin' alone, as the song says, is all I've ever done well.'

'Your song? Sorry, luv, I've not been keeping track.'

'Nanci Griffith. Found an echo. Sometimes other people take the songs right out of your head.'

'Aye,' Willie said. He took a long, assessing look at her as she sprawled in a fat easy-chair with a loud pattern of big yellow marigolds. 'You look good,' Willie said. 'But you look tired.'

'I don't know why. All I've done is wandered around and talked to people. Yeah, I'm knackered. Must be the air.'

'Air's not what it was,' said Willie. 'Fancy a biscuit? Cheese butty?'

'No, thanks.' She closed her eyes. 'It's nice in here. I could go to sleep in this chair.'

'Feel free.'

'No.' She forced her eyes open. 'You've got trouble here, Willie. Your ma. Like, I realize it's not my business, but I think she's got some private war on, you know?'

'Oh, aye. I know that all right. I . . .' He hesitated, refilling her teacup. 'How long you been here? I were looking out for you at Matt's funeral.'

'I was being low-profile,' Moira said. 'But I saw the business with the witch bottle, if that's . . .'

'Oh . . .' Willie sat down and crossed his legs, started up a staccato finger-rhythm on the side of a knee. 'I don't know. Sometimes I think we're living inside a bloody folk museum.'

'It's no' a museum,' Moira said. 'I just watched her out on the Moss. There's kind of a dead tree out there.'

'Bog oak,' Willie said. 'That's all it is.'

'Then why're your fingers drumming up a storm?'

'Shit,' Willie said. 'Shit, shit, shit.'

'Come on.' Moira dragged herself out of the chair. 'Let's go and talk to her.'

Moira's left foot was feeling cold and wet. She stamped it on the cobbles. 'Went out on the Moss with no wellies. Stupid, huh?'

Rainy afternoon in a small village, nobody else about, no distractions, and they were both on edge. The hush before the thunder.

It's in the air. A damp tension.

So quiet.

'Catch my death.' Moira smiled feebly.

Both of Willie's hands drumming. It happened to Willie through his fingers. People said it was nerves. But what were nerves for if not to respond to things you couldn't see?

'Hey, come on,' Moira said softly, 'what's wrong here, Willie?'

'I don't know.' He sounded confused. 'Nowt I can put me finger on.'

They'd hammered on Ma's door. Waited and waited. All dark inside.

Willie started blinking. The only noise in the street was the rapid rhythmic chinking of his fingers on the coins in one hip pocket and something else, maybe keys, in the other. It echoed from the cobbles and the stone walls of the cottages. Willie's fingers knew something Willie didn't.

'Willie, quick, come on, think, where would she be? Where would she go if she was scared?'

He looked swiftly from side to side, up and down the street. 'Willie . . . ?'

Hands wet with the once-holy spring water, white with powdered plaster. Wind blowing through her head. Mind a-crackle with shredded leaves and lashing boughs. No thoughts, only shifting sensations, everything shaken up like medicine gone sour in the bottle. Air full of evil sediment.

Sky white, trees black, church tower black.

Twisted legs and malformed feet crabbing it through the bracken and the heather.

Broken owd woman going back to her useless bottles.

'Let me help you, Mrs Wagstaff, for God's sake.' Long, striding legs, head in the clouds. Wanted to help for appearances' sake; wouldn't look good if he buggered off and owd Ma fell and broke a leg.

'*Gerroff me!*' she shrieked.

'You've got to turn away from all this! Make your peace with Almighty God. It's not too late . . .'

Screeching through the gale in her brain, 'What would you know? It's long too late!'

Wretched gargoyles screaming along with her from the church's blackened walls.

At the churchyard gate, relief for both of them, him going one way, to *his* church, not looking back; Ma the other, down towards the street. Sky like lead crushing her into the brown ground.

Top of the street, Ma stopped and squinted. Two people. Willie and a woman. The woman from the funeral, the woman from the Moss, the woman with the Gift.

Bugger!

Couldn't be doing with it. Questions. Concern. Sit down, Ma, have a cuppa, put thi' feet up, tell us all about it. Tell me how I can *help*.

Pah!

Ma turned back up the street, waited at the opening to the

brewery road till they'd gone past then took the path round the back of the cottages so nobody else would see the state of her.

'This?'

Water trickled dispiritedly from under the rock and plopped into the pool.

'Used to be a torrent,' Willie remembered.

'This is the holy well?'

The pool looked flat and sullen in the rain.

'There should be a statue,' Willie said.

'Of whom?'

'The . . . Mother. On that ledge. She had her hands out, blessing the spring. There's a ceremony, every May Day. Flowers everywhere. You can see it for miles. Then the lads'd come up from t'brewery, fill up a few dozen barrels, roll um down the hill. At one time, all the beer'd be made wi' this water, now it's shared out, so there's a few drops in each cask.'

Willie kicked a pebble into the pool. 'I'm saying "now". Gannons'll've stopped it.'

'Aye,' Moira said, 'there's no life here.' She bent down, dipped her hands in the pool. It felt stagnant. If Ma Wagstaff had come up here hoping for some kind of spiritual sustenance, she'd have gone away pretty damn depressed.

'Used to take it all wi' a pinch of salt,' Willie said. 'I mean . . . bit of nonsense, really. But we come up here. Every May Day we'd come up here, whole village at one time, all them as could walk. Then back to The Man, couple o' pints . . . bite to eat . . .'

Willie smiled. 'Good days, them, Moira. When you think back on it.'

'Hang on,' Moira said. 'There's something here.'

With both hands, she lifted it out, the spring water dripping from her palms. Dripping like tears from the eyes of the battered plaster head of the Mother of God.

'Oh, hell,' Willie said sorrowfully.

'The Mother?'

Willie nodded. 'There's three of um. Three statues. The young one, the Virgin, she's brought up on Candlemas – St

Bride's day, beginning of February. Then the Mother – this one – at Lammas. Then, at All-Hallows, they bring the winter one.'

'The Hag,' Moira said.

Willie nodded.

'The Threefold Goddess,' Moira said. 'Virgin, Mother, Hag.'

'Summat like that. Like I say . . . pinch of salt. Women's stuff.'

'Your ma . . . she'd never be taking it with a pinch of salt.'

'No,' said Willie.

'What about Matt?'

'He were different,' Willie said, 'when he come back. When we was lads it were just the way things *were*, you know? One of us'd be picked to collect stuff for t'seasonal crosses, collate it like, sort out what were what. We didn't reckon much on it. Bit of fun, like.'

'As it should be,' Moira said, pushing her sodden hair back to stop it dripping down her jacket. 'How else d'you get kids into it if it's no' fun?'

'Matt come back . . . wi' a mission. Know what I mean? Horridges had sold off brewery to Gannons and Gannons didn't want t'pub – it were doing nowt, were it? Local trade and a few ramblers of a Sunday. Perked up a bit when t'bogman were found, but not for long – nine day wonder sorta thing.'

'So Matt returns to buy the pub. Local hero.'

'Ex*act*ly. Spot on. Local hero, I tell thi, Moira . . . honest to God, he were me mate, but I wish he'd not come. You know what I mean?'

'I do now,' Moira said, hearing the tape in her head. 'He was an emotional man. An impressionable man. An obsessive man.'

Willie snorted. 'Can say that again.'

'But not a bad man,' Moira said.

'Oh no. I don't think so.'

'So somebody – or some*thing* was using him. He was a vessel. Willie, this bogman . . . ?'

'Oh, bugger.' Willie looked up into the sky, now putting down water with a good bit more enthusiasm than the Holy

Spring. The coins in his pocket chinked damply. 'I'm saying nowt. You've gorra talk to Ma.'

He heard her creaking into the hall below. 'Gerrout from under me feet, Bobbie.'

The cat.

Heard her feet on the bottom stairs and slid himself into a room which, as he'd ascertained earlier, was a box room full of rubbish, tea-chests, heaps of old curtaining, a treadle sewing-machine shrouded in dust.

Took her a long time and a lot of laboured breathing to reach the top of the stairs. Heard her in the bathroom, the dribble and the flush and the old metal cistern filling up behind her with a series of coughs and gasps.

He brought a hand to the crown of his head, felt his emergent, urgent bristles one last time, for luck. Luck? You made your own. He put his glove back on. For a moment, a while back, someone hammering on the front door had flung him back to that night last summer in the stolen car. The police! But then he'd concentrated – go *away* – and the knocking had stopped.

Flexing and clenching his powerful, leathered hands, he moved out onto the landing as the old woman sighed and braced herself to go downstairs.

Not much left of her. Old bones in a frayed cardigan. Hair as dry and neglected as tufts of last summer's sheepwool caught in a wire fence.

Some witch, he thought, rising up behind her.

Quite slowly – although he knew he'd made no sound – she turned around and looked up at him, at his fingers poised above her bony, brittle shoulders. Then at his face.

And he looked at hers.

They'd always said, in the village, how fierce her eyes were. How she could freeze you where you stood with those eyes, turn you to stone, pin you to the wall.

Shaw Horridge grinned. Come on, then.

Wanting her to do that to him. Focus her eyes like lasers. Wanting the challenge, the friction. Wanting something he could smash, like hurling someone else's Saab Turbo into a bus shelter.

Wanted to do it and *feel better*.

But her eyes surprised him. They were as soft and harmless as a puppy's.

For a moment, this froze him.

'Come on,' he said, suddenly agitated. 'Come on, witch.'

She stared calmly at him, heels on the very edge of the top stair. Wouldn't take much of a push. That was no good.

He said, 'Where's your magic, eh? Where's your fucking magic now?'

She bit her worn-down bottom lip, but otherwise didn't move. 'Don't you know me?' she said. 'Do you not know me?'

He shook his head. 'You're going to die,' he said. 'Don't you realize that?'

The withered old face crumpled into an apology for a smile. 'I'm dead already, lad,' Ma Wagstaff said, voice trickling away like sand through an egg-timer. 'Dead already. But it's nowt t'do wi' you. You'll be glad of that, one day.'

Her ancient face was as blank as unmarked parchment as she threw up her arms, hands wafting at the air. Her body seemed to rise up at him, making him lurch back into the landing wall, and then she flopped down the stairs, with barely a bounce, like an old, discarded mop.

CHAPTER V

The gypsy guy with the beat-up hat and the Dobermanns wasn't too sure about this. Still looked like he'd prefer to feed the stranger to the dogs.

'No,' Macbeth said. 'I don't even know her name.' Had to be easier getting to meet with the goddamn Queen. 'All I know is she isn't called Mrs Cairns.'

The guy's heavy eyebrows came down, suspicious. 'Who wis it told you where to come?'

'Uh, Moira's agent. In Glasgow. Listen, I'm not with the police. I'm not a reporter.'

'OK, well, you just stay here, pal,' the gypsy guy said, and to make sure Macbeth didn't move from the gates of the caravan site he left the two dogs behind. Macbeth liked to think he was good with dogs, but the Dobermanns declined to acknowledge this; when he put out a friendly hand, one growled and the other dribbled. Macbeth shrugged and waited.

The gypsy was gone several minutes, but when he returned he'd gotten himself a whole new attitude. Unbolting the gates, holding them back for the visitor. 'Wid ye come this way, sir . . .' Well, shit, next thing he'd be holding his hat to his chest and bowing. Even the Dobermanns had a deferential air. Macbeth grinned, figured maybe the old lady had sussed him psychically, checked out his emanations.

Whatever, in no time at all, here's Mungo Macbeth of the Manhattan Macbeths sitting in a caravan like some over-decorated seaside theme-bar, brass and china all over the walls.

'I'll leave ye then, Duchess . . . ?'

'Thank you, Donald.' Lifting a slender hand loaded up with gold bullion.

She was Cleopatra, aboard this huge, gold-braided Victorian-looking chaise longue. She had on an ankle-length robe, edged with silver. Had startling hair, as long as Moira's, only dazzling white.

'Well, uh . . .' This was bizarre. This was an essentially tacky situation. Awe was not called for. And yet this place was already answering questions about Moira that he hadn't even been able to frame.

She said, 'Call me Duchess. It's a trifle cheap, but one gets used to these indignities.'

Didn't look to be more than sixty. Younger by several centuries, he thought, than her eyes.

'And you'll come to the point, Mr Macbeth. Life is short.'

He blinked. 'OK.' Swallowed. Couldn't believe he'd come here, was doing this. 'Uh . . . fact of the matter is . . . I spent some time with your daughter, couple nights ago.'

'Really,' the Duchess said dryly.

'No, hey, nothing like . . . See, I . . .' This was his first meeting with Moira all over again. Couldn't string the words together. 'Can't get her off of my mind,' he said and couldn't say any more.

'You poor man.' The merest shade of a smile in the crease down one cheek. 'How can I help?'

Acutely aware how embarrassingly novelettish all this was sounding, how like some plastic character in one of his own crummy TV films, he said solemnly, 'See, this never happened to me before.'

The Duchess had a very long neck. Very slowly she bent it towards him, like a curious swan. 'Are you a wealthy man, Mr Macbeth?'

'One day, maybe,' he said. 'So they tell me.' Thinking, if she asks me to cross her fucking palm with silver, I'm out of here.

'The feeling I'm getting from you . . .' Those ancient, ancient eyes connecting with his, '. . . is that, despite your name, you've always been very much an American.'

'Is that the truth,' Macbeth confirmed with a sigh. 'All we got to do now is convince my mom.'

The Duchess smiled at last. 'I think I like you, Mr Macbeth,' she said. 'We'll have some tea.'

Later she picked up on the theme. 'You're really not what you appear, are you?'

'No?'

The Duchess shook her head. Tiny gold balls revolved in her earrings.

'This worries you. You feel you've been living a lie. You feel that all your life you've tried to be what people expect you to be. But different people want different things, and you feel obliged, perhaps, to live up to their expectation of you. You feel . . .' The Duchess scrutinized him, with renewed interest, over her gold-rimmed bone china teacup. 'You feel you are in your present fortunate position because of who you are rather than what you can do.'

Macbeth said nothing. He hadn't come here for this. Had he?

'Sorry to be so blunt,' the Duchess said.

'No problem,' Macbeth said hollowly.

'This is your job perhaps. People think you can open doors?'

'Do they just,' said Macbeth.

'Now you've woken up, and you're thinking, am I to spend my life . . . serving up the, er, goods . . . ? As a form of restitution? Paying back, even though I might be paying back to people who never gave me anything, or do I go out on my own, chance my arm . . . ?'

There were subtle alterations in her voice. Macbeth felt goose-bumps forming.

The Duchess said, 'Is there something more out there than piling up money? Even if that money's not all for me, even if it's helping the economy and therefore other people who might need the money more than me? Are there . . . more things in heaven and earth than you get to read about in the *New York Times*?'

Christ. He was listening to himself. By the time she sat back to sip more tea, he'd swear the Duchess had developed a significantly deeper voice and an accent not unlike his own.

Ah, this is just a sophisticated act. This is a classy stage routine.

'No it isn't,' the Duchess said crisply.

He almost dropped his cup. '*What* . . . ?' His hand shook.

'No, it isn't . . . going to rain,' the Duchess said sweetly. 'Although it was forecast. But then forecasts are seldom reliable, I've found.'

He guessed she'd never been to college. He guessed she hadn't always talked so refined. He guessed her life-story would make more than one mini-series.

Then he guessed he'd better start keeping a tighter hold on his thoughts until he was someplace else.

'I'm not a fortune-teller, you know,' she said, like some women would say, what do you think I am, *a hooker*?

'I, uh . . . Moira never said you were,' Macbeth said uncomfortably.

'I appear to be able to do it. Sometimes. But I don't make a practice of it.' She poured herself more tea. 'So why did I let you in here?'

Macbeth didn't know.

'Because I'm worried about the child,' she said. 'That's why.'

He said, 'I can understand that.'

'Can you?'

'I'm, uh, a Celt,' he said, and she started to laugh, a sound like the little teaspoon tinkling on the bone china.

'To be Celtic,' she said, 'is more an attitude than a racial thing. Like to be a gypsy is a way of life.'

'What about to be a psychic?'

Her face clouded. 'That,' she said, 'is a cross to bear. She'll tell you that herself. It's to accept there's a huge part of your life that will never be your own. It's to realize there are always going to be obligations to fulfil, directions you have to go in, even though you can't always see the sense of it.'

'That's what she's doing right now?'

The Duchess nodded. 'She has things to work out. Oh, I don't know what she's doing and I wouldn't dream of interfering, she's a mature person. But I am her mother, and mothers *are* always inclined to worry, so I'm told. I was only thinking – coincidence – just before you arrived, I wish she had someone who cared for her. But she's a loner. We all are, I fear. We learn our lesson. We don't like other people to get hurt.'

'You're saying you think Moira needs someone with her?'

The Duchess shrugged her elegant shoulders. 'Someone looking out for her, maybe. When Donald told me there was a man at the gate asking after Moira, I wondered if perhaps . . .'

Then she gave him the kind of smile that was like a consolatory pat on the arm. 'I don't really feel you're the one, Mr Macbeth.'

Sometimes, when he interviewed would-be film-directors, there was one nice, bright-eyed kid he could tell was never going to make it. And trying to let the kid down easy he'd always start out, 'I don't really feel . . .'

'Look, Duchess . . .' Macbeth felt like he was about to cry. This was absurd. He started to tell her about the night at the

Earl's castle, about Moira singing 'The Comb Song', and how it ended.

'Yes,' the Duchess said impatiently, 'I know about that.'

'So am I right in thinking Moira caused all that, the deer heads and stuff to come crashing down?'

The Duchess looked cross. 'The question is . . . pouff! Irrelevant! How can anyone ever really say, I did this, I caused this to happen? Perhaps you are a factor in its happening, perhaps not. I'll tell you something, Mr Macbeth . . . nobody who's merely human can ever be entirely sure of the ability to make *anything* happen. Say, if you're a great healer, sometimes it works . . . you're lucky, or you're so good and saintly that you get helped a lot. And sometimes it doesn't work at all. I once knew a woman called Jean Wendle . . . but that's another story . . .'

She lay back on the chaise and half-closed her eyes, looking at the wall behind him. 'Or, let us say, if you're a bad or a vengeful person, and you want to hurt somebody, you want to curse them . . . in the movies, it goes . . . *zap*, like one of those, what d'you call them . . . ray guns, lasers.'

He heard a small noise behind him, turned in time to see a plate, one of a row of five with pictures on them, sliding very slowly from the wall.

The plate fell to the floor and smashed. Macbeth nearly passed out.

From a long way away, he heard the Duchess saying, 'Doing damage, harming people is much easier but that's unpredictable too. Sometimes people dabble and create a big black cloud . . .' Throwing up her arms theatrically, '. . . and they can't control *where* it goes.'

Numbly, Macbeth bent to pick up the pieces of the plate. Maybe he'd dislodged it with the back of his head. The ones still on the wall had pictures of Balmoral Castle, where the Queen spent time, and Glamis Castle, Blair Atholl Castle and the Queen Mother's Castle of Mey.

He held two pieces of the broken plate together and saw, in one of those shattering, timeless moments, that they made up a rough watercolour sketch of the familiar Victorian Gothic façade of the Earl's place.

'Accidents happen,' the Duchess said. 'Leave it on the floor.'

Macbeth's fingers were trembling as he laid the pieces down. He needed a cigarette more urgently than at any time since he quit smoking six years ago.

'I never liked that one anyway,' the Duchess said.

Doubtless psyching out that Macbeth could use more hot tea, and fast, she filled up his cup and added two sugars.

He drank it all. She was offering him an easy way out. She was saying, what just happened – the plate – also, the skulls on the wall . . . this is kids' stuff . . . this is chickenshit compared to what a person could be letting himself in for if he pursues Moira Cairns.

Mungo Macbeth, maker of mini-series for the masses, thought maybe this was how King Arthur laid it on the line for any mad-assed knight of the Round Table figuring to go after the Holy Grail.

He'd often wondered about those less ambitious knights who listened to the horror stories and thought, Well, fuck this, what do I need with a Holy Grail? Maybe I should just stick around and lay me some more damsels, do a little Sunday jousting. How could those knights go on living with themselves, having passed up on the chance of the One Big Thing?

He said, 'Earlier, you said . . . about when a guy gets to wondering how much his life has really been worth and if there isn't more stuff in Heaven and Earth than he's reading about in the *New York Times* . . .'

The silent girl who'd brought the tea came back and took away the tray.

After she'd gone, he said, 'Duchess, why? I only met your daughter once, never even . . . . Why? Can you tell me?'

Instead, the Duchess told him the story of a man who fell in love with the Queen of the Fairies and all the shit that put him into. Macbeth said he knew the songs. Tam Lin, Thomas The Rymer, all that stuff? But that wasn't the same thing, surely, Moira Cairns was a human being.

'That's quite true,' the Duchess said gravely. 'But remember this. Wherever she goes, that young woman . . . she's bound to be touched with madness. Now, who is the white man?'

'White man?'

'I thought perhaps you might be his emissary . . . White-skinned man? I don't think I mean race. Just a man *exuding* a whiteness?'

'Somebody *I* know?'

'You don't?'

'I don't know what you mean.'

'I believe you don't. All right. Never mind.'

Macbeth asked, 'Do you know where Moira is?'

'Oh . . . the little Jewish person, Kaufmann, tells me she's in the North of England.'

'Bastard wouldn't tell *me*.'

'You he doesn't trust. Strange, that – I find you quite transparent.'

'Thanks.'

'There was a man called . . . Matt?'

'Jesus, you intuited that?'

The Duchess sighed in exasperation. 'She told me.'

'Right,' Macbeth said, relieved. 'Matt, uh . . .'

'Castle. She thinks he was her mentor. I rather suspect she was his.'

'Right,' Macbeth said uncertainly.

'He's dead. She'll have gone to try and lay his spirit to rest.'

Macbeth squirmed a little. Was this precisely what was meant by things you couldn't find in the *New York Times*? Was this what Mom meant about uncovering his roots? He thought not.

The Duchess smiled kindly. 'You can leave now, if you wish, Mr Macbeth. I'll have Donald see you to the gate.'

'No, wait . . .' Two trains of thought were about to crash, buckling his usual A to B mental tracks. 'This, uh, white person . . .'

'A thin man with white hair and a very white complexion.'

The castle. The bones. White-faced man with a cut eye.

'Shit, I don't believe this . . . you got that outa my head. You pulled it clean outa my head.'

'Mr Macbeth, calm down. Two or three weeks ago, a man of this description came to consult me. As people do . . . occasionally. He didn't get in. Donald is my first line of defence, the dogs are the second, and Donald told me the dogs disliked this man quite *intensely*. On sight. Now . . . dogs can't *invariably* be trusted, they may react badly to – oh – psychic disturbance in a person, or mental instability. But when a man arrives in an expensive car and seems very confident and the dogs hate him on sight . . .'

Stanhope, Macbeth thought. Stansgate?

'And when Donald conveyed my message that I was unwell, he was apparently quite annoyed. He sent a message back that he had information about my daughter which he thought I would wish to know. I suggested Donald should let the dogs have him.'

'What happened?'

'He left.'

Stanley? Stanmore? 'Duchess, you think this guy meant her harm?'

'Two people arrive within a short period to talk to me about my daughter. One the dogs dislike. How did the dogs take to you, Mr Macbeth?'

'I wasn't invited to play rubber-bone, but I seem to be intact.'

The Duchess nodded. 'I don't know how you found me – no, don't explain, it's not important. I didn't mention the man to Moira, she has enough problems, I think. But if you wanted to help her, you might keep an eye open for him. If there was a problem and you were to deal with it, she need never know, need she?'

Macbeth started thinking about the knights and the Holy Grail.

And this guy . . . Stanton? Stansfield?

PART SEVEN

ANGELS

From *Dawber's* Secret *Book of Bridelow* (unpublished):

THE HISTORY OF BEER

BEER, OF COURSE, WAS brewed in Bridelow long before the seventeenth and eighteenth centuries. Ale was the original sacred drink, made from the water of the holy spring and the blessed barley and preserved with the richly-aromatic bog myrtle from the Moss.

Nigel Pennick writes, in his book *Practical Magic in the Northern Tradition*:

'Cakes or bread and ale are the sacrament of country tradition. The runic word for ale – *ALU* – is composed of the three runes *As*, *Lagu* and *Ur*. The first rune has the meaning of *the gods* or *divine power*; the second *water* and *flow*, and the third *primal strength*. The eating of bread and drinking of ale is the mystery of the transmutation of the energy in the grain into a form where it is reborn in our physical bodies.'

It follows, therefore, that, to some local people, the sale of the Bridelow brewery and the detachment of the beer-making process from its ancient origins, would seem to be a serious sapping of the village's inherent strength, perhaps even a symbolic draining away of its lifeblood.

CHAPTER I

'S he's got to be in. I can hear the kettle boiling.'

And boiling and boiling. Whistling through the house. The kettle having hysterics.

'I've got a key,' Willie said, bringing out the whole bunch of them.

A dark, damp dread was settling around Moira. She took a step back on the short path leading to Ma Wagstaff's front door. Held on to a gatepost, biting a lip.

'What the f—' The door opening a few inches, then jamming and Willie putting his shoulder to it. 'Summat caught behind here . . .'

'Hey, stop, Willie . . . Jesus.'

Through the crack in the door, she'd seen a foot, black-shod and pointing upwards. She drew Willie gently back and showed him.

'Oh, Christ,' Willie said drably.

He didn't approach the door again. He said quietly, 'Moira, do us a favour. Nip across to t'Post Office. Fetch Milly.'

'What about a doctor?'

'She wouldn't thank you for a doctor. Just get Milly. Milly Gill.'

Moira didn't need to say a word. Milly Gill looked at her and lost her smile, shooed out two customers and shut up the post office. Ran ahead of Moira across the street, big floral bosom heaving.

When they got to the house, Willie had the front door wide open and tears of horror in his eyes. Milly Gill moved past him to where the old woman lay in a small, neat bundle at the bottom of the stairs, eyes like glass buttons, open mouth a breathless void, one leg crooked under her brown woollen skirt.

The body looked as weightless as a sparrow. Moira doubted she'd ever seen anything from which life was so conspicuously absent. A life which, obviously, had been so much more than the usual random mesh of electrical impulses. Even when it was moving, the little body had been the least of Ma Wagstaff.

This was a big death.

Willie Wagstaff stood in the front garden looking at his shoes, drawing long breaths. His hands hung by his sides, fingers motionless. The kettle's wild whistling ended with a gasp, and then Milly Gill came out and joined them. 'You'll need a doctor, Willie, luv.'

His head came up, eyes briefly bright, but the spark of hope fading in an instant.

'Death certificate,' Milly said softly. She took his arm. 'Come on. Post Office. I'll make us some tea.'

The street was silent, but doors were being opened, curtains tweaked aside. Shadowed faces; nobody came out – everybody sensing the death mood in the dusky air.

Moira thought bleakly, *They don't die like this, people like Ma Wagstaff. Not at a time of crisis. They don't have accidents and sudden heart attacks. They know when it's over, and they go quietly and usually in their own time.*

At the Post Office doorway, Milly Gill called out to the street at large, 'It's Ma Wagstaff. Nothing anybody can do.' She turned to Willie, 'No point in keeping it a secret, is there, luv?'

Moira heard Willie saying, 'I was only with her this morning.' The way people talked, facing the mindless robbery of a sudden death.

And I saw her less than an hour ago, and she was in some state, Willie . . . she was in some state.

'I'd guess it couldn't have been quicker,' Milly Gill said unconvincingly, leading them through the Post Office into a flowery little sitting room behind. 'She's still warm, poor old luv. Maybe she had a seizure or something, going upstairs. Sit yourselves down, I'll put kettle on and phone for t'doctor.'

'This is Moira Cairns,' said Willie.

'How d'you do. Plug that fire in, Willie, it's freezing.'

Scrabbling down by the hearth, Willie looked up at Moira through his mousy fringe, fishing out a weak smile that was almost apologetic.

'I should go,' Moira said. 'Last thing you need is me.'

Willie got to his feet, nervously straightening his pullover. 'I wouldn't say that. No.'

She thought, Poor Willie. Who's he got left? No mother, no Matt, no job maybe, no direction. Only fingers drumming at the air.

'Is there only you . . . No brothers, sisters . . . ?'

'Two sisters,' Willie said. 'There's always more girls. By tradition, like.'

Moira sat on the end of a settee with bright, floral loose-covers. The carpet had a bluebell design and there were paintings and sketches of wild flowers on the walls.

'Ah,' Willie said, 'she had to go sometime. She were eighty . . . I forget. Getting on, though. Least she dint suffer, that's the main thing.'

Oh, but she did, Willie . . . She couldn't look at him, her worried eyes following a single black beam across the ceiling. Two bunches of sage were hanging from it, the soft, musty scent flavouring the atmosphere. Homely.

'No hurry,' Milly Gill was saying in another room, on the phone to the doctor. 'If there's sick people in t'surgery, you see to them first. See to the living.'

When she came back into the sitting room, there were two cats around her ankles.

'Bob and Jim.' Willie's eyes were damp. 'Little buggers. Didn't see um come.'

Moira said, 'Your ma's cats?'

Willie smiled. 'Not any more. Cats'll always find a home. These buggers knew where to come. They'll not be the only ones.'

'This lady's with the Mothers' Union, right?'

Willie said, 'You know about that, eh?'

'I knew about this one when she first come in,' said Milly Gill. 'We'll have to have a talk sometime, luv.'

Her watchful, grey eyes said she also knew that women like Ma Wagstaff did not fall downstairs after having unexpected strokes or heart attacks. Willie's fingers had known that too, had felt it coming, whatever it was.

'Soon, huh?' Moira said.

Joel Beard said, 'Here? In my . . . in the churchyard?'

He and the policeman were standing in the church porch, the wet afternoon draining into an early dusk.

'It's a possibility, vicar,' Ashton said. 'It's something we have to check out, and the sooner we do it the less likely we are to attract attention. You haven't had any Press here, I take it?'

Joel Beard shook his curls. 'Why would they come here?'

'They would if they knew what we were proposing to do, sir, and these things have a habit of leaking out. So . . . I don't know if you've had experience of an exhumation before, but what it involves is screening off the immediate area and confining it to as few people as are absolutely necessary. You can be there yourself if you like, but I assure you we'll be very tidy. Now, the lights . . .'

'Lights? You mean you want to do it tonight? I thought these things took . . .'

'Not much more than a phone call involved these days, sir. We're under quite a lot of pressure to find this thing, as you can imagine.'

Joel said, 'It all seems so unlikely.'

It didn't, though. It connected all too plausibly. 'Inspector, how do you suppose that this was actually done? Without anything being seen?'

'This was what I was planning to ask you. Country churchyard, even at night somebody sees something, don't they? Perhaps they saw and they kept quiet, mmm? When was the grave dug?'

'I don't know,' Joel said. 'I imagine the day before. The Rector was in charge then, but he . . . he's in hospital. He's had a heart attack.'

'That's unfortunate,' Ashton said. 'No, you see, what's been suggested to us is that the grave was dug deeper than is normal and then the body was brought here and covered with earth and then the funeral went ahead as normal, with Mr Castle's coffin laid on top of the bog body.'

'That's preposterous,' Joel said.

It wasn't, though. Somehow there was a link here with the old woman and the bottle she'd been attempting to secrete into Castle's coffin.

'You see, our information is that there was a request from some people here for the body to be returned to the bog. And when it seemed unlikely that was going to happen, somebody decided to pinch it. Would you know anything about that, Mr Beard?'

'Good Lord,' Joel said. 'No, I certainly wouldn't. You

know, I think, on the whole, that I should like to be there when you . . . do it.'

'I thought you might,' said Ashton.

Moira felt weary and ineffectual, and she had a headache. Walking, head down, into the Rectory drive, she was speared by lights.

Cathy parked her father's VW Golf crookedly in front of the garage.

'How is he?'

'He's OK,' Cathy said quickly, unlocking the front door. 'I'm sorry, I didn't leave you a key, did I? I'm hopelessly inefficient.'

About her father – Moira saw she was playing this down.

Cathy unloaded plastic carrier bags and her long university scarf on to the kitchen worktops, all stark, white butcher's-shop tiling. 'I went into Manchester afterwards. Had to get away somewhere crowded, to think. Got loads of cold things from Marks and Sparks. You don't mind, do you? Pop sees to the cooking as a rule. I'm a disaster in the kitchen. Did you get to see Ma Wagstaff?'

'Yes,' said Moira.

'Did she talk to you?'

'No,' Moira said. 'I'm afraid not.'

Then Cathy discovered the sugar bowl was empty and went into the pantry, the little room under the stairs, for a new bag. 'Oh,' she said. 'The little scumbags.'

'Huh?'

Moira peered over her shoulder. Cathy was holding a brick. There was a small window in the pantry and the brick had clearly been used to smash it.

'Little bastards,' Cathy said. 'You know, this never used to happen. I know people say that all the time . . . "Oh, things were different when I was a kid and you could get in the cinema for sixpence. None of this vandalism in those days, kids had respect." But it's true. Even – what? – six months ago it was true in Bridelow. They *did* have respect.'

Cathy put the brick down on the floor. 'Now there's graffiti in the toilets at the parish hall. A week or two ago somebody had a . . . defecated on the seat inside the lych-gate. Can you believe that? In Bridelow?'

'You better check the house,' Moira said.

Cathy had a cursory look around the downstairs rooms. Everything seemed to be in order. 'Little sods. Everybody knows Pop's in hospital.' She looked at Moira. 'Oh. Yes. That's another thing. They're sending him to a convalescent home.'

'I thought it wasn't too serious.'

'Coronary,' Cathy said despondently. 'That's serious. They're sending him – committing him is how he sees it – to this Church nursing home down in Shropshire. At least a month. Which means Joel's got to move in here.'

'With you?'

'You're joking,' Cathy said. 'Even if I could bear to have him in the house, he's much too proper to countenance it. No, I'll go back to Oxford. Come up at weekends and see Pop. I mean, I expect you'll be wanting to be off, won't you?'

Moira said. 'Look, you got any hardboard in the garage or somewhere? We can block up this window.'

'Never mind, Alf Beckett'll fix it tomorrow.'

Moira said, 'Cathy . . . um . . . something bad's happened.'

Because of the Post Office's strict security regulations, Milly Gill's front door had two steel bolts and a fancy double lock, which she'd always thought was damn stupid in a place like Bridelow. Tonight, though, first time ever, Milly was glad to turn the key twice over and slide the big bolts. Even though she knew there were some things no locks could keep out.

The urgent banging on the door shook her. Willie Wagstaff never used the knocker. Willie would beat out his own personal tattoo with his fingers.

'Oh, Mother,' Milly Gill said, clutching her arms over her breast. 'I'm not going to be up to this.'

It was an hour since the doctor'd had Ma taken away, across the Moss. He'd said there might have to be a post-mortem, probably no more than a formality; it was most likely natural causes. But if there was reason to think she might have fallen accidentally, there'd have to be a public inquest.

Pity Bridelow didn't have a resident doctor any more; this was an Asian gentleman from Across the Moss who couldn't be expected to understand. Milly had pleaded with him not to let them cut Ma up if there was any way it could be avoided. It was important that all of Ma's bits should be returned to Bridelow for burial, not tissue and stuff left in some hospital wastebin.

More crashing at the front door.

'Who is it?' Milly shouted. Didn't recognize her own voice, it sounded that feeble.

'It's me. Alf.'

Milly tut-tutted at her cowardice. Why she should think there might be something abroad because something that happened to hundreds of pensioners every week had happened to Ma Wagstaff . . .

She undid the bolts and turned the key twice. 'I'm sorry, Alf. Not like me to be nervy.'

But, if anything, Alf Beckett looked worse than she felt. There was a streetlamp outside the door, a converted gaslamp with an ice-blue bulb. Its light made Alf look quite ill, eyes like keyholes.

'Milly,' he said. 'We're in t'shit.'

'Come in, luv,' Milly said. Her responsibility now, this sort of problem, keeping up community morale.

She sat Alf down on the floral settee. He was ashen.

'Now then, come on,' Milly said. 'It's all right. We'll get over this. We've had bad patches before.'

'No . . .' Alf shook his head. 'Listen . . .'

'It's my fault,' Milly said. 'We always left too much to poor old Ma. We thought she were immortal. Thought we could sit back, everybody getting on with their lives, foreign holidays, videos. Didn't seem to matter like it used to. And then when Ma started getting gloomy, we all thought it were just her age. Even me, daft cow. And now everything's happened at once, and it's shaken us. But we'll be all right, honest, luv.'

She got up to put the kettle on. 'I've sent Willie to t'Man

316

for a pint. Life's got to go on, Alf. Just means we'll have to have a bit of a get-together. Soon as possible. Sort this lad Joel Beard out for a start. Then we'll see what else we've got to tackle. Mrs Horridge, that's another thing . . .'

'Milly!' Alf Beckett's hearthbrush moustache looked bent and spiky. 'Police've come.'

'Eh? Because of Ma? Have they found summat?'

'No, no . . . Listen to me, woman, for Christ's sake.' Alf sat up on the couch, hands clasped so tightly together that his knuckles were whiter than his cheeks. 'It's t'grave. They're coming to dig Matt's grave up.'

In the narrow doorway to the back kitchen, Milly froze, filling it.

Alf said, 'Some bugger's told t'coppers as t'bogman's in theer.'

Milly felt sick. All churned up inside. Ma gone, the Rector in hospital. And her at the wrong time of life to cope with it all. She covered up her face with her hands and looked at him through her fingers.

'Lord,' she whispered. 'What've we done, Alf? What've we done in Brid'lo to deserve this?'

Cathy said to Moira, 'If Pop hears about this, he's going to do something stupid.'

She'd told Cathy only about Ma's death. Not about seeing the old woman out on the Moss fighting a dead tree.

She said, 'Like what?'

'Like discharge himself,' Cathy said glumly. 'Moira, I don't know what to do. They ran this place between them, Pop and Ma Wagstaff. They hardly ever met, but they had an understanding, you know?'

They were in the sitting room. Cathy had lit the fire. She was sitting on the sofa where Dic Castle had sprawled. She'd taken off her shoes and her thick woollen socks were planted on an old rag hearthrug dark with scorchmarks from stray coals.

'He doesn't talk much about it, but it was obviously really

tough for Pop when he first came here. He was pretty young – younger than Joel. And a Southerner. With a funny German name. Hell of a culture shock. Series of shocks, I suppose.'

'Like, when he finds out they're all heathens?'

'Is that what we are?'

Moira smiled. 'It's no' that simple, is it? I was up on the moor with Willie Wagstaff earlier. We saw the holy well. Who's that dedicated to? The goddess Brigid? St Bride? The Mother Goddess? Or the Holy Mother of God?'

'Gets confusing, doesn't it?' Cathy said.

'And the cross that was in the church, made out of twigs and stuff.'

'The Autumn Cross.'

'And there's a Winter Cross – yeh? – made of holly and mistletoe and stuff, and then a Spring Cross, made of . . .'

'You've got it.'

Moira said, putting it all together finally, 'They can't make up their minds *what* they are, can they?'

Cathy folded her legs on to the sofa. 'Like I said, you need to talk to Mr Dawber, he can put it into an historical context. But the first Church in Britain was the Celtic Church, and by the time they came along I like to think Celtic paganism was pretty refined, with this give-and-take attitude to nature and animals and things.'

'In parts of Scotland,' said Moira, 'particularly some of the Western Isles, it's not been so much a takeover as a merger. Like, nobody could say the teachings of Christ were anything less than a hell of a good framework for, say, human behaviour, the way we treat each other. But . . .'

'. . . in isolated areas, there were aspects of life it didn't quite cover,' said Cathy. 'Maybe still doesn't. And this area was always very isolated. Cut off. Self-sufficient. Immune from outside influences. We got electricity later than everybody else. Piped water was a long time coming. Television signals are still so lousy that most people haven't got one yet.'

'Yeh, but look . . .'

'. . . now it's a brick through your window and "Sheffield United are shit" on the walls, and somebody has one on a public seat – that's outside influences for you. Be a rape next.'

'Cathy, this bogman . . .'

'Oh, *he's* all right.'

'No, he's not. Matt Castle was besotted with him. The Man in the Moss. Matt was seeing him in Biblical terms – sacrificial saviour of the English Celts.'

'He died to save us all,' Cathy said. 'Gosh. Isn't that a terrible piece of blasphemy? Can you imagine the sleepless nights Pop had over this? The bogman: was he some sort of Pennine Jesus?'

'Or the anti-Christ, huh?'

Moira thought of the black, snaking branches of the tree on the Moss. Her head throbbed, as if the thing were lashing at her brain.

'OK,' she said hurriedly. 'Let's leave that be for a while. When they built the first Christian church here, they put it on the old sacred site and it's dedicated to Brigid, or Brigantia, now known as St Bride. And the ministers here have always had a kind of agreement with the priestess and her attendants who, in time, become known as the Mothers' Union, right?'

'All the Anglican Churches have Mothers' Unions. Young Wives' groups too.'

'Yeah, but most of them, presumably, don't recognize the symbolism: the mothers and the hags. The hags being the ones over the menopause.'

'When you're over the Change,' Cathy said, 'you go on to a new level of responsibility. Well . . . so I'm told. How do you know all this?'

'I read a lot of books. Now, OK, the bogman turns up again. The willing sacrifice. The pagan Jesus-figure who supposedly went to his death to save his people. That's one powerful symbol, Cathy. Regardless of what else it might be, it's a heavy symbol. It churns things up.'

'I've told you, he's all right.'

'What d'you mean he's all right? Somebody's *stolen* him. I'm telling you there are people around who will *do things* with a relic as powerful as that.'

'Look, it's OK, that's sorted out.'

'Sorted out?' She had to stand up, walk away from the fire, although she was shivering and it hurt when she swallowed.

'Moira, come on, sit down. I promise you, it's OK.'

'Why?' Moira demanded. 'Why is it OK, Cathy?'

'Because,' said Cathy simply, 'the bogman's had a full Christian burial.'

CHAPTER II

By now the sky was the colour of police trousers, Ashton thought prosaically, and damn near as thick. 'Tent would've been better,' he said as the rain started up again, steel needles in the arc lamp. 'Does it matter if he gets wet?'

'Depends what state he's in.' Roger Hall was struggling with his umbrella.

'Glad to see you're still sure he's down there.'

'Count on it,' Hall said.

Ashton's lads had erected a grey canvas screen, about seven feet high, around the grave; still just a mound of soil, no headstone yet, that saved a bit of hassle.

'Anyway, you've brought your own coffin, have you?'

'I wouldn't call it that,' Hall said. 'My assistant has it, over there.' Pointing at Chrissie White, shivering in fake fur, a plywood box at her feet.

'What's that white stuff inside then, Dr Hall?'

'Polystyrene chips. Shut that lid properly, Chrissie, we don't want them wet. We've also brought a few rolls of cling-film, Inspector. We wrap him in that first, so we don't lose anything.'

'Like a frozen turkey,' Ashton said. 'Anyway, it's good to see we haven't pulled a crowd. Yet. Let's just hope we can get this sorted before anybody knows we're here. Now, where's that gravedigger bloke?'

The big, curly-haired clergyman came over. Wearing his full funeral kit, Ashton noticed. Long cassock and a short cape like coppers used to have on point-duty in the good old days. He looked nervous. Might he know something?

'This is Mr Beckett, Inspector. Our verger.'

Little pensioner with a big, stainless-steel spade.

'You dig this grave first time around, Mr Beckett?'

'Aye, what about it?'

'Usual depth?'

'Six feet, give or take a few inches. No need to measure it, sithee, when tha's done t'job a few score times.'

'And when Mr Castle was buried, did you notice if the earth had been disturbed?'

'It were bloody dark by then,' said Mr Beckett uncompromisingly, patting his chest, as if he'd got indigestion.

But actually smoothing the bulge in his donkey jacket.

For, in its inside pocket, shrouded in household tissue, lay a little brown bottle.

Be his job, this time, to get the bloody bottle into Matt Castle's coffin, which they'd have to get out of the way before they could get at the bogman.

This was a new bottle. Alf had gone with Milly Gill to Ma Wagstaff's house, and he'd stood guard while Milly made it up, all of a dither, poor lass. 'I'm not doing it right, Alf, I'm sure I'm not doing it right.'

'It's thought as counts,' Alf had said, not knowing what the hell he was on about. 'Ma always said that.' Standing at the parlour door, watching Milly messing about with red thread and stuff by candlelight.

'Alf.'

'What?'

'Go in t'kitchen, fetch us a mixing bowl.'

'What sort?'

'*Any* sort. Big un, I'm nervous. Come on, hurry up.'

Alf handing her a white Pyrex bowl, standing around in the doorway as Milly put the bowl on the parlour floor, feeling about under her skirts. 'Well, don't just stand there, Alf. Bugger off.'

The door closed, only streetlight washing in through the landing window, ugly shadows thrown into the little hall, the bannisters dancing. Milly's muffled muttering. And then the unavoidable sound of her peeing into the Pyrex.

THE MAN IN THE MOSS

Alf, trying not to listen, standing where Ma's body must have landed. Looking up the stairs into a strange, forbidding coldness. Him, who'd patrolled the empty church on wild and windy nights and never felt other than welcome.

'Hurry up, lass. Giving me t'creeps.'

'This is Ma's house.' The sound slowing to a trickle. 'There's not a nicer atmosphere anywhere.'

Alf deliberately turning his back on the stairs.

'Aye. But that were when Ma were alive.'

This time Moira went off to make the tea. Gave her time to think.

She'd asked Cathy who was left in the Mothers' Union, apart from Milly Gill. Cathy had looked gloomy and said, don't ask.

Moira lifted the teapot lid and watched the leaves settle. Seemed the Mothers' Union wasn't what it used to be. Ma Wagstaff used to say they'd let things slide a bit, Cathy said.

Moira put the teapot on a tray with a couple of mugs. Some dead leaves hit the window. From the doorway behind her, Cathy said, 'Ma thought there was something out there trying to get in. She said the air was different.'

'How do you know all this, Cathy? Do you have to be a mother to be in the Mothers' Union?'

Cathy grinned. There were bags under her eyes and her hair looked dull in the hard kitchen light. 'They'll even take virgins these days.'

'Are you?'

'A virgin?'

'A mother.'

'Pop's an enlightened clergyman,' Cathy said, 'but not *that* enlightened.'

Two young coppers helped Alf with the spadework, which was a good bit easier – just when you didn't bloody need it – than he'd have expected under normal circumstances.

He was ashamed of this grave, the soil all piled in loose, big lumps, nothing tamped down. But he'd rushed the job, as rattled as anybody by that ugly scene between Ma Wagstaff and Joel Beard, and then Lottie Castle screaming at them to get her husband planted quick.

Three feet into the grave, getting there faster than he wanted to, he could see Joel peering down at them. Unlikely the lad'd know yet about Ma Wagstaff's death, nobody rushing to tell him after the way he'd been carrying on.

Thing was, Joel probably had no idea what he was up against. Just a bunch of cracked owd women.

Which, Alf conceded, wasn't a bad thing for him to think just now; at least he didn't suspect Alf, and he wouldn't be watching him too closely.

'The problem is,' Cathy said, 'that it's become more of a way of life than a religion.'

'Is that no' a good thing?'

'Well, yeah, it is for ordinary people, getting on with their lives. This sort of natural harmony, the feeling of belonging to something. It's great. Until things start to go wrong. And your brewery gets taken over and most of the workforce is fired. And your village shop shuts down. And your local celeb arrives to save your pub from almost certain closure and he's dead inside six months. And your placid, understanding Rector develops quite a rapid worsening of his arthritis, which Ma's always been able to keep in check. Except Ma's losing it, and she doesn't know why.'

Cathy looked at Moira's cigarettes on the chair-arm. 'How long's it take to learn to smoke?' She waved an exasperated hand. 'Forget it. Oh, this place is no fun any more. Atmosphere's not the same. People not as content. I've been home twice since the summer and it's struck me right away. Maybe that's the same all over Britain, with this Government and everything. But Bridelow was always . . .'

'Protected?'

'Yeah. And now it's not. I mean, somebody like Joel would never have got away with what he's done – ripping down that kid's cross. And Our Sheila . . . I mean, we've had these religious firebrands before, maybe even my old man was a bit that way when he first arrived, but . . . something calms them down. Ma Wagstaff used to say it was in the air. Shades. Pastel shades. You know what I mean?'

'The old Celtic air,' Moira said. 'Everything misty and nebulous. No extremes. Everything blending in. You can sense it on some of the Scottish islands. Scotch mist. Parts of Ireland too. Maybe it was preserved here, like the bogman, in the peat.'

Cathy said, 'You're not going to rest until I tell you, are you?'

'And I do need to get to bed, Cathy. I feel terrible.'

Cathy sighed. 'OK. They stole the bogman back. They buried him in Matt Castle's grave before Matt went in.'

'Jesus,' said Moira. 'Who?'

'We're not supposed to know. But . . . everybody, I suppose. They're all in it. They've done it before. A few bits of bodies have turned up in the Moss over the years, and that's what they do with them. Save them up until somebody dies. And curiously, somebody always does – even if it's only an arm or a foot turns up – somebody conveniently snuffs it so the bits can have a Christian burial. Well . . . inasmuch as anything round here is one hundred per cent Christian. But this body . . . well, it's the first time there's been a whole one.'

'And the council discovered it, didn't they? So no way they could keep this one to themselves.'

'And then the scientific tests, revealing that this had been a very special sacrifice.'

'The triple death.'

'Mmm.'

'So Ma Wagstaff and Milly Gill and co. and . . . Willie? Is Willie in this?'

'Willie used to be a carpenter.'

'He did too.'

'And he's good with doors and locks. And then there's that mate of his, the other chap in the band . . .'

'Eric.'

'He works for a security firm now, in Manchester. The

same firm, as it happens, that was hired to keep an eye on the Field Centre.'

'Bloody hell.' Moira slumped back in her chair. 'It's beyond belief. It's like one of those old films, where everybody's conspiring. *Whisky Galore* or something. So the body's back home, in Bridelow soil.'

'It didn't go *completely* right. Milly says that right at the last minute Ma started getting funny feelings about it going in Matt Castle's grave.'

'I'm no' surprised.'

You've got to purify yourself. Of course.

'So she made up this witch bottle to go in Matt's coffin. It's got rowan berries in it, and red cotton and . . . the person making up the bottle has to pee in it.'

Moira said, '*Rowan tree, red thread / Holds the witches all in dread.*'

'What?'

'It's a song,' Moira said.

'Well, it's the wrong way round. Mostly it was the witches themselves who use the bottles, to keep bad spirits at bay. The spirits are supposed to go after the red berries or something and get entangled in the thread. It's all symbolic.'

'So she wanted to save Matt from evil spirits?'

Or maybe she wanted to save the bogman from something in Matt.

'I don't know,' Cathy said. 'I'm the Rector's daughter. I'm not supposed to know anything. We turn a blind eye.'

'But the bottle never got in the coffin, did it?'

'I don't know.'

'The supposed contaminant remains.'

'I don't *know*, Moira.'

He stood at the edge of the grave looking down. Forcing himself to look down.

Sometimes when he prayed he thought he heard a voice, and the voice said, You have a task, Joel. You must . . . not . . . turn . . . away.

Sometimes the voice called him Mr Beard, like the voice on

the telephone, a calm, knowing voice, obviously someone inside the village disgusted by what went on here.

One day, Joel hoped, he would meet his informant. When he encountered people in the street or in the Post Office, he would look into their eyes for a sign. But the women would smile kindly at him and the men would mumble something laconic, like 'All right, then, lad?' and continue on their way.

He stepped back in distaste as a shovelful of grave-soil was heaved out of the hole and over his shoes. Surely they had to be six feet down by now. He wondered whether, if they kept on digging, they would reach peat – the Moss slowly sliding in, underneath the village.

Insidious.

He looked over his shoulder and up, above the heads and umbrellas of the silent circle of watchers, at the frosty disc of the church clock, the Beacon of the Moss.

The false light. The devil's moon.

Perhaps that had to go too, like the pagan well and the cross and the monstrosity above the church door, before the village could be cleansed.

'More light, please.'

One of the policemen in the grave.

'You there yet?' The Inspector, Ashton. 'Swing that light round a bit, Ken, let's have a look.'

'Deeper than we expected, sir. Maybe it's sunk.'

'That likely, Mr Beckett?' The light swept across the verger's face.

'Aye. Happen that's what . . . happened.' Alfred Beckett's voice like crushed eggshell.

Ashton said, 'Right, let's have this one out, see what's underneath.'

Ernie Dawber had returned after dark from his weekly mission to the supermarket in Macclesfield, bringing back with him a copy of the *Manchester Evening News*, a paper that rarely made it Across the Moss until the following day.

The front-page lead headline said,

MASSIVE HUNT FOR BOGMAN

A major police hunt was underway today for the Bridelow bog body – snatched in a daring raid on a university lab. And a prominent archaeological trust has offered a £5000 reward for information leading to the safe recovery of The Man in the Moss.

'We are taking this very seriously indeed,' said . . .

'Oh, dear me,' Ernie Dawber said to himself, the paper spread out on the table where he was finishing his tea – toasted Lancashire cheese. 'What a tangled web, eh?'

Trying to keep his mind off what the doctor'd had to say. Well, what right had he to complain about *that*? Least he'd got a doctor of the old school who didn't bugger about – while there's life there's hope, medical science moving ahead at a tremendous rate; none of that old nonsense, thank the Lord.

Might just drop in and see Ma Wagstaff about it. Nowt lost in that, is there?

The doorbell rang.

Ernie didn't rush. He folded up the *Manchester Evening News* very neatly, preserving its crease. If it was Dr Hall, he didn't know what he'd say. As an historian he was glad the experts had got their hands on this particular body, been able, with their modern scientific tests, to clarify a few points. But equally Ma Wagstaff, with her instincts and her natural wisdom, had been right about putting the thing back.

Thank God, he thought, pulling at his front door, for instinct. All too aware that this was not something he himself possessed. Bit of psychological insight perhaps, now and then, but that wasn't the same thing.

So it had to be done, putting the bogman back in Bridelow earth. Commitment fulfilled.

All's well that ends well.

Except it hasn't, Ernie thought, getting the door open. It hasn't ended and it's not well. Lord knows why.

'By 'eck,' he said, surprised. 'And to what do I owe this honour?'

On his doorstep, in the rain, stood four women in dark clothing – old-fashioned, ankle-length, navy duffle coats with the hoods up or dark woollen shawls over their heads.

A posse from the Bridelow Mothers' Union, in full ritual dress. Could be quite disconcerting when you saw them trooping across the churchyard against a wintry sunset. But always a bit, well, comical, at close range.

'Can we talk to you, Mr Dawber?' Milly Gill said from somewhere inside whatever she had on.

Ernie identified the others in a second: Frank's wife, Ethel, Young Frank's wife, Susan. And Old Sarah Winstanley, with no teeth in. Probably the only remaining members of the Union fit enough to go out after dark this time of year.

He felt a warm wave of affection for the curious quartet.

'Now, then,' he said cheerfully. 'Where's Ma?'

No instinct, that was his problem.

'Thought you knew everything,' Milly Gill said in a voice as cold and dispiriting as the rain.

'I've been out,' Ernie said, on edge now.

Milly said quietly, 'Ma's died on us, and the churchyard's full of policemen digging up Matt's grave. Can we come in, Mr Dawber?'

Matt Castle's coffin came up hard.

It was like a big old decaying barge stuck in a sandbank; it didn't want to come, it wanted to stay in the dark and rot and feed the worms. They had to tear it out of the earth, with a slurping and a squelching of sodden soil and clay.

'Hell fire, you'd think it'd been in here years,' one of the coppers muttered, sliding a rope under one end, groping for one of the coffin handles.

Alf Beckett stayed on top, hands flat on the lid, knowing it hadn't been nailed down, knowing that if it slipped they could tip the corpse into the mud.

Thinking, *get it over, get it over . . . get the bloody thing found and have done with it.*

And wondering then if by any chance he was standing on the squashed brown face of the bog body. *Oh, what a mess, what a bloody mess.*

'All right,' the Inspector said as two men on the surface took the strain. 'Take it easy. Come out now, please, and keep to the sides.'

Alf scrambled out after the coffin. He was covered in mud.

'Lay it over there, please, don't damage it. Now, Roger . . . Dr Hall . . . time for you to take over, I reckon.'

'Right!' Dr Roger Hall strode into the lights, beads of water glinting in his beard. 'Now we'll see.'

Without ceremony, they dumped the coffin behind the piles of excavated earth, up against the canvas screen, well out of the light. Matt Castle: just something to be got out of the way, while everybody crowded round to gaze into the grave.

Except for Alf Beckett who shuffled behind the others, squatted down on the wet grass by the coffin, put a muddy hand inside his donkey jacket and brought out the witch bottle.

Whispering, 'Forgive this intrusion, lad,' as he felt along the muddy rim of the soil-slimy casket, hands moving up to its shoulders, thumbs prising at the lid, bracing himself for the stench, a sickening blast of gasses.

Some bloke barking, 'No . . . *no.* Not like that. Look, let *me* come down.'

Alf breathing hard, snatching at the lid as it suddenly sprang away. 'God help us.' Could he do this? Could he put his hands in there?

'Mind yourself, Dr Hall, bloody slippy down there.'

'. . .'s all right. Get that bloody lamp out of my eyes. Give me a light, give me a torch. Thanks.'

Alf thought it was worse that there was no light. He might not be able to see the body, but he'd have to touch it. Feel for the cold, rubbery hands . . . would they be rubbery or would they be slippery or flaking with decay? He didn't know, but he'd find out, prising the fingers apart to get them to hold the bottle.

Voice raised, muffled. Voice out of the grave.

'. . . Got to be . . . Chrissie, the trowel . . . pass me the trowel!'

'Take your time, Dr Hall, you won't get another chance.'

Hand inside, Alf could feel the quilted stuff and the stiff, lacy stuff, the lining. Felt more like nylon than silk.

Sweat bubbling up on his forehead to meet the rain, his moustache dripping.

The smell from inside the box was dank and rotten. Alf wrenched his head aside, looked away from the blackened hump of the coffin towards the people gathered round the open grave, Joel Beard singing out contemptuously, 'You see . . . *nothing*. Are you really surprised?'

Alf propping himself on his right arm, the hand splayed into the grass.

'Ashton, it *has* to be. I refuse to . . .'

It hit Alf Beckett, in a sudden burst of bewilderment. *The bogman. They can't find it . . . why can't they find it?*

And then his stomach lurched, hot vomit roared into his throat. His supporting arm collapsed, the nerves gone, and his mouth stretched into a scream so wide it seemed it'd rip his lips apart.

The scream was choked by the vomit.

His left hand, the one inside Matt Castle's coffin, had slipped, all five fingers dropping into a soft, cold and glutinous mess. A thin and viscid slithering thing was pulsing between them.

CHAPTER III

'This time,' Sam Davis said, 'you won't stop me.'

He'd already dressed by the time Esther awoke.

'Lights?' she said. 'Lights *again*?'

Sam nodded. Cradled in his arms was his dad's old twelve-bore shotgun.

'Get that out!' Esther shouted. 'I'll not have that thing in my bedroom.'

'Fair enough,' Sam said, patting the pockets of his old combat jacket.

'I *will* stop you,' Esther said, sitting up in bed, rubbing her eyes. 'If you go out with that gun I'll've called the police before you get to the end of the yard.'

'Please yourself.' Sam broke the gun. 'Man's got to look after his own.' He pulled a handful of cartridges from his jacket pocket and shoved a couple into the breech.

Esther started to cry. 'Don't waste um, luv,' Sam said. 'We tried your way. Big wanker. "Oh, Satan, get thee gone, I'm giving thee notice to quit."' Sam snorted. 'Now *I'm* giving um notice to quit. Wi' this. And they'll listen.'

'You're a bloody fool, Sam Davis,' Esther wept. 'You're a fool to yourself. Where will I be wi' you in jail for manslaughter? Where will your children be?'

'Shurrup, eh?' Sam said. 'You'll wake um. I'll be back in half an hour. Or less. Don't worry.'

'Don't *worry* . . . ?'

'I'll show it um. Happen I'll fire it over their heads. That's all it'll take.'

Sam Davis moved quietly out of the bedroom, and his wife followed him downstairs. 'I've warned you. I'll ring for t'police.'

'Aye.' Leaving the lights off, Sam undid the bolts on the back door. It was raining out, and cold enough for sleet.

When he'd gone, Esther, shivering in her nightie, said, 'Right,' and went to the phone.

The phone was dead. He'd ripped out the wire and pulled off the little plastic plug. Esther ran to the back door and screeched, 'Sam . . . *Sam*!' into the unresponsive night.

The nights were the worst times, but in a way they were the best because they hardened Lottie's intent to get out. By day – local customers drifting in around lunchtime, nice people – she got to thinking the pub was an important local service and there weren't many of those left in Bridelow and if she didn't keep it on, who would? And Matt. Matt would be so disappointed with her.

But at night, alone in the pine-framed bed which kept reminding her of her husband's coffin, enclosed by the still

strange, hard, whitewashed walls, she felt his stubborn obsess-
iveness in the air like a lingering, humid odour. And she knew
she'd paid back all she owed to Matt, long since.

If indeed he'd ever given her anything, apart from head-
aches and Dic.

She lay down the middle of the bed, head on a single white
pillow; for the first time entirely alone. Dic had gone off –
relieved, she knew – to his bedsit in Stockport; back on
Monday to the supply-teaching he was doing in lieu of a real
job. Dic looking perpetually bewildered all day, saying little,
mooching about rubbing his chin. Offering, in a half-hearted
way, to stay here until Sunday night, but Lottie briskly waving
him out – fed up with you under my feet, moping around, time
I had some space for myself.

To do what, though?

Well . . . to try and find a buyer for the pub, for a start.
That would be a picnic. Best she could hope for was to flog it
to some rich Cheshire businessman with romantic yearnings,
for conversion into a luxury home with an exclusive view of
peat, peat, peat.

Bloody peat. In the mornings she'd draw back the bedroom
curtains and the first thing she'd see would be black peat and
on to the scene her mind would superimpose Matt in his
wheelchair, sinking into the Moss and fighting it all the way,
and every bloody marsh-bird banking overhead would be
imitating the Pennine Pipes of blessed memory.

All I want is Bridelow Moss behind me. To be able to draw
back the curtains on to other people's gardens, parked cars, the
postman, the milkman, no hills in view over the tops of the
laburnums. (In other words, the view from the bedroom
window in Wilmslow which Matt had despised and which she
carried in her mind like a talisman of sanity.)

With the bedside light on, she gazed unblinking at the
ceiling, a single hefty black beam bisecting it diagonally so that
half the ceiling was light, half shadow.

'*Ma . . .*'

'*. . . aye, gone.*'

'*. . . agstaff . . . dead . . . you didn't know?*'

'*. . . God, no . . .*'

If walls could record voices and mood and atmosphere, The Man's ancient stones would have been crumbling tonight under the dead weight of suppressed emotion. The death of Ma Wagstaff: the underlying theme below all the trivial tap-room chat about Manchester United and the sodding Government, and the more meaningful analyses of working conditions under Gannons.

Lottie saying nothing, playing barmaid, pulling Bridelow Black for those committed to preserving the brewery and lager and draught Bass for those who'd been made redundant.

So Ma Wagstaff had gone.

Well, she was old, she was half-baked, she'd clung to her own loopy ideas of religion; let them be buried with her.

Not that anything stayed buried round here. The bogman rising again after who could say how many centuries, to cause torment and to haunt Matt's latter days. And now poor Matt himself rising again to help the police with their inquiries.

Which – jaw tightened, both hands clenching on the sheet for a moment – was none of her business, and none of Ma Wagstaff's any more. Just let it be all over. Just let them have found what they wanted and put Matt back in his grave and stamped down the soil.

What they wanted. She knew, of course, that it had to be the bogman. How honoured Matt would have been to know he'd be sharing his grave with his illustrious ancestor.

Most likely, she conceded, he *did* know. Matt always could keep a secret. Even from his wife.

Especially from his wife.

And that does it, Lottie thought. I'll talk to estate agents first thing Monday morning.

She put out the lamp and shut her eyes.

She was not lonely.

She was relieved at last of the horror and the pity of Matt and his illness and his all-consuming passions.

And relieved, too – now that Moira had been here, now that she'd received his taped begging letter – of the responsibility of overseeing the completion of Matt's magnum opus, his Bogman Suite. Moira's responsibility now. Poetic justice: one obsession taking care of another.

Not that Moira, presumably, had ever wanted to be Matt's obsession.

Lottie opened her eyes and stared searchingly into the darkness.

Or perhaps, obscurely, perversely, Moira *had*. She kept her ego under wraps, but it was there; it existed.

Maybe it *is* poetic justice.

You've been relieved. You're free to go.

The lino was as cold as flagstones under Ernie's bare feet, and although his bedroom slippers were under the bed, he didn't fetch them out; the cold was better.

I don't want comfort. I want the truth. An answer. What must I do? What is there left I can do?

Through the window, he could see the churchyard, gravestones wet with rain and blue under the Beacon of the Moss. Be one for me, happen, this time next year.

He couldn't, from here, see Matt Castle's grave, but he'd heard about all that from Alfred Beckett, who'd come pounding on his door while the dregs of the Mothers' Union sat dispiritedly drinking tea in his study. What can we do, Mr Dawber? Who's going to explain?

Me, he'd stated firmly. I'll explain, if necessary.

He'd never seen the Mothers in such a state and never imagined he would. Old Sarah Winstanley, with no teeth, just about said it all. No Ma. No teeth. No hope.

Not for me now, neither, with Ma gone.

'Everything's changing,' Millicent had said. 'Hardening. And now we've lost the Man, for good and all. They'll take him back to London this time, no question about that. Bad luck on this scale, Mr Dawber – it's not natural. Mary Lane died, did you hear? Pneumonia. Fifty-three, God forbid.'

Shades, Ma had said. *Them's what's kept this place the way it is*. They started talking about shades again, and it was not really his province. He'd promised Ma Wagstaff that he'd get the Man back, and now it was all falling through, and it was his responsibility. What was there *left*, in the time he had?

And then Milly had told them about Liz Horridge.

'I forgot all about it, wi' Ma being found not long after. I found her up Ma's front path. First time she's been seen in t'village for months. Well . . . she were in a *shocking* state, banging her fists on Ma's door – "please, please", like this, whimpering, you know? I put me hand on her shoulder and she nearly had hysterics. "I want Ma, I want Ma." I says, "Ma's not here, luv. Come and have a cuppa tea," I says. She just looks at me like she doesn't know who I am, and then she pushes me aside and she's off like a rabbit. I rang the Hall to tell somebody, but Shaw's never there, is he?'

And Moira Cairns staying with young Cathy, in the Rectory, at the very heart of the village.

He looked down at the graves. Why had she come so secretively? And why hadn't she gone away again? He'd seen her walking down from the church this morning. Strikingly good-looking lass. Probably in her late thirties, looking it, because of that white strand in her hair, like the light through a crack in the door of a darkened room.

But what did they know about her?

'Nowt,' Ernie said aloud to the silent graves.

Should he say owt to the Mothers? He wasn't a stirrer, he wasn't a gossip, he'd always known more than he passed on, just as *Dawber's Book of Bridelow* was only ever a fraction of what the Dawbers knew about Bridelow.

Who'd take over the *Book* from him? No more Dawbers left in Bridelow. Happen it really was the end of an era. Happen the Bridelow to come wouldn't have the distinction that warranted a book of its own. Ernest Dawber, last of the village scribes. Chronicler of the Fall.

Alf Beckett's arrival had saved him. If Alf hadn't turned up, one of them, or all of them, would surely have sensed he had worries and sorrows of his own.

By 'eck, he'd been scared, had Alf Beckett. So scared, as he'd told them, that he could hardly keep his spade level when the time came to shovel the soil back on Matt Castle's coffin.

After finding no trace of the bogman.

'*They didn't find it?*' Milly Gill up on her feet in a flash, for all her weight. Alf shaking his head dumbly.

'What's it mean, Milly?' Frank's wife, Ethel, dazed.

'I don't know.' Milly's voice hoarse. 'I don't understand.'

'But it's good, isn't it?' the youngest of them, Susan, said. 'We dint want um to find it.'

'Of course it's not good,' Milly said. 'You don't suddenly get a miracle like that in the middle of a lot of bad. It's not the way of things. What frightens me: if he's not there, where in God's name is he?'

She broke off for a sip of tea. 'I'm sorry, Mr Dawber. I should've told you earlier. It were finding Ma. Knocked me back. Strange, though, isn't it? Everything's so terribly strange all of a sudden.'

When they'd gone, Ernie had telephoned the Hall himself. No answer. He'd go up there tomorrow, a visit long overdue.

'It must be deliberate, you know, all this,' Milly had said. 'An attack. Village is under attack.'

'Eh?'

'Like I said, things go in waves, Mr Dawber. Good times, bad times. We're used to that.'

'Aye . . .'

Ma had said, *What this is . . . it's a balancing act.*

'But this is an attack,' Milly said.

Ernie had been flummoxed for a minute. 'You mean the curate? Joel Beard?'

'Well, he's part of it. We let them disturb the Man in the Moss. We didn't do right by him. Now we've no protection. All sorts are coming in. Unsuitable people. Aye – people like him.'

'All my sources tell me,' Ernie said, 'that Joel's ambitions are being fuelled by the new Archdeacon, who fancies him summat rotten.'

'Joel Beard's gay?'

'Not as I know of, but the Archdeacon certainly is.' Ernie noticed old Sarah looking mystified. 'No, Joel Beard's incorruptible, I'm afraid. Whatever he's doing, he thinks he's doing it for the good of mankind.'

'They'll all be coming in soon,' Milly said despondently. 'Look at all them strangers at the brewery. Three of ours sacked, one of theirs brought in. Rationalization, they call it.

We don't see it till it's happened. Sometimes I think all we see is . . .'

'Shades of things. Aye.' Then Ernie had fallen silent, thinking of a woman in a black cloak at Matt's funeral. Moira Cairns, former singer with Matt Castle's Band.

Alf said, 'That bloke, Hall, he wouldn't accept it at first. Said he were convinced it were theer and if he had to dig all night he'd get it out.'

'Aye,' Milly said grimly. 'Happen somebody told him. Somebody wanted that grave dug up so *we'd* know there was nowt down there, apart from Matt. Oh, Christ. Oh, Mother, I don't like this.'

Alf sat down on the footstool Ernie would rest his feet on while thinking. 'This Hall, he even wanted to open Matt's coffin. Thought happen bogman were in theer.'

'God in heaven,' said Ernie.

'Joel Beard – he started kickin' up then. Wouldn't let um go near. Said they 'ad no permission except for t'take coffin out, like.'

'Quite right too,' Ernie said.

'Alf,' Milly said anxiously. 'The bottle. You did get the bottle in?'

'No.'

Milly Gill closed her eyes and clasped her hands together in anguish.

'Couldn't do it,' Alf said. 'Seemed no point.'

Milly said angrily, 'Did you even try?'

'Oh, aye.' Alf's hands had been dangling between his legs as he squatted on the stool. Ernie saw that both hands were shaking. 'I got lid off, no problem. Nobody were watching, thank Christ.'

They were all looking at him now. Alf Beckett, soaked to the skin, moustache gone limp, eyes so far back in his head that they weren't catching any light from Ernie's green-shaded desk lamp.

'Weren't theer!' Alf suddenly squealed. 'Matt weren't theer! Nowt in t'coffin but bloody soil!'

There'd been a silence you could've shovelled into buckets.

Ernie could still hear it now, as he stood looking over the graveyard, glittering with rain and the blue light of the Beacon of the Moss.

'And worms,' Alf had said finally, shaking on the little wooden footstool, staring at the floor. 'Handfuls of big, long worms.'

At the window, Ernie Dawber sighed very deeply.

Moira awoke with this awful sense of doom set around her like a block of ice.

She was hot and she was cold. She was sweating.

And she was whimpering, 'Mammy. Oh, mammy, please . . . don't let them.'

She'd dreamed a version of the truth. She was a little girl again, living with her daddy and her gran in the almost posh Glasgow suburb, catching the bus to school, Gran's warning shrilling in her ears, '. . . and you just be sure and keep away from the old railway, you hear?'

On account of the gypsies were back. The gypsies who still came every autumn to the old railway, caravans in a circle like covered wagons in a Western when the Indians were hostile.

Coming home from school, getting off the bus, the two darkskinned gypsy boys hanging round. 'Hey, you . . . Moira, is it? The Duchess wants tae see ye . . .'

'You leave me alone . . . Get lost, huh.'

'We're no gonny hurt ye . . .'

'You deaf? I said get lost.'

'Ye gonny come quietly, ye wee besom, or . . .'

Dissolve to interior. A treasure cave, with china and brass and gold. And the most beautiful, exotic woman you ever saw. 'My, you're quite a pretty child . . . Now, I have something . . . Think of it as a family heirloom . . . Tell no one until you're grown . . . Guard it with your life now!' This rich, glowing thing (which would be dull and grey to most people) heavy in your hand.

'You must remember this day, always. You *will* remember it, for you'll never be a wee girl again.'

And that night she had her first period.

Guard it with your life.

Moira sprang from her bed, snapped on the light. The guitar case stood where she'd left it, propped between a mahogany wardrobe and the wall. She dragged it out, lay it flat on the worn carpet, the strings making wild discordant protest as she threw back the lid, feeling for the felt-lined pocket, where might be stored such things as spare strings, plectrums, harmonicas.

And combs.

The door was tentatively opened, and Cathy appeared in rumpled pyjamas. 'What's wrong?'

Moira was shivering in a long T-shirt with Sylvester the Cat down the front.

'*Moira, what's wrong?*'

Moira's voice low and catarrhal, growly-rough, 'The broken window. Wasny just vandals.'

'You're cold.'

'Damn right I'm cold.'

'Come downstairs. I'll make some tea.'

Thrusting her hand again and again into the harmonica pocket. Nothing. She pulled out the guitar, laid it on the bed. Turned the case upside down. Picked up the guitar and shook it violently, and listened to nothing rattling inside.

When, slowly, she straightened up, her back was hurting. She felt arid, derelict. She felt old but inexperienced, incompetent. She felt like an old child.

Numbly, she reached behind the bedroom door for her cloak, to cover her thin, goosebumpy arms.

The cloak was not there. They'd taken that too.

Sam stumbled no more than twice. He knew his ground. Didn't need no light, although he had the powerful police torch wedged in his jacket pocket, case he needed to blind anybody.

It was pissing down. Sam wore his old fishing hat, pulled down, head into the rain.

Never been raining when these buggers'd been up here before. They wouldn't like that. Be an advantage for him, two years windblasted, rained on, snowed on.

There was a moon up there, somewhere buried in clouds, so the sky wasn't all that black. When his eyes had adjusted he could see the outline of the hill, and when he got halfway up it he could make out a couple of faint lights down on the edge of Bridelow.

But no lights above him now.

Moving round so he'd come to the circle from the bit of a hump behind it, he climbed higher, a lone blue-white disc floating into view, vague through the rain and mist. Beacon of the Moss.

Bloody church. Bugger all use they'd been, pair of um.

When he came to the bracken, Sam stopped, stayed very still, listening. Thought by now he'd have seen their lights, heard some of the chanting, whatever they did.

Sam went down on his haunches, the rain spattering the bracken. Quietly as he could, he snapped shut the breech of the gun, jammed the butt under his elbow and crouched there, waiting.

The rain coming down hard and cold, muffling the moor, seeping through his jacket. Might've brought his waterproof, except the thing would have squeaked when he moved. Have a hot bath when he got in, slug or two of whisky.

Sam hefted the twelve-bore. His mouth felt dry.

They were here. He could feel it. They were close.

Bastards. Stay aggressive. Aggression generated heat and aggression was better than fear.

Right. Sam moved in closer. He reckoned he was no more than twenty yards from the circle; couldn't see it yet. Just over this rise.

They were there; no question. But were they lying low, expecting him? Had they somehow heard him coming?

Sam pulled in a deep breath, drawing in rainwater and nearly choking. He stuck his finger under the trigger guard and went over the rise like a commando, stopping just the other side, legs splayed.

'All *right*, you fuckers!' he bawled. 'Nobody move!'

And nobody moved. Nothing. Not even a rabbit in the grass. Only the sound of the rain battering the bracken.

Holding the gun under his right arm, Sam fumbled for his

torch, clicked it on, swirled the beam around, finding one, two, three, four, five stubby stones, a circle of thumbs jabbing out of the moor.

'Where are you? Fucking come out! I'll give you your bloody Satan!'

Not frightened now. Bloody mad. *'Come on!'*

He thought about firing a shot into the bracken, case they were flattened out in there. But it wasn't likely, was it?

No, they'd gone. He switched off the torch, pushed it back in his pocket and did a 180-degree crouching turn, with the gun levelled.

Behind him, up on the moor, he glimpsed a fleeting white light. Didn't pause to think. Right. They're on the run. Move it.

Half-aware that he was departing from his own useless piece of moorland, Sam set off under a thickly clouded night sky with little light in it but an endless supply of black water; his jacket heavy with it and his faithful fishing hat, which once had been waterproof, now dripping round his ears like a mop rag.

He thought of his bed, and he thought of his kids and his wife, who he supposed he loved really, and he thought this was the stupidest bloody thing he'd do this year and maybe next, but . . .

. . . but them bastards were not going to get away with it, and that was that.

He tracked the light. Just one light, hazy, so probably a fair distance away. Heather under his boots now, waterlogged but better than the bracken, and the light was getting bigger; he was closing in, definitely, no question.

Two, three hundred yards distant, hard to be sure at night but the way the rain was coming down, crackling in the heather, there was no need to creep.

Sam strode vengefully onward.

Maybe it was due to forging on with his head down and his eyes slitted to keep the water out . . . maybe this was why Sam didn't realize for a few seconds that the light was actually coming, much more quickly, *towards him*.

A shapeless light. Bleary and steaming and coming at him through the rain . . . faster than a man could run.

'Hey . . . !' Sam stopped, gasping, then backed away, bewildered. His index finger tightened involuntarily and the gun went off, both barrels, and Sam stumbled, dropping it.

Something squelched and snagged around his ankle like a trap. He went down, caught hold of it – curved and hard – and realized, sickened, that he must have put his foot through the ribcage of a dead sheep.

Pulling at the foot, dragging the bones up with it, he saw the light was rising from the moor in front of him, misty and shimmering in the downpour.

And it seemed to him – soaked through, foot stuck in a sheep – that the light had a face, features forming and pulsing, a face veiled by a thin muslin curtain, the fabric sucked into a gaping mouth.

Sam's mouth was open too, now; he was screaming furiously into the rain, wrenching the torch from his pocket, thumbing numbly at its switch, until it spurted light, a brilliantly harsh directional beam making a white tunnel in the rain and mist, straight up into the face.

Where the tunnel of light ended suddenly. A beam designed to light up an object eighty yards away, and it shone as far as the rearing figure of light, a matter of four, five feet away.

Where it died. In the beam, the figure of light turned into a shadow, a figure of darkness and cold.

'No . . .' Sam Davis wanted chanting townies in robes and masks. He wanted sick, stupid people. Wanted to see them dancing, getting pissed wet through. Wanted to hear them praying to the fucking Devil, with their fire hissing and smouldering in the rain. Didn't want this. Didn't want it. No.

When the shadow stretched and the torch beam began to shrivel, as if all the light had been sucked out, leaving only a thinly shining disc at the end of the torch, Sam felt his bowels give way.

All the rage and aggression slithered out of him like the guts of a slaughtered pig, and the void they left behind was filled with a cold, immobilizing fear.

★

Lottie Castle came awake in swirling darkness.

Awakened by the cold air on her own body, exposed to the night, the sheets and blankets thrust away, her nightdress shed.

Her body was rolling about on the bed, drenched in sweat, arms and legs and stomach jerking and twitching with electricity, nipples rigid and hurting.

What's happening, what's *happening*?

She was ill. Her nervous system had finally rebelled against the months of agony and tension. She was sick, she was stricken. She needed help, she needed care. She should be taken away and cared for. She should not be alone like this, not here in this great shambling mausoleum.

Lottie began to pant with panic, feeling the twisted pillow sweat soaked under her neck as it arched and swayed. She couldn't see anything, not her body, not the walls, nor even the outline of the window behind the thin curtains.

It couldn't be darker. But it wasn't silent.

And fright formed a layer of frost around Lottie's heart as she became aware that every muscle in her body was throbbing to the shrill, sick whinny of the Pennine Pipes, high on the night.

CHAPTER IV

At 8 a.m., the Sunday sky hung low and glistened like the underside of a huge aircraft.

It didn't menace Joel Beard, God's warrior, skimming across the causeway, hands warm in his gauntlets, deep and holy thoughts protected inside his helmet, his leathers unzipped to expose the cross.

Nourished by little more than three hours' sleep at Chris and Chantal's place in Sheffield, he felt . . . well, reborn. Talked and prayed and cried and agonized until 2 a.m. Old chums, Chris and Chantal. Born Again brethren, still with the Church of the Angels of the New Advent. Still strong in their faith.

'I sometimes wish I'd never left.' Joel reaching out for reassurance.

'Why? It was your great mission, Joel – we all knew that, it's terrific – to carry our *commitment*, all our *certainty*, into the straight Church.'

'But it's just so . . . lonely, Chantal. I didn't realize how . . . or how corrupt. That there were places where the Church allowed the evil to *remain* – real evil – for a *quiet life*. A quiet life – is that what it's come to? I mean, tonight, going back to the church, after this fiasco with the grave, it was there for anyone to see. The ghastly light from the clock that isn't really a clock, and all the sneering gargoyles and the place over the door where this revolting *Sheelagh na gig* thing used to be . . . And you realize . . . it's *everywhere*. How many country churches have these pagan carvings, the Green Man, all kinds of devil-figures? Demons. Twisted demon faces, everywhere, grinning at you – it's *our* Church!'

Yes . . . yes . . . yes . . . the pieces of so-called character clinging to old churches like barnacles to a wreck, the very aspects of ancient churches that tourists found so picturesque . . . 'Oh, yes, I've always been fond of old churches.' As if this was some sanctified form of tourism, when really they were soaking up the satanic.

'What it means is that the Church has been sheltering this filth, pressed to its own bosom, for centuries. What everyone finds so appealing about these old parish churches are the things that should not be there. *Am I the only one to see this?*'

They'd brought him food and coffee. Made up a bed for him in the sitting room. Sat up half the night with him. Prayed with him in his agony.

'I've had visions. Dreams. I've been tested. All the time I'm there I'm tested. It tries to twist me. How can I handle this? I'm only one man.'

'No. You're not only one man, Joel. We're here. We're in this together. Tens of thousands of us. Listen, you were our emissary. You've seen and you've come back. We hear you, Joel. We hear you!'

Yes.

He slowed for the cobbles, bumping up the street towards the church, its stonework black with age and evil.

'Say the word, Joel. Just say the word. We're with you.'

'I'm tired. I've only been there a couple of days, and I'm exhausted.'

'You'll sleep tonight, Joel. We'll cover you with our prayers. You'll sleep well.'

And he had. Even if it was only for a few hours. He'd awoken refreshed and ready for his first morning worship at St Bride's, no prepared sermon in his pocket, no script, no text. He would stride into that pagan place and cleanse it with the strength of his faith. His sermon would be unrehearsed; it would almost be like . . . speaking in tongues.

Cathy said, 'You look really awful.'

'Thanks.'

'I've been trying to understand it,' Cathy said.

'Don't. It won't do you any good.'

Cathy pushed the fingers of both hands through her hair. 'I mean, they broke in here, in this really obvious, unsubtle way and they didn't take the telly or the video, or even your guitar . . . just this comb. Does it *look* valuable?'

Moira broke the end off a piece of toast and tried to eat it. 'Looks like one of those metal combs you buy for grooming dogs, only not so expensive and kind of corroded. Like a lot of stuff over a thousand years old, it looks like junk.'

'Look,' Cathy said reasonably. 'Is it not possible it just sort of slipped out when you were bringing your stuff in? Should I search the garden?'

Moira shook her head, gave up on the toast.

'Should we call the police?'

'No . . . No, this is . . . Only guy I ever took the thing out for was . . . Matt Castle, and I never wanted to. Look, I'm sorry. Your father's had a coronary, you've got this Joel Beard moving into your house and I'm rambling on about a damn comb. What time are you leaving?'

'This afternoon – sooner if I can.' Cathy said she'd wait for the cleaner, to tell her to put Joel Beard in the room Moira had slept in and to get Alf Beckett to fix the pantry window. Then she'd pack a couple of suitcases for her father and drop them off at The Poplars, this home for clapped-out clergy. And then think about going back to Oxford.

'What are you studying at Oxford?'

'This and that,' Cathy said. 'Where will you go? Home?'

Moira didn't answer. Where was home anyway? Glasgow? The folk circuit? She felt motiveless. The white-tiled rectory kitchen looked scuffed but sterile, like a derelict operating theatre. Getting to her feet was an effort. The view from the window, of graves, was depressing. The sky was like a crumpled undersheet, slightly soiled.

'I don't know what to do,' Moira said, and the words tasted like chewed-out gum. 'When something dreadful's going down and you don't know what it is or how you connect . . .'

'Why do you have to connect? You just came to a friend's funeral. You can go home.'

'Can I?'

'Just take it easy, that's all. You can't drive all the way to Scotland without sleep, you'll have an accident. Why don't you book in somewhere for a night?'

'I look that bad?'

'You look like somebody walked off with your soul,' Cathy said with this shockingly accurate perception.

Holy Communion, by tradition, was at 9, but by 9.15 nobody had arrived.

Joel went to pick up a stray twig in the aisle, a piece of the Autumn Cross the cleaners had missed. He took it outside, through the churchyard, and dropped it on the cobbles outside the lych-gate. Depositing it safely on secular ground.

On his return he glanced above the doorway, where the *Sheelagh na gig* had hung, half afraid the thing would have left some murky impression of itself on the stonework beneath, but there was only dust. He'd sent the vile plaque to be locked away in the school cellars until such time as a museum might be persuaded to take it.

He waited, in full vestments, in the vestry doorway, looking over the backs of empty pews towards the altar. Yesterday evening he'd had Beckett bring the wine up from the cellar room and then had the room locked, and he'd taken the key and hurled it away across the Moss.

The church clock gave a single chime for 9.30. When nobody came to Holy Communion. It didn't really surprise him. How could anyone here kneel at the altar, accepting the blood and body of Christ – knowing what they knew?

Knowing that stipends and student grants added up to bugger-all, she tried to give Cathy some money for the two nights' accommodation.

Cathy laughed. 'After you were burgled?'

Moira didn't think she looked too convinced about the comb. Understandably, perhaps.

They were standing by the front gate of the Rectory. She felt weak and washed out and cold without her cloak. The raw air hurt her cheeks and made her eyes water.

Cathy said, 'You look like you're coming down with something. Hope it's not this Taiwanese flu.'

Moira looked down the hill towards The Man I'th Moss. Either side of the cobbled street, the cottages looked rough and random, like rocks left by a landslide. She said goodbye to Cathy, kissed her on the cheek. Cathy's cheek felt hot and flushed, Moira's lips felt cracked, like a hag's. She was remembering the day the Duchess had given her the comb. How she'd stood before her wardrobe mirror and the old comb had stroked fluidly through her short hair, like an oar from a boat sailing with the tide, and the hair had seemed suddenly so lustrous and longing to be liberated, and that was when it began, the five-year war with her gran, who thought children should be seen and not heard and not even seen without their hair was neatly trimmed.

'. . . if that's what you were thinking,' Cathy was saying in a low voice.

'Huh?'

'I said . . .' raising her voice, '. . . it wasn't Dic.'

'What wasn't?'

'Whoever broke in. You've been indicating it was a personal thing. I mean, how many people would know about that comb anyway?'

'I didn't say anything.'

'You didn't have to. You thought it was Dic. Well, he wouldn't do a thing like that and anyway he . . . he's away teaching.'

'Where's he teach?'

'I'm not telling you,' Cathy said. Her pale eyes were glassy with tears. 'Please, Moira, it wasn't him. It wasn't.'

Moira thought, What's happening to her? What's happening to me? When she picked up her fancy, lightweight suitcase and her guitar case they both felt like they were full of bricks, and her hair felt lank and heavy, suffocating, like an iron mask, as she made her way over the cobbles to the church car park.

In the room directly over the Post Office, Milly Gill brought Willie Wagstaff tea in bed.

'Shouldn't've bothered,' Willie grumbled.

Milly said, 'I'm your mother now.'

'Don't say that.'

Balancing her own cup and saucer in one hand – the Mothers were supposed to be good at balancing things – she got gracefully back into bed with him. She was wearing an ankle-length floral nightdress tied over the breasts with an enormous pink bow. She looked like a giant cuddly rabbit, Willie thought, never more grateful for her than he had been this past night.

'I'm everybody's mother now,' Milly said miserably. 'Who else is there? Old Sarah?'

'Shit,' said Willie. 'I don't want it to be you.'

Milly shrugged her big shoulders and still kept the cup balanced on the saucer. 'I've lived opposite Ma for twenty years. I've studied her ways, best I can. I've been . . . well . . . almost a daughter-in-law.'

'I was always led to believe,' Willie said, 'that Ma was

supposed to announce her successor. "There's one as'll come after me." And it weren't you, luv, I'm sure of that.'

'No,' said Milly. 'But Ma thought she'd be around for another ten years yet. I know that for a fact. Ma thought she'd see in the Millennium.'

'Who can say owt like that? Who the hell knows how long they've got?'

'Ma knew.'

'Aye. But she were bloody wrong, though, weren't she?'

Milly squeezed her lips tight.

'Makes you wonder,' Willie said bitterly, 'if it's not a load of old garbage, all of it, the whole caboodle. Makes you bloody wonder.'

'I'll not have that from you, Little Man,' Milly chided, 'even if you are in grief. That's part of the problem. That sort of talk's like decay.'

'Realism, more like,' Willie said, his fingers waking up, stretching themselves, then batting the side of his teacup in a soft chinking rhythm.

'Drink your tea. You're upset. We all are. I just wish I could get some insight about the Man.'

'Aye,' Willie said. 'And where's bloody Matt? Don't bear thinking about, this lot. Makes me think I'll happen have Ma cremated.'

'You never will!' Milly sat up so suddenly she actually spilled some tea.

'Nowt as goes in yon churchyard ever bloody stays down,' Willie protested. 'Aye, all right. I mean, no, I'll not have her cremated, settle down. Will you talk to Moira?'

'I don't know,' Milly said. 'Wasn't there talk of her getting into bad magic some while back?'

'Aye, and she got out again,' Willie said. 'You met her last night. How did she seem to you?'

'All right, I suppose,' Milly said grudgingly. 'But you can't tell. I should be able to tell, I know, but . . . Oh, Willie . . .' Her shoulders started to shake and she collapsed against him. 'I'm out of me depth. Why did she have to die like that? Why did she leave us?'

349

'Because she had no choice,' said Willie, almost managing to get his arm all the way around her. 'It's no good us keep getting worked up about it. What's done is done.'

But his fingers didn't accept it; they set up a wild, uncontrollable rhythm on Milly's arm, just below the shoulder. *Ma was killed . . . Ma was killed . . . Ma was. . . .*

'Stop it!' Milly sobbed. 'I know. I bloody *know*! But what can we do?'

'Talk to Moira,' Willie said.

The church clock chimed, for 10 a.m.

'Be late for church,' Willie said.

'Not going,' Milly said. 'Means nowt to me now, that place. He's destroyed it. In one day.'

'Aye,' Willie said. 'And the well.'

'You *what*?'

'Him or somebody. I never told you, did I? I forgot – what with Ma and everything. Me and Moira went up there looking for Ma, and the well had been wrecked. Statue smashed, right bloody mess.'

Milly rolled away from him, mashing her face into her pillow in anguish.

'I'm sorry, lass,' Willie said. 'I just forgot.'

Sunday morning and the whole village was unaccountably silent. Moira walked to the church car park and loaded everything into the BMW.

It was coming up to 10.45, which probably explained the silence. This would be the time of the Sunday morning worship.

She walked across to the public notice board next to the lych-gate.

SUNDAY:
>   HOLY COMMUNION 9.0.
>   MORNING SERVICE 10.30
>   UNLESS OTHERWISE NOTIFIED

Life will go on. Unless otherwise notified.

She no longer felt observed. She wasn't worth it any more:

a thin, bewildered Scottish woman coming up to middle age and her hair turning white.

Everything was unreal. The clouds were like stone. Her head felt as if it was set in concrete. She needed to get away, to sleep and think and sleep.

And then, maybe, to find Dic, track the little shit down, deal with this thing.

She'd see Willie and then leave. She didn't feel like talking to him – or to anybody. But Willie was the other link; there were things Willie could tell her.

And he was a churchgoer, or always used to be. She was probably going to have to wait until they all came out.

She slipped through the lych-gate. It began to rain, quite powerfully. The gargoyles glared down at her. She moved quietly into the church porch, but there was no feeling of sanctuary here now. The sense of walking into the womb had gone with the *Sheelagh na gig*. It was merely shelter now, from the rain and nothing else.

Moira stopped, hearing a voice, a preacher's lilt, from the body of the church.

'. . . *Dearly beloved brethren, the Scripture moves us in sundry places to acknowledge and confess our manifold sins and wickedness, and that we should not dissemble nor cloak them before the face of Almighty God . . .*'

It was cold in the porch, colder than outside. She hugged herself.

And there was something wrong with that voice.

'. . . *Wherefore I pray and beseech you, as many as are here present, to accompany me with a pure heart and humble voice, unto the throne of the heavenly grace, saying after me . . .*'

The door to the church was closed. She would wait for a hymn and then go in.

'*Almighty and most merciful father, we have erred and strayed from thy ways like lost sheep . . .*

'*We have offended against thy holy laws . . .*

. . . and there is no health in us . . .'

Cathy had been right. She was coming down with something, a cold, flu. Wasn't just shock. She was shivering again. Should go back to the car, turn up the heater.

And then it came to her, what was wrong.

There should be *responses*. All these lines the minister was intoning were supposed to be repeated by the congregation. He was leaving the spaces.

'*To the glory of thy holy name . . .*'

But nobody was filling them. Not one person in this congregation was participating.

'*Amen.*'

Nobody repeated amen. He might have been talking to himself.

Holy Jesus.

'*We shall sing . . . Hymn number six hundred and three. "Round The Sacred City Gather."*'

She waited for the organ or the harmonium or whatever. That sound they always made, like they were drawing breath for the first chord.

There was silence. Only that hollow gasping ambience these places had. And then the singing began.

> '*Round the sacred city gather*
> *Egypt, Edom, Babylon.*
> *All the warring hosts of error,*
> *Sworn against her, move as one.*'

A strong and strident tenor. One voice.

This guy was singing on his own.

And that was very seriously eerie. Moira began to feel scared.

> '*Get thee, watchman, to thy rampart,*
> *Gird thee, warrior, with thy sword . . .*'

Trembling, she pushed gently at the swing-door, opening it just an inch, just enough to peer in . . . and let out the voice, louder.

> '*Watch to prayer lest while ye slumber,*
> *Stealthy foemen enter in . . .*'

She almost screamed. Let go of the door, letting it swing back into place with an audible *thunk* that seemed to echo from the rafters.

I'm away. I'm out of here.

As she ran out of the porch, into the bleakly battering rain, she could still see him, fully robed, statuesque but crazy-eyed, arms flung out, balanced there on the steps before the altar place, singing to all those empty pews. All those completely empty pews.

She walked back along the cobbles, to where she could see down the street as far as The Man I'th Moss.

Not a soul.

But the silence was more sorrowful than sinister, hung down like her confidence, somewhere around the soles of her shoes.

She looked along the blank windows of the cottages. The only sign of presence was some chimney smoking cheerlessly. Maybe all this had something to do with the sudden death of Ma Wagstaff. A big death.

And the stealing of the *Sheelagh*, the removal of the candles, the toppling of the Autumn Cross. Like they didn't feel welcome in the church any more, these bewildered people who no longer knew where they stood in relation to their God or their Goddess.

She turned into the alley which led to Willie's house and she hammered on his door, her body flattened against it. Come on, Willie, come *on*.

Deserted. She tried, a little nervously, a couple of raps on the front door of the curtained cottage at the top of the street where Ma Wagstaff had lived and died. Finally, she found an old envelope in the car and wrote a careful note, walking back down the hill to push it into Willie's letter-box.

Willie, I suppose we need to talk sometime about what we're going to do about Matt's music on the bog body. I don't suppose you feel any more like it than me at the moment, so I'll get in touch in a few weeks' time. I have to go home now . . .

Home. Where the hell was home?

Home is where the heart is, and I haven't got a heart, I haven't got a soul.

I have been burgled.

She stood in the street and looked from window to window, up and down, in search of life, and did not find it. But then, what the hell business was it of hers if the people of Bridelow wanted to lie low and boycott St Bride's and its unsympathetic new minister?

And turning on her heel, summoning energy from God knew where, she walked crisply, with determination, clop, clop, bloody clop on the cobbles, back up to the lych-gate and the car.

Almost falling into the arms of the Angel bloody Gabriel in white as he strode through the gate, his desperate solo service abandoned.

'I'm sorry,' he snapped. And then, with his hands still on her shoulders to separate their bodies, he began to stare at her. Seeing what she figured must be this sad, sluttish face, no make-up, hair awry, maybe a low and useless anger burning fitfully in the eyes.

His hands dropped away from her. His fists clenched. He began to tremble. He said, 'Who are you?' Golden curls tight to his head, Van Helsing-size cross looming out at her as his white linen chest swelled.

'*Who are you?*'

'Doesn't matter,' Moira said tonelessly. 'I'm leaving now.'

He blocked her path to the car, legs apart, this real big bastard in full Sunday vestments, humiliated in the sight of his God. Profile like Michelangelo's 'David' or something, a good head taller than she was and bellowing out, 'In the name of God . . . WHO ARE YOU, WOMAN?'

'Look, would you please get outa my way,' she said tiredly. Like she didn't have enough problems of her own.

'It's Sunday morning.' He was snarling now, through gritted teeth, rage choking him. 'And my church is empty. There is no congregation. No sidesmen. No organist.'

'Maybe it's just your sermons are crap,' Moira said. 'Look . . .'

He said, in a kind of wonder, backing off, his surplice billowing like a sail, 'You're *taunting* me.'

354

'Please . . .'

'I know who you are.' He was screaming it at the village. 'I know *what* you are!'

'Yeah, I'm sure you do, but would you please just get the hell out of my way?'

And knew, as she was saying it, that she shouldn't have used the word hell.

His face glowed red, bulging with blood.

She saw it coming but she didn't move. She took it from his massive open hand across the side of her face, from forehead to lower jaw. It would have hurt her less if she'd fallen, but she wouldn't do that. She stayed on her feet and she stared into his incandescent eyes.

Abruptly he spun away and strode back through the gate; she heard his footsteps crunching the gravel and then hitting the path. Finally she heard the church door crashing into place with an echo that didn't seem to fade but went on smashing from one side of her skull to the other as she moved unsteadily to her car.

CHAPTER V

Being Sunday, he could park in the street right outside and wait for some movement.

It was a dull, cold day in Glasgow, and a light gleamed out of the second floor of Kaufmann's scuffed tenement, which indicated Fiona had got it right. 'See, he often works on a Sunday, catching up with his VAT and stuff. But, Mungo, you tell him where you got this from I'm out the door; long as you realize that . . .'

Lucky he'd kept Fiona's home number. He owed the kid another dinner.

This Sunday morning convinced Macbeth that being a private investigator had to be about the most tedious occupation you could have outside of accountancy. The first hour, the car radio kept him amused with some bizarre soap-style drama about country folks in which nobody got killed, nobody seemed to be balling anyone else's spouse but two guys nearly came to blows in an argument about milk quotas. Only in Britain.

The second hour Macbeth fell to contemplating the futility of his life so far, the hopelessness of his quest, etc.

And then, just after 1 p.m., Malcolm Kaufmann came out of the building and spent some time locking the door behind him.

Kaufmann had on a long black overcoat over a pink polo shirt. Macbeth followed him to a crowded, chromium pub where Kaufmann ordered chicken sandwiches and, to Macbeth's dismay, sat down to eat them with two other guys he obviously knew.

Macbeth said shit a few times under his breath, ordered up a sandwich and a beer, sat as far away from Kaufmann as he could while still keeping him in view, and began to eat very slowly.

There were many women in the bar. Macbeth passed some time debating which one he'd make a move on if he hadn't been an investigator on a case. There was one in a dark blue velvet top who had to be wasted on the guy she was with; he was drinking too much and talking to other guys, she was on Diet Coke and probably only here to drive him home.

She had long, dark hair. Which, of course, was nothing at all to do with Macbeth picking her out, no way.

He was getting to thinking he *would* make a move, if only to make the woman's lunchtime more memorable, when Malcolm Kaufmann came swiftly to his feet, said a rapid goodbye to his pals and made an exit, weaving through the crowd with such practised agility that Macbeth almost lost him.

Couldn't be sure Kaufmann wouldn't get into a car or taxi and head off home, so he called after him in the street, and Kaufmann turned at the edge of the sidewalk and raised an eyebrow.

'Mr Macbeth. How very strange to see you.'

'We have to talk, Malcolm,' Macbeth said, trying to sound tough.

'Of course. We must arrange a time.'

'Like, now.'

'Oh, dear,' said Kaufmann. 'This sounds serious. What *can* the fair Moira have been up to?'

Macbeth walked right up to him. There was a cab idling not ten yards away, and he was taking no chances. 'We need to talk about a man,' he said, 'name of John Peveril Stanage.'

Ashton thought he should tell her himself, maybe test the water a bit. Also, he liked a pint around Sunday lunch when he got the time – unable, despite his divorce, to shake himself out of the feeling that Sunday lunchtime was special.

And he couldn't deny he was becoming quite fascinated by this place, a bit of old England only twenty miles from factories and warehouses, muck and grime and petty crime.

He drove across the Moss in his own vehicle, the Japanese sports car which was his first independent purchase with the bit of money left over after paying off his wife. A gesture. Ashton realized now that Gillian was probably right, it was bloody pathetic to buy a car like this at his age. Lump of flash tat, and he could never even remember what bloody make it was.

'Oh,' she said, looking up to serve him. 'It's you.'

No curiosity, he noticed. But then, if they *had* recovered anything from that grave, be all over the village, wouldn't it?

'Just thought I should officially inform you, Mrs Castle,' he said confidentially, across the bar, 'that we didn't find what we were looking for. I'm sorry we had to put you through this.'

There were no more than a dozen customers in The Man. None had looked up when he came in. Made a change; most pubs, they could smell a copper the same way he could scent illegal odours amidst tobacco smoke. Always somebody in a pub with something to hide, whether they'd been flogging nicked videos or their MOT was overdue.

'You have your job to do,' Lottie Castle said. She seemed weary, strained, nervy. Still looking good, though, he'd not been wrong about that. Tragedy suited some women. Something about recent widows, murder victims' wives especially;

357

stripped of all need for pretend-glamour, they acquired this harsh unadorned quality, the real woman showing through. Sometimes this excited him.

Must be getting warped, price of thirty years in the job.

'I had the feeling yesterday,' he said, 'that you thought we *might* have found something.'

She said, 'Wouldn't have surprised me either way. The bog body, wasn't it?'

'Somebody told you.' He wondered why she should make him think of murder victims' wives.

'Call it intuition,' Lottie said. 'What you having?'

'Pint of Black?'

'You'll be the only one,' she said.

When he raised an inquiring eyebrow she told him another bunch of jobs had gone, working men replaced by men in white coats brought in from Across the Moss. Rumours that Gannons might even close the brewery altogether, transferring all production of Bridelow Black to their new plant outside Matlock.

'Never,' said Ashton. 'How can you brew Bridelow Black in Matlock?'

'How can you brew German lager in Bradford?' said Lottie. 'People don't care any more. They've got the name, that's all that matters.'

'Thought the lads here were looking a bit cheesed.' Ashton nodded at the customers.

Lottie said, 'Gannons have apparently got tests showing the local spring water doesn't meet European standards of purity. Cost a substantial amount to decontaminate it. Added to which the equipment's antiquated. Where's the business sense in preserving some scruffy little dead-end village brewery on the wrong side of a bog?'

'Bloody tragic,' Ashton said, and meant it. 'Just about finish Bridelow, I reckon.'

'People've got to have work,' Lottie said. 'They'll move out. School'll shut. Church'll be operating every fourth Sunday. Still want this?'

'Better make it a bottle of Newcastle,' Ashton said. 'I wouldn't like to cause an incident.'

'The rot's already set in, I'm afraid,' Lottie said, pulling a bottle from under the bar. 'General store closed last week. Chip shop's on its last legs. How long the Post Office'll keep a sub-office here is anybody's guess.'

'Not good for you either. Dozen customers on a Sunday?'

'Be a few hikers in later,' Lottie said listlessly.

'I was told,' Ashton said smoothly, raising his voice a little, 'that some folk reckon all the bad luck that's befallen this village is due to that bogman being removed from the bog.'

Behind him, conversation slowed to a trickle.

'That's stupid,' Lottie said.

'You see, that's why we thought somebody might've had the idea of bringing it back to Bridelow. And where better to put it than at the bottom of an existing grave? Done it before, apparently, according to my source.'

'And who might that be?' asked Frank Manifold Snr from behind his half of draught Bass.

Ashton didn't turn round. 'Surprising as it may seem, Mrs Castle, I can understand it, the way people might be feeling. Problem is, we're talking about a prize specimen here. Experts from all over the world'd made plans to come and see it. It's almost unique. Invaluable. And so, you see, the police are under quite enormous pressure to get it back.'

There was no reaction from Lottie Castle. He was pretty sure now that she knew nothing.

'Well . . .' Ashton sucked some of the creamy froth from his Brown Ale. 'I suspect we're going to have to disrupt people's lives something terrible if we don't find it soon.'

By this time, the silence behind him sounded thick enough to sit on.

'Of course,' he said, 'if the bogman *was* in Bridelow or, say, back in the Moss . . . and somebody was to tell us, anonymously, precisely *where* . . . Then, personally, I can't see us taking it any further.'

Ashton felt that if he fell off his stool the silence would probably support him.

'Now, another piece of information that's come my way, Mrs Castle,' he went on, 'is that a certain gentleman has agreed to provide sufficient money to create a permanent exhibition centre for the bogman. And that this centre might well be established here in Bridelow, thus ensuring that the bogman remains in his old home. And that the hundreds of tourists who come to see him will spend a few bob in the village and perhaps have a drink or two in this very pub. Perfect solution, you ask me. What's your own feeling, Mrs Castle?'

'My feeling?' Lottie began to breathe hard. She started to straighten glasses. To steady her hands he thought.

'Yes,' he said. '*Your* feeling.'

Lottie didn't look at Ashton, nor past him at the other customers, just at the glasses.

'I hope you never find it,' she said in a voice like cardboard.

He said nothing.

'Caused enough upset.' She started to set up a line of upturned glasses on the bar top.

'And, you know . . . I don't really think I care what happens to this village. I'll tell you . . . *Mr Ashton* . . . Anybody wants this pub, they can have it. For a song. You fancy a pub? Supplement your police pension? Bit of country air?'

He could see tears in her eyes, hard as contact lenses.

'Views?' she said. 'Lovely views?'

'Mrs Castle,' he said. 'Please. I'm sorry.'

'Peat?' she shrieked, slicing a hand through the line of glasses so that the last two instantly smashed against the beer-pumps. 'You want peat? Peat, peat and more fucking peat?'

Cassock wind-whipped around his ankles, Joel stood looking down the village street, his back to the church notice board, his face soaked by rain and by sweat. The sweat of rage and humiliation.

He shouldn't have struck her. It was unpremeditated, but it was wrong. And yet, because the woman was an incarnation of evil, it was also rather unsatisfactory.

. . . *shalt not suffer a witch to live*. Until the arrival of the sound-drenching rain and wind, he'd contemplated delivering his sermon from the middle of the street, denouncing the denizens of Bridelow to their own front doors.

What a damning indictment of Hans Gruber this was. Hans who packed the church at least twice on Sundays, a stranger who had been accepted by the villagers as one of their own.

One of their own!

Hans turning a blind eye to the lone, black-clad figure in the churchyard before the funeral – the hooded figure clearly exuding not respect, nor monastic piety, but a heathen arrogance.

And Gruber, the quisling, screaming at him, Joel, '*Put it back!*' as he snatched the bottle from the coffin.

Joel looked down the street towards Mrs Wagstaff's cottage. Its curtains were drawn, upstairs and down. This was another deliberate insult: '*I'll come to church for Hans Gruber's services, but I'll not even leave my bed for yours.*'

He began to shake with rage. Obviously, after the incident at the well, the harridan had poisoned his name in Bridelow.

The street was deserted. He strode to the telephone kiosk in front of the Post Office. The answer was clear. If, as a Christian, he had been rejected by the resident congregation, then he must summon his own.

'Just get me out of here, get me across those hills and you can break down,' she said. 'Or do what the fuck you like.'

She had this sore throat now.

Cathy had been talking about some kind of Taiwanese flu. Whatever the hell that was, it sounded like the BMW had it too.

'I get across these hills,' Moira told the car, 'I'm gonny book you into a garage and me into a hotel that looks sufficiently anonymous, and then I think I'm gonny die quietly.'

Out of the corner of an eye – the BMW making noises like Kenny Savage in the lavatory the morning after – she'd seen the dead tree on the Moss again. It didn't move but it didn't look so obviously dead any more, a white light shining like a gemstone in its dragon's eye.

She'd closed her own eye, the eye which was letting in the

image of the tree, and this hurt. It was the side of her face Joel Beard had slapped. Maybe the eye had gone black; she couldn't bring herself to look in the mirror.

I can't *believe* he got away with that. Normally I'd have torn the bastard's balls off.

The BMW retched, like it was about to throw up its oil or something.

'Maybe you didn't understand me.' She gripped the wheel, shaking it. 'Maybe you only understand German. In which case you'll never know that if you don't get me to that hotel . . . I'm gonny trade you in, pal . . .'

In the driving-mirror, through the rain coming down like sheet metal now, she could see the spikes of St Bride's Church, maybe two miles back across the Moss.

'. . . and you'll be bought at auction by some loony, tear-arse seventeen-year-old looking for something fast and sleek to smash up and get killed in, yeah?'

Yelling at the car because she didn't want to hear anything else coming at her through the rain and the engine noise. Didn't want to touch the radio-cassette machine on account of there was a tape inside with the late Matt Castle on it, Matt coming seriously unspooled.

Her head ached and her hair felt heavy and greasy, just awful. She pushed it away from her eyes. The Moss had gone from the mirror, it was all scrubby moorland with dark, unfinished drystone walls like slippery piles of giant sheep-shit.

She came to a signpost and hesitated, then pointed the car at the place that sounded biggest and closest.

Buxton. Some kind of inland resort. With hotels. Listen, hen, what you do is you book into the biggest, plushest hotel they have there – like the Buxton Hilton or whatever – and you take several aspirins and you get a night's sleep and then you do some hard thinking. You *can* still think, OK, you *can* still function. The comb is merely an artefact invested with symbolism by you and by your mammy and however many other gypsies have had it in their gold-encrusted fists – but to claim it holds part of your spirit, your essence, your living consciousness is just ridiculous sentiment. Right?

Sure.

The Buxton road doubled back round the Moss to the Bridelow moors in a steep, curving climb, with what seemed like a sheer cliff going up on one side and another sheer cliff going down on the other with just a low drystone wall between Ms Moira Cairns and a long, long drop into what, being largely invisible through this sheeting rain, might just possibly be Hell.

Come on, come . . . *on*.

The BMW was faltering, its engine straining, like the big rubber band that powered it was down to its last strand.

Sweating, she flung the damn thing into third gear and then to second, revving like crazy.

Except the engine didn't.

It stalled.

In the middle of a twisting, narrow road, barely halfway up a hill that looked about three times as steep now the BMW wasn't actually ascending it any more, this bastard stalled.

'Oh, shit' – hauling on the handbrake – 'I'm really screwed this time.' First time any car had broken down on her for maybe ten years.

Also, coincidentally, the first time she'd had flu or whatever the hell it was in maybe five. And worst of all . . .

Worst of all the handbrake couldn't hold it.

Now, *look* – treading hard on the footbrake – it isn't that the cable's snapped or somebody's been messing with it, it's just stretched too far. Garage'll have it fixed in ten minutes.

What you have to do now, assuming you get to the bottom of this hill OK, you have to shove this car into the nearest grass verge then get out and walk through the filthy rain – without, OK, the benefit of a mac or an umbrella – until you come to a phone box or somebody's house.

Malcolm was always on at her to install a car phone. No way, she'd said. Malcolm said, When you want to be incommunicado you can just switch it off. She said, Incommunicado is my middle name, Malcolm, so where's the point in paying out fifty quid a month? But it's tax-deductible, Moira . . .

She wanted to scream with the terminal frustration of it: if

363

she managed by some miracle piece of driving to deposit this magnificent piece of Kraut technology at the bottom of this bottomless hill, that was when her *real* problems would begin.

She didn't scream; her throat was hurting too much already.

Gently, oh, so bloody gently, she let out the brake and allowed the car to slip backwards down the hill, which now seemed almost fucking *vertical* . . . twisting her neck round over her shoulder to try and track the curves in the streaming wet road. Not much to see anyway but rain and more rain. She was no damn good at this; never been able to master that mirror-image coordination you needed for reversing.

Thing is to stay well into the left, hard against the sheer cliff – OK, steepish hill, that's all it is – the one going up.

And, God, if I can make it to the bottom in one piece I will walk through this filthy, blinding rain for ten miles, hear me?

This roaring in her ears, it had to be the blood, flushed up there by concentration and the flu.

Letting out the brake, going backwards in short bursts, then jamming on, feeling the wheels lock and slide on the rain-filmed road. OK . . . easy . . . you're OK . . .

Just as long as nothing's coming up behind you!

Then, alarmingly, she was going backwards in a sudden spurt, and when she jammed on the brakes it made hardly any difference, and the breath locked in her swollen throat.

Staring, helpless, as the car's rear end suddenly slid out into the middle of the narrow carriageway, skimming over the central white line, the tail end skidding off, aiming itself at the crumbling stones, no more than two feet high, set up between the road and Hell.

'Oh, my . . . *Christ!*'

Scared now . . . like *really* scared, Moira tried to jam both feet on to the footbrake, straightening her legs out hard, heaving her back into the seat until it creaked, the pressure forcing her head back and around until she was staring out of the front windscreen, the car slipping back all the while.

It was like going up the down escalator in one of those panicking nightmares, only with the thing on at triple speed and a wall on one side and an endless, open liftshaft on the other.

And the brakes were definitely full on . . . and gripping . . . while the car was sliding backwards on the rain-slashed road, and Moira's ears were full of this dark turbulence, turning her vision black.

Black, black, black.

Black, it said.

BRIDELOW BLACK

. . . across the cab of the massive, dripping truck powering down on the BMW like some roaring prehistoric beast.

Oh . . .

. . . Christ . . .

. . . Get it into first gear . . . !

She was starting to scream out loud, plunging the clutch down, grinding the gearstick. But there was nowhere to go, the windscreen full of black, the truck's engine bellowing then scornfully clearing its throat as, with no great effort, it prodded the little car and Moira Cairns through the disintegrating drystone wall and the shimmering curtain of rain and over the road's edge into the endless mist beyond.

CHAPTER VI

The old clergyman across the lounge was deeply asleep in his chair, head back, mouth open.

'Lifetime of begging, you see,' Hans Gruber explained to his daughter. 'He's turned into an offertory box. You go over there, drop a pound coin in his trap and it'll suddenly snap shut. Clack! Another quid for the steeple fund.'

Hans smiled.

Cathy said, 'You're feeling better, then.'

'Until I stand up. And a stroll to the loo is like the London Marathon. But it's always better when you get out of hospital. Even coming here.'

The Poplars was a Georgian house with a modern, single-storey extension set amid flat, tidy, rain-daubed fields where Cheshire turned imperceptibly into Shropshire. There were all kinds of trees in the grounds except, Cathy had noted, actual poplars.

'Nearly as exciting as Leighton Buzzard,' Hans said. 'Makes me realize how much I love Bridelow. Its hardness, its drama.'

Cathy said nothing. Right now Bridelow had more drama than Beirut could handle.

Hans leaned forward in the chair, lowered his voice – even though, apart from the Rev. Offertory Box, they were alone in the lounge. 'I'm finished, aren't I, Cathy? I'm out.'

'Bollocks,' Cathy said, with less conviction than the choice of word implied.

Hans shook his head. 'Really wouldn't mind so much if it was going to be anybody but Joel. Thinks he's a New Christian, but he's actually more set in his ways than that poor old sod.'

Cathy squeezed his hand. 'You'll be back in no time.'

'No. I won't. Joel, you see . . . he's like one of those chaps in the old Westerns. Come to clean up Bridelow. Vocation. And Simon Fleming sees Joel as *his* vocation, and as long as he's archdeacon . . .'

'Joel might have bitten off more than he can chew, Pop. He put on his first Sunday service this morning, and nobody came.'

'You're not serious.' Cathy watched her father's mouth briefly wrestling with a most unChristian, spontaneous delight.

'Honest to God, Pop. A totally unorganized boycott. You know what Bridelow's like. Sort of communal consciousness. Apparently a few people started to drift along, got as far as the churchyard, realized the usual merry throng was not gathering as usual – and toddled off home. Does your heart good, doesn't it?'

'Certainly not,' said Hans, recovering his gravitas. 'It's actually quite stupid. Just get his back up, and then he'll do something silly. I don't mean go crying to Simon or the bishop or anyone, he's too arrogant. He'll want to sort it out himself. Damn.' Hans looked gloomy. 'That was really quite stupid of them. I can't believe Ma Wagstaff allowed it.'

'Ah.' Cathy lowered her eyes. Hans was wearing tartan bedroom slippers; somebody must have had a battle to get him into those.

'What's wrong?'

'I'm sorry, Pop,' Cathy swallowed. 'Something I haven't told you.'

Hans went very still.

The customers didn't stay long after Lottie had her flare-up. Led by tactful Frank Manifold Snr, they drank up smartish.

'What about you, pal?' Frank said to Inspector Ashton as he deposited his empty glass on the bar top. 'Haven't you got some traffic to direct or summat?'

Lottie said, 'It's OK, Frank. It's me. I'm overwrought.' She turned to Ashton. 'Have another. On the house.'

'No, this chap's right,' Ashton said. 'You've enough problems without me.'

'No,' Lottie said. 'I want your advice. I've had . . . intruders.'

When Joel arrived to take up residence at Bridelow Rectory, he found Alfred Beckett replacing a broken window in the pantry.

He stood over the little man. Perhaps, he ventured sarcastically, some explanation was due.

'Well.' Mr Beckett thumbed a line of putty into the window-frame. 'I *would* have been theer, like. Never missed a morning service in thirty year. Except in an emergency.'

Like this problem here. Which, as Mr Beard could see, he was at this moment putting right before it started raining again causing everything in the pantry to be soaked through and ruined.

'Mr Beckett,' Joel snarled. 'You are the *organist.*'

'Aye,' said Mr Beckett uncomfortably. 'That's true, like, but . . .'

'But nothing! You *knew* there would be no congregation. You knew no one would come.'

'Nay,' said Mr Beckett. 'Nobody come? Well, bugger me.'

Joel felt a red haze developing behind his eyes. He wondered briefly if the hypocritical little rat hadn't smashed the

Rectory window himself as a lame excuse for his non-appearance.

'Bloody vandals,' Mr Beckett said, expertly sliding in the new pane of glass. 'Never used to get no vandalism in this village, and that's a fact, Mr Beard.'

Joel stared at him.

You're nobbut a thick bloody vandal wi' no more brains than pig shit.

Joel snatched the ball of putty from the window-ledge and sent it with a splat to the pantry floor.

'Mrs Wagstaff,' he said icily. 'Mrs Wagstaff is behind all this.'

'Nay,' said Mr Beckett.

'Why can't *any* of you people tell the truth?' This devious little man was the only villager who derived a small income from the Church and doubtless could not afford to lose it. 'When I came past her cottage not half an hour ago, Mrs Wagstaff had not yet deigned to draw back her curtains. What, pray, is your interpretation of that?'

Mr Beckett scraped up his ball of putty.

''Cause she's bloody dead,' he said. 'Why d'you think?'

Feeling his holy rage congealing into a hideous mess, Joel walked numbly through the kitchen, down the hall and into Hans Gruber's study.

Had the old woman spoken to neighbours of her encounter yesterday by the pagan shrine? He remembered, with no pleasure now, the gratification he'd allowed himself to feel as he left her in the churchyard and watched her stumping angrily away. The feeling that he finally had her on the run.

Had she run hard enough to bring on a stroke? To give her a heart attack?

Was there a general feeling that he, Joel, was responsible for her death? And for Hans's collapse at the graveside? Was that what this was all about?

Joel sat bowed across Hans's desk, his fingers splayed over his eyes. Was this to be his reward for following his Christian instincts, reacting fiercely and publicly as God's blunt instrument?

Was it?

Joel lowered his hands and saw a tower of books before him on the desk. Amidst the acceptable, routine theology, he saw such inflammatory titles as *The Celtic Ray* . . . *The Virgin and the Goddess* . . . *Pagan Celtic Britain* . . . *The Celtic Creed* . . . *The Tenets of Witchcraft.* Evidence of Hans's attempts to rationalize this evil, the way one might seek to explain crime in terms of social deprivation.

When it came to basics, Joel had no great illusions about himself. He was not a scholarly man. His strength was . . . well, literally that. His strength.

He wasn't going to be able to work in this study. He'd lock the door on Hans's collection of pornography, just as he'd locked the dungeon door behind him. Ante-rooms to hell, both of them.

With a sweep of his arm which sent the books in the pile spinning to the four corners of the room, he experienced again the sublime grace of movement he'd felt as he leaned from the ladder and slashed the cord which bound the Autumn Cross.

Bound to be casualties. But he would go on. He must.

She led him out of the back door to an old barn of a place only a few yards from the main building. Unlocked the door.

'How did they get in?' Ashton asked.

'I don't know.'

'No windows forced?'

Lottie shook her head, bewildered.

'What's been taken?'

Lottie still shaking her head. 'Nothing. Nothing I can see.'

Ashton looked hard at her and let her see that he was looking. Was this a wind-up? Or was there a mental problem?

He didn't think so. She was standing in the middle of the barn, hands on hips, the sleeves of a bulky Scandinavian-type cardigan pushed up to the elbows.

She had firm, strong arms.

'Mrs Castle . . .'

'I know. You think I'm off my head.'

'I didn't say anything . . .'

'Well, me too, Mr Ashton. I think I must be cracking up.'

'Gary,' he said. 'And I'd like to help. If I can.'

'You not got better things to do? One of the lads was saying there's a big police hunt up on the moors.'

'That's South Yorkshire's,' Ashton said. 'Our manor finishes just this side of the Moss. We'll help if we're asked, but we've not been asked. I'm off-duty anyroad.'

'Who're they looking for?'

'Farmer. Don't ask me his name. Went off after some trespassers last night and didn't come back. Had his shotgun with him, that's the worry. Why? You think it might be the same hooligans broke in here?'

Lottie shook her head again. It wasn't so much a denial, Ashton thought, as an attempt to shake something out.

'But then,' he said gently, 'there wasn't a break-in here, was there, Mrs Castle?'

'There had to've been,' Lottie said, quietly insistent. 'There's no other explanation.'

Ashton sat down on the edge of a dusty old couch next to a black thing that made him think of a dead animal, all skin and bones. He saw Mrs Castle glance at it briefly and recoil slightly.

'What's this?' Ashton was curious. There was a flute bit sticking out of it, with airholes.

'That?' Lottie said. 'That's the Pennine Pipes, Mr Ashton. Primitive kind of bagpipe. My husband's instrument. Woke me . . .' She hesitated. 'Woke me up, Mr Ashton. About two o'clock this morning.'

'What did?'

'Them. The pipes. Somebody down here playing the pipes. You think I could mistake that noise after living with it twenty-odd years?'

Ashton experienced a sensation like the tip of a brittle fingernail stroking the nape of his neck.

He said, 'What did you do?'

'Well, I didn't go down,' said Lottie. 'That's for sure.'

'Perhaps somebody wanted to frighten you, Mrs Castle.'

She said, 'When you got Matt's coffin out, did you . . . ?'

'No,' Ashton said. 'We had no reason and no right to disturb your husband.'

She said, 'Do you mind if we go outside?'

'After you,' Ashton said. He pulled the wooden door into place behind them, quite thankful to be out of there himself. Place was like a mausoleum without a tomb.

Lottie Castle sniffed and one side of her mouth twitched in latent self-contempt. 'You know what it's like when you're alone. Or maybe you don't.'

'Yes,' he said. 'I do.'

'Things that would otherwise seem totally crazy go through your head.'

'True.'

'And with you lot digging up his grave, I thought . . . Well, it was as if he was . . .'

Lottie Castle thrust open the kitchen door. Ashton followed her in, quietly shut the door behind them and stood with his back to it.

'I didn't catch that,' he said. 'As if he was what?'

'As if you'd let him out,' Lottie Castle said in a parched monotone, looking down at the flags. 'And he'd come back. For his pipes.'

She turned her back on Gary Ashton and walked over to the stove.

'Listen,' Ashton said, wondering if he was cracking up. 'This piping. Was it, like – I'm sorry – any particular tune?'

'No,' she said. 'No particular tune.' She was silent a moment, then she said, 'When Matt used to get the pipes out, he'd flex the bag a bit, get the air circulating, make all these puffing, wheezing noises and then a few trills up and down the scale. Warming up, you know? Getting started.'

Lottie placed both palms on the hot-plate covers. 'Matt Castle getting warmed up,' she said. 'That was what I thought I heard.'

Hans moistened his lips with his tongue. Cathy got up. 'I'll fetch you a cup of tea.'

'No . . .' Her father moved in his chair, winced. 'No, it's all right. I . . .' He looked quietly down at his knees for a while. Then he said, 'They were talking about a plastic one. Back at the hospital, you know. I said to leave it a while. I said I was seeing a very experienced private therapist.'

Cathy smiled. 'Wasn't working though, was it?'

'No.' Hans sighed. 'She was talking, the last time I saw her, about something getting in and sapping her powers. Perhaps it was intimations of mortality. That was her way of expressing it – that she was coming to the end of her useful life. And maybe she could see the end, as well, of over a thousand years of tradition. And *I'm* wondering, too, if this is going to be the end of it.'

Cathy said nothing.

Hans said, 'Bit of a rag bag, the Mothers, aren't they? Now? Nobody to really take over. Nobody with Ma's authority. Milly Gill? I don't think so, do you? Nice woman, but too soft – in the nicest way, of course. And the rest of the village – well, modern times, modern attitudes. General loss of spirituality. I blame the eighties, Mrs Thatcher, all that greed, all that materialism. Some of it had to find its way across the Moss sooner or later.'

'It's still a good place, Pop, in essence.'

'Yes . . . as long as that essence remains. I'm very much afraid the essence has gone.'

Cathy thought they'd never come as close as this to discussing it. He'd always been too busy organizing things, fudging the issue. The issue being that the parish priest in Bridelow must become partially blind and partially deaf. This also was a tradition.

In the old days – which, in this instance, meant as recently as last year – it wasn't possible to get to Bridelow Brewery without passing the Hall.

The Hall was built on a slight incline, with heathery rock gardens. Ernie Dawber could remember when the old horse-drawn beer drays used to follow the semi-circular route which took them under the drawing-room window for the children to admire. The Horridges were always proud of their shire horses; the stable block had been a very fine building indeed, with a Victorian pagoda roof.

Now it was decaying amid twisted trees grown from hedges long untrimmed. No horses any more; it was heavy trucks and different entrances, no obvious link between the brewery and the Hall. Liz Horridge, Ernie thought, must be feeling a bit bereft. He shouldn't have left it so long. There was no excuse.

The Hall itself, to be honest, wasn't looking too good either. Big holes in the rendering, gardens a mess. Arthur Horridge would have a fit. Ernie was merely saddened at another symptom of the Change.

Gettin' a bit whimsy, Ernest?

Leave me alone, Ma. Give me a break, eh?

Fifty yards below the house, the drive went into a fork, the wider road leading to the brewery.

'By 'eck,' Ernie Dawber said, stopping to look.

For suddenly the brewery was more impressive than the Hall.

In the past it had always been discreet, concealed by big old trees. But now some of the biggest had been felled to give the Victorian industrial tower block more prominence.

Gannons's doing? Had they made out a case for the brewery as an historic building and got a Government grant to tart it up?

Bloody ironic, eh? They sack half the workforce, talk about shifting the operation to Matlock, but if there's any money going for restoration they'll have it. Happen turn it into a museum.

They'd even finished off repairing the old pulley system for the malt store, briefly abandoned last . . . May, was it? How soon we forget . . . when a rope had snapped and Andy Hodgson had fallen to his death. Accidental death – official coroner's verdict. No blame attached.

Don't want to put a damper on things, Ernest, but summat's not right.

Go away, Ma.

He had to stop this. Snatches of Ma Wagstaff had been bobbing up and down in his brain ever since he'd awakened,

373

like an old tune that'd come from nowhere but you couldn't get rid of it. Reminding him of his commitment. *Get him back.*

And if I don't? If I fail? What then?

He could only think of one answer to that. One he'd thought of before, and it had made him laugh, and now it didn't.

Well. Nagged from beyond the grave. You wouldn't credit it. Ernie straightened his hat, girded up his gaberdine, turned his back on the brewery, which suddenly offended him, and hurried up to the Hall.

He pressed the bell-push and heard the chimes echo, as if from room to room within the house.

Even as he pressed again, he knew there was nobody inside.

So she doesn't come down to the village any more . . . Well, she's always been a bit aloof. Not a local woman. Only to be expected with this bad feeling about the brewery. She supposed to subject herself to that when it wasn't her fault?

But you, Ernest . . . Nowt to stop you going to see her.

Ma . . .

. . . *She were in a shocking state, banging her fists on Ma's door* – '*please, please*', *like this* . . .

'Please, Liz.' Ernie, sheltering under the overhanging porch as the rain came harder. 'Answer the door, eh?'

He remembered attending her wedding back in . . . 1957, would it be? This high-born, high-breasted Cheshire beauty, niece of Lord Benfold, on the arm of a grinning Arthur Horridge, boisterous with pride – free ale all round that night in The Man. 'Sturdy lass,' Ma Wagstaff had observed (they were already calling her Ma back in the 'fifties). 'Never pegged her own washing out, I'll bet.'

Ma talking then as if Eliza Horridge were nowt to do with her. As if there was no secret between them.

It was years before Ernie had put two and two together.

. . . *put me hand on her shoulder and she nearly had hysterics.* '*I want Ma, I want Ma . . .*'

Oh, Lord, Liz. Answer the bloody door. Please.

*

Hans said, 'I realized a long time ago where the essence was. That a real centre of spirituality was what was important – that what *kind* of spirituality it was was, to a large extent, irrelevant.'

'You say you realized . . .' Cathy said slowly. 'Did that come in a blinding flash, or were you . . . tutored, perhaps?'

'Both. They started work on your mother to begin with. Through the well-dressing. She was always interested in flowers.' Hans laughed painfully. 'Can you imagine? Doing it through something as utterly innocuous as *flower arranging*? Millicent Gill it was taught her – only a kid at the time, but she'd been born into it. Flowers. Petal pictures. Pretty.'

'Yes,' Cathy said.

'Then flowers in the church. Nothing strange about that But in this kind of quantity? Used to look like Kew Gardens in August.'

'I remember.'

'And the candles. Coloured candles. And the statues. I remembered commenting to the bishop – old Tom Warrender in those days, canny old devil – about the unexpected Anglo-Catholic flavour. "But they still turn up in force on a Sunday, do they, Hans?" he said. And then he patted me on the shoulder, as if to say, don't knock it when you're winning. Of course, even then I knew we weren't talking about Anglo-Catholicism – not in the normal sense, anyway. And then, when we'd been here a few years, your mother went into hospital to have you and Barney . . .'

'Which reminds me, Pop, Barney called from Brussels – he'll be over to see you before the end of the week.'

'No need. Tell him . . .'

'There's no telling him anything, you know that. Go on . . . When Mum was in hospital . . .'

'I was approached by Alf Beckett, Frank Manifold and Willie Wagstaff. They said the house was no place to bring babies into, far too dismal and shabby. Give them a couple of days and they and a few of the other lads would redecorate the place top to bottom. Be a nice surprise for your mother – welcome-home present from the village.'

'I didn't know about that.'

'Of course you didn't. Anyway, I said it was very good of them and everything, but the mess . . . Don't you worry about that, Vicar, they said. You won't even have to see it until it's done. We've arranged accommodation for you.'

'Ah,' said Cathy.

'They'd installed a bed in the little cellar under the church,' said Hans. 'The place had been aired. Chemical toilet in the passage. Washbowl, kettle, all mod cons. Of course, I knew I was being set up, but what could I do?'

Hans paused. 'I spent . . . two nights down there.'

'And?' Cathy discovered she was leaning forward, gripping the leatherette arms of her chair.

'And what? Don't expect me to tell you what happened. I came out, to put it mildly, a rather more thoughtful sort of chap than when I went in. Can't explain it. I think it was a test. I think I passed. I hope I passed.'

'But you didn't want Joel sleeping down there?'

'God, no. The difference being that I'd been there a few years by then – I was halfway to accepting certain aspects of Bridelow. They knew that. Somebody took a decision. That the vicar should be . . . presented. To Her. I think . . . I think if I hadn't been ready, if I hadn't been considered sufficiently . . . what? Tolerant, I suppose. Open-minded . . . then probably nothing would have happened. Probably nothing would have happened with Joel. But I didn't want him down there. I don't want to sound superior or anything, but that boy could spend fifty years in Bridelow and still not be ready.'

Cathy said, realizing this wasn't going to do much for her father's recovery, 'Suppose . . . suppose he *did* spend a night down there. And he was already worked up after that business at the funeral. And he stirred something up. Brought something on. Suppose he was tested – and failed?'

'Well,' Hans said. 'There's an old story Ernie Dawber once told me. About what really happened when that bishop spent a night down there in eighteen whenever. They say he went totally bloody bonkers.'

Hans patted Cathy's hand. 'But then,' he said, 'wouldn't have been much of a story at all if he hadn't, would it?'

There was a loud, urgent rapping on Willie's front door, which could only be Milly.

Who knew the door was hardly ever locked – certainly not when Willie was at home – but who'd knock anyway, for emphasis, when it was something important.

Willie had been re-reading Moira's note. It had been a relief at first; didn't think he could really apply himself to Matt's bogman music, not right now, not the way he was feeling.

But what did she mean, *I have to go home*? Why did she *have* to go so quickly she couldn't wait to say ta-ra?

'Aye,' he shouted. 'Come in, lass.'

'Willie.' She stood panting in the doorway, her flowery frock dark-spotted with rain.

'I were just going to make some toast for me tea. You want a slice?'

'Willie,' she said. 'Come and see this.'

''s up?'

'You've got to see it,' Milly gasped.

'It's pissing down. I'll need me mac.'

'Never mind that!' She pulled him out of the door, dragged him up the entry and into the street. 'Look.'

'It's a bus,' said Willie.

A big green single-decker was jammed into the top of the street outside the Post Office. Thin rivers of rain were running down the cobbles around its back wheels. On the back of the bus it said, *Hattersley's Travel, Sheffield*.

'Coach tour?' Willie said, puzzled. Coaches would come to Bridelow quite often in the old days. In summer, admittedly, not on a wet Sunday at the end of October.

'Look,' Milly said.

About forty people had alighted from the coach, mostly young people in jeans and bright anoraks. A small circle had gathered around the unmistakable, golden-topped figure of Joel

Beard. They stepped forward in turn, men and women, to hug him.

'Praise God!' Willie heard. As he and Milly moved further up the street, he heard the phrase repeated several times.

Willie looked at Milly through the lashing rain. 'What the bloody hell's this?'

Milly nodded towards two young men unwrapping a long, white banner. Gothic golden lettering explained everything – to Milly, anyway.

'Who the bloody hell,' said Willie, 'are the Angels of the New Advent?'

'They've got a church in Sheffield. Me cousin's daughter nearly became one about a year ago. They're fundamentalist Born Again Christians, Willie. They see the world as one big battleground, God versus Satan.'

'Like the World Cup?'

'It's not funny, Willie.'

'This is what you've dragged me out to see? A bloody Bible-punchers' outing?'

'You're not getting this, are you, Willie luv?' Milly's greying hair was streaming; her dress was soaked through. Willie noticed with a quick stirring of untimely excitement that she wasn't wearing a bra.

'What I'm saying, if you'll listen,' Milly hissed, 'is that they're God. *And we're Satan.*'

A short time later, Milly heard a small commotion and looked out of the Post Office window to see a group of people assembled in the centre of the street between the lych-gate and the Rectory.

One of them was Joel Beard. Someone held up the trumpet end of a loud-hailer and handed a plastic microphone to Joel.

'GOD IS HERE,' he blasted. 'GOD IS HERE IN BRIDE-LOW. YOU ARE ALL INVITED TO A SPECIAL SERVICE AT EIGHT P.M. TO REDEDICATE THE CHURCH IN HIS NAME.'

Milly felt a terrible trepidation. Obviously none of the villagers would turn up. But what effect was it going to have, all these no doubt well-meaning but dangerously misguided people stirring up the atmosphere?

'THIS IS AN OFFICIAL ANNOUNCEMENT. BRIDE-LOW HAS TONIGHT BEEN FORMALLY REPOSSESSED BY THE LORD.'

'Heathens out!' someone yelled.

'HEATHENS OUT!'

PART EIGHT

JOHN PEVERIL STANAGE

From *Dawber's* Secret *Book of Bridelow* (unpublished):

MEN

WHAT PART HAVE men really played in the history of Bridelow?

Not perhaps, if we are honest, a distinguished one, except for our late friend the Man in the Moss, who – we are told – gave his life for our community.

We have, I suppose, dealt with the more mundane elements: the business matters, employment, the sustenance of a measure of wealth – enough, anyway, to keep our heads above the Moss.

And we – that is, male members of the Dawber family – have acted as local chroniclers. Albeit discreet ones, for I am sure that if this present manuscript were ever to see the light of day our so-far hereditary function as the compilers of the dull but worthy Book of Bridelow would cease immediately to be a tolerated local tradition.

But as for the important things in life (and death), well, all that traditionally is the preserve of the women, and as far as most of the men have been concerned they are welcome to it. We are, in the modern parlance, a Goddess-orientated society, although the role of the Christian deity is more than politely acknowledged. (Thank You, Mother – and You too, Sir, is one of our phrases.)

However, men being men, there have been occasional attempts to disrupt the arrangement. And when a man is possessed of abilities beyond the normal and a craving for more, then, I am afraid, the repercussions may be tragic and long-lasting.

CHAPTER I

Macbeth pumped money into the coinbox, all the loose change he had.

A young female voice said, 'This is . . . hang on, I can't make it out . . . two four oh six, I think. I don't live here, I've just picked up the phone.'

Macbeth could hear a lot of people talking excitedly in the background. He said, 'Can I, uh, speak with Moira? Moira Cairns?'

'This is Bridelow Rectory.'

'Sure. I need to speak with Moira. Can you get her to the phone?'

'I'm sorry, I'm pretty sure we haven't got a Moira. We've got a Maureen. Would you like to speak to her?'

The glass of the phone booth was streaked with rain. It was going dark; all he could see were the lights of a fast-food joint over the road. Didn't even know which town this was. He'd just kept stopping at phones, ringing this number. First time anyone had answered.

The young female voice asked, 'Are you still there?'

'Yeah, yeah, I'm still here. Listen, ask around, willya? Moira Cairns, I . . . Chrissake, she *has* to be there.'

There was a long pause, then, 'I'm sorry,' the female voice said coldly. 'Your speech is profane. Goodbye.'

And hung up on him.

Hung up the fucking phone, just like that!

Macbeth raced out of the booth and across the street, bought a burger with a ten-pound note and got plenty of change. The burger was disgusting; after two bites he tossed it into a waste bin and took his change back to feed the phone.

He wasn't about to waste this number, all the time it had taken to obtain it. The call to the Earl, the waiting around for Malcolm Kaufmann, the blackmail.

'I called the Earl this morning, Malcolm. You remember the Earl? The man who asked if this Rory McBain, who was booked to entertain his guests, could perhaps be replaced by Moira Cairns? This coming back to you, Malcolm? The way the Earl was prepared to, uh, oil the wheels?'

This last item was a lucky guess, the Earl having denied any suggestion of making it worth Kaufmann's while.

None the less, it had gone in like a harpoon, spearing Malcolm to the back of his executive swivel chair.

'See, the longer it takes for me to find her, Malcolm, the more likely it seems I'm gonna have to reveal to Moira the extent of your co-operation in this, uh, small deception.'

At which Malcolm had pursed his lips and written upon his telephone memo pad a phone number. All he had. He swore it. Moira had phoned yesterday, left this emergency-only contact number, along with a message: no gigs until further notice.

'She done this kind of thing before?'

'All too often, Mr Macbeth.'

On top of the coinbox, Macbeth had three pounds and a couple of fifty-pence coins. He dialled again.

This time it was a different voice, male.

Macbeth said, 'Who's that?'

'This is Chris.'

'Chris,' Macbeth said. 'Right. Listen, Chris, I need to speak with Moira. Moira Cairns. You know her?'

'Oh,' said Chris. 'You rang a few minutes ago. You were abusive, apparently.'

'Je—!' Macbeth tightened his grip on the phone, calmed

himself. 'I'm . . . sorry. Just I was in a hurry. It's kind of urgent, Chris. Please?'

'Look,' Chris said. 'We're strangers here. Why don't you speak to Joel? Just hang on.'

Macbeth fed a fifty-pence coin into the phone. Presently a different guy came on. 'This is the Reverend Joel Beard. Who am I speaking to?'

'Uh, my name is Macbeth. I was told I could get Moira Cairns on this number, but nobody seems to know her, so maybe if I describe her. She's very beautiful, has this dark hair with . . .'

'With a vein of white,' the voice enunciated, slowly and heavily.

Macbeth breathed out. 'Well, thank Christ, I was beginning to think I'd been fed a bunch of . . . what?'

'I said, what did you say your name was?'

'Macbeth. That's M . . . A . . . C . . .'

'Ah. That's an assumed name, I suppose. I'd heard you people liked to give yourselves the names of famously evil characters as a way of investing yourselves with their – what shall we call it – "unholy glamour".'

'Huh . . . ? Listen, friend, I don't have time for a debate, but it's now widely recognized that the famously evil, as you call him, Macbeth was in fact seriously misrepresented by Shakespeare for political reasons and, uh, maybe to improve the storyline. He . . .' – shoving in a pound coin – 'Jeez, what am I doing? I don't want to get into this kind of shit. All I want is to talk with Moira Cairns, is that too much to ask? What the fuck kind of show you running there?'

A silence. Clearly the guy had won himself an attentive audience.

'The woman you're seeking' – the voice clipped and cold – 'has been driven away. As' – the voice rose – 'will be all of your kind. You can inform your disgusting friends that, as from this evening, the village of Bridelow, erstwhile seat of Satan, has been officially repossessed . . . by Almighty God!'

'YEEEESSSS!' The background swelled, the phone obviously held aloft to capture it, a whole bunch of people in unison. 'PRAISE GOD!'

And they hung up.

Macbeth stood in the rainwashed booth, cradling the phone in both hands.

'Jesus Christ,' he said.

Back in his hire-car, windows all steamed-up, he slumped against the head-rest.

Is this real?

I mean, *is* it?

The Duchess had indicated Moira had gone to this North of England village for the purpose of laying to rest the spirit of her old friend Matt Castle, whichever way you wanted to take that.

Whatever it meant, it had clearly left the local clergy profoundly offended.

But while Macbeth's knowledge of Northern English clerical procedure was admittedly limited, the manner of response from the guy calling himself The Reverend Joe-whoever and what sounded like his backing group was, to say the least, kind of bizarre.

Wherever she goes, that young woman, she's bound to be touched with madness.

Yeah, yeah, can't say I wasn't warned.

But there is a point at which you actually get to questioning yourself about how much is real. Or to what extent you are permitting yourself to be absorbed into someone else's fantasy.

But not unwillingly, surely?

Well, no. Not yet.

Truth is, it's kind of stimulating.

The time was 5.15. Macbeth left the car and returned to the diner across the street, on the basis that one sure way of restoring a sense of total reality would be another attempt to consume a greasy quarter-pound shitburger and double fries.

About an hour ago, before leaving Glasgow, he'd found a Sunday-opening bookshop where he bought a road atlas and a paperback.

He laid the paperback on his table next to the shitburger.

The cover showed a huge cavern full of stalactites and stalagmites. The angle of vision was roof-level, and way down in the left-hand corner was a small kid with a flashlight.

The book was called *Blue John's Way*. From inside the title page Macbeth learned it had been first published some thirty years ago, and this was apparently the seventeenth paperback impression.

On the inside cover, it said,

THE AUTHOR

John Peveril Stanage has emerged as one of the half-dozen best-loved children's writers of the twentieth century.

Basing his compelling stories on the history, myths and legends of the Peak District and the Southern Pennines, of which he has an unrivalled knowledge, he has ensnared the imagination of millions of young readers the world over.

Mr Stanage's work has been translated into more than fifteen languages and won him countless awards.

Not over-enlightening, and there was no picture. But then, Macbeth thought, the guy didn't exactly look like a favourite uncle; maybe the publishers figured he'd scare the readers.

But then again, that was obviously part of his intention, if *Blue John's Way* was typical.

A quote on the back from some literary asshole on the London *Guardian* said the book conveyed a powerful sense of adolescent alienation.

The bookseller had told Macbeth a growing number of adults were hooked on Stanage's stories for kids; apparently he was becoming a minor cult-figure, like C. S. Lewis.

'In America, I'm told,' the bookseller said, 'his books aren't even marketed as children's fiction any more.'

'That so?' Macbeth, whose reading rarely extended beyond possible mini-series material, had never previously heard of Stanage. 'He live down in – where is it? – the English Peak District?'

'He's publishing under false pretences if he isn't.'

'You got any idea precisely where?'

A shrug. Negative.

This morning, under pressure, the Earl had admitted to Macbeth that he personally had been unfamiliar with the work of Moira Cairns until a member of The Celtic Bond steering committee had drawn his attention to it. Yes, all right, *forcefully* drawn his attention . . .

'*So it was Stanage who was insistent Moira should be hired for this particular occasion?*'

'*He was keen, yes . . .*'

'*How keen?*'

'*He's a great admirer of her work.*'

'*Tell me, Earl, why is Mr Stanage on your steering committee?*'

'*Well . . . because he's a great authority on an aspect of Celtic studies – the English element – which is often neglected. And because he's . . . he's very influential.*'

And also rich, Macbeth thought. That above all. The crucial factor. The reason you're taking all this shit from me, Earl, the reason you deigned to accept this call at all.

Macbeth propped the paperback against a sauce bottle and re-read the blurb.

> John Clough is an unhappy boy growing up fatherless in a remote village in the Northern hills.
>
> He has never been able to get on with his mother or his sisters who live in a strange world of their own, from which John, as the only male, is excluded. At weekends, he spends most of his time alone in the spectacular limestone caverns near his home, where he forms a special bond with the Spirits of the Deep. With the Spirits' help, John discovers the dark secret his mother has been hiding – and sets out to find his true identity.

Macbeth went back to the counter, ordered up a black coffee and opened up the road-atlas.

'How long you figure it would take me to get to . . . uh . . . Manchester, England?'

'Never been, pal. Five hours? 'Pends how fast you drive.'

*

Last night Macbeth had called his secretary in New York to find out how seriously they were missing his creative flair and acumen. His secretary said he should think about coming home; his mom was working too hard. Which meant his mom was working *them* too hard and therefore enjoying him being out of the picture.

So no hassle.

Five hours? A short hop.

But they claimed Moira had been given an assisted passage out of town. *The woman you're seeking has been driven away.*

So she might no longer be in that area.

But she would not be the easiest person to get rid of if she still had unfinished business.

Macbeth was getting that Holy Grail feeling again. The One Big Thing.

What the fuck . . . He climbed back into the Metro, started up the motor.

CHAPTER II

'Right, let the dog see the rabbit. That the photo, Paul? Ta.'

'Got to be him, Sarge.'

'Not necessarily, lad, all sorts come out here purely to top umselves. I remember once . . .'

'It is, look . . .'

'Aye, well done, lad. Never've thought he'd have got this far in last night's conditions, no way. But where's the gun?'

The body lay face-up in the bottom of the quarry, both eyes wide as if seeking a reason from the darkening sky.

'Hell fire, look at state of his head. Must've bounced off that bloody rock on his way down. You all right, Desmond?'

'Just a bit bunged-up, Sarge. Reckon it's this flu.'

'Hot lemon. Wi' half a cup of whisky. That's what I always take. Least you can't smell what we can smell. Hope the poor bugger shit hisself *after* he landed.'

'What d'you reckon then?'

'Harry, if you can persuade your radio to work, get word back to Mr Blackburn as he can call off the troops, would you? And let's find that gun, shall we? I don't know; be a bloody sight simpler if we hadn't got his missus bleating on about him charging after Satanists.'

'Haw.'

'Ah now, don't knock it, Desmond. If you'd seen some of the things I've seen up these moors. All right, more likely poor sod'd been trying to find his way back home, *terrible* bloody conditions, gets hopelessly disorientated, wandering round for hours – what's he come, six miles, seven? – and just falls over the edge. But this business of intruders, somebody'll want it checked out, *whoever* they were, *whatever* they was up to . . .'

'Or if they even existed.'

'Or, as Paul says, if they even existed, except in the lad's imagination. I'd let it go, me, if we find that gun. Accidental, and you'd never prove otherwise, not in a million years. What we supposed to do, stake out the entire moor every night till they come back for another do?'

'Poor bugger.'

'Aye. Glad we found him before it got dark, or we'd be out here again, first light. Well, look at that, what d'you know, it's starting raining again, Desmond.'

'Yes Sarge.'

'Hot lemon, lad, my advice. Wi' a good dollop of whisky.'

'Oh Lord, we're asking you to intercede, to help us sanctify this place, drenched for centuries in sin and evil. Oh Lord, come down here tonight, give us some help. Come on down, Lord . . . shine your light, that's what we're asking . . . come on . . .'

'SHINE YOUR LIGHT.'

'Yes, and into every murky corner, come on . . .'

'SHINE YOUR LIGHT.'

'Through every dismal doorway . . .'

'SHINE YOUR LIGHT.'

'Into every fetid crevice . . .'

'SHINE YOUR LIGHT.'

And Willie shouted it too.

'SHINE YOUR LIGHT.'

It was easy. It was just pulled out of you, like a handkerchief from your top pocket. Nowt to it.

At first he'd felt right stupid. Felt bloody daft, in fact, as soon as he walked in, wearing his suit, the only suit in the place, so it was obvious from the start that he wasn't one of *them*.

Not that this had bothered them. They'd leapt on him – big, frightening smiles – and started hugging him.

'Welcome, brother, welcome!'

'Good to see someone's been brave enough to turn his back on it all. What's your name?'

'Willie.' Gerroff, he wanted to shout, this is no bloody way to behave in church. Or anywhere, for that matter, soft buggers.

'Willie, we're so very glad to have you with us. To see there is one out there who wants to save his soul. Praise God! And rest assured that, from this moment on, you'll have the full protection of the Lord, and there'll be no repercussions because you'll be wearing the armour of the Lord's light. Do you believe that? Is your faith strong enough, Willie, to accept that?'

'Oh, aye,' said Willie.

'No,' Milly Gill had said flatly and finally, when Mr Dawber wanted to go. 'It's got to be you, Willie. Mr Dawber looks too intelligent.'

'Thanks a bunch.'

'You know what I mean. You look harmless. It's always been your strength, Willie luv. You look *dead harmless*.'

'Like a little vole,' said Frank Manifold Snr's wife Ethel in a voice like cotton-wool, and Milly gave her a narrow look.

'Just watch and listen, Willie. Listen and watch.'

'What am I listening for?'

'You'll know, when you hear it.'

What he'd heard so far had left him quite startled. They sang hymns he'd never encountered before, with a rhythm and gusto he associated more with folk clubs. He felt his fingers begin to respond, tried to stop it but he couldn't. Felt an emotional fervour building around him, like in the days when he used to support Manchester City.

It had started with everybody – there'd be over fifty of them now – sitting quietly in the pews, as Joel Beard led them in prayer.

But when the hymns got under way they'd all come out and stand in the aisle, quite still – no dancing – and turn their faces towards the rafters and then lift up their hands, palms open as if they were waiting to receive something big and heavy.

When the hymn was over, some of the younger ones stayed in the aisle and sat there cross-legged, staring up at the pulpit, at their leader.

'Some of you,' Joel Beard said soberly, 'may already have realized the significance of tonight.'

Joel in full vestments, leaning out over the pulpit, the big cross around his neck swinging wide, burnished by the amber lights which turned his tight curls into a helmet of shining bronze.

A bit different from downbeat, comfortable old Hans with his creased-up features and his tired eyes.

But no Autumn Cross over Joel's head.

No candles on the altar. All statuary removed.

And despite all the people in their bright sweaters and jeans, with their fresh, scrubbed faces and clean hair . . .

. . . Despite the colourful congregation and despite the emotion, the church looked naked and cold, and gloomy as a cathedral crypt.

Joel said, 'Every few years, the realms of God and Satan collide. The most evil of all pagan festivals falls upon the Lord's day. Tonight, my friends, my brothers, my sisters, we pray for ourselves. For we are at war.'

Bloody hell, Willie remembered, it's . . .

'It is Sunday,' Joel said quietly. 'And it is All-Hallows Eve.'

New Year's Eve, Willie thought.

Time was when they'd have a bit of a do down The Man.

Except that always happened tomorrow, All Souls. Bit of a compromise, reached over the years with the Church. And a logical one in Willie's view. Imagine the reaction, in the days of the witchhunts, to a village which had a public festival at Hallowe'en. So they had it the following night, All Souls Night. Made sense.

Wouldn't be doing much this year, though. Bugger-all to celebrate.

'We have recaptured this church,' Joel Beard proclaimed, 'for the Lord.'

Sterilized it, more like, Willie thought, feeling a lot less daft, a lot more annoyed. Despiritualized it, if there's such a word.

'And it is left to us . . . to hold it through this night.'

'YES!'

Oh, bloody hell, they're never!

'PRAISE GOD!'

'We'll remain here until the dawn. We'll sing and pray and keep the light.'

'KEEP THE LIGHT!'

It's a waste of time, Willie wanted to shout. It's a joke. Apart from the Mothers doing whatever needs to be done – *in private* – Hallowe'en's a non-event in Bridelow. Just a preparation for the winter, a time of consolidation, like, a sharing of memories.

'I would stress to all of you that it's important to preserve a major presence here in the church.'

Nay, lad, give it up. Go home.

Joel said, 'If anyone needs to leave to use the toilet, the Rectory is open. But – hear me – go in pairs. Ignore all distractions. And hurry back. Take care. Make your path a straight one. Do not look to either side. Now . . . those who thirst will find bottles of spring water and plastic cups in the vestry. Do *not* drink any water you may find in the Rectory; it may have been taken from the local spring, which is polluted, both physically and spiritually.'

Willie was stunned. This was insane. This was *Bridelow* he was on about.

'And of course,' Joel said, 'we shall eat nothing until the morning.'

'PRAISE GOD!'

Willie slumped back into his pew next to a girl with big boobs under a pink sweatshirt with white and gold lettering spelling out, THANK GOD FOR JESUS!

'Have we been taken over, though?' Milly said. 'Have we lost our village? Gone? Under our noses?'

'Bit strong, that,' Ernie Dawber said with what he was very much afraid was a nervous laugh. 'Yet.'

They were in Milly Gill's flowery sitting room.

He'd set out for evensong, as was his custom; if there was a boycott it was nowt to do with him, damn silly way to react, anyroad.

She had caught up with him, suddenly appearing under his umbrella, telling him about the Angels of the New Advent. Time to talk about things, Milly said, steering him home, sitting him down with a mug of tea.

'You're the chronicler, Mr Dawber. You know it's not an exaggeration. You've watched the brewery go. You've seen people fall ill and just die like they never did before. You know as well as I do Ma didn't just fall downstairs and die of shock.'

'It's common enough,' Ernie said damply, 'among very old people.'

'But Ma Wagstaff?' Milly folded her arms, trying for a bit of Presence. 'All right? Who's taken the Man? Who's taken Matt Castle from his grave? Come off the fence, Mr Dawber. What do you really think?'

'You're asking me? You're in charge now, Millicent. I'm just an observer. With failing eyesight.'

'There you go again. Please, Mr Dawber, you've seen the state of us. We're just a not-very-picturesque tradition. What did I ever do except pick flowers and dress the well? And we meet for a bit of a healing – this is how it's been – and Susan says she can't stop long because of the child and it's Frank's darts night.'

'Young Frank needs a good talking to,' said Ernie.

'That's the least of it. They're all just going through the motions, and nothing seems to work out. It's like, we're going into the Quiet time – this is last midsummer – and Jessie

395

Marsden has to use her inhaler twice. We can't even beat our own hay fever any more. It'd be almost funny if it wasn't so tragic.'

The image speared Ernie again. Ma showing him the Shades of Things and making him promise to get the bog body back. And him failing her, in the end. But need this be the end?

'Happen you need some new blood,' he said finally.

'I don't think that's the answer, Mr Dawber. The strength is in the tradition. New blood's easy to get. Remember that girl who showed up a couple of years ago? Heard about Bridelow – God knows how – and wanted to "tap the source"? Place of immense power, how lucky we were, could she become a . . . a "neophyte", was that the word?'

Ernie Dawber smiled. 'From the Daughters of Isis, Rotherham, as I remember. Nice enough girl. Well-intentioned. You sent her away.'

'Well, Mr Dawber, what would you have done? We couldn't understand a word she was saying – all this about the Great Rite and the Cone of Power.'

'Come off it, Millicent. You knew exactly what she was saying.'

'Well . . . maybe it seemed silly, the way she talked. Made it all seem silly. It does, you know, when you give it names, like the Cone of Power. New blood's all right, in this sort of situation, when you're strong enough to absorb it. When you're weak it can just be like a conduit for infection.'

'That, actually,' Ernie said, 'was not quite what I meant by new blood. Let's try and look at this objectively. Everything was ticking over quite nicely – not brilliant, bit wackery round the joints – but basically all right, given the times we're in. Until this bog body turns up. The Man. It all comes back to the Man.'

'You think so, Mr Dawber? The Man himself, rather than what people have made of him?'

'It's all the same,' Ernie said. 'That's the whole point of a human sacrifice.'

Milly stood up and went to the window, opaque with night and rain. 'How long's it been raining now, Mr Dawber?'

'Over a day non-stop, has to be, and coming harder still.

Stream's been out over the church field since teatime, and the Moss . . . the Moss will rise. It does, you know. Absorbs it like a sponge. In 1794, according to the records, the Moss rose three feet in a thunderstorm.'

Ernie laughed.

'See, that's me. The chronicler, the great historian. Head full of the past, but we don't learn owt from it, really, do we? The past is our foundation, but we look back and say, nay, that was primitive, we're beyond that now, we've evolved. But we haven't, of course, not spiritually, not in a mere couple of thousand years. It's still our foundation, no matter how crude. And when the foundation's crumbled or vanished, we've got to patch it up best we can.'

Milly Gill didn't seem to be listening.

She said, 'I prayed to the Mother tonight. Sent Willy off to the church to learn what he could and then I went up to the Well with a lantern and knelt there in the rain at the poolside with the Mother's broken-off head in me hands, and I asked her what we'd done and what we could do.'

Milly fell silent. Ernie Dawber looked round the room, at the grasses and dried flowers, at Milly's paintings of flowers and gardens. At Milly herself, always so chubby and bonny.

For the first time, she looked not fat but bloated, as if the rain had swelled her up like the Moss.

'And what happened?' Ernie said after a while. He thought of himself as one of the dried-out roots hanging in bundles from the cross-beam. Shrivelled, easy to snap, but possessed of certain condensed pungency. Put him in the soup and he could still restore the flavour. He looked closely at Milly and saw she was weeping silently.

'Well?' he said softly.

'If she was telling me anything,' Milly said, 'I couldn't hear it. Couldn't hear for the rain.'

Shaw said, 'What have you got on under that cloak?'

'Not a thing.' Sitting at Shaw's mother's dressing table, Therese had rubbed some sort of foundation stuff into her face, to darken her complexion, and painted around her eyes. 'But it's not for you tonight. You can get excited though, if you like – make him jealous.'

Shaw touched her shoulder through the black wool.

She turned and looked at him, her eyes very dark. The look said, Get away from me.

Shaw winced.

He looked over at the bed, at his mother's well-worn dressing gown thrown across it. He was surprised she hadn't taken it with her.

'Therese,' he said, 'how was she really? When she left.'

'Your mother? Fine. She'll be enjoying the change.'

'I'm not *over*-happy about it. She's a dismal old cow, but . . .'

'Relax. Or rather, don't relax. Look, she didn't *want* to be here. She's really not very sociable these days, is she? Especially where the brewery's concerned.'

He watched Therese's eyes in the mirror. She could always, in any circumstances, make things happen. Yesterday, his mother had been almost hysterical when he said he'd be bringing the Gannons chairman over for drinks. This morning the old girl was missing but Therese – miraculously, shockingly – was in Shaw's bed, and Therese said, 'Oh, I popped in last night, and we had a terrific heart-to-heart, Liz and I. She's become far too insular, you know, losing all her confidence. Anyway, I persuaded her to go to the Palace in Buxton for a couple of days. Packed her case, ordered her a taxi before she could change her mind. Wasn't that clever of me?'

Yes, yes, he'd been so relieved. The old girl would have been suspicious as anything if he'd suggested it. He remembered the Malta idea. Hopeless. But trust Therese to win her confidence.

Trust Therese. Drifting around the house rearranging things; how the house had changed in just a few hours, a museum coming alive.

'What've you got there?'

She'd picked up a black cloth bag from the dressing table, tightened its drawstrings and set it down again.

'Hair.' She turned the word into a long, satisfied breath. 'Beautiful, long black hair.'

'Hair?'

'With a single gorgeous strand of white. I had to use a wig for so long. But there's no substitute for the real thing.'

'Can I look?'

'Of course not. Don't you learn *anything*? If it's taken out now, it loses half its energy. That was why it was important to leave her as long as possible. And it's nicely matted with blood, too, now, which is a bonus.'

'It's all moving too fast for me,' said Shaw. 'That comb . . . does that tie in?'

'Well, the comb was a problem at first, actually. It's had to be sort of reconsecrated. We're not touching that either until the moment comes.'

She stretched. Her slim arms – leanly, tautly muscular – emerging from the folds of the black cloak. 'Then I shall uncover the hair and run the comb through it. You know how combing your hair can generate electricity? If you comb it in the dark, looking into a mirror, you can sometimes see blue sparks. Ever done that?'

'With *my* hair?'

Therese laughed. 'Poor Shaw. One day, perhaps.'

Shaw said, 'I'm sure it must have grown another quarter of an inch since I . . . you know, since Ma Wagstaff.'

'There you are, you see. First you simply felt better. Now you even *look* better. And after tonight . . .'

Shaw said, 'I'm not sure I really want to be there. I'll be so scared, I'll probably screw up or something.'

'Nonsense.' Therese lifted the hood of the cloak. 'How do I look?'

Her voice had a husky, slightly Scottish edge.

Shaw shuddered.

CHAPTER III

Mungo Macbeth figured at first, irrationally, that he must have reached the coast.

Came over the hill through rain which was almost equatorial in its intensity, and there was this sensation of bulk water below and beyond his headlights. Too wide for a river – assuming Britain didn't have anything on the scale of the Mississippi in flood.

And there was a lighthouse across the bay. The light was a radiant blue-white and sent a shallow beam over black waves he couldn't see. Only, unlike a lighthouse, it wasn't rotating, which was strange.

Macbeth stopped the car and lit a cigarette. He'd pulled in for gas near Macclesfield, looked up into the hard rain and the lightless hills and abruptly decided, after six years, to take up smoking again. Thus far it was not a decision he'd had cause to repent.

He turned off the wipers and the headlights; the rain spread molecules of blue light all over the windshield.

The sign had said Bridelow, so this had to be it.

Or rather, *that* had to be it.

The road carried on straight ahead and from here it looked likely to vanish after a few yards under the black water. Which was no way to die.

Macbeth finished his cigarette, slid the car into gear – still not used to gears – and then set off very slowly, headlights full on, thinking of Moira, how mad she was going to be when he showed up. Wondering what her hair would look like in the rain.

Moira Cairns: the One Big Thing.

The later it got, the harder it rained, the more frightened Lottie became of the night and what it might hold.

Not that she was inclined to show this fear. Not to the customers and especially not to herself. Every time she caught sight of her face in the mirror behind the bar, she tightened her lips and pulled them into what was supposed to be a wry smile. In the ghostly light from Matt's lovingly reconstructed gas-mantle, it looked, to her, gaunt and dreadful, corpselike.

Lottie shivered, longed for the meagre comfort of the kitchen stove and its hot-plate covers.

'All right, luv?' Stan Burrows said. 'Want a rest? Want me to take over?'

Big, bluff Stan, who'd been the brewery foreman – first to lose his job under the Gannons regime. If she could afford it, it would be nice to keep the pub, install Stan as full-time manager.

And *then* clear off.

Lottie shook her head. He must have noticed her agitation. She thought of a rational explanation to satisfy him.

'Stan, it isn't . . . *dangerous*, is it? You know, with all this rain getting absorbed into the Moss. Doesn't flood or anything?'

'Well, I wouldn't go out theer for a midnight stroll.' Stan made a diving motion with stiffened fingers. 'Eight or nine foot deep in places. You might not drown but you'll get mucky. Still, I'm saying that – people *have* died out theer, but not for a long time. Don't think about it, best way.'

'Hard not to,' Lottie said. 'Living here.'

'Used to be folk,' said a retired farmer called Harold Halsall, 'as could take you across that Moss by night in any conditions. Follow the light, they used say. Beacon of the Moss. All dead now.'

'Fell in, most likely,' said Young Frank Manifold. 'Bloody place this is, eh? Moss on one side, moors on t'other, wi' owd quarries and such. Why do we bloody stay?'

Frank and his mates had spent the afternoon helping in the search for Sam Davis, found dead in a disused quarry just before dusk.

'Bad do, that, Frank.' Harold Halsall had picked up the reference. 'Used to be me brother's farm, that. Never did well

401

out of it, our George – salesman now, cattle feed. Is it right that when they found yon lad's shotgun he'd loosed off both barrels?'

'Leave it, Harold,' said Stan Burrows, flicking a quick glance at Lottie. They'd spent nearly an hour discussing the Sam Davis incident before Harold had come in. Stan probably imagined that was adding to Lottie's nerves: the thought of being all alone here while whoever Sam had been chasing when he went over the quarry was still on the loose.

If it was only that . . . Lottie turned away.

'Tell you what.' Young Frank'd had a bit too much to drink again. More than one person had been saying it was time he went out and found himself another job. 'I wish I had a bloody shotgun. Fire a few off outside t'church, I would.'

Lottie groaned. Tonight's *other* topic of conversation.

'Soon bring that bastard out,' said Frank. 'Him and his children of God. Then I'd fill him in, good.'

'Don't think you would, Frank,' Stan Burrows said. 'He's a big lad, that curate. Once had trials for Castleford, somebody said. Nay, he'll quieten down. Let him get it out of his system. All he's doing's making what you might call a statement.'

'Twat,' said Frank.

'Don't rise to it,' Stan said. 'Best way. Mothers'll not . . .' Stan realized he'd uttered a word Lottie preferred not to hear in her bar. 'Aye,' he said. 'Well.'

It went quiet. Not sure what they were allowed to talk about. Be better for everyone, Lottie thought, when I've gone.

She heard running feet on the cobbles outside and the gaslight sputtered as the door was thrown open. The porch lamp showed up rain like six-inch nails.

All the lads looking up from their drinks.

'Jeez.'

He wore a sweater and jeans. He shook raindrops out of black, wavy hair. Lottie didn't recognize him.

'Wet enough for you?' she said. Nobody drove out for a casual pint at The Man I'th Moss on dark autumn nights, and he certainly wasn't dressed like a rambler.

'Wet enough for Jacques Cousteau,' he said and grinned,

brushing droplets from his sweater. It was, Lottie noticed, a very expensive soft-knit sweater. Cashmere, probably.

Lottie laughed. 'What would you like?'

'Scotch,' he said. 'Please. Any kind. No ice.'

'Oh,' she said, surprised. 'You're American. Sorry, I didn't mean to say it like that.'

'Bloody hell,' Young Frank Manifold called over. 'I know visibility's bad out there, mate, but I think tha's missed thi turn-off for Highway 61.'

It began just like any normal hymn – well, normal for them.

Sort of hymn Barry Manilow might have written, Willie thought. Slow and strong, with a rolling rhythm and a big, soaring chorus, undeniably catchy. One of the Angels of the New Advent was playing the organ, backed up by a portable drum machine with an amplifier set up under the lectern. Willie couldn't prevent his fingers going into action on his blue serge knees.

Didn't reckon much to the words. Modern language, but humourless. No style.

He glanced at the girl in the Jesus sweatshirt. Her eyes were glazed and unfocused. She had a certain look Willie had seen before, but usually on people who were on something.

High. She was high on God.

As he watched, slow tears rolled down her white cheeks.

The hymn soared on. Joel Beard stood in his pulpit, apparently soaring with it, eyes closed and palms upturned. Willie thought of his mother, now lying in a chapel of rest in Macclesfield. How was he supposed to make funeral arrangements when the service would have to be conducted by this pillock?

The drum machine stopped and then the organ trailed away, but the voices went on, and the words were no longer trite, no longer actually made any sense. Were, in fact, no longer what you might call words.

Willie listened to the girl.

'Holia . . . holia . . . amalalia . . . awalah . . . gloria . . . hailalalala . . .'

He was bewildered. All around him voices rose and fell and rose and swelled, ululating together in a strange, enveloping coda.

Everyone singing different words.

'*Ohyalala . . . holy . . . holy . . . malaya . . . amala . . .*'

He looked up at Joel, presiding Angel, and Joel was smiling, with his eyes closed.

For a while Willie closed his own eyes and was at once carried away on it, drifting, aware that his fingers were stretching, feeling as if they were coming directly out of his wrists, nerves extending. His fingers moved very lightly against his thigh, sometimes not quite touching it.

Something fluttering like a small bird in his own chest and rising into his throat.

'*Mayagalamala . . .*'

That was *me*.

Willie stopped, stood very still for a moment, opening his eyes and taking in the scene. All those upturned palms. All those eyes, closed or glazed.

He sighed and slid quietly out of the pew and down the aisle to the church door. It was bolted, but nobody heard him draw back the bolts and slip out into the teeming rain.

Standing in a spreading puddle at the edge of the porch, Willie looked up at where Our Sheila used to hold open her pussy. He closed his eyes against the cold dollops of rain.

'Speaking in tongues,' he muttered. 'Speaking, chanting, singing in tongues.'

Language of the angels. Open up your hearts to God and He'll fill your mouth with rubbish.

'It's a block,' he said to Milly Gill and Ernie Dawber. 'They're blocking everything out. They're surrounding umselves with sound and emotion. But it's like blanket emotion – you feel good, you feel you're being drawn into something. It's just like candyfloss. You know what I mean? Like . . . *psychic* candyfloss.'

Ernie couldn't remember when he'd heard such a long speech from Willie Wagstaff. Always such a shy lad, in and out of class. You kept forgetting he was Ma's son and therefore, even in a Goddess-oriented society, he must have picked up a few tips.

'It's stirring things up, though,' Milly said. 'And that's not good at All Hallows. You've got to be very careful at All Hallows.'

'We probably asked for it,' Willie said. 'Whole congregation going on strike like that.'

'He provoked it,' Milly said. 'He destroyed things dear to us. He provoked us. Were we supposed to sit there and listen to his pious ramblings after that?'

'Perhaps,' Ernie said reasonably, 'that was what he wanted to do. Provoke a confrontation. It's no great secret, if you know what you're looking for, that the religious practices in Bridelow are not as elsewhere. His brand of Christianity views it with very serious disapproval, not to say abject horror.'

'Hans could've said no to him,' Milly Gill said, 'Hans could've said he didn't want a curate.'

'Hans was a sick man, Millicent. He *did* need the help. And Bridelow does change people, you know. Straightened out, a lad like Beard could even be an asset. It's just everything happened so quickly. Left on his own in what he sees as an evil, pagan parish . . . The way he is now, everything's either black or white. Which is what Ma warned me about. Beware of black, she said, and beware of white.'

'Aye,' Willie said. 'But where's the black coming from?'

'Mr Beard thinks we're the black,' Milly said.

Ernie almost smiled. There she was in one of her endless wardrobe of floral dresses sitting on her flower-patterned sofa with her flower pictures on the walls, bundles of dried flowers and herbs dangling from the beams. She was life, she was colour. Flowers were all the children she'd never had.

Even if the flowers were wilting.

'You keep saying that,' Willie almost snapped. '"He's God, we're Satan". You're avoiding the bloody issue. There *is* bad here. Real bad. Ma saw it coming, and we all said, Ah, poor old woman's off her trolley. We ignored the signs. Look at that bloody tree as suddenly appears out on t'Moss. Did anybody really check that thing out?'

'I never go on the Moss,' Ernie admitted.

'No, you don't, Mr Dawber. You like t'rest of us – we can't turn it into allotments, so we ignore it. And when somebody like Matt comes back and he looks out there and he says, *That's where we're from* . . . Well, we pat him on the back; we know he'll settle down. That's the trouble, see, we've all bloody *settled down* . . . even the Mothers've settled down. This is not a place you can totally settle down, you've always got to keep an eye open and perhaps Ma was the last one who did.'

It's a balancing act, Ernie Dawber heard in his head, Ma nagging him again. Willie was right. Even this morning, going up to find Liz Horridge, he was telling her to go away, leave me alone, Ma, get off my back.

'I were out there,' Willie said, 't'other morning. Wi' t'dog. Young Benjie kept going on at me – "Oh, there's a dragon out there, Uncle Willie." "Nay," I said, "it's bog oak." But I went out t'ave a look, just to satisfy him, like. Dog come wi' me . . . and *he* knew what it were about. And what did I do? I buggered off sharpish. I dint listen to t'dog and I made fun of Ma. I made fun of Ma over Matt's coffin and the witch bottle – scared stiff she'd ask *me* to do it. I dint mind helping pinch t'bogman back, bit of a lark, that were. But opening Matt's coffin . . .'

Willie shuddered. 'Wimp,' he said. 'That's me.'

'She was right,' Milly said. 'Matt wasn't protected. We were putting him in as the Man's guardian. What use is a guardian without a sword?'

As usual, Ernie Dawber, schoolteacher, man of words, man of science, was floored by the exquisite logic of all this.

'Who . . . was it?' he asked delicately. 'Who dug them up?'

Milly's sigh was full of despair. 'I can't begin to guess, Mr Dawber. So many signs. We could see them, but we couldn't see a pattern. I've been praying to the Mother for a pattern. Can't seem to get through, even to meself. It's like all the wires are crossed. Or there's a fog.'

'There's a fog in the church,' Willie said. 'They're making one. White fog. You can't get through because it's like all your lines of communication've been pulled down. The holy well, the church. Ma. It's like the white and the black have joined forces to crush us.'

'And what are we supposed to do?' There was no colour in Milly's cheeks. 'What can we do when we're so weakened, and we don't know who we're fighting or why?'

Ernie Dawber thought, So many sad, bewildered, frightened people. An invisible enemy. An ancient culture feebly fighting for its soul.

He noticed that all of Willie's fingers lay motionless on his knees.

'You know what I think,' Ernie said calmly. 'I think we need another sacrifice.'

CHAPTER IV

Milly Gill shifted on the sofa. It creaked.

'Eh?'

Ernie Dawber smiled in a resigned sort of way. He was sitting on a straight-backed chair, still wearing his old gaberdine mac, his hat on his knees.

'I don't know the story of the Man in the Moss,' he said, 'any more than anybody does. Some say he came all the way from Wales, or even Ireland. That he was sent as a sacrifice. Well, that seems likely, but we don't really know for certain *why* he was sacrificed.'

Willie said, 'I thought . . .' Then he shut up.

'Some historians speculate it was to keep the Romans at bay,' said Mr Dawber. 'But we don't *know* that. And in the end the Romans weren't so bad. They were a relatively civilized people. Bit stiff and starchy, like Joel Beard, but nowt wrong with them really. They taught us how to build proper roads and walls and useful things like that, but I like to think we taught them a lot as well.'

'We?' said Willie.

'The Celts. The earliest real civilization in Europe. Cultured, spiritual. Knew how to fight when it was needed, but not military like the Romans. The Celts never sought to impose order, only to recognize the order that existed around them.

And the moods of nature and the atmosphere. "Shades of things," Ma said.'

'Aye,' said Willie, remembering. 'Shades of things.'

'Moderation,' said Mr Dawber. 'Equality. Respect for each other, nature, animals. For religions. A simple, logical philosophy and one I've tried to pass on to generations of schoolkids, just like my forefathers did. And do you know . . .'

'Aye,' Willie said. 'It worked. It always worked. Kids leave school, bugger off to the cities, rebel against their parents and their parents' values and that. But there's summat about Bridelow. What we learned here, we didn't reject. I suppose . . . 'cause it was so *different*. Radical, like, in its quiet way.'

'Little island, Willie. Sacred island of the Celts. Little island of moderation in an ocean of extremes. Takes some protecting that. A balancing act.'

Mr Dawber turned his hat round on his knees. He's nervous, Willie thought.

'I've written a new edition of *The Book of Bridelow*. What you might call the unexpurgated edition. Just for me own benefit really. Just to reason things out. You'll find it in a blue typing paper box on top of the big bookcase in my study.'

Willie said, 'Why're you telling us that?'

'Maybe it should be printed. Just one copy, to be kept in safekeeping, for posterity. As a reminder of how Bridelow was and *why* it was what it was. To look back on when everything's changed, when the outside world's absorbed us.'

Willie looked hard at the stately old chap, trying to remember what Mr Dawber had been like when he was young, when he'd taught him for four years. He couldn't.

He glanced at Milly, who was silent, pensive. 'Mr Dawber,' he said, 'why are you telling us now?'

'You see, that's the obvious explanation to me,' said Mr Dawber, looking down at his hat. 'That's what he died to save. Not to prevent anything as transient as another Roman invasion. He died to protect a way of life, a whole attitude. The Celtic way. Something worth dying for, don't you think?'

'Happen,' Willie said cautiously.

'I think I'd like to die for that,' said Mr Dawber.

Milly Gill leaned forward on the floral sofa and lifted one of his liver-spotted hands from his hat brim. 'What are you trying to say, Mr Dawber?'

The old chap said, 'Difficult times, lass. The outside's invading us. The White. The Black. Joel Beard. Gannons.'

'Yes,' Milly let go of his hand, 'it *is* an invasion. The worst kind. The kind you don't notice until it's on you.'

'You see, I don't quite know how it's done,' Mr Dawber said, matter-of-factly. 'I thought you might.'

'How what's done, Mr Dawber?'

'Why, the Triple Death, of course.'

'I don't like the way you're talking, Mr Dawber.'

'You see, I wouldn't like to cause any trouble for anybody. That is, I wouldn't like it to look like *murder*. So what I'll do is happen retire to the seaside. Health reasons. The owd chest's never been good. Got relatives in Bournemouth, you know.'

'Bournemouth,' Milly repeated.

'Aye, and nobody'll be interested enough to prove otherwise. I've packaged up the deeds and stuff, of the house, and I've left them with the manuscript, to go to Hans when he returns. With instructions that the house should be let, peppercorn rent, to somebody as needs one. Happen a new historian. Won't be called Dawber, but that wasn't much of a tradition, was it? Anyroad, I've tied things up very nicely, actually. I'll've gone. To the seaside.'

'Aye,' Willie said. 'You sound like you could use a holiday, Mr Dawber. Good long rest, eh?'

'I'll have that all right. In the Moss.'

Wearing a chilling half-smile, he carried on talking as if he couldn't see the pair of them staring at him, frozen.

'You know, when I first read the British Museum report it sounded quite horrific, but the more I thought about it . . . Well, the garrotting bit and the cutting of the throat – that was mostly symbolic. He wouldn't have felt any of that because they'd have tapped him on the head first, you see.'

'Mr Dawber . . .' Milly stood up. 'I can't believe what I'm hearing and I'll not have you talking like this in my house any more.'

'I'm an owd man, Millicent. I've done me bit, had some good times.'

'And you'll have some more.'

'No.' He shook his head. 'There'll be no more good times for any of us, unless we do summat drastic. They've taken the Man in the Moss. This is far worse than the University or the British Museum taking him. He's gone to the dark. And it's All-Hallows. The Celtic New Year's Eve.'

'I know what day it is,' Milly snapped. 'I'm supposed to be a bloody witch.'

'Time of change. Time to look back, store what's useful and important, discard the old stuff as isn't. Time when worlds overlap. Time to *act*. Sit down, Millicent.'

'Act?' Willie came aware of the power of the sheeting rain, could hear it smashing at the roof slates. A power surge brought a quiver to Milly's tulip-shaded standard lamp.

The lady bartender said, 'Stan, *would* you take over, I'm sorry,' and steered Mungo Macbeth into a back room, a big, chilly-looking kitchen.

'Who *are* you?' she demanded.

He told her his name again. He insisted he was a friend of Moira's. He repeated what he'd said in the bar, that he needed to talk to her. Urgently.

'She's not here. Why did you think she would be?'

The woman was good-looking with a strong face, but she also looked like she was carrying a lot of trouble, her eyes vibrant with anxiety. She crossed the flagged floor to a big iron stove and laid her hands on it.

Macbeth said, 'I didn't think she'd be *here*, specially. Not this inn. This was the first place I came to, is all. With lights on. After I crossed the bridge.'

'What bridge?'

'Over the water.'

'It's a bog,' she said. 'It's not water.'

'I'm a stranger. Never came this way before. I'm sorry if I seem ignorant, Mrs . . .'

'Castle,' she said.

'Oh, Jesus,' Macbeth said. 'I guess that means you're Matt Castle's . . .'

410

'Widow.'

'I'm sorry.'

'Why should you be?' she said sharply. 'You didn't know him, did you?'

All you could hear in the kitchen was the sound of rain splashing on the yard outside with the force of a broken fire-hydrant.

'No,' he said. 'I knew that Moira . . . thought a lot about him.' Shit. What'd I walk into here?

'Yes.' She bit her lip. 'Look, the last I heard, Moira was staying at the Rectory.'

'I called the Rectory. There were quite a few people there. They said she was, uh, no longer around.'

'The Born Agains, that would be. What would they know? How far've you come?'

'From Glasgow.'

'*Glasgow?* You drove all the way down from Glasgow? In this? Well, Mr . . . I'm sorry . . .'

'Macbeth.'

'Yes. Well, I suppose it isn't too surprising. Quite a few blokes have done crazy things for Moira Cairns.' A faint smile penetrated the anxiety. 'Look, we'll make some phone calls, shall we? See if we can find out where she is. There's a chap called Willie Wagstaff who might just know. It's funny he's not in tonight, actually. I'll give him a ring.'

'You're very kind. I'm sorry. I just had no idea who you were.'

'That's all right.'

'Is this your inn? What I mean is, you, uh . . .'

'Do you need somewhere to stay tonight, Mr Macbeth?' She gave him a look that was almost a plea.

'I guess I do,' he said. 'You have a room?'

'Yes,' she said gratefully. 'I have a room.'

'I've spent the last couple of days studying and thinking,' Mr Dawber said. 'In the end, you see, I'm a man of logic.'

Christ, Willie thought, preserve us from logic.

411

'Bridelow's is a peculiar logic, but logic it is. But our grasp of it has been gradually weakened.'

'Can't build a wall,' Willie said. 'Can't keep the modern world out for ever.'

'We did have a wall,' Milly said despondently. 'But I don't think I was cut out to be a brickie.'

Willie longed to give her a cuddle. For his benefit as much as hers. Longed to build up the fire, with crackling logs to block out the rain. His kind of wall. He thought about Joel Beard and his born-again mob, exulting and singing in tongues in the dying church: *their* kind of wall.

Mr Dawber picked up Milly's chubby hand and held it. 'Tonight, lass. If this wall finally comes down, it'll most likely be tonight, because somebody has the Man and they'll use him for evil. And that'll finish it.'

Old bugger's spent more than a couple of days on this, Willie thought. Ma's been schooling him. *They're looking for openings. Looking for cracks in t'wall. Been gathering out there for years, hundreds of years.*

Mr Dawber looked steadily at Milly. 'You've got to replace the Man, my dear.'

'*Her?*' Willie spluttered. '*She* has?'

'Ma would have taken charge, but sadly, she's not here. Which puts you in the firing line, Millicent, I'm afraid, and you've got to be strong. You're a big girl, if you don't mind me saying so. Big enough to wield the knife.'

Milly screamed and dragged her hand away.

Mr Dawber said, 'I know it'll hurt you more than it hurts me, and I'm sorry, I really am, lass.'

He stood up and straightened out the skirts of his mac. 'When I said I didn't go out on the Moss any more, I wasn't being strictly truthful. I spent a lot of time out there last summer after the Man was found, working out where he lay in relation to the village and also in relation to the path marked out by the Beacon of the Moss. Result is, I know just the place to do it.'

'Nay,' Willie said. 'Moss'll have shifted. Besides, there were no beacon in them days.'

'You mean there was no church clock. The beacon was a

412

real beacon on the hill where the church now stands. And the Moss was more like a lake. Water to reflect the light.'

Willie stood up. 'Look, Mr Dawber, we'll forget you ever said all this if you will.'

Mr Dawber put on his hat. 'I'll leave you two for a bit. Perhaps you might summon the Mothers, what's left of them as are well enough to come out on a night like this, and have a chat about it.'

'Hey, come on,' Willie said. 'Get some sleep, Mr Dawber, eh? We'll see you tomorrow, have a proper chat. All right?'

'No, I'll not sleep. I've a few things to sort out. Few private things to burn. Letters and such.' He looked at his watch. 'It's ten to nine now. I'll be back for you soon after eleven.'

Milly shrank away from him. 'Mr Dawber, you don't seriously . . .'

'I *do*,' he said sternly. 'And it's got to be tonight. Tonight has the power. The word is Samhain, Millicent, although I realize the Mothers have gradually dropped the old terminology. And on a practical level, the Moss is swollen with rain; when it goes down, things will be absorbed again, taken in.'

'Mr Dawber,' Milly Gill whispered, 'don't do this to me. Please.'

'Perhaps, before I return, something'll have happened this night to make you see the sense of it. Ma dead? That young lad up on the moors? How many do you want? Where, for instance, is . . . ?' He pulled down his hat. 'Never mind.'

He turned round at the door, and a broad smile was channelled through the wrinkles, from the corners of his mouth to his eyes, and his face lit up like a Christmas tree.

'I'm not unhappy, tha knows. Be a lovely thing.'

Mr Dawber turned the key in the double lock and unbolted the front door to the fierce rain and the night.

CHAPTER V

'You been there before? The house?'

'Mmmm.'

'I suppose,' Chrissie said, 'I should be flattered. It's possibly our first official date.'

'What did you say?' His eyes flicking over to her then back to the road, quick as the windscreen wipers.

'You haven't been listening to anything I've been saying, have you?'

'Of course I have.'

'Doesn't matter. You're obviously preoccupied.'

She hadn't wanted to come with him anyway, being actually in the process of trying to lose his attentions without losing her job. Even if he *had* been comparatively spectacular in bed of late.

'Did you say something about a date?'

'I said it was possibly our first official one. Where we're actually seen together without a collapsible coffin between us. I was being flippant, Roger.'

'You're here as my assistant,' he said coldly.

'Oh, thanks very much. You'll be paying me, then.'

Actually, there was no real need to be especially nice to him. No way he could get her fired, knowing what she knew about him and his dealings behind the scenes with the man they were going to meet.

'What a bloody awful night,' she said. Now they were up in the hills it was coming down so hard the wipers could hardly keep up. 'I wonder what witches do when it's pissing down.'

'What?' Almost a croak.

'Witches.'

'What about witches?'

'It's Hallowe'en. I was wondering what witches do when it's raining this hard. Whether they call it off. Or do it in the sitting room. Can't dance naked in this, can you? Well, I

414

suppose you *could*. You're on a pretty short fuse tonight, Roger.'

'No, I'm not,' he snapped.

'Why don't you just tell me what's bothering you. Apart from the usual, of course.'

He didn't reply.

Sod this, Chrissie thought. 'Anyway, it was my understanding that your friend John Peveril Stanage lived in Buxton or somewhere. Why, pray tell, is he holding his Hallowe'en party in Bridelow?'

'Look.' It was too dark to see but she could tell his hands were throttling the steering-wheel. 'It's not a party. It's just a gathering. A few drinks and . . . a few drinks.'

'But not a party.' She was starting almost to enjoy this.

'And the reason it's in Bridelow . . . the Bridelow Brewery's been bought by Gannons Ales, right? And it now emerges that Stanage has been a major Gannons shareholder for some years and recently increased his holding, oh . . . substantially. Is now, in fact, about to become Chairman of the Board.'

'I suppose he's got to do something with all his book royalties and things. Apart from setting up bogman museums.'

Roger didn't rise to it, kept on looking at the road, what you could hope of see of it. 'Seems Shaw Horridge – that's the son of the original brewery family – is about to become engaged to Stanage's niece. They own Bridelow Hall. Which is where we're going.'

'I'll probably be underdressed,' Chrissie said, putting on a posh voice, 'for *Braidelow Hawl*.'

If it was *that* innocuous, why was Roger so nervy?

'Where's your wife tonight?'

'Working.'

'How are things generally?'

'So-so.'

'Everything all right in bed these days?'

'Chrissie, for Chr—' He hurled the car into low gear and raced up a dark, twisty hill.

'No clammy, peaty feelings any more?'

'What the hell's the *matter* with you tonight?'

415

'What's the matter with *you*?'

When they crested the hill she saw a strange blue moon. 'What on earth's that?'

'It's the Beacon of the Moss,' Roger said in a voice that was suddenly tired. 'Look, I'm sorry. Sorry I ever got committed to Stanage. I admit I'm in too deep, all right?'

She saw the bog below them. In the headlights it looked like very burned rice-pudding.

'It's as though he owns a piece of me,' Roger said. 'Bought me just as surely as he's bought Gannons Ales. I mean, last weekend, when I went to London . . . Chrissie, I didn't go to London. I was at Stanage's place.'

'In Buxton?'

'In Buxton, yes. That's where . . . Look, I'm a scholar, an academic, not religious, not impressionable. I'm basically a very sceptical person, you know that.'

Chrissie stifled it. 'Absolutely.' She allowed herself a deep, deep breath. 'But tell me this: who gave the bogman a penis?'

Roger slowed down for the causeway across the Moss. He seemed to slump on the wheel; she could have sworn she actually heard him gulp.

'I did.'

Ha!

'I used a piece of gut, what they thought was part of the duodenum.' He sounded relieved to be telling someone. 'Moulded with peat and something Stanage gave me . . . a . . . a stiffening agent.'

How ridiculously sleazy it sounded. Hadn't done much laughing, though, had she, when she saw the thing lying there projecting its bloody great menacing cock into the lights?

Actually, it was pretty sick.

They set off very slowly across the causeway. It seemed to be raining harder than ever here.

'Why?' she said. As if she really didn't know. Scholar. Academic. Sceptic. Not impressionable. Ha.

'He insisted it'd . . . you know . . . do the trick. Said I'd obviously become very close to the bogman, and the bogman had – this sounds very stupid – power. And I should use it.'

'And you didn't laugh in his face because you needed him. And his money.'

'No! I didn't laugh because . . . because he isn't a man you can laugh *at*. You'll know what I mean when you meet him. Look, do you really think I'd go discussing my private difficulties with . . . well, with anyone? I mean, my bloody wife's a *doctor*, and I couldn't talk to her about it. Of course, I did think things would be different with you.'

'Because I was a bit of a slag, I suppose. And not very bright in comparison with Doctor Mrs Hall. And because I was impressed with this big glamorous archaeologist who was on telly a lot, and flattered.'

'No, of course not, what do you think I . . . ?'

'Stick to honesty, Roger, you were doing very well. So you discussed your little . . . problem with Mr Stanage.'

'I didn't intend to. Well, obviously. He just seemed to know. He looked at me . . . *into* me, almost. Smiling faintly. As if he'd decided to find something out about me that I didn't want him to know. And then he said, "Try something for me, would you?" Sympathetic magic, he called it. I knew if I didn't give it a go, he'd know somehow. And if anyone saw it, I'd just blame the students. But then . . .'

'But then it started to work,' Chrissie said. Or something had. Probably the power of suggestion.

'As you know,' he said.

'You must have been half-dismissive and half-elated. And half-frightened, I suppose. I know that's three halves, but I'm not very bright, as we established. God almighty, Roger, what *have* you got yourself into?'

'He's . . . a strange man. His knowledge is very extensive indeed. But, yes, there *is* something I can't say I like.'

'Some of his books are very weird, Roger.'

'I haven't read his bloody books.'

'You should.'

'Just keep your mouth shut when we're there, that's all.'

'At the party?'

'*It's not* . . .'

'What is it, then?'

Roger drove up off the causeway, past the entrance to the big stone pub, The Man I'th Moss, and into the main village street. Halfway up the street, greasy light seeped out of a fish and chip shop, but it seemed to have no customers; not surprising in this weather. The blue moon turned out to be shining out of the church wall – must be a clock with a face each side of the steeple. But no hands, no numerals. How strange.

The clock lit up the inside of the car and Roger's bearded face. Chrissie began to feel uneasy.

'*Come on, then, Roger.*' As if the blue clock was lighting him up for interrogation. 'What else are you hiding?'

'Yes.' He turned right before the church, back into darkness. 'I'll tell you. Stanage says he can get the body back.'

'Oh, yes. Who from?'

'I don't know.'

'How?'

'I don't know.'

'What *do* you know?'

'He says we should all get together, those of us who've been close to him.'

'Him?'

'*Him.*'

Chrissie lit a cigarette. 'Turn round,' she said.

'What?'

'Turn the fucking car round, Roger, I'm not having anything to do with this.'

He stopped the car abruptly in the narrow road and it skidded into the kerb. The rain drummed violently on the roof and splashed the dark windows. It was savage and relentless, like a thrashing from God.

'Chrissie, please . . .'

She blew smoke in his face.

He choked back a cough. 'Chrissie, I don't want to go on my own.'

'Grow up, Roger.'

'Listen, I'm just a little bit scared too, can't help it. If only for my . . . for my reputation.'

'Well, naturally.'

418

'But *I* can't *not* go, can I? And say goodbye to everything. And make him, you know . . .'

'Make him what?'

'Angry,' he said pathetically.

She couldn't see his face; she didn't want to. She gritted her teeth. 'Turn it *round*, I said.'

'Lay off, eh, Frank?'

'I wanna know. Come on, he can't just fucking show up, middle of the night, and not tell us why. Don't want no more fucking mysteries in this place. Had it up to here with fucking mysteries.'

'Go home, Frank, you've had too many.'

'Too many what? Listen, fart-face, you're not my fucking foreman no more. Not your pub, neither. What's your name, mate?'

Macbeth had had too many bad experiences of telling his name to guys in bars. 'Kansas,' he said. 'Jim Kansas.'

'. . . kind of fucking name's that?'

'Frank, if you don't go home . . .'

'Aye? Go on. Finish sentence, Stan. What you goin' do if I don't go?'

'I shall pick up that big bottle of Long John,' said Mrs Lottie Castle, appearing in the doorway, 'and I'll use it to bash out all of your front teeth, Frank Manifold. That's for starters. *Out!*'

'It's raining,' Young Frank said.

And he giggled. But he went.

Macbeth started to breathe again.

'Sorry,' the barman Stan said to him. 'Everybody seems to be on edge tonight.' The other guys in the bar were draining their glasses, coming to their feet. 'We'll leave you to it, Lottie, I think. Shut the place, I would. You'll get no more custom tonight. Not in this.'

Now Stan looked meaningfully at Macbeth. Lottie said, 'He's staying.' Stan nodded dubiously and didn't move. 'He's an old friend of Matt's,' Lottie said. 'Couldn't make it for the funeral.'

'Right.' Stan accepted this and shrugged into his overcoat. ''Night then, Lottie. Good night, Mr Kansas.'

Macbeth was curious. This woman didn't know him from Bill Clinton and here she was letting her regular customers and the help go and him stay the night. Normal way of things, the woman being a widow, this would've been no big surprise, he had to admit. But she was a very *recent* widow. Also, she didn't seem to have even noticed what he looked like.

She looked tired. Drained. Eyes swollen. She dragged out a weary smile.

'Mr . . . Mungo. I've located Willie Wagstaff. He doesn't know where Moira is, but he says he doesn't mind talking to you if you don't keep him too long. He's at his girlfriend's – that's the Post Office. About a hundred yards up the street, same side.'

'Right. Uh, what did you . . . ?'

'I told him I thought you were all right. I hope you are.'

Macbeth said, 'Mrs Castle, what's going on here? Just why is everybody on edge? Who're all these people at the Rectory?'

'Ask Willie,' she said. 'And just so you know, he used to play the drums in Matt's band, so he's known Moira a long time. Do you want to borrow an umbrella?'

'Thanks, I have a slicker in back of the car. What if I'm late?'

'I'll still be up,' Lottie Castle said. 'Whatever time it is. Just hammer on the door.'

Lottie bolted the door behind him, top and bottom. Then she went through to the back door and secured that too.

She put on some coffee, partly to combat the rain noise with the warm pop-pop-pop of the percolator.

Earlier she'd pulled through a three-seater sofa from the living room that never got lived in. There was a duvet rolled up on the sofa.

Tonight's bed. Would have been, if she'd been alone in the pub. She'd put the American in Bedroom Three, the one Dic used when he was here. Soon as he'd left yesterday she'd changed the bedding, aired the room. It was just across the passage from her own.

Were bad dreams somehow stopped at source when you were no longer alone in the building?

That, of course, would depend on whether they *were* dreams.

On the refectory table was a local paper with the phone numbers of two estate agents ringed, the ones that specialized in commercial properties. Give that a try first, see if anyone was interested in a loss-making pub, before resorting to the domestic market.

Former village inn. Full of character. Dramatic rural location. Reduced for quick sale.

Well, did she have a choice? Was there any kind of alternative?

Lottie poured coffee, strong but with a little cream which she left unstirred, thin, white circles on the dark surface, because black coffee was apt to make her think of the Moss.

She left the cup steaming on the table, stood in the centre of the room for a moment with her sleeves pushed up and hands on her hips. 'Matt,' she said, 'you know I didn't want to come, but I didn't complain. I supported you. I gave up my lovely home.'

Strange, but all the time he was dying he never once allowed a discussion to develop about her future. But then, they never actually talked about him dying; just, occasionally, about him being ill. And yet he obviously wasn't afraid; he was just – amazing, when you thought about it – too preoccupied.

'You were always a selfish bastard, Matt,' she said.

Standing on the flags, hands on hips, giving him a lecture.

'Don't see why I should feel ashamed, do you?'

Feeling not so unhappy, because there was someone to wait up for.

She left on a wall-lamp in the kitchen, went through to the bar, leaving the door ajar. Switched the lights off one by one at the panel beside the mirror, leaving until last the disused brass gas-mantle which Matt had electrified.

The porch-light would stay on all night, gilding the rippling rain on the window. Lottie moved out into the darkened, stone-walled bar, collecting the ashtrays for emptying.

Wondering what Willie would make of the American with the silly name who'd driven down from Glasgow on the wettest Sunday of the year to find Moira Cairns.

Matt would have done that. Matt would have killed for Moira, and there was a time when she would have killed Moira because of it, but it didn't seem to matter any more.

When the gaslight came back on behind the bar, Lottie dropped all the ashtrays with a clatter of tin.

The gas-mantle was fitted with an electric bulb under the little gauzy knob thing and it looked fairly realistic. Or so she'd thought because she'd never seen the original gas.

Until now.

Oh, yes. This was gas, being softer, more diffused; she almost felt she could hear a hiss. Did they hiss? Or was that Matt?

Matt, whose face shone from the mirror behind the bar, enshrouded in gaslight.

Lottie stood with her back to the far stone wall. Her hands found her hips. Against which, untypically, they trembled.

She said, very quietly, 'Oh, no.'

Ernie Dawber knew that if he allowed himself to think about this, he would at once realize the fundamental insanity of the whole business.

He would see 'sense'.

But Bridelow folk had traditionally answered to laws unperceived elsewhere. Therefore it was not insane, and it required another kind of sense which could never be called 'common'.

So he simply didn't think about it at all, but did the usual things he would do at this time of night: cleaned his shoes, tidied his desk – leaving certain papers, however, in quite a prominent position.

Love letters, they were, from a woman magistrate in Glossop with whom Ernie had dallied a while during a bad patch in his marriage some thirty years ago. He'd decided not to burn them. After all, his wife had known and the woman was dead now; why not make one little bequest to the village gossips?

In the letter he was leaving for Hans, he'd written: 'Let the vultures in, why not? Let them pick over my bones – but discreetly. Let it be so that nothing of me exists except a name on the cover of *The Book of Bridelow*.'

Suddenly he felt absurdly happy. He was going on holiday.

He made himself a cup of tea and set out a plate of biscuits, wondering what archaeologists two thousand years hence might make of this.

. . . the stomach yielded the digested remains of a compressed fruit not indigenous to the area but which may have constituted the filling for what nutritional documents of the period tell us were called 'fig rolls'.

Ernie Dawber chuckled, ate two biscuits, drank his tea and sat back in his study chair, both feet on his footstool. He did not allow himself to contemplate the kind of knife which might be used to cut his throat or the type of cord employed for the garrotting or whether the blow to the back of his head would be delivered with a carpenter's mallet or a pickaxe handle.

But, feeling that he should at least be aware of what had happened on this particular day in the world he was leaving behind, he switched on the radio for the ten o'clock news.

Not such a bad time to be leaving. Chaos behind what used to be the Iron Curtain, more hatred between European nations than there'd been since the war. A psychopath killing little girls in the West Country.

But then, at the end of the national news, this:

Police who earlier today found the body of a man after a nine-hour search of the South Pennine moors say they've now discovered a woman's body, less than a mile away, in the burned-out wreckage of a car.

However, they say there appears to be no link between the two deaths. The first body, found in a quarry, has now

423

been formally identified as a 27-year-old farmer, Peter Samuel Davis.

The woman's body, not yet identified, was badly burned after the car, a BMW saloon, apparently left the road in wet conditions, plunged over a hundred feet into a valley bottom and burst into flames.

Ernie switched off the radio, his fingers numb, picked up his telephone and rang the Post Office.

Perhaps, before I return, something'll have happened this night to make you see the sense of it.

Sense, he thought, feeling cold all of a sudden. It's all gone beyond sense.

CHAPTER VI

Chrissie shrieked, 'Come on, come on, *come on!*' and beat with both fists on the door until it shook.

She was wearing a short mac said to be showerproof, but that depended what you meant by shower and she'd taken no more than two minutes to run like hell down the street and she was panting and absolutely bloody *soaked*.

When the door opened, Chrissie practically fell inside. 'God!' Shaking water out of her hair.

Expecting glasses chinking, laughter, maybe the clunk-ding of a one-armed bandit. Certainly not silence and dimness and a red-haired woman with lips drawn tautly back and pain-filled, frozen eyes.

'I'm sorry . . . I mean, this *is* a pub, isn't it? You're still open aren't you? I mean if you're not, I only want to use the phone. To call a taxi.'

'Box,' the woman said in a strangled whisper, as if she had a throat infection. 'Up the street.'

'Yes, I know, but I've no change, I . . . excuse me, but are you all right?'

'Really don't know. Better come in.'

'Thanks. God, what a night.'

'Car . . .' The woman cleared her throat. 'Excuse me. Your car broke down?'

'Actually, I had a row with my boss . . . boyfriend. Well, both. Although probably not either after tonight. I just got out of his car and walked off. Well, ran off, with this weather. I mean, isn't it awful? I'm making a puddle on your floor. Sorry.'

When she rubbed the rain out of her eyes, Chrissie saw she was indeed in what seemed to be a public bar. Nobody here, apart from her and the woman. 'Hey, I'm sorry. I really thought you were open and the door had just jammed or something and . . . You're really not well, are you?'

The woman had her back to the bar which was dark, only the shapes of bottles gleaming. 'Can you . . .' She gripped the edge of a table as if to steady her voice. 'Excuse me, but can you see a light-fitting, like an old gas-mantle, side of the bar?'

'Er . . . yes. Yes, I think so.'

'Is it on?'

'Well, no.' *Could she be blind?*

Then the woman just sort of folded in on herself as if afflicted by some awful stomach cramp or period pain, and Chrissie's brain dried out quickly. The Man I'the Moss. This was Matt Castle's wife. 'Hey,' she said, 'come on, sit yourself down. You on your own?'

Mrs Castle nodded and Chrissie led her to a corner seat opposite the bar and bent down to her. 'Make you a cuppa tea?'

She shook her head. 'I've got coffee. I'm OK. Honestly. Just a shock. I've had a shock.'

'Can I send for anybody? Relatives? A doctor?'

'Please,' Mrs Castle said. 'Just don't go, that's all. Come through. Phone's in the kitchen.' She got up and walked to the bar, and when she reached it a tremor seemed to pass through her and she pushed quickly through a door in the back wall.

Chrissie followed her into a big farmhouse-type kitchen, taking off her sodden mac and tossing it into a corner, useless thing. Underneath, she was wearing her navy-blue suit over a light blue silk blouse and pearls. Classy and understated for John Peveril Stanage's soirée, she thought with a sardonic shudder.

'Just go on talking,' Mrs Castle said. 'I'll be all right in a minute.' She was wearing a big, sloppy Icelandic-type sweater, but she still looked almost blue with cold and she hunched herself over the stove. Chrissie went and stood next to her and folded her arms.

'Well, this chap I was with, called Roger. Married, of course. I'm his bit on the side, except that's not as frivolous or irresponsible as it sounds, for either of us . . . well, it never is, is it, really?'

Mrs Castle was just looking into space. There was a full coffee cup on the table, but the coffee had gone cold, a whirl of cream almost solid on the top like piped icing.

'Roger's a prat,' Chrissie said. 'There's no getting around that. He's got a terrific opinion of himself and yet at the same time he's obviously a bit intimidated by his wife – she's a doctor. He wanted something else, less demanding. Which was me. One slightly shopsoiled divorcee off the bottom shelf – flattering, eh? High-powered wife, so he's looking for something cosy and undemanding and, worst of all, a bit cheap, you know what I mean?'

Mrs Castle nodded and struggled to smile, a little bit of colour in her cheeks. She was actually very attractive, good bones.

'I mean, you talk about undemanding, he didn't even have to go anywhere to pick me up. We work in the same office, I'm his secretary-cum-personal assistant – soon found out what *that* meant.'

Realizing she'd never talked to anybody about her and Roger before. Maybe this could turn out to be unexpectedly therapeutic.

'But at the end of the day,' Chrissie went on, 'his biggest love – I mean, listen to this – his biggest love, who's far more important to Roger than either me or his wife – is a squidgy little brown man who's been dead about two thousand years and came out of a bog. Now, can you . . . ? Ow!'

A kind of mad revulsion in her eyes, Mrs Castle had

suddenly swung round from the stove, grabbed hold of Chrissie's wrist and was digging her nails into it.

As if, Chrissie thought, pulling away, cold, to make sure I'm actually flesh and blood.

'I tell you what, Mrs Castle. I reckon you're the one who would benefit from talking about it.'

'Where are we going exactly?'

'Rog, mustn't be so *anxious*, m'friend! Mind holding the umbrella? Oops! Two hands, please, or you'll lose it.'

Huge golf umbrella; anything else would have been turned inside out by the sheer force of the downpour. Hard, vertical, brutal rain.

'There, that's stopped 'em from dithering.'

'I wasn't d—'

'Surrounded by *ditherers*! Don't worry, I like 'em. Shaw used to be a ditherer, didn't you, Shaw? Ditherer, stammerer, cowardly little bastard. Fixed it, though, didn't we? Fixed *everything*. Right, then, if we're all ready, in we go. Been here before, Rog?'

Darkness. Cold.

'Never. Pretty chilly, isn't it?'

'Chilly? This? Hear that, Tess? Poor Roger thinks it's chilly. This is Tess, my niece, aren't you, darling? And what shall we say about these others? What they are is a bunch of unfortunates befriended by the lass, she's *so . . . good . . . hearted*.'

'Uncle, please . . .'

'Apologies, my love. Yes, up the stairs is where we go. Onwards and upwards. Into the Attic of Death, do you like that?'

'Not really.'

'Relax, relax. Relax*ation*. The key to everything, Shaw knows that, don't you, m'boy? Up again. Ought to be a lift, be totally cream-crackered, time we get there. How you feeling now, Rog?'

'A touch light-headed, now, actually. How many drinks did I have, I can't . . .'

'Just the one, Roger, just the one. Famous for our cocktails, aren't we, Tess?'

'What's that smell?'

'New one on you, is it, Rog? What a terribly sheltered life you must have had, m'boy.'

'Oh, *dear God*.'

'Ah, now, let's not bring *that* chap into it, Roger.'

'I'm going to be sick.'

'No you're not, you're going to get used to it. No time at all. Now relax, the dead can't harm you.'

Don't look at it, don't look at it, don't . . . Oh, Lord, what's happening to my head?

'No, actually, I'm lying again. That's a common myth perpetuated by morticians. You're quite right, the dead can *indeed* harm you, in the most unexpected ways. The dead can harm you *horribly*.'

Laughter. Laughter all around.

By the time Macbeth walked into the room behind the Post Office the sense of there being something deeply wrong in this rain-beaten village – *everybody seems to be on edge tonight* – had become so real it was starting to affect the air; the atmosphere itself seemed thin and worn and stretched tight like plastic film, and faces were pressed up against it trying to breathe.

Two faces. One chubby and female that ought to have looked healthy and a small, male face under a brown fringe, a face out of *Wind in the Willows* or somesuch.

Both faces pressed up against the tight air of a small and crowded room full of flower pictures, flower fabrics and flowers.

Macbeth finding it hard to introduce himself. 'I, uh . . .' Harder still to explain what he was doing here. 'Mrs Castle – Lottie, right? – thought maybe you could tell me where I could find a . . . a friend of mine.'

'Aye,' the little guy said. 'Look, can I ask you, how close were you to Moira, lad?' A slow, kindly voice, but Macbeth felt the damp behind it.

'I guess I'd like to be closer,' he said frankly.

Rain from his black slicker dripping to the floral carpet.

Rain making deltas on the window and small pools on the sill.

Rain coming down the chimney and fizzing on the coalfire.

And yet all the flowers in the room – on the walls, in the pictures, on the woman's dress – contriving to look parched and dead.

The woman said bleakly, 'Since Willie spoke to Lottie we've had a phone call.'

'Moira?'

The woman's wise eyes were heavy with a controlled kind of sorrow.

A hammer inside Macbeth's brain beat out *no, no, no*.

'Sit down, lad,' the little mousy guy said, pulling a chair out from under a gate-legged mahogany dining table. On the table was a bottle of whisky, its seal newly broken; beside it, two glasses.

'Well, of course I don't believe in it, you see, Chrissie. I never have. All right, maybe it's not a question of not believing. I mean, is there a name for a person who just simply *doesn't want to know*?'

Chrissie warmed both hands around her coffee cup. 'For that matter, is there a name for a man who professes to be above all that superstitious nonsense but is more than happy to let it cure his impotence, and then he can go back to not believing in it again?'

'I think "bloody hypocrite" would be one way of putting it,' Lottie said. 'But . . .'

'But tonight . . . God, am I really saying this? Tonight you saw the ghost of your husband.' Chrissie shuddered; *it really did go all the way up your spine*. 'Wasn't going to use that word. Never liked it.'

'Ghost?'

'What does it mean, Lottie? Was he really there? I mean his . . . ?'

'Spirit? Was his spirit there?' Lottie's voice rose, discordant like a cracked bell. 'Yes. I think it was. And crushed. His spirit crushed.'

She thrust a fist to her mouth, swallowing a sob, chewing her knuckles.

'Let it come,' Chrissie said, and Lottie wept some hot, frightened tears. 'Yes, he *was* a man of spirit, always . . . endless enthusiasm for things, what first attracted me. But there's a negative side to enthusiasm, isn't there?'

'Ob . . . session?'

Lottie sniffed. 'First there was the woman. Moira. Not only beautiful, but young and – worst of all, worst of *all*, Chrissie – talented. The thing I couldn't give him. Support, yes. But inspiration . . . ?'

'You're beautiful too,' Chrissie said ineffectually.

'Thanks,' Lottie said. 'Was. Maybe. In the right light. Doesn't mean a lot on its own, though, does it? Don't get me wrong, it never . . . *flowered*, this thing over Moira. They never actually *did it*. I know that now. But I think that's worse in a way, don't you? I mean, the longing goes on, doesn't it? The wondering what it *might* have been. Maybe I should have let him work it out, but I gave him an ultimatum: her or me . . . and his son. Dic. He'd have lost Dic, too. It coincided, all this, you see, with an offer she got to join another band. He made her take it. It was "the right thing to do".'

'Martyrdom,' Chrissie said.

'He didn't get over her exactly. He just went in search of a new obsession and ended up reviving an old one. Which was coming back to Bridelow. Not my idea of heaven on earth.'

'Not tonight anyway,' Chrissie said, looking over to the window. It was like staring into a dark fishtank.

'Naturally, I encouraged him. Sent him up here at weekends with Dic and a picnic lunch. Safe enough – I just didn't think it would ever happen. Then they found that blasted bog body and he just went nuts over it. Kept going to see the damn thing, like visiting a relative in hospital or prison or somewhere. Next thing, he hears the brewery's been flogged off and this place is on the market, and I was just carried along, like a whirlwind picks you up and you come down somewhere else you never wanted to be.'

Lottie stopped, as if realizing there was little more to be said. 'And then he got ill and died.'

She nodded at the door to the bar. 'That gas-mantle. He worked for hours on it. Place was a tip, plastering needed doing, but all he was bothered about was his precious gas-mantle. Bit of atmosphere. Matt all over: tunnel vision.'

'I read once . . .' Chrissie hesitated. 'An article in some magazine at the dentist's. This chap said there were certain things they came back to. Gh . . . dead people . . . Christ, that sounds even worse. Anyway, things they'd been attracted to in life.'

'Aye. Makes sense he'd come back to his bloody gaslight, rather than me.'

'I didn't mean it that way. Sort of landmark for them to home in on. Like a light in the fog. You could always have it taken down.'

'He'd go daft. He'd hold it against me for ever.'

'What did he look like? His old self, or what?'

'He looked terrible.' Lottie started to cry again. Why can't you ever learn to button it, kid? Chrissie told herself.

'It was very misty,' Lottie said through a crumpled hand-kerchief. 'He kept fading and then . . . like a bad TV picture in the old days, remember? As if – I suppose your chap was right – as if he was trying to hold on to his old gas-mantle, for comfort, and something was trying to pull him back.'

'Back where?'

'Into the darkness behind the mirror. He couldn't see me, I'm sure he couldn't *see* me at all. Am I going mad, Chrissie?'

'No more than any of us. Do you want me to stay with you tonight? I've nowhere else to go.'

Lottie's hands clutched each other, began to vibrate. She's wringing her hands, Chrissie thought. I've never seen anybody actually wring their hands before.

'The truth is,' Lottie said, 'I hated him by the end. There was nothing *left* but the negative side. No enthusiasm, *only* obsession. He was, when it comes down to it, a very nasty man.'

Lottie stared into her empty coffee cup as if trying to read a message in the grains. 'But he was also dying, you see, and you aren't allowed to hate dying people, especially if the

431

nastiness is to some extent out of character and therefore, you think, must be connected with the dying.'

Chrissie lit another cigarette. 'When my mother was dying, towards the end, I wanted it to be over. For her sake. But, if I'm honest, partly for my sake too.'

'I don't think we're talking about the same thing, luv. Christ almighty . . .' Lottie covered her ears – '. . . isn't this bloody rain *ever* going to stop?'

'Listen to me,' Chrissie said. 'When you thought . . . when you saw this . . . when he was in the mirror, tonight . . . did you hate him then?'

'No. I felt sorry for him. Don't get me wrong, I was very frightened, but at the bottom of that there was a pity. It was the gas-mantle. Putting that together, wiring it up, was about the only innocent, gentle thing he did here. I was irritated at the time, but when I look back . . . It's the only thing makes me want to cry for him.'

Chrissie stood up. 'I don't know why, but I think we should put it on. The light, I mean. The gas thing.'

'Why?'

'Because if that represents the nice, harmless side of him, perhaps you should show him you recognize that. I don't know, maybe it's stupid. But perhaps he wants your forgiveness, perhaps he wants to know you remember that side of him. The gentle side. So maybe, if you gave him a sign that you understood, then he . . . he'd be . . . you know . . . at peace. Isn't that what they say?'

'Who?'

Chrissie shrugged. 'Old wives, I suppose.'

'Old mothers in this village. OK.' Lottie came wearily to her feet. 'Let's try it.'

'Might make you feel better.'

'Might, at that.'

They went through to the darkened bar and Chrissie lifted the flap and went round to the customers' side, so they were standing either side of the brass mantle. In the arrow of light from the kitchen, she could see it was on a hinged base screwed into the wooden frame of the bar and projecting about eighteen inches. Behind it, on Lottie's side, was the mirror in a Victorian mahogany frame. Chrissie made herself gaze into the mirror and saw only her own dim reflection, looking rather pale and solemn.

'Perhaps we should say a prayer, Lottie.'

'No, thanks,' Lottie said.

'Well, at least think of him as you press the switch. Think of the good times.'

'My memory isn't what it was,' said Lottie. 'No, I'm sorry. You're doing your best. All right. Matt, listen, if you can hear me . . .'

At the end of the gas-mantle a feeble glow appeared.

'Switch it off a second, Lottie, let's get this right.'

'I didn't . . .' Lottie said, in a voice which rose in pitch until it cracked, '. . . switch it on.'

'Merciful God,' Chrissie pulled from somewhere in her past, 'please . . .'

The small light at once flared to a dazzling, magnesium white. Huge shadows reared. Lottie screamed once and backed off into the kitchen.

When the bulb exploded, with a crack like snapping bone, Chrissie found herself at the far end of the bar trying to hug the stone wall.

CHAPTER VII

'Listen,' Macbeth said, clutching Milly's plump arm, 'let me call the cops. Maybe it wasn't her car.'

'Don't make it worse, lad,' Willie Wagstaff said, his eyes hollowed out with grief. 'I've already been on to um. I said me wife were out in a BMW and I were worried sick after hearing the news. I didn't want to get involved in identification or owt, so in the end I said the wife's car were red and they said this one was grey – *had* been grey – and give me the registration, and I went off, sounding relieved. Relieved. Jesus.'

'I don't understand.' Macbeth stared desperately around the room. 'These things don't happen. I just don't fucking *understand*.'

'They do happen,' Willie said hopelessly.

'Especially here.' Milly was looking hard into the fire. 'Especially now.'

'Shurrup,' said Willie gruffly. 'How far you come, lad?'

'Glasgow.' The One Big Thing, he thought. God damn. And closed his eyes against the pain.

'She was special,' Willie said. 'We all knew that.'

'Yeah,' he whispered.

'Special like your mother,' Milly said. 'I think we knew that too. And now they're both dead.'

'Leave it, luv. It's coincidence.'

'Is it?'

Macbeth opened his eyes. Something badly wrong here, but did he care? And what could he do anyway? One week. Before that, Moira Cairns had been a face on an old album cover.

One week. A chance meeting, an inexplicable cascade of bones, a talk on the terrace in the aftermath.

There'd be another album now. The Best of Moira Cairns. In memoriam. Even if he'd never met her, he'd be grieving. In one week, she'd become the core of his existence – a woman whose last glance at him had said, fuck off.

'There was a guy,' he heard himself saying, 'who meant her harm.'

Donald told me the dogs disliked this man intensely. On sight.

Willie Wagstaff and his girlfriend were both staring at him.

'The Duchess wanted me to look out for her, you know? The Duchess said wherever she went she'd be . . . touched with madness.'

'Who's the Duchess?' Willie asked. Macbeth noticed that the fingers of Willie's left hand had struck up a rhythm on the side of his knee. He seemed unaware of it.

Macbeth said, 'Her mother.'

'The gypsy?'

Macbeth nodded. He looked out of the window. A big van with a blue beacon and an illuminated sign had stopped down the street. The sign said, Ambulance. 'Is this rain never gonna ease off? Is it normal?'

'No,' Milly said. 'It's not normal. Who was the man? You said there was a man. Who . . . meant her harm.'

434

Macbeth's mind slipped out of gear for a moment. He panicked, clutched at the air.

The air in the room, so dense. The rain bombarding the roof. The Duchess said, *If there was a problem and you were to deal with it, she need never know, need she?*

And how badly he'd wanted to deal with it and *wanted* her to know, and now it was too late to deal with it and, sure, she would never know.

'John Peveril Stanage,' he said.

And the other two people in the room slowly turned and looked at each other, and Willie blanched.

The fingers of both hands were slamming into his knees and this time he *was* aware of it but seemed unable to stop it.

When the ambulance arrived at the chip shop for Maurice Winstanley, both Maurice and his wife, Dee, were in a state bordering on hysteria.

'I knew summat like this'd happen. I never wanted to open, me,' Dee shrilled, a skinny little woman – how could you work in a chip shop and be that thin? It fascinated one of the ambulancemen for a couple of seconds until he saw how badly burned Maurice was.

They had to treat his arm best they could, but there wasn't a whole lot they could do on the spot, what with Maurice gawping around and then kind of giggling with pain, and his wife going on and on like a budgie on amphctamines.

'I says to him, Who's going to come out for chips, night like this? He says, What about all them young people up at t'church, they'll be starving before t'night's through. I says, All right, I says, you want to do it, you can do it on your own.'

The ambulanceman had fancied a bag of chips himself, specially after that drive over the hills and across the Moss: gruesome – he'd been driving and felt sure he could see the bloody peat rising and sucking; put one wheel in there you'd have had it.

'All right, Mr Winstanley, if we can get you out this way . . .'

'Where's your stretcher, then?'

'He can walk, can't he, Mrs Winstanley? I was going to say, we need to get him in as quick as we can. He might need to go to the burns unit.'

But chips would never be the same again. How gut-churning an appetizing smell like that could become when, on top of battered cod and mushy peas, there was the subtle essence of frazzled flesh, the result of Maurice Winstanley's right arm blistering and bubbling in the fryer.

'Lucky you haven't got a heart attack case, as well,' Dee said. 'He let out such a shriek.'

'I'm not surprised, luv. Any of us'd've gone through the roof.'

'Oh, this were *before* he stuck his arm in t'fat. I says, Now, what's up, I says. And he turns round, white as a sheet, I says, Whatever have you done? And *then* he does it. Thirty years frying and he shoves his arm in. I don't think he knew what he were doing at all.'

In the ambulance, racing back across the Moss, Maurice shivered and shook a lot, a red blanket round him, his arm in about half a mile of bandage. 'Never believe me, lad, she never will. I wouldn't believe me.'

'Don't matter how long you've been at it, Mr Winstanley, you can always have an accident.'

'No, not that.' Now Maurice *looked* like a chip shop proprietor. Maurice was a fat man. Maurice's big cheeks had that high-cholesterol glow about them and there were black, smoky rings around his eyes.

'She had to believe that, naturally,' Maurice said. 'She seen it happen. Fact it were only t'bloody agony of it brought me round, see, and I couldn't even feel that at first. I were looking at it a good two seconds. I thought, what's that pink thing in t'bloody fat?'

'Don't think about it, Mr Winstanley. We'll not be long now. What d'you reckon to United's chances, then?'

'I don't want to talk about *United*, lad! I hate bloody soccer. Listen, no, it weren't *that* she'll not believe, I've allus been a clumsy bugger. No, see, what it were as caused it in t'first place, I'd just seen summat as frickened life outer me. Froze me to t'spot, you know? Numb, I were. Numb.'

'Sounds like my mother-in-law.'

'Oh, Christ,' said Maurice Winstanley, subsiding into his pain. 'What's the bloody use?'

Even though Deirdre Winstanley opened all the windows into the rain, the smell of fried skin wouldn't go away; only seemed to get stronger.

When she opened the door, Susan Manifold, having seen the ambulance, ran across the street through the torrent, asking Dee what was wrong, could she help.

'His own fault,' Dee said. 'Silly bugger. Thirty years, I don't know.'

'Will he be all right?'

'Will any of us?'

'I'm sorry?' Susan Manifold stepped inside the chip shop, to escape the wet, wrinkling her nose at the smell.

'Well, look at it.' Dee gestured at the water, now level over the cobbles and the drains weren't taking it. She seemed more worried about that than Maurice's injury, or perhaps she was looking for something to take her mind off it.

'Will it flood?' Susan asked.

'Never has before, but there's always a first time. Look at them drains. Is there nowt you can do?'

'I'm not a plumber,' said Susan.

'No,' said Dee. 'But you're a Mother.'

'Oh, come on!' Susan flicked back her ash-blonde fringe. 'We can't alter the weather.'

'Could've, once. Not you, maybe, Susan. Happen before your time.'

'Old wives' tale,' Susan said carelessly, and the full horror of what she'd said came back at her like a slap in the mouth. She was betraying Milly Gill and the memory of Ma Wagstaff. But, God help her, *Mother* help her, she had no belief in it any more.

Upset, she walked back across the drowned cobbles. Frank

wasn't home yet from the pub. When he did arrive he'd be drunk and nasty. Another problem the Mothers were supposed to be able to deal with.

Dee Winstanley slammed the door. That was stupid, what she'd said. Stupid what Susan had replied. Stupid what Maurice had done. Stupid to have lived behind a stinking chip shop for thirty years.

Stupid, stupid, stupid.

And the smell wouldn't go away; the layer of fat, from fish and pies and peas and fried human skin, hung from the ceiling like a dirty curtain, and the fluorescent tubelight was a bar of grease.

Dee threw up the flap, stumbled behind the counter, slammed down the chromium lid on a frier full of flabby chips congealing together like a heap of discarded yellow rubber gloves.

Couldn't clean that tonight. Just couldn't.

'Cod and six pennorth o' chips. Please.'

The nerve of some people. 'We're closed,' Dee yelled into the thick air around the high counter.

'. . . and six pennorth o' chips.'

Dee sighed. Some people still thought it was funny to demand six pennorth o' chips, same as what they'd asked for in old money when they were kids.

'We've had to close early,' she explained patiently. 'Maurice's had an accident. Gone to hospital. All the chips are ruined.'

She peered through the shimmering grease at this persistent customer. Recognized the voice straight away, just couldn't put a name to it.

'. . . pennorth o' chips. Please.'

The customer clambered through the lardy light and she heard the clatter of coins on the glass counter.

'You deaf or summat, Matt? I can't serve you. It's Maurice . . . they've taken Maurice off in th'ambulance. He's had a . . .'

'. . . and six pennorth . . .'

*

At first there was no sound in the crowded, flowery sitting room, except for the endlessly percussive weather and Willie Wagstaff's fingers on his jeans picking up the same rapid rhythm.

'John Peveril Stanage,' Macbeth repeated in a stronger voice, because the name'd had the same effect as throwing three aces into a poker game.

Doing this for the Duchess.

Willie said, 'Never heard of him,' about a second too late to be convincing, and Macbeth, suddenly furious, was halfway out of his chair when there were four hollow knocks at the front door, all the more audible for being way out of synch with Willie's fingers and the rain.

'Mr Dawber,' Milly Gill said tonelessly, but made no move to answer the door.

CHAPTER VIII

Milly Gill half rose and then sat down again and looked at Willie and then at Mungo Macbeth.

'I'm sorry, Mr Macbeth. Sorry to've given you such awful news. But . . .' Spreading her hands: what else can I do?

Telling him to get the hell out in other words.

Macbeth stood up but made no move toward the door. 'I don't think so,' he said.

The hollow knocking came again, a little faster this time, a little closer to the tempo of Wagstaff's restless fingers.

'Why d'you do that?' Macbeth said, in no mood for tact. 'With your fingers.'

Willie looked non-plussed, like nobody ever asked him that before.

'He has a problem with his nerves,' Milly Gill said hastily. 'If you don't mind, Mr Macbeth, there's a gentleman come to see us.'

So they know who it is. Knocking comes at the door, latish, and they know what it's about before they open up.

439

'Sure,' Macbeth said. 'Thanks for your time.' Maybe he *should* go. Cancel his room at the inn, drive out of here, head back north. Maybe organize a flight home. And call on the Duchess? Could he ever face the Duchess again?

He nodded at Willie Wagstaff, followed Milly Gill to the door.

'Good luck,' he said, not sure why he said that.

And then something told him to turn around, and he found Willie on his feet, a whole series of expressions chasing each other across the little guy's face like videotape on fast-forward.

'Look.' Willie was clasping both hands between his legs like a man who badly needed to use the john. 'It's not nerves. It's . . .'

'Hey.' The big woman pulled back her hand from the door catch. 'A few minutes ago you were telling *me* to shut up.'

'I know, lass, but happen we've kept quiet too bloody long. This . . . Moira. Dead. Finished me, that has. Too many accidents. Going right back to that lad who fell off top of the brewery. Too much bad luck. And when I hear Jack's name . . . Hang on a minute, lad. Milly, let Ernie Dawber in.'

Milly said, 'If it's Jack – which I . . .' She swallowed. 'If it is, we've got to sort it out for ourselves.'

'Oh, aye. Like we've sorted everything else out. *Let him in.*'

This Ernie Dawber was a short, stout, dignified-looking elderly guy in a long raincoat and a hat. He didn't look pleased at being kept waiting in the rain. He looked even less pleased to see Macbeth.

'This bloke's a friend of Moira's,' Willie Wagstaff explained.

'Mungo Macbeth.'

Old guy's handshake was firm. Eyes pretty damn shrewd. 'My condolences,' he said. 'I'm sorry.'

'Mr Dawber,' Willie said, 'I'll not mess about. This lad – Mungo – reckons Moira . . .' He took a breath. 'He reckons there's a connection with Jack. With . . . John Peveril Stanage.'

Willie's voice was so thick with loathing that Macbeth had to step back.

'Not possible,' Ernie Dawber said. 'I know what you're saying, but it's not possible.'

'No?' said Willie.

'He was banished, Willie. In the fullest sense. Forty-odd years ago. In all that time he's never once tried to come back. And if your ma was here now she'd go mad at you for even saying his name.'

'Aye. But she's not. She's dead.' Willie's voice hardened. 'Suddenly. Under very questionable circumstances.'

Ernie Dawber shook his head. 'You're clutching at straws.'

Milly Gill said, 'Leave it, Willie. We've problems enough. Jack couldn't set foot in this village . . .'

'While Ma was alive!' Willie shouted.

'He's a rich man now, Willie, he's got everything he needs. And like Mr Dawber says, he's never once tried to get back in. Why should he?'

'Aye,' said Willie. 'Why should anybody want owt to do wi' Bridelow? Why's Bridelow suddenly important? Why's it on everybody's lips when things here've never been so depressed? Why? – Mr Dawber'll tell you, he's got the same disease.'

'Willie, stop it off!'

Willie brought a hand down on the gateleg table with a crack. 'Bogman fever! That little bastard's contagious. Look at Matt, he got too close for his own sanity. How close did you get, Mr Dawber, that you want to die for it as well? Did you ever think it'd got at *your* mind . . . staid, cautious old Ernie Dawber, man of letters?' He turned away. 'Ernie Dawber, human sacrifice. Don't make me laugh!'

'Stop it!' Milly Gill advanced on Willie like she was figuring to pull him apart. 'How dare you, little man? There's things we *never* can laugh at. Maybe something's turned *your* mind.'

'Jesus.' Macbeth stepped between them. 'Bogman fever? Human sacrifice? What kinda shit *is* this? Guy in the bar said everybody was on edge tonight, I figured he was making small-talk. Back off, huh?'

Removing his hat, Ernie Dawber stepped further into the room, leaving the door ajar behind him. No visible ease-up in the rain. 'Could I ask you, Mr . . .'

'Macbeth. Like the evil Scottish King, had all his buddies iced.'

'That's as maybe,' Ernie Dawber said. 'But could I ask you, sir, what precisely is your interest here?'

'I got nothing to hide.' Macbeth let his arms fall to his sides. 'I fell in love with a woman.'

The noise from outside was like Niagara.

'And now she's dead,' Macbeth said. 'Some bastard's keeping secrets about that, maybe it's time for me to research a few ancestral vices, yeah?'

He shifted uncomfortably. Starting to sound like some steep-jawed asshole out of one of his own TV shows.

'Perhaps,' said Ernie Dawber, 'we should all calm down and discuss this. And for what it's worth – history being my subject – despite the Bard's best efforts to convince us otherwise, Macbeth was actually quite a stable monarch.'

'Ernie . . .' Macbeth pulled out a chair. 'I wasn't so pissed about this whole thing, I could maybe get to like you.' He sat. 'Now. Somebody gonna tell me about John Peveril Stanage?'

Only Milly Gill still looked defiant. She folded her arms, pushed the door shut with her ass.

'Oh, hell, tell him, Willie,' Ernie Dawber said.

It had been novelty value, and now it was wearing off.

Chris wasn't stupid; he wasn't blind, being born-again to God didn't blind you to common sense.

Most of them were young. They sought, Chris conceded, a vibrancy and an excitement in religion which the Church had failed to give them. They found it at outdoor rallies, in marquees and packed rooms that were more like dancehalls. And now they were back where, for many of them, it had begun first time around in the stoneclad starkness of an old-fashioned church. To defend it, Joel had told them. Against evil. But an evil they could not see, nor comprehend.

And Chris, an elder of the Church of the Angels of the New Advent, was asking himself: is this man, this figure of almost prophet-like glamour, this embodiment of the biblically angelic, is this man *entirely sane*?

'Joel.' Chris shambled over to the lectern, a lean, bearded man in a lumberjack shirt. 'Er, how many hours has it been exactly?'

'Are you counting, Chris?'

'No, but . . . I know the heat's on in here, but it's still pretty cold. Bit of an ordeal for some of these kids.'

'You're saying their faith isn't strong enough?'

Like the PE teacher he used to be, Chris thought. Loftily disdainful of youngsters shivering on a wintry playing field.

'Of course not,' Chris said. 'But don't you think . . . don't you think this church is *clean* now?'

'This thing is deep-seated, Chris.' Joel clutched at the lectern for strength, the muscles tautening in his face. 'You think you can eradicate centuries of evil in a few hours?'

He looked down at the wooden pedestal lectern, as if seeing it for the first time, and then sprang back. 'Look! Look at this!'

The lectern was supporting a black-bound Bible, open across spread wings of carved oak.

'It's an eagle,' Chris said. 'Lots of them are eagles.'

'This is not an eagle.' Joel's hands retracted as if the lectern were coated with acid. 'Look.'

Chris didn't understand.

'An owl is a pagan bird,' Joel intoned calmly, like a bomb-disposal expert identifying a device. 'Step away from it. Go down and open the door.' He closed his eyes, breathed a brief, intense prayer for protection, gently detached the Bible, carried it to a choir stall.

And then hefted the lectern in both arms, as though uprooting a young tree.

'Door!' Joel gasped.

Feeling less than certain about this, Chris preceded him down the aisle. Hesitantly, he held open the church door and then the porch door until Joel had staggered out and, with an animal grunt, hurled the lectern far into the rainy tumult of the night.

They heard it crash against a tombstone.

'Filthy conditions.' Joel stumbled back into the church, slapping at his surplice, a strange, fixed look on his face. 'Is this natural, all this rain? Is it *natural*, Chris?'

443

'It's only rain, Joel.'

'You're not seeing this, Chris, are you? You're not seeing it at all.'

All heads were turned towards him as he walked back up the aisle. Chris sensed an element of uncertainty among their devotion. Perhaps Joel was slightly aware of it too, for he raised his eyes to the altar. 'Oh Lord, give them a sign. Give them proof!'

He stood where the lectern had been, his coronet of curls looking dull, as if tarnished by the rain. Chris found himself praying silently for deliverance from what was becoming a nightmare.

'It was . . .' Joel spread his big hands helplessly the width of the aisle, '. . . evil. Don't you see? It wasn't an eagle, it was an *owl*. A symbol of what *they* would call "ancient wisdom". It was a *satanic artefact*. Can't you understand? It had to be removed.'

'Praise God,' someone called out, but only once and rather feebly.

A man in a white T-shirt drifted up to Joel as if to congratulate him, shake him by the hand. When Joel opened his arms to embrace his brother, he felt a blast of cold air against his chest.

Puzzled, he looked down and saw that his pectoral cross was missing. Must have become hooked around the lectern, and he'd thrown it out of the door as well. He felt angry with himself. Now he had to *visualize* the cross. But he saw his brother Angel's open arms and he smiled.

His brother was smiling back. His brother's eyes were brown and swirling like beer-dregs in a glass.

'Thank you,' Joel said. 'Thank you for your support. Thank you for your faith.'

Couldn't recall the name. But he knew the face, although he'd seen it only once before.

'Joel,' Chris said, 'you OK?'

Seen the face by lamplight and edged with lace in a violated coffin.

Joel's eyes bulged. He felt his jaw tightening, his lips

shrinking back over his teeth, his throat expanding under pressure of a scream.

But he didn't scream. He would *not* scream. Instead, he stretched out his arms and grasped his terror to his bosom.

'Joel!' A voice behind him. Chris? But so far away, too far away, a dimension away from death's cold capsule in which Joel embraced a column of writhing darkness comprised of a thousand wriggling, frigid worms.

'Begone.' But it came out breathless, thin and whingeing, from between his clenched teeth.

He tried to project the missing pectoral cross in front of him, a cross of white fire.

Gasping, 'In the name . . . name of God.' As the cold worms began to glide inside his vestments and to feed upon him, to devour his faith. 'In God's name . . . *begone!*'

'Joel, stop it.' Hands either side of him, clutching at his arms.

The cross of fire had become a cross of ice.

Joel roared like a bull.

They were pinioning his arms while the cold worms sucked at his soul. His own brothers in God offering him as sustenance for the voracious dead.

'*Aaaaargh!*'

A boiling strength erupted in his chest.

In the centre of the silence, the black bag was brought to the woman.

From the bag, a thick, dark stole uncoiling. A slender vein of silver or white.

Winding it around her hands like flax and holding it up and showing it to the corpse, twisting it in the candlelight.

Hair. Human hair, two feet of it, three, bound together, with a strip of grey-white hair rippling through it.

The woman's hands moving inside the tent of hair with a certain rhythmical fluidity, as the pipes moaned, an aching lament. The watchers mumbling and, out of this, a single voice rising, a pale ribbon of a voice singing out, '*I conjure thee.*'

And winding back into the mumbling with the winding of the hair.

'He's coming.

He's coming and he's strong.'

Up against the vestry wall, four of the men around him so he couldn't break away, he wailed in despair, 'Whose side are you *on*?'

Blood in the aisle. One man sitting up on the flags, head in his hands, semi-concussed.

Chris pressing a tissue to a burst lip. 'Joel, it's all gone wrong. You're seriously scaring people. Some of the women want to leave, get out of here.'

'They can't. They can't go out there now. Not safe, do you not see?'

'Joel, I'm sorry, they're saying it's probably safer out there than it is here with . . . with you.'

'Lock and bar the doors. Go on. Do it now. LOCK AND BAR THE DOORS!'

'Joel, please, they're saying *you* . . . All that screaming and wrestling with . . .'

'With evil! The infested dead!'

'. . . with yourself, Joel! Oh, my God, this is awful. Somebody wipe his mouth.'

'Where *is* he?'

Joel flailed, but they held him.

'Where *is* he? The spirit. Was he expelled? *Tell* me.'

'Let's go back to the Rectory, shall we? Have a cup of coffee? Come back later. When we've all, you know, calmed down.'

'What's happened to your face?'

'You hit me, Joel.'

'No.'

'Yes! You were like a man poss . . . We couldn't hold you. Please, Joel. You've been under a lot of stress.'

'. . . fighting it . . . fighting for our souls. Stinking of the grave . . . filthy womancunt . . . let me . . .'

'Come on. You're scaring people. Let's get some air. Please.'

'Matt Castle. Spirit of Matt Castle. Soiled. *Soiled spirit.*'

'Joel, Matt Castle's dead . . .'

'And was *here*!'

'Look, Declan's hurt. I think he hit his head. He needs a doctor. Please.'

'Illusion. Temptation. They *want* you to open the doors and let them in. If you don't do it of your own free will, they'll get inside you, fill you up with worms, make you think things that aren't true. Let me go, I command you to let me go.'

'Let him go.'

'Chris?'

'Just let him go. We can't hold him all night.'

'Matt Castle. Its face was Matt Castle's. But I looked into its eyes and its eyes were the eyes of Satan.'

'Yes. Yes, but it's gone now, Joel. I swear to you it's gone. You . . . you defeated it. You were more powerful. You . . . you threw it to the ground and it . . . sort of disintegrated.'

'Ah.'

'Yes, we saw it. We did. Didn't we, Richard? So, Joel, come back to the Rectory, OK? You need a coffee. And a lie down. After your exertions. After your . . . Oh God, help me . . .'

'. . . was it wearing?'

'. . . your struggle.'

'What was it *wearing*?'

'I . . . Well, it wasn't . . . I mean, too clear. Not from where we were standing. A . . . a shroud, was it? And glowing. Sort of glowing?'

Joel felt his face explode. '*Liars!*'

His chest swelled, arms thrashed. One man was thrown across the vestry like a doll, spinning dizzily around until the stone wall slapped into his nose; they heard him squeak and a quick crack of bone, and then Joel's white surplice was blotting up bullets of blood.

'Come on! Let's get out now. Don't go near him.'

'What about Martin?'

447

'Pick him up, come *on*. Oh, my God. It's all right. It's all *right*! Somebody stop them *screaming*.'

Joel heard scrambling and scuffling, stifled shouts and squawks and screams, bolts being thrown, the soulless slashing of the rain and a shrilling from inside of him, something squealing to be free.

At first he wouldn't move, paralysed with dread. Then he began to laugh. It was only the mobile phone at the leather belt around his cassock.

He pulled it out and inspected it. A deep fissure ran from the earpiece to the push-buttons. He had difficulty dragging out the aerial because its housing was bent.

The phone went on bleeping at him.

He tried to push the 'send' button, but it wouldn't go in. Joel became irrationally enraged with the phone and began to beat it against the wall. Went on beating it when the bleeps stopped and a tinny little faraway voice was calling out, '*Mr Beard*.'

Would have continued until it smashed to pieces in his hand, had he not recognized the voice.

'*Mr Beard, can you hear me?*'

'Yes.'

'*Are you all right, Mr Beard?*'

'They've all gone.'

'*Who?*'

'The Angels.' He giggled. 'The Angels have flown.'

'*As angels are apt to do. You won't run away from this, will you?*'

'Never!'

'*Mr Beard, I told you once – do you remember? – about the Devil's light. How no one could cross the Moss at night except for those for whom the Devil lit the way.*'

'Yes. I remember. Isn't it time you told me who you were?'

'*I'll do better than that, Mr Beard. I'll meet you.*'

'When? Where?'

'*Tonight. Stay in the church. Be alone.*'

'No choice, have I? And yet I know . . .'

448

'*You could always run away from it.*' Teasing.

'I'll never do that. I'm not afraid, you know. I . . . tonight I've embraced evil and I know . . . I know that I am never totally alone.'

'*Well said, m'boy. Together we'll put out the Devil's light.*'

'Thank you,' Joel said. 'Nobody else believes in me. Thank you. Thank you for everything.'

He started to weep with the joy of the sure knowledge that he was not alone.

PART NINE

FEAST OF THE DEAD

From *Dawber's* Secret *Book of Bridelow* (unpublished):

SAMHAIN. (i)

IN BRIDELOW, NEW YEAR is celebrated twice. Once in late February, at Candlemas, the feast of Brigid (and St Bride), when we look forward to the first signs of Spring. And also, of course, at Samhain – now sadly discredited as Hallowe'en – the Feast of the Dead.

This remains the most mysterious of Celtic festivals, a time when we remember the departed and the tradition bequeathed to us. A time, also, when the dead may be consulted, although such practices have been actively discouraged because of the inherent danger to the health and sanity of the living.

CHAPTER I

It was bad, what he learned about John Peveril Stanage. So bad it made Macbeth wonder how the hell the creep had ever gotten published as a writer for children without some kind of public outcry. And yet he felt there was something crucial they weren't telling him, something they were edging around.

'It was, I believe, an incident with the cats that was the first indication,' Ernie Dawber was saying. 'Because that was the first direct attack on Ma . . . not your ma, Willie, the old Ma.'

'Bob and Jim,' Willie said sadly. 'They was always called Bob and Jim.'

Very slowly Macbeth had been building up an image of this village as somewhere arguably more Celtic, in the ethnic and religious sense, than any known area of Scotland, Wales, Ireland or even upstate California.

And because he'd never seen the place, except at night and through equatorial rain, this image was clearer and more credible than it ought to have been.

He'd learned that Ma Wagstaff, some kind of matriarchal figure, had died under what the people of Bridelow, if not the medics, considered questionable circumstances.

He'd learned the significance of the Man in the Moss, about which he recollected reading a downpage item in the *New York Times* some months back.

Altogether, he'd learned more than it might normally have been considered wise for them to tell him, and he guessed they'd opened up to him for two basic reasons – A: because they saw what Moira's death had done to him. And B: because they and most other sentient beings in Bridelow had good reason to believe they were in some deep shit.

'What'd he do to the cats?' Macbeth asked, not sure he really wanted to know.

'More a question of what he *would* have done,' Willie said,

454

'if Old Ma hadn't caught him with his magical paraphernalia and his knife and the poor cat tied to a bread board. He'd be about twelve at the time.'

'Little swine,' Milly said. There were two cats on her knee, one black, one white.

'I can just about remember it,' Willie said. 'I were only a little kid. I remember Old Ma shut herself away for a long time – most of a day. Just her and the cats – one had white bandages on its front paws, thanks to Jack, but it was better than no head. And none of us was allowed to go near, except them as was summoned.'

'Always the practice at a time of crisis,' said Ernie Dawber. 'I remember, not long after I became a teacher at the school, Walter Boston, who was vicar then, he shuffled in one fine morning and called me out of class. I was to go and present myself to Old Ma at once. Well, I wasn't entirely sure in those days of Old Ma's role in the community, but I knew enough not to argue, so it was "class dismissed" and off I went.'

Ernie Dawber was sitting in a stiff-backed chair, his hat on his knees and a cup and saucer balanced on the crown of it.

'So, in I go, and there's Old Ma, sitting like you, Milly, cats on knees. And our Ma was there, too, still known as Iris in those days, although not for much longer. Anyroad, they said I was to go back and talk to each of the children in turn and find out if any of them had had . . . dealings . . . with Jack.'

Macbeth said, 'We talking about what I think we're talking about?'

'Depends,' Milly Gill said. 'Nowadays what they call ritual child-abuse is mostly just a cover for paedophile stuff. For Jack, the abuse was incidental, the ritual was the important bit.'

'Let's put this in context,' Ernie Dawber said. 'The Bride-low tradition is very much on the distaff side, and most of us accept this. It's a gentler, softer kind of, of . . .'

'Witchcraft?' Macbeth said.

Milly said, 'We don't like that word, Mungo. It implies you want to use it to *do* something. All we wanted was to keep a

455

balance. It's more like, you know, conservation. That's why women have been best at it; not got that same kind of aggression, not so arrogant as men.'

'In general.' Ernie Dawber sniffed once. 'But what I wanted to say was that you don't get a tradition carried on this long unless there's a certain . . .'

'Power,' Milly said. 'Immense power.'

'. . . concentrated here,' said Mr Dawber.

'Power?' Macbeth was still sitting at the gateleg table. There was a small amount of whisky left in his glass. 'What kind of power we talking about?'

Milly rearranged the cats. 'Let's just say that if you wanted to *do* something you'd do it a lot better in Bridelow than you might elsewhere.'

Willie said, 'For most of the lads here it's no big deal. We used to say it were women's stuff – back in the days when you were allowed to talk like that. So it were a while before anybody realized that Jack . . . Stanage, I'll call him that, though that's just an invented name he writes under . . . that Jack Stanage had been, like . . . studying.'

'He always had a girl,' Ernie said. 'Any girl. Any girl – or woman – he wanted. This'd be from the age of about thirteen. Bit more precocious in those days than it might seem now.'

'Yes,' Milly said, and they all looked at her. Milly looked down at the cats and said no more.

'I didn't notice that so much,' said Willie hurriedly, 'him being a few years older than me. What I noticed was the money. He always had lots of money. He was generous with it too, if you went along with what he wanted you to do. He could show you a good time, could Jack.'

Milly didn't look up. 'Not when you're ten years old,' she said.

'Uh . . . yeah.' Macbeth reached over to his slicker, pulled out the paperback, *Blue John's Way*. Ernie Dawber picked it up with a thin smile.

'You read it?'

'Leafed through it. In light of what I just heard, I wondered if maybe . . .'

'Not so much an allegory, Mr Macbeth, as . . .'

'Mungo.'

'When I know you better, Mr Macbeth. Not so much allegory as a case of "only the names have been changed".'

'So let me get this right . . .' Macbeth was cautious. 'This is a guy who gravitates towards the, uh, arcane. A guy who might like to try and harness other people's powers, maybe.'

Willie looked up. 'What are you thinking about?'

Macbeth finished up his whisky. It made him feel no better. 'I'm thinking about Moira Cairns,' he said soberly. 'And I'm thinking about a comb.'

To Joel Beard, former teacher of physical education, the issue had always seemed such a simple one. If good was to triumph over evil then good required strength. Good needed to work out regularly and get into condition. Indeed, he found a direct correlation between the heavy pectoral cross and the powerful pectoral muscles needed to support it.

But he couldn't find the pectoral cross.

He'd found the wooden lectern, one of the owl's wooden wings missing, smashed up against the Horridge family tomb. Now he was down on his hands and knees in the sodden grass, the rain pummelling his back.

Not that he felt powerless without the cross, not that he felt like a warrior without his sword; he could stand naked and know that his spiritual strength came from within, but . . .

'Mr Beard . . . are you here?'

Joel stopped scrabbling in the grass, felt his back stiffen.

The fluid, tenor voice had curled with ease around the tumult of the night. It was, he realized suddenly, the voice of a man who might have been a priest.

It's all around you, Mr Beard . . . you'll see the signs everywhere . . . in the church . . .

Joel stood and was drawn towards the voice and the question which had tormented him for so many months.

'Who are you?'

They stood opposite each other at the porch door. Joel thought he was the taller, but only just. He couldn't see the man's face under his black umbrella.

457

The man stepped inside the porch and lowered the umbrella. 'You don't know me?'

'I've never seen you before,' Joel said, water cascading down his face. Sweet, refreshing rain? Rain out of darkness was not so sweet.

The man waited, languid, in the doorway under the porch lantern. He wore a loose, double-breasted suit of black or charcoal grey.

'It's many years since I was here, Mr Beard. It's changed, thankfully. Otherwise I simply wouldn't have been able to come in.'

Joel said, 'I took it upon myself to remove certain offensive artefacts.'

'Well done, m'boy.' The man's face split into a sudden grin, revealing large teeth, unexpectedly yellow in his candle-white face.

'Who are you?' Joel said. 'Why are you doing this?'

'My name,' said the man, extending a long, slender, white hand, 'is John. And I was born here.'

Joel took the hand firmly. He had developed a manly handshake which some recipients apparently found crushing. This hand, he found when his fingers closed on it, was not crushable; it was like high-tensile steel.

He recognized strength.

'May I come in?' he asked politely.

'M' dear boy . . .' The man called John stepped to one side. 'Interesting weather, have to say that. Washes away the murk of the past, perhaps.'

'Did you find it was . . . murky . . . when you lived here?'

'Mr Beard, it was layer upon layer. Tell me – small point – what are your views on the ordination of women?'

'I deplore it,' said Joel from the heart. 'I shall always deplore it.'

'Well said. Probably hasn't escaped your notice that the so-called spirituality of this place has been steered for generations by women.'

'They call *this* spirituality?' Joel gestured towards the space where the pagan abomination had spread her legs.

John lifted his hands. 'My point entirely. Expressed, in

various ways, many years ago. Before I was made to leave. Not much more than a boy at the time. Excluded. And then sent away. Do what they like, these close-knit communities.'

'Made to leave? Because you stood out against their witchery?'

John shrugged.

'It's barely credible,' said Joel.

'I'll be quite frank with you, Joel – may I call you Joel, I feel we've known each other so long now – I'll be quite honest, I promised myself that one day, I'd see them and their way of life destroyed. Can you understand that?'

'"Vengeance is mine sayeth the Lord." However, in certain circumstances, we're all tools, are we not? I've always seen myself as a tool.'

'Quite.' John pulled open the inner door into the church itself and stepped through into the amber-lit interior. He moved like a partially blind man, feeling his way. He kept touching things, placing his hands on the walls, the pillars, the pew-ends, as if surprised that he was not receiving electric shocks.

'It's been cleansed,' Joel said. 'But it's still vulnerable. Was Hans Gruber here in your time?'

'Who? Oh, the collaborating minister. No, I left many years before he arrived. Fellow called Boston in my day. But much the same, y' know. Much the same.'

'A quisling?'

'They're all tamed within a remarkably short space of time. Which is why I thought *you* should be alerted.'

'How did you know I'd come here?'

'Dear boy, could you have *resisted* it? Besides which, there *was* Archdeacon Flemming.'

'Oh.'

'Friends of friends, y' know.'

Joel was vaguely disappointed. He'd seen his mission to Bridelow in terms of divine orchestration rather than human machination. And yet, could not the two be interlinked?

'Gone mostly unchallenged for centuries y' know,' John said. 'And so when local papers were passed to me, relating your adventures in Sheffield, it was clear you were The Man for The Job, as it were. All the namby-pamby clerics around. All the airy-fairy, New Age nancy-boys. No. Anybody could rattle them, Joel, it was going to be you.'

John walked slowly up the nave. Even the amber lights failed to colour the pallor of his skin or the snow-white hair receding in ridges from his grey-freckled forehead.

'Used to have crosses here, made of twigs and things, dangling down. Kiddies would be sent out to collect the entrails.'

'Gone. I dealt with it. And their nasty little shrine at the edge of the moor.'

'But your friends have chickened out. Why was that?'

'There was . . .' Joel shook water from his curls, '. . . a manifestation of evil. Some of them couldn't . . . cope. John, I have to know . . . are you a priest?'

John's yellow teeth reappeared. 'Joel,' he said. 'I've told you as much as I can about me and more than I should.'

'I thought so,' said Joel. He paused. 'It isn't over, is it? If it were, you wouldn't be here.'

'Well deduced, Joel, m' boy. Have you ever been up to the lamp?'

Joel stared at him. He felt an almost chemical excitement in his stomach. 'The so-called Beacon?'

'I said we'd put it out, didn't I? I said between us we'd put out the Devil's Light. So. After you, m' boy.'

'Where?'

'To the stairs. Do you have a hammer?'

'I believe there's one in the shed, bottom of the churchyard.'

John looked at his watch. 'No time, old lad. Witching hour approaches. Have to make do with what we've got.'

He grinned, affable, relaxed and not quite like any priest Joel had ever encountered.

'Stanage fixed it,' Macbeth said, 'so Moira would be performing at the Celtic convention. He also requested that she play a certain song, called "The Comb Song", which was of, uh, personal significance to her.'

'I know.' Willie Wagstaff started to pour out more whisky, then changed his mind and capped the bottle. 'I was there, must be ten years ago, when that song was recorded. My contribution seems to have been chopped in the final mix, but she wanted friends around her during the session. She invited Matt and me, but Matt couldn't come, I think probably Lottie wouldn't let him.'

Macbeth was a mite dismayed. 'Said she hadn't told anyone the background to that song before.'

'She didn't, lad, far as I know. She just wanted us to be there. She never told us what it were about and I didn't ask.'

Macbeth felt a small pinprick of tears. Quickly, to cover up, he began to tell them about the deer-head incident.

'See, just before it happened, it grew real cold in that room and real tense, like a thunderstorm's on the way. Afterwards, this guy – who I now know to be Stanage – is close up to Moira, and he's bleeding from one eye. Probably got hit by a shaft of bone. Looking back, I get the feeling there was some kind of contest – that's too mild a word, some kind of struggle, battle of wills . . . and that's what caused it. I started thinking of two stags locking horns. But there was so much . . .'

'Energy.' Milly Gill was nodding. 'So much energy that it exploded in the atmosphere and brought down all these . . . things.'

'See, another thing, Moira felt pretty negative about the deer heads, the idea of guys like the Earl blasting off at defenceless animals for kicks and then hanging the heads on their walls. Not the old Celtic way, she said, to boast about, I dunno, the superiority of one species over another. Or maybe I read that someplace.'

Ernie Dawber chuckled. 'The Celts were more likely to display *human* heads. But even then, as you say, not gratuitously.'

'It does sound, doesn't it,' Milly said, 'if what you say about him bleeding is correct, that if there *was* a contest, then Moira won it.'

'He wouldn't like that,' Willy said. Macbeth sensed that beneath the table the little guy's fingers were beating bruises into his knees. He found his own fists were clenching.

'But why'd he target Moira, that's the question? What'd he want with her?'

Willie said, 'Well, it's no coincidence, is it?'

Ernie Dawber looked up at the wall-clock, hand-painted with spring flowers. 'I don't want to hurry you, but I'm not sure where this is getting us.'

Willie stood up suddenly. His nose twitched in disgust. 'Getting us a damn sight further than talk of sacrifice, Mr Dawber.'

Macbeth said, 'Sac . . . ?' and Ernie Dawber put a finger to his lips.

'Don't you think, for his own good, it would be better if Mr Macbeth were to leave us?'

'Bollocks to that.' Willie's eyes flashed and he thumped a hand down on the table.

Milly Gill said, 'Willie . . .'

'And bollocks to your daft ideas, Mr Dawber. We might have taken some bullshit off you when you was headmaster, but not any more. If Jack's behind this, least we know what we're up against.'

'And you think that makes it any better, Willie?' Ernie Dawber shook his head. 'No, this is a man who was a danger to us all at the age of sixteen. Now he's rich and powerful, he's had half a lifetime of indulgence in esoteric studies of what you might call the most dubious kind. He's got a hatred for Bridelow inside him that's been fermenting for about half a century. And you're saying we don't need drastic action to protect us?'

'If John Peveril Stanage is in some way responsible for the death of Moira Cairns,' Macbeth said grimly, 'please, just point me in the right direction and I will go bust this bastard's ass.'

Willie and his woman looked at each other, stark hopelessness in their eyes.

'I hope you're not trying to tell me,' said Ernie Dawber, with dignity, 'that our American friend is in some respect *less* irrational than I am?'

'I wouldn't try to tell you anything, Mr Dawber, you're the schoolmaster and I know my place.'

'Willie!'

'I've had it, lass. I've had enough of this crap. If you want to go out on the Moss and kill Mr Dawber, just do it.'

He stopped because the door had opened. Macbeth saw there was another woman in the room, standing quite still, watching them.

She was young, maybe mid-twenties. Rain sparkled in her thin, blonde hair and there were big globules of it like tiny winking lights against the dark blue of her duffel coat.

'You left the Post Office door unlocked again, Milly. You'll have armed robbers in.'

'Cathy.' Ernie Dawber stood up, his hat in one hand, the cup and saucer balanced on the other. 'I thought you'd gone back to college.'

'You really think I could leave at a time like this, Mr Dawber? Sit down. Please.'

The girl walked into the room, glanced at Macbeth and thought for a moment, then apparently decided to go ahead anyhow.

'Am I right in concluding, Mr Dawber, you've been offering yourself as a replacement for the Man in the Moss?'

Macbeth closed his eyes, wondering briefly what the prospects were of him awakening in his hotel bedroom in Glasgow with a real lulu of a hangover and Moira Cairns still alive someplace. When, with a sigh, he opened them again into the slightly tawdry light of Milly Gill's many-petalled parlour, Milly was saying, 'How long have you been on the other side of that door, Cathy?'

'Long enough.' The girl turned back to the old man. 'Mr Dawber, let's get one thing cleared up. The Man in the Moss was in what, in his day, would have been considered the prime of life. To us, he'd be a young lad.'

Ernie Dawber placed his cup and saucer on the table and took his hat in both hands.

'He was fresh meat, Mr Dawber,' said Cathy. 'Whereas you – and I trust you won't take offence – are dried-up, wizened and probably as tough as old boots. What I'm saying is, you wouldn't be much of a sacrifice, Mr Dawber.'

Ernie Dawber cleared his throat. 'In the last War, Catherine, when Hitler was planning an invasion of these shores from occupied France, the, er, pagans of southern England . . .'

'. . . held a ritual on the beach at Hastings or somewhere in cold weather, and an old man went naked and allowed himself to die of exposure, thus setting up a barrier against the Nazi hordes. I don't believe that old story either, Mr Dawber.'

Macbeth could tell by the way Ernie Dawber was turning his hat around in his hands that the poor old guy was close to tears.

Cathy said, 'I know you love Bridelow more than any man alive . . .'

'Any*one* alive, young lady.'

'Sorry. But throwing your life away isn't going to help anyone, least of all the poor devil who's got to do the deed. You won't accept this, I know you won't, but you're like a number of people who got too close to the Man in the Moss, you're drawn almost into another world. You contemplate things that under normal circumstances . . .'

'Cathy, lass, these are *not* normal circumstances.'

'Yes, but *why* are they not? Why's everything been allowed to go haywire? You've got to ask yourself when all this started and how. I've spent a long time talking to Pop, and . . .' Cathy pulled damp, pale hair out of an eye. 'Look, you know they've been seeing Matt Castle in the village.'

Willie Wagstaff jerked and stiffened and went white. Macbeth couldn't take any more. He got up, walked over to the window and listened hard to the rain until it turned the girl's steady voice into white noise, crazy disconnected phrases seeping out, like when you drove into a new state and your car radio was catching some stray police waveband.

'. . . and when she looked into the fryer, the fat had all congealed and gone black. Black. Like peat.'

Macbeth pushed his forehead up against the window, rolling it repeatedly on the cold, wet glass.

He was too tired for this but couldn't imagine how he'd ever sleep again.

From *Dawber's* Secret *Book of Bridelow* (unpublished):

THE TRIPLE DEATH

THREE WAS A SACRED number for the ancient Celts.

I don't know why. Nobody does, obviously.

But think of Christianity – the Holy Trinity. Now think of the Celtic triple goddess – maiden, matron, hag.

Think, if you like, of the Law of Three, as taught by the cosmologist Gurdjieff. '. . . One force or two forces can never produce a phenomenon,' writes his colleague, P. D. Ouspensky, going on to explain about (i) the positive force, (ii) the negative force and (iii) the neutralizing or motivating force.

I like to think of a three-pin plug, for the safe performance of which the third force, the Earth, is so essential, although I don't know if this is an adequate analogy.

Whatever the explanation, the Celtic gods appeared to have demanded a sacrifice in triplicate before the necessary energy might be released.

And sometimes the cycle of death seemed to operate according to some pre-set cosmic mechanism. For instance,

the eminent Celtic scholar Dr Anne Ross has described the
legendary demise of the sixth-century Irish king Diarmaid,
whose triple death – by weapon, drowning and burning – was
foretold by seers. Diarmaid poured scorn on this until his
enemies struck at the Feast of Samhain, when the hall was
set ablaze and Diarmaid run through with a spear. Seeking
safety from the flames, the king plunged, fatally, into a vat of
ale.

The Celts have always had a great sense of comic irony.

CHAPTER II

*D*eath. No peace in it.
    *You struggle towards the light and the light recedes, or
maybe it's the bastard darkness has grabbed hold of your
feet, hauling you back. Cloying, sweating darkness. Darkness like
a black suit that's too small for you. Darkness like . . . black peat
. . . the kind of dark you don't come out of until you're long, long
dead and even then it's somebody's mistake.*

*Anything's better than this kind of darkness. Forget about
Heaven, Hell would be better.*

Joke.
    *So, OK, this guy, he goes to Hell, right, and it's not what he
was expecting, no hot coals and stuff, just all these other guys
standing around drinking cups of tea – up to their necks in liquid
shit. And they pass him a cup and he's thinking, hey, you know,
this could be a lot worse.*

*And then the Devil himself strolls in – horns, cloven hoofs,
spiky tail, the whole getup, plus a big smile – and the guys' faces
all drop.*

*And the first guy thinks, Hey, what's the problem, the Evil One
seems affable enough? And then the Devil beams at them all and he
says,*
    'OK, boys, teabreak over, back to your tunnelling . . .'

This could be the secret of the damned universe. Teabreak over, boys, back to the fucking tunnelling.

Oh, Jesus, help me. I'm cold and sweating and dead.

Timegap.

And you wake up into it again and there's the light in the middle distance, only this time the light doesn't back off, the light comes right at you, a big dazzling explosion of light and all you can think is, leave me alone, huh.

Just leave me alone, let me go back into the shit.

Into the black peat.

I'm not afraid of the dark. I'm crying, but I'm not afraid.

The minister's daughter, Cathy Gruber, pushed through the multitude of the Born Again, into the Rectory drawing room. Mungo Macbeth following, wondering how come she didn't throw all these jerks into the street.

A fire was blazing in the hearth, a sofa pushed close to the heat, a woman stretched across it; she had her eyes shut and she was breathing hard. Her long, dark hair hung damply over an arm of the sofa. A small group of people was clustered around. One guy was on his knees; he held an open prayer-book.

It looked as still, as solemn and as phoney as a Pre-Raphaelite death scene, Macbeth thought, as Cathy knelt down next to the guy with the prayer-book.

'How is she now?'

'In and out of sleep.'

'Has she spoken about it? She has to, you know, Chris. If she keeps all the details bottled up, it's going to cause a lot of trauma.'

Chris said, 'Who is this man?'

'I believe we talked on the phone.'

'Oh. The American. I passed you on to Joel, didn't I?'

467

'Some asshole zealot,' said Macbeth, and Cathy frowned at him.

'I'm sorry to say poor Joel's still in there,' Chris said. 'Still in the church.'

'Best place for him,' Cathy said. 'Let him cool his heels for a while. Chantal, can you hear me?'

The woman on the couch moved, eyelids twitching like captive moths. Cathy held one of her hands. 'This really is a wonderful lady,' Chris said to Macbeth. 'I don't know what we'd have done.'

'Cathy?'

'Makes you think you underestimated the benefits of an old-fashioned Anglican upbringing. She's not at all fazed by any of this.'

'Why I'm sticking close to the kid,' said Macbeth. 'I was fazed clean outa my tree some hours back.' He nodded at the sofa. 'This lady your wife?'

'We're united in God,' Chris said as Chantal's eyes opened and then shut again.

'What happened to her?'

'She was raped,' Chris said baldly.

Chantal moaned. Macbeth focused cynically on Chris, who looked to be about his own age and still had the remains of that bland, doped look you could guarantee to find on a proportion of fundamentalist Christians, Children of God, Mormons and sundry Followers of the Sublime Light.

Cathy stood up. 'Keep her warm. Call me if she wants to talk.' Maybe sensing the tension, she led Macbeth away.

The house seemed stuffed with men and women feeding their bland, doped faces with biscuits and potato-chips, and drinking coffee from paper cups. They were in small groups, many holding on to each other, and they weren't talking much, although a few were praying silently, heads bent and palms upturned against their thighs.

Macbeth decided this was probably better than mass hysteria.

'You want coffee?'

Cathy shook her head. He followed her into the hall; she

brought out keys, unlocked a door, led him into an unoccupied room with book cases and an upright piano.

Macbeth said, 'Cathy, reassure me. That woman really was *raped*? In addition to everything, we got a rapist on the loose?'

The girl pushed the door into place, stood with her back to it. 'She *thinks* she was raped. Seems she'd gone back alone to the church to plead with Joel to come out. Says she was thrown across a tomb and had sensations of . . . violation.'

Cathy looked him in the eyes, unsmiling. 'I'm afraid that what we have on the loose is something that used to be Matt Castle.'

The room was silent, apart from the rain on the window, which, by this time, Macbeth hardly registered.

'You believe that.' Already he knew better than to make it a question.

'It's a lot for you to swallow in one night,' Cathy said, 'but Bridelow used to pride itself on having a certain spiritual equilibrium. And now somebody's turned the place into a battlefield. Opposing forces. Black magic, as I understand it, doesn't work quite so well without there being something equally extreme to ignite it.'

'Like, opposites attract.'

Cathy nodded. 'My old man is an ordinary, old-fashioned country clergyman who's learned not to ask too many questions. Joel Beard's an extremist – same background as this bunch. Somebody engineered it that Joel should come to Bridelow with a mission to wipe out the remains of some very innocuous, downbeat paganism. We thought there was an understanding in the diocese that you don't put unstable fanatics into Bridelow, but I'd guess somebody was simply blackmailing the Archdeacon.'

'This is the boss-cleric.'

'As you say, the boss-cleric. Simon. Who's gay. And who's been more than a bit indiscreet in his time.'

'And the blackmailer? Stand up, John Peveril Stanage?'

'This is the one man whose name is never mentioned in Bridelow. The one writer whose books you will never see on the paperback rack in Milly's Post Office.'

'You were outside when I told them about that stuff with the bones in Scotland?'

Cathy went on nodding. She looked very young. Still had on her damp duffel coat and a college scarf wound under her chin. 'Mungo, I can't tell you how sorry I am about Moira. I sincerely blame myself. I should never have let her drive away in that state.'

He felt his eyes narrow. 'State?'

'I think I must have been the last person to see her alive. She was very down, I'm afraid. She'd picked up a bug of some kind. And she was upset over the burglary – someone broke in here and stole some things from her. Including this . . . famous comb. Which she kept in a secret pocket in her guitar case.'

'They stole the case?'

'Just the comb. Seemed silly. I'm afraid I didn't really believe her about that, at first.'

'Shit.' Macbeth clenched his fists. 'How would this sonofabitch know precisely where she kept the comb?'

'Mungo . . .' Cathy hesitated. 'She told me she'd only shown one person where she kept that comb.'

'Wasn't me.'

'No,' said Cathy. 'It was Matt Castle.'

'The ubiquitous Matt Castle. What was her relationship with this guy?'

'She was in his band. And that was all. She was always very insistent about him never touching her.'

'Yeah, but I bet he wanted to.'

'I *know* he wanted to. He was crazy about her. Men tended to . . . Oh, gosh, I'm sorry.'

'The irony of it,' said Macbeth, 'is I never got to touch her either.'

'But I doubt,' Cathy said, not without compassion, 'if you're of quite such an obsessive temperament.'

'Something hurts, is all. Maybe it's self-pity. I, uh, thought she was gonna change my life.'

'Maybe she has.'

'You mind if we get off this subject? Tell me about Castle.'

'Yes.' Cathy sat on the arm of what must have been her father's wing-backed fireside chair. 'Matt's son, Dic, reckons his father's lust . . . unrequited lust . . . for Moira, just got progressively worse with age. Eventually developing into almost a . . . perversion? About women with long, dark hair.'

Macbeth was seized, for the first time, by the reality of something more potentially soul-damaging than either grief or anger.

He said, 'That woman in the room across there . . .'

'Yes,' Cathy said calmly. 'I noticed that too.'

This was more like it. This was much more like Hell.

'Christ, I feel just awful.'

Pain in the head, behind the eyes. A growling pain. Put me back. Put me back into the nice, warm shit.

'You've got to come with me,' the Devil urges.

Hot coals roaring and crackling all around. The inside of a furnace, but without the pretty colours. A black furnace with one cold, flashing, piercing flame.

'Piss off, leave me alone.'

'Look, I haven't got much time.' Stabbing her through the eyes with his needle of light.

'You've got all the time there is, pal, all the time there ever was and all the time there's ever gonny be. That no' enough for you?'

'Please. For Christ's sake.'

'Listen, will you get rid of the damn light?'

'Sorry. I forgot you'd been in the pitch dark so long. I'll put it under my jacket, that any better?'

'Yeah. You're OK, Satan, you know that?'

'Try and sit up.'

'Get your fucking hands off me!'

'Listen to me, you have to get moving.'

'Who is this?'

'It's me. Dic. Dic Castle.'

Light on his face. Dark red hair, Matt's jawline, Matt's stubborn lips.

She coughed. It made her head ache. She said, all she could think of to say, 'Was it you? Was it you took my comb?'

'No,' he said. 'No I didn't. I know who *did*.'

'Who?' Her back hurt as she sat up. Like it mattered now.

'Bloke called Shaw Horridge. But that's not important right now.'

'No.' The name didn't seem to mean anything to her. 'Look, Dic, I don't want to seem stupid, but what are you doing here? What am I doing here? And where in Christ's name *is* here?'

Maybe they were *both* dead. Maybe he'd been sent to offer her a cup of tea.

'It's a storage building, back of the brewery.'

'Brewery?'

'Bridelow Brewery. You have to come now, Moira. Please. I'm supposed to have gone for a pee, that's all. They're going to start wondering where I've got to, and then we could be in a lot of trouble.'

She stood up. There was mist to struggle through, thick grey mist. A monster rose over her and opened its jaws.

Bridelow. Bridelow Black.

Her hands fiddled with her clothes. Sweater. Jeans. She seemed to be fully clothed. She felt naked and raw.

'Thought I was fucking dead. Dic, why am I no' dead?'

'They've had you on drugs.'

'Sure as hell wasn't speed, was it?'

'I don't know. I really don't know much about drugs.'

'Bridelow Brewery,' she said. 'Why's that scare me? Bridelow Brewery. Bridelow *Black*.'

On her feet now, panting, leaning against something, maybe a wall, maybe a door. He'd put out his light. They were just a couple of voices. 'Bridelow Black,' she breathed. 'Ran me off the road. Ran me over a damn precipice.'

'No precipice. There was a flat area over the wall next to the road. Then a slow drop after that. There was a lot of mist. They took you out . . .'

'Fat guy with a half-grown moustache.'

'Yeah. Name's Dean-something. Calls himself Asmodeus, after some biblical demon. Looks like a dickhead, but he isn't.'

'He hit me. Also, some big bastard in a dog-collar hit me. Everybody hits me.'

'Can you walk?'

'Three of them in the lorry. They were dragging me away. Who the hell are these people?'

'They all work at the brewery. Gannons fired the local men, brought in these people. Occult-followers from Sheffield and Manchester. Small-time, no-hope urban satanists. You can practically pick them up on street corners. Doesn't really care any more who he brings in, any low-life shit'll do.'

'Who's this?'

'Stanage.'

'Sorry, my head's, like, somewhere else. I'm not following this. Who's . . .'

'Can you walk?'

'Guess I can. Question is, do I want to?'

'Then walk out of here. Do it now. You walk out of here in a straight line until you get to the road. No, look, I'll come with you as far as the entrance, OK, then I've got to get back or I'm dead. I'll give you the lamp, but don't use it till you're out of sight of the brewery. Go to the Rectory. You remember where the Rectory is?'

'Rectory. Yeah. Near the church.'

'You remember Cath?'

'Dic,' she said, 'what's that noise? I was thinking it was the hot coals.'

'Coals?'

'Never mind.'

'It's just the rain, Moira. The rain on the roof. It's raining heavily, been like this for hours. You're going to get wet, can't be helped. OK, I'm opening the door. You see anybody . . . *anybody* . . . run the other way. Tell Cath . . . are you taking this in?'

'Doing ma best, Dic.'

'Tell her they're going to put out the light. In the church. The beacon.'

'Who's "they"?'

'Moira, listen, they've got my dad propped up in there. And his clothes. And the pipes. And me. And . . . you. Please, just go!'

'What did you just say?'

A shuddering creak and he pushed her out, and it was like

473

THE MAN IN THE MOSS

somebody had thrust her head down the toilet and flushed it. She gasped.

'Come on.' He took her arm. She could make out the shapes of trees and a sprinkling of small lights among the branches.

'Not that way.'

'What's that tower?'

'Part of the brewery. Can't you go any faster? I'm sorry. They catch you, I'm telling you, they'll kill you.'

She'd stopped. She was shaking. Somebody was pouring bucketfuls of water directly into her brain. She clapped her hands to her head.

She screamed.

'Christ's sake, shut up!'

'Dic. *My hair!*'

Voices. Lights.

'Moira, run! Take the lamp.' Thrusting it into her hands, heavy, wet metal. 'Don't use it till you're away from here.'

Running footsteps.

'My hair's gone!'

He pushed her hard in the back and then she heard him take off in the opposite direction, shoes skidding on the saturated ground.

'Dic?'

'Run!' He was almost howling. 'Just run! Don't lose that lamp!'

'Dic, what have they done to my hair? *Where have they taken my fucking hair?*'

CHAPTER III

S urprising how vulnerable you felt in a tomato-coloured Japanese sports car up here on a night like this. Ashton took it steady.

He wondered: how much water can a peat bog take before it turns into something the consistency of beef broth?

Not his manor, the natural world. The *un*natural world was

more like it. A number of the people with whom Ashton conversed at length – usually across a little grey room with a microphone in the wall – were creatures of the *un*natural world.

As for the *super*natural world . . .

I don't know why, Ashton told himself as he drove towards Bridelow Moss, but in a perverse sort of way this is almost invigorating. To be faced with something you can't arrest, matters which in no way can ever be taken down and used in evidence.

Completely out of your depth. He looked down at the Moss. There was an area of Manchester called Moss Side, in which the police also sometimes felt out of their depth, so choked was it with drugs and violent crime. Did the name imply that once, centuries ago, it had been on the edge of somewhere like *this*? And, if so, how much had changed?

Not the kind of thing policemen tended to think about.

Gary Ashton, facing retirement in a year or two, spent an increasing amount of time trying to think about things policemen did not tend to think about. Intent on not becoming just 'a retired copper' working as consultant to some flash security firm and regaling people who couldn't give a shit with his personal analysis of the criminal mind and endless stories about Collars I Have Felt.

Just lately, Ashton had been trying to talk to people as people, knowing that in a very short time he would be one of them.

A well-controlled tremor in her voice. *'Inspector Ashton, I'm extremely sorry to bother you at this time of night, but you did say if anything else disturbing occurred, I should let you know immediately.'*

Yes, yes, Mrs Castle, but I meant in the nature of a break-in. Unless a crime has been committed or is likely to be, I'm sorry but this is not really something the police can do anything about.

Except, he hadn't said any of that.

What he'd said was, 'Yes, I'll come, but as long as you understand I won't be coming as a policeman.'

Turning off the telly in his frugally furnished divorced

person's apartment, reacting to a peculiar note of unhysterical desperation in a woman's voice and getting into practice for doing things *not* as a policeman.

Surprising how vulnerable you felt not being a policeman on a very nasty night proceeding in an easterly direction across a waterlogged peatbog in a tomato-coloured Japanese sports car to see a woman about a ghost.

'Well,' Ernie Dawber said finally. 'I think it must be obvious to all of us where they are.'

Willie said, 'Macbeth wasn't fooled, you know. He knew we was keeping summat back.'

'Let's hope Catherine keeps him out of our way. Come on, Willie, there's nobody but us going to see to this.'

Milly Gill was hugging Bob and Jim and looking, Ernie thought, a bit like his mother had looked when she'd switched off the radio after the formal declaration of World War Two.

'What are you going to do?'

'Well, I know we're only men, Millicent, but we're going to have to stop this thing. Don't know how, mind. Have to see when we get there.'

Ernie put on his hat.

'Where?'

'The Hall. The brewery. By 'eck, I wish I'd listened to my feelings. So used to them coming to nowt, see, that's the problem. I remember examining the list of Gannons directors – last summer, this was, just after the takeover was mooted.'

'I know,' Willie said. 'J. S. Lucas. Occurred to me too, just momentarily, like, but I thought I were being paranoid.'

Milly looked blank.

'Lucas were t'name of Jack's father. Not many folk'd know that.'

Ernie watched Willie struggling into his old donkey jacket with the vinyl patch across the shoulders. Not seen that for some years. Lad had put on a few pounds in the meantime.

Milly Gill slid the cats from her knee. 'Well, all I can say is you seem determined, Mr Dawber, that one way or t'other, you'll not see tomorrow's sun.'

476

'Time comes, Millicent, when being an observer is no longer sufficient.'

'And what about you, Willie? Feller who liked to pride himself on his cowardice.'

'True,' Willie said. 'But this is family.'

'I'm just praying,' Ernie said, 'as they've not done owt to Liz Horridge.'

Willie grinned. 'Always had a bit of a thing for Liz, dint you, Mr Dawber?'

'She could've done no better than Arthur Horridge,' Ernie said generously.

'And might've done a good deal worse, eh?' Willie was over by the window. 'Not slackening off at all, bloody rain. Moss'll be treacherous for weeks.'

'We're not going to the Moss,' said Ernie. 'We're not going anywhere near the Moss.'

He was still thinking furiously about what young Catherine had said about obsession. That he himself had been trapped just as surely as Matt Castle and Dr Hall. That there was indeed something powerfully emotionally disruptive about the bogman.

Ernie glanced at Milly Gill, who was not, he reassured himself, in Ma's league. Not yet.

Determined that one way or t'other you'll not see tomorrow's sun.

Aye, well, Ernie Dawber thought, we'll have to see about that.

The tapping on the study door was firm but polite.

Cathy opened it. They were coming out anyway, though without much direction. At some point, Macbeth had suggested they simply call the cops, but Cathy said the cops must already be looking into Moira's death; how were they supposed credibly to plant the idea that the accident was in some way unnatural?

Chris stood in the doorway. 'We've come to a decision,' he said. 'Thank you for your hospitality, but we want to go back.'

'Back?' Cathy said.

'To the church.'

'Oh,' Cathy said. 'But you can't.'

477

Chris smoothed his beard. 'We're deeply ashamed, Cathy. We had no faith. We watched Joel struggling with the demon, and we thought he'd gone mad.'

'He has,' Cathy said tautly.

'And now this attack on Chantal. She was the only one of us whose belief in Joel was sustained when the chips were down. She went back and she was physically and spiritually attacked. Could have been killed. We let that happen.'

'Open up, did she?'

Chris stared at her in horror.

'I mean to you,' Cathy said irritably. 'Did she tell you exactly what happened to her?'

'Come on, Chris,' a woman's voice called from behind. 'It's only half an hour to midnight.'

'I'm sorry,' Chris said. 'God protect you. God protect you both.'

Cathy flung the door wide. There was a whole crowd of them gathered behind Chris.

'Let me spell it out for you. All of you. You've all been used. Joel was used. Somebody wanted to break down the church's defences – these are defences built up over centuries.'

'Yes,' said Chris. 'We were the last line of defence.' Not understanding, unlikely to be *capable* of understanding. 'And we were afraid. We lost faith in our brother, Joel. We deserted him when he most needed us, and it took the violation of our sister . . .'

'Sister?' Macbeth said. 'She's your goddamn wife!'

'And Joel was right too . . .' Chris backed away, 'about *this* man. Turn him out, Cathy. Turn him out and come with us.'

'Of course I'm not going to bloody turn him out! He's got good reason to be angry; a friend of his died tonight.'

Chris didn't blink.

'Come *on*, Chris. In God's name,' the woman behind him cried.

'I'm coming.'

Cathy grabbed his arm. 'What I'm saying to you, Chris, is that it's not safe for you to go back in that church. Any of you. You won't do yourselves any good and you'll probably do us all a lot of harm.'

Chris said pityingly, 'Our trust is in Almighty God. In whom, to our shame, we temporarily lost our faith. And for that we have much to make up. Whatever happens in there will be His will.'

'He gave you a brain, Chris. To think with, you know? Have you given up thinking for yourselves? Letting Him do all your thinking now, is it?'

Chris pulled his arm away, eyes full of drifting cloud. 'Pray for us, Cathy.'

'Yes,' said Cathy when they'd gone. 'But who am I supposed to pray *to*?'

Because he was used to making a recce before venturing in, Ashton drove once up the village street, turned around on the parking area by the church and drove slowly back towards the pub.

Just as well he was driving slowly. Twice, people hurried across the street, two men together and two women individually, flapping like chickens in the blinding rain.

There were lights in most front rooms, lights in the chip shop but a 'closed' sign on the door. Water gushed down the sides of the road, down the hill. Where did it all go? Into the Moss?

Ashton followed the water as far as the pub, where the only light was the hanging lantern over the front porch, illuminating the sign, *The Man I'th Moss*. No picture. What would it have shown? Why had they given the pub that name, possibly a couple of hundred years ago, when nobody could have guessed there was an ancient body in the bog?

Or could they?

Ashton pulled on to the forecourt and dashed for the door. Lottie Castle. He could spot a liar in seconds. He could also tell when people were deluded. And he could, of course, spot people who were daft or innocent enough to be led up the garden path.

But this Lottie Castle.

Now, here's a cool, intelligent woman who is definitely not

lying; a woman you could, with confidence, put in a witness box in front of George bloody Carman QC.

And here's a woman claiming to be haunted. You know why I half believe this? Ashton still quizzing himself as he huddled on the doorstep in his trench coat, ill-fitting slates in the porch letting water trickle down his collar.

Because this is a woman who sincerely *doesn't want* to believe it.

And is also, yes, an attractive widow. Well, what's wrong with that?

The woman who answered the door, however, was not Lottie Castle. But if Ashton the human being was disappointed, Ashton the copper was back on duty the second he identified her.

'Miss . . . er . . . Mrs White.'

'Chrissie.'

'Aye,' he said. 'Chrissie. And is Dr Hall here too?'

'Not exactly *here*, Gary . . . is it Gary tonight?'

'Hard to say,' Ashton said, stepping inside. 'Hard to say, now.'

Her own smooth, smoky voice taunting her as she struggled through the dripping wood, booming out from the old, disused recording studio in her head, the voice sneering,

> *Never let them cut your hair*
> *Or tell you where*
> *You've been, or where*
> *You're going to*
> *from here . . .*

Everything leaking out now from that slashed and razored head, raw thoughts exposed at birth to the cold and spitting night.

For a bad long time she'd stood alone among some trees and wept and sobbed and cursed and refused to believe it. *They can put it back, can't they? Christ's sake, they can sew people's arms back these days.*

First the horror, then the anguish. And then the horror and anguish and the rage, all shaken up, this wild, combustible cocktail.

'Who?' she screamed to the invisible sky. '*Who?*'

Them.

Dic had headed them off. They'd gone after Dic and she was alone in the filthy night, everything rushing back with nerve-searing intensity, the savage rain smashing it into her naked head along with the insistent bump, bump, bump of the taunting mental Walkman.

And the things Dic said.

Stanage.

Of course, yeah. The Celtic expert. The writer. John Peveril Stanage. Never read his books, too young for me, by the time I'd heard of him.

But I'm going to kill that man. That man is *dead*.

Memories.

On the plane to Dublin for a gig. Matt holding up a paperback, *The Bridestones*. '*Should read this. Tell you where I'm coming from.*' Moira politely looking up from Joseph Heller or somesuch. Mmm? Sure. Get around to it someday.

And then the American, Macbeth, at the Earl's Castle. '*This writer – Stanton, Stanhope? Is he* mad . . . *this guy's face is white.*'

John Peveril Stanage. The pale predator at the castle.

The comb-hunter.

The hair-surgeon.

Moira clung to a tree, its mesh of leafless branches keeping most of the rain off her. But when her head penetrated a jagged tracery of twigs, she could actually feel them graze her scalp.

She screamed in despair.

Last one, OK? Last scream. Last curse. Then you start to think. God, you drift through life listening to your conscience and your instincts and premonitions, all your airy-fairy feelings, and you never *think*.

Moira, listen, they've got my dad propped up in there.

Meaning an effigy? A dummy representing the spirit they wanted to conjure?

Necromancy. The black side of spiritualism. You collect, in the appropriately drawn and consecrated circle, the most intimate possessions of the dead person, those things . . .

. . . *his clothes.*

carrying his smell, his sweat. And those things . . .

. . . *the pipes.*

he would most hate to leave behind. And those . . .

. . . *me.* Dic.

people who were close to him. And . . .

And you.

the things after which he craved.

Moira moved deliberately out from under the tree, stared up into the sky until she was blinded by the rain, and then hung her head and let the night drench her.

They took the comb.

They cut off my hair.

They have me. They have my essence.

They have used these things to summon Matt Castle from the grave.

CHAPTER IV

How Young Frank Manifold had ended up at the brewery he didn't exactly remember.

What he did remember was his anger reaching gale-force as soon as the cold rain hit it. Slung out again! Slung out like a kid from the only pub in Bridelow.

Settle down, Frank.

Cool it, eh, Frank.

Don't you think you've had a couple too many, Frank?

Int it past your bedtime, Frank?

They'd say it once too often. In fact tonight they *had* said it once too often.

What Frank remembered first was bunching his fists on the pub forecourt and looking around for somebody to hit and seeing only rain and smeary lights in the windows of houses of folk as wouldn't come out in it merely for the pleasure of being filled in by Young Frank.

Another thing he'd thought about was hitting a wall, but he'd done that once before and his fist remembered and wouldn't go through with it.

The soft option would've been to go straight home and have a row with the wife. But if Susan didn't feel like a row she wouldn't let you have one, simple as that. Susan, who insisted that being in the Mothers' Union was just something you agreed to so as to keep the numbers up, but who could look at you through slitted eyes and take the anger out of you easy as letting tyres down.

Don't want that, he remembered thinking. Want to keep the anger.

Raging through the rain in just his jeans and his ordinary jacket, sopping wet-through in minutes.

Deciding at one stage, I know what I'll bloody do, I'll go up the church and duff over a few Born Again Christians.

Nowt against Christianity, *as such*. Nowt against Hans Gruber, a southerner but a straight-up bloke. Just that when it came to that big prat Joel Beard; when it came to T-shirts with JESUS SAVES on the front and grinning tossers stopping you in the street to asking how well you knew God; when it came to getting accosted by tasty women with PRAISE THE LORD across their tits . . .

When it came to it, truth was Frank didn't hate Born Again Christians anywhere near as much as he hated Gannons.

Which, he supposed, must be why he'd ended up pissing hard and high against the main door of the brewery, thinking maybe he could kick a couple of windows in before he sobered up.

Which was how come he saw the lights.

And how come he found the main door wasn't locked.

Well, this were a bit of a turn-up. Frank stood a while getting rained on and stared upwards. Summat weird about this. Light coming out the sides of the wooden boards on the topmost windows, the owd malt store as was.

From what Frank had heard from his ex-workmates and his

dad, that malt store hadn't been used in twenty years. When Gannons had the winching system repaired on the outside of the building there was no suggestion it had been for winching sacks all the way up to the top again, because the owd malt store'd been shut and boarded up. Make it look authentic for tourists, this was what everybody thought.

Frank wandered around to the side of the building, and there was the platform thing . . . right at the top.

Summat had been winched up there tonight. Obviously.

Fucking cowboy brewers. Happen the owd malt store'd been *refurbished*. Happen they was having a little cocktail party up there for the directors.

Right then. See about that.

Frank went in.

She knew, sure, how ill she was, soaked through and shivering, feverish, temperature racing up the thermometer, about to ring the little bell.

Knew also that she could never look into a mirror again. Not *ever*.

And yet her mind had never seemed so clear. A cold searchlight, ruthlessly spearing into dark and musty corners.

Felt weak as hell and sore, and she walked with difficulty through the leafless, waterlogged wood. But her mind was an athlete, leaping chasms of dark thoughts. Her mind was an engineer constructing complex bridges.

'What we're looking for,' Moira mumbled, stopping, moving closer to the stocky, blistered trunk of an oak, switching off the lamp, 'is something long-term.'

Like a long-term connection between Matt and Stanage.

This had happened before; Matt's enthusiasms were unstoppable. If Matt finds interesting echoes in a book, Matt goes in search of the author.

Take this as fact. Matt meets Stanage. Matt and Stanage find so much common ground that secrets are shared . . . at least on Matt's side.

Nobody other than Matt could have told Stanage about Moira Cairns and the comb. Say that by the time these two men meet, she's – stupidly – recorded 'The Comb Song' and both Matt and Stanage are scenting magic. And Stanage has stored all this away for future reference.

Moira sank down against the fat, scabby treetrunk, finding an almost sheltered spot between two huge protruding roots, enclosing her like legs. Sheets of rain on three sides; like crouching in a cavern behind a waterfall.

OK.

If Stanage has learned about the comb he's learned a whole lot more of Matt's secrets, maybe passing on a few tantalizing but useless bits of information of his own about the old Celts and the Pennine Pipes in return. Worth it, because he sees such terrific potential in Matt, the most wonderful raw material for his own research.

Because Matt, maybe like Stanage, is ruled by his compulsions. Only Stanage is cleverer.

She closed her eyes and she was back in the ballroom of the Earl's castle.

His face is an unhealthy white. He has light grey eyes and grey freckles on his expanse of forehead. There's a whiteness all about him, growing into arms like the branches of trees. Like antlers.

He is linked to the skulls on the walls. He is the horned god, the hunter of heads.

He has taken her hair.

And she sees it all with such brutal clarity, detached from her wonderful, magical comb-reared hair, her earliest, most important expression of individuality and free thought.

Hands to her head, couple of inches left, less in places. Aw, what the hell, you're alive, what d'you want, huh?

Revenge? She shivered with fever and fury.

Hands inside the guitar case. Stanage is feeling for the comb. He is feeling for your soul.

Two hundred miles away Matt Castle is lying in wait for death. Maybe Matt, in the last morphine minutes of his life, is also reaching out for you. Those arms of sick smoke coiling out of the baronial fireplace.

If Stanage gets access to your soul, to the core of Matt's craving . . .

485

. . . then Stanage will have a link with Matt that extends beyond death.

Stanage will have a hold on Matt's spirit.

With the comb and the cloak and the . . .

'Long-haired girls. Always the long, dark hair.'

Dic.

'After a charity gig. She was waiting for him in the car park. About twenty-one, twenty-two. About my age. Long, dark hair.'

The craving kept alive in the darkness of shop-doorways and the backs of vans.

And manipulated. And moulded and twisted.

Stanage has recreated me as spirit-bait for Matt. He's taken my soul and thrown away the husk.

But why, Moira wondered, so physically, achingly tired now, enclosed in the roots of a malformed oak tree, an electric lamp on her lap, *why can I think so well?* Why can I see all this so clearly, unless that's to be my final torture?

That and a dawning, unquenchable hatred for Matt Castle.

Frank made his way, quietly as his shoes would allow, up the narrow iron stairs, past the deep fermenting-tanks. Up another flight, past the coppers. It were bloody dark, but Frank had been up here that many thousand times it didn't matter. And the smell, the lovely, familiar smell. Better than sight, that smell. Better than women.

Halfway up the third flight leading to the mash tuns, Frank choked back what he thought was going to be a hiccup but turned out to be a sob. He stopped in a moment of despair. How was he going to live the rest of his life without this wondrous rich, stale, sour, soggy aroma? How was he going to survive?

He clambered to the top, staggered out on to the deck clutching for support at the thick copper pipe connecting the malt mill to the mash, the big tuns around him, his old mates. Get um out, a voice was rasping in his gut. Gannons. Get the bastards out. Get the brewery back for Bridelow.

He leaned, panting, over the side of one of the tuns and his breath echoed in its empty vastness.

One more flight. He went three-quarters way up to a door that'd always been kept locked for safety's sake for as long as he'd worked there.

Voices behind it.

'. . . not terribly subtle. What time is it?'

'Coming up to eleven-fifteen.'

'No time for that, then. Really, I' – a light laugh, half-exasperated – 'just can't get over what you've done. I really didn't think you were that clever. Now, look. You know, presumably, that we mustn't actually kill you. Not yet, anyway.'

'Don't care. Do what you want. You're just a slag. Couldn't give a . . .'

A crash. A moan. A rolling on floorboards.

'All right, come on, pick him up. Sit him next to his dear daddy. Let him have a good whiff. Bind his arms very firmly, palms up, OK? And at approximately ten minutes to twelve . . . are you listening? At ten minutes to twelve, you can open his wrists.'

Frank was in a fog. He heard it all but couldn't make sense of the words and some kept repeating on him.

Kill . . . whiff . . . palms up . . . open his wrists.

It was a woman's voice, not a local accent. More words tumbled down the steps, Frank's brain tripping over them. Sometimes he seemed to hear the key words before they joined actual sentences.

Trickle.

'Don't go mad. Just want a trickle at first. Steady plop, plop, plop. We'll be well into it by then. Once you get the trickle going, you come back and join us. Very quietly. You say nothing.'

Blood to blood.

'What if he screams?'

'He won't. If he does, you can cut another vein. Slow release is best. I mean, I was going to do this anyway; this way we get an instant connection, blood to blood.'

blood to . . .

'Oh, yeah? And who would it have been if this one hadn't suddenly become available?'

. . . blood?

'Oh. *Right.*'

Frank's hands were sticky on the iron stair-rail. Brain couldn't handle it. Past his bedtime. Turn back, go home, sleep it off, eh? But there was a voice he recognized, the voice that said it didn't care, the voice that called the female voice a slag. The voice of the owner of the wrists which would be opened at precisely ten to twelve, but just a trickle unless it screamed.

Frank screamed. Frank was screaming now.

As all the lights went on, Frank screamed, *'Dic!'* as a figure shimmered in the doorway at the top of the steps and a new smell mingled with the malted air, a smell just as warm, just as rich, just as moist, but . . .

The new smell went up Young Frank's nose and forced his mouth wide open like a bucket. He belched up half a gallon of beer and bile, which spouted up in a great brown arc and then slapped down on the metal steps.

'Manifold. You dirty, uncouth lout. Should have guessed.'

Frank looked up into supercilious, wrinkling nostrils.

He began dumbly to move up the steps, his shoes skidding on his own vomit, his hands trying to make fists, his chest locked tight with hatred, his drink-rubbery lips trying to shape a word which eventually came out like another gob of harsh sick.

'. . . *Horridge* . . .'

Gonna have you, said the rough voice in Frank's gut. This time gonna take you apart, you smarmy twat.

He slipped, and his hands splashed on the steps.

Shaw Horridge stood quite relaxed in the doorway, a shred of a smile on his lips. 'You are an absolute oaf, Manifold.'

Frank's fists turned into claws and he took what he imagined to be a great leap up the final three iron steps towards Horridge's throat.

Horridge didn't move at all until Frank's head was on a level with the top of the stairs, at which stage a foot went almost idly back. And then – momentarily – on top of the mellow aroma of malt, the sour stench of vomit and the sweet-rancid essence of rotting flesh, Frank experienced the absurdly pure tang of boot-polish as Shaw's shoe smashed through his teeth and was wedged for a second in his gullet.

Choked, retching, he threw up his arms to grab the foot, but the foot was . . . receding, just like the rest of Shaw Horridge.

Young Frank realized he was flying slowly and almost blissfully backwards.

It seemed a long time until he thought he heard a metallic *ching* as his head connected with something solid (metal everywhere in a brewery) and a dull, fractured *crump* somewhere inside his brains, wherever they might be splattered.

CHAPTER V

There was a rustling over the tumbling water noise; this was what awoke her (how could she have slept, how *could* she?) And half a second later there was a light in her eyes and people moving behind it.

Two of them.

Moira reared up, back to the tree, a spitting cat. 'Come on. Come on, then . . .'

Hands curling into claws. Pray that one is Stanage.

Because she would die before they'd take her back. She'd die raking his face.

One of them gasped.

The other said, 'By 'eck.'

He'd heard it before, so it was no big surprise. The hackneyed country and western, with chorus.

Leave your sor-row
Come and join us
Shed those sins,
Find the joy within . . .

One time, Macbeth had directed this made-for-TV picture about the crooked evangelist Boyd C. Beresford the Fourth. Spent a whole ten days cruising the Bible Belt, stuff like this churning out of the car-radio, out of hotel-room TV sets, out of mission halls and marquees – until even arid atheism began to look like a safe haven.

So he was not impressed. Not even when they started singing in tongues, because he knew how easy this stuff was to fake, even while you were convincing yourself you weren't faking it. And all the healing that lasted just long enough for the relatives to throw in a two-hundred-dollar donation. *You feeling better, sister? Or maybe your faith isn't yet strong enough for you to be healed?*

'Go away. Begone, heathen!'

This real big Born Again Christian on the church door. Stained jeans and a grungy parka. Tattoos on both wrists, one involving what looked like it used to be a swastika on fire before it got reprocessed into a bulky crucifix. Fascist punk finds God. It happened. Classic demonstration of what Cathy had said earlier about one extreme igniting another.

'Listen, I don't plan to cause any trouble,' Macbeth said wisely. 'All I want is to talk with Joel Beard. I would like for you to bring him out here. That too much of a problem?'

Cathy had said, 'Mungo, you have an open, honest face. You've got to get to Joel, talk some sense into him. Long as you go easy on the casual blasphemy, he has to listen to you – you're not from Bridelow and you're not a woman. Tell him what you like, but get him to evacuate that place. They think they're safe in there . . . they're just so naive, they're children . . .'

The big guy with the ex-swastika said, 'You got five seconds to get them filthy heathen feet the other side of this sacred threshold.'

Beat up on a pagan for the Lord. Jesus.

'Listen,' Macbeth said urgently. 'Go tell Joel that Pastor Mungo Macbeth of the, uh, East Side Evangelical Mission, would like to speak with him.'

'You're lying,' Swastika said, but with audibly less conviction than a moment ago.

'God will forgive you for that,' Macbeth said. 'Maybe.'

'He's not there,' Swastika blurted out.

'He is everywhere,' said Macbeth.

'No, Joel. I mean Joel. When we got here we couldn't find him. He's vanished.'

'What do you mean, vanished?'

'He's just gone.'

'Well, where'd he go, for Chr . . . Where might Reverend Beard have gone?'

Flash of fear in the guy's small eyes. 'Why d'you think we're praying so hard?'

'So your friends have returned.'

John stood bathed in blue light.

The blue was in the old glass around the enormous lantern. Round panes, set in the four exterior walls, were frosted white.

There wasn't much to it; Joel had expected more, perhaps the remains of a clock mechanism, but there was no sign of there ever having been one.

'I knew they would,' Joel said. 'I knew it was impossible for them to forsake their God for very long.'

John smiled, his teeth shining blue.

'Still,' Joel said, 'I won't say I'm not relieved. Shall I go down? Tell them what we're going to do?' He moved towards the top of the stone steps.

'Lord, no.' John's face grew solemn. 'They've fled once.'

'Yes,' Joel said. 'I'm sorry.'

The room was about nine feet square. In any other church it would be the belfry; here it was the lamphouse. The lantern hung from the pinnacle of the roof. It was perhaps five feet in diameter.

There was lead around the rims of the glass circles in the walls, but no remains of numerals; it had clearly never been a clock.

Inside the bluish milky glass set into an old iron frame, he could make out the incandescent shapes of three big electric bulbs.

John said, 'Used to be an oil lamp, you can tell. Big candles before that, probably. A lure for the spirits of the Moss.'

Joel remembered his nightmare in the cellar room, imagining the lantern laying an ice-blue beam over still water.

Channels of rain glistened like icicles on the glass. The light was quite ghastly, dehumanizing. John, with his pale, flat face, looked almost demonic. Joel glanced sharply away, afraid of the illusions this evil light could evoke. Though they'd been up here over half an hour, he became aware for the first time of a small door in the shadows to his left.

'What's in there, do you know?'

'Let's see, shall we?' John moved lightly across the boarded floor, pushed and twisted at a handle. 'No . . . 'fraid it's locked.'

Joel closed his eyes and listened to the singing. The hymn was trailing into a drone of tongues, male and female voices flowing into a bright river of praise. He tried to let it flow into him.

On all sides of them, up here in the tower, the night sky was roaring with rain.

'How long?'

'Little under ten minutes. Impatient, are we, Joel? Excited?'

'Why can't we just switch it off and go?'

'You see a switch anywhere, m' boy? Be on a circuit. Time-switch. Anyway, what good would that do? No. Have to smash it. Violence, I'm afraid. Strength. What you're about, isn't it Joel? Strength. Might. No room for namby-pamby, nancy-boy clerics on the Front Line, mmmm?'

'Yes,' Joel said. 'You're right. I'm ready for that. Midnight, then.'

Back at the Rectory, Macbeth said, 'What could happen to those people? Spell this thing out.'

Reaching the front door, he'd heard Cathy, on the hall phone extension, saying, 'I don't know, I'll call you back.' Putting down the phone to let him in.

Now, in the study, sitting on the edge of the piano stool, she said, 'How can I say what could happen? You're nowhere in this game until you accept that nobody can ever say for certain what's going to happen and anyone who thinks he can, or that he can manipulate it, is due for a hell of a shock one day.'

Macbeth said, 'What game?'

'Game?'

'You just said "in this game".'

Cathy shrugged. 'Life, I suppose.'

But he wasn't aiming to back off. 'OK, so what's the bottom line? What's the worst thing could happen? Before you answer, bear in mind what I saw in Scotland and that Moira is dead and that I don't believe I have a great deal I care about left to lose.'

Cathy said calmly, 'I've lived in Bridelow all my life. I've acquired knowledge of certain things, OK? And most of today I've been talking very seriously to my father who's had to deal with things most clergymen don't even read about.'

'Sure,' Macbeth said impatiently. 'What's your point?'

'Put it this way, if it was Pop in there, I'd be less worried.'

'So what you're saying is, in the great metaphysical ball-park, these guys are strictly little-league.'

'Let's say they're hardly ready for what they're up against. They create their own universe, you see, these people. In this little universe everything is down to the Will of God and all evil can be defeated fast as a prayer. When *real* evil shows its hand, it can be so traumatic they'll . . .'

'Flip?'

'Flip is right,' Cathy said. 'Flip is the least of it.'

'Real evil?'

'Stanage is the man no one here ever talks about. Stanage is evil beyond what ordinary people care to envisage.'

'OK,' Macbeth said. 'First thing, you can't stay here alone, case these people come back with some even more screwball ideas than they had when they left.'

She looked kind of suspicious. 'What's the alternative?'

'I reserved a room at the inn. You take that. I'll stay here.'

'Oh,' said Cathy. 'I see. The big macho bit. Mungo, how can I say this? You're the one who shouldn't be here on his own.'

'What you want me to do, drive outa here? Things didn't work out with Moira, let's draw a line under all of this? OK, we'll both stay here. I'll take the sofa. I'll call Mrs Castle.'

'Mungo, I'm not going to stay here. I'm going to Milly's. We have things to discuss and it's women only, I'm afraid. My advice is, take your room at The Man, get some sleep. You look all-in. If there's anything you can do, we'll ring you.'

'Oh,' Macbeth said.

'I promise.'

'Sure.'

This was Moira all over again. *Macbeth, just go away, huh?*

'I dint recognize you.' Willie was almost in tears. 'God help me, I didn't know who you were.'

'I think there was a similar problem,' Mr Dawber said drily, 'in the Garden of Gethsemane, on the Third Day.'

Willie could tell Mr Dawber was almost as pleased as he was, but there was a shadow across it.

Mr Dawber said, 'Seeing somebody you thought was dead, there's bound to be an element of shock. Take her home, Willie. Take her to Millicent.'

'Cathy,' Moira said, unsteadily on her feet, Willie's donkey jacket around her shoulders. Willie reckoned she also was in shock. 'Whatever you like,' he said. 'I can't believe this. I just can't believe it. It's a miracle. It were on t'news. They found your car, bottom of a bank.'

'I'll tell you about it,' Moira said.

'It *was* your car?'

'Oh, aye.'

Willie said, his voice rising, 'There were a body in it. Police found a woman's body!' He stared hard at her in the torchlight. He wondered if she knew where she was. He wondered if she knew what had happened to her beautiful hair.

He was glad that when he'd touched her, putting his jacket around her, she'd been stone-cold and damp, but solid.

494

Mr Dawber was silent. If he had any curiosity about the body in the BMW he was keeping it to himself.

'Let's not hang about,' Willie said. 'Mr Dawber?'

'You go,' the old man said quietly. 'I'll carry on.'

'You're never going up there on your own, Mr Dawber, no way.'

'I'll go if I want to,' Mr Dawber said, and there was a distance in his voice. 'Nobody tells the headmaster what to do. Remember?'

'Aye, and if I arrive back there without you, Milly'll kill me, you know that much, Mr Headmaster, sir.'

Mr Dawber said mildly, 'This lass'll be catching her death if you don't be on your way.'

'Please, Mr Dawber.'

'Dic.' Moira's body pulsed. 'Either of you seen Dic Castle?'

'Not since the funeral,' Willie said. 'Gone off teaching, Lottie said, in Stockport or somewhere. You seen him, Mr Dawber?'

There was no reply. Willie swung his torch round.

'Mr Dawber!'

Mr Dawber had gone.

Roger Hall asked, 'Is he mad?' The effects were wearing off; he didn't feel so elated, he did feel quite relaxed. He did *not* feel there was anything bizarre about this, why on earth should he?

Therese arched an eyebrow. She was not beautiful, but she was compelling. He wouldn't kick her out of bed.

'Well, of course he's mad,' she said. 'Didn't that occur to you?'

'He knows so much. How can you know so much, be so learned, and be insane?'

The candles around the circle were half burned down. The other people squatting cross-legged – the people Therese was 'helping', the people who did what they were told – gazed dull-eyed into the candle flames and never spoke.

'Look at it this way, Roger,' Therese said. 'You're quite a learned man yourself. Would you say *you* were insane?'

Matt Castle slumped in his chair. He wore a white T-shirt and was quite obviously and horribly dead, but he didn't offend Roger Hall any more.

Roger laughed. 'But Stanage . . . I mean, he does know what he's doing?'

Dic Castle, something as primitive as chloroform administered to him on a rag, was bound and taped into a metal-framed chair with his wrists upturned. This did not offend Roger either. Nor did the hypodermic on the table.

'He's done it before,' Therese said. 'Many years ago he dug up a corpse, dead no more than a week, to tap her knowledge. It is, as you've gathered yourself, all about knowledge. I thought that was just wonderful – he went into Bridelow churchyard at night and dug the old girl up with the sexton's spade. He was about nineteen at the time. He just, you know, has absolutely no fear. That's half the battle, when you think about it.'

'Yes.' She was right. Conquering fear was the vital first step. Fear of being caught out. Fear of the law. Fear of humiliation.

'Look at Shaw,' Therese said. 'Shaw was a fantastically good subject because he was so utterly screwed up, so socially backward to begin with. Six months ago, Shaw was scared to walk into a pub by himself; now he's killed two people and he's never been happier. He's out there now, and if anybody tries to disturb us, he'll . . . you know . . . without a second thought.'

'And you're telling me all this.' He wanted to pinch himself; he wanted to find the smell of Matt Castle nauseating. And he couldn't.

'You're one of *us*,' Therese said generously. 'You've been one of us for months. We'd never have got the Man out of the British Museum without your help, and you'd never have had the balls to get him out without ours. Come on, it's time. Have another drink.'

'I mustn't,' Roger said coyly, accepting a glass. 'One final question. Therese . . . what would have happened to Chrissie if she'd come to the house with me?'

'Who . . . ? Oh, the secretary. The divorced secretary with

no immediate family in the area. *That* Chrissie. Don't ask, Roger. Don't ask and you won't be told the truth.'

Therese poured them all a drink from an unlabelled brown wine bottle. 'Cheers,' said a dull, empty-looking woman called Andrea. Therese moved to a bench in the corner of the room opposite Matt and slipped a cassette into a black ghetto-blaster.

From the largest of several black bags, she withdrew the Pennine Pipes and laid them at Matt's feet.

From the portable ghetto-blaster seeped the weeping, far-away, opening notes of 'Lament for the Man'.

Dic squirmed.

From one of the bags, Therese took a pencil-slim plastic-handled craftsman's knife, which she handed to Owen, a weedy, expressionless man.

'I'll give you the signal,' Therese said. 'If it disturbs you, you may tape his mouth.'

CHAPTER VI

Refusing a whisky, Gary Ashton said, 'I'm not saying I don't believe this, ladies. I've seen too many weird things, put away too many weird people, we all do. Sometimes, you're face-to-face with real evil, and you're laughing it off. You laugh off criminals – blaggers, toe-rags. You don't think too hard about it, you're a copper. Not a shrink. Not a priest. You nick the buggers, put them away, that's where it ends.'

'Meaning you can't help us,' Lottie said.

'Far as the law's concerned, Mrs Castle, there's one crime been committed here. Somebody's pinched an archaeological relic.'

He'd sat there and he'd drunk coffee and he'd sympathized. He'd trusted them, too, both of them. They were frightened, more than if they'd been robbed. Although he knew bugger-all about wiring and such, he'd been and examined the electrified gas-mantle and fitted a new bulb, and, sure enough, it didn't come on. Fuse probably, he'd said. Where's the fuse-box?

And Lottie had said, never mind.

Truth was, the bloody thing had fused at the wrong time and put the shits up two women who were already mentally stressed.

Ghost in the mirror? Pipes in the night?

Strange atmosphere? Aye, there was. There was a strange atmosphere all over this whole village tonight, it hit you soon as you crossed the Moss. Too much rain, for a start, as if it was nature's attempt to cool something down, to put out a fire somebody was busy stoking under this place.

Put that in a bloody police report. Show that to the Superintendent. Strange atmosphere. '*There was a very strange atmosphere, boss.*'

And then Chrissie White said what he'd been faintly hoping she might.

'What if I knew who'd stolen the bogman?'

'Ah. Then I'd have a lot more leverage, wouldn't I, Chrissie?'

Chrissie said, 'Have you heard of a writer called John Peveril Stanage?'

'My kids used to read him avidly.' He glanced at Lottie. 'One grown up, now. The other still lives with his mother and her new feller. Aye, John Peveril Stanage. What about him?'

'He's got plans to fund a permanent museum for the bogman. As you know, Roger would run it. Stanage would have permanent access to the bogman.'

'So why would he nick it? I presume you are saying he nicked it. Or had it nicked.'

'I don't know,' Chrissie said. 'I just think he has.'

'Why?' Ashton began to feel less hopeful.

''Cause he's invited Roger to some sort of gathering at Bridelow Hall and he's told him he might be able to find out where it is.'

'That's not the same thing, Chrissie. Also, it's presumably only what Dr Hall's told you.'

'Well, that's right. I suspect there's a lot more to it than that. Can't you get some of your blokes and, raid it or something?'

'Oh, aye,' Ashton said. 'The police are always raiding

private parties at the homes of the rich and influential. Matter of course, Mrs White. Normal procedure. Happen the Chief Constable'll be one of the guests. Or the MP?'

'What if they're doing – I don't know what to call it – black magic, or something?'

'Well, it's not basically against the law, luv. Matter of religious preference, in the eyes of the British legal system. Unless it involves children or animals, of course. You think it does?'

Chrissie said, 'Roger's been messing about with the bogman.'

Ashton tried not to laugh. 'I really don't think that'd have them cancelling leave at the Vice Squad. Mrs White . . . Chrissie. And Mrs Castle . . . I sympathize, you know I do, or I wouldn't be here. If you want me to do anything as a policeman, I've got to have something hard, solid and preferably nothing at all to do with the supernatural.'

Lottie said angrily, 'You think I . . .'

Ashton held up a hand. 'No, I don't. That's why I came. You're a nice woman, and things are happening to you that you don't understand and don't particularly want to understand. I admire you, Mrs Castle.'

'But I'm wasting your time. All right, I'm sorry. You'd better get off home to your . . .'

'Flat,' said Ashton. 'What I said was, there was nothing I could do as a copper. As things stand. However, I also attempt to be a bit of a human being, on the side. Anything I can do in that capacity, I'll be happy to do it, just as long as it's not illegal and doesn't mean saying ta-ra to me pension. How's that?'

'Thanks,' Chrissie said despondently. 'But we're all of us semi-qualified human . . .' Breaking off at a hammering on the door. Lottie looked up sharply. Initial alarm, Ashton noted, soon subsiding into weariness.

'Oh, hell, I'd forgotten about him. I've not even made up his bed.'

'Who's this?'

'An American chap. Moira's boyfriend. Better let him in before he gets soaked.'

'I'll go,' Ashton said. 'Never know what else it might be this time of night, do you? Moira's your daughter, is she?'

Milly had given up on security. The Post Office door was on the latch. Cathy burst through it, throwing off her coat.

'Where is she?'

'I'm here. Just don't look at me.'

Milly had built up the fire with great cobs of coal. Moira was hunched over it, feet on the red-tiled hearth, a glass of Guinness between them. Her jeans and sweater hung from a wire line under the wooden mantelpiece. She wore a dressing gown of Milly's with a design of giant daisies. There was a pink towel around her head.

Cathy grinned helplessly.

Moira said, 'Take more than death to kill me, huh?'

Is that it? Ernie Dawber wondered. Determined not to see tomorrow's sun? And will anyone? Will we ever even see the sky again?

Getting a bit whimsy, Ernest?

Aye, I am that, Ma. Been whimsy all night. Offered meself as a sacrifice, Ma. Wanted to go out on the Moss and not come back. Bit pathetic, eh?'

He walked with a measured pace towards Bridelow Hall, shining his torch, making no attempt to conceal his approach.

Well, what would you have done, Ma? Doctor tells you it could be two years, could be six months. Or less. You start to think, where am I going to be when it happens? Where would I like to be more than Bridelow? Bridelow as it is now. With the shades of things and the balance. Where else could I go and actually be any bloody *use*?

His saturated hat was moulded to his head, the sodden brim as heavy as a loaded teatray.

Little problem in the brain, Ma. That's why I was thrown a bit when your Willie lost his rag and raised the issue of my mental state.

Ernie chuckled. I suppose you'd have seen the black glow on me too, eh, owd lass? And said nowt.

But did you see it around yourself?

Happen not.

Ernie became thoughtful.

He didn't need his torch lit when the Hall came into view. For the Hall was all lights, upstairs and down, and brought back, with a momentary thrill, a picture of the old days when Arthur and Liz held open house for the brewery workers and their relatives and friends. Which amounted to the whole village in those days. Liz in a glittery gown, Arthur permitting his stern eyes a twinkle behind those forbidding horn-rims.

And Shaw.

Shaw was never there on such occasions. Shaw, they said, was shy. Shaw could never say the headmaster's name. Mr Der-der . . .

'*Mr Dawber*,' Shaw said easily.

He stepped out from the brewery entrance gate, the stem of a stylish golf umbrella propped elegantly across his left shoulder. His dark suit was perfectly dry.

'Good evening, lad,' Ernie said heavily. 'I've come to see your mother.'

'Small problem there, Mr D. Mother's spending the week-end at a hotel in Buxton. Autumn break.'

'Brave of her, lad. Conquered the agoraphobia, then, has she?'

'She hasn't got agoraphobia, Mr Dawber. She's simply rather a retiring person. Shy, even.'

'As you were yourself, Shaw. Perhaps it's an hereditary problem. Dealt with yours, though, didn't you, lad?'

'One alters. As one gets older.'

Shaw Horridge, sheltered from the downpour, was smirking. It brought out the headmaster in Ernie.

'Perhaps heredity says it all.' Standing his ground, dripping. 'I'd like a chat, Shaw Horridge, and I'd like it now.'

He'd almost said, My Office. At once.

For a second, Shaw looked disconcerted.

Ernie pocketed his torch. 'I won't go away.'

'Won't you?' Shaw's smirk vanished and was replaced by an expression Ernie didn't recognize but which he found surprisingly menacing.

'Come up to the house, then,' Shaw said.

Two phone calls was all it took. One to Headquarters, one to the doctor's house. At least this was something Ashton could do – they'd given him a name in connection with an incident under investigation; he could check it out.

'Thanks very much, Doc,' Ashton said. 'Owe you one.'

Lottie was over by the stove again, deep lines in her face, the permanent frown. Years of Matt Castle in the making, Ashton reckoned, but not irreversible.

The American, Macbeth, was sitting at the kitchen table, watching him in silence, black hair stuck to his forehead, tension coming off him like vapour. Chrissie White was watching the American; what was coming off her wasn't quite seemly under the circumstances.

'Well, then,' Ashton said, putting down the phone. They were all staring at him now. 'Your Miss Cairns. I suppose I'm right in assuming she was nowhere near her middle-fifties?'

Macbeth breathed out in a rush. 'God damn.'

'Grey hair?' said Ashton. 'Somewhat overweight?'

'But . . .' Macbeth sat down next to Chrissie. 'But it was her car?'

'Clearly. With another woman's body in it. What's that say to you? Mrs Castle? Any other women missing?'

'God!' Macbeth had his head in his hands. His body sagged. Relief. No way you could fake that.

Chrissie smiled thinly. 'Well,' she said, '*that's* all right, then.'

Lottie said, 'What did she look like?'

'She was badly burned, apparently. As I say, mid-to-late fifties. Plumpish. Grey hair, quite short. So who is she? And what was she doing in Miss Cairns's car?'

Macbeth looked up. There were tears in his eyes.

Ashton let his gaze rest on the American. 'There is, of

course, another question. Two, perhaps. Where *is* Miss Cairns? And what does she know about this woman's death?'

'Hey,' Macbeth said. 'Come on . . .'

'Has to be asked, sir.' And other questions. Like, what's brought this American all the way from Glasgow in the worst driving conditions of the year so far, and what's he doing in this country anyway?

Macbeth said, 'How official is this?'

'Well, now,' Ashton said, 'that depends, doesn't it?'

Macbeth said nothing for nearly half a minute, then he spread his hands. 'OK. How much you know about a guy name of John Peveril Stanage?'

Chrissie gasped, and Ashton allowed himself a sigh of manifest satisfaction.

Moira was choking.

'Jesus, what the hell is this stuff?'

'Shurrup and get it down,' Milly said.

'Yeah, but what . . . ?'

'Ma Wagstaff's Crisis Mixture,' said Milly. 'Last bottle.'

'Tastes like something scraped off the floor at a foot clinic.'

Cathy said seriously, 'Drink it, Moira. We need you.'

She drank it. She drank it all, every last nauseating mushroom-coloured drop. All the time watching Cathy over the glass, the girl's narrow face taut with concentration.

'Dic.' Moira let Milly take the glass away. 'Thank you. Cathy, what are we going to do about Dic?'

'I told you, didn't I?' Cathy said. 'I said it wasn't Dic who took the comb.'

'Aye, you did. I'm sorry. But why's he with Stanage? How'd he get into this? And the girl. The woman.'

'Therese. Pure poison. Lady Strychnine.'

'But Dic was *helping* them.'

'Dic was helping *us*,' Cathy snapped.

'Us?'

'The Mothers.'

'You told me . . . Hang on, I'm confused, you said you weren't one. You said your father wouldn't . . .'

'I didn't know you well enough. I lied. It's OK to lie sometimes. Except to yourself.'

'Sure.' Moira sighed.

'Dic lied to himself a lot. He lied about his father. He lied about not hating his father.'

'I know. Maybe we all lied to ourselves about Matt.'

'Aye.' Willie Wagstaff was sitting on the arm of the sofa. 'I never wanted him to come back to Bridelow, me. He were too . . . disruptive, you know?' He paused. 'Like our Jack.'

'How it happened,' Cathy said, 'Dic read Stanage as a kid. His dad was all for it. Imaginative stuff, full of Celtic reverberations.' She looked up at Willie in appeal. 'They didn't *know*, you see. Matt had been away too long. He didn't know Stanage was Jack Lucas. Not at first.'

'Makes sense,' Willie said. 'It were a long time before any of us found out. Peveril. Stanage. Derbyshire place-names. Peveril of the Peak. Nothing too local. How *should* we know? He were never on telly, never give interviews to t'papers.'

'So, like a lot of kids,' Cathy said, 'Dic wrote him a fan letter. *Un*like a lot of kids, he got a reply inviting him to visit the great man. Beginning of a beautiful friendship. It was Stanage who persuaded Dic to learn the Pennine Pipes. Matt was delighted, as you'd imagine, Dic having always rejected traditional stuff.'

'Why would Stanage be so interested in Dic?' Moira asked.

'He wasn't. He was interested in Matt. They'd known each other as kids, obviously, and Stanage was looking for ways into Bridelow. That was *his* ruling obsession, to get back at them.'

'At . . . ?'

'At Bridelow. Specifically at the Mothers. The Bridelow establishment. The keepers of the Bridelow tradition. The keepers of . . . I don't know.'

'The balance,' Milly said. 'The keepers of the balance.'

'God knows,' said Willie, 'they tried to sort him out. They tried everything. He were just . . . just bloody *bad*, what can you say? And when he like . . . finally overstepped the mark, he had to go. He were halfway gone by then, anyroad, gone off to university, smartest lad ever come out of Bridelow. Can say that again.'

Moira said slowly, 'How do you mean, overstepped the mark?'

Willie looked at the others. Milly nodded. Willie said bitterly, 'He desecrated a grave.'

'Spell it out, little man,' Milly said softly.

'He dug up Owd Ma. That were me granny. Ma's ma. Been dead a week.'

'He had it all timed,' Milly said. 'The right day, the right hour, the right position of the moon, all this. He had to *know*, you see. He had to know what was being denied to him because he was a man.'

A gout of rain came down the chimney. On the fire, a red coal cracked in two with a chip-pan hiss.

Moira said, 'He did this? Necromancy? He tried to get information out of a dead woman?'

Willie reached for Milly's hand. She said, 'I was only a youngster. I only know what I was told later, by Ma. She said there were things he knew, things he threw in her face . . . that he couldn't possibly have learned from anyone else. So either Old Ma told him stuff on her deathbed, which is so unlikely as to be . . .'

Moira started to feel sick, and it wasn't Ma Wagstaff's Crisis Mixture. 'Willie, sooner or later Matt would know about this guy. What he was.'

'We never talked about it, lass. But, aye, sooner or later. But he'd be too far in, maybe, by then. To be charitable. In the end, though, it's two of a kind. Exiles wanting in.'

'Men,' said Milly. 'Men wanting knowledge.'

'And now he's doing it to Matt. What he did to your gran. Dic told me, he said, "He's got my dad." How can . . . ?'

'We know,' Milly said. 'Matt's coffin's full of soil.'

Cathy said, 'Listen, the night Dic brought you to the Rectory, afterwards he had a few drinks, got a bit . . . mixed up. He was approached. There was a sexual approach. He thought it was you.'

'What a compliment.'

Cathy frowned. 'Next day he told me about it. He's always told me things. He was in a hell of a state. He needed . . . calming down. You can tell how easily they get people.'

Moira nodded. She knew well enough.

'I said you were with me the whole time,' Cathy said, 'so it couldn't have been you.'

'Thank you.'

'And then we talked about it for ages. It was *our* only way in. For Dic to go along with it, see what happened. I think he saw it as a way of getting out of the influence of his dad and Stanage and the whole thing.'

Moira started shaking her head. Lamb to the slaughter.

'He's been through hell.' Cathy's eyes looking hot with sorrow. 'Yes, they've got Matt's body. Yes, they've been . . . arousing him.'

Moira covered her face with her hands.

'There's Stanage and this Therese. Calls herself Therese Beaufort. He claims, apparently, that she's his niece. That's crap. All kinds of people've been attracted to him over the years. He's, you know, he's . . . magnetic.'

'I know.' Moira rubbed her eyes. 'I know his kind. Who else?'

'Detritus. There's a Satanic-type cult based in Sheffield that's been holding rituals on the moors, in the old Bronze Age circles. Been going on for years. They move as close as they can to Bridelow – it's got a reputation in the occult world, as you can imagine. Place of power.'

Moira felt herself back in the churchyard, deformed stone across the moor, hopping like a toad, a quick splash of blood . . .

'Therese,' Cathy said. 'Tess – she's Tessa-something, Dic says, she came up from the Welsh border – Tess brings them along. They're revolting. That farmer – there was a farmer killed on the moor, Sam Davis – he came to see Pop last week. Lights in the night, rams killed. His wife reckoned they were even sacrificing babies.'

'It's not unknown,' Moira said. 'I believe some of these cults are actually breeding babies for sacrifice. How did this guy die?'

'Fell down a quarry at night. How do you know that, about the babies?'

'Read it in the *News of the World*,' Moira said quickly.

'Look, you say they get as close as they can to Bridelow. But they can't get *in*, right? You told me the other night there were defences. The kind you can't see.'

Milly said, 'Jack could let them in. Down in Cambridge, Jack was mixing with all kinds of people. Jack was learning all the time. We had to do something or else Bridelow'd be . . . just like everywhere else. Soiled. Only more so, because . . .'

'. . . because it was a place of power. Right?'

'We had to do something,' Milly said. 'Or Ma did. Ma was the only one could do it.'

'Why?' Moira hunched forward, hands clasped. 'I mean, what? What could Ma do?'

Milly looked down into her lap where Willie's hand lay.

'Come on, Milly,' Moira said almost angrily. 'What is it you're not telling me? Cathy, do *you* know?'

'Yes,' Cathy said. 'I think so.'

CHAPTER VII

Ernie had taken off his hat, placed it on the hallstand, where it was still dripping five minutes later when Shaw Horridge shouted, 'Get out. Get out, Mr Dawber. Get out before I kill you!'

Six months ago Ernie would have had a regretful laugh at that. Six months ago, Shaw wouldn't have been able to say it without a hell of a struggle. Now it was quite apparent that Shaw would indeed like to kill him and certainly could. And it wouldn't be his first time.

Feelings. Ernie had ignored his feelings, his whimsy. They were never specific enough, never quite *accurate*. He was a man and also a scholar in his own small way, and feelings, in Bridelow, were what women had.

And now, when it was probably too late, he was finding out what feelings were for.

He stood by the hallstand. Over his head hung a leaded lantern in a wrought-iron frame. Tasteful; one of Liz's earliest purchases.

'Your mother's no more in Buxton, lad, than we are now.'

'She *is*!' Shaw seemed about to stamp his foot. With his folded umbrella he prodded the air an inch or two from Ernie's eyes.

Ernie didn't move. 'Nearest she got to Buxton is a BMW motorcar at the bottom of a bank. She's in a police mortuary, lad. That's where your mother is.'

Known it as soon as he and Willie had found the Cairns lass. Known it, really, for most of the day. That she was dead.

'You're off your head, Mr Dawber.'

'Not yet, lad. Soon, happen. But not yet.'

'I've told you once to get out. I won't tell you again.' Shaw's eyes glittered like broken glass.

'Kill me, eh?'

'You think I won't?'

'No, I know you would.' Ernie picked up his wet hat, held it in front of his chest like a breast plate. Took a big, long breath. Saw before him the little lad in Class I of the infants. Fair-haired, fair-complexioned, tall but slightly built. Brought to school that first morning by stocky, swarthy Arthur Horridge, Arthur's dark brown hair already greying at the temples.

Ernie looked into Shaw's pale, malevolent eyes. 'Just like you killed your granny, eh, lad?'

Shaw drew back across the hall. His mouth twisted up and opened on one side, his face alternating between a sneer and a stare of more than slightly crazed, vacant incomprehension.

'What's this? What's this nonsense? What are you babbling about? You're an old fool, Mr Dawber.'

'Haven't they told you, Shaw? Hasn't your father told you?'

'My father's dead.'

'I only wish he were, lad.'

'I . . . You . . .'

'Your father's Jack Lucas. John Peveril Stanage.'

'That's . . . that's absolute crap.'

'You want to hear about this, Shaw?'

Shaw had backed up against the flock-papered far wall, his mouth twisting noiselessly from side to side, both hands over his head, hovering half an inch above his baldness.

'When I was a little lad' – Ernie leaned his back against the hall stand, relaxed – 'there was a bit of a kerfuffle in Bridelow. Minor scandal, soon hushed up, years before I learned the details. Anyroad . . . Ma Wagstaff . . . Iris Morris in those days, young lass, bit of all right, too. But wild. Nowt anybody could tell her. Wasn't going to stay in little Bridelow, was she? Off to the city, our Iris, most weekends. Met a feller, as you'd expect. Educated smooth-talker, name of Lucas.'

Shaw Horridge was standing with his legs apart, panting a little.

'Came back pregnant. Wouldn't be the first one. Prospective father buggered off soon as he found out. The old story, and folks in Bridelow's always been liberal enough about that kind of thing. Except Iris was a bit special. Direct line, see. Presented to the Mother same week she was christened. Expected, somehow, to have a daughter.'

'This is nonsense,' Shaw said. 'I'm going to kill you.'

'Hear me out first, eh?'

'I killed someone else tonight. I killed Manifold. Young Frank. I killed him . . . just moments ago.'

'I don't think so,' Ernie said uncertainly. The idea of Shaw Horridge coping with Young Frank with a few drinks inside him was still a bit laughable. Wasn't it?

'I did. I'll show you.'

'Let me finish, lad, eh? Where was I? A daughter, yes. They expected she'd have a daughter first, that's the way it is usually. But no, it was a boy, and a most peculiar child. White. All over.'

'No!'

'Yes! Folks said, it's retribution. She sinned. Sinned not so much against God but against her heritage. And the child? A changeling, they said. Know what that is, Shaw? Child of another . . . species, shall we say. A cuckoo. That was the word they used, changeling's my word, as a folklorist – all nonsense, of course, happen just a genetic throwback. But "cuckoo" was what they said. Not out loud, of course. Whispered it, though, when Iris wasn't about. But then she got married to Len Wagstaff and had three more, and the family closed ranks a bit and the things John did later were covered up. At first. Until it wasn't possible to cover them up any more.'

'What things?'

'Pranks, at first. Not the worst you could say about them, but if you were being charitable you'd call them pranks. Cruel pranks.'

'Perhaps they made him feel better,' Shaw said.

'Eh?'

'You do something brave, you push yourself. And you start to feel better.'

'Do you?'

'Yes. You can do anything if you push yourself into places you wouldn't normally go.'

'Oh, aye?'

'Look at this, for instance. How do you think I got this?'

He was doing it again, letting his hands hover half an inch from the bald part of his head.

'I don't understand,' Ernie said.

'Can't you see?' Shaw leapt about flinging switches until the hall was blazing with lights. Wall lights, ceiling lights, lights over five mirrors reflecting his bounding figure. 'Look. *Look!* I was completely bald at the front. Even two weeks ago, I was bald.'

'Aye?'

'Well?' Shaw bent his head towards Ernie. It threw off light like a steel helmet. 'Well?'

'Well, what?' Ernie said.

Shaw straightened up. 'Know when it began to grow again? When I agreed to get rid of the old lady.'

'Your grandmother.'

'That's crap. You come here, you give me all this bullshit. How stupid do you really think I am, Mr Dawber?'

Ernie thought very carefully before he spoke.

'Stupid enough,' he said, stepping away from the hallstand, bracing himself, 'to think your hair is growing again.'

The fire hissed again. There was a visible bubbling among the coals.

'Have to get Alf Beckett to fit you a cowl on t'chimney,' Willie Wagstaff said prosaically to Milly.

Moira moved her legs closer to the fire, feeling she might never be truly warm again.

'Your brother? He's your brother?'

'Half-brother,' said Willie. 'But it counted for nowt. Once he'd gone he were never spoke of again. And after that, Ma never looked back.'

'And there was a new respect for Ma,' Milly Gill said. 'That she was able to do it.'

'Do what? What did she do?'

'Personal banishing rite,' Milly said. 'She walked around the village boundary three times within a day and a night. She walked barefoot, placing stones. Calling on . . . elements not usually invoked. But he was a strong presence, even then.'

'Be July of that year when he come back,' Willie recalled. 'End of his second year at Cambridge. Arrived in a fancy sports car.'

'Wherever he went,' Milly said, 'he could make money or get people to give him things.'

'There's an owd tree,' Willie said, 'just this side of t'Moss, 'fore you get to t'pub. Jack piled his car into that. Broke both arms. Elsie Ball, as were landlady of The Man in them days, she dint recognize Jack at first. Went out to help him, but Jack wouldn't come out of his car, *couldn't* come out. Just sat there until the ambulance come. Ma were standing at top of street, she knew who it were. Too far apart to see each other's faces, but I remember Elsie saying clouds were coming down, hanging low, like a thunderstorm were about to burst.'

'And then Jack went away,' Milly said, 'and we never saw him again. He knew he'd never get back in, long as Ma were . . .'

'Alive,' said Willie, and Moira saw the fingers of his left hand beginning to crawl up the side of his knee.

'So,' Moira said, 'if he *wanted* to get back . . .'

'Why should he? He were rich. He were becoming famous. He had everything he could wish for.'

'Except his heritage,' Moira said.

'He tried to *destroy* his heritage,' Milly insisted.

'No. He tried to restructure it, surely. He tried to rebuild it around himself. It was a placid, earth-related, female religion, and he wanted to harden it into something he could use.'

Milly looked at her with suspicion.

'I've encountered it before,' Moira said. 'No. He was never going to walk away from that. All the time he'd be building up his armoury of contacts inside Bridelow. Matt and Dic we know about. There are probably others.'

'Shaw Horridge.' Willie's fingers were drumming hard. 'The brewery. He'd bought into Gannons. He must've done that purely to get hold of Bridelow Brewery.'

Who took the comb?

. . . bloke called Shaw Horridge, but that's not important right now . . .

'Yes,' Moira said.

Willie's fingers going like hell, both hands now. 'The bloody *scale* of the thing! Too big for us to see. Maybe we never wanted to see it. He'd gone. Right, Ma says, that's it. Never mention him again and you'll never see him again. And we never have.'

'Except,' said Milly, 'in Shaw.'

Willie looked at her. Moira watched his eyes widen.

'It was a Mothers' thing,' Milly said. 'Never talked about. I think Mr Dawber knew, but that's all. Probably not many people remember now, and I was just a child, but when Eliza McCarthy first arrived in Bridelow it was as Jack's girlfriend. All Jack's girlfriends were from wealthy backgrounds. Liz didn't last long, I don't suppose she was beautiful enough. It was probably just the family link with the Duke of Westminster that interested him.'

Milly pulled one of the cats on to her lap, began to stroke it from neck to tail. 'What happened, I believe, is that they had a row and Jack just drove away and left her in tears in the street. Which was where Ma found her. This was before the banishing.'

'Aye,' Willie said, something dawning. 'She spent the night with us. It were the year before me Dad died. He'd gone to The Man, he were in t'darts team, and I remember lying in bed and hearing Ma and this lass talking for hours.'

'Probably what you heard was Ma warning her off Jack. Next day, when Jack didn't come back, Ma introduced Liz to

Arthur Horridge and two months later they were engaged. Well . . . four days before the wedding, Liz is hammering on Ma's door in a terrible state. She's pregnant.'

Milly hauled the second cat on to her lap as if she needed reinforcement. 'Jack. Jack on the outside. He can't get into Bridelow but he can still get to his ex-fiancée.'

'Bastard.' Both of Willie's hands fell away from his knees.

Cathy shook her head in distaste. 'How could she?'

'You didn't know him,' Milly said. 'When I was nine years old, Jack took me and two other little girls for a walk on . . . Oh, you don't want to hear, it was nothing by comparison with what else he's done. But he could walk in and even if you didn't really like him he'd get what he came for. Liz – it wasn't rape, as such, you could learn to live with that. Anyway . . . Ma had a long chat with Arthur Horridge and Shaw was born, and he was Arthur's son and nothing more was ever said.'

'I can't believe all this,' Willie said. 'Can't believe we never *thought*. We didn't think of the bugger any more – better not to. Wrote his books under the name John Peveril Stanage, we knew that, so it was as if the Jack Lucas we knew had gone for good.'

'Pouring all his worst fantasies into his books, huh?' Moira said.

'Something like that. Takes that American lad to come in here and drop Jack's name in our laps before we put two and two together.'

'Oh,' said Cathy. 'Mungo! He still thinks . . .'

Moira spun so fast the towel unwound from her hair. Cathy's hand went to her mouth but failed to stifle a cry.

'They did that to you? They cut off all your . . . ?'

Moira let the towel fall.

'Oh, Moira!' Tears sprang into Cathy's eyes.

Deliberately calm, Moira said, 'They needed my hair to entangle Matt's spirit. They locked me in an outhouse in the dark. They couldn't kill me because that would have released *my* spirit, defeating the object. So they kept me in this sensory vacuum, sedated with mogadon or some shit that turns you into a comatose non-person so that your energy, your personality, your essence can be . . . stolen.'

513

Moira stood up, reached under the mantelpiece for her stiffening jeans. 'Cathy, I . . . You invoked the awful word "Mungo".' Disgusted to feel a tiny smile pulling on the muscles at the corners of her mouth.

'He still thinks you're dead,' Cathy said. 'He's over at The Man. I'd better call him.'

'Uh huh.' Moira shook her head. 'I don't know how Macbeth got here or why, and I don't have time to find out. I'm starting to see everything. Clear as hell.'

Her mind burning up with it.

They stood either side of the Beacon of the Moss, heads bowed.

Joel had asked, 'Shouldn't we pray?'

'We should meditate,' John had said.

Joel stood in the blueness of it and tried to concentrate his mind, to absorb the rise and fall of Tongues from beneath, to achieve a holy stillness. But his thoughts lumbered ape-like around the shadowed walls of the chamber. He could not see John's face, could only sense the man's awesome containment.

'It's time,' John said very quietly, raising his head.

Reaching up, beyond the top of the great lantern, he examined the chain by which it hung from the thick, long-ago-smoke-blackened beam. 'Come beneath it, Joel. Catch it when I release it.'

And while Joel crouched, arms full of light, John reached up and unhooked the chain.

The lamp was unexpectedly heavy. Joel stumbled but held it, pulling down several feet of electric flex which had been coiled between the beam and the wall. The lamp did not go out.

'Good,' John said. 'Now lower it to the floor.'

They both stood back. The pointed top of the lantern was on a level now with Joel's groin.

'Kick it in,' John urged.

Joel tried to see his face but saw only the bared blue teeth and blue steel ripples of hair.

He couldn't move.

'This is the pagan light. This is the lure. *Very few people* dared cross the Moss, Mr Beard, except those for whom the Devil lit the way. Have you heard that legend? Have you heard it?'

'Yes . . . !' Joel panicking. 'I heard it from you. You told me.'

'And do you believe it? Consider the evidence.'

'I believe,' Joel intoned, 'that this is a place of pagan worship. I have seen the signs. I have seen the woman with the spread cunt. I have *dreamed* of her. And I have seen the dead walk.'

'And you know that this night is Samhain, the Feast of the Dead, and that the light is shining out across the peat to welcome the dead to this place.'

'It shall not happen.'

Joel lifted his foot, aware as never before of its size and its weight, and he plunged it, with a shattering, through the glass of the lantern and watched the shower of shards, blue and then white, pierce the tumbling shadows.

'The bulbs, Joel. Now the bulbs!'

Joel felt his lips stretched tight as his foot went back again and again, lightbulbs exploding, all of them, whorls of jagged colour, and then there was the creak of a door opening, a rapid clumping of footsteps and his neck was wrenched back and the last thing he saw before the last bulb blew was John's luminescent teeth as the man held up a scimitar of white glass, nine inches long.

Joel bit rubber, and felt his knees buckle before he was even aware of the single dull, heavy blow on the back of his head.

For a long time there was only night, and then there was a lake and a naked woman on a hill, and the woman smiled with a sorrow deeper than the lake and Joel wanted to scream, *I recognize you. I recognize you now, for what you are . . .*

But the woman was gone and there was only a void of dark sorrow and John's voice, coming very quickly, words running together, some in an archaic and alien language, and a few that he could understand.

'. . . *that by the laying down of the blood . . .*'

Another, deeper male voice joining John's in fractured counterpoint.

'. . . *and shall be recompensed for that which we have borrowed* . . .'

Joel trying to speak, his arms pinned behind him, confusion and humiliation turning to a savage anger as his chest swelled and his elbows jerked and there was a grunt behind him and he spat out the rubber and jerked his head forward and inside him he let out a great roar of rage.

And only a liquid gurgle came out, and he felt his very soul was pouring out through his throat and something heavy thrust into the small of his back and there was a shattering explosion and Joel was out into the flooded sky and falling through the slipstream of his blood.

PART TEN

MOSS

CHAPTER I

Nobody in the house had been able to get to sleep anyway, because of the rain, and then The Chief started to howl, a terrified yelping sort of howl, sending Benjie hurtling down the stairs and his mam screaming from the landing, 'He'll go in a kennel, that dog, I'm warning you!' And The Chief carried on howling, even with Benjie's arms tight around his neck, and Benjie shouted back up, 'It's that dragon again, Mam!'

Heard his mam snort from the landing.

Mumbling into the dog's fur, '. . . same as killed me gran.'

And Benjie thought he should get dressed and take The Chief out into the street so his howling would wake up the whole village and everybody would be able to escape before the dragon came out of the Moss.

Moira was already dressed when they heard Alfred Beckett shouting in the Post Office, 'Shop! Shop!'

Milly brought him through and Alf stood there, getting his breath back, raindrops glittering in his moustache.

'They've put it out!' he gasped, holding on to the back of the sofa. 'Bastards've put out the light.'

Willie pushed past him and dashed through the office to the front door. 'He's right.'

'Beacon of the Moss,' Milly explained to Moira.

'What's that mean? That it's out?'

'It's happened before, obviously, power-failures and such, but with all the rest of it . . .'

'You're saying it's cumulative, right?'

'I'll go up,' Willie called back.

'No,' Moira snapped. 'There's been too much rushing in, far's I can see. Cathy, the Mothers – how many *are* there?'

'It's a ragbag,' Milly said.

'How d'you call a meeting?'

'The old days, used to be said we never needed to call them at all.'

'Well, how about we try the phone, huh?'

'They'll all be in bed.'

'Jesus wept! If I had any hair I'd be tearing it.'

Dic Castle knew that a common way of committing suicide was to cut your wrists while lying in a bath of warm water and that it was largely painless, letting life seep away.

He was not in a bath of warm water, but he supposed sedation had the same effect in that he was aware of *not* trying to scream through the sweating adhesive tape across his mouth but just sitting there, bound by string and wire to his chair, wondering how long before it was over.

His hands were painlessly numb, cloth tourniquets around both wrists so that the blood flow was regulated, like an egg-timer.

He wasn't even resentful any more. He'd got Moira out. He'd led them away from her and they didn't know she'd gone, the sound of the rain muffling her hysteria. Him? They thought he'd just chickened out and run away, and now they'd caught him, and maybe this was what they'd intended for him all along.

Blood to blood.

He watched their faces: Philip, the glum satanist; Owen, the ex-nurse who'd given him valium through a vein; Andrea, the care-in-the-community mental patient who'd killed but not exactly *murdered* two small boys many years ago; Therese, who thought she was already halfway to being a goddess; Dr Roger Hall, who just wanted to meet the Man in the Moss.

Real evil, Dic realized, was a bit bloody pathetic.

Outside, the apprentice at the gate, was feeble Shaw Horridge, probably more inadequate than any of them because he had had money and privileges on a scale incomprehensible to most of the others.

Over in the loft at the church, Dean – also known as Asmodeus – had been hiding for hours with Terence, the hulking occult bookseller from Salford, awaiting their mentor, the revered John. Slaveringly eager for whatever grotesque experience he'd prepared for them, the more perverse the more sensuously exciting.

Dic had ceased some while ago to be shocked. He'd already seen in his father the damage caused by the perversion of a Utopian dream. He was twenty-four. He'd seen Matt Castle's jolly, infectious pioneering spirit shrivel to a sour fanaticism. And then he'd died.

And now, because of his father, Dic would die too. Taped into a wooden chair with the blood draining slowly from his wrists.

Blood to blood.

Dic was staring across the circle, with a vaguely surprising sense of pity, into his father's eyes, when a movement made him turn his head. Therese had shuddered.

Therese was sitting cross-legged, although her legs were hidden in cloak and shadow. There were candles, ordinary white candles, in glass jars because of the draught, seven of them arranged around the circle, which had been painted on the wooden floor in white and was actually two concentric circles a yard apart. In the space between the circles they all sat, like shadowy partygoers gathered for charades.

Dregs.

But Therese had shuddered.

'Yes,' she breathed. 'He's done it. Can't you feel it?'

And as if she'd signalled to them, the inadequates started mumbling, some far back in their throats, making unintelligible noises as though trying to disengage their dentures.

Revolting bastards.

In time, the mumbling became more intense and seemed to encompass the figure sprawled, rotting and stinking, in the wooden armchair.

Dic could look at it now with little sense of shock and no sense of relationship. At the withering lips drawn back, the yellow of teeth, the stiff, spouting hair above eyes wide open but glazed like a cod's eyes on the slab.

His father.

*

Of course, if you'd suggested to Chris that it was a game, a recreation like golf or squash or amateur theatricals, Chris would have been most resentful and his reply would probably have been – as he would now admit – somewhat pompous and self-righteous.

Born in Hemel Hempstead, Chris was an accountant in Sheffield. He was thirty-seven, had had his own house, on what was now a minimal mortgage, since the age of nineteen. So that when he married Chantal four years ago life had not exactly been an uphill struggle, with foreign holidays and two cars from the beginning. And the fact that God had not yet seen fit to bestow upon them a child, well, perhaps that indicated God had other work for them.

Chris had always been a churchgoer. However, as he'd intimated in passing to the American, Macbeth, the Anglican faith had long since ceased to satisfy his intense need for a more dynamic relationship with his deity.

Baptism into the Church of the Angels of the New Advent, with its full-throated, high-octane worship and its promise of *real religious experience*, was the fulfilment of what Chris had been anticipating all his thinking life.

Within eighteen months, he'd become an elder of the Church, dealing with its finances, investing its reserves, getting the best deal for God.

It filled his life. *God*, therefore, filled his life.

And God was not a hobby.

The validity of the Church of the Angels of the New Advent had been confirmed by the acceptance at theological college of one of its founders, Brother Beard, who had been called by God to go out into the 'straight' Church and reform it from within.

God's reasoning had become all too clear to Chris when Joel had been called to Bridelow.

His appearance at their house last night in search of sanctuary had made Chris – and he was sure he could also speak for Chantal – feel very honoured and (he would have admitted this now) very excited.

When Joel had spoken of his discovery of the symbols of pagan devil-worship in the Lord's house, Chris had been, on the surface, appalled, and underneath (he might not yet have admitted this) thrilled.

And when Joel had telephoned them this morning with a dramatic plea which said, more or less, Bring in the troops, the war has begun, Chris's blood had begun to race.

It was not a recreation. It was not a hobby. It was not just an unusual and stimulating way of spending Sunday, hiring a coach and everyone piling in, prepared to fast through the night (bar the odd cup of coffee) to bring light where once was darkness.

It was a war.

When the initial joyous element had been rather dispelled through exhibitions of mental stress by, first, Joel and then (perhaps influenced by Joel's rather overheated display) Chantal, Chris, the Lord's accountant, had decided that a more precise and ordered approach was required if they were to avoid further humiliation.

When they'd returned, a little shamefaced, he'd taken it upon himself to bar the church doors and state that there was to be no more wandering in and out for coffee and anyone experiencing anything irregular should simply clasp the hand of his or her brother or sister and pray for it to pass.

And there had been hymns and prayers (without handclapping, since they had learned that some faiths considered there to be a demonic element in this), and the familiar flow of exhaltation had once more been attained.

Until Chris himself had heard a distant crash from somewhere above and foolishly disregarded it until the reality of their struggle became distressingly (at first) evident.

He heard and felt it begin.

It began with a cooling of the air and a creeping change in the tone of the chant.

Hoooolyamallaaagloriagloriamalalaglorytogodglorytogod

The girl next to him had been singing melodiously, her voice high and pure and sweet.

And then too sweet.

Cloying, in fact, with an acrid saccharine aftertaste, which he was actually beginning to taste in his own throat. And then becoming simpering and childish. Peevish and playground-rhythmical.

> *holygod holygod holyholyholygod*
> *goldyhod goldyhod golyhold holygold*
> *godlyhole godlyhole godlyhole . . .*

And then it happened very quickly . . . sort of *whooooosh*, like a small hurricane of bad breath. There was a wafting sugary smell which soon became sweetly putrid, like the bad orange at the bottom of the bowl, as the chant, the pure song of Tongues, suddenly was sounding raucous and guttural, women cackling hideously (enticingly) and men making grunting, retching, foul pig noises.

We're doing it, Chris thought, in a kind of euphoric dismay, as a slimy earth taste arose in his throat. *We are exorcizing the Evil*.

Just that nobody had told him it would be quite so unpleasant (and stimulating).

When Paul, their musician – who had, admittedly, never been all that proficient – began to force a vicious, grinding discordance through the organ pipes, Chris stepped out into the aisle and ran up the steps of the pulpit from where he observed that at least five Angels of the New Advent had begun hurriedly to divest themselves of their apparel.

He also saw three men, one a kind of albino with a cherub's mouth, emerge from the vestry and calmly let themselves out of the church by the main door.

They were laughing.

There was still no sign of Joel.

Joel?

Who *was* this Joel?

Chris saw no more, for he was attacked by one of his squealing sisters and his face clawed and he enjoyed it *immensely*.

Mungo Macbeth had specialized for over ten years in the downmarket kind of TV-movie in which people fell wildly in love and moved heaven and earth to find fulfilment in some-one's arms.

Between times he'd done cop movies, about hard-bitten, cynical cops who, underneath it all, had feelings same as anyone else.

However, apart from the ones who'd given him parking and speeding tickets, Macbeth had never before met a cop who was not being played, at unreasonable expense, by some asshole with a beach house and security gates.

Love stories did not end, before they had even begun, with the death of the love object. And cop movies were never about cops who sat in your car in an endless monsoon, which, by the way, was becoming seriously frightening, and said, 'Well, I'm buggered if I know how to handle this, mate.'

They were parked up by the church in Macbeth's car on account of the grey-haired, weary-looking cop wasn't even sure his would stand up to the conditions.

Macbeth, also pretty tired, said, 'How about you just call up the precinct house and have a bunch of uniforms directed this way?'

Ashton said, 'How about you get sensible, pal?'

'I apologize.'

'Look,' Ashton said, 'it seems very likely a crime *has* been committed. But what scares the living shit out of me is that the possible criminal element in all this does not seem to be the worst aspect, if you get my meaning.'

'Yeah.'

'And if I were to contact my headquarters and somebody there did actually take me *seriously*, their first instruction – I know this much – would be: do nothing.'

Ashton scrubbed at the misted windshield. 'I'm not in the mood for some shiny-arsed politician telling me to do nowt. There's summat nasty here. I don't know how to react, but I *have* to. Right?'

'I dunno,' Macbeth said. 'It was different, somehow, when I thought Moira was dead.'

'How do you know she's not?' Ashton demanded, blunt as a sledgehammer.

'What are you saying?'

'Christ, I'm saying, *help me*. I'm saying I'm not playing this by the book because there's no book I know of covers it. I'm saying that normally, as a copper, I'd want nothing at all to do with you because I don't know you from Adam. But at least you look a bit too soft and innocent to be a villain, and if I'm not playing it as a copper I need some help and you're all I've bloody got.'

'OK,' Macbeth said reluctantly. 'First question: you equipped with a piece?'

'Eh?'

'Are you armed?'

'Are you thick?' Ashton said. 'Or just American?'

Macbeth shrugged and started up the car. 'OK,' he said. 'Let's crash the party.'

Hoping Moira would be there but not . . .

. . . not *involved*.

'OK, Lottie said fifty yards from the church, make a right, so if I reverse . . .'

He never got to do it. The hire-car was surrounded by people; they were banging on the windows and the roof.

Shortly after Shaw Horridge stopped screaming, Ernie Dawber tried to get past him to the front door, and this proved to be a bad mistake. His second bad mistake.

For a long time, Shaw had been tearing around the hall clutching at his head. He'd have been tearing his hair if there'd been enough to get a grip on.

It was a squarish hall with a high ceiling and these five mirrors, three of them full-length, put there by Liz to spread the light.

It had not been the place to break the spell.

How could the lad *ever* have convinced himself that his hair was growing again, when the opposite was true? Hadn't he looked in a mirror recently? And if he had, what had he seen?

Certainly not what all five mirrors had reflected tonight before Shaw's tenuous self-control had snapped and he'd picked up a chair of Victorian mahogany and swung it above his head around the walls, and his shining baldness was reflected a thousandfold in the hail of flying glass, as Ernie cowered on his knees by the hallstand, protecting his face with his hat.

When he made a dash for the door, Shaw was on him in one bound, his sharp, pale. face aglitter with blood and glass bright as jewellery. 'How did you do it? How did you do it, old man?'

It was some minutes before Ernie came to understand that the poor, crazed boy was holding him responsible for the disappearance of his hair.

'Listen to me,' Ernie said gently. 'They lied to you, lad. They lied about everything. Your hair, the brewery, your poor mother. They . . .'

Bewitched him? Twisted his mind? Before Ernie could choose the least inflammatory words, Shaw's face convulsed. He snatched up the chair again and smashed it down on the hallstand an inch from Ernie's ear, snapping off two legs.

'Get it back!' Shaw shrieked. *'Get my hair back!'*

And if this was a dream it didn't matter. There'd be no awakening anyway. Dic thought about his mother, all she'd had to put up with from the bastard. She should have married a secondary-school head or a bank manager in Wilmslow, or an airline pilot working out of Ringway. All that grit gone to waste on a two-bit musical maverick committed to a primitive instrument you could barely get a proper tune out of.

Made him want to weep.

The candles were burning low. Either this or his vision was going.

. . . blood to blood.

He tried to catch the eyes of the bitch, Therese, as she cried, 'I conjure *thee*, Matthew! Empowered by the Highest Strength, I *conjure* thee!'

The candles guttered. The Pennine Pipes, lying like a dead cormorant in his father's rotting lap, began to throb and to squirm as though they were full of maggots.

527

'I *conjure* thee, Matthew, under penalty of being burned and tortured in the fires for ever and ever, I *conjure* thee to appear before me and to answer my questions . . .'

Air farting through the Pennine Pipes until they squeaked and heaved, in their wrapping of black hair with a single white streak.

'I *conjure* thee, Matthew, by the power of thine own base desires, to appear before me in a pleasant and human form and to present to me the spirit of thy father of the Moss . . .'

Slipping in and out of dream. Samhain, and they said the walls were thin as paper. He thought he saw a quiver on the yellow, peeling lips of his father's corpse.

'. . . I *conjure* thee.'

A man with a knife.

Nothing ornate or ceremonial. Just a cheap craftworker's knife with a red plastic handle.

One of the untouchables bending over Dic and huffing and panting.

'By the Highest Power and by the Angels of the Firmament . . .'

The numbing power of the drug fell away from Dic like an old raincoat, leaving him naked, all his nerves singing, his cheeks bulging like a trumpeter's with a vast scream taped into his face for ever.

'Mmmmmmm!' he screamed into the adhesive tape.

'. . . and by the Angels of the Deep and with the blood that was *thy* blood and shall be *again*, Matthew . . .'

The knife cut through the tourniquets at his wrists and Dic closed his eyes, feeling nothing in his numb, etiolated arms, and yet feeling the blood rise in fountains.

'I CONJURE THEE!'

CHAPTER II

'*Hey . . . stop this bloody car . . . come on.*'

Big, shambling guy Macbeth recognized as Stan, the bartender. But Stan wasn't interested in Macbeth.

'You're the copper, aren't you?'

'Happen,' Ashton said warily.

There was Stan and some of the other guys who'd been in the bar when Macbeth arrived, but not the kid who'd figured to punch him out. Also, there was Willie Wagstaff. Macbeth leapt out, grabbed the little guy by the arm.

'Willie, hey, listen up. The body in the car . . . this was not Moira.'

'Oh,' said Willie; his mind was clearly elsewhere; he kept glancing over his shoulder towards the church and around the street. Stan was bawling into the car window at Ashton.

'Bloody hooligans. Fanatics. You're the police, get um out!'

'Willie, that means she's not dead, you hear me?'

'I'm only one policeman, sir, and I'm off duty.'

'You knew, Willie. You *knew*, goddamn it.'

'They don't *know* you're on your own,' Stan said. 'Supposed to be flaming Christians, should've heard the language. Just knock on t'door and tell um t'sling their hooks. What's the problem? We're getting wet.'

Macbeth said, 'Goddamn it, you *know* . . . Willie, where is she?'

Gary Ashton, annoyed, was out of the car, slamming the door, holding both hands up. 'All right! Quieten down. What's so important?'

Macbeth backed out, looked around the small assembly. 'Cathy know about this?' Willie nodded urgently.

Eight or nine of them now, almost a mob. Macbeth said, 'Gary, there's a bunch of well-meaning but seriously misguided people in there. Take it from me, these guys aren't shitting you, they need to be got out.'

'And we need to get in,' Stan said soberly. 'Just don't want more trouble than we can handle.'

Ashton stood in the rain pulling on his jaw. 'OK,' he said eventually. 'If I can clear this church out for you, maybe you can do something for me afterwards, all right?'

Stan shrugged, causing his old-fashioned plastic raincoat to crackle. Willie said something about Mr Dawber, looking upset, his fingers compulsively chinking the coins in his pocket.

'And another thing,' Ashton said. 'I'm not a policeman. You've never *seen* a policeman here tonight. You got that?'

Moira pulled on the navy blue duffle coat. 'Jesus, haven't worn one of these in years. This makes me a Mother?'

'Mother, maiden, hag,' Cathy said. 'It's all the same in Bridelow.'

'Just as well,' Moira said. 'I don't qualify as any of the above. Where are we going?'

Milly led her out into the street. 'Not far. Mind you don't drown in the gutter.'

Not far turned out to be Ma Wagstaff's little stone terraced cottage, its step awash but still gleaming white in the beam of the lamp Dic had given to Moira.

'Listen, I'm getting worried about Dic,' she'd said a few minutes earlier to Cathy.

'Me too,' Cathy said. 'But they couldn't kill him, could they? For the same reason they couldn't kill you. Surely?'

'No,' Moira had said dubiously. 'But sometimes you can do more harm to someone than killing them'd be, you know?'

Milly unlocked the front door and put on lights. Moira took in a tiny and ancient parlour with more bottles than a pharmacy. Or maybe this *was* a pharmacy. There was a light glaze of sadness over the room.

'I don't know where to start,' Milly said.

'Well, we don't have much time. Where'd she keep her . . . you know, recipes and stuff?'

Milly smiled wryly. 'In her head.'

'Oh, shit.' Moira began to open cupboards in the sideboard

and found more bottles. There were a few dozen books; maybe there'd be papers stuffed inside one of them. 'What's upstairs?'

'Her bathroom. Her sewing room. Her bed.'

'Are we *sure* she copied it down?'

'I remember seeing a map, a plan, kind of. I know I did. Keeping Jack out, it wasn't something you went into lightly, you know.'

Moira felt a light breeze on one side of her face. It smelt vaguely of sage.

'Something that hadn't been done for centuries,' Milly said. 'And it had to be exact. I don't know what to say, maybe if . . .'

Moira turned very casually around and looked back through the doorway into the hall.

Where she saw a little woman in misty shades of grey and sepia, a little woman who might have been formed – had it been daylight, had there been sun – by the coalescence of dustmotes.

The little woman slowly shook her head.

And disappeared.

Moira turned back into the room. 'It's not here,' she said softly. 'Ma Wagstaff had no map.'

Chris picked up the pink T-shirt and held it up in front of him and started to laugh.

Across the front of the T-shirt was inscribed, THANK GOD FOR JESUS.

He looked at it for long seconds. It made no sense to him. No sense at all any more. It was gaudy. It was trite. It was meaningless. The girl, who was called Claudette, looked a whole lot better without it, curled up asleep under the pulpit wrapped in velvet curtains torn down from the vestry.

Nice tits, Chris remembered. Paused. Wasn't that a pretty bloody sinful thing to contemplate in the House of God?

Yeah, well . . .

She'd be pretty cold, though, Claudette, when she awoke. It was getting bitter in here. Those amber-tinted lights created a completely false impression of warmth, making the pillars seem mellow.

The communion wine had helped a bit. Gerry, the solicitor from Rotherham, had found two bottles in the vestry. Well, why not? It was a so-called pagan place, wasn't it? It wasn't a sin to drink heathen wine.

Sin. Chris shook his head. So trite.

Only problem was, after that wine, he wanted a pee.

'Forget it,' he'd decreed automatically about a quarter of an hour ago. 'Nobody goes out.' Although for the life of him he couldn't remember *why* nobody should go out. Except that while it might be cold in here it was extremely wet out there. Frankly, Chris reckoned he could probably use a piss, a pint and a bag of chips in that order.

Stupidest thing they'd done had been to let the bloody bus go. That was Joel again, silly sod. Burn your boats, he'd instructed them. Well, it was all right for him, he'd cleared off somewhere. Least he could have done was left his mobile phone around; they could have got Reg Hattersley out of bed and bribed him to fetch his coach back.

Chris surveyed his little band, all forty-seven of them, The Angels of the New Advent. High-flown name, eh, for an assorted bunch of misfits whose sole connecting factor was the conviction that their lives were one course short of a banquet. Only *one* course, note, they all had their own houses and decent cars and dishwashers, etc.

Some of them were wandering around, rubbing their heads. A couple had lit cigarettes. His watch told him it had gone midnight. This was getting ridiculous.

He remembered the singing breaking up into self-parody, and a few of them had torn clothes off, mostly the ones clad in propaganda clobber like this silly T-shirt. And then there'd been isolated outbursts of anger and resentment, mostly towards Joel Beard, who'd brought them to this dump and then abandoned them – but not before going berserk and assaulting Martin, who'd lost a tooth, and Declan, who was convinced he was suffering delayed concussion. And, of course, convincing Chantal she'd been raped by an evil spirit.

'I ask you . . .' Chris said scornfully, aloud.

When someone started banging on the door, he wandered across, suspicious.

'Whosat?'

'Who am I talking to?' An authoritative kind of voice.

'Yes?' Chris said, equally peremptory.

'This is the police,' the voice said levelly. 'I don't know who you are but I have to inform you that you have no legal right to occupy this building and I'm suggesting you vacate it immediately. If you unbolt this door and everyone comes out without any trouble, I can promise you that no further action is likely to be taken. If, however . . .'

'Yeah?' Chris said. This really *was* the police?

A distant voice berated him, his own voice within his chest. He heard it say, *Get thee hence, tempter,* what he might well have said out loud an hour ago. What a plonker he'd been.

'I do strongly advise you, sir, not to play silly-buggers. Open this door, please.'

Chris gazed at the oak door, probably six inches thick, at the iron bolts, four inches wide.

Where is your power? the inner voice bleated pathetically at the policeman. *Blow it down, why don't you, with your foul, satanic breath.*

Must've been nuts, Chris thought. All of us. Mass hysteria.

'Yeah, all right,' he said resignedly and drew back the bolts.

There were cheers of relief from the brothers and sisters sprawled among the pews.

Although glances were exchanged, Milly didn't ask her how she knew there was nothing in the house. There was silence, then Milly said, 'What are we going to do now?'

'Don't know about you,' Moira said. 'But I think I'm gonny cry.'

'Moira.' Willie was in the doorway, about a yard from where Ma's ghost had stood.

Milly shook her head. 'It's not here, little man.'

Willie nodded, unsurprised. 'She weren't much of a filer-away of stuff. 'Cept for foul-smelling gunge in the bottom of owd bottles.'

'Don't knock it,' Moira said. Less than half an hour after forcing down Ma's Crisis Mixture, she was, inexplicably, feeling stronger than she had in some while.

'Moira . . .' Willie glanced behind him to where the rain bounced off Ma's moon-white doorstep. 'Don't you think . . . ?'

'Yeah,' Moira said. 'I know. I know.' She sighed. 'OK. Come away in, Macbeth.'

Suddenly self-conscious, she found herself mindlessly reaching for the duffel-coat hood to cover the desolate ruins of her hair. 'Ach,' she said, and let her hands fall to her sides.

When he stumbled over the threshold, this Mungo Macbeth, of the Manhattan Macbeths, he was looking no more smooth and glamorous than the average drowned-rat hiker from the moor.

Willie had told her briefly how the guy had driven all the way from Glasgow with three crucial words: John, Peveril and Stanage.

'Mungo,' she said, her voice unexpectedly husky, 'I just don't know what I'm gonny do with you, and that's the truth.'

Macbeth smiled, a soft, stupid, wet-faced smile; she could tell he hadn't even noticed her hair.

'The one big thing,' he said, almost in a whisper, and it made no sense.

It fact it was all crazy, Moira thought. Horrifically crazy. He shouldn't be here. He didn't know what the hell he was into. He didn't have a chance.

And did any of them?

CHAPTER III

Eventually, Benjie had persuaded his mam to let him take The Chief to his bedroom, where the German Shepherd squeezed himself into the gap between the wardrobe and the wall, sat there with his ears down and panted a lot.

'Come on, lad,' Benjie whispered, sitting up in bed in his old ninja turtle pyjamas. But The Chief wouldn't move. He kept himself in this dark corner and there was pleading in his sad, brown eyes.

Above the noise of rain, Benjie could hear other village dogs howling in the distance. When he lay down and shut his eyes he realized that the way The Chief was panting meant he was *really* howling too, but The Chief was smart, the last thing he wanted was to have himself taken out to the shed.

When Benjie opened his eyes again, he saw light-beams flitting across the curtains, like car headlights.

Which would have been all right, only the back of the house overlooked the Moss and there were no cars on the Moss, except months ago when the lorries and JCBs had been out building up the road and they'd found the bogman.

Benjie scrambled to the end of his bed, leaned over and stuck his head through the gap in the curtains.

He gasped.

It were like Fireworks Night out there.

Lights all over the Moss, like smouldery bonfires. Lights shwooshing like rockets, through the rain, from one side to another, sometimes going across each other.

But no noise except for the howling dogs and the rain.

The lights lasted no more than ten seconds and then it was all gone and Benjie couldn't see anything apart from the water rolling down the glass.

But when he lay in bed, the light showed up in the space between his eyes and his closed eyelids. He saw the Moss lit up greenish now, all green and glowing, except for the Dragon Tree.

And that was *twice* as big now, its branches, all gnarled and knotted and black among whirling, spinning lights, two of them spiking up into the sky . . . arms like giant horns with groping claws on the end. And the whole thing was breathing, dragging up big, soggy lungfuls of peat, and soon it was going to burst and its arms would gather up the whole village.

Benjie felt a scream coming on and chewed the bedclothes instead, not wanting to be put out in the shed with The Chief and get gobbled up first.

*

Macbeth watched Chris and Chantal sink side by side into the sofa at the Rectory. They didn't seem like the same people. 'I really am tired,' Chris said. 'I'm shagged out.'

And then, clearly shocked at himself, he looked up at Cathy. 'I'm sorry. I don't know what I'm saying. Catherine, has something got inside me? Am I possessed?'

Cathy waved it away. 'Chris, you've got to tell me very quickly, no evasion. *What happened in there?*'

Chris tugged at his beard. 'I just don't know. First of all, it was fine, we felt . . . how we used to feel. Holy. Special. And then it all went wrong . . . *really* quickly. It went . . . dirty.'

'It was like baptism,' Chantal said, hugging herself with goosebumpy arms. 'Only in reverse. In our baptism . . . our *re*-baptism, we throw off some of our outer clothes – symbolically – and we're submerged in water. It could be a river, or we'll hire a public pool for an afternoon, and you come up cleansed and purified.'

'That's *it*,' Chris said, eyes full of agony. 'That's right. Only this was like being submerged and some of us threw off our Christian clothes and we came up not so much dirty . . . well, yes, dirty – but worse, really. Like it was *before*.'

'People smoking,' Chantal recalled. 'In church. But it didn't *feel* like church, it didn't feel like anywhere.'

'Yeah, and blaspheming in an everyday sort of throwaway fashion. And we drank . . . God forgive us, we drank the Holy Communion wine, like it was any old pop. It didn't matter. We were like the mass of godless people out there, we didn't need religion any more, we had no use for it. Catherine, I'm so confused. We'll burn in hell for this, I think we've already *started* to burn.'

'It's OK,' Cathy said soothingly. 'The fire's out, now.' She turned to Moira and Macbeth. 'It's obvious, isn't it? It was the final sterilization.'

'Well . . .' Moira said. 'You can't just drain the power of centuries out of stone, you can only take it out of people. So you let them absorb it through their mindless, passive rituals and then you snuff out the light, blow their shaky faith up in their faces and leave them empty and when they walk out, totally knackered like this guy here, they've drained out everything that was left in the church.'

'Forgive me,' Macbeth said, 'why'd they wanna do that?'

'Because the church is the sacred centre of the village,' Cathy said. 'It's got to be neutralized before you can . . .' She stopped for breath and couldn't go on.

'Replace it with something black and horrible,' Moira said.

'What . . . what can *we* do to help?' Chris asked, rather feebly.

Cathy rounded on him. 'You can keep your bums on that settee, call in all your friends and *don't move* until your coach comes for you. And then you can go away for ever.'

'Steady, Cathy.' Moira took her arm.

'Wants to know if he's possessed?' Cathy said with a sharp laugh. 'Well, of course he's possessed. Possessed of a very slow brain. Moira, look, there's a copper out there who wants to go up the Hall with Stan Burrows and a bunch of his mates and do some sorting out, as they put it.'

'So stop him,' Moira said.

'*You* try and stop him!'

'Look, they go up there mob-handed, God knows what could happen. It's pretty damned obvious – and we're looking at something planned months ago – that Stanage has shut down the church to deflect a lot of energy towards the second natural focus, the second-highest building in Bridelow. The brewery, right? And what's at the very top of the brewery building?'

'Th'owd malt-store,' Willie Wagstaff said impatiently. 'Disused. Moira, happen this is over me head, but why don't we go up there mob-handed and flush the buggers out?'

'Because you can't fight this thing with primitive violence. I swear to you, Willie, those guys go up there they'll wind up killing each other. It's like, how come you can put a bunch of ardent, Bible-punching born-again Christians in a *church* and they come drifting out an hour or so later with this amazing born-again *apathy*?'

'He's right, though, Moira,' Cathy said. 'We can't just stand around doing nothing. *Somebody* ought to go up there.'

'It's what I've been trying to *tell* you!' Willie cried, all eight fingers beating at his thighs. 'Somebody *has*. Mr *Dawber*'s up there. And Mr Dawber's been in a mind to do summat daft.'

'OK,' Moira said. 'Come on, Willie.'

'We'll go in my car,' Macbeth offered, moving to the door.

'Ah . . . not you, Mungo.'

'*What . . . !*' Macbeth counted three seconds of silence before he tore off his black slicker and slammed it to the Rectory lino with a noise like a gunshot. Willie jumped back. On the sofa Chris and Chantal gripped hands.

'Now listen up!' Macbeth snarled. 'Everybody just fucking *listen up*! I have *had* it. I have had it up to *here* with getting told to butt out. I am *sick to my gut* with being treated like some goddamn halfwit with a stupid name who had the misfortune to be born five generations too late to be part of any *viable heritage*. Either I'm in, or I start figuring a few things out for myself, and maybe I'll kick the wrong asses and maybe I won't, but that's your problem not mine.'

It all went quiet. Shit, Macbeth thought. Which reject script did that come out of? He picked up his slicker and put it on.

'OK,' said Moira carelessly. 'You drive, Mungo. Cathy, I don't know what to say, except *please* keep that cop off our backs for as long as you can. And maybe if you can get the Mothers together in one place, that might be best. Would everybody fit into Ma Wagstaff's parlour?'

Some of what happened next Macbeth did not follow. Several times he wished he'd never left Glasgow.

Once, he wished he'd never seen Moira Cairns.

Twice Ernie Dawber had said his throat was very dry and would it be possible to get a drink of water?

He was sprawled in a corner between the hallstand and the front door. There was broken glass all around him. He thought he'd sprained his ankle when he fell.

'When you ter-tell me.' Shaw Horridge was still standing, feet apart, amidst the wreckage of the mirrors. His mouth looked permanently twisted because of a cut which extended his lower lip. There were stripes of blood down both cheeks. Freckles of glass still glittered either side of his thin nose.

'What *can* I tell you?' Ernie croaked. 'He planted his seed in Bridelow and that seed turned out to be you. Was Ma going to have your mother turned away, same as they did with your father, and leave Arthur Horridge humiliated three days from the altar? 'Course she wasn't, she'd been in the same situation.'

'I cer-cer . . . I cer-cer-can't accept it, Mr Der-Der . . . Aaagh!' With both fists, Shaw began to beat his own head. Ernie felt his agony, the way he used to experience the lad's frustration all those years ago, when Shaw was the best reader in the class and couldn't prove it.

'They never told you, because not many outside the Mothers' Union knew about it. Me, I put two and two together after a bit, but I said nowt. It was none of my business. Ma kept an eye on you but she'd never go too close. She never wanted you to be *tempted* or to get too close to the shadow side. For your own good. Please, lad . . . a cup of water?'

'If I ter-turn my ber-back on you, you'll be . . . out.'

'I don't think I can even walk, lad.'

'How der-der-do I know that? Ker-ker-keep talking.'

Ernie swallowed. 'I . . . remember once, Arthur came to see me. Arthur knew, of course. Arthur was inclined to link your stammer directly to the circumstances of your conception. And he said, Ernie, he said, why doesn't she do something? Ma? Why doesn't she cure the poor lad's stutter? Arthur, I said, if you knew how much pain that causes Ma, her own grandson . . .'

'Ger-grandson!' Angry tears joined the blood on Shaw's cheeks. 'I used to stand outside wer-with the other ker-ker-kids, der-daring each other to look into the wer-windows. She'd cher-chase us all off. Wer-wer-witch. Owd witch!'

'She was frightened, Shaw. Frightened for you. Scared that one day she might have to banish you as well because of what might be in your blood. Didn't want you exposed to the shadow side. That's why after your . . . after Arthur died, she'd never come up to see your mother, even when Liz became agoraphobic and wouldn't come down to the village. She didn't want to go near *you*. She didn't want you ever to know who you were or to become drawn to the shadow side.'

Which, in the end, he thought, you were. You were a sitting duck.

Wanted to ask, What happened to your mother? What happened after she forced herself to come down to the village and scream for sanctuary outside Ma's door? While you were inside, presumably. For who else would it be? Who else could destroy Ma's defences so surely? Who else would Ma allow to push her downstairs?

'I didn't ker-kill her, you know,' Shaw said suddenly. 'She said she was der-der-dead already. Dead already!'

And at that moment, directly above Ernie's head, the door chimes played their daft little tune and there was a banging on the glass panels and, 'Mr Dawber! Ernie!'

Shaw jerked from the waist, as if the electric doorbell had been connected to his testicles. 'Ger-go away!'

Ernie grabbed a breath and raised his voice. 'It's Willie Wagstaff, Shaw. Let him in, eh?'

'Mr Dawber!'

'Come on, Shaw!' Ernie shouted. 'You know Willie!'

Across the hall, the front door shuddered as a boot went into it, flat, under the lock. Shaw leapt across the hall and threw himself against the back of the door as the foot went in again, and then he sprang back, lurched towards Ernie, face full of blood and glass, terror, confusion and fury. He turned, tore open a white-panelled door on the other side of the hall and flung himself into the passage beyond as the front door heaved and splintered open.

Willie was alone. His eyes flickered under his mousy fringe in the bright lights. 'Ernie.'

'Give us a hand, Willie. Done me ankle, I think.'

'Where's the lad?'

'Let him go, eh? He's got a lot to think about. We need to get to the brewery, if it's not too late.'

'Never mind that.' Willie got a hand under Ernie's armpit. 'Can you . . . that's fine. That's excellent, Mr Dawber. Hang on to me. The brewery . . . Moira's seeing to that.'

'That lass? By 'eck, Willie, you're . . .'

'She's not just "that lass", Mr Dawber, take my word. Anyroad, Mungo's with her, the Yank. He give me his car keys; we need to get you back. You're our last hope, Mr Dawber. Come on. I'll tell you.'

The body was up against a huge metal tub. There was the smell of beer, the smell of vomit and a smell Macbeth would soon recognize again as the smell of blood.

'I don't know him,' Moira said. 'I've never seen him before.'

Macbeth covered his mouth with his hand. This was it. The final proof he'd half-imagined he was never going to get, that this affair was real, life and death. Bad death.

'This is crazy, Moira.' He grabbed hold of the iron railing, for the coldness of it. Only it was slick with something and he jerked his hand away. 'I never saw a stiff before. Never saw a dead relative. Never went to a funeral with an open coffin.'

Moira had nothing to say to this. She turned her lamp on the man's face. His whole head was a weird shape, like it had been remoulded. Violently. There was blood over the face and down from the rim of the big tank. Macbeth felt his gut lurch. He leaned over the side of the huge beer vat and he threw up, shamed by the way it echoed around the scrubbed metal.

He turned back to Moira, wiped his mouth. She was kind enough to direct the beam of her lamp away from him. Real macho stuff, huh? Either I'm in this with the rest of you or I'll go solo, start kicking asses.

Or maybe I'll just throw up the shitburger I had near Carlisle.

'I'm sorry,' he said. 'That was unavoidable. Thing is, I *do* recognize him. His name is Frank. He was in the pub earlier. He was pretty smashed.'

'He certainly looks pretty smashed now,' Moira said. Sounding harder than he liked to hear. He was shocked.

'He fell?' Looking up the steps, all slimy with something that stank.

'You could convince yourself of anything, Macbeth. OK, then – after you.'

'Up there?'

'Well, we're no' going back now.'

Oh, shit. Please. Get me outa here.

'OK. You stay down here, then. Wait for me.'

'No! Jesus. But, like, I mean, what if they're waiting for us?'

'There's nobody here, Macbeth.'

'How'd you know that?'

'I was . . . listening. And watching. And . . . you know.'

No, he didn't fucking know. But he wasn't going to make an issue of it. He went slowly up the metal steps. She stayed at the bottom, lighting his way, until he reached a blank wooden door.

He hesitated, looked back down the stairs at where the beam bounced off the white walls and cast a soft light on her. She looked smaller than he remembered inside this bulky duffel coat, too big for her by a couple of sizes. And yet she seemed strangely younger, without most of her hair.

Well, shit, of *course* he'd seen that, soon as he'd walked in out of the rain. It was the most awful mutilation, like slashing the *Mona Lisa*, taking the legs off of the *Venus de Milo*. It was a goddamn offence against civilization.

But was it *self*-mutilation? Was it like a novice nun cuts off all her hair to give herself to Christ?

And this was why he'd never even mentioned it. This was why, Willie being in the car too, all he'd said to her by way of explanation for him being here was, 'The Duchess asked me to look out for you.'

To which she'd made no reply.

Moira's face creased sympathetically now in the white light.

'Look, Mungo . . . fact is, if the sight of this poor guy made you chuck your lunch, you're not gonny find it too pleasant in there. There's no shame in that. Willie's pretty squeamish, too, which is why he was glad to go off in search of the old schoolmaster guy. So . . . if you . . . what I'm saying is, this isn't your problem. You really don't have to put yourself through this.'

'And you do?'

'Yeah,' she said. 'I'm afraid I do. Me more than anybody.'

He just stared down at her.

'Goes back nearly twenty years. This is the consequences of getting involved with Matt Castle.'

'He's dead.'

'Yeah,' Moira said.

Macbeth said, 'People here keep seeing his ghost. That's what they say. You believe that?'

'Yeah,' Moira said.

'What am I gonna find behind that door?'

'You don't ever have to know, Mungo. That's what I'm trying to tell you.'

'Aw, shit,' Macbeth said. 'The hell with this.' He scraped hair out of his eyes, opened them wide and pushed open the door with his right foot.

CHAPTER IV

Willie's youngest sister was in her dressing gown, making tea. 'Sleep through this weather? Not a chance. Our Benjie's messing about up there, too, with that dog. I've told him, I'll have um both in t'shed, he doesn't settle down.'

'Where's Martin?'

'Working up Bolton again. Takes what he can. Bloody Gannons.'

'Right,' Willie said. 'Well, if you can get dressed, our Sal. You've been re-co-opted onto t'Mothers.'

'Get lost, Willie. I told Ma years ago, I said I'll take a back seat from now on, if you don't mind, it's not my sort of thing.'

Aye, well, no arguing with that. Certainly *wasn't* her sort of thing these days. Sal's kitchen was half the downstairs now, knocked through from the dining room and a posh conservatory on the back. Antique pine units, hi-tech cooker, extractor fan. All from when Horridges had made Martin sales manager, about a year before Gannons sacked him.

'Anyroad,' Sal said. 'Can't leave our Benjie. God knows what he'd get up to, little monkey.'

'Well, actually,' Willie said, 'I wouldn't mind getting the lad in as well. We're going to need a new Autumn Cross, a bit sharpish.'

'Be realistic. How can a child of his age go out collecting bits of twigs and stuff on a night like this?'

'Aye, I can!' Benjie shouted, bursting into the kitchen, already half-dressed, dragging on his wellies. 'I *can*, Uncle Willie, honest.'

'Get back to bed, you little monkey, if I've told you once tonight, I've . . .'

'Lay off, eh, Sal. We need everybody we can get.'

'Is this serious, Willie? I mean, *really*?'

Willie said nothing.

'What's in that briefcase?'

'This and that.'

'Uncle Willie,' said Benjie, 'T'Chief's been howling.'

'They're all howling tonight, Benj.'

'And t'dragon. T'dragon growed, Uncle Willie. T'dragon's *growed*.'

When Milly caught Cathy's eye over the heads of the assembled Mothers they exchanged a look which said, this is hopeless.

Altogether there were seven of them squeezed into Ma's parlour, standing room only – although at least a couple were not too good on their pins and needed chairs.

'Susan!' Milly cried. 'Where's Susan?'

'Staying in with the little lad,' Ethel, Susan's mum, told her. 'Frank's not back. Likely on a bender. She won't leave the little lad on his own on a night like this.'

'Wonderful!' Cathy moaned. 'Hang on, what about Dee from the chippy? Needs must, Ethel.'

'She's had a shock, what with Maurice, she won't even answer the door.'

'Well, get somebody to bloody break it down. And if Susan's got to bring the kid along, do it, though I'd rather not. That'll be nine. Willie! How's it going? Any luck?'

'We found it, I think.' Willie came in clutching Mr Dawber's old briefcase. 'Here, make a bit of space on t'table.'

'How is he?'

'He's resting. Had a bit of a do wi' Shaw Horridge.' Willie was spreading out sheets of foolscap paper. 'Thank God for Mr Dawber, I say. Anything to do with Bridelow he collects. Whipped it off Ma 'fore she could put it back of t'fire.'

'Looks complicated.'

'It's not as bad as it looks. They're all numbered, see, and they join up, so we've got a complete map of t'village wi' all the key boundary points marked. Ma did um all barefoot. But that were summer. What you want is one woman at each, and each to take a new stone. Alf's got um ready for consecration, like, end of his yard.'

'How big are they, these stones?'

'Size of a brick, maybe half a brick. Some of um *are* bricks, come to think of it. Ma used a wheelbarrow.'

'We'll never do it,' Milly said in despair. 'Are you proposing to send old Sarah out to the top of Church Field with half a brick?'

'She could do one of the closer ones,' said Cathy. 'If you or I take the Holy Well . . .'

'We still haven't got enough.' Milly lowered her voice. 'And what kind of commitment we'll get out of half this lot I *don't* know. Ma was right. We've been hopelessly complacent. We let things slide. We haven't got a chance.'

'There's always a chance,' Cathy said, and even Willie thought her voice was starting to sound a bit frail. She was overtired, lumpy bags under her eyes, thin hair in rat's tails.

'What?' said Milly, approaching hysteria – and Willie had never seen *that* before. 'Against a feller who's spent half a lifetime stoking up his evil? Against that hideous girl? Against all them practising satanists?'

'They're idiots,' Cathy said. 'Any idiot can be a satanist.'

'Aye,' said Milly, 'and any idiot can make it work if they've got nowt to lose.'

'All *right*.' Cathy turned to Willie. 'How's Alf getting on?'

'Moaning,' Willie said. 'Reckons cement won't hang together wi' all the rain. Stan Burrows and them've fixed up a bit of a shelter for him. I told him, I says, you can do it again proper sometime, Alf, just make sure it sticks up tonight. I called in at Sal's, too, and young Benjie'll be along wi' a pile of stuff for a new cross. Reckon you can fettle it?'

'Aye,' said Milly. 'I suppose I can.'

'Don't you start losing heart, lass. Hey, our Sal's on her way too, what about that?'

'Never!' said Cathy. 'Ceramic hob on the blink, is it?'

'I'm persuasive, me, when I put me mind to it.'

'That'll make it ten, then,' Cathy said. 'Still, not enough. But we're getting there. Please, Milly, *please* don't go negative on me now.'

Macbeth closed the door behind him, as if to prove he wasn't really a wimp and could handle this alone, and he didn't come out for a long time, maybe half a minute, and there was no sound from him either. And Moira panicked. *I was wrong. They're all there. They're waiting for us.*

'Moira,' he called out, more than a wee bit hoarse, just at the point when she was about to start screaming. 'I think I need some help.'

At the foot of the final stairway, the air was really sour, full of beer and vomit, blood and death. She took a breath of it, anyway. She was – face it – more scared than he was, and whenever she was really scared, she went brittle and hard, surface-cynical. A shell no thicker than a ladybird's.

She wanted a cigarette. She wanted a drink.

She wanted *out* of here.

'Hold your nose,' Macbeth advised, opening the door. He sounded calm. Too calm. He was going to pass out on her any second.

And of course she didn't hold her damn nose, did she, and the stench of corrupted flesh nearly drove her back down the steps.

'I covered that one over,' Macbeth said. 'Couldn't face it.'

A circle within a circle. Candles burned down to stubs, not much more than the flames left, and all the rearing shadows they were throwing.

'Watch where you're walking,' Macbeth said.

The attic light was brown and bleary with sweat, grease, blood. Several chairs inside the circle. Two of them occupied.

One was a muffled hump beneath old sacking. 'All I could find,' Macbeth said. 'I don't think you should uncover it. I don't think *anybody* should. Not ever.'

A yellow hand poked out of the sacking.

She stared at it, trying to imagine the yellow fingers stopping up the airholes on the Pennine Pipes.

'It's this one,' Macbeth said behind her. 'Moira? Please?'

Moira turned and took a step forward and her foot squelched in it.

Congealing blood. Bucketsful.

'You don't have to do anything like that,' Cathy said. 'It's not as if I'm asking you to bare your breasts or have sex with anyone under a full moon or swear eternal allegiance to the Goddess.'

'Pity,' said the blonde one, trying, and failing, to hold her cigarette steady.

'All you have to do,' Cathy said, 'is believe in it. Just for as long as you're taking part.'

'I don't, though, luv,' Lottie Castle said. 'And I can't start now.'

However, Cathy noticed, she couldn't stop herself looking over their shoulders towards what was probably the gas-mantle protruding from the side of the bar.

Cathy had heard all about the gas-mantle, from the policeman, Ashton, who was standing by the door at this moment. Observing but keeping out of it because – as he'd pointed out – there was no evidence of the breaking of laws, except for natural ones.

'Yes, you do,' Chrissie said. 'You've always believed in it. That's been half the problem.'

'And how the hell would you know that?'

'Oh, come *on*. The last couple of hours I've probably learned more about you than anybody in this village. And you more about me than I'd like to have spread around.'

547

'Yes,' said Lottie. 'I suppose so. And how do you come into this, luv? Always struck me as an intelligent sort of girl, university education. Oxford, isn't it?'

'That's right, Mrs Castle, Oxford.'

'No polite names tonight. It's Lottie.'

'And I'm Chrissie,' said the blonde.

'You know about your husband,' Cathy said. 'You know what they've done.'

'Cathy luv, he ceased to be my husband the night he needed somebody else to close his eyes for him. Well, a fair time before that, if truth were known. I've had half a lifetime of Matt Castle, and that's more than *anybody* should have to put up with, and I can say that now, because I can say *anything* tonight, believe me.'

As soon as Cathy had walked in she'd spotted the two glasses, smelt the booze.

'All right,' she said. 'Forget your husband. Let's talk about your son.'

Lottie's face hardened immediately into something like a clay mask.

'Dic? What *about* Dic?'

'Just I don't think he's dead,' Macbeth said.

'Oh, Jesus. Jesus.' Moira put down her lamp in the blood, the light tilted up at Dic's face.

But they couldn't kill him, could they? For the same reason they couldn't kill you. Surely.

'Willie was right, Mungo. We should've been up here, mob-handed. Thought I was being clever. Being stupid. *Stupid!*'

But sometimes you can do more harm to someone than killing them'd be, you know?

'Tights,' Macbeth snapped. 'You wearing tights under there?'

'Huh . . . ? No. What's . . . ? Oh, Jesus . . . *Dic . . . please don't be dead.*'

'Shit,' said Macbeth. 'Handkerchief?'

548

'I dunno what's in these pockets, it's no' my coat . . . yeah, is this a handkerchief?'

'How big is it? OK, tear it in half. Fold 'em up. Make two tight wads.' Macbeth was peeling off the thick adhesive tape binding Dic's arms to the chair-arms. Both arms were upturned, palms of the hands exposed. Veins exposed. There was a welling pool of rich, dark blood at each wrist and it was dripping to the floor each side of the chair. There was a widening pond of blood, congealed around its blackened banks. Late-autumnal flies from the roofspace crawled around, drunk on blood.

'OK, now you hold his arm above his head. You're gonna get a lot of blood on you.'

'I got more blood on me than I can handle,' Moira muttered. 'You sure you know what you're doing, Mungo?'

'I never did it for real before, but . . . Ah, you don't need to hear this shit, just hold his arms. Right. Gimme one of the pads. See, we got to hold the . . . this is a pressure pad, right? So you push it up against the wound with both thumbs. Like *hard*. Idea is, we stop the blood with the pad, then I wind this goddamn tape round just about as . . . *tight* . . . as I can make it.'

'Is he breathing?'

'How the fuck should I know? Now the other arm. Hold it *up*, over his head . . . And, shit, get the tape off his mouth. Chrissakes, Moira, didn't we *do* that?'

The tape across Dic's mouth stretched from ear to ear. Moira tore it away, and Dic mumbled, 'Do you . . . have to be so rough?'

Moira jumped away in shock. Macbeth yelled, 'Keep hold of that fucking arm, willya?'

'Aw, Christ. You're no' dead.'

'I'm no' dead,' said Dic feebly, and he giggled.

'Don't talk,' said Moira. 'You're gonny be OK. Mungo?'

'He's lost a lot of blood.'

'Don't I know it. I'm paddling in it.'

'He needs to go to a hospital. This is strictly amateur hour. Can't say how long it's gonna hold. Far's I can see, they cut

549

the vein. If they'd cut the artery this guy'd be long gone. They cut the vein, each wrist, taped his arms down. The blood goes on dripping, takes maybe a couple hours to drain the body. How long they had you like this, pal?'

'Not the faintest,' Dic said. 'I was on valium, I think. Intravenous. So I'd know what was happening but wouldn't care.'

'That's good. See, the dope slows down the metabolism and that goes for the blood flow too. This is weird stuff, Moira, this left me way behind a long time back.'

Moira said, 'Do you know why, Dic?'

Dic nodded at the hump under the sacks.

'Do me one favour,' Macbeth said. 'I saved your life, least you can do is let me keep that fucking thing under wraps.'

'That's Matt, isn't it, Dic?'

Dic nodded. He was lying back in his chair, both arms still flung over his head and black with dried and drying blood. Moira didn't recall ever seeing courage on this scale. Maybe the valium had helped, but it was more than that.

'Suppose you know,' Dic said, 'where they've gone.'

'We have to get you to a hospital.'

'When you're on valium and you're still terrified, you know it must be pretty awesome.'

'Looks pretty cruddy to me,' Macbeth said.

'We'll get you down the steps, OK? We'll get you out of here.'

'He's not sane, you know. I don't reckon he was all there to begin with, lived in his own fantasy world. Like Dad. And that guy Hall.' He closed his eyes. 'Bloody Cathy. The things you do for love, eh?'

'Mungo,' Moira said. 'How about you go downstairs to one of the offices, find a phone? Get us some transport for Dic.'

'You'll be OK?' Macbeth looked like he couldn't get out fast enough.

'Sure. Get hold of Cathy. You got the number?'

'Called it enough times from the phone-booth.' He hesitated in the doorway, Dic's blood on one cheek.

'Go,' Moira said.

550

When they were alone, she said, 'Dic, I need to ask you
. . . Matt . . .'

'I gave him blood,' Dic said. 'And you . . .' He nodded at
the thing in the other chair.

Moira sighed. Sooner or later she had to face this.

She hooked a finger under a corner of the sacking.

The dead couldn't harm you.

'You get used to him,' Dic said with a dried-up bitterness.
'You start to forget he ever looked any different.'

She pulled away the sacking. The smell was putrid. It was
the kind of smell that would never entirely leave you and some
nights would come back and hover over you like the flies that
were clustering around Matt's withered mouth, the lips already
falling from the teeth.

'I was afraid to look at him in his coffin,' Dic said. 'Mum
said there was no shame. No shame in that.'

'Dic,' Moira said. 'What's that in his lap?'

'The pipes.'

'That stuff wrapped *around* the pipes.'

'You know what it is.'

Moira reached out with distaste and snatched the bundle
from the lap of the corpse. Air erupted from the bag and the
pipes groaned like a living thing. Or a dying thing. She cried
out and dropped the pipes but held on to what had been around
the pipes, black hair drifting through her fingers in the
flickering candlelight. A glimmer of white.

'Which of them did it?' Her voice so calm she scared
herself. 'Which of them actually cut it off?'

Dic said, 'The woman, I'd guess. Therese. They wanted
him strong and . . . driven. You know?'

His eyes kept closing. Maybe he was about to pass out from
loss of blood. She didn't know what you did in these circumstances. Did you let him rest or did you try to keep him
conscious, keep him talking? He seemed to need to talk.

'I gave him blood,' he said. 'Blood feeds the spirit or
something like that. Blood's very powerful in magic. And
so . . .'

He winced, coughed, nodded at the hair.

'. . . so's desire.'

'And what,' Moira said, staring into Matt Castle's impenetrable, sightless eyes, stuffing the hair into a pocket of the duffel coat, 'did he get from the bog body?'

'Wrong question.' Dic's eyes closed and didn't open for several seconds. Moira was worried. Dic said, 'I think you should be asking . . . what it got from him.'

His eyes weren't focusing. 'Listen, I don't know whether they got what they were after. All kinds of noises were coming out of . . . that.'

Moira picked up the sacking, tossed it over Matt with a shudder.

'Hall was trying to talk to it. Had a few phrases in medieval Welsh. I don't think it made any sense. In the end he was screaming at it. Stanage was screaming at Therese. It didn't go how they hoped.'

'Does it ever.'

'I can't believe these people.'

'I can,' Moira said. 'What went wrong?'

'Couldn't find the comb was one thing. Stanage was furious.'

Moira bent over him. His eyes were slits. 'Dic, why couldn't they find the comb?'

'Because I'd . . . taken it. I think. Earlier on. I took it out of the bag. Knew they were saving it for the climax.'

'Where is it now?'

He tried to shake his head. 'I'm sorry,' Moira said. 'We'll get you out of here. Listen, if I leave you now . . . can you bear it? Mungo'll be back in a minute. Only I want to get away on my own. Dic, can you hear me?'

Dic's eyes were closed. He was half-lying in his chair, hands still thrown back behind his head. There seemed to be no more blood seeping under the tape.

Didn't they say that your blood stopped flowing when you died?

Dic's canvas-seated wooden armchair still stood in the pond of his blood, mostly congealed, like mud, like the surface of a peatbog.

'Dic?'

No reply. But he was still breathing, wasn't he? She touched his fingers; they felt cold, like marble.

'Dic, tell Mungo . . . tell him not to worry. Tell him . . . just tell him I've gone to meet the Man.'

CHAPTER V

There was a strange luminescence over the Moss, as though the rain itself was bringing down particles of light. She could see its humps and pools, and she knew there were people out there, could hear their voices, scattered by the rain. The Moss was swollen up like a massive pincushion and every heavy raindrop seemed to make a new dent.

She walked openly to the door of The Man I'th Moss and hammered on it, shouted 'Lottie!' a few times. All the lights were on, lights everywhere, in the bar, in all the rooms upstairs.

But nobody here.

OK.

She switched on her lamp and walked around the back to the yard where the stable block or barn place was, Matt's music room. Its door hung open, the hasp forced. They hadn't even bothered to disguise their visit when they came to borrow the Pennine Pipes.

Switching off her lamp, Moira went quietly in. She put on no lights. The air inside seemed to ripple with greens and browns, like sealight.

Mosslight.

The carpets on the wall tautened the air. Dead sound. No echoes.

She took off her coat, found the old settee, the one with its insides spraying out. Sat down, with the lamp at her feet, and thought peacefully of Matt and felt no hatred.

All gone.

Released.

*

It had taken her nearly ten minutes to get here. Ten minutes in which the rain had crashed down on her sparsely matted skull, and she'd yielded up her anger with a savagery even the night couldn't match.

Screamed a lot. Cursed him for what he'd done, all those years of lies and craving, abuse of Lottie, abuse of Dic, abuse of her from afar, divulging to the crazy Stanage the secret of the comb, letting Stanage set him up, set her up in Scotland.

Letting Stanage into his weaknesses. So that the long-haired girls appeared on cue. This Therese playing the part with an icy precision, drawing out of Matt the thin wire of desire by which they could anchor him.

I used to think she was . . . a substitute. Me own creation. Like, creating you out of her . . .

While he was no longer sure that this was not, in essence, Moira.

. . . I should've known. Should've known you wouldn't leave me to die alone. I'm drawing strength from the both of you. The bogman and you . . .

Had Stanage known that Matt was dying? Was Matt chosen *because* he was dying? So that his spirit, chained to Stanage and Therese, chained willingly to Bridelow by the old Celtic magic, could be controlled after his death?

So it could be used as a conduit.

To reach the Man, the spirit of the Moss, the guardian of the ancient Celtic community at the end of the causeway.

Moira walking quickly down from the brewery, finding her way quite easily this time back into the village. Avoiding the car racing with full headlights up the brewery road, probably in answer to Macbeth's summons. Avoiding any people she happened to see on the street – especially women.

This, God help me, is my task.

Go over it again. Get it right.

Here's what happened.

The villagers steal the Man to do with him what's been done so many times with bits of bodies found in the Moss: give him a good Christo-pagan burial at the next public funeral.

But this isn't just another bit of body. This is the complete perfectly preserved remains of the original sacrifice, laid down with due ceremony after undergoing the Triple Death.

This is powerful, this will reverberate.

And wise old Ma Wagstaff – realizing, presumably, just *how* powerful – mixes up her witch bottle with a view to protecting Matt's soul from any dark, peaty emanations.

Not realizing that it's the *Man in the Moss* who needs protection – against the tortured, corrupted, *manipulated* spirit of Matt Castle.

Got to get him back. Got to get him out of their control.

Got to lose all the hatred because that's *their* medium. Hatred. And lust. And obsession.

When Stan the bartender and Gary the cop came for Dic, Macbeth was pacing the room, trampling in the blood. Where is she, where the fuck *is* she? Almost ready to shake the poor guy, get some sense out of him.

'God almighty!' he heard from the bottom of the steps. 'It's Young Frank!'

'Don't touch him. You can't help him now.'

'He were three-parts drunk. Fighting drunk. Drunk most nights since he lost his job.'

'Maybe he fell, maybe he didn't. Either way, I'm having this place sealed off, so watch where you're treading, Stan.'

'Hey, come on willya,' Macbeth shouted. 'There's a guy up here *isn't* dead. Yet.'

'We're coming,' Gary the cop said. 'And I don't like that smell one bit.'

Thirty seconds later, he's pulling the sacking from the stiff – 'Fucking *Nora*!' – while Macbeth's demanding, 'Moira. You seen *Moira*? Lady with very, *very* short hair . . . Chrissakes!' And Stan's staring at all the blood, looking sick, and Dic's shifting very feebly in his chair.

'Right!' said Gary the cop. 'Who is *this*?'

Macbeth slumped against the wall. 'It's Matt Castle.'

'Thank you,' said Gary. 'At least we know *he's* not been murdered. Let's get an ambulance to this lad. And a statement later, I think.'

At which Dic came round sufficiently to start yelling, hoarsely, '*No!* I'm not going to hospital! I won't!'

'Hey, hey . . . All right, we'll not take you to hospital, but you can't stop here.'

'Take me to Cath,' Dic said, and Ashton looked at Macbeth. Macbeth nodded, and Stan got his arm behind Dic and helped him to his feet.

'Keep his arms over his head,' Macbeth said, 'else he's gonna start bleeding again.'

In back of Stan's ancient station wagon, Macbeth said quietly to Dic, 'Moira. Where's Moira go? Come on, kid, talk to me, I saved your goddamn life.'

'Said to tell you,' Dic mumbled, 'that . . . she'd gone to meet the Man.'

'Holy . . . *shit!*' Macbeth slammed his fist into the back of the seat.

'Yeah,' Dic said. 'I didn't like the sound of that either, but there wasn't much I could do.'

Drifting on an airbed of memories.

Hey, Matt, you remember the night the van broke down on the M1 and we put on a thank-you gig for the AA guys at three in the morning at the Newport Pagnell Services?

Blurry light coming off the Moss through the rain. They're out there, OK. And it's cold and it's wet and the Moss is filthy and swollen. No place to be, Matt. No place to commit yourself for all eternity.

Or until you might be summoned by those to whom you mortgaged your soul.

Hey, remember when you left the pipes in the hotel room in Penzance and Willie ran all the way back from the hall and I went on stage alone? And I only knew four solo numbers, and I'm into an encore of the first one before Willie dashes in with the pipes?

The slimy mosslight from the high windows awakening the

barn, finding the womanly curves of the old Martin guitar. This was your place, Matt, this was where you put it all together, this was your refuge.

. . . So I wanted . . . I wanted in. To be part of that. To go in the Moss too . . .

But you don't now. Do you?

It's warm in here. (Aw, hell, it's freezing; you just better wish it warm, hen, *wish* it warm until you can feel it.)

She picked up the lamp from the floor at her feet and took it across to a wooden table. She switched it on, directing its beam to the centre of the settee, picked up Matt's Martin guitar, went back and sat in the spot, with the light on her face.

She strummed the guitar. The strings were old and dull and it was long out of tune. One of the machine-heads had lost its knob, so she just tuned the other strings to that one.

It would do.

She sat back, closed her eyes against the lamp's beam, although the battery was running out and the light was yellowing. She imagined the Moss, black and cold and stagnant.

Now you're out there, you know the terrors the Moss holds, the deep, deep, age-old fear.

Death doesn't have to be like that, Matt.

Come on. Come on back. Come to the warm.

She pictured Matt as he'd been once. Stocky, muscular, vibrant with enthusiasm.

Come . . .

. . . come to . . .

to me.

And in a low and smoky voice, she began to sing to him.

The Mothers' Union was congregated in the high Norman nave of St Bride's Church.

Above the Mothers hung a ragged cross made of branches cut by Benjie from a rampant sycamore hedge at the bottom of the Rectory garden. The branches, still dripping, were bound with chicken wire and tangled up with hawthorn.

Cathy walked in, out of the rain, under the reassuringly gross, widened flange of the *Sheelagh na gig*, cement particles among the coils of her hair. Alf Beckett had also brought the statues out of the shed, and several long, coloured candles were lit.

He was up in the lamp room now, fixing up a high-powered floodlight supplied by Stan Burrows, who'd been in charge of the electrics for the Bridelow Wakes party which was usually held on the Church Field on May Day Eve. (Except for this year, when there was still too much media attention, due to the bogman.)

'*Twelve*,' Cathy said after a quick head-count. 'We're waiting for Moira.'

'She doesn't have to be here,' Milly said. 'If she's with us, she's with us.' Cathy was glad to see Milly had at last taken charge.

The assembly was not inspiring, including, as it did, women like Dee Winstanley, who'd declined to follow her mother into the Union on the grounds that they didn't get on, and two lesbians who ran a smallholding up by the moor and had never been allowed to become active members because their motives were suspect.

A pile of wet stones glistened on an old wooden funeral bier under the pulpit.

'All right!' Milly clapped her hands. 'Let's make a start, shall we? I want to begin by calling down a blessing on this church. If you'd all form a rough circle from where we've pushed the pews back.'

Milly wore a long, dark blue dress decorated by a single brooch in the shape of two intercurled holly leaves.

She closed her eyes.

'Our Father . . .' she began.

'And Our Mother . . .'

> . . . *sees herself in colours and*
> *she weighs her powers in her hand* . . .

'The Comb Song'. The song of night and invocation. In the singing of it, things happen.

And the comb, safe in its pocket in the guitar case, protects you from evil.

But this is not your guitar. This is Matt's guitar. Singing the song of invocation to the dead strings of Matt's guitar in Matt's music room, and *no* protection.

It was 1.30 in the morning.

The women filed silently out of the church, most of them muffled in dark coats, under scarves and hoods so Macbeth couldn't tell who was who.

There was a bulky one he figured was Milly. Two who were slightly built were walking together.

'Cathy?' he whispered. 'Cathy?'

Neither of the women replied.

Each clutched a stone.

They walked out of the church porch under a weird carving of a grotesque, deformed creature, all mouth and pussy. At this point they divided, some proceeding down the path toward the main gate, two moving up toward the graves, the others following a narrower path down into a field which disappeared into the peatbog.

'Moira? *Moira!*'

No answer. The rain continued.

'. . . the fuck am I gonna do?'

'Nowt,' said Willie Wagstaff. 'Nowt we can do. It's in the lap of the gods.'

Ernie Dawber was with him, leaning on a walking stick. They moved under the porch with Macbeth, gazing out toward the Moss. Nobody spoke for a while, then he said, 'Hallowe'en's over now, right?'

'Samhain, lad,' said Ernie. 'Let's not cheapen it. In Bridelow we used to celebrate Samhain on November first, so you could say our day is just beginning.'

'Or not,' said Willie. 'As the case may be.'

'Or not,' Ernie agreed.

Macbeth said, 'How deep is the, uh, Moss?'

'Normally,' Ernie said, 'no more than a few feet in most places. Tonight? I wouldn't like to guess. I don't think we've ever had rain this hard, so consistently, for so long, have we, Willie?'

'Could it flood?'

'Soaks it up,' said Ernie. 'Like a sponge. It's rivers that flood, not bogs.'

'There's a river running through it, isn't there?'

'Not much of one.'

'What are those women doing?'

'We never ask, lad,' said Ernie.

'Ever thought of becoming a local tour guide?'

Ernie shrugged.

Macbeth said, 'What are those lights?'

'I can't see any lights, lad.'

'It's gone. It lasted no time at all. It was, like, a white ball of light. It seemed to come out the bog. Then it vanished.'

'Didn't see it. Did you, Willie?'

'OK,' Macbeth said. He was getting a little pissed with this old man. 'Tonight, Mr Dawber, it's my belief you seriously offered your life for this place. I'm not gonna say that's extreme, I don't have enough of a picture to make judgements. What I would like to know is . . . that, uh, compulsion you had . . . has that . . . passed?'

Seemed at first like Ernie Dawber was going to ignore the question and Macbeth could hardly have blamed him for that. Willie Wagstaff didn't look at the old man. Rain apart, there was no sound; Willie was not performing his customary drum solo.

Then Ernie Dawber took off his hat.

'It seems silly to me now,' he said in his slow, precise way. 'Worse, it seems cowardly. I went to see the doctor t'other night. Been feeling a bit . . . unsteady for some weeks. They'd done a bit of a scan. Found what was described as an inoperable cyst.' Ernie tapped his forehead. 'In here.'

Willie's chin jerked up. 'Eh?'

'Could pop off anytime, apparently.'

'Aw, hell,' Macbeth said. 'Forget I spoke.'

'No, no, lad, it was a valid question. I've been writing a new history of Bridelow, one that'll never be published. Chances are I'll not even finish the bugger anyroad but it's about all those things I didn't dare put into the proper book. Maybe it's the *first* proper book, who can say?'

'I'd like to read that,' Macbeth said. 'One day.'

'Don't count on it, lad. Anyroad, I thought, well . . . it's given you a good life, this little place. You and a lot of other folk. And now it's in trouble. Is there *nowt* you can do? And when you're on borrowed time, lads, it's surprising how you focus in directions nobody in their right minds'd *ever* contemplate.'

He chuckled. 'Or maybe it's not our *right* minds that we're in most of the time. Maybe, just for a short space of time, I *entered* my right mind. Now there's a cosmic sort of conundrum for you . . . Mungo.'

'Thanks,' Macbeth said. He put out his hand; Ernie took it, they shook. 'Now, about those lights . . .'

'Aye, lad. I saw the lights. And that's another conundrum. The Moss is no man's land. No man has cultivated it. No man has walked across it in true safety. What we see in and on and around the Moss doesn't answer to our rules. I've not answered your other question yet, though, have I?'

Macbeth kept quiet. There was another ball of white light. It came and it went. In the semi-second it was there Macbeth saw a huge, awesome tree shape with branches that seemed to be reaching out for him. Involuntarily he shrank back into the porch.

'Is it past?' Ernie considered the question. 'No. If I thought it'd do any good, I'd be out there now offering my throat to the knife.'

He turned back toward the Moss. There was another lightball. Coming faster now.

'Quite frankly, lad,' said Ernie conversationally, 'I think it's too late.'

And in the chamber of the dead
forgotten voices fill your head . . .

It said, hoarsely, *Going to show me?*

Moira tried to stay calm but couldn't sing any more. She was desperately cold.

This famous comb.

This time she had no comb to show him.

But you never leave yourself open like that. You never confess weakness to them.

'What will you give me if I show you the comb?'

Six pennorth o' chips.

Laughter rippling from the corners of the room. The lamplight was very weak now in her face.

Behind the light, a shadow.

CHAPTER VI

They had told Chrissie to look out for a seat at the top of the church field. It wasn't hard. The church field was the piece of uncultivated spare land continuing down from the last of the graves to a kind of plateau above the Moss. Chrissie's torch found the seat on the very edge of the plateau.

What she hadn't expected was to find someone sitting on it.

Normally, this time of night, she'd have been scared to death of getting mugged. Somehow, holding this daft stone, that didn't seem a possibility.

She found herself sitting next to him on the wooden bench in the pouring rain. Someone had lent her a long, dark blue cagoule and she knew very little of her face would be visible.

It was like a dream. 'Hello, Roger,' she said.

He turned his head. His hair was flat and shiny, like tin. His beard dripped into the neck of his blackened Barbour.

He peered at her. He didn't seem to recognize her nose. 'Is it Chrissie?'

'It is indeed. Not a very nice night, Roger. One way and another.'

He was silent a long time. Then he said, 'I spoke to him.'

'Him?'

'*Him.*'

'That must have been nice for you both.'

'So it was worth it,' Roger said. 'In the end.'

'Was it? Was it really?'

'Oh, yes. I mean, it's knowledge, isn't it? Nothing is more valuable than knowledge.'

'What about love?' said Chrissie.

'I don't understand,' Roger said.

'No. I don't suppose you do. So what did he have to say to you?'

'Who?'

'*Him.*'

'Oh.' Roger stood up, drenched and shiny, and rubbed his knees as if they were stiff. 'Do you know, I can't really remember. I expect it'll come back to me.'

He didn't look at her and began, seeming oblivious to the rain, to stroll away along the path which led back from the plateau's edge and wound down towards the Moss.

Chrissie waited until he'd gone from sight and then gently placed her stone beneath the seat and stood very quietly and said the words they'd told her to say.

A curious thing.

Soon as Ernie Dawber admitted he too could see the balls of light, then they became clearer.

'It's a bit like ball-lightning,' Ernie said. 'There's been quite a lot of research, although the scientific establishment doesn't formally acknowledge it.'

Talking in his schoolmaster's voice, Macbeth thought, because it puts him on top of a situation he doesn't understand any more than the rest of us.

'They do seem to be a manifestation of energy anomalies within the earth's magnetic field. Often occur, I'm told, on fault-lines.'

'What's that mean?'

'And there's also a theory that they can interact with human consciousness. So that when we perceive them we actually bring them into existence, if that isn't back-to-front logic. What do you say, Willie?'

'I'm more worried about that tree-thing, Mr Dawber.

Young Benjie calls it a dragon. Bog oak, I thought it were. Come up out of t'Moss, all of a sudden like. Got a wicked kind of . . .'

Macbeth said, 'There are people out there, around the tree.'

'Daft buggers.' Ernie squinted through the rain.

Macbeth was watching a haze of light rising from the tree, as if someone had set fire to it. But the flames, instead of eating the wood, had risen through it, like one of those phoney log-effect gasfires.

The light had risen above the tree and its boughs looked to be clawing at it, as though to prevent it escaping, and the Moss itself seemed to rise in protest. Macbeth felt a thickening tension in his gut.

Mouth dry, he watched the haze of light spread out like a curtain and then hover over the Moss, maybe six or ten feet from its surface.

'This is . . . unearthly.'

The light was drifting towards the edge of the Moss, towards the hulk of a building near the peat's edge.

'All things are natural,' Ernie Dawber said with a tight-jawed determination. 'If some are . . . beyond our understanding.'

'What's that place?' Thought he was hearing distant screams.

'Back of the pub,' Willie said. 'That's th'owd barn back of the pub, where we used to rehearse wi' Matt.'

'The light's over it. The light's hanging over the roof.'

Ernie Dawber said, 'I don't think I can see it any more.'

Moira Cairns put down the guitar and turned towards the door.

Two of them.

The mosslight on the two tombstone speaker cabinets either side of the door.

Both of them standing in the entrance with the cabinets either side of them.

John Peveril Stanage and the girl, Therese.

'So kill me,' Moira said simply.

'You know we can't,' Therese said. 'Not until you give him back.'

Moira reached to the table and turned the lamp on to them. Not much energy left in it now but enough to show her neither of these people was wet. Had they been inside the inn all the time? Had they been expecting her? Or was this merely the nearest vantage point for the Moss?

'Who are those people out on the Moss, then?' Moira asked. 'With the devil tree.'

'Do you know, m'dear,' he said, 'I can't actually recall any of their names.'

She remembered him so well now. The dapper figure, the white hair rushing back from his grey-freckled forehead like breakers on an outgoing tide. The cherub's lips. A man as white as the bones tumbling from the walls.

'I can't believe,' she said, 'all the trouble you've gone to. Getting to know Matt inside out, all his little compulsions. What are we looking at here? Years?'

'We don't have time for a discussion,' Stanage said. 'We want you to release him. You can't hold him for much longer, you simply don't have the energy.'

Moira said, 'Where's the Man? Made a big mistake, there, you know, John. You stole him away, you took responsibility for him. You took responsibility for the vacuum. The Moss'll no' wear that. Was an old guy in the village tonight, he'd figured out the way to square things with the Moss was another sacrifice. Maybe that was right.'

'It was *absolutely* right, m'dear,' Stanage said with a sudden smile. 'Saw to that on the *very stroke*, I believe, of midnight. When the Beacon of the Moss was extinguished, so was someone's life. A young, fit, active life . . . a *jolly good* replacement for the Man, if I say so myself.'

'Who?' Moira felt her face-muscles tightening, also her stomach.

'Why . . . just like the original sacrifice . . . a priest. The Triple Death – a blow, a slash – and a fall. And then gathered up and offered to the spirit of the Moss – *our* spirit. All square, m'dear. All square.'

'The Reverend Joel Beard? You killed the Reverend Joel Beard?'

'And consigned him to the Moss. Well, *hell*, sweetheart, don't sound so appalled. No friend of yours, was he? He struck you, word has it.'

'I suspect he mistook me for your friend,' Moira said. She let her gaze settle on Therese. Worryingly young. Black hair, perhaps dyed, sullen mouth. And the cloak. *Her* cloak.

'This is the wee slag, then, is it, John? Doesny look a lot like me. Did she wear a wig before she got hold of the real thing?'

'She's angry *enough*, Moira,' Stanage said less cordially. 'Don't make it worse.'

'*She's* angry? With *me*? Aw, Jesus, the poor wee thing, ma heart goes out. She's no' satisfied with ma hair now? Would she like to cut off ma leg? Would that make her happy, you think, John?'

Therese hissed and uncoiled like a snake and took a step towards Moira. Stanage laid a cautionary hand on her arm. Emerging from his dark sleeve the hand looked as white as an evening glove.

'This is futile,' Stanage said abruptly. 'Leave us, Tess. Would you mind awfully?'

'I can take her,' Therese spat. 'She's old. Her sexuality's waning. She can't hold him. I can take him from her. Watch me.'

'Tess, *darling*, no one is questioning your lubricious charms, but I suspect this is not about sex. Leave us.' Steel thread in his voice. 'Please?'

Therese gathered up her cloak and left without another word. Stanage closed the door and barred it. Moira instinctively moved into a corner of the ruptured settee, clutching the electric lamp to her breast.

'Right. Bitch.' Obviously a man who could shed his charm like an overcoat that'd become too heavy. She became aware of a scar about an inch long under his right eye, a souvenir from Scotland.

And he was aware she was looking at it.

The barn seemed to shift on its foundations, and there was

a crunch and a series of flat bangs. She didn't let her eyes leave him; she knew what it was: books falling over as a shelf collapsed. The shelves were all makeshift, held up by bricks.

Neither of them had moved.

'Don't make *me* angry,' Stanage said.

'We seem to be a little short of bones in here,' Moira said. 'That affect your performance, does it? Books just don't respond so effectively. Maybe you just don't have that same affinity. I borrowed one of yours from ma wee nephew one time. Thought it was really crap, John. Lacked authenticity, you know?'

John Peveril Stanage was tightening up inside, she could tell that, could feel the contractions in the air. Mammy, help me. Mammy, wherever you are, I'm in really heavy shit here, you know?

'You want me to sing to you, John? Would that help your concentration?'

She began to sing, very softly.

> . . . *for the night is growing colder*
> *and you feel it at your shoulder* . . .

She could feel Matt Castle at her shoulder, a wedge of cold energy.

And more.

'*Shut up*,' Stanage said.

Could smell the peat in him now.

Pulling the blue plastic lamp between her breasts until it hurt. Feeling the shadow behind her, huge and dense and pungent with black peat. *Don't turn around. Don't look at him.*

But John Peveril Stanage was looking. Stanage was transfixed.

All at once there was complete quiet.

'The rain,' Macbeth said. 'The rain stopped.'

Damn futile observation; everybody here could tell the rain had stopped.

He found he was in the middle of a crowd under the smiling snatch people called Our Sheila; been so busy watching the weird lights on the Moss he hadn't noticed the Mothers returning. Without their stones.

One of them standing next to him, shaking out her hair. 'Where's Moira?' It was Milly.

'She's not with you?' Cold panic grabbed his gut. 'You're telling me you haven't *seen* her?'

'We couldn't wait for her. We had thirteen stones to put down. Cathy's had to take two.' Milly glanced around. 'Cathy not back yet?'

'Listen . . .' Macbeth grabbed her shoulders. 'Moira told Dic she'd gone to . . . meet the Man. I figured that meant she was part of your operation.'

Milly shook her head. 'I'd be *terrified* to meet the Man. I don't know, Mungo. I really don't know what she meant. I'm sorry.'

'You all right?' Willie demanded.

'Tired. Exhausted. We've done all we can. Willie. That's the most I can say. I doubt it'll be enough.'

'Oh.' Mr Dawber, looking out across the Moss. 'Oh, good God.'

In the centre of rainless stillness, there came a noise overhead like deep, bass thunder. Like the exploding of the night. Like the splitting of the sky.

And they all saw it.

The reason they all saw it was that Bridelow Moss was suddenly lit up like a football ground.

The Beacon of the Moss was back, not blue this time but ice-white and a thousand times more powerful.

'It's Alf's arc light,' some woman explained. 'Knew he'd have it fixed before long. What was that b . . . ? Oh, Mother. Oh, Mother, help us! What's *that*?'

At first, Macbeth was simply not able to believe it. There was no precedent. It was outside the sphere of his knowledge.

First thing he saw, snagged in the floodlight, was the malformed tree with branches like horns. The horns of a stag-beetle, he thought now. Because an insect was what the tree resembled.

Or a bunch of brittle twigs.

Insignificant compared with what was growing out of the Moss, beyond, behind and far, far above it.

It was happening on the edge of the light, at what was surely the highest point of the Moss. Macbeth thought of a mushroom cloud. He thought of Hiroshima. He thought of Nagasaki. He thought in images on cracked film in black and white.

He heard shrill screams from the Moss and he thought, *Shit, it's the end of the goddamn world.*

Mushroom was wrong. More like a dense bunch of flowers. Or a cauliflower. A gigantic, obscene black cauliflower burgeoning monstrously from the bog.

The silent air was dank with a smell like the grave.

And, up close, the sour smell of primitive, bowel-melting fear.

'What is it?' Milly screeched. 'What is it, Mr Dawber?'

'It can't be . . .'

'What? *What?*'

People clutching at one another.

Ernie Dawber said hollowly, 'It's burst.'

Macbeth just stood there watching the liquid vegetable form in a kind of slow motion.

'The bog's burst,' Ernie Dawber cried out, aghast. 'It's bloody *burst*! Everybody . . . into the church! *Fast!*'

'Where's Cathy?' Milly shrieked above the tumult of spreading panic. 'She went down to take the last stone.'

'Where? Where to?'

'To the pub. The back wall. Under the old foundation stone. It's the last one.'

As the air started to thicken, Macbeth began to run, down through the graveyard towards the street, and by the time his feet hit the cobbles, a wall of cold, black, liquid peat was thundering into the village like volcanic lava.

'What have you *done*?'

'I obviously have an affinity . . .' John Peveril Stanage grinned, '. . . with the Moss.'

'You are a fucking insane man.'

'What is sanity?' Stanage said, as the high windows blew out and the whole roof of the barn was smashed down by the blackest of nights.

From *Dawber's Book of Bridelow*:

THE BOG BURST

THE SCALE AND SEVERITY of the Bridelow Bog Burst has caused widespread shock and disbelief, although it was not without precedent.

Such phenomena have occurred infrequently within recorded history, usually after a period of inordinately heavy rainfall when the surface layer of vegetation becomes too weak to retain the liquefied mass of peat beneath.

Several minor bog-slides have been reported in recent decades. After a midsummer thunderstorm in 1963, a peat-slide affected a large area of Meldon Hill bog in the Northern Pennines, leaving two scars in the blanket peat about 230 metres long and 36 metres wide.

Many centuries earlier but closer to the site of our own disaster was the eruption of Chat Moss, near Manchester, which Leland, an historian in the reign of Henry VIII, records as having '*brast up and destroied much grounds and much fresche water fische therabowt and so carried stinking water into the Mersey and carried the roulling mosse to the shores of Wales, part to the Isle of Man and sum into Ireland.*'

One cannot but suspect a certain exaggeration in this account. But those of us who experienced the horror of that night, those who lost friends or loved ones or only their homes will carry with them to their own graves the smell, the texture and, for some, the very taste of the black and ancient vegetable matter we call peat.

From *Dawber's* Secret *Book of Bridelow* (unpublished):

Celtic comb
(Irish?)
scots?   E.D.

A TALL ORDER, owd lad.

To try and unearth the truth from the Black. To make sense out of what happened. To consider whether my beloved Bridelow has a future. And, if so, what kind.

I thought at first to put it off until after the official Government inquiry, from which there'll obviously be a report for public scrutiny. However, that's not likely to emerge for months, and when it does it's bound to be a dry Civil Service document full of scientific guff and a list of safety recommendations for communities which happen to be situated on the edge of large, unstable peatbogs.

'Ernie,' you said, 'you're the only man who can put all this into any sort of human and historical perspective. You must get it down while it's fresh. Before it becomes part of Bridelow Mythology.'

What you really meant was, While you're still with us, Ernie.

'And who'll read it, owd lad?'

'Let's hope,' you said sadly, 'that nobody outside of Bridelow will ever have to.'

So I'm writing this in your study at the Rectory while you're up at the church, conducting your first evensong since the Burst. Thanks to your charity, I've been sleeping (whenever the Lord permits it) in the little spare room at the top of the house.

Emergency accommodation. My own house, exposed up by the school, being one of the first destroyed.

Seemed, when it was happening, like Armageddon: most of what we knew and loved engulfed by a dreadful destructive force . . . perhaps the merciless anger of the Lord, which we had brought upon ourselves by clinging to our primitive Christian paganism while all those around us (them Across the Moss) had long since been converted and embraced the Light.

Embraced the light? Don't make me laugh. There's more black out there than you'll find in Bridelow even now, under its dark blanket of peat.

Peat preserves.

The Moss preserved the ancient dead and two millennia of fear, violence, sickness and dread. And other things of which we do not speak, of which we *cannot* speak. Of which Matt Castle, all those years ago, could not speak, only let it pour away, out of the pipes, as he wandered in his agony upon the Moss.

It has absorbed all our overflowing emotions, this Moss, like a gigantic psychic cesspit. It has preserved and it has neutralized. An archaic chemical cathartic.

Ignore me, Hans, I'm getting too deep. Or too whimsy, as Ma Wagstaff would sometimes rebuke me, poor owd lass.

Avoiding getting to the simple physical horror of it.

Thousands of tons of the filthy stuff. Liquefied peat. Stink? I don't think I'll ever get rid of it from the back of my throat. And certainly not from the back of my thoughts. Not as long as I breathe.

Cowering in the choir stalls, we could hear it descending all around the church, still hearing the echo of that cataclysmic thunderclap in aftershocks of rumbling and roaring, and we thought the church would implode, the walls collapse in upon us with a shattering shower of stained glass.

But the church held. The makeshift Autumn Cross swayed and rustled, the lights went out and came on again, bar the one above the door, but the church held.

More than my house did. Reason it went: it was on the wrong side of the street. The first explosion, the actual burst, sent the fountaining filth hundreds of feet into the air . . . why, bits of it were found on the moor, five or six miles away.

But when it settled into a mere tidal wave – a bit, they say, like the tip slide which killed all those poor kids in South Wales – it was the buildings on the west side of the street that took it: the Post Office, the chip shop, Bibby's General Stores (poor old Gus Bibby couldn't have known a thing; his flat over the shop was filled up in seconds with liquid peat as dark and evil-looking as the comfrey oil in one of Ma Wagstaff's jars).

Naturally, The Man I'th Moss, the most westerly building in the village, on the very edge of the bog, is now under a great morass of muck. Selling it won't be a problem for Lottie Castle now; just a question of collecting the insurance, more than enough for a semi in Wilmslow.

At least thirty people died in the village that night; how many were simply victims of the Bog Burst may never be established. Which is, you will agree, just as well.

Quite a few are believed to have perished instantly out on the Moss, although, again, an exact number will probably never be known. Perhaps, over hundreds of years, the bodies will be disinterred, perfectly preserved no doubt, like our Man. Museum pieces – although perhaps not, because the Burst will be part of *recorded* history, so people will understand.

Or will they? Do any of us, even now, know precisely what happened, or why?

Except for Dr Roger Hall, who was seen by his assistant, Mrs White, to be heading for the Moss a short time before

THE MAN IN THE MOSS

the Burst, most of those who died out there, in conditions which recall what I've read of the black horrors of the Somme, will remain unidentified. Many were likely to have been men and women long estranged from their families or disowned by their relatives because of the unacceptable practices in which they indulged themselves.

I know very little about so-called 'satanism', whether this is simply a convenient name we have given to those who seek personal power over others through supposedly supernatural means. Whether, as some say, they sacrificed newborn babies out on the moor in order to 'reconsecrate' the stone circle, I certainly don't know *that*. I do not *want* to know.

All I do know is that extremism of any kind has never taken root in Bridelow, where a practical paganism and a humble Christianity have comfortably linked hands for so long. Many of the dead, sadly, were members of the fundamentalist Christian group called, if I have this right, The Church of the Angels of the New Advent. A large number of them, including their leaders, Mr and Mrs Christopher Montcrieff, heard the mighty thunder-roar and – believing it to be the dawning of the Day of Judgment, as forecast in the Book of Revelations – rushed out of the Rectory into the street with arms and (I would like to think) hearts upraised.

And, in seconds, were buried alive.

Not that many would have remained alive for long under that glutinous mess, most being crushed or drowned or suffocated very rapidly, mouths and noses and lungs clogged for ever. Some of those who did survive had been trapped in pockets of air under beams or walls or other protective bullwarks – although just as many were killed by masonry which was crumbling like crisp toast under the weight of hundreds of tons of peat.

The first death, largely overshadowed by what was to come, remains officially unexplained.

The body in the BMW motor car did indeed prove to be that of my old friend Eliza Horridge. There will be an inquest, and it will probably record an Open Verdict, for Liz appears to have died not of injuries sustained in a car accident and the subsequent fire but some hours earlier and of hypothermia, due to exposure.

There is no question that Liz was suffering from an agoraphobia exacerbated by the fear that her presence was no longer welcome in Bridelow following the sale of the brewery to Gannons (I feel, therefore, that none of us who knew her is exempt from blame) and that, fearing the imminent reappearance of her old lover, John Lucas (whom I shall henceforth, to keep him at a distance, refer to by his adopted *nom-de-plume* of John Peveril Stanage) courageously overcame her illness to seek the aid of her one-time protector, Iris Wagstaff.

And when Ma – who then had herself but a short time left to live – failed to answer her door, Liz, feeling she dare not return home, became confused and wandered out on to the moor. I cannot bring myself to contemplate those cold, wet hours of mental agony and desperation before she succumbed to fatigue and lay down to the sad sleep from which she would never awaken.

I can only assume that her body was discovered on the moor by the sick, satanic brethren recruited by Stanage and his temptress and conveniently employed, most of them, by Gannons. And then (remember, we are not dealing here with wholly rational people) someone decided to put Liz's body into the car, from which they had removed Miss Moira Cairns, before destroying it. As the police could establish no link whatsoever between Liz and Miss Cairns, it was assumed the car had been stolen, but inquiries, I am told, are not yet complete.

As to the part played in this affair by the brewery . . . Well, as the economic heart of the village, it was obviously a target for someone with malice in mind.

I realize now that perhaps the very first death of what we might, quite justifiably, call Bridelow's War, was that of Andy Hodgson, the young worker who 'fell' to the ground during the reassembly of the rusted pulley-and-platform mechanism used originally for winching sacks to the highest level of the brewery . . . that old malt store which was to become the unholiest of temples.

It is my belief that Andy Hodgson was himself a foundation-sacrifice to consecrate the malt store, in one of several corruptions of Celtic ritual performed in an effort to crumble the edifice of our tradition. The platform was later used, there can be no doubt, to winch up the body of Matt Castle, stolen from its grave for despicable necromantic purposes.

It was early days, though, and Andy's death was clearly less elaborate than that of poor Joel Beard, for whom I shall always have a certain respect, whose body remains buried somewhere out on the Moss, and perhaps far more deeply now than was ever intended.

The brewery, in an eastern corner of the village, much shielded by trees, was unaffected by the Burst. When a certain police officer paid a discreet visit the following morning he did not find what he apparently had been expecting. The remains of Matt Castle and Young Frank Manifold had disappeared.

A mystery? Not, I suspect, much of one. I think, if I were to question a few former regulars of The Man I'th Moss, particularly the estimable Mr Stanley Burrows, I might discover that, in the aftermath of the Burst and all the panic and confusion, the number of bodies in the bog had been surreptitiously supplemented.

The aforementioned policeman, an untypically thoughtful and philosophical officer approaching retirement, wishes it to be recorded that he was *not* in Bridelow on the night of the disaster and is unlikely to return. Although, I am informed, this officer has been undertaking some private 'stress-counselling' with a certain widow, in his own time.

It was to be two days before the other bodies were discovered at the brewery. I shall come to this.

Those of us, including Benjie's dog and Ma's cats, who sought sanctuary in the church remained unharmed, although it was terrifying to feel the building almost rocking around us.

Surrounded by rescue-squads in the wan light of early dawn, we could see peat four or five feet deep in parts of the churchyard, like an obscene black parody of snowdrifts.

Most of the graves had disappeared, just the heads of crosses showing. Our Sheila remained in position, looking perhaps more disgruntled than usual with her most public parts gunged up with peat.

Although their yards and gardens were submerged, the houses on the right of the street, had been spared the worst, and these included Ma Wagstaff's cottage, wherein we came upon something inexplicably strange.

Dic Castle was sitting in Ma's old rocking-chair in an atmosphere of unexpected tranquillity. He had been brought to the house at his own request after Stan Burrows and a certain policeman had been unable to find Cathy Gruber. Curiously calm, Dic had insisted they leave him alone, and with so many horrors competing for their attention they didn't argue for long.

And so the lad sat himself down in the rocking chair and slept through all the roaring and the screaming, and he dreamed of an old lady rather irritably bandaging his wounds, continually assuring him that she had better things to do.

I myself have seen those wrists. Now, still within a week, the scars are scarcely visible.

I am a schoolteacher and an historian, a man of facts. I make no comments upon this.

The American, Mr Macbeth . . . Mungo, why not? . . . could so easily have followed the rest of us into the church and saved himself, but instead displayed exceptional and foolhardy courage.

I doubt if he himself knew whether it was Cathy or Miss Moira Cairns he thought he could save. But in his desperate race down the village street he must have felt himself to be close to the epicentre of an earthquake, drenched by the insidious black liquid, with cobs of semi-solid peat falling like bombs all around him and the crackling roar of collapsing buildings on the western side.

Eventually, the young man reached The Man I'th Moss, and must have been horrified by what he found.

For the pub began with the second storey, its ground

floor buried under a black avalanche, the lantern over the front door half submerged but still eerily alight.

Mungo knew the peat would be far too deep to enable him to reach the rear of the building in the normal way, so he waded out to the boundary wall – now no more than a foot above the surface – clambered on to it and moved perilously, like a tightrope walker, around the forecourt until he reached the yard at the rear, at the end of which was the remains of the barn which had been used by Matt Castle for his music.

An ante-room to hell.

. . . Oh, Jesus . . . the fuck am I gonna do? I can't handle this. There's nobody alive here. There . . . is . . . nobody . . . *alive*.

Clawing at his eyes, filling up with the black shit.

And what if I find her body? You expect me to deal with that, Duchess? You sent me down to here to bring her body back, that it? Well, fuck you, Duchess, f . . .

Hold it.

Voices. Close up.

Maybe these were echoes of voices from before the deluge, peat preserving the last blocked screams of the dying.

'Drop it. Darling . . . simply drop it. It'll pull you down. Drop the stone – listen to me, now – drop the stone and wade away because – believe this – another four or five paces and you'll be in over your head, and it won't matter. Drop the stone and back away now and save yourself. All you can do, m'dear.'

'Get *stuffed*!'

Cathy.

Macbeth saw that after the rain, after the blast, there was a lightness in the sky, still night but somehow drained of darkness. A phoney dawn, bringing things and people into visibility.

Cathy was waist-deep in the peat, her fine, fair hair gummed to her skull. She was looking up, but not at the rained-out sky.

Above her, balanced upon a fallen roof-spar, an apparition glowing white, or so it seemed, undamaged by the night or the storm of peat, was the writer, John Peveril Stanage.

Macbeth crouched on his wall.

It was clear that Stanage knew exactly why Cathy was holding, above the level of the peat, a single grey boulder, the kind from which these tough drystone walls had been constructed.

And it was clear also that he believed – part of the psychological mesh he'd helped weave, the mystical dynamic he'd set in motion long ago – that if this boulder should be put in place, in some *particular* place, he'd be able to proceed no further in the direction of Bridelow.

He *believed* this.

In the air, a glimmering, light on metal.

Stanage had hold of a length – five feet or so – of copper pipe.

This was not mystical.

Even as Macbeth struggled to his feet, the pipe began to swing.

'No!'

As he fell from the wall, the pipe smashed into Cathy.

Macbeth rolled into three feet of liquid crud and came up like a sheep out of the dip, found it hard to stand upright, the stuff up around his waist and it was so goddamn *heavy*, filling up the pockets of his slicker; he shrugged out of the slicker, stood there, breathing like a steam engine, black shit soaking into his fucking useless Bloomingdale menswear department cashmere sweater.

'Cathy . . . where the f . . . ?'

'Who are *you*?' said Stanage.

Macbeth scraped peat out of his eyes. 'It doesn't matter,' he said.

He heard Cathy spluttering beside him, glanced briefly at her – something oozing out the side of her head, something that wasn't peat. He pushed himself in front of her, slime slurping down the front of his pants; cold as hell.

'Cathy, just do as he says and get outa here, willya.'

Cathy's hands came out of the mire with a kind of sucking

sound and they were still clutching the grey stone. He saw her grinning, small white teeth in a small blackened face.

'Go!' Macbeth screamed. 'Get the fuck outa here!'

He heard the wafting of the copper pipe through the moist air and he threw himself forward and met it with his body, hard into the chest, and his skin was so cold and numb that if it cracked a rib, or maybe two, he didn't even feel it.

He wrenched hard on the pipe and heard a grunt and then Stanage was tumbling from the end of his roofspar and, breaking the surface of the Moss with a splat, and Macbeth went under. And when he came up, the peat felt a whole lot colder and he couldn't even cough it out of his lungs because of the long fingers like a wire garotte around his throat.

From *Dawber's* Secret *Book of Bridelow* (unpublished):

MUNGO MACBETH HAVING instructed her, in his distressingly restricted New York parlance, to remove herself, Cathy realized she had little choice but to do as he said. The girl cannot swim – even if anyone could in liquid of this consistency and temperature – and her only hope was to get help.

You must remember that Cathy was in a state of some bewilderment; she had not seen the bog burst, only heard the thunder roar, and, like most of us, could have had no concept of the scale of the devastation.

But the village must have looked very different, shockingly so, with the converted gaslamps on one side of the street protruding no more than a few feet from the murky surface of what had now become an extension of the Moss. And the poor girl must have been appalled by the sight of the collapsed cottages, the telephone box protruding from the peat like a buoy and the Post Office in ruins behind it.

She waded frantically back to the wall, placed the grey stone on top, hauled herself up after it and sat there a while, shattered by what she had seen and half-stunned by the blow from the pipe which had landed on her shoulder and rebounded on to the side of her head. She knew there was blood there, mingling with the rivulets of peatwater from her hair, but she did not touch the wound, preferring to remain ignorant of its extent and severity so long as she could function.

Cathy tells me – rather ashamed – that her mind at this point had simply blanked out Mungo Macbeth and what might be happening to him at the cold hands of John Peveril Stanage. She sat on the wall, with the grey stone on her knees. Beyond pain, beyond fear, beyond fatigue, beyond thought . . . even beyond prayer.

And when all feeling had gone, apart from a sense of failure and despair, something came to *her*.

Now . . .

Problems.

It is not my place to be credulous and speak of 'vision'. Nor would I wish to use the clinically dismissive term 'hallucination'.

Of course, I have read the stories, the 'eyewitness testimony', from Lourdes to Fatima to Knock and Walsingham, and occasionally I have been impressed and heartened but most times left cold and more than a little sceptical.

I have *heard* of similar eyewitness reports from the edge of bubbling streams in the Peak District of Derbyshire and – yes – from our own Holy Well above Bridelow. And these have not been chronicled at all, for, in the view of devout Roman Catholics, *Our* Lady is hardly considered to be the same figure as *Their* 'lady', although both have been 'seen' to shine with a silvery aureole, as of the moon rather than the sun.

Well. Cathy's Lady – you'll laugh, or perhaps you won't – wore a duffel coat.

She appeared to be sitting next to the lass on the wall. She was not beautiful, Cathy says, but her aura of feminine grace was so powerfully calming that the air became still and soft and moist, and even the rugged stones beneath her felt like cushions.

She remembers hanging her head, her chin upon her chest, and the lady stroking her hair. Or at least it *was* stroked.

*

581

About the duffel coat.

My researches tell me that the priests and priestesses of Ancient Britain – the shaman class, if you will – would usually be attired for ceremonial purposes in a loose, hooded garment of blue wool. Quite when the duffel coat, as we know it, reappeared I don't know; my knowledge of social history has never extended to fashion trends, but it has always struck me as curiously meaningful that, while most coats are fastened with plastic buttons or zips, the duffel is secured by pegs of wood. Or (even more interesting) of horn.

But I digress.

The next thing Cathy remembers is standing at a point halfway between the end of the pub forecourt and the first of the ruined cottages. The peat was up to her knees.

Our Lady of the Duffel Coat was gone.

And so was the stone.

Cathy says she felt nothing; neither relief nor the old despair. She was an empty vessel. It was not until later that she would recall the lady in any supernatural sense. She had been as real as the stone, which Cathy had no memory of depositing.

Now there was only the practical problem of avoiding death on the drowning side of the village.

The Beacon of the Moss was alight again, courtesy of Alf Beckett and his floodlight. It threw a strange glimmer on the black surface of a new river flowing between great banks of peat down the middle of the street. From out of a mound of peat, a stiffened arm protruded, the fingers curled and black.

From behind her, Cathy heard voices. She turned her back on the street and waded towards the sound, coming at last to the most southerly part of the village which ran down to the Moss near the causeway and where, she remembered, Lottie Castle was to have placed her stone.

It was here that Cathy became the last person to see Shaw Horridge and Therese Beaufort – later formally identified as one Tessa Byford – alive.

The effects of the Burst at this southern point were

somewhat less marked. Although the Moss had overflowed the causeway in places (which was to cause serious delays for the rescue service vehicles) it had not reached a life-threatening depth for an adult.

The man and woman were thigh-deep at the edge of the causeway, and Cathy was about to call out to them when she realized who they were. Lady Strychnine, as she'd referred to Therese, was hissing at Shaw to get back and leave her and attempting to disengage his hand from around her wrist. Shaw, it appeared, was trying to drag her back towards the village and laughing in a voice which Cathy has described to me as surprisingly coarse and cruel.

'Come on,' Shaw was shouting, almost gleefully. 'Come back. You can do it. You'll feel *so much better*.'

He kept repeating this phrase, hitting her with it, Cathy says, and pulling at her arm, and Therese was screaming shrilly and at one stage actually vomiting with fear.

'Lottie's stone, you see,' Cathy is telling me. 'Therese couldn't go past the stone. And it was then that I realized' – Cathy shakes her head in incomprehension – 'that it had worked. That we'd done it. That the Bridelow Mothers' Union was able to function.'

And knowing what she knew about the woman (not half of what we now know) Cathy felt no great pity when Shaw Horridge quickly let go of Therese's wrists and suddenly delivered an enormous blow to her face with his fist.

All this time Cathy had been backing away up the street towards the village centre, and she turned around just once to see Shaw Horridge walking very slowly and deliberately up the street with Therese's slender body hanging limply from his arms.

As I recorded earlier, it was two days before the corpses were found. This happened when an executive of Gannons accompanied the company's insurance assessor into the brewery to see what minor damage had occurred.

They would hardly have bothered to go into the malt loft even it had not been firmly locked and no keys apparent. As it was, they progressed no further than the second level where the 'coppers' stand.

These are the huge tanks in which the 'wort', as the initial preparation is known, is mixed with the hops (or bog myrtle in old Bridelow Brewery days) which preserve the beer and give it that all-important bitter quality.

It appeared that Shaw, quite methodically, had lit the oil-boiler and gone about the beer-making process on his own, something which, to my own knowledge, he had been able to do since the age of twelve under the paternal eye of Arthur Horridge.

The operation must have taken Shaw several hours, by which time the village was teeming with urgent life: fire and ambulance personnel, moorland rescue teams, television crews; at least two helicopters overhead. I wonder, what state was Therese in during this period? Was she conscious? Did she know what was to happen? Was she – already forcibly conveyed beyond a boundary which she had been psychologically incapable of crossing unassisted – in any state to object?

The copper, by the way, is also known as the 'brew kettle' because in it the hops are boiled into the wort preparatory to the addition of yeast.

They say the insurance assessor passed out after finding the bodies of Shaw and Therese, which must have boiled for nearly two hours before the boiler, reaching danger-level, had automatically cut out.

Was this, I wonder, another example – drowning, boiling and perhaps, in Therese's case, simultaneous strangulation – of that ancient mystery, the Celtic Triple Death?

What was Shaw's state of mind? Was he angry? Embittered? Remorseful? Or a dangerous brew of all three?

'Tell me,' I ask Cathy. 'When you heard them on the edge of the Moss, was Shaw stuttering, as he used to do? You know . . . *You'll fer-fer-feel ber-ber-better?*'

'No,' she says. 'I'm pretty sure he wasn't.'

'I'm glad,' I say.

*

Poor Mungo.

His larynx full of peat, his eyes staring up in terminal terror into the eyes of the madman Stanage, his mouth no doubt full of flip New York obscenities which he now knew he would never utter.

Poor lad.

The stranger in a strange land. Thrown upon the Scottish shore with the instruction, I am told, to discover his 'roots'.

By 'eck. How gullible some of these Americans are apt to be.

And the winds of fate . . . nay, the *typhoons* of fate, can sometimes pick you up and put you down precisely where you wanted to be. Only when you look around, do you realize it's the very *last* place you wanted to be.

He found his Celtic roots, all right. We might not wear kilts or speak a different language or owt like that, but I reckon we've been closer in Bridelow to the true Celtic way – *Shades of things, Ernest!* (Aye, thank you, Ma) – than you'll find in any lonely hamlet in Sutherland or Connemara.

And I think it will survive. I think the Mothers will watch over the rebuilding of a stronger Bridelow. I doubt they'll ever again 'let things slide'.

Cathy won't let them.

Did you know, Hans, by the way, that your daughter was coming to the end of her second and final year at a very reputable theological college outside Oxford? I bet you didn't. I bet she just kept telling you she was doing 'postgraduate research' or something of that order.

But Ma Wagstaff knew. Ma Wagstaff spoke more than once of the 'one who'll come after me' and everybody laughed because it sounded so quaintly biblical.

They have a fund, you know, the Mothers. A bank account in Glossop or Macclesfield or somewhere, to which unexpected windfalls and bequests are added from time to time, and there was sufficient money in that to put Cathy through theological college without anyone knowing.

If all goes well, it'll be The Reverend Cathy soon. And in

a few years, all things being equal, Bridelow will have its first woman minister. Oh, aye. You can count on it. You really think the Archdeacon won't give us his full backing in ensuring that the lass is appointed? By 'eck, lad, we've got enough dirt on that bugger to buy his soul off him, and we're not afraid to use it!

Makes you think though, doesn't it. Another giant step for mankind in little Bridelow: probably the first official Anglican clergyperson (as we'll have to say) equipped to serve both God and the Goddess.

By 'eck.

Could've given Macbeth twenty-five years at least, this bastard, his face white as a skull, white as the skulls that tumbled from the walls in the Earl's castle so long ago, in another time, another life.

But so goddamn strong. His hands so hard, so tight around Macbeth's throat that Macbeth figured one finger must have been driven, nail first, through the skin, through the flesh and up his windpipe where it had lodged and swollen to the size of a clenched fist.

He fought to breathe, but there was no air left, not anywhere in the world.

Stanage's eyes had receded into his skull as he thrust Macbeth's head down under the water once, twice. Second time he came up, Macbeth's eyes were popping too far out, probably, for eyelids to cover, and he was seeing nothing through the black water. Only his inner eyes saw everything, with a helpless clarity:

. . . *this is how it happens, this is how you drown*.

His lungs hard as concrete, his whole body filled up with peat.

. . . *gonna be preserved. For all time. For ever*.

'I remember you now,' he heard Stanage saying. 'Scotland, yes? An American. Followed the Cairns creature around like a bloody lamb.'

Stanage must have known the last question, the one Macbeth couldn't speak, the one which even his blacked-out eyes could no longer convey.

He said, almost gently, 'She died.'

And Macbeth stopped resisting, surrendered to the limitless night.

'Bloody unfortunate, really. Didn't want her dead at a crucial stage. But it'll be OK, I suppose; she won't be doing much yet. They're very bewildered, you see, m'boy. At first. It can take about three days – well, weeks, months, years in some cases. Oh, she was doubtless better prepared than most, but however developed they are, it's three days, minimum, 'fore they can do *damage*.'

Stanage wore a black jacket over a white shirt. The shirt was spotless; suddenly this was the worst thing, a spiritual travesty; Macbeth, dying, felt sick at the injustice of it.

'Caught her unawares, I think, when it came, m'boy. Even though she certainly did have a spirit. Damn well caught *me* unawares on one occasion, as you saw. Bitch. But the Scottish business, that was really . . .'

Forcing Macbeth under the dark water again; this time no struggle, get it over . . .

But Stanage brought him up again.

'. . . just a small clash of egos, in comparison. Small clash of egos. This, though . . . this is a splendid shake-up. Past and present, worlds colliding . . .'

Macbeth's eyes cleared a moment; he saw a big yellow grin.

'. . . roof coming in, I was expecting it, threw myself under a table. Central beam – oak beam – came down on her. If she'd had all her hair – ironic, really – I wouldn't have seen it happen. Not in quite such exquisite detail . . . crrrrrrunch. Like an eggshell.'

Eased his grip a fraction, so that a thin jet of air entered Macbeth's lungs. He used it.

'*Motherfucker*.'

Stanage laughed. 'What? Lord, no. You ever *see* my mother?'

Closed up Macbeth's throat.

'Fucked a sister or two. That was fun. For a while. Strengthens the old family ties. Goodnight, m'boy. Don't suppose *your* passing will cause much of a vibe on the ether.'

Last thing Macbeth saw, with gratitude, was some dark shit on Stanage's shirt.

Must've sprayed it out with 'motherfucker'.

From *Dawber's* Secret *Book of Bridelow* (unpublished):

THEY HAVEN'T FOUND his body and happen they never will.

Peat preserves.

Oh, aye, it does that. But how much of what peat preserves *should* be preserved?

It's not natural, that's the problem. Dust to dust. All things must pass. All things must rot. For in rotting there's change. That's the positive aspect of physical death. All things must *change*.

Nothing changes much in the peat; so peat, in my view, works against natural laws. Living on the edge of it, Bridelow folk have always been aware of the borderline between what is natural and what isn't.

This is not whimsy. But all the same, I've had a bellyful, so I've decided, on balance, that I won't die here. Happen my soul'll find its way back, who can say? But, the Lord – and Willie Wagstaff – decided one rainy night that the peat was not for me, so I'm taking the hint and I'll pop me clogs somewhere else, thank you very much.

Also, to be realistic, I think I need what time's left to me to do a bit of thinking, and I reckon Bridelow is too powerful a place right this minute to get things into any sort of perspective.

So.

I'm off to Bournemouth, owd lad.

Don't you dare say *owt*. And don't anybody panic either; when I say Bournemouth, I mean Bournemouth – I've a cousin runs a little guest house up towards Poole Harbour.

Your Cathy says she'll come and see me and bring Milly, and they'll try their hand at a spot of the old Bridelow healing. 'Doctors!' Cathy says. 'What do *they* know?'

Aye. What *do* the buggers know?

We'll see.

He could taste the peat on her face. Nothing ever tasted as good. He wanted to believe it. He didn't.

Wherever she goes, that young woman, she's bound to be touched with madness.

He thought, If we're *both* dead maybe I got a chance *this* side.

'I . . .'

'Don't talk. Not if it hurts.'

There was light in the sky; this time maybe the real thing: dawn.

All Souls Day.

His ass was wet. Everything was wet.

No.

The Duchess said, *Now, who is the white man?*

'No!' Macbeth screamed. 'Fuck you, Duchess!'

'She won't take too kindly to that.'

'No,' he said. 'Please. No tricks. No more tricks.'

He opened his eyes. Shut them tight again. 'Stanage, you motherf—'

'He's gone. Believe me. He's the other side. He can't get across. Whether he's alive or dead, he can't get across.'

Macbeth opened his eyes. Kept them open. Kept staring and staring.

'Eggshell,' he said. 'Said her head was smashed like an eggshell.'

'Whose head?'

'Yours? When the roof came in?'

'I hope not,' Moira said, putting a hand for the first time to the remains of her hair. She wrinkled her nose. 'But I sure as hell kept bloody still underneath that beam until he'd gone. Can you walk? I mean, can you stand up?'

Macbeth leaned his back against the wall and did some coughing. Coughed his guts up. Felt better. Not a whole *lot* better, and the way his goddamn heart was beating . . .

He got his eyes to focus on her.

'Are you real?'

'Do I no' look real?'

Her slashed hair was in spikes. Her face was streaked with black peat and blood. He couldn't tell what she was wearing except for peat.

'Uh . . . yeah,' he said. 'I guess you look real. 'And I . . . Did we come through this?'

'Come on,' Moira said. 'We need to move.'

Holding on to each other, Macbeth still feeling like he was dream-walking, they made it back across the forecourt to where the peat came no higher than their thighs.

And then Moira's plastic lamp went out, which seemed to bother her a lot. 'Just hang on, Mungo, thing's coming to pieces.'

'That's OK.' His brain felt like it was muffled. Mossy. 'We don't need a light any more. Sun's here. Someplace.'

Figured that even if she walked away from him at the top of the street, even if she walked away for ever, he had all the light he'd ever need.

'No,' Moira stopped. 'Been through a lot, me and this lamp. There's blood on it. Is it mine, or Stanage's?'

Macbeth panicked then. He spun around in the peat, saw the roof of The Man I'th Moss, the caved-in roof of the barn, spars and serrated masonry projecting jaggedly into the half-light.

'He's gone,' Moira said.

'You sure he's gone? How can you be *sure*? Someone like that, he can go that easy?'

He stared down into the peat, like a pair of hands might break and drag him down. Or even worse, if there were hands *down there, underneath* . . .

'Please God . . .' Macbeth breathed as a hand went around his arm.

'It's OK, Mungo.'

'Is it? Is it OK? Are you still real? Oh, Jesus . . .'

He started to weep.

'Mungo,' Moira said. 'Wasny that easy.'

Clawing at his hard, white face, at his nose, his teeth, going at him like a madwoman. Blood oozing, greasy, warm blood. And once I saw his eyes, never really seen his eyes before.

In his eyes is this, like, languorous amusement. The damage I'm doing is superficial, and he's laughing at me.

Behind him, there's a shadow on the moss. The shadow isn't moving.

Behind me . . .

This warm breath on my neck. I don't even have to turn around to know how putrid this breath is. Death-room breath.

But I do turn around. I turn my back on John Peveril Stanage, and Matt Castle is there.

Matt Castle is crouching on the Moss. He is very still, still as stone. Still as the bounding toadstone on the moor before it leaps.

His feet do not touch the peat. He's maybe five yards away but I can smell his breath. He is breath, all breath, a mist on the Moss. He's in his element is Matt Castle.

'I don't remember this,' Mungo said. 'I don't remember any of it.'

'These things sometimes happen out of time, you know?' Moira looked up at where the Beacon of the Moss shone down, not blue, somehow pale gold, like an early sun. 'In a twinkling.'

She looked down at the plastic lamp, its back piece hanging off where you put the batteries in. 'Dic gave me this when he rescued me from the outhouse. It's just a wee, cheap thing, made in Taiwan, where the flu comes from. It had gone out, and then it came on, and when it came on Matt's . . . essence, spirit . . . began to squirm, like Dic was sending him a message, you know? And I turned around and . . .'

. . . the light shines into the eyes of John Peveril Stanage and Stanage backs off, backs off too far. He's starting to scream – agony, bitter frustration, and somehow I'm hitting him with the

591

light, the finest, brightest light ever came out of Taiwan . . . and his eyes are this orangey colour floating further back, further away, like the diminishing tail lights of a car disappearing into the night . . .

'Kept hitting him with the light, Mungo, but he'd gone over. Gone out of the Bridelow circle. Maybe a couple of feet was all it took. Like an electric fence, you know? Shock just hurled him back. Maybe he drowned. Was no' my problem.'

She was still fiddling with the lamp, trying to put it back together.

'And then there was just the two of us. You puking your guts out, Mungo. I don't know what happened. Maybe we're talking Providence, maybe . . . Here, hold on to this a wee minute.'

She gave him the plastic base and two batteries fell out and plopped into the peat. Then something else fell out after them and she caught it.

What this was, Macbeth saw, was a little metal comb. Like a dog comb with a whole bunch of teeth missing.

'Dic.' Moira stared at the comb. 'He stole it back. He told me, but I . . .'

Moira Cairns started to laugh. Mungo Macbeth never heard anyone sound quite so elated. Laughing fit to cause ripples in the peat. Laughing enough to bring on another goddamn bog blow-out.

She fell down in the swirling street with a filthy splash and she dragged him down on top of her, both arms around his neck, the comb in one hand, and she was kissing him hard on the mouth and the peat on her lips tasted like maple syrup.

When eventually they came to their feet, she linked her arm into his and started to lead him along the western side of the street to where the Beacon of the Moss flashed a tired signal to the sun. The black peat was quite deep around them, but it was feeling cool, now, and good.

'Teabreak's over,' she said, turning towards him, the peat around her hips. And she started to laugh again, in lovely big peals. *'Teabreak's over, boys. Back to your tunnelling, yeah?'*

Mungo Macbeth said, 'Huh?'

From *Dawber's* Secret *Book of Bridelow* (unpublished):

HANS.

Before I go . . .

I can understand your feelings about the death of the young farmer, Sam Davis, but I don't think you should blame yourself; from what you've told me he was a head-strong lad and if he'd listened to you in the first place he'd have left well alone and might be alive today.

Easy for me to say, but it's what I believe.

And at least his stories of night activity among the circles on the moor were our pointer to the location of the bog body. It was obvious what they would do with him: switch him from the sanctity of the churchyard to the poisoned earth of a once-holy place which had systematically, over a long period, been reconsecrated in the name of evil.

Cold storage. Nowhere colder.

The policeman, I understand, expected to find him in the loft at the brewery, but his body was never taken there. I suspect that even Stanage knew that his ancient spirit would be impossible to confront unless it was diffused through Matt Castle. Matt Castle, who they thought they could command.

We are all so stupid, are we not, to believe that anything beyond the physical can ever truly be controlled by mankind?

So we all went up there, that's me and the Mothers and a few lads to do the labouring. Went by day, stroke of noon, with as much brightness in the sky as anyone has a right to expect this time of year.

You know, that place still reeks so much of evil that it could be an environmental and spiritual menace for centuries. I don't know what they'll be able to do about *that*.

Anyroad, Willie Wagstaff and Stan Burrows went in and dug up the bogman and dumped him in a wheelbarrow, and we brought him back to Bridelow.

Where he now lies in what I think you will agree is a place of ultimate safety.

R.I.P.

IRIS WAGSTAFF.
AND
FRIEND . . .

No witch bottle. We didn't want to insult her.

CLOSING CREDITS

CONCEPT: Carol Rickman. The Man in the Moss was formally unearthed when my wife, who'd just read a book on Lindow Man, said, 'I think you should do one about a bog body.' Cleverly, she said this in front of the right witnesses – my ever-helpful agent Andrew Hewson, and eagle-eyed editor at Pan-Mac, Bill Scott-Kerr – at one of those power lunches you hear about. She also kept a cool sub-editor's eye on the whole operation.

TECHNICAL ADVICE

(i) PEAT: Biologist Dr Fred Slater, curator of the University of Wales Llysdinam Field Centre at Newbridge on Wye, Powys, told me about bogs, bog-myrtle and bog oak, and, producing several key scientific reports, introduced the mind-boggling concept of a bog burst.

(ii) CELTIC LORE: Britain's premier Celtic authority, Dr Anne Ross, author of the seminal *Pagan Celtic Britain*, discussed some of her own experiences and referred me to Anthony Myers Ward, Celtic investigator and mysteriologist, who lives dangerously close to Bridelow and to whom I and the Mothers' Union owe a great deal. Paul Devereux put me on to David Clarke, author of the excellent *Ghosts and Legends of the Peak District* (Jarrold Books), who was good enough to make me a copy of a crucial videotape.

(iii) RELIGION: The Revds Ernie Rea, of the BBC, and John Guy, the vicar of Y Groes, got me out of a couple of potentially nasty ecclesiastical traps.

(iv) BEER: Jeremy Blundell showed Carol and me around the Three Tuns Brewery at Bishop's Castle in Shropshire, where quality real ales are produced with no evidence of supernatural intervention, and Iain Loe of CAMRA provided some useful background material.

(v) MEDICAL: Dr Viv Davies talked about heart conditions, Geraldine Richards and my dad, Arthur Rickman, about arthritis and Pamela

Baker, reflexologist and former nursing sister, explained (very colourfully) the drawbacks of wrist slitting.

My US agent Stuart Krichevsky (of the Madison Avenue Krichevskys) was good enough to vet certain aspects of Mungo Macbeth.

Nigel Pennick's *Practical Magic in the Northern Tradition* (Aquarian Books) helped to clarify certain important points, as did the British Museum's compendium report: *Lindow Man – the Body in the Bog*. Thanks also to Graham Nown, Kate Fenton, Rick Turner and Gordon Green's bog-snorkelling fraternity at Llanwrtyd Wells without whom I may never have appreciated just how unpleasant liquid peat can be.

Due to the demands of fiction, virtually none of the background information has gone unmolested, so remember, IT'S NOT THEIR FAULT.

Phil Rickman
Candlenight £4.99

From the outside, the Welsh village of Y Groes looks idyllic. When his wife inherits an old cottage there, Giles Freeman eagerly grabs the chance of permanent escape from London.

But there is a menacing magic at work in the apparently peaceful valley. Ancient secrets lie buried; the corpse-candle remains alight; and the Bird of Death beats its wings at the window.

Too late Giles discovers the powers of darkness gathering around him . . .

Only his American friend Berry Morelli senses the terrible threat. Through his love for the village schoolteacher Bethan, he is drawn into a climactic struggle with the monstrous forces of Celtic legend.

'A tautly written and nervy horror story with something important to say . . . grimly sinister, written with blood-curdling aplomb'
GEORGE MACBETH, SUNDAY TELEGRAPH

'No shortage of excitement . . . the supernatural thriller has never been a favourite genre of mine but *Candlenight* was exciting enough to overcome my prejudices' RUTH RENDELL, DAILY TELEGRAPH

'A brooding first novel . . . an impressive debut which credibly fuses Celtic myth with contemporary Welsh politics'
CONRAD HILL, SUNDAY TIMES

'Authentic shudders with some wonderful touches of the bizarre'
KATE SAUNDERS, EVENING STANDARD

Phil Rickman
Crybbe £4.99

In Crybbe, only strangers walk at twilight . . .

For four hundred years, the curfew bell has tolled nightly from the church tower of the small country town, Crybbe's only defence against the evil rising unbidden in its haunted streets.

Radio reporter Fay Morrison came to Crybbe because she had no choice. Millionaire music tycoon Max Goff came because there was nothing left to conquer, except the power of the spirit.

But he knew nothing of the town's legacy of dark magic – and nobody really felt like telling him . . .

In Crybbe, death isn't necessarily the worst thing that can happen . . .

'Wonderfully spooky . . . utterly compelling . . . You must read it' JILLY COOPER

'Gripping throughout . . . a powerful book and a thoroughly good horror story. Classic stuff' GUY BURT, THE TIMES

'I don't like horror novels, but I loved this one. I believed in the people and relished the wit' JOANNA TROLLOPE

'Gothic evil at breakneck pace . . . rip-snorting supernatural fun' CHRISTOPHER FOWLER, TIME OUT

'A massive, ambitious novel tight with atmosphere and thick with latent violence . . . brilliant' PETER JAMES

All Pan Books are available at your local bookshop or newsagent, or can be ordered direct from the publisher. Indicate the number of copies required and fill in the form below.

Send to: Pan C. S. Dept
              Macmillan Distribution Ltd
              Houndmills Basingstoke RG21 2XS

or phone: 0256 29242, quoting title, author and Credit Card number.

Please enclose a remittance* to the value of the cover price plus £1.00 for the first book plus 50p per copy for each additional book ordered.

*Payment may be made in sterling by UK personal cheque, postal order, sterling draft or international money order, made payable to Pan Books Ltd.

Alternatively by Barclaycard/Access/Amex/Diners

Card No.

Expiry Date

Signature

Applicable only in the UK and BFPO addresses.

While every effort is made to keep prices low, it is sometimes necessary to increase prices at short notice. Pan Books reserve the right to show on covers and charge new retail prices which may differ from those advertised in the text or elsewhere.

NAME AND ADDRESS IN BLOCK LETTERS PLEASE

....

Name _____

Address _____

_____

_____

_____

6/92